BACKED BY LOVE

A Turkey Earthquake Anthology

Gwyn McNamee   Scarlett Finn   Katrina Marie   Liz Durano

Evey Lyon   D. Kelly   Dakota Willink   Jocelyne Soto

Imani Jay   S.M. West   Carrie Lomax   D.L. Gallie

S.L. Sterling   Vi Summers   Claire Hastings   Lyra Parish

Eve Pendle   Kimberly Quinn   Echo Grayce & Melissa Ivers

Lauren Stewart   Tara Wyatt   Lee Savino   Cadence Keys

January James   Alix Key

Introduction

On February 6, 2023, a devastatingly powerful 7.8 magnitude earthquake and strong aftershocks decimated parts of Turkey. We've all watched, helpless, as rescuers tried to reach those trapped in the rubble, and the death toll continued to rise.

25 romance authors have banded together to try to make a difference by releasing this anthology with 100% of royalties going to a reputable charity helping those in affected areas-- the Turkish Red Crescent (the Turkish arm of the Red Cross).

Enjoy these stories of hope and love and help us support those affected by the earthquake by backing them with love.

Featuring stories from:
Gwyn McNamee
Scarlett Finn
Katrina Marie
Liz Durano
Evey Lyon
D. Kelly
Dakota Willink
Jocelyne Soto
Imani Jay
S.M. West
Carrie Lomax

DL Gallie
S.L. Sterling
Vi Summers
Claire Hastings
Lyra Parish
Eve Pendle
Echo Grayce and Melissa Ivers
Tara Wyatt
Lee Savino
Lauren Stewart
Cadence Keys
Kimberly Quinn
January James
Alix Key

Made to Order

Gwyn McNamee

Chapter One

FUCK.

Flopping down onto the mattress—alone—is like fucking Heaven right now.

Exhaustion permeates deep into my bones. I'm not even sure I could get it up right now if I tried. No amount of tugging, sucking, or fucking right now would rouse my soldier.

How fucking depressing is that?

My poor dick is so over-used, it's practically ready for a coffin and burial. Six straight nights of dates. Six straight nights of fun but meaningless sex with six different women—over and over and over and over...

Against a wall, on a desk, in a pool, in the backseat of a car, bent over the sink in a bathroom at a restaurant, in an alley behind a nightclub...

Pretty much anywhere and everywhere you can fuck, I did this past week.

Most men would be thrilled and probably call me a fucking pussy for complaining about too much sex. But I need a breather, at least for one night.

Just give me a little time—away from the women, and away from the Goddamn filet mignon.

If I don't see another tiny, round piece of steak in my life, I would die a happy man. These women all think they're funny and clever serving it to me when we eat at their homes or ordering it if we eat out on our dates.

Yeah, real original.

I would roll my eyes, but I'm too fucking tired for even that minuscule movement.

But I need to know what time it is. I didn't expect to be coming home this late, or early rather, since it was already well after midnight when I finally left her place.

That woman was an animal tonight. Four...no five rounds of hot, sweaty, hair-pulling, hip-slamming, nail-scratching, fucking exhausting sex. And she probably would have wanted to go again if I hadn't managed to sneak out when she finally dozed off. But there are rules, and rule number one is no spending the night...no matter how utterly exhausted I may be.

With some concerted effort, I roll onto my side and check the clock on the nightstand.

2:30 taunts me in bright red numbers.

Christ. I roll onto my back and close my eyes.

Thank God it's Monday. A night with the guys to unwind, and a few beers at The Bottle is exactly what the doctor ordered. Jason knew what he was doing when he required us all to take Mondays off. You can't do this job without a scheduled break of some kind, it's too physically and emotionally taxing.

But I can't enjoy that respite for another seventeenish hours.

I first have to try to get a couple hours of sleep so I can make it through my two motion hearings this morning, and then a full afternoon of client meetings. But at least there's a light at the end of the tunnel.

No dates until Tuesday, and as of right now, my Saturday night is still free. I can't even remember the last time I had a weekend night off.

Fridays and Saturdays are prime nights, and my rates are double those nights for that very reason. Women don't want to attend parties alone. And with Made to Order offering escort services, they don't have to anymore.

Tonight was an anomaly. Sunday dates are usually low-key—a walk in Lincoln Park, maybe a stroll through the Field Museum. But this lady...sweet fuck was she feisty. I had barely knocked on her door before she was dragging me inside by my lapels and smashing her mouth on mine. It was immediately clear this was not going to be a casual mid-afternoon date, but rather an all-day and all-night fuck session.

I normally wouldn't mind, but after my dates Friday and Saturday, I had kind of been looking forward to something a little less, well, physical.

Who would have ever thought I'd be tired of having sex? Not me. But after almost two years, and countless women, it's starting to get real old, real quick. The faces all blend together, and I'm pretty sure at least half of them give fake names anyway. Having a hot, wet pussy wrapped around my cock always feels incredible—how could it not? —but just once, it would be nice to spend some time with a woman who wants to actually spend time with *me,* not with "Lewis."

I stare at the ceiling and try to will myself to get off the bed.

A scalding hot shower would probably be prudent right now. The scent of her flowery perfume and our mingled sweat still clings to me, but I don't have the energy to make it to the bathroom, let alone stand for ten minutes to scrub the filth off. I'll just change my sheets tomorrow.

Right now, the only thing I'm going to do is sleep.

Sleep and dream about my night off and away from the sexually crazed, desperate women of Chicago.

JOSETTE

It's taunting me.

The damn calendar entry is a constant reminder of how pathetic my life truly is. Well, maybe not pathetic. But definitely lacking in social engagements. At least, ones that aren't work-related.

The retirement party for one of the founding partners is Saturday.

And it's shaping up to be another blown opportunity to demonstrate to the partners I'm stable and reliable enough to be considered as a new partner. After busting my ass for them as a clerk during law school, and another five years as an associate, I've brought in more business than some of the damn partners.

Yet, they still don't take me seriously as a partner candidate. The misogyny runs deep. These old codgers don't believe a young, unmarried woman is partner material, no matter how good I am at my job or how much money I make for them.

Assholes.

I could sue them for sexual discrimination, but aside from the misogynist shit, I actually like working here. I have great co-workers, great benefits, and I'm free to do pretty much whatever I want. I don't want to throw away all the hard work and long hours I've put in to establish my client base. But I need to do something. I can't bust my ass for another five years of my life knowing there's no potential for advancement. There's no way I'm moving up in the firm without at least a stable relationship.

Which means I'm screwed, because it's not like I have time to date.

Hell, I can't even remember the last time I went on one. It was probably Jake whatever his last name is, and God, that had to be...*what*...eighteen months ago? Working eighty hours a week doesn't really leave time for relationships. Other than the one I have with my BOB.

Which reminds me...I need more batteries.

I drop my face in my hands. God, I am pathetic. My life revolves around work and a battery-operated boyfriend.

Something needs to change.

I let my hands fall, and my gaze returns to the calendar. Only this time, it's not the party reminder my eyes are drawn to, it's a phone number scrawled along the side margin.

When Ginger told me about Made to Order, I thought she was full of shit. How in the world is there a male escort service in Chicago? Do women actually use it? I mean, what kind of woman pays a man for sex?

And I figured she had to be fucking with me when she told me her boyfriend, Dylan, used to be employed there, as something *other* than a butcher. He seemed perfectly normal when I met him at The Brown Bottle when Ginger dragged me there for dinner after work one night. Ginger got a kick out of my disbelief and assured me it was true, and that she actually met him because her sister booked her a date through Made to Order.

I'm glad things worked out for her, I really am. Dylan seems like a really amazing guy, and I love seeing her so happy. But come on, I'm a fucking lawyer.

I know escort services are legal as long as nothing sexual occurs, but hiring somebody to be my date is just so...I don't know...sleazy. Plus, there's no way sex *isn't* happening with these guys. Ginger confirmed as much for me. So, getting involved with Made to Order, even for just a date, would be putting me in concert with illegal activities. And that is so not kosher.

Besides, even if I did book a date, no way I could pass off an escort as a legitimate romantic partner. My bosses would never buy it...would they?

Ginger insists the level of "cuts" they have is unlike anything I could ever imagine and that I'll be surprised by their "quality." But I can't say I believe it. How could anyone I would actually be able to pass off as a date work as an escort?

When she slipped the menu underneath my office door this morning, I almost shit myself. It's one thing to mention it to me over lunch—far, far away from the office—but she actually brought that thing into the firm. She's lucky she's an amazing assistant, otherwise I would smack her upside the head for bringing it here.

Instead, I quickly perused the menu and scribbled the phone number along the side of my calendar before I shredded the evidence.

Good thing my industrial shredder doesn't leave anything for the cleaning crew to piece back together…

Dammit.

I don't want to do it. Just thinking about calling and actually paying for a date has my stomach churning worse than before final exams in law school. But I don't have a choice. It's this or slave away for another five to ten years and maybe never make partner.

My hand shakes as I pick up the phone from my desk and then immediately slam it down.

Jesus Christ, I almost called from the work line.

Epic face-palm.

I'm not cut out for this cloak and dagger criminal shit.

Instead of using the phone on my desk and potentially leaving incriminating evidence, I pull out my cell phone. After pressing the numbers into the keypad, my finger hovers over the send button so long, the screen blacks out, and I have to reenter my password to bring it up again.

It's now or never, Josette. Time to grow a pair and just make the call.

Chapter Two

JOSETTE

I THOUGHT I WAS NERVOUS calling Made to Order to place my "order," but that was nothing compared to the acid climbing up my throat waiting for my date to arrive.

Date...ha! Can you call it that when you pay for it? And I mean *pay* for it...a lot.

Filet Mignon seemed like the most prudent choice even though he was by far the most expensive. I chose him specifically because it said he has extensive higher education and can charm even the most difficult crowds.

Please God, let him be able to hold an intelligent conversation with the partners at the party.

Otherwise, I'm royally fucked, underwent all this stress, and spent my money for nothing.

I just need to get through this night.

All I need is *one night* of them taking me seriously as a partner candidate. The rest, I can figure out later. This will at least show them I'm capable of having a relationship, even if it is fake.

Everyone needs a man, after all.

The eye roll is only seen by me in the mirror, but I can't stop it. It's the twenty-first century, and

I still need a man to advance in my career. What an absolute dinosaur-size load of shit.

Chill, Josette.

I need to tamp down my anger and annoyance if I want to make a good impression tonight. It's so damn easy to control my emotions in the courtroom, but anywhere else, I tend to wear my heart on my sleeve.

And that won't fly tonight. We need to be the perfect, happy couple if there's even a rat's chance in Hell of convincing the old farts that our "love" is real. I need to play the part perfectly.

A layer of mascara turns my practically clear lashes into long, black, elegant ones. I step back and give myself a final look in the long mirror on the back of the bathroom door. The shimmery black cocktail dress is definitely going to turn some heads tonight. But it's tasteful, not over the top. And my highlights are perfect platinum thanks to a trip to the salon earlier today.

At least I know I look good tonight. Hopefully, he's as handsome and charming as Ginger's boyfriend. Having to spend a night pretending to be a couple with a guy I have zero attraction to or who is a total bore would be pure torture.

The doorbell rings, and I take a deep breath to steady my fraying nerves.

I check the clock. It has to be him. At least he's prompt. With one last glance at myself in the mirror, I grab my clutch and head toward the front of the house.

For some reason, the walk to the door feels more like I'm walking down death row toward my electrocution than to answer the door to—hopefully—an attractive date.

A look through the peephole doesn't help much. All I can make out in the dim porch light is a dark head of hair on a very tall man.

Here goes nothing.

My shaking hands smooth down my dress before I throw the door open, and my breath catches in my throat.

Wade Saxon.

You have *got* to be kidding me.

WADE

If you would have given me a million guesses to figure out who would be opening the door for my date tonight, the last person I would have named is Josette Westmore.

The perky blonde is a damn shark in the courtroom.

I've noticed her.

It would be impossible not to, with the way she commands a room and always appears so confident in her sky-high heels and expensive, tailored suits. The woman is an absolute powerhouse, and from what I hear, she pretty much wipes the board in every case she handles. This is a woman who is always in control and always comes out on top.

But right now, she's anything but confident and in control. If anything, she looks like she's going to puke. Her alabaster skin is even whiter than normal—something I would never have imagined possible. It only makes the pink flush of embarrassment spreading across her chest and cheeks even more apparent.

Shit. She's beautiful when she's flustered.

I wait for her to say something, but the uncomfortable silence just continues to linger between us while we assess the situation analytically, like we are both trained to do. This has to be even worse for her than it is for me.

Traffic whizzes by on the busy street behind me, and I shift my weight from one foot to the other.

Fucking awkward.

Someone has to say something. It might as well be me, I guess.

"Uh, hi Josette. I didn't realize..."

How could I have known? She told Jason her name was "Jo." That could be short for anything. And there's no way she could have known it would be me. I try to maintain *some* anonymity by using my middle name, Lewis, when I go on dates.

Still, what are the fucking odds...

One lawyer working as an escort; one lawyer hiring one. This could not be more fucked up.

She finally pulls her jaw up from off the floor and narrows her blue eyes on me.

"You've got to be fucking kidding me."

I concur, counselor.

What else can I do but shrug? Until she tells me to get lost, I'm committed to be her date for the evening, for whatever she wants. She sure as hell paid for it. "I wish I was, Josette."

Christ, I really, really wish I was.

This could be so horrifically, fucking bad for me. One report to the Attorney Registration and Disciplinary Committee about what I'm doing, and my law license is fucking toast. Even if I argue that there were no sexual activities happening, which would be perjury, just being associated with an escort service is enough to end my career.

Her head shakes from side-to-side, sending her blonde bob swinging just under her chin.

"But...but how? Why?"

She squeezes her eyes closed and pinches the bridge of her nose momentarily. When she returns her gaze to me, the questions still linger in those blue orbs. Keeping her eyes on me seems almost like a physical struggle at this point; they bounce behind me to the street, across to the neighbors, and then down to her feet while she waits for my response.

We would need several hours and a couple bottles of good bourbon before I could fully answer those questions. And it would probably be less painful if she submitted them in interrogatory format so I can just type them out instead of having to verbally answer and relive the last two years of my life.

I look down at my watch—anything to avoid maintaining eye contact with her when she so obviously doesn't want to look at me.

It's only been five minutes? I feel like I've been standing here for an hour already.

"Do we need to be anywhere? Your instructions said to be here promptly at 7:30."

"Shit!" Her head jerks up, and she looks over her shoulder at a clock hanging in the entryway of her condo. "Shit. Shit. Shit. Yeah, we gotta go. We can discuss how fucking awkward this is later."

Awkward doesn't even begin to describe it, even though that's the word that's been rattling around in my head since the moment she opened the door. This is epically, totally, and royally fucked-up.

Chapter Three

BY DISCUSS THIS LATER, I meant never. Because really, if this is embarrassing for me, it must be ten times worse for Wade. He's a goddamn lawyer moonlighting as an escort. How the hell does that even happen? He has to know he could be disbarred for this. There's no way the bar would let this fly. Even if all he's doing is dates, which I *highly* doubt given what was told to me about Made to Order, that's more than enough to raise questions of ethics.

So, I'll just get through the night, and we can pretend like this never happened.

Our ride to the party is, thankfully, short and silent. Wade has a nice car, a *really* nice car. The supple leather hugs my body and the low hum of the engine almost manages to soothe my frayed nerves.

Is he doing this for the money?

He's an amazing lawyer; he should be making enough to support himself unless he's one of those douche nozzles who has to have the best of everything so he can show off.

But Wade never struck me as an arrogant man.

Confident, yes. Arrogant, no.

Hell, maybe he's just doing it to get laid. *That* wouldn't surprise me. He is a man, after all.

Wade fucking Saxon. Why did it have to be him? Why couldn't it have been some perfectly nice guy like Dylan? One who I don't have to see all the time around the courthouse.

We pull up beside the valet stand outside the Art Institute. By the time the valet has assisted me out of the car, Wade is already at my side offering me a half-hearted smile.

"Shall we?" He holds his elbow out for me. I hesitate briefly.

It's necessary, Josette.

I never thought I'd have to give myself a pep-talk to take the arm of a handsome man. One who I have noticed more than once around the courthouse. Leave it to fate to fuck with me like this. How many damn men are there in Chicago? Why does he have to be Filet Mignon?

When we reach the stairs, he removes his arm from mine and slides his hand down onto my lower back. A tingle races up my spine at the gesture. He ushers me up, and with every step, the warmth of his palm through my dress is a constant reminder of how long it's been since I've had sex.

With a person, that is.

Wade halts me at the top of stairs with a hand on my shoulder. I turn to him and raise an eyebrow in silent question.

He offers an apologetic smile. "What's our story?"

Shit, I hadn't thought about that.

I shrug and check out the area around us to ensure no one is close enough to overhear us conspiring. "What would you suggest?"

His eyes travel down my body before returning to mine. The corner of his mouth quirks up. I'm sure the half-smile is meant to be reassuring, but instead, it sends my already starved libido galloping faster than American Pharaoh.

He takes my hand in his and kisses the back of it.

Who the hell does that anymore?

That half-smile turns into a grin. "I guess, given the circumstances, we met at the courthouse and have been seeing each other for a couple months?"

Easy. Straightforward. Believable.

I nod my agreement to the story and take his arm again.

We're about to walk into the lion's den. Thankfully, we're both trained liars.

WADE

Why the hell does a woman like Josette need an escort for a work party?

Men should be lining up to spend time with her. Every male lawyer I know has a real hard-on for her. Any one of them would have given their left nut to be the man at her arm tonight.

Instead, she's paying me...

Without need.

I would have gladly accompanied her if she'd only asked. What is so important about this party that she had to spend that kind of money to ensure a date?

After twenty minutes inside, I have the answer. Every old goat in the joint has expressed their surprise to Josette. Apparently, her showing up with a date, a boyfriend, none the less, is a bit of a shock. From the way they talk, I'm surprised a couple haven't dropped dead from a heart attack at the mere sight of me with my arm around her.

What a bunch of misogynist pricks. No wonder she didn't want to come alone. They're more interested in discussing our "future" together than anything else, and they've barely let her get a word in. All the attention is on me—my career, my plans for us.

Normally, I wouldn't mind. A room full of lawyers isn't intimidating for me. It's home. But knowing we're lying and this is all a big scam is making me uneasy. It wouldn't be an issue if she were some random woman and this were some random work party. But these are my colleagues, people I have to see professionally every day for the next fifty years.

Well, I'll be practicing for another fifty years to pay off my student loans; these old fucks will be dead in less than ten if their appearance is an indication of their health.

As if their condescension weren't enough, my empty tumbler only aggravates me more. I need another drink, and given the look in Josette's eyes, she does too. They're narrowed at one of the partners, Godfrey Mason, as he rambles on about his "courtship" of his late wife, Justine. He's just reached the "she was a good little lady who stayed at home, never complaining, barefoot and pregnant in the kitchen" part of his story. Basically, the exact same thing we've already heard from every other partner tonight.

How Josette manages not to haul off and slap them senseless is a testament to her self-control. But mine is starting to slip. More alcohol would be a big help.

A hand on my shoulder has me turning away from Josette and the douchebag partners.

Holy shit!

"Dylan? What are you doing here?" I never thought I'd be so happy to see my former co-worker from Made to Order.

He smirks and hands me a glass I'm praying contains something very strong. "You looked like you could use one of these."

"You're right." He always was insightful. Much to my benefit tonight. I tip the glass back and savor the burn of whatever mid-level whiskey they're serving at the bar.

"Ginger works for Goldberg, Mason, and Quinley. She's actually Josette's secretary."

What the hell?

I survey the room, and sure enough, Ginger's in the corner chatting with some other attorneys I recognize from the courthouse. When her eyes meet mine, she winks and holds a glass of champagne up in my direction.

Christ.

"You could have given me some warning, man."

He chuckles, and I follow him to a less populated area of the room. This isn't exactly a conversation to have where others can eavesdrop. "Sorry, dude. I didn't know until we were almost here. Ginger said she gave Josette the menu when she needed a date, but apparently Josette never told her she actually *booked* anyone until earlier today."

"You boys better not be talking about me." Ginger slides her arm around Dylan's waist, and his goes around her shoulders.

I glare at her, trying to convey just what a shit situation she's put me in. It's not that I don't want to be out with Josette, because I do. I just don't want her to have paid for it. "Jesus, Ginger, you could have warned me Josette was my date tonight."

She sighs and tosses her long brown hair over her shoulder before offering an apologetic smile.

"Look, I didn't even know she had gone through with it until a couple hours before the party, and by then, it was too late for her to find another date. She needs this, Wade. Like, really, really needs it. She's been gunning for partner and working eighty-hour weeks. And they flat out told her she's not 'stable' enough because she hasn't settled down yet."

"Well, shit." I suspected as much given how they've been talking and acting, but for the assholes to actually *tell* her that to her face...

They have some fucking balls.

Though they are probably shriveled and wrinkly by this point.

Now I understand why she needed me so badly tonight. I just wish I were here with her under other circumstances. She looks fucking smokin' in that dress.

Chapter Four

JOSETTE

I'M NOT SURE WHAT GINGER and Dylan said to Wade, but when he seeks me out after their little powwow, any awkwardness that had existed between us seems to vanish the moment he put his arm around me.

The menu didn't lie.

"Lewis" can charm the pants off anyone, including the partners. He's gracious, flirty, friendly with everyone, and a grade-A schmoozer. He's also somehow managed to keep my temper from flaring while listening to the partners. It can only be winning me points, especially since he seems intent on spending his time lauding how amazing I am—in and out of the courtroom.

"The first time I saw Josette, she was arguing a summary judgment motion in front of Judge Cocher. It only took about two minutes of me witnessing the way she tore apart any argument the plaintiff tried to put forth before I was a goner. I think the only person more stunned than the judge was me."

He glances over at me with those damn bourbon eyes, and the flare of heat in their depths almost makes me believe he's telling the truth.

Stop it, Josette.

I force myself to take a half-step farther away from him. Just standing that close to him, feeling the heat radiating through his perfectly tailored tuxedo has me considering things good girls don't think about. He gets paid to give women attention and make them feel appreciated and loved. That's all this is.

Bill and Kevin chuckle at Wade's description and then turn their focus to me. "So how did he end up winning your heart, Josette?"

Well, shit.

Lying to my bosses about having a steady boyfriend is one thing, but delving too deep into any specifics of our "relationship" will only lead to future issues. I know what happens when people develop elaborate stories to try to cover up the truth. They fuck up. They get caught. They end up in deep shit. And sometimes in jail.

"Oh, you know, he charmed me with his briefs."

A round of drunken chuckles ensues, and Wade casts me a look that sends a ripple of warmth through my limbs, straight to my core.

And now I'm picturing him in tight as hell boxer briefs...with a massive bulge.

Shit.

At least it seems to satisfy the bosses, and they move back to grilling Wade about his law practice instead of his "love" for me. He launches into a discussion of his practice focus, and I release a sigh of relief. It seems the portion of the evening where they cross-examine us has concluded, and with no blood spilled. It couldn't have gone better. I don't think I've ever had a *real* boyfriend who was so gregarious and charming.

But this is going to be a *long* night now that I can't get the image of him undressed out of my head.

WADE

Christ.

How is it possible for Josette to have gotten more beautiful as the night went on?

It's not from the alcohol. I only had three drinks and was stone cold sober when we left the party. No, it's not from booze, it's because now I've actually spent time with her and know it's not just beauty on the outside.

There's always been something about her. But tonight, I finally figured out what it is. She's just real. There's no façade; there's no act; there's no different person in the courtroom in her real life. She's the same firecracker whether she's arguing a motion or discussing the latest episode of Law & Order with her work colleagues. And fuck if it isn't the sexiest thing I've ever seen.

Walking up the stairs to the small porch of her condo, I can't keep my eyes off the way her dress hugs her firm ass. I want nothing more than to take her inside and show her just how fucking gorgeous she really is.

And given the way she's been looking at me all night, I'm pretty sure she'd let me. But then again, it's been a while since I've been alone with a woman who wasn't paying for my company.

Isn't that a bitch...

Josette pauses at the door and turns to face me. "Thanks for tonight, Wade. I know it can't have been comfortable for you."

It certainly wasn't easy on my cock. I must have had a raging hard-on for about half the night.

I grin at her and take a step closer. "I have no idea what you're talking about. I had an amazing time with you this evening."

She quirks an eyebrow at me, and I close the distance between us until we're a mere hairsbreadth apart. I lean in, intent to show her just what a great time I really had, but her hand on my chest stops me. She backs away a step until her body is pressed against the door.

"What the hell are you doing?" Her ice-cold eyes are nothing like the warm pools I've been swimming in all night.

Seriously?

I thought it would be obvious.

"Kissing you."

I don't even see it coming, just feel the sharp sting of her slap across my left cheek.

My hand instinctively moves up to cover my tingling flesh. "What the hell was that for?"

Red colors her cheeks, and her fists clench and unclench at her sides. "You're a real asshole, Wade. I can't believe you thought I would pay you to have sex with me."

Wait, what?

I'm so stunned by her accusation that, by the time I gather my thoughts enough to reply, she's already inside and slams the door in my face. I stare at the dark brown wood of the door for several moments, trying to get my head around what she said.

What the hell just happened?

How could she not understand that tonight was genuine, and that I actually like her—a lot. This was never about the payment—well, at least not once I knew she was my date for the night.

I guess it doesn't matter. All she sees me as is a fucking whore.

Chapter Five

WADE

S HE WON'T EVEN LOOK AT me. Twenty minutes of sitting across from each other in the courtroom, waiting for our cases to be called, and not once has she bothered to even glance over here.

As far as she's concerned, I don't exist.

I get paid to sleep with some of the most beautiful and classiest women in Chicago, but the only one I want won't even look at me. Because I'm a whore.

This is the first time in almost two years I really feel slimy about what I've been doing.

And ain't that a bitch.

"Wheaton vs. First State Insurance Company, case number 17L205."

My case being called finally breaks what was probably a little bit of creepy staring at Josette. The scheduling conference should only last five minutes.

But I can't manage to avoid checking Josette out from the corner of my eye while I'm at counsel's table.

I catch her watching me at least once. That's a good sign, right? It offers me a little hope that she might hear me out. All I'm hoping for is for her to give me a chance to explain myself and what happened Saturday night. I don't think that's asking for much, but given the cold shoulder she's giving me today, I may have my work cut out for me.

When I finish my case and turn my eyes to meet hers, she blushes then looks down at a paper on her lap and scribbles furiously.

Probably something about what a big douche I am—definitely not "I love Wade Saxon" with little hearts doodled around it.

Instead of leaving, like I should, to get back to the office and do some actual work, I pop a squat on the bench outside the courtroom and wait. I'm gonna make Josette talk to me no matter how much she may be trying to avoid it.

I can't go through another night like the last two. I've barely slept—thankfully, not because I had a date last night, though. Jason wasn't happy when I cancelled my Sunday "social engagement." But after Saturday night, there's no way I could do it. My mind replays what happened on Josette's front steps on a constant loop. It's pretty much all I've been able to think about, so putting on a game face to go out with another woman, and potentially have to fuck her, just wasn't happening.

How could it have gone so horribly wrong with Josette?

I thought I'd made it pretty clear throughout the evening how much I liked her, how attracted to her I was.

Maybe my game is off?

It's possible I've grown rusty in the whole "assessing a woman's interest" thing in the last two years. But I could have *sworn* she was reciprocating with the flirting.

Maybe she's just being cautious. If that's it, then I can't say I really blame her. She doesn't know me, not really. All she knows is she paid for a date with "Lewis," and I showed up on her doorstep. But her aggressive reaction to my attempt to kiss her Saturday night just doesn't sit well with me. That was more than being cautious. That was flat-out anger. And Josette is *not* a woman I want mad at me.

I've seen her chew up and spit out attorneys who have been doing this for forty years like it was nothing. That earned her my respect well before we ever met. A confident woman who doesn't let the old boys' club mentality of the Cook County Courts intimidate her deserves admiration. The fact that she's breathtakingly beautiful is only an added bonus.

Fuck.

Why didn't I ask her out? Why didn't I make a move?

Because she's older, more experienced, and I thought she certainly had a man wrapped around her finger. It may be too little, too late. But she needs to know how pure my intentions were...not that I didn't want to get her in bed, but that wasn't my goal. I just wanted to get to know her and be close to her. She needs to know my interest is real. She needs to know how totally and completely wrong she was. She needs to understand the truth.

JOSETTE

Of all the goddamn courtrooms in Cook County, he has to be in the same one as me this morning.

Fate is one mean bitch.

All I want to do is get through my motion, get the fuck out of here, deny I ever saw him, and forget everything that happened Saturday night.

Jesus...

I can't believe he thought I would pay him for sex.

What an asshole.

I managed to avoid looking at him while we waited for our cases, but once he was on the record, and I heard that low, gravelly voice, my eyes flicked over to him of their own accord.

Of fucking course he caught me looking, too. The heat spreading across my face only confirmed for him that I'd been scoping him out.

How embarrassing. He doesn't deserve my attention, not after what he did.

It's time to push him to the back of my mind, once and for all, so I can concentrate on my work again.

My motion goes smoothly despite my inability to get Wade out of my mind, no matter how much I try. Another mark in the win column. I'm going to need as many of those as possible if I want the partners to forget the fact that Wade isn't a part of my life anymore.

I fly out the door of the courtroom with plans to hightail it back to the office, but instead, I come face-to-face with Wade sitting across the hall just staring at me.

Goddammit.

Why does he have to look so damn good in a suit?

And be such an amazing lawyer—competent and passionate in the court room. All it does is make me think about how those skills will transfer into the bedroom.

Why? Why? Why? Why?

And why the hell do I have to be attracted to him?

This would be so much easier if he were ugly. And dumb.

But he is a jerk.

He climbs to his feet, his perfectly tailored suit moving with him, clinging in all the right places. "Josette, we need to talk."

I walk past him without a pause. If I linger even a second, it will mean the end of my resolve. "There's nothing to talk about, Attorney Saxon."

His footsteps follow me down the marble hallway. "There most certainly is. We clearly had a misunderstanding on Saturday."

Misunderstanding, my ass!

Fighting my natural instinct to look back at him when I reply is nearly impossible, but somehow, I manage. "No, there wasn't. It was perfectly clear what happened."

He grabs my elbow to stop me and turns me to face him. I'm tempted to slap him again, but there are people bustling up and down the hallway, including several other lawyers who are now eyeing us speculatively.

"Will you stop litigating for a second and just listen to me?"

His eyes plead with me, and despite my anger, I can't find it in my heart to say no to him.

Pushover.

Something about him draws me, like a moth to a flame. He will burn me, no doubt, but I need to at least give him a chance to say whatever it is he wants to tell me. If I don't, he'll never leave me alone, and this awkward tension between us will linger for the remainder of our careers. It could make for some very uncomfortable days in court.

So, with reluctance, I nod. "Fine. But not here. Meet me at my place at seven tonight."

We'll put an end to this nonsense then.

Chapter Six

WADE

MY STOMACH IS LODGED IN my throat before I even knock on her door. Standing in the exact spot she slapped me Saturday night makes me second-guess the wisdom of being here.

I've never been nervous for a paid date, a motion hearing, hell, even a trial, but this woman has me tied in knots.

The three raps of my knuckles against the door sound more like a foreboding warning instead of announcement of my presence.

Shit. Pull yourself together.

Thirty seconds feels like five minutes, but the door finally opens.

Her icy blue eyes are wary, but she moves aside to allow me in without a word. I follow her and force myself to keep my eyes on our surroundings instead of her ass in the tight yoga pants plastered against her skin.

She's trying to kill me.

The moment she steps into the den, she bee-lines for the small bar in the corner. "Want a drink?'

Hell, yes.

"Uh, sure." Alcohol will probably help numb the inevitable pain this conversation will bring.

She holds up a bottle of Maker's Mark. "Bourbon good?"

I smile and nod. She even has decent booze. Could she be any more perfect for me? "Perfect."

With her back to me, it's impossible to tell what she might be thinking. But if it's anything like my current thoughts, it's a cluster of about a thousand different things. I want to tell her everything—why I started doing this, how I've been wanting out and just didn't realize it, how she was...*is* different. But I have no idea where or how to start.

Every way I've gone over it in my head sounds wrong. How can you make a woman like Josette understand taking money for sex?

She turns back to me and hands me a glass. I raise it in a silent toast before I take a sip. The spicy heat burns my throat in the best way possible and gives me an excuse to take a couple moments to gather my thoughts.

After an awkward minute, Josette drops onto the couch and watches me expectantly. "You wanted to talk, so talk."

I release a sigh and run my free hand back through my hair, considering my words. "I think you got the wrong idea on Saturday. I wasn't coming on to you because you paid for my company. I was coming on to you because I like you."

She pauses with her drink halfway up to her mouth and frowns, a crease forming in her forehead. I'd give anything to know what she's thinking right now.

"How can you expect me to believe that? You're just saying it now because we have to see each other professionally and don't want it to be weird."

The words are said with such conviction, it's clear she really believes what she said. Exactly what I feared.

"Not true." I move toward where she sits on the couch but stop a few feet away, not wanting to crowd her or make her feel uncomfortable. "I noticed you the first time you came into the courtroom when I was a newbie. I just figured a woman like you would be taken, so I never approached you."

Something I'm deeply regretting right now.

Her eyes sharpen and narrow on me, and she rises from the couch. "I don't believe you. You lie for a living, Wade, and I bet you're pretty damn good at it."

JOSETTE

He recoils slightly at my words, but I didn't say anything I don't believe to be true. A good lawyer can convince someone of anything. And Wade is a *great* lawyer. I need to be on guard at all times around this man. If I'm not careful, he'll weasel his way past my carefully constructed barriers and get to me in a way I can't fight.

When he closes the distance between us, my first instinct is to step back. But I don't, because I'm apparently a glutton for punishment. And being this close to Wade Saxon is pure agony on my neglected libido. The same musky, masculine scent he wore on Saturday envelops me again.

It's like pure sex.

And it's not fair, not at all.

His hand slides over mine, and he takes my glass from me. After setting both glasses on the end table, he returns to stand in front of me, his whiskey colored eyes burning into mine, but not with anger, with something much more dangerous.

"Does this feel like a lie?"

Before I even have time to react, his lips are on mine, kissing away any ability to form coherent thought or voice any protest.

Not that I *would* protest.

It's not a kiss. No. It's more of an all-out assault on my mouth and my senses. His tongue seeks entry, and, instead of stopping him, I moan against his lips and open for him. Because, *Christ,* Wade can fucking kiss.

Our bodies surge together, and his very real interest presses against my stomach. *Jesus, it's been too long.* And he feels so damn good.

Just as quickly as it started, he pulls away and steps back.

What?

My eyes fly open and meet his. They blaze at me, but he keeps his distance. "Tell me you don't believe I really want you, and I'll go."

I drive my hands back through my hair and tug on the ends in frustration. "Oh, I believe you want me. That's not a problem."

That's not the problem at all.

Confusion flits across his face. "Then what is?"

Well, he asked...

"Besides the fact that I work so much I don't have time for a relationship? How about the fact that you're a prostitute?"

He recoils harder than when I slapped him on Saturday night. I instantly regret using that word, but that's what he is, isn't it? He dates and sleeps with women for money. What else could I call it?

His eyes close, and he takes several deep breaths. I've never seen him rattled in the courtroom, but my words have clearly thrown him. After a moment, he sighs. "That's not what I do. I mean, yes, I sleep with women who pay for my company occasionally, but the vast majority of my dates are just lonely women who want someone to spend time with. You're the first one I've ever really wanted to be with. I never expected to feel so dirty for doing this because it never affected my life before. I just needed to do this to keep my firm afloat."

My questions about his car and financial situation loom again.

"Yeah, we never really got around to talking about that. How the hell did you end up working at Made to Order, anyway?"

He sighs and runs a hand back to his hair again. "Well, when I went to law school, it was with the intent to go to work for my grandfather's firm when I graduated. He had a very successful practice, and I used to help there during summers. But the old man died six weeks before I graduated. Instead of inheriting his firm and clients, or even part of his estate, all I got was his sports car and all the rest of his estate and money were donated to Northwestern Law School. He left me a letter saying that he had built his firm from the ground up and it made him a better lawyer and that's what he wanted me to do. And I tried, I really did, but I just didn't have the number of clients I needed to pay my overhead. This is an expensive town. My buddies from college own Made to Order and offered to let me come to work for them. I thought it sounded fun."

I cringe at the admission.

"And it was fun for a while. It's not anymore."

My heart wars with my common sense. I believe him, but that doesn't change the situation. I may be able to eventually forget what he did. We all have pasts, after all. But it sounds like he needs to keep doing this. "Are you saying you want to give it all up to be with me? After one date? One that I paid for?"

Chapter Seven

WADE

D O I WANT TO GIVE *it up? The money? What will I do with the firm? What will happen to Made to Order? They need the income as much as I do.*

A thousand questions race through my head. But there's only one answer.

I reach out for her and tug her against me. "Yes."

Her eyes widen, and she pulls her lower lip under her teeth for a moment before releasing it. "Really?"

A storm rages in the blue depths, and I know it will take some time to convince her things with us are different. But I'm willing to put in the time and the effort. She's fucking worth it. I just hope she gives me the chance to show her how serious I am.

Made to Order is my past. She's my present and future.

Finally.

No more waiting. I kiss her, pouring everything I want to say into the single action. Her tongue tangles with mine, and this time, her fingers curl into my shirt, and she drags me even closer. Whatever reservations she may have had, they seem to have been supplanted by the fire burning between us, at least for the time being.

My hands slide down her small frame until I'm gripping her thighs. She doesn't need any encouragement. She jumps up and wraps her legs around my waist, grinding her core against my rock-hard cock.

Sweet fuck...

I don't want to tear my lips from hers, give her any reason to stop doing what she's doing to me. But there's information I need. Important information. So, I pry myself away from her. Her eyes fly open and search mine.

"Bedroom?" I grin at her, and she laughs, nodding her head backward toward a hallway behind her.

It's all the direction I need.

Every step I take toward her bedroom crushes my cock against her heat. Even through our clothes, it's scorching. I can't remember the last time I wanted a woman this badly. The last two years have made me forget what it's like to truly *want* someone. It's a heady mix of unrestrained lust and uncontrollable frenzy.

I stumble halfway down the hall, our kiss fogging my head and making walking nearly impossible. Pushing her against the wall seems like the best course of action if I want to stay on my feet. Although, the floor of the hallway would work for what I have in mind...maybe a bit tough on the knees, though.

Wall seems to be the lesser of two evils, plus it's closer.

She gasps when her back hits the drywall, and she breaks our kiss to pull back and look at me. "Why'd you stop?"

"Because I can't wait another ten feet to be inside you."

JOSETTE

His words, along with the friction against my clit from his walk down the hallway, almost have me coming on the spot.

I don't know if it's just been too long since I've had sex, or if it's because of the way Wade throws me off balance, but any reservations I had about being with him have flown the coop. It's probably not smart. As a lawyer, I should be more analytical. But I'm sick of analyzing Wade and his motives.

The only thing that matters right now is my very wet pussy and his very hard cock. Everything else can wait until later.

My hands move to the button of his jeans in a split-second, and his mouth descends on mine again.

Dammit.

Why are these damn buttons so fucking hard to unhook?

He chuckles against my lips and pushes me harder into the wall with his chest before moving his hands down to assist me. I clutch his hips between my thighs until his palms return to support my thighs.

Lips connect with the heated skin on my neck, and I grind against him. He sucks against the throbbing pulse there, and a bolt of electricity shoots straight to my clit.

One of his hands moves down to the waistband of my yoga pants. "We need to get these off you."

I nod my agreement and wiggle my hips to assist him as he pulls the fabric down my thighs.

My feet fall to the floor just long enough for him to bend and fully remove them and then shove his jeans and boxers down before I'm back up and pressed against the wall with his mouth on mine. The length of his dick presses against the very thin material of my thong. I reach down and capture it in my hand.

Holy hell.

I know I haven't seen or felt a dick in a long time, but this is far from average. Not that anything about Wade is. Just the thought of having this hunk of meat inside me has my core pulsing and clenching.

He groans against my lips then moves his mouth across my cheek to my ear. "God, Jo, you are so fucking beautiful. You're driving me crazy."

My lips find his ear, and I lick around the lobe, savoring the twitch of his cock in my hand and the shudder that rolls through his body. "Ditto, counselor."

"Fuck!" He pulls his head back and takes my face in his hand. "Say that again."

"Say what?"

He grins and tilts my head back, then presses his lips to mine. "Call me counselor."

The giggle tumbles from my mouth, and I can barely get the words out. "Whatever you want, counselor."

With a chuckle, he pulls back slightly and quirks an eyebrow at me. How the hell does he make that look so damn sexy? "Whatever I want? That's a dangerous statement, Attorney Westmore."

Chapter Eight

WADE

JOSETTE'S BREATH CATCHES, AND SHE gulps. Watching her throat contract has my cock jumping in her grip again. All I can think about is what it will feel like to have her swallowing my dick and my cum.

Christ.

If I don't get myself under control, this will be over before it even starts. Control has never been an issue for me. At least, not since I was a teenager. But Josette seems to hold a power over me. And I'm happy to let her wield it.

I urge her to set her feet on the floor again then jerk my shirt off over my head. She takes the hint and pulls off her tank top, letting her perfect breasts sway freely.

Oh...fuck me...

They call to me like beacons in the night, but I force myself to bend down to snatch a condom from my jeans. The last thing I expected was to be using one tonight, but in my profession—at least the now-former secondary one—I need to have them at the ready at all times. I've never been so happy to be prepared.

Her eyes follow my hand, and then she glances down the hallway. "Are you sure you don't want to go to the—"

My mouth on hers silences the question. Yes, we will make it to the bedroom...eventually.

But not now.

I push the condom into her hand and hook my fingers into her panties. *Fuck.* They're soaked. If there was any question about whether she wanted me as much as I want her, these are proof she needs it as badly as I do.

While I drag them down her legs, she tears the package open. There's no way I can resist having her pussy right in front of my face. As much as I want my cock buried inside her, I want to taste her more.

She uses her free hand to tug on my arm, encouraging me back up, but I ignore the gesture, instead focusing all my attention on the beauty before me.

The carpet matches the drapes.

And fuck, she is beautiful.

With an approving groan, I lean in and press on her thighs, urging her to spread them wider. She complies, and I waste no time diving in and slipping my tongue into her wet heat.

Jesus fucking Christ.

It's like I'm a thirsty man stranded in the desert who finally found a fucking oasis. And I can't drink enough. My tongue probes and flicks, and her whimpers assure me I'm doing something right. Fingers dig into my scalp, and she pleads. "Please...Wade...I need..."

"What?" My murmur against her heated flesh sends her writhing against the wall. "Tell me."

"I need to come."

Don't we all...

As much as I want to feel her come apart against my mouth and on my tongue, I don't want to tease her any longer. It's time for both of us to get what we want. And that's only going to happen once my cock is buried deep inside her pussy.

Slowly, I rise to my feet, letting my tongue trail across her hips, over her flat stomach, and up to her pointed nipples. I grin at her wide-eyed stare and suck one into my mouth. She bucks and her hand finds my hard flesh again. Her fingers roll the condom down my straining cock, every touch along the sensitive skin pushing me closer to the edge of my control.

When her hand circles the root of my dick and she uses it to tug me against her core, the sound that tumbles from my lips is more animal than human.

I reach down and slide my hands under her ass, helping her get her legs up and wrapped around my waist again. She reaches down and aligns my cock with her swollen pussy, and with one thrust of my hips, I impale her, slamming her back against the wall.

"Oh...God..." The words tumble from both our lips in unison.

So fucking tight...wet...hot...no, scorching.

Instead of pulling out and driving into her like a madman, which is precisely what every fucking atom of my being is begging me to do, I pause. Her eyes fly open, and her nails dig into the back of my neck. "What are you doing? Go!" She flexes her cunt around my cock, almost as if to spur me into action.

"I'm savoring the moment, darling. Don't worry, I plan on very thoroughly fucking you."

JOSETTE

Thoroughly fucked sounds like Heaven right now, but I'm in Hell. Because he...isn't...moving.

I squeeze his cock and rock my hips, dig my nails into his skin, and press my lips against his...*anything* to get him moving again. His mouth on my pussy almost made me come undone, but he stopped just short of my release, and now, he's torturing me with his cock.

It stretches and fills me completely. The sweet burn of his intrusion was quickly replaced with the thundering need to be hammered...hard.

I've never been one to desire the rough and fast kind of sex. Slow and sweet has always been more my style. But not with Wade. And if he doesn't fuck me soon, I may kill him. At least if I get an understanding female jury, I can get an acquittal based on justifiable homicide.

Just GO!

Our tongues tangle—almost fighting each other for control. I don't know who wins, but finally, *sweet Lord, finally*, he pulls back and then shoves into me again.

My head smacking against the hard wall at my back should probably bother me, but with Wade's hips slamming against mine while he pumps into me, there is nothing but pleasure.

His cock stretches me, and the head of his amazing dick drags against just the right spot with every thrust and retreat.

I dig my nails into his shoulders and my heels into his ass, driving him deeper with every thrust. The hot flutter of his breath against my neck makes me shudder around him. He finds my pulse point again and sucks in rhythm with his hips.

Holy shit.

The orgasm that was building while his mouth was at my core surges back to life. My thighs burn from clutching his wildly driving hips, but it's nothing compared to the burn in my veins when I finally come. Wildfire rages through my body and fireworks explode behind my eyelids.

He groans against my neck. "Jesus fucking Christ..."

Then he pulls his head back, and his forehead drops against mine. He continues to pump into me while my core milks his cock. Just as I'm starting to regain my sense and return from the incredible hazy high of my orgasm, he groans and shoves into me—hard and deep—and comes.

Chapter Nine

WE DID EVENTUALLY MAKE IT to the bedroom. And three rounds later, Josette passed out and I quickly followed.

The soft light seeping in through the partially opened blinds finally forces my eyes open. It's been years since I woke up next to a woman. That was always a rule—no sleepovers. They could have me as many times and as many ways as they wanted, but I always went home and slept in my own bed. Now, there's no place I'd rather be than right where I am, in Josette's.

Right here.

My fingers itch to touch her blonde hair splayed across the pillow, but my left-hand lays precariously close to her exposed breast. Tough choice. My cock is also screaming at me to make a repeat performance of last night.

Instead of teasing her nipples like I want to, so damn much, I drag my arm off her chest and slowly push the sheet down until her entire body is exposed in the hazy morning sunshine. Despite my throbbing cock, my focus right now is her.

I want her to fall apart again. I need to taste her.

The sheets shift as I slowly slide down until I'm in the prime position to give her the perfect wakeup. She stirs slightly when I use my palms to spread her legs open, but she doesn't wake. Her flesh is faintly swollen from last night's activities. I'll have to be gentle.

No problem. I can do gentle.

The first taste of her this morning is just as incredible as it was last night. I slip my tongue along her pink folds, and she moans and shifts, opening her legs even wider for me.

"Am I dreaming right now?" Her voice is low and husky, and fuck if it isn't the sexiest thing I've ever heard.

"Hmmm." I hum against her clit in response, and her body jerks. Her hands find my head, and she pushes down, urging me to continue my early morning explorations. I probe into her pussy with my tongue while my thumb rubs slow circles around her clit.

She bucks and whimpers, digging her fingers in my hair and tugging. Now that she's good and wet, I work my way back up while slipping two fingers inside her.

Curling my fingers into her upper wall elicits a strangled gasp from her, and her entire body shudders under me. "Yes, right there."

With a groan, she shifts and begins thrusting her hips in time with my sucking lips and pumping fingers. My own hips rock instinctively, and I send up a silent prayer I don't come all over the sheets before I can get inside her.

It won't take much longer. Her thighs are already quivering, and her breathing is nothing more than desperate pants.

"Wade...fuck...I...I'm gonna come."

She wasn't kidding. When her orgasm hits her, she bows up off the bed, driving herself against my face while her pussy grips and shudders around my fingers. My cock throbs so hard, I almost come at the sensation of her falling apart around me.

There isn't anywhere in the world I'd rather be than right here.

Hands shove at my head, forcing me away from her, and I look up. From her position propped up on her elbows, she assesses me with lust-glazed eyes.

"Well, that was a new way to wake up."

I shift up and climb over her until she relaxes back into the mattress. "Mmm, good new way?"

Her laughter bubbles up and makes my heart race.

Such a beautiful fucking sound.

My hard cock presses against her drenched core. She shifts and rocks until the entire length is coated in her release.

"Great way. But now I need to ensure you're awake too."

JOSETTE

His responding grin clears the remaining post-orgasmic fog from my head. I never got to taste him last night. We were too busy fucking like rabbits to really slow down and enjoy a thorough exploration of each other. That was fine, but now, I want nothing more than to suck his cock and watch him fall apart.

I reach around his hips and urge him up. "Come up here."

As he shifts up, his cock drags across my sensitive clit, causing a shudder to roll through me. He chuckles and settles his knees outside my shoulders, placing him in the perfect spot for me to explore and savor him.

My first lick down his cock causes a litany of curses to tumble from his puffy lips. That mouth is so damn talented—in the courtroom and the bedroom. A silver tongue for sure.

He moves his hands up to the headboard and grips it so tightly, the creak echoes in the room. I've barely touched him, and he's already struggling for control.

A + work, Josette.

His dick is this hard just from going down on me and getting *me* off. That's a real boost for a girl's ego.

I wrap my hand around the base of his cock and concentrate my attentions to the head. Swirling, licking, sucking, I drive him to the brink before I back off and blow lightly across the wet, throbbing flesh.

The headboard creaks again, and I glance up to find him drilling me with dark, lust-filled eyes. His jaw is clenched so tightly, I'm afraid he may crack a tooth.

With just the tip of my tongue, I work my way up and down his entire length...over...and over...and over...until his muscular thighs shake next to my ears. I grasp his balls in one hand and work them while I wrap the flat of my tongue around his length and wet him root to tip.

"Jesus...fuck, Jo."

Torturing him is fun, but I would rather watch him come than play with him anymore.

Without breaking eye contact, I open my mouth and slowly suck him down —inch by glorious inch—until the head of his cock bumps against the back of my throat. I don't have a gag reflex, so when he groans, shuts his eyes, and sucks in a breath, I know my next move will send him over the edge.

And I will enjoy watching every moment of it.

I wait a few seconds until his eyes open and meet mine again, and then I tilt my head back and swallow, letting the muscles of my throat milk his release from him.

"Holy motherfucking...shit!" His orgasm hits him, and he shoves his dick even further down my throat in tight, sharp thrusts. I grasp his ass and hold him steady as he spills down my throat with his eyes clenched shut.

When he's finally spent, he groans and slowly withdraws from my mouth. Those hazy amber eyes find mine, and I grin and lick my lips.

"What...the hell...was that?" The question comes between panted breaths, and I can't stop the laughter from bubbling up from my chest.

He leans down until we're practically sharing oxygen, but stops short of kissing me.

"Seriously, Jo, that was..." He sucks in and releases a deep breath and then shakes his head slowly. "The most incredible thing I've ever experienced in my entire life."

I quirk an eyebrow at him and grin. "Oh, was it? I just call that a Morning Alarm Clock."

Chapter Ten

WADE

"**I**F THAT'S HOW YOU PLAN on waking me up every morning, then I'm moving in today."

What?

"You want to move in?"

I shake my head and grin. "It was just a joke. I'm not trying to rush anything. All I wanted was for you to give me a chance to prove to you that *you* are what I want, nothing and no one else. As long as I've done that, I'm happy where we are."

One corner of her mouth tips up as she tries, unsuccessfully, to conceal a smirk. "While I do think it's a bit early to be discussing living arrangements, I'm willing to admit I may be enjoying your company...a little."

"A little?"

Liar.

She can't maintain her straight face any longer and breaks into a grin. "A tiny bit."

I shift so my growing erection presses between her legs and she groans. "Tiny?"

Her hands thread into my hair, and she pulls my lips down to hers. "Minuscule."

A thrust and roll of my hips elicits a moan from her. I capture it with my mouth. She kisses me back and removes one hand from my head to shove it between our bodies. When her fingers curl around my cock, I grunt against her lips.

She grasps me with a firm grip and strokes the length of my shaft—up and down, up and down, up and down—until I'm practically humping her hand.

No, not like this.

"Stop." I jerk my hips back and grab her wrist to still her hand.

A knowing smile spreads across her face. "What?"

"I'm not coming in your hand. I'm coming inside you. It can be another morning tradition."

She giggles as I lean over to the nightstand to grab a condom. The pile of empty wrappers makes me smile to myself. And to think, a week ago, I was complaining about too much sex.

Never again.

As long as it's with her, I'll have sex a hundred times a day.

I suit myself up in record time while she lays back looking epically breath-taking in the early morning light.

How am I ever going to be able to look at her in court again without picturing her like this? I'll have a perpetual hard-on.

"Turn over. On your knees."

Her eyes twinkle, and I think she's about to challenge me, but, instead, she licks her lips and flips over. When she raises her luscious ass into the air toward me, I have to bite my lip to keep from saying something very ungentlemanly. That's for the future. I can't scare her off now with talk of backdoor encounters.

I settle behind her and press my cock between her thighs, against the wet heat of her pussy. She shudders and shimmies further back, brushing my length against her clit.

"Mmm."

We did hot and heavy and hard last night. This morning, I want to give her long, slow, and torturously sweet.

JOSETTE

He presses the head of his cock against my core and grips my hips. Instead of shoving into me hard, he ever so slowly eases his way in—inch by glorious inch.

"Holy fuck." In this position, he's longer, thicker, and deeper...so much deeper. He drags out gradually and sets an unhurried pace.

The languid drag of his cock is wholly unexpected after last night's hard and fast sessions, but *damn* does it feel incredible.

So fucking good.

I clutch the pillows between my forearms and press my cheek flat against the mattress, angling my ass even higher and shifting his position slightly.

"Fuck yes!" He leans an arm down next to me and lowers his chest against my back. His warm breath flutters the hair hanging around my face. Fingers brush it away from my ear, and he slowly sucks the lobe between his lips before kissing my neck and retreating.

The long, lazy thrusts start a gradual building heat that spreads out from where we're connected. His fingers dig into my hips harder, and I know he's hanging on to his restraint by a thin thread.

He wants to unleash, but he's holding back to give me what he thinks I need.

But what I need is for this orgasm to come, not linger on the edges just out of reach.

"Go!"

There's a slight stutter in his rhythm at my words, but then he groans and slams back into me with enough force to rock me forward on the bed.

Yes!

It doesn't take long for my orgasm to wash over me like a tidal wave. I cry out and clench around his cock. Four deep, hard strokes later, he follows me over the edge.

He collapses next to me and drags me onto my side, pressing his chest to my back.

"Wow." It's the only word I can manage to get out.

He barks out a laugh and rolls me onto my back before pushing up on one elbow. "I concur, counselor."

I giggle, and he catches it with his lips, sucking out any breath I have left with the passion in his kiss.

Damn.

This man has managed to work his way into my heart in a matter of days. I just hope I'm not making a tremendous mistake.

He pulls back and frowns. "What just happened?"

"What do you mean?"

A hand moves forward to brush some hair away from my face. "You were here, then you were gone."

Shit.

I don't want to tell him what I was thinking. I've hurt him with my words enough already. But it seems I don't need to voice my concerns.

He drops his forehead against mine and presses a chaste kiss to my lips. "I'm done with that, Jo. I'm calling Jason today and telling him I'm retired, okay. It's just you and me from now on."

You and me.

No sweeter words have ever been spoken. Although, if things continue down this road, I may be hearing the word "partner" said soon.

"You know, we are going to need a story about how we met."

He grins and shakes his head. "No, we don't. What I said at the party was true. You blew me away in the courtroom and caught my attention. We just won't mention the way you blow me away in the bedroom, too."

"So, you're done with Made to Order for good?"

He shakes his head, and my heart sinks a little. "No, what if we need some filet mignon?"

Thank you for reading *Made to Order*. I hope you enjoyed Wade and Jo's story. For more from Gwyn, make sure you're signed up for her newsletter here: www.gwynmcnamee.com/newsletter and check out her website here: www. gwynmcnamee.com.

About the Author

Gwyn McNamee is an attorney, writer, wife, and mother (to one human baby and one fur baby). Originally from the Midwest, Gwyn relocated to her husband's home town of Las Vegas in 2015. Gwyn has been writing down her crazy stories and ideas for years and finally decided to share them with the world. She loves to write stories with a bit of suspense and action mingled with romance and heat. When she isn't either writing or voraciously devouring any books she can get her hands on, Gwyn is busy adding to her tattoo collection, golfing, and stirring up trouble with her perfect mix of sweetness and sarcasm (usually while wearing heels). Gwyn loves to hear from her readers. Find her here:

Newsletter: www.gwynmcnamee.com/newsletter
Website: http://www.gwynmcnamee.com/
FB Reader Group: bit.ly/GwynMcNameeRG
Facebook: bit.ly/GwynMcNameeFB
Tiktok: bit.ly/TikTokGM
Instagram: bit.ly/GwynMcNameeIG
Twitter: bit.ly/GwynMcNameeTwitter
Goodreads: bit.ly/GwynMcNameeGR
Bookbub: bit.ly/GwynMcNameeBB

Forbidden Fruit

Scarlett Finn

Chapter One

B ROGAN CHASE.

She swallowed.

Of all the men her husband could've brought to their bed, why did it have to be Brogan Chase? He wasn't the first and wouldn't be the last. This one, this guy, stung. Fate wasn't smiling on her. Not that it ever did. But this joke was cruel.

Her past. Her present. Her fantasy and reality. Further evidence that her life wasn't her own.

Sitting on the padded bench in the middle of the closet, she listened. As always. Kept her ears open to the men in the adjoining bedroom waiting for her cue.

"What the fuck is this, Manzani?" Brogan Chase demanded.

"Your debt."

"You need me in your bedroom to settle our debt? No fucking way, old man. Whatever you got in mind, you can go fuck yourself."

"That's how you talk to me? We made a deal."

"Yeah, one I'm starting to regret," Brogan snapped.

"Then I'll call the cops and have him arrested."

"You? The cops?" he snickered. "I don't fucking think so."

"Trust me, Chase," Silvio Manzani said, his voice deep and emotionless. "Pray I call the cops. 'Cause if I deal with this the Manzani way..." Silence lingered a few seconds. "You took on Chico's debt so I wouldn't slit him open. You going back on your word?"

"No, but I won't scratch any itch for you either, old man."

"Don't be so quick to judge."

"What are you—"

The light in the bedroom dimmed, cutting Brogan off. Her cue. Rising, she touched the single knot in the belt of her silk robe. The sheer white fabric clung to her skin, leaving little to the imagination. The demonstration proved her body was for the pleasure of men, her face didn't matter.

The first time her fingers had curled around the closet door to step out and perform her designated role, her heart had pounded while anxiety raged. Since then, she'd been numb to her husband's expectations. Until then anyway. There, in that moment, her pulse thumped hard, like her heart begged escape.

Brogan Chase.

By the door, probably ready to run.

Silvio had his back to her, but he'd know she was there. She behaved and fulfilled her role every time he demanded compliance.

Beneath Brogan's low brows, there was definitely a flicker of surprise. "Ma'am," he said in acknowledgement of her before switching the scowl to Silvio. "We'll finish this later."

"Don't forget who you're talking to," Silvio said, sauntering past Brogan to lock the bedroom door. "Go sit on the bed."

"What the fuck is—"

"Sit on the fucking bed or tell Chico's mom why she's burying her son."

Climbing onto the bed, she crawled to the center on her knees and waited. That was her job. To be available as her husband demanded. Boy was it a role she'd learned well.

"The bed? What kind of shit is this?"

"You afraid of a beautiful woman?" Silvio asked, familiar superiority dripping from his mocking words. "She's a quarter your size. You could snap her like a twig." Her husband's eyes cut to her. "Could be a game for later."

Like clockwork, she provided the expected smile. She didn't ever look right at him; it wasn't allowed. She'd learned to absorb a lot even while her chin was low.

Silvio Manzani could do anything he wanted. With her. With any woman. Any man too. Except possibly Brogan Chase.

"I'm not afraid of the woman, but I ain't here for your entertainment."

"She's here for yours," Silvio said, strolling to the wingback chair by the fireplace.

The chair that faced into the room, faced the bed.

"Can't please your own woman?"

"Go sit on the bed and you'll find out why you're here. Ask one more question or object again and you won't get another chance." Silvio took a cigar from his pocket and clipped the end. "My men are tailing Chico as we speak. If I call 'em home, they'll bring a body with them."

On a nasal inhale, Brogan came and sat on the edge, his back to her. Like she didn't exist. Maybe she didn't. Wasn't like she'd never considered the possibility. Maybe she'd died in some horrific and bloody accident and this was her hell. Why did Brogan Chase have to be in her hell?

"Dolly."

And that was her cue. Damn. Did it have to be him?

It had been a long time since she'd been nervous. The flutter in her chest, the tension that bordered on panic, proved she was still capable. Not a welcome reminder. That wouldn't help her do her job.

Clearing her mind, she exhaled. That was it. Life. Breathe. In. Out.

On her knees, she went to him, touching the back of his neck with a fingertip. Tracing it around, she settled next to him, leaning in as her finger went lower.

The body beneath that warm fabric was hard. She could feel the line of his pec, the ridges of his abdomen and just as she reached the buckle of his belt—

He snatched her wrist. The slap and grip jolted her. Surprise? Fear? No. Her breath caught as her lips parted. Arousal.

How was it possible?

"What is this shit?" Brogan demanded, but not of her. Tossing her arm aside, he shot to his feet. "I don't need to pay for it."

"She does," Silvio said. "She doesn't earn her way here, she's put on the open market. You want that on your conscience as well as your cousin's death?" Pause. "Sit your ass down and let the woman work."

Another huff, but he did sit down. What did he want? What got a guy like Brogan Chase off? Strong, confident, he wasn't the type of guy women could miss. For the first time in that bedroom, she wanted to impress. Wanted a man, this man, to feel her, see her. He wouldn't. They never did. She was an instrument in her husband's orchestra, a weapon in his arsenal. A thing, an object. Not a person, a robot, programmed to achieve a singular aim.

Slipping her palm down his body, her own curiosity thrummed. This time when she got to his belt buckle, he let her continue. On an inhale, his chest expanded as she cradled his length concealed in denim. This was a man in control. But she'd done this too many times before.

Massaging his cock woke it to her. Good. Just like any other guy. She unbuckled his belt. No objection. Probably because he needed the freedom, that much was obvious from the depth of his breathing. Measured, quick, deep. Was he the type to take control? She'd bet he was. If the situation was mutual.

Don't think like that. What did it achieve? Nothing.

This was any other guy. Same old, same old.

With her eyes almost shut, she held her breath as her hand curled around his shaft. Thick, hard, pulsing in her palm. A shiver went through her. Thank God she wasn't allowed to look.

When his jaw moved, she slithered lower, resisting her urge to break the rules. She didn't break the rules. None of them dared. Kissing his head, she swirled her tongue around him. Shit. Squeezing her eyes closed did nothing to dampen the excitement whirlpooling in her gut. He was big. Magnificently big. So much so, she doubted her ability.

Taking him into her mouth was easy. But it wouldn't be enough.

"Shit," he hissed, and scooped her hair into his fist, holding it tight at the base of her skull.

Mmm. She almost purred. Need was familiar. Not hers, but theirs. Oh, but that sting. Licking the length of him, she did her best, but swallowing him would be impossible. Maybe with practice.

Unfortunately, that wasn't her call.

"Don't play with him, Dolly," Silvio chanted from the other side of the room.

No, that game was reserved for specific dolls. Her role was simple. Easier than most. For that, she was grateful. She retrieved the condom from her pocket to roll it onto him. Would it fit? Maybe. Almost. She could only do her best.

Rising, she slid a leg across his lap, using his shoulders as support. He was right there, on the edge of the mattress, making her perch precarious. Right up until he locked a forearm beneath her ribs, forcing her posture upright. Her body jerked against his and her eyes leaped up. Oh, wow, the darkness swirling around his pupils sucked her in. She wasn't supposed to look. Eye contact was against all the rules. Oh, but it rooted itself in her. That could be the last moment of true human connection she ever experienced.

Lost in that instant, it was the sharp shock of his blunt head stretching her that snapped her back. Wincing, impulse wanted to retreat.

"Do it if you mean it," he said, the drone of his voice ripping through her.

Relaxing her thighs, she took another shot. She slung an arm around his neck, silencing her discomfort, pressing her body tighter to his. Damn, that joy, that heat, her ability to feel wasn't lost. Ripples of desperate desire shimmered from that point of pleasureful pain. Goddamnit, she wanted him.

"Hmm," he exhaled a sound of calm encouragement.

And his mouth came closer; the nudge of his nose on hers tempted it higher. This time, her eyes closed of their own accord, absorbing the sensation of longing on instinct. This was what it felt like to be in bliss.

"She's so delicate," Manzani said, shattering the cocoon of their intimacy. Imagined or not. "Have you found your limit, Dolly? Are you going to disappoint me?"

No. That was a death sentence.

She had to do it. Do what she was told. Forget fantasy. This was reality. Not what she made up in her head. She descended again. Brogan's forearm stayed at her back, but his hand dropped to her hip, steadying her.

Her jaw loosened at the wonder of it. Fullness. To be satiated in every way. Her thirst quenched. Her hunger satisfied.

When she thought he was in, that they were there, he just kept on coming. Her lips curled for just a flash. But it wasn't allowed. Rules. Follow the rules.

His pleasure mattered, not hers. Was she capable? Squeezing him within her, she rose and fell until her thighs ached. Brogan Chase. If she had a fantasy man, he was it. So much had changed. About her. In her life. For all the shit she'd gone through, Brogan Chase was the reward. Maybe he'd be the last one she ever got. And it was fleeting. He clenched his jaw, and she sank down. All the way down, savoring the moment of completion. Nothing in life was guaranteed, especially one like hers. Stealing the happiness when it came was all she could do.

If only she could call out, ask for more or beg for pleasure.

The pressure building in her could only be one thing. As she slickened from the friction, she sped up, her desperate body wished for—

"Fuck."

He grabbed her hips and yanked them down as his thrust up.

That was a look she knew. All good things came to an end. Sometimes too quickly.

She licked her lips and climbed from his lap, back onto the bed.

"Away, Dolly."

A command she expected and one she followed by rote.

"That's it? You just send her away?"

Hopping off the opposite side of the bed, she returned to the closet, pulling the door over without closing it all the way. Again, as was the routine.

"What do you care?" Silvio asked. "You got yours. Now fuck off."

"What?" Brogan demanded, the buckle of his belt rattling. "What the fuck? That's your favor? I fuck your girl and we're square?"

"We're far away from that," Silvio said. "You do as you're told now, when you're told."

"You said that when you told me I was working security for you. You didn't say nothing about this."

"Think of it as a perk."

"Why would you want to watch another guy fuck your woman?"

"She fucks herself, every time, because she's a hungry little slut."

"That it? That what you think?"

"None of your fucking business."

"When will the debt be settled? How long will this shit go on?"

"So long as I say. Now get the fuck out of here!"

He didn't get it. Brogan thought it was possible to settle the debt and please the master. Neither would ever be true. If Silvio Manzani got his hooks in, they were there for life.

The closet door opened. Silvio filled the frame, rolling his cigar between his thumb and forefinger.

Fixated on her, he whistled once. Dashing over, she stopped in front of him, expecting her breasts would get most of his attention. He didn't disappoint and squeezed one then skimmed his hand across to the other.

"You broke the rules," he snarled. His hand came fast across her face, snapping her head to the side. "Want me to send you down to the pit?" Her nose ran. Was it tears or just the pain that was so easily absorbed? He grabbed her jaw tight, forcing her head up. But she wasn't allowed to look him in the eye. "Do you?"

Keeping her gaze away, she did her best to shake her head while in his grip. Tears slipped free. God, she resented the shit out of the pleasure he got at exerting his power.

He came even closer. "You enjoyed it." Spittle from the words hissed through his teeth struck her face. "You did." Her nostrils flared. She couldn't look at him. Couldn't speak. He just loved to taunt. "You're disgusting. So fucking eager to swallow him. You're a whore, nothing but a whore. He's forgotten you already." Maybe. Did it matter? Thrusting her face back, he grabbed the belt of her robe, tearing the fabric away from her body to toss it into the bedroom. "You stay in here tonight. I don't want to hear you. Petty will put you to work tomorrow."

Petty's job was to put them to work. The routine varied, but it always ended the same.

Just to emphasize his point, he shoved her, grabbing her arm as she stumbled to force her onto the floor. "Your place is on your knees," he growled. "Don't forget it again."

Striding out of there, he slammed the door, and the lock clicked.

If life wasn't so pathetic, she'd laugh. He didn't need to lock the door. She had no desire to leave the closet. At least in the closet, she was safe. For however long that lasted.

Chapter Two

L IES EXISTED TO APPEASE CONSCIENCES.

If there were consciences to be appeased.

Smile. Be pretty. Dumb. Silent. Be admired. An object. That was her. And the other women circulating Silvio's party. His monthly casino night, a guy's night, of excess and machismo. Silvio's dollies weren't the only ones there. Strippers served drinks and danced, in public and in private.

Could she do it? What would it be like to go home at the end of a shift? To be safe? It wasn't worth thinking about.

"You're a dirty fucking slut," Silvio's words warmed her ear. She hadn't even seen him approach, but there he was behind her, scotch scenting his breath. "You ashamed of yourself?"

The music blended from one tune to the next.

Snatching her arm, he jerked her a quarter turn, staying behind her. What was she meant to see? What was...? Brogan. By the door. Dressed in black, just like the other agents protecting the guests... More accurately, protecting the Manzanis.

"Guy can't do his job, can't take his fucking eyes off you." Was that true? She'd never know; she wasn't allowed to look anyone in the eye without permission. "If he can't do his job, he's useless to me." His teeth scraped her ear. "You know what happens when people aren't useful to me."

Yes, she did. Brogan would too if he didn't get his head in the game. Of course, this was Silvio's story, that didn't make it true. Games were his forte.

The playing pieces might look like people to anyone else. To him, they were objects on the game board to be manipulated.

"You're gonna fix this."

How was she going to do that? His grip clamped tight on her upper arm; he dragged her through partygoers to the exit in the far corner. With his phone in his other hand, he continued down the corridor to the restroom at the end.

Swinging her around, he tossed her into the room and slammed the door behind them. A short wall opposite the door doubled as the end of the long vanity. The mirror stretched the entire width above the counter. She hated the light. Hated to look at herself in its harsh luminescence.

Her eyes closed and her head dropped to the side. Whatever he wanted, he'd get. They couldn't be more alone. Even with people just on the other side of the door, with servers and caterers and all the other service providers moving up and down the corridor, it didn't matter.

They were alone.

Bracing her hands on the cool marble, she didn't react to him opening her dress zipper. Why should she? If he wanted every man in the building to take turns, that's exactly what would happen. And what would she do? Take it. She was Silvio's possession to maneuver at his will.

Just as he hooked his fingers under the straps of her dress, the door opened. Shit. Brogan Chase.

"Close the damn door," Silvio said, stalking over to thrust it back into the frame.

"What the fuck is going on?" Brogan demanded. "What the fuck are we—"

"She's gonna apologize." Silvio folded his arms. Brogan still seemed bewildered, but it didn't matter. "Dolly."

Sit. Stay. Beg. It was all commands.

"No," Brogan said, backing up until he hit the vanity. "No, we're not doing this again."

"It's her fault. Apologize, Dolly."

"That's not her fucking name."

"You think she remembers her name? That's long gone. We don't name toys."

She opened Brogan's pants, and his willing cock sprang out. The rest of him wasn't as receptive. He pushed her hands away and stuffed himself back into the fabric.

"We are not doing this again."

Bowing her shoulders forward, the front of her dress fell, spilling her breasts against him. He did a double take, but there was no mistaking that he noticed. Did he like what he saw? It shouldn't matter.

Taking his hand, she guided it to her breast. He needed to take over, to respond. If he didn't, Silvio's patience wouldn't last.

Not that she enjoyed forcing herself on anyone. The games could only go on for so long.

When his thumb rasped across her nipple, she almost smiled in sheer relief. Untucking his shirt, she ran her hands up his body, as much as she could, and ducked to kiss his stomach, his groin, his shaft.

"Shit," Brogan hissed. His girth swelled as he grew hard beneath her mouth. God damn, she wanted to look up, to watch his response. Was he enjoying her or was it an involuntary reaction? "No." He pushed her head away. "No."

There was nowhere for him to turn with the counter at his back.

"You rejecting her?" Silvio asked.

She licked her lips.

"What? Fuck," Brogan barked. "Yes! Enough with this bullshit."

"Gimme the dress."

And there it was. Her greatest triumph was her ultimate failing. There was some kind of irony in that.

Pushing it down over her hips, she slipped it from her legs, still sitting on the floor. She toed off the shoes too. They weren't hers. Nothing belonged to her.

"What the fuck are you doing?"

"Get one of your guys to take her to the pit."

"What?" Brogan asked. "The pit is—"

"Her home for however long she survives it."

Silvio spat on her leg and said something in Italian.

God, like she didn't already feel disgusting.

"No," Brogan said. "You are not gonna—"

"She's useless. She can't suck a dick. What other use I got for her?"

"I didn't say she couldn't—this is not about her."

"She's a toy to be played with. When a doll breaks, she goes out with the trash."

"She's not broken," Brogan growled.

"If she can't turn a guy on, she's broken. Get up." He kicked her before she even got to her hands and knees. "Fucking move!"

"Enough!" Brogan retorted, putting himself in front of her, facing off with Silvio. "You want me to fuck her? I'll fuck her."

A pity fuck. How had this become her life?

Using the vanity for support, she pulled herself onto her feet. Naked and feeble compared to the stature of the men, it wasn't easy to stand proud.

Like before, she braced her weight on her hands against the vanity. Someone swept her hair from behind her shoulder to in front. Squeezing her eyes closed, she resisted the temptation of looking, of responding to the almost caress. That was the closest she'd had to affection in... how long?

Sound opened her eyes, and a condom appeared on the counter in front of her. Silvio provided no doubt, but it was Brogan who leaned over to grab it. For a second, the weight of his chest on her back... odd the things people took for granted. What she'd taken for granted before... Was there a before?

A warm, rough hand skimmed onto her hip. "You okay, baby?"

Was that—a question for her?

Silvio laughed. "She won't look at you, she won't talk to you. This bitch is trained to—"

"I'm trying my fucking best to forget you're in the fucking room, old man."

"Only way this happens is with me in the room."

The way Brogan started to turn forced her hand up to catch his on her hip. He couldn't hurt Silvio. No, well, he definitely could. Then what? What happened to the guy who went after one of the city's most dangerous crime bosses? Nothing good.

No matter what, they were in a no-win situation.

Without looking up, she could feel his eyes on her. His hand slid back to its position and that pressure... Oh, it ached, but that insistence was like an insurmountable desire. Their bodies might not fit well together, but the need was too great to resist. As he pushed in, she pushed back, relishing the delicious stretch of her body around his.

He didn't stop. Even when there was resistance, he pushed on, filling her up, allowing her body to consume him.

A hum of pleasure lodged in her throat. Shit, the rules. Silvio was right there, watching every second.

The exhale from the man behind her was almost enough to help her forget. It was something to know he wasn't immune to the need. That sound, that moment, was just what she needed. Brogan Chase.

His cock slid back, right to the threshold of her body. Clinging to his hand, the unconscious maneuver betrayed her want, not only to him, but to her as well. She'd never...

He slammed back into her. With a sure grip on her hips, he moved her body to complement his. Yes. She wanted to scream. It took every ounce of willpower to silence that wish. It had to be a dream. It was a dream. The hot, hard man behind her, fucking himself inside her, was a fantasy cooked up by her insanity.

Brogan Chase.

Inside her.

Fucking her.

She bit her lip as he propelled himself into her hard one last time.

Oh.

It was over.

He froze for a few seconds then slid away, leaving that hollowness inside her once again.

"Signore!" came a call from beyond the door. "Your son is here."

"Fuck," Silvio muttered and pointed at her. "Stay here."

Yeah, because what else was she going to do while Silvio still had her dress in his hand? She could go out there, but it would be easy pickings. Vex, as Silvio's son was known on the street, brought mayhem wherever he went.

Still bent over the vanity, she caught her face in both hands.

"What's your name?" Brogan. Instinct wanted to move her hands, but then what? Would he expect her to look at him? She wasn't allowed to look at him. "Manzani was bullshitting when he said you wouldn't talk, wasn't he?" With her face in the cradle of her hands, she shook her head. Gesture was the only allowed method of communication. "You won't look at me." Except she'd already broken that rule. "The other night, our eyes met, you broke the rules."

Yes, she had. And, in truth, Brogan could say anything he liked to Silvio. They would believe the man over her.

Exhaling, she turned around to lean on the vanity, but kept her chin down.

"You're allowed to look at me," he said, frustration flavoring his tone. "I say you're fucking allowed. Jesus, we've fucked twice and you can't even look at me." He stepped back. "It's wrong. I should've... I didn't want you to go to the pit. You don't know that place; no woman wants to go there. Sounds like bullshit to say I did it for you. I'm sorry—"

She grabbed his wrist, her eyes wide as they flashed to his. And, shit, they snagged right there. Fuck, he was beyond formidable. He could squash Silvio like a bug, yet he'd kept his cool. He couldn't know how she appreciated his action.

His large hand slid up over her jaw to her cheek. When he tightened his grip and stooped lower, she had to avert her gaze again.

"No kissing either, huh?" She shook her head. "Why do you live like this? Why do you let him—he's got you over a barrel too. You owe him something and this is the price." He exhaled. "Always fucks like Silvio Manzani that come out on top."

His wrist was thick, strong. Why was she still holding it? Touching him. There was no need for it, but she couldn't bring herself to let go.

"Guess there's only one thing I can fix."

Her? Was it—he grabbed her hips to sit her on the vanity. What were they...? What was going on?

Her legs parted as he moved between them.

"Any time you tell me to stop, I'll stop, okay?" She nodded, but wasn't really sure what she was agreeing with. His fingertips trailed up her thighs, rough, bold, masculine in a way she hadn't experienced.

One hand went around to the small of her back, the other—her breath caught when he grazed her clit.

"Hey," he said, rubbing in gentle circles, warming her up slow. "Up here."

She must've blinked twenty times. As the tumble of hormones rolled beneath her ribs, heat rushed to her head. Their eyes met. He winked, and her teeth caught her lip. They couldn't talk, it wasn't allowed. She shouldn't even be looking him in the eye.

Her hips moved. It was impossible not to squirm against the pleasure of his —shit; he pushed a finger into her and her ass lifted from the vanity. Shit, that felt good. Pushing her head back into the mirror, her body writhed against his fingers.

She wanted to call out for him. Brogan Chase.

Something slick met her folds. Bringing her head down, it was... Shit, he was down there, crouched between her thighs. If Silvio walked in—fuck Silvio, it felt too good.

One of her hands jumped from the vanity to sink into his hair. The other braced her weight, so her hips stayed off the marble.

"That's it, baby," he growled against her, licking her clit again, circling and tormenting it with the tip of his tongue before dropping lower to fuck her with it. "Fuck, you're amazing."

She was amazing? Her ears rang.

"Ah," a sound, just a single syllable, croaked from her throat.

Shit, be careful. They had to be careful.

Snaking his hand up her body, he squeezed her breast, tracing her nipple with the tip of his thumb. "I've got you, baby. I love how you move."

And she was, her hips, her waist, her legs, all of her moved in tune with the rhythm of his indulgence.

God, it was better than... God. Scorching endorphins ripped through her and she froze. Locking in the moment as her climax washed over her. It took every atom of her being not to call out for the man who'd pampered her like no other.

Silvio would kill them both if he found out.

Brogan planted his palm on the vanity by her hip. "If he wasn't watching, your pleasure would come first every time."

Another shiver went through her. Maybe an aftershock he'd set on a timer, or it was the dark determination in his eyes.

Still locked on to that connection, she grabbed his belt.

"We got time?" he asked, skimming his hands up to her waist. "Shit, you're beautiful." That startled her to a complete stop. Beautiful? She wasn't—why would he say that? "I couldn't take my eyes off you tonight."

Which was the source of the problem. Supporting her jaw on the side of his forefinger, he stopped her from looking away and drew slow, lazy lines on her chin with the edge of his thumb.

She needed to tell him. To somehow convey that... She could lose herself forever in his eyes. Was it just because a connection like that was against the rules or was it special? The second was more attractive, but that was kidding herself.

The door opened. Brogan backed up to check who was there, and crossed to plant a hand on the wall, blocking the person's way.

"You get out here," a male said. "The woman can stay."

The woman. That wasn't Silvio and Brogan had barred his entry. Protecting her modesty?

He glanced back to wink, then disappeared with the other person. A bathroom. Well, she'd hung out in weirder places. Someone would come for her... eventually.

Chapter Three

TEN CAME AND WENT. Eleven passed her by. The hours of her life dwindled away, disappeared into the ether, as she lay in that bed, staring up into the canopy crown laden with expensive silks. Opulence. Luxury. The Manzanis could afford the finer things in life. Families who made a habit of purchasing people's souls didn't want for anything material.

Brogan Chase. Where was he? A week had passed since she last saw him and there she was, thinking of him again. He'd probably forgotten her. But she hadn't forgotten him. She should. Holding on to hope and any glimmer of happiness, even fleeting and illusionary, was dangerous.

She couldn't sleep. Not at night. Before midnight was harder, unless she was performing. So far there hadn't been sounds from elsewhere in the wing. Didn't necessarily mean anything. Women who weren't allowed to talk didn't often make noise.

Shit. Sleep. Just sleep.

Breathe in.

Breathe out.

Bang.

She sat up. What was that sound? Another. And another. Shit. Leaping out of bed, she stilled at the next sound. Gunfire. That was an automatic weapon.

What should she do? The closet wasn't bulletproof. Neither was the bathroom. If she went out there... she'd more likely get shot than escape.

There could be dozens of assailants. Maybe scores. What did they want? Silvio, or money? No one would rob the Don in his own house.

But it couldn't be cops. They didn't use machine guns. Unless maybe they did against decked out mafiosos.

Wasn't like the Manzanis were short of weapons or men of their own to defend their base.

When the bedroom door burst open, she braced, expecting havoc. But it wasn't intruders or even strangers.

Brogan Chase.

Alone.

He strode to her, gun in hand. "Anyone else here?" She shook her head and sucked her bottom lip as his eyes trailed down her nude body. "Where are your clothes? Where's the closet?" She pointed, and he snagged her hand to lead her into the adjoining room. Nothing hung on the racks. He let go of her to search the drawers, but there was nothing there either. "You're not allowed clothes?"

She shrugged.

Appropriate moments granted them the right to wear clothes. Which didn't include while they were alone in bedrooms.

"Shit, baby," he said, grabbing the side of her head. "You can talk to me. Silvio will never know."

Easy for him to say. Being in the habit of remaining mute, she didn't want to break the seal for fear it wouldn't close again.

Putting the gun on the vanity, he grabbed his hooded sweatshirt at the back of his neck to tug it off and thrust it at her.

"Put this on." Shaking her head, she pushed it away while backing off. "Don't worry about the consequences." But she kept shaking. "There's at least twenty guys in the lobby and more covering the exits. I don't know what this is yet, but I don't want anyone coming up here, seeing you like this." Her modesty? Dignity? That was a joke. How long had it been since she had either? "If they see you like that, they'll touch you. They'll hurt you. Is that what you want? Them taking turns?" Because she was the dirty whore who'd tempt them to it. "I'm not saying you'd want it, but it'll happen." He thrust the sweatshirt at her again. "Please."

Figuring him out would take longer than they had.

Suspicion wanted her to resist, but she accepted it because his eyes... They were the only eyes that saw her.

"I'm going to find out what's happening," he said, picking up the gun. "You want the weapon? Will you use it?"

She shook her head. Truth. Silvio was clear that she wasn't to do anything without his instructions. Her thoughts were invalid. Her wants irrelevant.

Anything men wanted, she was to give, providing her husband got something out of the deal.

Slowly, his brow descended. "Will you protect yourself?" She didn't speak. "Will you fight?"

He really didn't understand anything. Brogan Chase. Her ideal man. Her fantasy. Was completely clueless.

Another reason they could never be anything real. He would never understand. A man like him couldn't and shouldn't have to.

A gunshot came from somewhere in the building. His head turned, then her hand was on his cheek, bringing it back around. His eyes. Alert. Ready. Keen.

"Don't worry, baby," he said, laying his hand on hers to draw it down. "I'll do it for you."

He kissed her knuckles and then was gone. Out of the closet, heading into the dangerous fray.

Left alone with his hoodie, she raised the fabric to her nose, absorbing what he'd left of himself. If Silvio saw it, he'd punish Brogan. Somehow.

And she wouldn't allow that. Wrapping the fabric around her shoulders, she nestled in the corner with her knees pulled up. She'd hold it close for just a second, then secret it away.

The next bang was closer. Shouting. Someone was shouting.

Life, such as it was, would trundle along. Tomorrow the sun would rise, and she would go on... or not. If the higher powers were smiling on her, maybe she wouldn't wake up to see it.

The closet door startled her awake.

Each night sleep captured her eventually. Oblivion lasted only as long as her husband allowed. Just like always, without time to adjust, her eyes opened, and her head rose. She had to be on for... something. Without delay. Without hesitation. Was it time to perform? Silvio didn't care about sleep or comfort.

"Come here."

Blinking into the cold air. That wasn't her husband's voice. Who was...?

Brogan Chase.

"Where's the sweatshirt?"

His—yes, his hoodie. Getting with it, she sprang back and pulled out the lower drawer to lift the board beneath. Her hiding slot. She retrieved his apparel and handed it over to put the lid back. Before the drawer was closed, he startled her by pulling the hoodie on over her head.

She shifted, blinking in confusion as he fed her arms into it.

"It's not safe for you to stay here."

Not safe? Yeah, and it hadn't been safe for a long time.

"Can you walk?" he asked, guiding her to her feet as he closed the drawer with one of his.

Why wouldn't she be able to walk?

"We've gotta go, babygirl, but you've gotta move fast."

Go where? Why? She hadn't been out of the Manzani mansion in... she didn't even know the date.

As he took her to the threshold, she pulled back. Leaving? Punishment would be the pit. If Silvio didn't kill her himself.

"Things are going to shit. Vex is a time bomb. You can't be around here; it's a war zone. People are already dead. I don't want you to be next."

And who could she trust? What did he want? Brogan. Was he on her side?

"This will be easier if you work with me, but I'll carry you out if I have to."

From anyone else, that could be interpreted as a threat. Despite the low gravel of his voice, it didn't inspire fear.

Trusting him was a risk, but a worthwhile one.

What did she have to live for?

Drawing in a breath, she nodded once, and they got moving.

His experience of the house and situation was greater than hers. No matter which way he went, she followed. Most of the house layout was a mystery. Toys like her had their place and no choice but to stick to it. They were always under supervision or lock and key.

Not that night. Or if there had been either, Brogan had taken care of it.

"Wait," he said, jerking her into a perpendicular hallway, putting her back to the wall, and crowding in close.

In the darkness, she couldn't see much of him, but that didn't matter. She could feel him. Not just the steadying hand on her waist, but the heat of his body cocooning hers. She closed her eyes, resisting the urge to lean in, to wrap her arms around him or rest her face on his body.

Brogan Chase's motive may be a mystery, but the prospect of him was too alluring to ignore.

Her libido wanted things it could never have. Just because he'd pleasured her to climax once didn't mean he'd do it again. Maybe it was all a manipulation and he planned to sell her or take her to the pit for brownie points. Whatever it was, there was no going back.

They went all the way down to exit through the basement. He scooped her up to put her into a beat-up truck, easing her head down to keep her out of sight as they left the grounds.

"We're gonna be okay," he said after a few minutes. "You can sit up now." She slouched but raised her head. "You're safe."

And when his hand slid onto her knee, she wanted to believe him. Brogan Chase wasn't an easy guy to read. Or maybe he was, and she'd just forgotten how to trust her gut. They drove and drove, but their destination didn't matter. Silvio would find her eventually. This chance to breathe free air was one she'd savor while it lasted.

Many minutes and miles later, he drove down an alley, around the back of a dark building and stopped.

"Wait there," he said.

Following instructions was her forte, so she did exactly that.

She didn't expect him to open the door and pick her up to carry her into the building. They went up three floors. He only put her back on her feet to fish out keys and unlock a door. He stepped back to usher her inside. Shadows cast over the couch and the kitchen they bypassed to go through another door.

A bedroom.

What else did she expect?

This was familiar.

"The bathroom's in here," he said, turning on the light of an adjoining room.

Were they going to bed? Who needed the bathroom? Did he want her to clean up?

First thing... she eased the neck of the sweatshirt off her shoulders to let it fall to the floor. Either he'd saved her life or neither of them would see sunrise.

She went to the bed. This she knew. This was—

"Get some sleep, babygirl." Her knee rose to the bed. "There's an extra blanket in the closet."

Without so much as looking at her, he disappeared, closing the bedroom door behind him.

Extra blanket in the closet. Sanctuary hadn't changed much.

Chapter Four

"SHIT."

The exclamation came a second before someone scooped her up from the floor.

What was—Brogan Chase.

And she was just still asleep enough that she turned her face toward his broad chest like it was okay to savor him.

"When I said in the closet, I didn't mean in the closet," he said, dumping her on the bed, then going over to slide the closet door shut. "Shit, you scared me." She scared him? Sitting up, her head tilted in question. "Why won't you talk to me, baby, huh?" He came to sit on the edge of the bed. "We're the only ones here. No one will hurt you. I promise you, it's safe."

And she wished she could show what it meant to her that he believed that. Silvio would come for her. Unfortunately, that was just a fact.

Scooching closer, she kept her eyes down and pointed a fingertip on the back of his neck. It trailed around the side of his neck to his chest an—

"No," he said, catching her wrist like he had before their first time. "That's not what this is. I don't want your routine, I want your trust." It wasn't possible to give him that when she couldn't even trust herself. "Talk to me." His hand went into her hair to cradle the side of her head. "Did he hurt you? Is it physical? Can you speak?" It had been so long since she'd uttered a word that it wasn't certain she'd remember how. "I want to hear your voice. I want to know your name."

Silvio taught all his toys that their mouths were for one thing only.

If they weren't going to have sex, she shouldn't be on the bed anyway. Slinking off, she went to her knees between his feet, pushing her palms up his thighs and—

This time he caught both of her wrists.

"That's not what this is," he said, stern to the point of scowling. "You think that's why I brought you here? For sex? Baby, I was getting it at Silvio's house anyway. Why would I risk my life just to screw you in my bed?" Screwing in his bed sounded good. Screwing without a witness would be a dream come true. "Guess we've gotta go right back to basics." Guiding her onto the bed again, he swept her hair from her shoulder. "Close your eyes." Hmm. "You follow instructions, right? Do as you're told?" She nodded. "So close your eyes."

Okay. But it was weird and not the kind of thing Silvio would order her to do at all. She closed them and quickly peeked from one. He laughed. Which opened her eyes in surprise.

"Close them and keep them closed, baby," he said, caressing her cheek. "Please."

Another thing Silvio would never say. This time when she closed them, they stayed closed.

Her whole body tensed when the whisper of his lips touched hers. Quickly drawing back, she shook her head.

"You've gotta trust me, baby," he said, snatching her head to pull her closer. "No one will ever know what happens in this room. This is you and me. Only you and me."

Secrecy? Privacy? His lips were perfect, his tongue had pleasured her and —he pushed his mouth to hers, demanding acquiesce. How she wanted to surrender, how she wanted this. The sweet, slick joining of mouths that so many took for granted was her forbidden fantasy.

Kissing wasn't allowed. For her anyway. For the other girls, maybe, but Brogan Chase? That was an entire football field away from allowed.

Maybe she was a slut. All this time Silvio had been saying it and she heard it but never listened.

Shame dropped her chin almost to her chest.

"Did that feel wrong?" he asked, still holding her head with one hand. "Didn't feel wrong to me."

This had to stop. Her boundaries were loosening. It had taken so long to get to her position in Silvio's house. To be allowed a room and food and no punishment. All of that would go to hell if she lost her focus.

Grabbing for that routine, she tried to climb into his lap, but he caught her waist, holding her back.

"Is that how it goes?" His grip tightened on her waist. "Like with us. Is that the script?" Was he mad? She couldn't tell. "What did he make you do, baby?" But she couldn't answer. His grip slid up to her cheeks. "No sex until I know it's what you want. Until I hear it from your lips."

And that may never happen. His lips. Their lips. Somehow, he sensed her need and leaned in to marry their mouths again. Brogan Chase.

Any second Silvio's men could burst in and put bullets in both of them. How come assuming the worst comforted her? If it was all going to be over in a few seconds anyway, what did it matter how she spent them?

The balm of his kiss soothed her. It laid to rest every fear and worry. No other man gave her permission to be free. Try as she did to resist the allure, the possibility was too much.

Running her hand into his hair, her mouth loosened, and his tongue slid over the threshold of her lips. It had been so long since she'd sunk into the delight of a kiss, let alone one with a man who ignited fire in her every atom.

Clutching the back of his neck, she steadied herself as he put her on her back and came down with her, never breaking their kiss.

Time. Feeling. It was all the same thing. The same erupting force that echoed within her, drowning everything else out.

This kiss.

This man.

"Brogan."

"Yes, baby."

Yes? His lips touched hers again, smudging one way than the other. Had she said that aloud?

"Chase." That was her voice in the tiniest whisper. Another kiss. "Brogan Chase."

Grabbing for his shoulders, their eyes locked. Speechless took on new meaning. It wasn't that she couldn't, she just had. Without thought, without choice, the words had escaped her. That was dangerous. Very dangerous. All of him had the power to break her, to steal her sense and survival instinct.

Looking at him. Kissing him. Speaking to him? All against the rules.

One side of his mouth lifted. "My full name?"

She swallowed. Hard. Her fingertips floated to his cheekbones, his jaw, and up to his brows.

"It's how I hear it," she whispered, "in my head."

"My full name?" he asked. She nodded. "Then I gotta return the favor. What's your name, babygirl?"

Did she remember it? Yes, but it had been a long time since she'd thought of herself as that person. Was there any of her former identity left?

"Dolly."

"No," he said, tucking her hair behind her ear. "That's not who you are anymore. You're not his toy."

"I'm yours?"

"No," he said, rolling to his side next to her. "You're yours. Tell me your real name." Again, she shook her head. "You don't trust me?"

Trust was relative. Her fingertips met his lips. "I haven't kissed a man for…"

"Too long. But I can't say I'm sorry to break the trend. Was it him, Silvio? Was he the last?" More head shaking. "I want to understand." To save her. Petty was right. Silvio too. "Talk to me, baby. You've gotta know I'd never hurt you."

Trust.

It was hard won for a reason. She'd trusted the wrong man before and look where that got her.

Sucking her lips, ridding them of their kiss, she wriggled toward the edge of the bed.

He caught her wrist to hold her back. "Where are you going?"

The closet. Stupid as it may sound to him, the closet was her only haven. His was small. So small that she had to sleep lying beneath his rack of clothes, but she had to still comply somehow.

"Don't shut down on me," he said, tugging her arm. "Look at me, baby."

"It's against the rules," she whispered like if she was quiet enough maybe the words wouldn't count.

"No, it's not. Those rules, Silvio's rules, they might count with him and the people he brings to you. But here, I'm not one of his people. No one brought me here. I'm here because I wanna be here. I wanna be here with you."

Unable to help herself, she gazed into him. "He'll come for me."

"And I'll tell him where to get off. No one's dragging you back there against your will."

Except that was the real kicker. Her will wasn't the issue.

"You owe him something." Because they'd talked about it that first night. "And I owe him something too."

"He'll get back whatever he's owed, babygirl." Sitting up, he cradled her face again. "That won't include you."

"It's all I have," she said, tucking her legs under her as she settled next to him on the bed again. "My body is all I have to give him."

"I'll pay him. Whatever your debt—"

"It's not my debt," she whispered, her focus floating away. "I'm the payment."

"You were…" He sat up slowly, his grip loosening from her wrist.

"Someone bartered you?" That was one way to put it. "Who? Tell me who the fuck—"

She touched his lips. "I'm a toy."

"No, you're not."

"You can't owe him for me too."

"Watch me."

She shook her head. "No, what I mean is, you have nothing more to give him. What you owe him for Chico, it's already your life. You can't settle the debt. It's impossible to repay it. He makes you think it can, but it can't. You belong to him, just like I do. We don't get more credit, from the moment you made that deal until the moment you die, you are his."

"No."

"Yes."

"I won't take you back there."

"Even if he would let you keep one of his dolls, he'll play with you. I've seen it."

"Play with me?"

She licked her lips and shuffled a little closer, still keeping her voice quiet. "He brought you to my bed."

"Yeah."

"I'm not the only doll," she said.

"You think he'll force me to fuck other women?"

"I know he will."

"Why?"

"Because it would hurt me." If they stayed together, they'd fall deeper into whatever was between them. If they didn't, she'd end up back at Silvio's anyway. "Because it would hurt you. That's his pleasure..." She sighed. "One of them anyway."

"How can—"

"Because I've seen it. You made a deal with the devil. It's never fair. There is no equal or end. And he has dolls for everything; we're each given a role. He has a sub, a domme, the ass girl, who's also the golden showers girl." Not a role she envied. "He even has a virgin."

"A virgin?"

She nodded. "Never to be touched."

Which may be worse. On top of all her rules, the no talking, looking, or kissing, his virgin had to endure no human touch at all.

"How do you know all this? How long have you been there?"

"I don't know."

"How many women does he have captive?"

With a shrug and another sigh, she lay down flat, resting her hands on her stomach. "I don't know. The number changes."

"It changes?"

Angling her head, she sought his eyes again. "Eventually he gets bored or a doll breaks."

"Breaks?"

"The rules."

"The pit," he said like he understood. "That's where they go."

"If she's lucky."

"You don't know the pit if you think that's lucky."

"You don't know the alternative," she said, closing her eyes.

Chapter Five

MAYBE IF SHE JUST breathed, everything would be okay. Somehow. Hope had no place in her life. In anyone's life.

Brogan's lips touched hers, jolting her in a knee-jerk retreat. "What's the alternative?"

She wasn't supposed to tell anyone. It was all whispers and eavesdropping anyway. And Petty. With the threats... the promises.

"It's not this. Not lying in bed with an attractive man like we have no cares in the world."

"I care," he said, sliding a hand over hers on her stomach as he lay on his side again. "I care about you."

"Why?" The question was valid. "Why me? Why would you care about me?"

"I can't answer that."

"You want my trust but won't give me yours."

A sign of their inequality. Something else familiar.

"Because I don't know," he said, his fingers curling around her jaw. "You're important. Have been since I first laid eyes on you that night in your room." Oh, if only he knew. "That's what I wanna see. Your beautiful smile." Huh, when was the last time she smiled? She shook her head, still in his grip. "You want my trust? I'll tell you anything you want to know."

"Your life. Your secrets."

"No secrets," he said. "I call Chico my cousin, but we aren't blood related. He's the younger brother of a guy who used to run in our crew. For years, I worked for the Manzanis and other families. I was a bad guy... maybe I still am. I don't know if that shit ever goes away."

"Why did you stop?"

"Jagg stopped. You know Jagger Dunn?" She nodded. "Jagg stopped and Ford stopped. It's different going out there when you don't have your family at your back. Jagg got the auto shop going, made money on customs, and gave all of us an out. All of us a home."

"So why come back?"

"Chico's an asshole. Not a bad kid, just not too bright. He got himself in some trouble. Stupid trouble he shouldn't have been near, but he's impressionable..."

"Wrong place, wrong time?"

"I wish it was as simple as that." The pad of his thumb descended the angle of her jaw. "He got roped into smuggling arms."

"Weapons?"

"Yeah and..."

"Silvio doesn't like disobedience." Or not knowing everything and giving orders. "Was it for him?"

"No, but he was involved. Chico was using Manzani shipments to bring the guns in." She winced. Bad plan. Very bad plan. "Yeah, that's how it went down."

"You saved Chico's life. And now you want to save mine. What about your life?"

"I have a... shady past."

"Is our past who we are?"

"You're not shady," he said. "Your heart is good."

Her past. Her present. Filled with so many shameful acts. She didn't deserve his kindness. Any kindness.

"You don't know," she whispered.

"Are you hungry?"

"I don't want food."

"Don't trust me not to poison you?"

"I haven't earned it."

"You don't earn shit around here. Around here you're a goddess."

Happiness didn't feel quite right in her gut, but laughter bubbled out of her. Giving herself to it, her body arched, and there he was, ready to accept her against him.

"That's funny? Thanks. Laugh at me for worshipping you?"

"You're Brogan Chase."

"Yeah, who'd you think you were getting?"

"I have to go to the closet."

Capturing her as she tried to wriggle away, he dragged her back. "No more closets." He kissed her head. "Let's get you something to eat. Let me take care of you."

With their fingers threaded together, he guided her out of the room. The apartment was open plan, kitchen to the left, tall skinny windows to the right. The couch was beat up, the entertainment unit distressed, nothing matched, and she didn't care. Brogan's apartment was worth a thousand of Silvio's fancy house.

He went around the narrow island to open the fridge in the corner. "I got eggs. Juice. I didn't know what you'd like."

"You went out?" she asked, going around to lean against the island, her hands hooked on the edge behind her.

"The fridge was empty. I had to stock up for you."

From one life to another, the gear change was jarring. "You didn't have to do that."

"You like coffee?"

Squirming, discomfort crawled across her skin. "No."

"You don't like coffee?" He glanced over his shoulder. "What's wrong?" he asked, closing the fridge, wearing a frown. "What's going on in your head?"

"You have to take me back."

He came in close. "Not a chance."

"He'll come for me, and it won't be pretty. He'll hurt you."

"And what will he do to you?"

If she went back or if she stayed? "He's my husband and—"

"You're married? How the fuck is that? I thought—"

"We're all his wives. All of his toys. His mistresses. He takes care of us. We're his wives."

"You're not his wife," he said, picking up her hand to wind her arm around his waist as he moved up against her. "And I'm not taking you back."

"It will be worse. This, just being here, talking to you, it's all wrong. He'll ask me. What happened. Where I've been and Petty—I can't be here. Every second here means a day of punishment there."

If she was lucky.

"How does he punish you?"

"You don't want to know."

"I do. Were you always this way or is it being there? Is it what they do to you there?"

"What way?"

"Scared. Worried. Tense."

Ready. Alert. On guard. "You don't know what it's like."

"Tell me," he said, his fingers drifting through her hair. "What is it like?"

Something else she'd never told anyone. Who would she have told?

"When they take you, it's... It happens fast. You're disoriented. They want it that way. They drug you and... At first, you're scared of the drugs. Then you realize it's better. It's better to be out. Time means nothing there. You don't wait for hours to pass, it's days. Weeks until you see someone. Even then it's dark and..." Laying her hands on him, it was easier to focus straight ahead than on anything else. "They keep you locked up for a year. That's what Petty says. No exceptions. You exist in this small space. In the dark. Every time you call for help, every time you scream... they do it again."

"What?"

"Reset the clock. That means no food. Barely any water. You're naked already, but it's so cold... I was cold for so long, I was afraid to be warm. Afraid of water that wasn't ice cold."

"They break you down."

"All that comes after the beatings. Sometimes they happen for no reason. They'll beat you if you raise your head when they bring you food or flinch when they inject you."

"Inject you with what?"

"I don't know. You don't ask questions. Whatever is in the needle, it puts you to sleep. They crush pills into the food too; sometimes you see the fragments. But you eat it, you're grateful for every bite. The rules serve a purpose. Silvio wants perfection. He has a clear idea of how a doll should behave and everyone complies." Her eyes rose to his. "Everyone, Brogan. If you break the rules, they reset the clock... or worse."

"What's worse?"

"The troublemakers, the washouts, the ones who resist..."

"What?"

"They inject them with something else, over and over until she's addicted and strung out..." And not only wholly compliant, but wholly dependent too. "Then they're given a choice, the pit for a hit or..."

"Or...?"

"They're sent to the hotel." She couldn't bear to think about that potential future. "The longer I'm gone, the worse it will be. If I'm lucky, Petty will reset the clock and I'll have to go through it all again from the very beginning."

"You think they'll keep you in the dark if you go back there?" He set his hands on the counter on either side of her. "They'll beat you and starve you..." His concern faded to a smile. "Do you think I'd let anyone hurt you like that and do nothing?"

"You can't do anything if you're dead. Or if they do the same thing to you."

Fear took on new meaning. At least she was aware of what her future held. It would be new for him. "You have to do as you're told. Everything. Every word. Listen. Don't speak. Don't argue."

"You think someone will try to lock me up?"

"You have value," she said, touching his face. "Not like us. The dolls. Our value comes in being meek and malleable. I know you'd have value sexually, but I've never heard of him doing that to a man." Though that didn't mean he hadn't or wouldn't. "If you fight back, it's worse."

"Don't be scared of him." He picked her up to set her on the island. "Don't be scared of anyone. I'll protect you, I promise."

On an exhale, tears stung her eyes. "I believe you mean that." Her fingertips traced his lips. "But he won't lose. He never loses. Silvio Manzani gets what he wants every single time."

"Until now. Maybe that used to be true, but if he tries to get between us, tries to hurt you again, I'll take him down, baby. Whatever it takes."

"If you had that ability, you'd have done it for Chico. No one is as strong as him. The Manzanis are untouchable."

"The McDades are stronger."

Wariness prickled her shoulders. "Don't replace one devil with another. You don't think Ire McDade would have the same uses for me, for both of us? You have to be careful. You shouldn't even be talking like this. If anyone knew—"

"No one will know. This is us. Just us," he said, sliding her to the edge of the counter. "My word means something. I will protect you. Just like I promise to take care of your needs..." His fingers coasted to her inner thighs. "As soon as you're ready."

He had a way of turning things around, of pretending everything was going to be just fine. Maybe that came with experience. Before her captivity and training, she'd been naïve to what horrors the world held. She hadn't believed that at the time. Retrospect had a way of righting perspectives, but their outlooks were so different.

"I've had so many fantasies about you," she murmured, sinking into a dream.

"Every single one of them will come true, baby." If only he could read her mind, maybe he'd make more sense of what was in there. "You got a list?"

And if maybe trust existed... Hell, any moment could be her last. Wasn't that her comfort?

"There's one thing I want. One act I've missed more than any other."

"Anything."

As her heart sped up, her thoughts slowed. Touching his waist, she pulled him close against her, tucking her head down to rest on his chest.

"Hold me tight."

"Shit, baby," he breathed in her hair as he put his arms around her to do as she asked. "No more horror."

A fantasy in itself.

Being held, feeling the warmth of another body on hers, she'd almost forgotten. Before Silvio, she hadn't given the simple act much weight, hadn't known its significance. His embrace, any genuine embrace, hadn't been a part of her life at the Manzani mansion.

Brogan Chase.

Keeping herself close, she tipped her chin higher, seeking his eyes. They lingered for a moment, then he dipped down to kiss her.

Just what she wanted. What she needed. Somehow, he intuited all of it.

Brogan Chase.

Her arms relaxed, but he kept his tight. Sliding her butt back, she slipped the leather of his belt from the buckle.

He broke the kiss. "Baby, we don't have to—"

"I want to," she whispered. "*When* hasn't been my choice for years. I was the seductress, always on top, but never in control. I want you inside of me because you want to be inside me. Not because Silvio commands it."

"You wouldn't believe how much I want you, how much I wanted you, even with that fuck in the room."

His jaw shifted as he clenched his teeth.

She gently stroked the muscle. "Do it if you mean it."

What he'd said to her their first time.

Except before either of them could do anything, his cellphone rang.

"Shit." He backed off to grab it from the opposite counter. "What?" he barked into it, turning his back to her. "No, I don't wanna—I don't give a shit what—fine. Fuck." He hung up and tucked the phone into his back pocket. "I have to go out."

"Silvio?"

He came back to her. "If I tell him to go fuck himself, he'll send guys over here." Silvio would send guys over there eventually, at some point. "Vex is being a dick, and he's distracted."

"He won't be distracted forever."

"Let me go figure out what the fuck is going on. Get a read on the room." When her head dropped, he crouched to snag eye contact. "Stay here, baby. I'm gonna figure this out."

Still so sweet that he believed that. "What if he already knows?"

"He'd come in all guns blazing."

"You know that but still want me to stay here? You should put me on a bus with twenty bucks if you value your life and really want to help me."

"I'm selfish. I want you with me. Will you stay?" he asked. She hesitated. "Trust. This is how we prove to each other we're as good as our word. Will you stay here? Wait for me?"

If he wanted to lock her in, he could. He could tie her to something or chain her up. Trust. An odd notion to consider.

"Can I use your shower?"

"Shower. Watch TV. Empty the fridge. Sleep. Whatever you want. Just do not answer the door. Don't order food. I don't want anyone coming to the door and seeing you when I'm not here."

Even a pizza boy could be on Silvio's payroll; it wasn't completely unheard of.

"I'll stay on one condition."

"Name it."

"You kiss me goodbye."

He smiled. "I'll kiss you, but it won't be goodbye. It's until next time."

If everything went their way and that definitely wasn't her experience.

Chapter Six

A DOOR CLOSED and her eyes opened. The TV was on. Until it went off. She turned her head to the man at the end of the couch, remote in hand.

"You fell asleep?" he asked, coming to scoop her up. "I'm gonna pretend it was accidental and not that you have something against the bed."

Still rousing from sleep, her voice stayed silent as he laid her down in the middle of his bed. The moment his arms slid away, and he started to turn, her hand leaped into his.

"Stay," she said into the darkness. "Please stay with me."

"You're safe here, baby." The back of his fingers grazed her jaw. "I've locked the door and I'll be on the couch—"

"Sleep here with me," she said, wriggling over to the furthest side.

"This another one of your fantasies?"

Something so mundane probably amused him, but he wasn't far from the mark. "Do you judge me?"

"Never," he said and rose to take off his sweatshirt.

After his boots and socks were gone, he turned like he intended to lie down.

"That all I get?" she asked.

Glancing at his tee-shirt, his brows were high when he looked at her again. "Couldn't help but notice that, uh..." In a backward nod, he gestured at her body with his chin. "You're naked."

Something completely normal for her. "Is that... bad?"

"Never bad," he said, yanking off his tee-shirt to toss it aside too. "We've never been naked together, you know."

They'd had sex, but never been naked together. He wasn't wrong.

"You afraid of me?"

The question was genuine, but he laughed.

"Baby, I don't want you afraid of me." Standing up, he took off his pants, but the boxer briefs stayed in place when he came down to gather her against him. "How's this?"

"Good." Reaching past her, he caught the comforter to drape it over them. "What happened at Silvio's?"

"Vex is being an asshole. Throwing his weight around with his guys. Him and Silvio are locked up in the office. Not sure if they're saving the world or bringing the apocalypse."

Could go either way.

"Did anyone hurt you?"

"No," he said, stroking her arm. "And no one mentioned a missing doll."

Didn't mean her absence wasn't noted. "They probably haven't told Silvio yet. The best way to handle Silvio is to solve the problem before bringing it to him. It's the only chance you have to avoid a bullet. He doesn't take bad news well. Some guys have the dolls do it just to avoid being in the line of fire."

"The more you tell me about your life there, the more sure I am, I'm never letting you go back. I don't want to be one of those asshole guys who gives his girl rules. You've had enough of that to last a lifetime. But, fuck, babygirl, don't ask me to do it. Don't ask me to see you back there dancing to his tune."

Sliding a leg over his, she drew it higher until her knee met his cock. His hard cock. Of its own accord, her fingers curled over it.

"You're hard."

"Since the minute I saw you, baby." He pulled her higher to kiss her head. "Ignore it. It will go away."

Turning her head, she kissed his chest. "I know a way to make it go away."

His gruff laugh was only semi-amused. "Which we'll get to when my girl-friend's ready."

His girlfriend?

Blinking, she lifted her head, still rubbing him through his underwear. "You asked about my fantasies..."

Climbing onto him, her legs opened around his, so she worked her clit against his erection. Damned fabric blocked her prize. Still, she rose, straddling him, working her hips, stimulating both of them.

"I think I figured one out." Before she could ask, he rolled over, sweeping her onto her back under him. So he was over her. On top. "No more on top for a while."

Tears actually stung her eyes as she ran her fingers through his hair. "Brogan Chase."

"But only when you're ready."

"I'm ready."

"No, my cock's ready. That's not the same thing."

But when he tried to move away, she locked her legs around him. "I haven't had sex with a man on top since before they dragged me to Silvio's basement. Don't ask me to wait another day."

Their mouths met on a harsh intake of breath. Somehow, he cradled her and pushed down his underwear at the same time. His weight on hers. The stability. That solid anchor of him shielded her from the whole world.

Brogan Chase wanted her.

Tongues coiled, hands roamed, but she was ready for more.

"Brogan," she whispered, her eyes heavy.

His matched them. "I want this to be real. It has to be real."

"It's real," she said, her pelvis rising.

"You want this?"

"I want this."

"Not because it's—"

"Brogan Chase," she said, her fingers curling around the back of his neck. "Do you want me to beg?"

"Never, babygirl. You're a goddess here. You get whatever you want."

"I want you."

"I'm yours, baby. All yours."

"Show me."

The whispered words curled the corner of his mouth, and he reached down between them to—

"Oh, wow," she said.

Her eyes closed as his mass invaded, conquering her. All of her. That was the first time she could show him with her body, with her words, just how incredible he made her feel.

"Open those eyes, I want you to see me." Elevating her hips, she pushed into his advance, desperate for all of him to occupy her. "Eye contact." Forbidden at Silvio's. "Who you with, baby?"

"Brogan," she said and whined when he pulled back to duck and kiss her.

"Gimme your voice, your kiss. I want all of it, baby."

"I want all of you."

Taking him deep still wasn't enough, yet she was sated. Filled full. Replete.

Gorged. Tightening her shoulders, her body moved beneath him. Still within her, he gave her just enough space to squirm and play, stealing her pleasure.

"It's for you," he said and stroked her hair. "Damn, baby, you're beautiful."

"I'm hot."

"You are."

"I want..." She gasped in a breath when he pushed down, massaging her clit with his groin. "Mm, keep doing that."

Panic opened her eyes. Had she just given him an order? That wasn't what she—

He rocked against her. "Tell me what you want, baby. Make demands. It's all allowed here. No punishment."

Which in itself was arousing. "Fuck me," she said. "Show me you want me."

Accepting that challenge, he eased out and in, slickening his way, easing the route as the friction gathered pace.

"Brogan!" she called, grabbing for his arms, her body moving with his. "Oh, please, baby!"

On a feral call of freedom, she gave herself to the pleasure that ripped through her being. It was impossible not to surrender. He'd given her every-thing she needed, everything he wanted, and rescued her from a fate she believed she'd never survive.

He took her up and over once and again, dishing out the delight for free. What was his price? Love? Fidelity? Living in the dream with him was seduc-tive, the forbidden fruit that maybe she was supposed to resist. Was he a test? If Silvio had sent him, she'd failed. Fuck, did it have to feel so good?

"Brogan!" she called to him again as he forced all of himself into her with a hissing growl of his own.

"Fuck, baby," he said, flopping down next to her. "Fuck, that was good."

"I think this is the easy part," she said, going to him when he opened his arm to her. "Sex with you has always been good."

"This was our first time without..."

Orders? A witness? Rules? Putting her paranoia aside, for that second at least, she was free. A woman lying in the arms of the man she worshiped. He called her a goddess, but he'd played in her fantasies. She'd dreamed of him. Imagined what she might do if given the chance to be near him. And that moment had arrived.

"What do we do now?" she asked, stroking his chest as he squeezed her body to his.

"We'll figure it out. Whatever comes next. We have each other. I believe in that. I trust in that. Can you?"

Could she? She wanted to, more than he could know. With nothing else to lose, giving herself to him was a Hail Mary pass. But this was her fantasy man. Her Brogan Chase, believing in him was a given.

TO BE CONTINUED...

Read more:
"Forbidden" Series Page.

Thanks for reading Forbidden Fruit!

Sign up for Scarlett's newsletter at:
https://www.scarlettfinn.com

About the Author

Check out all things Scarlett Finn on her website: **https://www. scarlettfinn.com**

Bestselling author of steamy romantic suspense and contemporary romance novels, Scarlett Finn loves to explore the mystery of love... and throw in a good plot twist!

Alpha heroes and strong, independent heroines lead the way through the drama and intrigue. Her raunchy novels jump into the action from page one and keep the reader on their toes all the way to the end.

Click here to take a look at Scarlett Finn's other titles!
Available on all platforms!

Gone Snowbound

Katrina Marie

Chapter 1

Tiffany

There must be a full moon, or something. The restaurant has been extra nuts. I can't remember the last time we had to have a wait list, and we aren't prepared for that. We're a small restaurant in a tiny building. What the hell was Dennis thinking about making me the manager? I'm not cut out for this. It would be bad if I called him and asked him to come in early and help, right?

I grab the tray of food, remembering those days when waiting tables was what I did all the time, before Dennis gave me a promotion. You've got this Tiff. Pull up your bad bitch panties and deal with it. Not bad as far as pep talks go. Let's hope it gets me through the rest of the shift. Only two hours to go. Dennis is taking over when I leave, and I can take a much-needed break from being on my feet.

With the food in hand, I back out of the kitchen, plaster a wide smile on my face, and act like it's not fake as hell. As much as I want to yell at these people to go home because it's too cold to be outside, all they see is a bubbly redhead ready to serve them.

"How are y'all today?" I ask the table in the corner closest to the window. A group of four women sit at the round top with shopping bags littering the floor around them. "Who had the southwest chicken soup?"

"Right here." The woman in the corner holds up her hand. I reach across the table and place the bowl in front of her. "Thank you." The same routine goes around the table until all the women have their meals.

"Do you need anything else?" I bring the tray down to my side and hold it in the same position you would a cute clutch.

"No, we're good." One of the women shakes her head and picks up her glass of water. "But, thank you."

"You're welcome." I turn and take a step. Except there's something caught on my foot. I fall to the floor, dropping the tray and barely getting my hands in front of me to keep me from hitting my face on the cold tile. A glance back tells me exactly what I suspected. One of their shopping bag handles got caught on the clasp of my boot. I wonder if Dennis will let me put a new shopping bag rule in place. I mean when we're this packed, it's honestly a hazard.

The woman closest to me at the table, slides out of her chair and to my side. "Are you okay?"

A part of me wants to revel in my bitchiness. I mean, I'm on the floor because I tripped over their crap. Of course, I'm not okay. But, I'm the manager and there's a certain decorum I need to maintain. "Yes, I'm fine. It's not the first time I've fallen, and I'm sure it won't be the last." Flipping over until I'm sitting, I reach forward and unhook the bag handle from my boot.

"I'm still so sorry. I told them we should have taken the bags to the car before eating." The woman glares at her friends. "Move those in the corner so nobody else trips over them.

"It's okay. At least I already delivered your food. Otherwise...this would have been a lot messier."

"Thank goodness for that," she smiles and holds out her hand to help me up.

"Thanks." I wipe off my clothes to make sure I don't have anything on me. "If you need anything else, let me know."

"We will," she sits down, "and, again, I'm sorry."

Waving off her apology, I head back to the counter to deposit the tray. Janie is covering her mouth with her hand, and I know the asshole is laughing at me. "Don't even start." I hold up my hand as if that will stop her commentary. It never does. She's grown on me, but that doesn't mean I like her all the time.

"I wish I would have gotten that on video. Dennis would find it hysterical." She's not wrong. He'd be laughing and wouldn't try hiding it.

"I'm sure one of his stupid cameras caught it. He'll get a nice little show when he checks them later." I lift my hand to one of the cameras and discreetly flip it off. There. He can have that parting gift as well. "Let's just get through the rest of this afternoon so we can go home. Your replacement should be here before Dennis shows up."

"Sure thing, Boss." She salutes me and grabs another order. She smirks as she passes by me. What the hell is that about? She only makes that face when she knows something I don't. Please don't let it be Dennis throwing even more obstacles at me.

There aren't many days I regret my life choices, but today is one of them. Had I applied myself, I could be working my own hours like Stella. Or in a cubicle with set days and times, like Audrey. But no, I chose to accept Dennis's offer of manager. It's usually a manageable day. It seems like the closer we get to Christmas, the more insane our foot traffic is. And, this year seems to be worse, even if it is good for business.

I open the door to my apartment that I share with Spencer and kick my shoes off before I close it behind me. It drives him crazy when I leave my shoes here, but I can't find it in me to care. They need to come off. That's the only thing that matters. My plans for the rest of the day include sitting on the sofa with a cup of hot chocolate and binge watching whatever catches my attention. There is absolutely nothing that will move my ass off the sofa.

There's a suitcase sitting outside the hallway before I even make it to the living room. What in the fresh hell is going on here? It feels like a stone is settling in the gut of my stomach, and I don't know if I can handle any other horrible thing happening today.

Instead of going to the sofa where I planned on planting myself and being a potato, I turn down the hall and toward our bedroom. Spencer comes out of the room just as I'm about to enter and I slam into his chest. "Oh, shit." He looks down and leans back until he can see my face. "Are you okay?"

I notice the second suitcase he's pulling behind him. This really doesn't look like it will be a good end to my day. I stiffen and point to the suitcases. "I don't know. Is it?" Before he has a chance to say anything, I step away from him. "Were you going to leave without saying anything?" I cross my arms over my chest and wait.

He furrows his brows in confusion. "What are you talking about?" He takes a step toward me and I scoot back again. My back hits the wall and I've run out of space.

"The suitcases, Spencer." I point again to reiterate my point. "Were you hoping I wouldn't be home when you split so you wouldn't have to explain anything." This is why I didn't do relationships. You inevitably end up getting hurt. "This is just the fucking cherry on my shit sundae day."

He moves before I can sidestep him. One hand is braced against the wall beside me, closing off all escape from this nightmare situation. He uses the other hand to gently lift my chin until we are eye to eye. "How could you ever think I'd leave you, Tiff?" He kisses my forehead, and it's the complete opposite of everything currently playing on loop in my brain. "You're it for me. I thought I'd made that pretty damn clear the entire time we've been together."

"But the suitcases," my voice trembles. It pisses me off that I feel so weak at the thought of him no longer being here, and confused as to what's going on. "That typically means leaving, and you didn't say anything about going out of town. What else am I supposed to think?"

He groans and leans his head against the wall, right beside mine. The memory of how we first got together flashes in my mind. It wasn't so unlike this. I was pissed off then, and we ended up in my bed. His voice close to my ear sends shivers down my spine. "I knew I shouldn't have listened to Dennis."

"Um, what does Dennis have to do with this?"

He moves until he's beside me and leaning against the wall. "I've been working in secret with your boss to get you a few days off so I could whisk you away for a romantic getaway before we are with your entire family for the holidays. I told him I should at least give you a hint, and he convinced me it should be a complete surprise." He glances at me and waves his hands in the air. "Surprise."

Oh, thank God. He's not leaving me. Not that I wouldn't be okay in the long run, but I legit can't imagine him not by my side. "Yeah, probably not the best way to handle things." Grabbing his hand, I lead us to the bedroom. It's the closest place to sit down, and I still need to wrap my head around the past few minutes. "I don't see how I can take off, though. Today was hella insane and I don't see it getting any better the closer we get to Christmas. Everyone wants somewhere warm to eat while taking a break from shopping."

Spencer pulls me into him once again, knocking us both off balance. We're laying on my side of the bed and his arm is wrapped around my waist. "Dennis has run that restaurant for years without you, he'll manage just fine. You need the break. Being manager doesn't mean you have to spend every waking second there."

Now that I think about it, I don't remember the last time I had a day off. I know it's not healthy, but I have to make sure everything is running smoothly. I can't do that if I'm not physically there. He's right, though. I do need a break. "You have a point." I nod toward the suitcase sitting by the door. "I'm assuming you packed for me."

"Yeah," he sighs. "I planned on being at the door with flowers before you got home, but you left earlier than I expected."

"It was a crappy day. We were slammed. I had to wait tables." I tap his stomach with each point I'm making. "And, I fell face first on the floor."

"That's what you should have led with." Spencer runs his fingertips along my arm, causing goosebumps to form. "Are you okay?"

"Mhmm. I was embarrassed, but nothing major." The idea of getting away for a few days is way more appealing than thinking about all the annoying shoppers we've dealt with the past few days. I cuddle into Spencer. "So, where are we going?"

"That will remain a surprise." He lifts up and turns until he is hovering over me. "For now, I think I need to make sure you didn't injure yourself with that fall."

"I like that idea." Though I'm not happy about the location of our vacation being unknown.

Chapter 2

Spencer

Telling Tiff, we were going on a vacation was a mistake. Dennis was right. I should have had the car loaded and whisked her away without any sort of explanation. She has asked me where we're going at least a thousand times.

"Soooo, when are you gonna tell me where we're going?" And that makes one thousand one times. She's loading her suitcase in the trunk of the car. She of course had to make some adjustments to what I packed and it hits the bottom with a loud thud. I swear she added enough clothes and hair products to last her a month. We're literally only going to be gone three days.

"Not until we get there." I wanted to go last night, hoping she would sleep a majority of the way and really be surprised. But that did not happen. She was exhausted from being on her feet all day and then her short burst of emotional turmoil, regardless of how inaccurate it was, I thought it best we wait until bright and early this morning. With the trunk now closed and both of us in our respective seats, it's time to start our adventure.

The sun is barely peeking over the horizon when I pull out of the parking garage. The oranges and yellows are picturesque even though they don't seem to fit in with the frigid air. They are colors you'd expect in summer or late fall. Tiffany is staring at the sunrise as if it's the most beautiful thing she's ever seen. She pulls out her phone and snaps a quick picture. Her awe of the world around her is one of the things I'll forever love about this woman. She makes me want to look at our surroundings through her lens.

"You should be driving and not staring at me."

"I'm not—"

"You are. I can feel you." She pulls on her seatbelt making sure it's secured around her body. "Also, that's how people get in wrecks."

"By looking at their hot as hell girlfriends?" Needling her is more fun than it should be, but it takes a lot to really piss her off.

"Exactly by doing that. Now, turn your face toward the road and drive." She grabs a pen and crossword puzzle book out of her bag and opens it up to the next puzzle. "Unless, of course, you want me to tell me where this mysterious getaway is, and I'll handle the driving."

"Absolutely, not." I shake my head and shift my focus to the road in front of me. "Don't worry your pretty head about where we're going."

"As long as it includes a coffee shop and breakfast, then I'll do exactly that." She pauses for a moment, tapping her pen on her book. "But seriously, I need caffeine. I'm not sure how I'm supposed to function this early without it."

She can't. It's something I've learned about her since we started dating all that time ago. She doesn't do mornings, and if she's forced to, she needs a pick me up. Her cousins are the exact same way, and I can't help but wonder how young they were when they were introduced to coffee. If I had to guess it was all Stella's doing.

All I know is I need to get her fed and caffeinated or it's going to be a long drive. I'd like to enjoy most of today at the cabin instead of being stuck on the road.

"Spencer?" Tiffany sounds like she's just woken up, but I know for a fact she hasn't gotten to sleep. "We're getting close to the gas station with the good bathrooms. Any chance we can stop?"

Damn. We've barely been on the road, but I'm not an asshole. "Yeah, we can stop. But in and out. No shopping for knickknacks."

"Fine," she rolls her eyes. "I guess I'll be a good girl. I really do need to pee though. I one hundred percent blame the coffee I guzzled down."

The laugh comes out with zero apologies. "Please tell me I can call Stella and tell her."

"Why would you do that?" I'm not sure why she's so confused about it.

"Because you and Audrey are always giving her crap about having to stop and go to the restroom," I wink at Tiff, "and look who needs to make a potty stop now when we've barely made it an hour on the road."

"If you even think about calling her, I will murder you in your sleep." She crosses her arms over her chest. "This is the one thing I can lord over my cousin and I will do it until the day I die," pointing out the window she adds, "you're about to miss the exit."

Shit. I don't miss the smirk she sends me. As if she just got a one up on me. It's her fault I can't pay attention. She's so damn feisty. It's hard not to interact. Especially when she's really pulled me out of my shell since I moved in with her. I was the quiet guy and didn't have many friends, but now I can give as good as I get.

Luckily, there isn't anyone in the lane beside me as I rush over to take the exit. It's a pain in the ass trying to go to the next exit and backtrack. I would do it in a heartbeat, though. Nice bathrooms are a requirement for her. She mentioned something about stopping at a sketchy gas station with her family as a kid and she made Audrey go in the bathroom with her. She described it as somewhere scary movies begin. I can't really blame her for being picky.

No matter what time of day you come, it's going to be busy. It's worth it. I find a spot close to the doors and put the car in park. Before Tiffany can get out of the car, I grab her arm. "No shopping. In and out."

"I know, Spence." She reaches for the handle. "Can I go pee now?"

"Smart ass." Both of us get out of the car and I lock it. It feels like the temperature has dropped a good ten degrees since we left this morning. I don't remember seeing anything about a cold front, but we rarely watch the news, or weather. We rush inside the store, and the warmth is what we needed after that frigid blast of air. I look at her. "Meet me back here in ten minutes."

"You got it, Boss." She rushes toward the bathroom. I feel like a dick for driving it home so much, but she has squirrel moments and next thing you know we're in this place for hours. I speak from personal experience. When her cousins are with her, all bets are off.

I just want to get to our location. I may have some ulterior motives with our surprise getaway. But I'll never get to reveal them until we get there. First stop for me is another cup of coffee. I feel like I've been going nonstop and the only thing that will keep me going is caffeine. There are a few other things I need to grab for snacks along the way. It's really not that far of a drive. It's actually not a huge distance from Stella and Johnny, but Tiff doesn't need to know that. Some of the snacks we love can only be found here. So, I need to stock up.

As the time to meet back at the register closes, I head that way. Tiffany is already waiting on me. "Jesus Christ." I can't help it. It's the only thing that comes out of my mouth. She has one of the small shopping carts full of things. "Did you grab one of everything the store sells?"

She shrugs and motions for me to add my stuff the cart. "You won't tell me where we're going and I wanted to make sure I'm prepared. Besides, you can never have too many sweets."

"If you say so." There's no use arguing with her. She's going to do what she wants. I watch as she places item after item on the counter. From barbecue sandwiches to fruits and veggies to fudge. She definitely has all the bases covered. I don't miss the flannel blanket she had hidden underneath everything. I should have known she couldn't resist getting something that wasn't food.

I can hear the people behind us groaning at the amount of stuff we're checking out, but I don't care. As long as my girl is happy, they can wait. Or, go to another line. Tiffany reaches for her card to pay, but I slide mine into the slot before she has a chance. This weekend was my idea, and I'm taking care of all of it. Even if she did get all the food she could manage.

With bags in hand, we rush back to the car. It's definitely getting colder. I hope it stops where it's at because neither one of us are very good at handling the cold. Tiff proved that when the temperature dropped at Stella's wedding. She made sure everyone had blankets to keep warm. I was the lucky guy that had to go pick them up from the store.

I press unlock before we're close to the car and start the car with the key fob. It won't be super warm but at least it won't feel like it does out here. I grab the bags from Tiffany so she can get in the car quickly. After putting everything in the backseat, I slide into the driver side, turn the heat up as high as it will go, and back out of the parking spot. Maybe now we can get this adventure underway without any more hiccups.

Chapter 3

Tiffany

"**A**re we there, yet?" I know I sound like a petulant child, but I'm so tired of being in this car. And...of not knowing where we're going. It's driving me crazy. I've never been good with secrets. Well, except about what went down between Audrey and Justin in high school. Other than that, I suck at keeping them. Surprise parties are also a no go with me. I sniff them out before they are done planning. It used to annoy the hell out of Audrey and Stella. They quickly gave up on trying to throw them.

"Not quite." He turns the radio up to hear the DJ. "What did he just say about the weather?"

I get out of my own head and long enough to hear them. "Everyone should get what they need and hunker down for the next few days. We're having an unexpected cold front. Well, colder than usual. We're going to get a lot of snow and ice on the roads."

"That sounds ominous," I joke from the passenger seat. They always say there's going to be bad weather. We all freak out and then nothing happens.

"Do you think we should turn around and go back?" Spencer tightens his grip on the wheel. "I mean we still have almost 2 hours to go and we really aren't that far from home when you think about it."

I laugh. "Of course, we aren't going back home. We already made it this far. Besides how bad can it actually get?" I look outside the window to see if there any snowflakes falling from the sky. There are none, big surprise. "They always do this. Over-exaggerate about how bad it's going to be, and then we are left looking like idiots."

"Are you sure?" I don't miss the nervous glance he sends my way. He seems pretty freaked out. But, he freaks out anytime it storms honestly. Especially, when there are tornadoes. As if we could do anything to actually get out of the tornado's path.

"I'm positive. If it comes to the worst, and were stuck inside for a few days, would that really be so bad? I mean I know we're living alone, but...this is the first time we've gone somewhere that doesn't include my cousins, or our families, and it would be nice for us to do something just for us over the next few days." Leaning over, I place a hand over his and slowly pull it away from the steering wheel, before interlacing our fingers. "Besides, where's your sense of adventure?"

His hand is clammy in mine and he chuckles nervously. "I don't know, maybe with the weather dude who said the roads were going to be covered in ice."

"And if they are, which I doubt they will be, we will stay snuggled wherever we are and find ways to amuse ourselves." I wink at him and he answers with a real smile. "I'm pretty sure we can think of a few ways."

"Oh, no doubt, me too." He gives my hand a gentle squeeze before bringing it to his lips and kissing it. "And they all involve your legs wrapped around me."

The car in front of us slams on their brakes and Spencer has just enough time to switch to another lane and avoid hitting him. I swear, anytime the word ice is even muttered, folks forget how to freaking drive. It's not like the roads have ice over them right now. "So, do you think we'll get to this mysterious place before this supposed cold front comes in?"

"As long as people don't start driving like assholes will make it there in plenty of time." That's reassuring because I am so ready to get out this car.

I know it's only been like thirty minutes since I've asked if we're there yet, but I'm bored out of my mind and ready to be wherever it is we're going. Also, I really need to go to the bathroom again. All the snacks probably weren't my best idea. I open my mouth to ask once again, but the sign we're passing makes me form another question. "Hey, isn't that the exit we take to go to Stella and Johnny's house?"

"Yes, yes, it is." He looks around as if he might see Johnny or Stella's car as we zoom along on the highway. "Johnny is actually the person who told me about this place I booked for our little getaway."

"And they know nothing about it?" Stella is pretty good at keeping secrets.

Although, she has a habit of letting little hints slip here and there. This is one of these things she definitely would have hinted at.

"No. They don't." He shoots me a satisfied grin. "I knew if I told Johnny, he would tell Stella, and then you would have figured it out. And, I could not let that happen."

"Well, why not? We always meet up with them when we are in the area."

"Because, Tiffany, I want these next few days to be special. I think we both deserve it after the amount of work we both have been doing, and all the preparations we had to do for the wedding." This must be a sore subject for him. He's not usually this defensive, and I'm kind of wondering if he's hiding something. Nothing nefarious, just something.

"Okay, I get that. But...could we maybe see them before we go home?"

He turns on his blinker to take the next exit. "For sure. That was one thing I did already plan for because I know you can't go without seeing your best friend when we are this close."

"Yay," I clap. "You, my adorable boyfriend, are the best."

"I have my moments." He squeezes my hand again. "Now, I need to focus on where we turn off this main road. It's a little tricky."

Even though the heater is running on high it feels like it's getting colder. Maybe the weather guy was actually speaking some truth. But that's all this is. A cold snap. Nothing is going to ruin our getaway. Not even Mother Nature.

About ten minutes off the highway, we finally make a left. The road is tiny, barely enough room for one car. It also feels like it's never going to end. The deeper we go into the wooded area, the more unease I feel. "Um, are you sure we aren't going to some house to be slaughtered by a serial killer? This is kind of giving off those vibes."

With the tree lined road, the sun is blotted out. It's dark and creepy. Something directly out of a horror film. "Yes, I'm sure." I can practically feel him rolling his eyes since I can't see them. His complete focus on the road in front of us. "I came out here while we were in town for the wedding. It's why we were late getting here."

"Wow," I nod in surprise. "You've been planning this for a while."

"Well, some of it, yes. But I didn't know the exact date until well, Dennis called me and said I needed to force you to get away. He was tired of seeing you at the restaurant."

Well, that's great. Both of them were conspiring against me. Maybe it's a sign that I have been working too much. That I haven't been giving Spencer the attention and time that he needs. Gah, have I really become that person that puts work over everything else? Look who ended up being more like Stella than anyone thought. I'll never admit it, though.

"Well, geez, tell me how y'all really feel." It's halfhearted after my sudden realization. "I'll get better about not working so much. It's just hard for me to trust that other people will do the job I need them to."

"You know, y'all could hire an assistant manager to handle things when you aren't there." It's not the first time he's mentioned it. Hell, even Dennis has said it. One day I will give in. Most likely when we get back. Even though I'm not sure I'm buying this whole I need a break story. It seems a little too clean. And I do, in fact, need one. It'll be good to rejuvenate the soul.

"Yeah, I kn—." The sentence dies on my lips because we are finally at our mysterious location. It's definitely in the middle of nowhere and absolutely breathtaking.

Chapter 4

Spencer

The look on Tiffany's face is one hundred percent worth the trip. But this is only the tip of the iceberg. I have so much more planned. Even if this cold weather is actually happening. Nothing will deter me from my objective.

"Do you like it?" Her reaction says she does, but I need to make sure. There aren't any houses around us for miles. I honestly didn't think places like this existed with the amount of development happening all over the state. It's a two-story log cabin with an almost wrap around porch. If it weren't for the satellite dish attached to the side, you'd think you stepped into an old book or tv show.

"It's amazing, Spence." She opens her door and begins to step out, but quickly pulls her foot back in. "Maybe I'll wait until we're parked next to the house. If it's possible, it's gotten even colder."

With that comment, I'm almost regretting the decision to not go back home. Almost. But, it's too late now, and this is something we need. "Okay, I'll park the car and make sure the house is warmed up before you come in." I keep driving forward down the driveway until I'm parked beside the front porch.

Even though I heard Tiff about the cold. I'm not prepared for it as I exit the car. A bad feeling settles in my gut. I don't think is going to be one of those times everyone looks like an idiot for freaking out about the weather. There isn't much I can do about it now. I hurry up the porch steps and look for the small rock the property managers said would be out here. I get why they use these to hide the key in, but do all the rocks have to look the same?

Finally, after picking up the fifth rock on the floral display sitting on a small table, I find it. My hands are shaky as I open it and let the key drop out. The cold makes my grip not quite as strong as normal when I pick the key up from the porch. I just hope they turned the heat on when they stocked the fridge. It's not normal for places to do this, but we were originally supposed to get here late last night and it's a service they offer for an extra fee. I took advantage of that because it would have been even harder to keep the location a secret if Tiff saw all the groceries in the car. I think she was expecting a resort experience. I went the opposite direction with a middle of nowhere vibe.

I slide the key in the lock and turn it before opening the door. Warm air greets me, and I breathe a sigh of relief. Even if we don't pay attention to what's happening with the weather, at least, it seems like the owners do. I leave the door ajar and hurry to Tiffany's side of the car. I pull the handle, opening the door, and stand in front of her to block as much of the wind as possible. "The house is warm. Go ahead and get inside. I'll get our bags."

"Are you sure?" She raises her eyebrows. "My bags are heavy as hell. It's not going to kill me to help you."

"You're practically shaking, Tiff." I reach for her hand. "I'm sure. Now go before I change my mind."

"Okay." She puts her hand in mine and allows me to help her out of the car. She places a quick kiss on my cheek and high tails it inside. I don't miss how she's favoring one leg. I think that fall yesterday may have hurt her more than she realizes. I'll look at her ankle once I'm down unloading.

Pushing the door closed, I pop the trunk and grab as many bags as I can. I don't bother trying to roll the suitcases. The uneven terrain makes it damn near impossible. Setting the bags on the porch, I turn to grab the last of them. It's just easier this way. When closing the trunk, I catch a glimpse of the five million snacks Tiffany got and her blanket. Looks like I'll have to make a third trip.

Tiffany meets me on the porch to grab some of our suitcases and carries them inside. I set what I have on the porch and get the plastic sacks out of the back seat. When I get back to the porch, she's there picking up her suitcase, struggling all the way to the door. I shift the snacks to one hand and grab the last two bags, carrying them inside.

"Your nose is bright red," Tiffany laughs as she pulls the bags of snacks off my arm. "Seriously, you could play the role of Rudolph."

"Gee, thanks." I set the bags on the floor and tap her on the nose. "I guess you haven't looked in a mirror, yet."

"I guess it's a good thing we're the only ones here and I don't have to impress anyone. Though I don't think I'd care much." She pulls out her package of gummy bears, shakes a few into her hand, and pops them in her mouth. "Now, enough talking about appearances. I want to explore the house."

The first thing she does is inspect the comfort level of the couch. She sits on each individual cushion until she finds the one she likes best. "I think this one will meld to my body well enough when we watch movies."

"Who said anything about watching movies?" I scratch my head in mock confusion.

"There is a giant television above the fireplace. One bigger than what we have. You can't tell me you don't want to watch some of your sci-fi shows on it." She pats her hand on the seat next to her. "Come sit, and see what you think."

I do as she asks, as if I wouldn't. She could tell me to walk after her off a cliff, and I would probably do it. She has to know just how badly I'm wrapped around her finger. "Okay, I see your point." I grab her hand. "Though we could also use this spot for something a little more intimate," I wiggle my eyebrows. "I mean it's pretty comfy no matter where you sit."

Tiff rolls her eyes and stands up. "You'll just have to wait. I'm not done exploring everything here." Instead of continuing down here, she takes the stairs two at a time. "Oh my gosh, there is an actual library up here."

When I checked the place out last time, I didn't bother going upstairs. The master bedroom is down here, and I didn't see a reason. But now, I might just venture up there. I take my time going up the steps, but come to a stop when I reach the landing. From downstairs it looks like it could be a game room, with a room off to the side. Mostly because the shelves aren't visible. It definitely makes for a nice surprise when you come up, though.

There's a lounge chair sitting in the middle of the room, and one of those chairs that look like a half moon off to the side. The shelves are stained a dark brown to match the walls of the house. Each bookshelf is floor to ceiling on the three walls. I imagine this is what everyone dreams of when they say they want a library. Reading physical books hasn't been at the top of my to-do list in quite some time. When I'm designing, I usually listen to a podcast or audiobook, and I'm kicking myself for that. I used to love the feel of flipping pages in a book. Though, I don't think I've ever seen Tiffany read. She must do it on her phone if she's this excited about it.

"This is impressive." I mutter into the quiet awe. I walk around the space, inspecting the titles. The owners of this house definitely didn't stick to one genre, either. There are romance novels, science fiction, fantasy, and books for teenagers. There are a few non-fictions and biographies, but if I'm looking for entertainment, I prefer to go into fantastical worlds. "Everything is so varied."

"It's pretty amazing," Tiff sighs. "Stella's friend Tonya would die if she knew this house had all these books. They do a monthly book club at the local coffee shop."

"That's actually cool." I run my fingers along the book spines until I'm standing by her side. "Who knows, maybe you can build a library like this one day."

"Eh, I prefer reading on my phone. It's portable and I can sneak in a few paragraphs when we're slow at work."

Well, that doesn't mean I can't get her an e-reader so she has something bigger to read on at home. I think I know what one of my Christmas gifts to her will be. I'll have to order later tonight when she's not looking to make sure it gets here on time. "I think that's a spare room," I point toward the door.

"I didn't even see it when I saw the books." She tugs on my arm and pulls me back toward the staircase. "I want to see what else is downstairs." I follow after her like the love-sick puppy I am.

Chapter 5

Tiffany

This place is like nothing I ever imagined. And, I don't think I've ever stayed in a log cabin. From the outside it looks like something you'd see in books, or even those beautiful shots you see on those home improvement shows. My cousins and I always talked about how we'd love to have log cabins like that, but it's not something you'd see in the city. At the time, none of us were looking to move out of Austin. But with Stella out here, I don't see why she couldn't own one. Although, there's no way in hell I'd give up the house she has right now. It's the epitome of small-town houses.

"Are we allowed to light the fireplace?" Not right now, but later after I'm done looking around the house.

"Yep. Just tell me when," Spencer says from behind me.

I let go of his arm, and make a left toward the only closed door down here. It has to be the master bedroom. I throw the door open and gasp. The bed is massive. It has to be a California king. It's framed by four tall wood posts. But, they aren't solid blocks. They look like pieces of branches that have been sanded down. It's totally not my style, but that doesn't take away from the beauty.

The back wall is floor to ceiling windows with a view of the wilderness beyond the house. The only thing that would make the view better is if there were mountains. Too bad this area of Texas is nothing but small hill and flat lands below that. "Are there any neighbors around here?" Because we're totally leaving those curtains open the entire time we are here.

"Not for miles," he grins. His mind must have gone exactly where mine did. We don't get this kind of freedom at home. If we left our curtains open, there would no doubt be a peeping tom in one of the buildings across the street.

"Good."

There's a sliding door on the wall next to the windows, and I push it open. The first thing I do is rush over to the bathtub sitting in the middle of the bathroom. It's huge and will fit both of us easily. The outside may look like it belongs in a different time, but whoever owns this house did a fantastic job decorating the inside. "Even though we're way out in the middle of nowhere, this tub is one hundred percent worth it."

"I'm glad you approve." There's another area where I'm sure a shower is, but I don't care about that nearly as much as I do this. "If you want to go put the snacks away and look in the fridge for what you want for dinner tonight, I'll get a nice warm bath started for you. You deserve it after the craziness of yesterday."

This is why I love this man. "That would be amazing." I turn to walk out of the room. "Do you need my help putting the suitcases away?"

"No, I've got them."

I'm almost at the door when I realize what he said about dinner. "Wait. Did you come down here earlier this week without me knowing?"

"Nope. I upgraded the service and they stocked the fridge with items I requested."

I clap my hands in excitement. "A girl could get used to this." I'm not lying either. I loathe getting groceries. Even when we have it delivered, there always seems to be items missing.

He follows me out of the room and stacks the bags on top of the suitcases before wheeling them to our temporary oasis. I head straight to the kitchen. It's an open concept and you can see the rest of the living space from the counter. This would be a perfect place to rent for the holidays with our families if there were more beds.

There's a reason he's the most adult person in our relationship. The fridge truly is stocked. All of the ingredients for some of my favorite foods fill the shelves. I look through the items and settle on spaghetti. It seems like a romantic idea for the first night of our getaway. I check the drawers to see if he got the vegetables for a salad. A smile crosses my face once I find them. This man truly thinks of everything. I want to be the one who cooks dinner tonight. One, because he planned all of this without me guessing. That takes a special kind of person. Two, because spaghetti and salad are one of the few things I can actually make.

The cabinets are well stocked and it doesn't take me long to find a bowl and cutting board. While he's putting the suitcases away and starting a bath, I can get started on the salad. It won't take long and by the time I'm done, the bath tub should be ready. Then we can properly break in this house for our short stay.

I'm sliding the salad bowl into the fridge when Spencer calls me from the other room. My timing is perfect as always. It's most likely the product of working in the food industry for so long. The amount of time it takes to make certain things is something I have down to a science. I grab a paper towel and wipe my hands on it before trashing it and making my way to the room.

The room is dark. The only light coming from the darkening sky outside. Another one of the reasons I loathe winter. There aren't any music festivals and the days are so short. It makes you want to go to bed when you get home rather than do anything productive. There's also light peeking from under the sliding door, but it doesn't look bright enough to be a lightbulb.

My steps are slow and measured as I make my way to the bathroom. Pushing the door aside, my eyes widen. Candles are placed on every countertop, filling the room with a warm ethereal glow. "Spencer, this...this is beautiful."

"Not nearly as beautiful as you." He stands and takes his time getting to me. Wrapping his arms around my waist, he pulls me toward him. "I know this place probably isn't what you were expecting, but I truly wanted these next few days to be special."

I lift up on my tiptoes and put my arms around his neck. Placing a succession of quick kisses along his cheek. "It already is," another kiss, "this house is perfect. I feel like a woodland princess."

He laughs. "You're more like a warrior than a princess, but I get what you mean."

I'm not sure if I should take that as a compliment or be offended. "Or, I could be a warrior princess like Xena."

"I like the way that sounds." He takes a step backward leading me toward the tub. "Any chance I can get you to wear the outfit?"

"Just tell me when," I grin. "There isn't much I wouldn't do for you. Maybe we can go to the next convention dressed as Xena and Hercules."

He backs away from me and looks at himself. "I'm in good shape, but not quite buff enough to cosplay Hercules."

"I don't think that's the point." I reach for the bottom of his sweater and pull it over his head. "Besides, I don't need you to be muscled out." Running a finger down his chest, I place kisses along his collarbone. "You're perfect. Just. The. Way. You. Are." I kiss him with each word so he knows I mean each and every word.

He grabs the hem of my shirt and pulls it over my head before bending down to slip my boots off my feet. His hands run a path up my calves, then my thighs, until his fingers are on the waistband of my leggings. His mouth is warm against my skin as he kisses right below my belly button. I grip his shoulders as he pulls my pants down and I lift one leg then the other until the fabric is in a pile on the floor.

My bra is the only fabric covering my body, and I reach back to take it off. But Spencer is standing now, and stops me. "I want to do it. You know since I've had all this practice now. I want to see if I can take it off with one hand."

"It'll be impressive if you do. I can't even do that." My laugh is real. In all the ways he can be possessive sometimes he's such a dork. Other people would probably mock the way we make jokes when we're having sex, but I don't care. It's one of the things that makes our relationship so special. I can be silly with him in ways I've never been able to with other men.

He holds my hands down between us with one hand and the other traces the outline of my bra until he reaches the small hooks in the back. His fingers fumble to get a grip and I attempt pulling my hands away to help him, but he tightens his grip. "I can do this."

Not a single word comes out in argument. He's determined. His tongue pokes out from between his lips and I know he's concentrating as hard as he can. It's one of his quirks that amuses me way more than it should. Finally, he pinches in just the right spot and the hooks are free of their clasps. My bra straps fall down my arms and he beams at me. "Told you I could do it."

"I never had any doubt." I reach for the button of his jeans but he pushes my hands away. "Um... if I'm naked, you have to be naked, too."

"I will be, but you're going to get in the bathtub first."

"But I want to be the one to undress you." I stomp my foot to punctuate my disappointment. It's childish, I know, but dammit. I always get my way. Especially when it comes to undressing the man I love.

"You'll just have to wait for another time."

"Tease."

His chuckle is low and deep as he helps me into the bathtub. As soon as I'm settled, he reaches for the button but pauses. I swear if this man doesn't get his clothes off in the next ten seconds, I'm going to murder him. Romantic getaway be damned.

Chapter 6

Spencer

There's fire in her eyes and I know she's not happy about my teasing. She does it to me all the time so it's only fair that I repay the favor. Slowly, I unbutton my jeans and slide them down, along with my underwear. She follows the movement every inch of the way down. I take my time pulling my socks and her fingers grip the edge of the tub. She's full-on glaring at me now. I better speed this up, or I'll have to face her wrath. Which, let's be honest, isn't all that bad. It's cute more than anything.

I barely have one foot in the tub, and she pulls me in the rest of the way. Water sloshes over the edge with the movement. "Someone is excited."

"No, someone is losing their patience because you decided to do a strip tease instead of hauling ass to join me." She pushes me to one side of the tub and climbs on top of me, rubbing her pussy against my cock. It has a mind of its own and twitches in response. "I mean, how often do we have access to a bathtub this big. The one at home barely fits me, and while I love shower sex, constantly standing after being on my feet all day tires me out sometimes."

Well damn. I never thought about that. "We could have less shower sex." I run my hands down her back until I'm palming her ass.

"I never said that," she pinches my nipple. She thinks she's punishing me, but it turns me on. "I'm just saying that this, right now, is a luxury for us and one we should take advantage of."

Not that I've asked, but I'm not sure many couples talk like this. At least not while having sex. Or, well, leading up to sex. To show my agreement, I lift her up until she slides over my cock and the tension, she had just moments before is gone. Her head falls to my shoulder and her hands hang over the edge of the tub. I can hear the water dripping off them as I lift her up and down over me.

Before long, her arms wrap around my neck and her hips are rolling over me. She's taken over the pace. Whether or not she wants to admit it, she likes being the person in control. Loves putting my body under her spell, until I lose it. Her movements are faster and my mouth trails along her neck until I get to her ear and kiss the spot she likes right below her lobe.

She's panting and oh so close. I am, too. Moments away from exploding, but I force myself to wait until I know she's ready. She lifts her head the tiniest fraction and I whisper, "let go." She moves quicker than before and I grab her hair pulling her lips to mine, swallowing her screams as she finds her release. I follow after her and lean my head back.

Her arms are still around me and she's leaning against my chest. I drop my hands to her waist and nuzzle into her. "Sorry I ruined what was supposed to be your relaxing bath," I mutter.

"If you apologize for that I'm going to bite you. That was exactly what I needed after being cooped up in the car most of the day." She slides off me and moves to the opposite side of the tub. "Though, I think we killed all the bubbles you had in here."

I can't help but laugh. "Sorry bubbles, I'd kill you a thousand times over. Totally worth it."

She lifts her feet and rests them on the edge of the tub. "Agreed." With a glance toward the window, she shakes her head. "I can't believe how dark it already is outside. If I didn't know any better, I'd think it's midnight."

"Do you want to get out?" I'm hoping she says yes. Not because I'm not enjoying sitting in here with her, but my fingers are getting pruny and that's never a feeling I've liked. It just feels so alien. Weird, I know, coming from someone who loves all things science fiction.

"Sure." Her stomach growls and I know why she wants to get out. "I'm getting hungry and want to get dinner started before it gets too late. I want to eat and cuddle up on the sofa with movies. Tomorrow we can explore." I know better than to get in the way of Tiffany and her food.

I stand and step out of the tub, looking for a towel. Damn, in my rush to get this all set up, I forgot to grab some. My feet slip on the cold tile floor as I hurry to the cabinet to grab a couple of towels. Her giggles are the only thing keeping me from cussing myself for forgetting. After wrapping a towel around my waist, I go back to the tub.

There's a mat for her feet, but it's soaked. I push my sweater next to it so she has something dry to step on. Once she's out I wrap the towel around her and inspect the damage we've done. It's not as bad as I thought it would be, but there's still water everywhere. "Why don't you get dressed? I'll clean this up and throw the towels in the dryer."

"Sounds good. I'll get dinner started, too." She gives me a quick kiss before rushing to the bedroom. "Don't be too long," she calls behind her.

It takes four towels to mop up the water. I'm freezing because of course; I haven't gotten dressed yet. I didn't want to put on clothes only to get drenched in the cleanup process. With the towels piled up by the bathroom door, I pull out my pajamas from the suitcase. I brought them in here, but I didn't unpack anything. My mind was on other things.

Tiffany's clothes are all over the bed, and I roll my eyes. Even when traveling she has the same habits. I scoop them up and deposit them in her suitcase so we have a place to sleep tonight. Otherwise, we'll have to do it later, and I don't want to mess with it. It's a good thing I love this super messy woman.

With my pajama pants and sweatshirt on, I grab the towels from the bathroom and head in Tiffany's direction. I have to cut through the kitchen to get to the small laundry room on the side. Rosemary and basil scents fill the room. It's one of my favorite parts of Italian food. Not only does it taste great, it smells amazing.

Tiffany is at the stove stirring the sauce as I pass by to the laundry room. I throw the towels in the dryer and start it. Hopefully it doesn't take more than one cycle to dry them. The last thing we need is for them to smell sour if we forget about them. Which both of us have done a time or two in the laundry room at the apartment. We set it there and went to eat only to come back hours later. I'll be happy when we can move into a place that has a washer and dryer in the actual space.

"How's dinner coming along?" I stand behind Tiff and wrap my arms around her.

"It's almost done." She smacks my hand when I try to taste the sauce. "Can you make yourself useful and put the garlic bread in the oven? The rest of the food should be ready by the time it's done."

"Sure thing." I move from behind her and grab the pan with the bread, putting it in the oven. This kitchen set up is pretty cool since the oven isn't attached to the stove. It makes it impossible for one cook to get in the way of another. "Where do you want me to set the table?"

There's a big family style table off to the side surrounded by windows. Or, there are barstools set up at the end of this counter. I just need her to direct me.

"Actually, I was thinking we could eat in the living room. Maybe watch a movie?"

"Sounds good to me." I search the drawers and cabinets for silverware and plates. I leave the plates on the counter, but take the silverware, some napkins and some wine glasses to the coffee table in front of the couch. The remote is on a side table and I grab it to see what's playing right now on TV. "Oh, hey, The Walking Dead is on. Want to watch that?"

I turn to see her reaction. From the way her face is screwed up, that's a definite no. "I'd rather not. It's gross to watch while we're eating. And, no offense, but I don't exactly want to watch a zombie show when we're in the middle of nowhere. It ratchets up the creepy vibe."

She has a point. "So, what are you in the mood for?"

"Anything that doesn't have death and gore is good with me."

The oven beeps and I hear the door open as she takes out the bread. I'm still scrolling for something that will keep both of our attention. It's close to Christmas so I settle on one of those warm-hearted romance movies. Not exactly what I love, but I know she watches them with her cousins. "Want me to start a fire."

"That would be awesome."

I get to work on getting the fire lit, and by the time I'm done she's setting our plates on the coffee table and a bottle of wine by the glasses. "I could have gotten my own plate."

"Shut up," she laughs, "it's not like I wasn't coming this way." She's not wrong. But I hate that she feels like she has to wait on me after doing it for others when she's at work.

"Let's eat. I know you're starving."

"Yep." She sits down on the floor and leans against the couch. After taking a bite, she points the fork toward the TV. "Thanks for choosing something tamer than zombies."

"It's not like I can't watch it whenever I want."

I sit on the floor next to her and we make quick work of dinner. Apparently, I was hungry, too. I've been so focused on making sure everything is perfect that I haven't eaten much all day.

Once we're done, I take the dishes to the sink and pull her up on the couch with me. She lays down in front of me with her eyes focused on the TV. "This weekend is going to be amazing."

"I hope so." I mutter into her hair. We both fall asleep to young couples falling in love over the holidays in their hometown.

Chapter 7

Tiffany

One minute I'm sleeping and the next I'm hitting the floor. "Ugh," I groan. I glance through my hair and see that I've rolled right off the damn sofa. Whose bright idea was it to fall asleep in here? Never again. "Why is it so bright in here?"

Using the sofa and coffee table to help me, I sit up to make sure I didn't spill the bottle of wine during sleep. Thank God it's on the other side of the table. Spencer is snoring, and I can't believe he's sleeping through my falling to the ground. I had to have made some kind of noise. I swear, this fool wouldn't wake up if there was a siren going off beside his ear.

Right now, though. I need to close the blinds because there is way too much light coming through. Groggily, I stand and make my way to the windows by the kitchen table, and my eyes widen. "Holy shit," I yell.

"What? What happened?" Spencer sits and pops up from sleeping like a vampire coming out of their coffin for the night. And of course, my shriek is what wakes him up. Not me falling to the floor right freaking beside him.

"There's snow." The last word is high pitched, and I don't mean for it to be, but we actually got snow. It almost never happens despite what the weather people say.

"Really?" He gets up and makes his way toward me, rubbing sleep from his eyes the entire time. "That's not just a little bit of snow. That's a lot."

"Yeah, it is," I clap my hands in glee. "Please tell me we're going to go play in it. Maybe build a snowman?"

"I don't know," he scratches his head, "neither one of us brought anything to wear for this type of weather." Oh no. He is not bursting my bubble. I open my mouth, but he puts his hand over it. "If you start singing that song from Frozen, I'm going to force you out there in what you're wearing now."

I glance down at my thin long-sleeved shirt and pants. Yeah, that's not happening. "If you come play in the snow, I won't sing it."

He shakes his head, but I can see the tiny grin he's trying to hide. "Fine. But let's go layer up. I also need to make sure there's detergent so we can wash our snow drenched clothes when we're done."

I don't give him a chance to argue. I rush to the room while he checks the laundry room. It takes me less than five minutes to put on multiple layers of clothes, including the fleece onesie I packed. I guess it's a good thing I added more clothes to my suitcase than what Spencer originally put in there. This is working out to my benefit.

Not bothering to wait, I go outside and figure he'll join me as soon as he's ready. It's so cold I gasp for breath. I didn't realize how much the temperature dropped last night. Which, duh, of course it did if we had snow, this morning. But I don't care. Snow days were my favorite as a child even though we barely got an inch. This is way more than that, and I can't wait to make my snowman and send a picture to Audrey and Stella.

What in the world is taking Spencer so long? I know he's not a big fan of outside in general, but come on. It is. Snow. In. December. How often does that actually happen in Texas?

The little angel on one shoulder tells me I should just wait until he comes out here before I go play in the white wonderland surrounding the house. But the devil...she is telling me to hide and get snowballs prepared. Decisions, decisions. It takes me a whole two seconds to decide I'm definitely going with the devil.

I walk as fast as I can down the porch steps without falling, an accomplishment in itself since it's slippery as hell, and hide on the other side of the car. It's a good thing we're on a hill because most of the snow has fallen down here, and it's pretty deep. Enough for my boots to sink to my ankles, and it's still coming down. My sock covered hands are freezing as I roll the snow into tiny balls and set them next to me. The key is easy access. I'd set them on the car, but that would be too obvious. At least it will be if he's paying attention.

There is a pile of about fifteen snowballs when I finally hear the front door open. "Tiffany? Where are you?"

I just need him to take a couple of steps outside the door and I can launch my attack. Too bad he doesn't seem to get the message because he's still standing with his whole body inside the house. I peek over the top of the trunk, and his eyes widened in surprise. "There you are. What are you doing over there?" Damn this bright red hair of mine. I feel like if it was a lighter color, I could've been a bit stealthier here. That's what I like to think anyway. Sneaky is definitely not how I roll most of the time.

"Oh, nothing." Hopefully he doesn't hear the mischief in my voice. The door closes with a thud, and snow crunches under his footsteps across the porch. I scoop up a handful of snowballs and prepare myself for when he gets closer. I mean, I could throw them now, but there's a good chance I wouldn't hit him. My aim isn't all that great. The few times we've gone to play paintball, I lose because I can't hit the broad side of a barn.

It feels like it's taking an eternity for him to make his way across the port. But, his footsteps sound considerably closer now. Counting to three, I pop up from where I'm crouching and launch one, two, three, four snowballs at him. The first two miss, but the third one hits in square in the chest. The fourth one gets him in the shoulder.

"What the hell?" This is the great part about him being so trusting, he never sees my devious ways coming. His mouth is wide open, and he's staring at me like I just took his favorite toy.

I wish I had my phone with me, I would totally take a picture of the face he's making. He is legit surprised that I actually threw snowballs at him. I mean, at this point, he shouldn't be. This is one hundred percent on brand for me. "You were taking too long."

"So, you throw snow at me?" I can't tell if he's really upset or still in shock that I did it.

"You can't tell me you've never had a snowball fight," I roll my eyes and bend down to pick up a few more.

He holds his hand out as if that will stop me. "Not that I can recall. It's not like we get a ton of snow in Austin. You should know that."

He has a point. But gah, what a boring childhood. Aside from the few times we had snow back home, we would always play in it when we'd go on our family ski trips. I take a few steps around the car, closing in on my prey. "Yeah, but it's like a rite of passage."

"Don't you throw another snowball at me." One hand is still up, but he bends to gather a fistful of snow in his other hand. He tries to roll it into a ball as I advance. "Tiffany, this isn't fair. I wasn't prepared."

"Eh, life's a bitch, sweetheart." I pelt him with two balls before he has a chance to stand up. "I'm pretty sure those people you play against in video games feel the same way when you sneak attack them."

"Totally different scenario." He responds. Instead of standing, he barrels toward me and tackles me to the ground. It's a good thing its actual snow covering the ground and not ice. Otherwise, that would hurt. "How did you like that attack?"

I wrap my arms around his neck, laughing. "Not so bad, Spence. Who knew you had it in you to actually tackle me?"

"Sometimes you have to play dirty." He leans over me and kisses the tip of my nose. "So, what exactly do we do in the snow?" All I can do is raise my eyebrows. This poor sheltered kid. He knows all the things about movies, books, and conventions, but nothing when it comes to playing outside. "I mean, is it pretty much what you see in the movies?"

"Yep." I roll until I'm hovering over him. "Except it's more fun because you have me as your guide." Standing up, I put my hand out to help him up. "We need to see if they have trash can lids or something."

"For what?" He uses my leverage to stand.

"To sled down this amazing hill."

"Oh no," he waves his hands in my direction. "I've seen Christmas Vacation. It didn't end so well for him."

"Quit being a baby," I grab his hand and pull him behind me. "That's a movie and severely over-exaggerated. This hill isn't even that steep."

"What if I choose life?" He tries to pull his hand out of mine, but I tighten my grip.

"You're going to live." I stop and turn to face him. "I'll wait at the bottom of the hill for you if that will make you feel better."

"Not really," he sighs. I can see when he decides he's going to do it. "But, I guess I'll try it."

"There's that adventurous side coming out."

"I think there are trash cans on the side of the house. I'll grab them and meet you at the top."

I watch him go around the house, patting his pockets as if making sure something is still in there. I really hope he didn't have his phone in his pocket. That wouldn't be good if it broke.

Part of me worries that I'm pushing him too hard. That he secretly hates that I want him to try new things. Life isn't worth living if you don't live it to the fullest, though.

Chapter 8

Spencer

This is such a bad idea. Why do I let this woman talk me into these things? Sure, the hill doesn't look so bad at first, but when you're sitting on a fucking trash can lid about to slide down it. It's terrifying. There's a reason I don't ride rollercoasters and this is it. I don't like not having control over what's about to happen. And let's face it. This could go horribly wrong. Especially when there's no way I'd be able to get the car up this hill with the amount of snow that's accumulated.

Tiffany is already at the bottom of the hill. She went first so she could show me how to do it. Where to place my hands and how to balance my weight. Honestly, I think I'd feel safer if we were using an actual sled, but I don't think people in Texas actually have those. There's no need when we only get snow like this once every decade or so.

She cups her hands over her mouth and yells into the falling snow, "You ready?"

Nope. Not in the slightest. There's no way I'm going to let her know how terrified I am. At least, not more than I already have. "Sure." There. That didn't sound too wobbly, right?

"Come on," she screams, "after this we can build a snowman then go inside for hot chocolate. I promise I won't make you do anything else death defying."

Yeah, because those last two words make me feel any better about this. I crisscross my legs on the lid, and grip one hand to the side. Inhale. Exhale. Inhale. Exhale. I can do this. I push off the ground with my free hand and then grip the other side of the lid like my life depends on it.

I'm speeding down the hill. The wind is blowing snowflakes into my face and it's hard to keep my eyes open. Bad idea. Bad idea. It's the only thing on repeat as I race to the bottom. Oh shit, I'm going to hit the car. Tiffany forgot to tell me how to stop. I'm going too fast and if I don't do something now, I'm going to crash, face first, into the trunk. I do what's probably the least logical thing and let go of the lid, throwing my body to the side.

The trash can lid flies up with the force of me moving. I have no idea where it goes, but I hit the ground hard. Snow hitting me in the face, and I know I'll be feeling this later. Rolling over, I check my surroundings and all my limbs making sure everything is where it's supposed to be. The lid is about ten feet away from me in the opposite direction. At this point, I should be happy it didn't hit the back windshield of the car. Or take out one of the windows on the house.

Tiffany isn't where I expected her to be. Which is by my side making sure I'm alright. No. She's still in the same exact spot, bent over her knees. Laughing. What the actual hell? Finally, she stands upright and makes her way to me. "What happened?"

"I was heading straight for the car." I point toward the thing in question so she knows how freaked out I am. "What else was I supposed to do?"

She plops down in the snow next to me. "Oh, I don't know. Lean your body to the side to change directions."

"But you didn't tell me that." I shake my head. "How was I supposed to know?"

"I figured you knew. I mean it's not too different from skiing, and you did that when we went to the resort last year." She slides her hand into mine and squeezes.

"And if you recall," I bump her shoulder, "I sucked at that too. I couldn't even make it down the slope little kids ski on."

"True." She leans her head on my shoulder. "Maybe we should stick with less exhilarating tasks from now on."

"Finally, we agree on something." I stand up and pull her up with me. "Want to go build that snowman now?" I've got to do something that makes me feel like less of a failure.

Tiffany tilts her head one direction. Then the other. "Is he leaning?" It's a two-foot snowman so it's entirely possible.

"Probably." My hands are frozen and I'm just ready to go inside. I pat my pocket again to make sure the box is still there. I slipped it in when I was layering up to come outside, but one thing after another keeps happening and I don't think I'll be able to find the right moment while we're outside. Even if it's the perfect backdrop.

She glances at the pocket I reached for moments ago. "Oh well. We'll just have a crooked snowman. Do you have your phone so you can take a picture? Mine's inside, and once I go in, I'm not coming out for a while."

Thank God for that. I'll be happy if we stay inside the rest of the time we're here. But Tiff embraces her inner child every chance she gets, and I'm trying to do the same. So, if she wants to come back out later, I'll follow. "Um yeah." At least the phone is in the same pocket. She must have been watching my actions, and I don't want her guessing the purpose of this vacation. Pulling the phone out, I hand it to her. "Snap away."

After snapping a few pictures, she hands the phone back to me, and starts toward the porch. "Hold on," I reach for her hand. "We have to get a picture with the little guy. It'll mark our first snowy vacation."

"But we had snow at the resort last year," she scrunches her eyebrows in confusion.

"Yeah, but this is unexpected snow, and it's only us here." I pull her toward the snowman, and we sit on either side of it. "It definitely needs to be memorialized."

She smiles up at phone while I take a few selfies. "You better be happy I didn't have my phone when we were sledding down the hill. That is something we should have on record."

"Nope," I shake my head. "It's really not." Talk about mortifying. I can only imagine what her cousins would say. Hell, Johnny and Justin would give me shit for years if they saw me in action. There was absolutely nothing fun about that ride from hell.

"Fine," she giggles. She stands and waits for me to join her. "We should definitely get inside and warm up. I think I lost feeling in my toes."

"I haven't been able to feel my face for a while."

We walk hand in hand to the house. I open the door and let her go inside before I do. Loathe as I am to admit it, despite almost dying on the makeshift sled, I did have fun this morning. More than I ever recall having as a kid. Maybe there is something to having adventures with Tiffany. I'm just hoping she'll allow me to have them with her for the rest of our lives.

Tiffany heads to the kitchen and pulls out a pan, filling it with water before setting it on the stove. Once she has the fire going underneath, she goes straight to the room. I follow behind her and she's digging through the clothes in her suitcase. "There they are." She exclaims when she finds yet another pair of pajamas. These are a heavy fleece and she grabs a pair of fuzzy socks before stripping out of the layers she has on.

I pull off my layers and shockingly only the first few are wet. The more I take off, the dryer my clothes are. But they still carry the bite of cold out from outside. I grab my flannel pants and a long sleeve shirt. Rummaging around in my suitcase, I search for another pair of socks, but I think I put them all on to go outside. A ball of pink flies at me. "Here."

"Will these even fit me?"

"They should," she shrugs. "At least, until your feet warm up." She walks by me, stopping to wrap her arms around me. Her fingers are freezing, but I don't move her away. "Thank you."

"For what?"

"For enduring what must be torture for you." Her mouth meets my bare chest and I know of a way we can warm up much faster. Another kiss and she leans back. "I'm going to see if the water is boiling yet. Hot chocolate sounds pretty great right now. And, I'm hungry since we went straight outside." She starts for the door. "Any chance you got bacon when you had them stock this place?"

"As if I could forget." She loves bacon.

"Awesome. Can you start another fire? My body is frigid and I want nothing more than to park my butt in front of it to warm up."

"Yep. Let me get dressed and get our laundry in the dryer then I'll start the fire."

"Thank you." With that she bounces out of the room.

And now I feel like an ass for making a big deal out of nothing when we were outside. And Tiffany's cousins call her dramatic. I think I win on that front today. Tiffany amazes me with how patient she is with me. I didn't have a lot of the experiences she did, and sometimes I freak out with what she throws at me.

I'm going to do my best to make the rest of the trip as complaint free as possible. Especially if I want her to answer a specific question.

Chapter 9

Tiffany

Spencer is lighting the fire and I'm working on the bacon. At least I'm wearing long sleeves. Whatever bacon they bought is popping grease like nobody's business. I can't imagine what it would be like if I was wearing anything but this. Even my legs and feet are protected in warm, comfy clothes.

I pause from bacon flipping to start a batch of fried eggs and put the biscuits in the oven. We'll see how multitasking works for me. I mean, the cooks at work do it all the time. How hard can it be? I crack one egg in the pan and wait for that side to cook. Spencer usually handles cooking the eggs so I hope he likes over-medium. It's the only way I know how to cook eggs. "How many do you want?"

"How many what?" He's still trying to get the fire lit. Last night the logs were already in place when we got here and he didn't have to worry about setting it up. Now, though...it looks like the firewood is getting the best of him. I would help, but that's not my area of expertise. Audrey always got our fire pit going when we were younger after I almost set the yard on fire. Our parents decided it just wasn't something I should be concerning myself with. Now, I wish she would have taught me. If we were ever trapped in the wilderness, I'd never survive.

"Eggs." I flip the one in the pan over.

"Three would be great." He glances up at me with a wide grin. "I worked up an appetite during my near-death experience sledding."

I roll my eyes. "It wasn't that bad." My goal before the snow goes away is to get him back out there and video the entire thing.

"If you say so." Finally, the wood in the fireplace catches fire and he high fives himself on a job well done. "Is something burning?"

"Shit," I screech. Apparently, it's really hard for me to do more than one thing at a time. "I'm so sorry." I pull the burnt bacon out of the pan and toss it on a plate. Honestly, I'm jealous of people that can cook multiple things at once. You'd think I'd be able to do it seeing as I manage a restaurant, but alas, that is not one of my super powers. One day, though.

Before I have time to register his presence, Spencer is standing beside me. "Do you need any help?"

I take the egg out of the skillet and put it on a plate before I fuck that up, too. I want us to have some semblance of an edible breakfast. "That would be great." I point the spatula toward the skillet I just emptied, "you want to take over egg duty?"

"Sure," he shrugs. He adds another egg to the pan and I put a few more pieces of bacon in the pan I'm using. "You know, you didn't have to start this by yourself, right? I planned on cooking for you all weekend."

"I know," I sigh. "I just wanted to put in some effort since you planned this entire trip. I feel weird just lazing about."

Laughing he nudges my shoulder. "That's not the way your cousins tell it. According to them, they do everything and you show up when you feel like it."

Ugh, my cousins can be such assholes. "Well, that's their side of the story. Not mine." It's like nothing I do is ever good enough.

"Honestly, I think your cousins still see you as a kid most of the time." He reaches around me for one of the burnt pieces of bacon and takes a bite. To his credit, he doesn't even make a face. I'm not sure how he isn't, but bless him for eating it. "Believe me, I know how that feels."

He's right on that. His mom treats him like he's five most of the time. Refusing to give up her baby. I get it. Spencer is an only child. Hell, my cousins and I are only children, but we had each other. He didn't have anyone. "True, but one day they'll see all of my potential and kick themselves for not giving me the credit I deserve."

"You are absolutely right." He kisses the top of my head and continues making the eggs while I work on the bacon. It's much easier focusing on this one thing. I glance behind me to check the timer for the biscuits. There's still eight minutes left. Looks like our brunch is going to work out splendidly.

"Any chance you got orange juice and vodka?" Breakfast at this time doesn't feel right without a screwdriver.

"Orange juice, yes." A frown mars his beautiful face. "Vodka, no. Sorry."

I stick my bottom lip out and pout. "It's okay. I guess I can drink a virgin screwdriver."

"You mean just orange juice?"

"Yes, if you want to be boring about it."

His only response is a laugh. I'm glad he gets my sense of humor. My cousins would have rolled their eyes and given me crap about it. Since Stella got married, I feel my relationship with them drifting. But not in a bad way. It's different. Like we're all growing up and getting on with our lives even though we'll always be there for one another. I was so scared that I'd lose my friendship with Stella when she got hitched. If anything, I look up to her even more. She has it all. Job, spouse, and beautiful house. Maybe one day I'll have that with Spence.

Spencer plates the last egg and I take the last few pieces of bacon out of the pan. The biscuits are all that is left. The white noise of the dryer suddenly stops and the oven beeps. That's not right. It should be going for at least another two minutes. When I look back at the oven, the display is blank. "Did a breaker blow?"

I walk to the oven and pull the door open. At least the biscuits are done enough to be edible. Spencer checks the dryer and punches the button repeatedly to restart it. "I don't think so, but I'll see if I can find the breaker box. It should be here in the laundry room somewhere."

He flicks the light switch up and down. Nothing happens. Oh no. That doesn't look like a good omen. "I'll go see if any of the lights in the other rooms come on."

I hit the switches in the living room...nothing. It's the same in the bathroom and bedroom. As a last resort, I walk back to the living room and try turning on the television. Son of a bitch.

When I said adventure. This isn't what I meant. Hiking through the woods, checking out the local scenery, and maybe finding a place to eat...those are the adventures I want to have. Not sitting in the cold without power.

"Do you think I should call the owners and ask them what we need to do?" Spencer looks worried and defeated at the turn of events. He shouldn't be, though. I'm the one that was like nope, this "snow weather" isn't going to be bad at all. Well, I was fucking wrong. So very wrong. We've been sitting without power for four hours.

"It might be a good idea. At least so we know that it's been reported since they do all that from phone numbers now." I only hope they answer.

Spencer searches through his recent contacts and my phone pinks with a message. Picking it up, I see the group chat with Stella and Audrey.

Audrey: Do you guys have power at your place? Ours just went out.

Stella: We lost it about five hours ago.

I debate if I should respond. I didn't tell either one of them I was out of town and totally forgot to send pictures of our snowman. Hell, I haven't even looked at my phone since we've been here. It's been a nice break from technology. A chance to completely unplug and enjoy the little moments so many of us take for granted. Except this power thing. This is not enjoyable in the least.

If I don't say anything, they'll freak out. Which means Audrey will make Justin get on the roads to come check on me. Or, they'll start blowing up Spencer's phone. And that's something we can't have right now while he tries to get in touch with the owners.

Audrey: Tiffany!!!! ARE YOU OKAY?!?

Tiffany: Yes. I'm fine. I'm actually out of town right now. We haven't had electricity for around four hours.

Instead of another text message, my phone rings and I'm on a group video call with both of my cousins. It's probably a good thing I'm not in Austin right now because if looks could kill, the frustration on Audrey's face would destroy me. "What do you mean you're not in town?"

Standing up I move across the room so I don't disturb Spencer while he's on the phone. We're both hunkered around the fire because the one thing master bedroom doesn't have is its own fireplace. "Spencer surprised me with a mini vacation. We're actually not too far from you, Stella."

"Oh, are you at the cute cabin?" She sighs, "I've been bugging Johnny to book us a weekend there, but we've been so busy with getting settled and his house ready to rent that we haven't had time."

"Stay on topic, Stella," Audrey snaps her fingers. "And y'all thought it was a good idea when they were predicting a massive snow storm?"

"That would be my fault." I raise my hand like I'm confessing something in school. "The snowy weather is never as bad as they say it's going to be. How was I supposed to know that this one actually would be?"

I take that moment to push the curtain aside and look out the window. The snow is coming down in droves. I've never in my life seen weather like this. Even when we go skiing the weather is mild. I mean, there's still snow on the ground, but it's not blizzard like conditions. "You have really got to start watching the news, little cousin."

"Eh, why would I want to? It's almost always doom and gloom."

"Because then you would be informed of stuff like this." I can see Audrey pacing back and forth in the kitchen she shares with Justin. "I've been checking social media and it looks like most of the state is losing power. Some places have started rolling blackouts."

"It'd be great if they roll those blackouts in this direction," I mutter. Spencer gives me a thumbs up motion and adds more wood to the fire.

"Are y'all at least staying warm?" Stella turns and I can see the fire lit behind her.

"Yes, there's a fireplace so we've been sitting in front of it." I can't recall if Justin's house has a fireplace. "What about you Audrey?"

"We're managing. Luckily, the stove here is gas so we've got the burners lit and closed off the rest of the house with blankets. We're also layered up."

"If things get too bad, call Dennis. He has a couple of generators and I'm sure he'd lend you one."

"I will." Audrey rubs her forehead. "Just promise me you'll be as safe as possible. I can't have you frozen like a popsicle. Either one of you."

"Yes, ma'am." I mock salute her. "I'm going to go join Spencer by the fire again, if you're done yelling at me."

"I'm done."

Stella finally speaks up. "If things get too bad, call us. We have a four-wheel drive and can probably make it to you."

"Will do. Be safe. Love y'all."

"Love you, too," they say in unison and we end the call.

Spencer pats the floor beside him and motions for me to come over. "I guess we'll just have to hang tight until the state gets their shit together."

"Yep." I'm just hoping it doesn't take too long. Not just for me, but for all those that don't have access to warmth or shelter.

Chapter 10

Spencer

Just like that, my special romantic getaway has turned into a frozen hellscape. At least we have a fireplace. We would have been freezing our asses off in the apartment had we stayed home.

Tiffany is lying on the floor, wrapped in three blankets we found in one of the closets, reading one of the books from the library upstairs. Her head is in my lap, hair splayed out like a halo. As cold as she must be, she looks relaxed. If anything, this trip made her take a break. Made her not worry so much about work and trying to keep herself afloat. "Are you comfortable?"

"Hmm?" She sets the book on her stomach and stretches her arms. She still hasn't been on her phone much to conserve the battery. But I've been playing games on mine and it's close to dead.

"I asked if you were comfy?"

"Oh, yeah. The only thing that would make it better is if I had a pillow." A quick glance at the decorative ones on the couch tells me all I need to know.

I gather her hair in one hand so I don't step on it when I stand. "Sit up really quick."

"What? No. You don't have to get one for me. I'm perfectly capable."

"It's fine," I laugh. "You keep being a potato. I'm going to grab the blankets and pillows off the bed and bring them in here in case the power stays off and we have to sleep in here."

"Good thinking." She sits up long enough to let me up. Grabbing her book, she rolls over, and turns herself into a human burrito. Leaning on her elbows, she continues reading. I'm not even sure what book she's reading, but I pull my phone out and snap a quick picture. I want it as a reminder that it's okay to slow down when she tries turning into a workaholic again.

Phone now in my pocket I hurry to the bedroom. It's cold without the warmth of the fire. I really hope this doesn't last longer than tomorrow. I didn't get a lot of food we could cook over the fire. Our saving grace tonight are the snacks Tiffany loaded up on. Words cannot express how grateful I am that she decided to splurge on them.

I fold the comforter up into a tidy square and grab the blanket off the chest at the foot of the bed. Our second night here and we've yet to take advantage of this massive thing. If the power ever comes back on, I plan on rectifying that. Next, I stack the pillows on the blanket pile. These have to be more comfortable than the ones on the couch.

There's only one more thing to get before going back into the living room. I open the drawer of the nightstand and pull out the box. This may not be the most opportune time to ask her, but we're unconventional like that. Hell, our whole relationship started with a one-night stand. When the moment feels right, I'll ask her.

Shoving the box in my other pocket, I grab the pile of blankets and pillows and head out of the room. The items hit the floor with a loud plop, and I hurry to close the bedroom door. I know closing it off when the main space is so open won't do much in containing the heat, but something is better than nothing.

When I turn around Tiffany has set her book aside and is laying the blankets out into a pallet in front of the fire. Not too close. We don't want to burn the place down when we go to sleep, but it's still close enough that we feel the full force of heat from the fireplace.

She notices me watching her and pulls down the edge of the top three blankets. "You have to be freezing after going into that room. Come lay down."

That's one thing I won't argue with. Waiting until she's under the covers, I slide behind her. "I'm sorry this has turned into a shit show."

"It's not your fault, Spence. You don't control Mother Nature," she eyes me skeptically, "unless, you're hiding a super power and you did this so we'd have no distractions."

"If only I was that amazing," I chuckle, "but really, this isn't what I envisioned when I booked this place. Though it doesn't sound as if we would have fared any better at home."

"You're right. We'd be freezing our asses off and wearing every piece of clothing we have." She snuggles closer to me. "We aren't equipped for this kind of weather, and neither is our apartment."

Leaning on one elbow, I use my free hand to comb through her hair, and feel her relax into me. "You're right." I pause for a moment. "Maybe we should look into a new place soon."

"That's not a bad idea." She yawns. That's one thing I've noticed. When there's no power, you constantly feel tired. There's no way to tell what time of day it is without looking at the phone. "Maybe we can find something off the beaten path. Something like this."

"Really?" That's hard to believe. She loves the accessibility of the city.

"Yep," she nods. "Can't you feel the difference out here? There's something so peaceful about the quiet stillness. There's no traffic on the roads. Horns and sirens aren't blaring at all hours of the day. Even when I lived with my parents, the town was just big enough to be annoying at times. Out here... there's nothing. Just you, me, and the beauty of nature around us."

This is why her cousins call her a free spirit. She finds the good in all situations and goes wherever her heart leads her. Hopefully her heart also leads to forever with me. This is my moment. The perfect time to ask her the one thing I've been wanting to for months.

"Tiff," I shake her shoulder to make sure she's awake. I don't want to disturb her if she's asleep, but I know if I don't take the leap right now, I'll never find the perfect time again.

"Yeah," she rolls over to face me.

I reach into my pocket and pull out the box. "I know this isn't the vacation I planned, or promised, but I wouldn't want to be here with anyone else but you." She opens her mouth to argue, but I don't let her.

I push the blankets off me and kneel in front of her. She follows suit, sensing there's something important I need to say. "I think I fell in love with you the first night we spent together after that concert. I knew I loved you when you came home early from that date, yelling at me for interfering in your life. And the moment you showed up at my parents' house dressed as Rogue, I knew I wanted to spend the rest of my life with you. This isn't the ideal place to ask you this. I had a hundred different scenarios planned. All of them outside, but that is clearly out of the question." I chuckle softly before taking a deep breath. Opening the box, I present it to her. "Will you cosplay with me, and go on a great many adventures with me, for the rest of our lives?"

She doesn't respond right away and I can't help but feel like I've royally fucked this up. That maybe I'm not as adventurous as she needs me to be. Or, maybe I'm too into my fantasy worlds. It takes a few seconds for me to realize tears are rolling down her cheeks. Before I have a chance to plant myself firmly to the floor, she launches herself at me.

We fall to the floor and I'm pretty sure her elbow just went into my ribs. "Of course, I'll spend my forever with you," she cries. The tears are coming down faster and if not for her reaction just now, I'd think she's breaking up with me.

"Are you sure?" Damn, that sounded desperate. But I need to make sure. I saw how freaked out she was when Stella got married, but I don't think that had anything to do with marriage itself. Although, she didn't say much about whatever she talked about with her cousin after the ceremony.

"I've never been sure of anything in my life." She leans down and presses her lips to mine before sitting up. "Even when it feels like nothing can, or will, go right, you're there to brighten my day. Do you seriously think I'd be handling this crazy ass weather as well as I have if I was with my cousins, or alone?" She doesn't let me respond and continues. "No. You are my peace and my calm. I know that no matter what, you'll always be in my corner and I can lean on you when life throws insanity at me."

"You're right, and I'll be there always. Until we're no more for this world."

She laughs, taking the box from my hand and sliding the ring on her finger before cuddling into me. "You sound like one of the guys in those fantasy movies you're always watching. But yes, it'll be us against the world."

Those words have made me the happiest man on earth. I lean up, crashing my mouth into hers. She opens her mouth the tiniest bit allowing me entrance. This really was the magical moment I've been waiting on. Everything is dark and silent around us as if we're the only people in the universe.

I tilt forward until I'm able to lay her down on the bed she's made for us. Pulling away from her for the briefest moment, I slide her layers of pants off her legs before taking my own off. All I want to feel for the rest of the night is being wrapped in her embrace. Making this the night we remember for the rest of our lives.

Epilogue: Tiffany

Why is it so hot in here? I scoot away from Spencer's body heat and move the hair from my face. Cool metal meets my cheek and I can't help the smile that comes over my face. I'm sure I look insane, but I don't care. Lifting my hand in front of me, I admire the ring on my finger. It's not your run of the mill diamond. It's a polished amethyst stone set on a silver band. He knew exactly what I would like. One of the many reasons he's absolutely perfect for me.

Sitting up, I groan. It's odd falling asleep to utter darkness and then it being so bright when you wake up. Those curtains are blackout curtains, and there shouldn't be any light peeking through them. Wait a minute. I look up and the living room light is on. "Hell yeah," I yell as loud as possible.

Spencer jumps up from his spot beside me. Guess he wasn't sleeping quite so hard. "What is it?"

"We have power, baby." I jump up and dance around the living room. My layers of sweaters come off with each movement until I'm in my long-sleeve shirt and underwear.

"Seriously," he looks around the room then up at the light. "Thank God. I'll never take electricity for granted again."

"You bet your sweet ass, we won't." I rush to the kitchen and pullout breakfast items. "But I was also serious when I said I want to move out of the city. Who knows...maybe I can talk Dennis into opening up another restaurant in a small town. Then Janie can run the one in Austin."

"I like the way that sounds." The good thing is, it won't affect him at all. He works from home. "I'll even help you bring the subject up with him."

"Nah," I wave his comment away. "I'm a big girl, I can handle it. Thank you, though, for the offer." He truly is the absolute best. I wasn't wrong when I said I knew he'd always be in my corner. That he even offered is why he's so amazing.

I pull a clean pot out of the cabinet and heat some water on the stove. I'm not sure if the water heater has had a chance to warm up and I need to wash the dishes from yesterday so we can cook breakfast. "Do you need some help in there?"

Taking a few seconds to think about it, I almost refuse him, but I don't want another bacon disaster like yesterday. "That would be great. You want to cook the bacon today?"

"I guess," he eyes me. "But why?"

"Because," I step around the counter. "I don't have on any pants and I'm not getting grease burns all over my legs."

"Good point." He gets up and joins me in the kitchen. He grabs a dish towel and dries the pans I've finished washing.

There's a knock at the door and we both freeze. My hands are covered in soap and Johnny is looking around the room as if that will give him some clue as to who could possibly be here. I whisper, "Do you think it's a serial killer?"

"In broad daylight? Naw," he shakes his head. "Besides, even serial killers have to be happy there's power again."

"Touché." I glance at all my clothes thrown around the room. "Maybe I should put on some pants after all."

"That's probably a good idea." He sets the pan he was drying on the counter and peeks out the dining room window. Groaning, he turns to me. "Did you have to tell them where we were?"

"Tell who?" I grab the closest pair of pants and pull them up.

"Your cousins." He points toward the window. "Stella and Johnny are on the porch."

"What?" Rushing to the door, I yank it open. Yep, my eldest cousin is standing right there, hand lifted in the air to knock again. "How the hell did you get here?"

She shrugs and pushes her way past me. Johnny follows after her, and I'm staring at both of them. "I told you Johnny had a four-wheel drive. We parked it up on the street."

"I hope nobody hits it. It's old, but that doesn't mean I'm ready to get rid of it," Johnny grumbles. He sets the bags he has on the kitchen table.

"So, you thought you'd pop in while I'm on vacation?" I should be annoyed, but honestly, I'm glad both of them are okay. It's nice to see their faces after all the snow.

"Yep." She pops the "p". "You should have known there was a chance we were coming. I had to see for myself that you were okay, and I wasn't sure if y'all got your power back yet."

"That's what phones are for, Stella."

She shrugs. "What kind of cousin would I be if I didn't make the trip in person." Her grin is wide and she starts pulling boxes out of the bags.

"I think you've been living in a small town way too long. Next thing I know, I'll find you giving advice to neighbors about how to spruce up their yards."

"Oh," Johnny laughs. "She didn't tell you? She already does that." My cousin glares at her husband.

"We were just about to cook breakfast," Spencer interjects before anyone can say anything else.

"There's no need." Stella waves him off. "We brought breakfast tacos. There's a little bit of everything. Y'all come eat."

Free food? And, I didn't have to cook it? I'm not going to argue with that, I grab some plates from the cabinet and set them on the table. "Thanks, guys."

Reaching into one of the boxes, I grab two tacos for me and two for Spencer. Before I can even reach for the hot sauce, Stella grabs my hand. "What is this?"

"That my dear, soon-to-be cousin in law, is an engagement ring." Spencer reaches for my free hand and gives it a light squeeze.

"Oh. My. Gosh. Congrats you two," she shrieks before rounding the table and throwing her arms around both of us. "It's about damn time."

"Let the insanity begin once again," Johnny laughs from his chair. "I'm happy for y'all."

"Stella," I pat her on the back. "I can't breathe."

"Oh, sorry," she releases us and takes a step back. "Am I the first to know? Please tell me I am."

"Yes, considering you barged in here."

"I cannot wait to tell Audrey that I knew first." She claps her hand and jumps up down. "She's going to be so pissed."

Oh great. I'll have to call her as soon as Stella leaves and tell her. If she hears it from me first, she won't be as upset. Stella goes to the fridge and opens the door. "Yes, you have orange juice." She glances around the counters. "Where's the vodka?"

"Y'all really are related," Spencer mutters to me. "We don't have any."

"Well," she sighs. "We'll have to celebrate with drinks at the house before y'all head back home. As soon as you can get your car out, I expect to see you."

There's no point arguing with her so I nod and take a seat. "She's about to take control of the whole thing, isn't she?" Spencer whispers in my ear.

"Yep." Hopefully we can reign her in. We aren't the traditional wedding sort of couple, and I'm sure she's going to balk at some of our ideas. But I'll let her have her fun...for now.

"We need to get you a wedding binder, and figure out a location." She pulls out her phone and starts listing notes of everything that needs to be done.

Leaning my head on Spencer's shoulder, I take in the scene before us. I was the wild child. The one my family thought would never settle down, much less get married. Spencer wraps his arm around me, cocooning me in his embrace. I can't wait to marry this man.

About the Author

About Katrina Marie

Katrina Marie lives in the Dallas area with her husband, two children, bonus child, grandchild, and fur babies. She is a lover of all things geeky and nerdy. When she's not writing you can find her at her children's sporting events, curled up reading a book, or binge watching her favorite shows.

Want to check see how Tiffany and Spencer met? Or, how her cousins found love?

Check out the Gone in Love Series: https://katrinamarieauthor.com/gone-in-love/

More Series by Katrina Marie

Out of the Ashes: https://katrinamarieauthor.com/out-of-the-ashes/

Taking Chances: https://katrinamarieauthor.com/taking-chances/

Find Katrina Marie online!

Facebook: http://bit.ly/2xRRsSE

Instagram: http://bit.ly/2xXp81t

Reader Group: http://bit.ly/2OWd6Nb

TikTok: https://bit.ly/2W59MHT

Newsletter: http://bit.ly/2BlDSsZ

BookBub: http://bit.ly/2VKs8sm

Goodreads: http://bit.ly/2TIncD6

Always You

Liz Durano

Chapter One

Pearl

"This is the worst night of my life!" My roommate Stella Carradine wails as I look up from the book I'm rereading for the tenth time. A senior at Hunter College like me, she looks amazing in a halter top dress, her open-toe high-heel shoes showcasing a fresh pedicure.

"What's wrong?" I ask.

"Tina was supposed to come with me tonight but she ate something bad for lunch and now, she's puking her guts out." She unwraps the long telephone cord she's managed to wind around her arm and hangs up the phone. "But I can't go to the club by myself," she adds.

"What about Martha?" Martha is another one of her nightlife-loving friends. The three of them usually stay up late, checking out discotheque and jazz clubs they hear about in the New Yorker.

"She's visiting her aunt in New Jersey." Stella pauses and turns to face me. "I know! You should come with me."

"No can do." I purse my lips toward the TV. "*Love Boat* is coming up next, and then *Fantasy Island*. And my parents are calling tonight. Jace is in town and he's going to jump in on the call so I need to be here. Apparently, he's home on vacation."

Jacinto "Jace" Vasquez is the oldest son of one of my parents' close friends and he and my older brother, Gael, are quite close. While Gael is currently stationed at Clark Air Base in the Philippines, Jace went into the Merchant

Marines. The last time I saw him was during Christmas break, and he was so fit and tanned that even my best friend Rosalie took notice.

"So have him get on the call next week," Stella says.

"I can't. He may only be home for a week," I say as Stella gets down on her knees and gives me puppy dog eyes.

"Please come with me, Pearl. Clint is taking me to one of the most exclusive, if not the most exclusive club in New York City tonight and I don't want to miss it. It's a once-in-a-lifetime thing. Pretty please?"

I set down my book on the couch. "But I have nothing to wear."

"You can wear one of my dresses. My mom sent me one last week I think will look way better on you since red isn't my color."

I make a face. "But what about my parents? They usually call after they finish dinner, which is ten or eleven my time."

She rolls her eyes. "I can't believe you buy the whole time-change excuse they give you as to why they call you so late. It's to make sure you're home on a Saturday night."

"Who's to say I don't leave the apartment after I hang up with them?"

"And how many times have you done that in the last four years you've lived in New York?" she asks as I flash her a guilty look. "Pearl, it's 1978. You need to let go a little bit or at least this weekend. You're such a good Catholic girl it's pathetic. And now the semester is ending and you've yet to experience New York nightlife." She grasps my hands together. "Please, Pearl. I've been looking forward to this night for the last two weeks but I also don't want to meet Clint and his friends at the club alone."

"Why don't you have him come pick you up?" I ask. "He is taking you out on a date, right?"

Stella rolls her eyes. "And have him come up to our apartment the size of a closet? Come on, Pearl. The guy lives in a townhouse in Midtown and our apartment fits in his living room. Would you want one of the richest guys in New York to know you live in a not-so-great part of the city where we have to have triple locks on our door?"

"So what? The rent is reasonable." But as Stella sighs, I see her point.

It's also no secret Clint Caldwell's world features finishing schools, vacation houses in Martha's Vineyard and the Bahamas, and private sports clubs. The latter is where Stella works during weekends as a server to make extra money, and it's where she also met Clint who asked her out two months ago. Tonight's supposed to be special. Stella thinks she'll finally get to spend the night at his place.

I sigh. "Alright, I'll go."

Her face breaks into a wide smile. "I'll make it up to you, I promise. And you'll have a good time tonight, I guarantee you that. You'll love meeting Clint's friends. They're the Who's Who of New York. Or more like the kids of the Who's Who of New York, which is just as good. One of them is even buddies with John-John."

I shrug. "So what about this dress?"

"Oh, you'll love it!" Grabbing my hand, she leads me into the bedroom where she rummages through the closet. "No plunging necklines or bare backs. Instead, it's got this flowing capelet that's too demure for me. Mom said it's a copy of a Halston piece but it makes me look like a good girl which I'm not." She pulls out a red dress on a hanger and holds it up in front of me, grinning. "But you are."

An hour later we're standing outside the hottest club in Manhattan on West 54th Street. It's not the best place to be, not with porn shops a few blocks down and questionable people milling about on the fringes. But judging from the crowd of people gathered around the entrance, all of them hoping to be among the lucky ones picked to go inside, the club might be as good as all the newspapers claim it to be.

Too bad Clint and his friends are nowhere in sight.

"Are you sure he'll show up?" I ask, rubbing my arms. I should have brought a coat but Stella assured me we wouldn't need it. Once we're inside, she said a coat would only be in the way.

"He'll show up." She stands on her tiptoes to scan the crowd.

A man wearing an electric blue leisure suit sidles up to us. "Hey, girls, trying to get inside? I can get you in. There's a back door–"

"Get the fuck out of here, dude," Stella says in her best New York accent. "You honestly think we'll fall for that?"

"Bitch," the man mutters as he walks away.

"Damn right I am," she counters, grabbing my hand so I'm right next to her. "You gotta learn to give attitude, Pearl. It's the only way you can survive in this city." Suddenly her face lights up when someone calls her name. "There he is!"

She pulls me through the crowd toward two men. Clint wears an all-white ensemble while his friend looks handsome in a red shirt under his dark vest and matching blazer and pants. But it's his eyes that transfix me most of all, blue with dark circles that frame his irises.

"Calista and her friends are running late," Clint says as he kisses Stella on the cheek. "They're going to catch up with us inside later."

"Pearl, these are my friends, Clint and Daniel. Daniel is a financial analyst who also trades stocks and is one of the best in the city–"

Clint laughs. "That's why he's my trader."

"And he's also one of the city's most eligible bachelors, too," she continues.

"Not if you ask Calista," Clint says as Daniel shakes his head, looking annoyed before turning toward me and shaking my hand. "It's very nice to meet you, Pearl."

"Pearl is my roommate," Stella adds. "She goes to Hunter, too."

Daniel's gaze lingers on me. "What are you majoring in?"

"Archaeology."

Clint chuckles. "Haven't we discovered everything already?"

"You don't have to discover anything new to study archaeology. It's the study of human history and pre-history through artifacts. I hope to specialize in Puebloan pottery," I add.

"What's that exactly?" Daniel asks, his brow furrowing.

"It's pottery made by the Anasazi Indians in North America," I explain. "Like the famous cliff dwellings in Mesa Verde."

"Ah, yeah," Daniel replies. "I've heard of them. Never been, though."

"Don't get her started talking about pottery this or pottery that or we'll never make it inside the club." Stella pulls me to her. "Pearl is from New Mexico. She's in her senior year like me."

"Are you pursuing a Master's?" Daniel asks and I shake my head.

"I'm going home right after I graduate."

Stella winks playfully at Daniel. "Unless some eligible New Yorker snags her first."

"We have to get in now," Clint says as a man by the door waves for us to come closer. "He's letting us in as a favor to Calista's dad and I don't want to give him a chance to change his mind."

As we walk through a smoke glass door that leads to a narrow walkway, I can feel Daniel's gaze on me. I smile, my cheeks flushing, heat pooling in my belly.

I've spent the last four years focusing on my studies, making every dollar my parents pay to have me study in New York worth their while. Sure, I'm on a scholarship, but there are expenses and so I do my best to keep them down which means I don't go out with Stella as much as I'd like unless it's to a concert at the park or something that doesn't require me to buy a drink. It means I don't get to meet guys as often as Stella does, the rich ones she says hang out at specific places in the city.

After a man behind a counter hands us our tickets, we walk through another narrow hallway where a chandelier above reflects laser lights all over the walls. It's like another dimension and for a moment, I lose myself in the energy that seems to emanate from the end of the hallway where loud music vibrates through the walls.

"Stella's going to be with Clint all night," I say as my roommate disappears through the doors. "I hope you don't mind but if you're not with anyone–"

"You're with me," Daniel says as he offers his arm and I lace my hand around his elbow. "Don't worry. I'll be your date for the evening."

"You don't have to be my date but..." The rest of my words is swallowed up by the music that reverberates through the walls the moment we walk through the doors. The club is something else. It's overwhelming and exciting. Strobe lights flicker across the dance floor and against the walls, and neon lights flash in various colors. In one corner, people lounge on leather couches and talk, drinks in hand while the dance floor is filled with people, some wearing the most outrageous costumes, or barely anything at all. On one platform, a woman wearing only a feather boa and a bikini bottom shakes her body to the music. It's a lot to take in, the sights, the sounds, the people.

As a familiar song plays, Stella laughs as Clint spins her around before kissing her on the lips. Her arms wrap around his neck and they disappear into the crowded dance floor.

"Would you like something to drink?"

Daniel's voice snaps me out of my thoughts and I nod, not knowing what else to do. I've stared long enough. As he takes my hand, a jolt of electricity catches me by surprise, traveling down my spine to the tips of my toes. I gasp and I pull away.

"Static electricity," he says, clasping my hand again and weaving through the crowd. This time, nothing happens but a fluttering in my stomach.

At the bar, he tells me he and Clint went to the same schools in Manhattan and eventually Columbia. It's difficult to hear anything above the loud music but somehow I hear every word Daniel says as he leans down to speak into my ear. Each time he does so, I catch a whiff of oak moss, patchouli, and juniper berries, musky and masculine. My stomach tightens at the nearness of him, and when he pushes a lock of hair that strays over my eyes, the fluttering in my belly turns into butterflies, a whirling, heady sensation that makes its way to my chest.

How come I never felt this way with Jace, not even when I saw him last Christmas, muscled and tanned from months spent at sea? He kissed me and said we should be exclusive but I told him finishing my degree came before anything else. Being "exclusive" would have to wait.

With Daniel, it's different. Being so close to him sends my world off-kilter, like a planet jolted out of orbit by a passing meteor and all I can do is find my way back.

Stella and Clint appear in front of us. "What are you guys doing standing there?" Laughing, she pulls me toward the dance floor. "Let's dance!"

The song is fast but I manage to dance to it without feeling too self-conscious, my body moving to the rhythm. When Daniel spins me around, I feel giddy. I love the way the dress feels against my skin, how the capelet drapes over my shoulders and arms. Sexy without revealing anything else.

Daniel has his moves down, too. The man can dance, and for the rest of the song, the world around us fades. It's just us and the way he watches me and touches me. The way he makes me feel seen.

"Red suits you," he whispers in my ear. "You look beautiful."

Before I can reply, a woman appears beside him. "Daniel, there you are! I've been looking all over for you."

As three other women join us, I figure they must be the friends who were running late. From the corner of my eye, I see Stella and Clint heading toward the couches.

"Pearl, this is Calista Gallo," Daniel says as he returns to dance in front of me. "Cal, this is Pearl, Stella's roommate."

"Nice to meet you." Calista's gaze sweeps over me before returning to Daniel. "Daddy would like to see you. He said it's important."

Daniel's expression turns serious. "Where is he?"

She points toward the far corner of the club, behind the couches. "He's in the private room."

As she leaves the dance floor, Daniel reaches for my hand but Calista's friends come between us and all I can do is follow right behind them as we weave through the crowd just as a group of people rushes toward the dance floor, eager to take the space that opened up.

Someone bumps into me and I feel myself falling but a woman behind me grabs my arm, stopping my fall. She's tall and dark, with a buzz cut and electric blue eyeliner. "You're okay, doll," she says as I regain my balance.

"Thank you."

I step off the dance floor and hurry toward a door where I'd last seen Daniel and Calista's friend heading. Two men guarding the entrance step in front of the door, blocking my way.

"Sorry, lady. VIP guests only."

"But I'm with them." I wave at Calista and her friends but they turn the corner before they can see me.

"As I said, lady, VIP guests only," the man growls, his face impassive.

I head to the lounge area where I last saw Stella and Clint but they're not there. I search for them on the dance floor but there's no sign of them either. Inside the ladies' bathroom, I stand inside a stall trying to think of what to do next until someone bangs against the door.

Fear sets in as I search for Stella and Daniel again, even asking the man guarding the VIP area again if I could go in but to no avail.

They're gone and I'm on my own.

Chapter Two

Daniel

One minute she was right behind me and the next, no one remembers they'd met her. But that's Calista for you. The only person who matters to her is her.

But it's not her fault. When you've been with someone for three years and suddenly they don't love you, you do what you can to preserve whatever you have left. And for Calista, that means anything that will keep me with her. It's been four months since we broke up and I should walk away, but how can I walk away when her world is also mine?

It's no secret that I wouldn't have made it into her circle of friends—the circle that once belonged to my father—without her help. Without her utter belief in my abilities and my talents. I have a lot to be thankful for, but I also know when it's time to leave, when the love that you thought you felt for someone is gone.

It wasn't sudden at all. It was gradual. One day I woke up and I felt empty. Somehow, somewhere along the way, I had fallen out of love with Calista though I tried so hard to find it again. We did the things we used to do together —quiet things like reading on a Saturday night instead of hosting the biggest party of the season or going Upstate on a weekend instead of attending the Met Ball. But none of them worked. In the three years we'd been together, we'd changed. We grew up. It didn't help that she acquired some bad habits along the way; habits proved to be the lines even I couldn't accept.

So if she's rude to the new girl—Pearl—I get it. But that doesn't mean I'm going to excuse it.

"Where are you going?" Calista asks as she grabs my arm. We've left the VIP section of the club where I got to speak with her father, Tommaso Gallo, and see what he wanted with me. After agreeing to meet him the following Monday, I'm back on the main floor, next to the row of couches where exhausted partygoers sit to catch their breath. Some are doing a few lines on the tables in front of them.

"I'm going to look for Pearl," I say, cocking my head toward Clint and Stella who are too busy kissing and fondling each other to notice anything else.

"She'll be fine," Calista says. "Come with me to the Rubber Room. I want to see if what they say about it is true."

"Get your friends to go with you." I walk away, not waiting for her to reply, losing myself in a sea of people dancing to Donna Summer moaning to the music. No one may remember the girl from New Mexico majoring in Archaeology, but I do. And I need to find her.

Ten minutes later, I decide to step out of the club. I'll risk not being able to get back inside but I've looked everywhere for Pearl, even mistook another woman dancing on the floor as her and earning the ire of her boyfriend. I just hope she didn't try to make it back home alone. The area isn't exactly the safest to be caught alone in. People like Pearl, the ones who didn't grow up here, don't know the city the way I do. She doesn't realize how bad it can be, how, behind the glittering lights and glamour, there's ugliness hiding between the cracks.

And it's all my fault.

I find Pearl standing in front of a lit sign next to the club, her arms crossed in front of her as two Tony Manero wannabes wearing ill-fitting leisure suits crowd her. One is wearing a ridiculous feather boa and a fedora, his loud voice calling her baby.

"There you are." I elbow my way between both men who protest, demanding who the hell I am. But all my focus is on Pearl, at the fear that's written on her face. "I thought I told you to wait for me by the door."

"Hey, man, she's with us," growls the man in the boa.

"Get out of my way," I growl as I wrap an arm around Pearl's shoulders possessively. She's trembling, the skin of her arms cold from the chilly night air but I know it's not from the cold. "Are you gonna move aside or do you want me to make you?"

The words that emerge from my mouth surprise me as the man with the ridiculous boa opens his mouth but says nothing. I've never been a man of violence. That's for my brothers, not me. I'm the money man in the family, the one with the brains as my mother would say. But as my hand forms a fist as they step aside, using my brain is the last thing I'm thinking about right now. I want to beat them to a pulp for scaring Pearl.

As I guide her away from the club entrance and away from the leering eyes that had undressed her minutes earlier, I vow never to put her in harm's way ever again. It's a weird feeling, being this protective and angry. I just met her but it's as if I've known her all my life, as if I've been waiting for her and I didn't know it.

"Are you sure you're all right?" I shrug off my coat jacket and drape it over her shoulders.

"I'm better now." She pulls my coat tighter around her. "I should've stayed inside but I couldn't find anybody. You guys disappeared."

"I'm sorry about that. I thought you were with us the whole time, but you're here now and you're safe."

"What about your girlfriend?"

I shake my head. "Calista is not my girlfriend. We broke up four months ago but we still go around the same circles. Her father is also my boss." As Pearl grimaces, I scan the crowd pushing against the velvet rope, trying to get the club owner's attention. "Would you like to go back inside?"

She shakes her head. "I want to go home. But don't worry. I'll take a cab."

"I'd be more comfortable if I took you home. Would that be alright?" I glance at my watch. "It's one in the morning and I'll feel better knowing you're home safe."

"But only to my door," Pearl replies, her expression sheepish. "I won't ask you to come inside."

"I wasn't expecting you to."

Relief washes over her. "Then I'd like the company."

I hail a cab and we get in. I catch the scent of her perfume as I slide next to her in the back seat. It reminds me of rose and jasmine but with cheap quality to it, like she's wearing a Chanel No. 5 knockoff, but I don't care. Together with the scent that is all hers, it's intoxicating.

We don't speak as the cab races down the street, stopping at each streetlight that seems to turn red every time. It gives me more time to be with her, but it's not enough. I'm not ready to let her go yet.

"Do you have to go straight home?" I ask as we near her apartment. "There's a deli on the way that's open 24 hours. I'd like to buy you coffee and talk."

She peers at me, surprised. "Just talk?"

"Just talk. I'd like to get to know you better, Pearl," I say. "Is that okay?"

The deli is quiet with only three patrons, a couple at a table near the window talking in whispers and a man reading a book while nursing a cigarette, a steaming cup of coffee in front of him.

"Did you really ditch your friends at the club for this?" she asks as she slides into the booth. "This isn't exactly exciting."

I grin. "I was serious about wanting to get to know you better."

"What do you want to know?"

"Everything."

She laughs. "Guess you're in the mood for a bedtime story then. My life is pretty boring."

Nothing could ever be boring with you, I almost say out loud but I hold off. This is all new to me, this feeling of giddiness at being alone with her. I'm not falling in love like the songs say. Maybe I'm curious to see what makes a small-town girl like Pearl tick. Maybe I just need a distraction.

"Try me," I say instead as a bleary-eyed waitress approaches our table.

For the next two hours, we talk and I learn that Pearl's family is from Taos, New Mexico, a town about an hour and a half away from Santa Fe and about two hours north of Albuquerque. Her father is a local potter and her mother holds cooking classes every month. Her older brother, Gael, got so tired of living in a small town that he enlisted in the Army right out of high school and is stationed at Clark Air Base.

She's attending Hunter College on a scholarship and is in her last semester. After she graduates, she plans on returning to New Mexico where she hopes to put her degree to good use. She could stay and earn a master's degree but besides the cost which her family would have to take on, she misses home like the wide-open spaces and the big blue skies, the scent of sage and piñon. There's also the Rio Grande where she goes fishing for walleye and large-mouth bass.

As she tells me how she learned how to fish, I wonder if that's why I'm attracted to her. I've never met anyone like Pearl, someone who unabashedly loves their hometown despite all the glamour and pizzazz of New York. She has a certain glow about her that nothing in the tristate area can replicate.

"No love lost between you and New York then?" I ask. We've moved on from cups of coffee and slices of apple pie to ice cream floats. Hell, if the waitress demands we order breakfast, I'd do it in a heartbeat if it means I get to be with Pearl a little longer.

"Maybe a little bit," she replies. "As they say, you can take the girl out of Taos but you can't take Taos out of the girl."

"If you were given a chance to stay in New York, would you?"

"I doubt it. There's nothing here that'll make me stay."

"Nothing at all?"

She shakes her head. "Nope."

"What if it's someone who'll miss you if you leave?"

A blush creeps on her cheeks and she lowers her gaze. My stomach clenches and the fluttering inside my chest intensifies.

Shit, I have it bad.

"You do know you're moving fast, right?" she asks, the corner of her mouth lifting.

"Yup."

"Aren't you afraid you'll scare me away?"

"Would you like me to slow down?"

She thinks for a moment, her brow furrowing, and shakes her head. "No."

I grin. "I'll keep going then."

Pearl laughs. "Please do. It's nice to feel important after being forgotten at a nightclub."

It's drizzling as we leave the deli two hours later and walk the rest of the way home. Her decision, not mine as she hugs my coat tightly around her shoulders. I've barely had anything to drink but I'm drunk on Pearl Anaya, the sound of her voice, the sight of her big hazel eyes, and her smile. I don't even feel the drizzle against my skin.

It's going to take all my willpower to keep my hands off her when we reach her door but I have to do it. I promised her I'd walk her home and that's all I intend to do. I'm a man of my word.

At least, I was until tonight.

"Have dinner with me," I blurt out as she retrieves her key from her purse. "Tonight."

"I have an early class tomorrow."

"I'll take you home right after."

She eyes me suspiciously. "Just dinner then."

I breathe a sigh of relief and nod. I think she said yes. "Just dinner."

"Seven o'clock. That way, I can get to bed early."

I grin. "Seven o'clock it is."

Tommaso Gallo's car is idling outside my apartment when I step outside at 6:30. The door opens and he beckons me to get inside.

"Calista said I'd find you here," he says. "I need to speak with you."

I adjust the collar of my coat. "Anything wrong?" I try to remember if anything had happened in the market today, but it's the weekend and there's nothing in the news to be worried about.

"I hear you're interviewing with the Becket brothers," he says as my jaw clenches. "I hope the word on the street isn't true."

"And what exactly is the word on the street?"

"You're leaving the firm. This interview with the Becket brothers is the second meeting which tells me it's serious," he continues. When I keep walking, he orders his driver to keep pace, ignoring the honking cars behind them. "If you're unhappy at the firm—anything—you know you can tell me, Daniel, right? We can fix it, whatever it is."

"Nothing's wrong at the firm."

"Then why are you leaving?" he asks. "You've been with me for three years and this is all so sudden. Is it because of Calista? I can tell her to ease off on you, but you and I both know she's having a difficult time since you guys broke up. You can't blame her for hoping. You are my golden boy, one of the best traders I've ever seen."

"Can we discuss this tomorrow?" I ask. "I'll be at the office first thing."

"Actually, there's something I need to talk to you about." His tone turns serious. "An opportunity to run your own firm."

I stop and turn to face him. "My firm?"

He nods. "It's not in Manhattan but it'll be yours."

"Why?" I can guess why. It'll mean I'll still be under his watch, but it's also an opportunity I can't ignore. My own firm would mean more money and more chances to prove myself on the big stage instead of working under Gallo.

"This one's in Long Island and you'll be closer to your mother and your brothers. That is if you consider that a positive," he says, chuckling. "But it will be all yours to manage." He pats the seat next to him. "Come in and we can talk more about it. It won't take long."

I glance at my watch. If I step inside his limo, I'll be late for my dinner date with Pearl. If I don't, I'm telling him that his offer isn't that important to me. Mr. Gallo can get me places faster than I can on my own. My accomplishments in the last three years working for his firm are proof of that. It got me places I never thought I'd be welcomed in. Calista's connection helped, too. Because of her, I was able to walk the same grounds as the very people who years earlier, didn't think my family was good enough to be among them. Instead, I now manage their money.

With my firm, I could do so much more.

A ticket to the big leagues in half the time it would take for me to do it on my own.

"What do you say, Wonder Kid?" Mr. Gallo's voice snaps me back to the present. "I could change your life."

"A few minutes," I say as I step inside the limo.

"I'll even drive you to your date so you won't be late." He extends his hand, grinning. "Is that a deal?"

I grip his hand. "Deal."

Chapter Three

Pearl

I glance at the clock again. 7:45 PM and he's still not here.

Daniel Drexel just stood me up.

So why am I still dressed?

I should change back into my PJs and make myself a sandwich because even if Daniel shows up, there's no way I'm going out now.

I should have known this would happen. It was simply too good to be true, him being so enamored with me he couldn't take his eyes off me all night.

Who am I kidding?

Daniel only felt bad that I got separated from the group at the club so he made up for it by offering to take me home and then wanting to get to know me better over coffee. Asking me out to dinner was icing on the cake. Another way to play with me.

Toy with me.

So why am I still sitting next to the telephone waiting for it to ring?

But what if he doesn't know my phone number? He never asked me for my phone number so he doesn't know it. But he could always ask Clint since Stella and I share one number.

I sigh. How naive of me to think Daniel was one of the good guys.

Thank god Stella isn't here to witness my humiliation. After spending the night with Clint at his apartment, she came home only to dress into something more comfortable to go to the movies, which means she'll probably be home soon.

As I step out of my dress, I can't believe I spent money on it. I didn't need to buy it but I did anyway, thinking it was about time I splurged on something. At least even if I won't wear it tonight, I know I'll wear it when I return home for spring break, maybe when I go out with Jace if he's in town.

I was home when my parents called this morning, worried about me after missing their call last night. I half-lied, told them I went to a friend's birthday party and got home at midnight, and went straight to bed.

"You missed talking to Jace, mija," my mother said. "He was looking forward to talking with you before he left for another six months on a ship."

"Maybe next time, Mama. I was looking forward to catching up with him, too," I said, pretending to sound disappointed.

The front door opens and Stella's high heels click against the floor before stopping abruptly.

"Why are you still here? I thought you were going out with Daniel," she says as I step out of the bedroom. "Please don't tell me you changed your mind and decided to stay home and reread your favorite book. What'll it be now? Tenth time?"

"Eleventh time, but no." I slip on my PJs and button the shirt. "He stood me up."

She stares at me. "No."

"He sure did."

She collapses on the couch, frowning. "That's weird because Clint told me he was raving about you today. Said you both talked for hours which is my idea of a very boring date."

"If this is your attempt at trying to make me feel better, you need to try harder." I settle on the couch beside her. "But did he really rave about me?"

"They met for lunch while I came home and showered." She kicks off her shoes and rubs her foot. "I'm shocked he didn't show up. Maybe he had something else come up. Clint told me he's so good at his job that other brokerage firms are trying to get him, a fact that's not lost on Mr. Gallo."

"Was that why he went all business on me the moment he heard Mr. Gallo was at the club last night?" Over coffee and slices of pie, Daniel had told me he worked at a mid-sized brokerage firm but he was hoping to move on to a more promising company. One day, he hoped to open his own firm but he still had so much to learn.

"Probably. Calista's really been talking him up to her dad. I suspect she wants him back. But I doubt that'll happen now. I saw the way he looked at you, Pearl. Like you were the best thing since sliced bread."

"Guess that bread got stale for him fast," I say, sighing. "Anyway, I have to remove my makeup and go to bed. I'm meeting my professor at seven tomorrow for my honors essay and I can't be late."

She joins me in the bathroom a few minutes later while I'm applying cold cream on my face. The hickeys on her neck stand out against her skin in the mirror as she wipes her lipstick off with a tissue.

"I'm so sorry about last night. I should have made sure you were still with us, but I couldn't leave the club to look for you because I didn't know if I'd be allowed back inside," she says. "Someone said they saw you with Daniel outside so I figured you were in safe hands."

"Don't worry about it, Stella. He was a gentleman."

She takes the tub of cold cream from the counter and dabs cream on her face. "But I don't like that he stood you up tonight. Something must have happened."

"Yup, something sure did. He made me out for a fool." I wipe my face with a tissue, removing every bit of cream and makeup from my skin. "But I will not let it bother me. After this semester, I'm returning home and I don't plan on coming back here."

She pouts. "But what about earning a master's degree?"

"With what? My good looks?" I scoff. "Besides, I miss home. It's not enough to go home for spring break or the holidays. I want to work as soon as I can, maybe get a job with the archaeological society and put my degree to work."

She nudges me with her shoulder. "Or you could find yourself a rich man and live happily ever after." As I sigh and shake my head, knowing how impossible Stella can be, she adds, "Why do you think I'm making sure Clint will never look at another woman? New York is where fairy tales come to die but not on my watch. You gotta hustle, baby, especially for love."

"Well, I hope you and Clint live happily ever after."

"If you ever decide to stay, you'll always have a place with me... and Clint." Stella giggles. "Who knows? I could be living in a penthouse with an amazing view of Manhattan soon. Goodbye, closet apartments. Penthouse of my dreams, here I come!"

I smile. "That would definitely make me reconsider."

I finish removing my makeup and wash my face. While Stella finishes up in the bathroom, I go to the bedroom and slide under the covers. As my head hits the pillows, I feel tired, my emotions on a rollercoaster I can't stop.

I can't believe I allowed myself to be carried away by a player like Daniel last night only to find myself waiting for a man who stood me up.

I reach for my favorite paperback and flip through the pages until I land on one of my favorite chapters to get lost in. As I start reading, memories of Daniel gazing at me from across the booth at the deli fade away, replaced by the hero on the page. The book isn't even a romance. It's a sweeping saga of adventure and political maneuverings featuring a South American son of a diplomat. There aren't romantic scenes between him and the many women he ends up with but somehow he checks all my boxes.

My hand moves lower and slides under my pajama bottoms as the hero on the page takes a woman from behind and calls her a name I can't imagine anyone calling me but I like it.

At least this one won't leave me disappointed.

The heady scent of roses greets me first when I return from my morning class. Its source is a dozen large ruby-red roses in a glass vase sitting on the kitchen counter.

"I knew he didn't no-show on purpose," Stella declares as she sets a Life magazine on the couch next to her and stands up. "He had an unexpected meeting."

"Did he tell you that?"

She nods. "He was at the door when I got home. Came with the delivery guy to make sure they brought it to the right apartment."

I set my book bag on the couch, doing my best to act nonchalant. "That was nice of him."

"He came by last night but you were already asleep and he insisted not to wake you. Believe me, I would have. But when I woke up, you were already gone," she continues. "He was very upset for missing your date."

I set my book bag on the couch. "He could've called and told you that."

"You never gave him your number, and he couldn't get a hold of Clint to get it."

When I shoot her a suspicious look, she adds, "Look, I'm not trying to make excuses for Daniel but you could at least give the man credit for trying." She cocks her head toward the flowers. "Aren't you going to read your card?"

I pluck the card from the arrangement and open it.

Dearest Pearl,

Please forgive me for last night. There's nothing more I want at this moment than to share the same space and breathe the same air with you. If you choose to give me another chance, tell me where and I'll be there.

Yours always,
Daniel Drexel

"Lord almighty, but the man has a way with words. He's like a real-life prince, I tell you. I'm swooning," Stella says as she fans herself with her hand. "Aren't you?"

I wish I could tell Stella I'm not feeling anything, not after getting stood up but I can't. The butterflies in my stomach are fluttering like crazy and I wish I could see him right now. My mind immediately goes to places where I can meet him again. The public library? The museum? Maybe another try at a dinner date?

But I also need to be realistic.

Daniel is good at this. Too good.

He's a big-city guy who can get any girl he wants, including me.

The ringing of the phone snaps me out of my thoughts. As Stella runs toward it, I get there first and block the phone.

"Don't! It could be Daniel."

"Or it could be Clint." She reaches behind me and snatches up the receiver.

"If it's Daniel, I'm not home," I whisper as she brings the receiver to her ear.

"Oh, hello, Daniel... You're looking for Pearl? She's right here. Let me get her," Stella declares cheerily and hands me the phone as I glare at her. "I have to run. I have a class."

As I bring the receiver to my ear, she grabs her book bag and clutches at her chest dramatically before running out the door. But before I can think of revenge, I hear Daniel saying my name.

I clear my throat. "Thank you for the flowers. They're beautiful."

"It's the least I can do for what happened last night," he says in his deep voice. "I was looking forward to having dinner with you but something came up and I couldn't get out of it in time."

"It's okay."

"No, it's not. I've never stood anyone up on a date and you're the last person I'd ever want to do such a thing to," Daniel continues. "I'd love to give it another try. Dinner, that is."

"Sorry, but I don't go out on school nights," I say, sighing.

"It doesn't have to be on a weeknight," he says. "It can be lunch or coffee. Tell me when and where and I'll be there."

"What about work? Your meetings?"

"I'll reschedule them for you. And this time, I will do it." He pauses. "Do you go straight home after your classes? We can meet nearby."

"It's not near the college at all but I usually go to the Village," I say.

"There's a bookstore that opened on the corner of Waverly Place and West 10th Street and I go there a few days a week."

"Are you going this afternoon?"

"Maybe."

"What time do you usually go?"

"At around three on Mondays and Wednesdays," I reply. "On Thursdays, I'm there around two."

"I'll be there."

"You mean today?"

"Yes."

"What if I change my mind?"

"Then I'll see you on Tuesday at two and if not, Wednesday at three."

I laugh. "You're serious about that? If I choose not to go any of those days, you'd still go?"

"I will," he says, my chest fluttering as his deep voice lowers. "I want to see you again, Pearl."

My stomach clenches at the unmistakable desire in his voice. "I think we're going about this too fast, Daniel. Why don't we play it by ear? If I see you, I see you. If not, that's fine, too. Anyway, I have to go."

As I say goodbye and hang up, I walk to the couch and sit down, my knees weak. My heart is racing and I'm breathless, my body in sudden need of release.

I force myself to get up and walk to the bedroom. Shutting the door behind me in case Stella returns home early, I pull open my lingerie drawer and retrieve a small vibrator massager tucked next to a copy of *The Sensuous Woman*, many of its pages folded to mark passages I've reread so many times. The massager comes with different attachments that the salesperson behind the counter at Sears assured me were for a variety of uses. General, facial, scalp, body, and callus massage, the back of the box states. But there's only one attachment that matters, one that fits a very sensitive spot.

Under the covers, I switch the vibrator on and press it between my thighs. Thoughts of Daniel fill my mind, his eyes, his smile, the deep bass quality of his voice that makes me shiver just thinking about it. No man has ever made me feel and do things I've never done before since meeting him.

For I want to do naughty things with Daniel.

Forbidden things.

Things a good girl like me shouldn't do.

Chapter Four

Daniel

She's browsing the books on a lower shelf when I walk into the bookshop. For a moment, I watch her. A goddess in a roomful of books oblivious to the world around her or the man who hasn't stopped thinking about her since he met her a week ago.

Wearing a loose red blouse tucked into a pair of tight bell-bottom jeans, the sight of her sends my heart racing. I want nothing more than to walk up to her, kiss her, and take her home with me. All I'm missing is a club and rudimentary language declaring my intentions and I'm no different from a caveman with primal needs.

"She's the perfect fling," Clint had said. "Maybe her father's right. Maybe you simply need to sow your wild oats right now. Get it out of your system and come back to Calista when you're done."

But Clint's wrong. Pearl is no casual fling, and I don't have any intention of making her one.

"Daniel, glad you're here," says a woman standing behind a counter. "A shipment of *The Ends of Power* arrived today and I saved you a copy. It will be right here when you're ready to check out."

"Thank you, Helene," I say before making my way toward Pearl.

My breath hitches when she looks up from the book she plucked from the shelf. Hazel eyes, rose-red lips, and thick black hair that falls down her back. Curves I want to dig my fingers into.

She's beautiful.

So achingly beautiful.

I don't regret the power she has on me. Since I've been coming here a week ago hoping to see her every time, I've bought over ten books so I don't look like I'm only here to meet someone. If books are the way to Pearl's heart, I'll buy the damn bookstore if I have to. As it is, I've already moved my lunch breaks to two on Tuesdays and three in the afternoon on Mondays and Wednesdays, hoping every time I came by to see her.

"Hi, Daniel," she breathes when I stand in front of her. "I had no idea you knew the owner."

I chuckle. "After coming here three times in one week, you start to stand out."

Her eyes widen. "I'm so sorry I couldn't make it last week."

"It's okay. We left it open," I say. "But can I say that you look absolutely beautiful?"

"Thank you." Her gaze lowers, her cheeks reddening. "You look pretty dashing yourself. Is that what you wear to work?"

I look down at my suit. "Every day."

"I love your tie. It highlights your eyes."

"Thank you." I swallow, words failing me as my gaze remains on her mouth. I'm ready to hang on her every word, in any language she wishes to use but just as she made me wait all this time, I remind myself to take it easy. Go slow. "Did you finish your essay?"

I'd called her twice in the past week but Stella told me Pearl was still at the college, working on an essay before spring break.

Pearl shakes her head. "Still researching."

"If there's anything I can do to help, let me know. Even if it's for moral support as I know nothing about archaeology."

She grins. "Only if you consider visiting Mesoamerican galleries with me exciting, then be my guest."

"I'd love to."

She rolls her eyes, skeptical. "Yeah, right."

"I'm serious, Pearl. Tell me when you'd like to go and I'll be there." When she doesn't say anything, I cock my head toward the book she turns face down in her hands and hides behind her. "What are you reading?"

"Nothing. At least, nothing like the one you ordered," she says. "*The Ends of Power* sounds pretty serious."

I shrug. "It's current events." I jut my chin toward the book she slips back on the shelf. "What were you reading?"

"Just something that caught my attention."

"Must be interesting if you picked it up."

She takes a deep breath. "If you really want to know, it's Harold Robbins' latest book. *Dreams Die First.*"

I reach down and retrieve the book from the shelf. "May I buy it for you?"

Pearl shakes her head. "You don't have to."

"I've been buying serious books since last week. Politics, money, investing," I say, grinning. "I need something that'll tell the owners I'm actually well-rounded."

"Be careful. I doubt being seen reading his books will elevate your image," she says, giggling. "Robbins' work isn't exactly considered high-brow."

"But you like it."

She nods sheepishly. "Stella thinks it's too macho. Or misogynistic, really, but the guy can tell a story."

"Didn't his books become movies?"

She nods. "One of them even starred Elvis, but the books are better."

I turn the book over and read the back cover. "You seem to know a lot about him. Is he one of your favorite authors?"

Her blush deepens. "No."

I laugh. "You're a terrible liar, Pearl, but that only means I'll have to expand my reading list."

She opens her mouth to protest but stops to step aside and give a customer room to check the books on the shelf in front of her.

I tilt my head toward the door. "Have coffee with me. Maybe you can tell me more about this not-favorite author of yours."

After paying for the books, we walk a few blocks to Fourth Street where we find a small intimate cafe and a corner table. This time, Pearl is the one with the questions.

Do I love my work? Yes. Do I have the rest of the afternoon off? Yes. Am I really into politics as the book reserved for me shows? Yes and no. My interest in politics is tied to its influence on the market.

And finally, the one I've been waiting for: What came up that night that was more important than our date?

"Advancement." I hate how the word slides off my tongue, how closely I took the bait. Who the hell would turn down a promotion that would have me earning over fifty grand a month?

"Did you take it?" Pearl's voice snaps me back to the present and I shake my head.

"No."

To say Tommaso wasn't disappointed would be an understatement. He honestly thought it was all in the bag, that I'd say yes to the offer of a firm of my own and more money than I could dream of as a 24-year-old stock trader. It would be understood that Calista and I would get back together, of course, another reason I'd be around.

"I hope it was worth blowing our date," Pearl says, grinning.

"No... and yes," I reply. "You're giving me another chance."

She arches an eyebrow. "Am I?"

"I'd like to think so," I say, my expression serious. "I haven't stopped thinking about you, Pearl. Every fucking day."

"What kind of thoughts?"

This time, it's my turn to blush, or I think I am blushing for it's the last question I expect to hear coming from her. My small-town girl. My goddess.

"Dirty thoughts."

She giggles, her cheeks reddening. "How dirty?"

Her laughter sends light through my very core. "Very," I reply, grinning.

"I like that."

I squeeze her hand. "And you?" I pause. "You can be honest with me."

She leans across the table. "Same."

"Dirty thoughts?"

Her answer is a whisper, her smile full of mischief. "Filthy."

I chuckle. "You're determined to make me suffer, aren't you?"

"You stood me up," she says, pouting before her face breaks into a smile.

"I deserve it then," I say, grinning. "But is there a tab somewhere? I need to know if there's still a balance due and if so, how much."

"Oh, there is a balance, all right."

"How will I know when it's fully paid?"

She thinks for a few moments, her eyes narrowing. "When you do something that blows my mind."

"There's a saying, and I'm sure you've heard of it," I murmur. "Be careful what you wish for. Not everything is like what you've read in your favorite books."

For the first time, her gaze drops to the table and I feel her confidence waver. It's as if the rules of the game she thought she'd been playing suddenly changed. "But what if everything I know is from the books I've read?"

"Then we'll have to make sure the real-life versions are a hundred times better."

I finish my coffee and set the cup down, studying her. I've been with a few women—not a lot, by Clint's standards—but no one has managed to inflame me the way Pearl has, and our conversation has only intensified every emotion going through me. It's as if she knows where my buttons are and has her fingers pressed on every single one.

And I never want her to let go.

We take a walk around the Village after we leave the cafe. It's getting crowded; people are getting out of work and stopping by their favorite clubs along the way. We browse the shops, pretending not to notice anything interesting as we approach an adult toy store, the Pink Pussycat Boutique. Just when she thinks I'm not looking she steals a glance and blushes when I catch her.

"Have you ever been inside?" she asks and I nod.

"A few times. You?"

She shrugs. "Maybe."

"What did you get?" I ask. "Or were you simply browsing with your boyfriend and letting him pick something for you?"

"I've never had a boyfriend."

I stop in my tracks and turn to look at her. "Are you serious?"

"A long-term one, that is. I kinda dated in high school but I have an older brother and he's very protective. After he joined the Army, his best friend kept an eye on me so I never really got a chance to have a serious relationship," she says. "When I moved here, New York men were so... so direct. Aggressive."

"I can understand how that could be scary," I say. "Your brother's best friend. Did he actually stop anyone from asking you out?"

She shakes her head. "Not to my knowledge. He's my best friend too."

I'm sure he is. "What does he do?"

"He's in the merchant Marines," Pearl replies. "I was supposed to talk to him last Saturday but I went to the club with Stella instead."

"Do you like him?"

"Not in the way you think, but he did kiss me when I came home for Christmas," she says sheepishly. "We ended up under the mistletoe."

"And?"

She thinks for a few moments. "It was okay."

"Not world-shattering?"

"Is it supposed to be?"

"Not all kisses are created equal," I say as she shrugs again.

"If it happens, it happens."

Not with him, it won't, I almost blurt out but I stop myself. If she's trying to make me jealous, it's working.

"Do you think it will? With him, at least?"

"I don't know. We grew up together and our parents kinda encourage us being together," Pearl replies. "Maybe because Taos is a small town and everyone knows everyone. Who's dating who, who broke up, that kind of thing. We end up dating local people."

"Do your parents have to approve who you date?"

She glares at me and crosses her arms in front of her chest. "Of course not. I'm 22 years old and I'm old enough to date whoever I want."

"Would you like to go on a date with me?" I ask.

"Aren't we on a date already?"

"This will be an official one," I reply. "Let's say dinner on Saturday? We can check out a jazz club or a poetry reading afterward. There's one this Saturday at the Ear Inn. Have you read Maureen Owen's work?"

Pearl stops and turns to look at me, her eyes wide. "Is she really doing a poetry reading this Saturday? I'd love to go."

"Then we shall."

An hour later, I walk her up to her apartment door. I've never gone this slow with anyone before but with Pearl, I don't mind. I like watching her open up to me, her trust growing with every word. I love watching her eyes light up when she's happy, the way her mouth widens into a smile that reaches her eyes, the dimple on her left cheek deepening.

"Thank you for a lovely time," she says as we stop in front of her door. "I appreciate you taking it slow. I hope you don't mind."

"I think we're going at the perfect speed."

I cup her face in my hand, my thumb stroking her jaw. As Pearl's lips part, I lower my head and kiss her. A soft and gentle kiss, like the touch of a butterfly's wings. She tastes of vanilla and oranges and summer walks in the rain.

As my kiss deepens, my tongue sliding between her teeth and tasting her, I feel myself falling, my heart racing inside my chest so loud I wonder if she can hear it, too.

Suddenly I pull away and Pearl looks up at me, her mouth still parted, breathless. There's a look of surprise in her eyes as she touches her lips with her fingers. "Wow," she whispers as I run my thumb across her lower lip. "Just... wow."

"Good," I murmur as I push a lock of hair behind her ear. "Because there'll be more of that on Saturday."

Chapter Five

Pearl

Daniel was right.

Not all kisses are made equal.

Some feel like you're kissing your brother while others feel like the world beneath your feet moved, shattering everything you thought you knew—even if everything I know about love, kissing, and sex come from the books I've read.

Still, none of them had prepared me for the exact moment Daniel kissed me. The tingle of excitement that shot up and down my spine, the fluttering in my chest that seemed to go down to my stomach, the weakening of my knees.

And I can't wait for more.

Only it hasn't happened yet and the evening is almost over.

Sure, he kissed me when he picked me up at the apartment. A peck on the lips that left me wanting more. With Stella already out on her date with Clint, we had every opportunity for a deeper kiss but no, with a knowing look, Daniel said dinner first and then the poetry reading at the Ear Inn, the oldest bar in New York City.

But he hasn't kissed me again. He's held my hand throughout dinner, yes. He even draped his arm over my shoulders for most of the poetry reading, but another kiss? Nothing.

And now we're leaving, his hand pressed against the small of my back as he guides me toward the door and I'm a desperate horny mess. Anticipating so much more...

"Would you like to come to my place for a nightcap?"

As soon as Daniel's words tumble out of his gorgeous mouth, I almost shout my answer, but I catch myself. No matter how much my body would want to betray me, I'm still a good girl.

Yet no book warned me about the overwhelming emotions threatening to take over all rational thought as Daniel's gaze moves from my eyes to my mouth and lower, to the V neckline of my dress. None of the books told me I'd be so turned on by the sound of his voice and the way he looks at me like I'm the only person in the world. Nothing else exists but us.

But if I'm supposed to be a good girl, I should say no. You don't go to a guy's place without knowing what's bound to happen next. Only I'm tired of being a good girl. I'm tired of watching Stella have all the fun and tell me all about it, and I'm tired of experiencing everything about love and sex through books.

That ends tonight.

"I'd love to," I reply as Daniel holds my hand and we walk past a group of people milling in front of a jazz club.

"Pearl! Daniel! Wait up!" We turn around to see Stella and Clint stepping out of the door. "Where are you guys off to?"

I stare at Daniel, panic filling me. "He... he was about to take me home," I blurt out, too embarrassed to tell her the truth. "We just attended a poetry reading."

Stella grimaces. "Please don't tell me you're going to be sitting by your phone tonight and waiting for your parents to call."

"You two should join us," Clint says before I can reply. "We're headed to Calista's for a party. Didn't she invite you?" he asks Daniel who nods. "Then come with us. My driver's on his way and we can all go together. You know how her parties are. The more the merrier."

Stella giggles as she kisses Clint on the lips. "I can't wait, babe. This will be my first time."

"Your first time for what?" I ask as a black Cadillac stops in front of us.

She laughs. "You'll see." When I hesitate, she sighs. "Pearl, don't be such a party pooper. Let's go. I promise you'll have fun."

"And don't worry. Daniel won't let you out of his sight this time," Clint adds as he pulls open the car door, and Stella slides in. "Will you, Daniel?"

Twenty minutes later, we step out of the car in front of a building in Midtown. Daniel and I follow Stella and Clint through the main doors, across the lobby, and head toward a private elevator.

"Are you sure you want to do this?" Daniel asks as we stop. "We don't have to."

"I know but I don't want to be a party pooper."

"Then we don't have to." He cocks his head toward the door. "We can go to my place."

"But I'm also curious."

Daniel exhales, his brow furrowing. "Just keep an open mind, okay?" he says as we join our friends in the elevator that only has three buttons: Penthouse, lobby, and parking garage.

Before I can come up with anything else to say, the elevator stops and the doors slide open. Laughter and disco music greet us as we step out of the elevator. A mirror ball hangs in the middle of the room with a lit-up dance floor that's occupied by people dancing.

"I'm going to grab a drink," Clint says. "You guys want anything?"

"We're not staying long," Daniel replies as Clint looks at him in surprise.

"Oh, man, the party barely started."

"I think what Daniel's trying to say, sweetheart, is they've got other plans," Stella says, laughing as my cheeks redden. She grabs my hand, pulling me aside. "Don't worry. I understand, especially with a man like Daniel. But before you go, let's check out the heated pool on the 50th floor. I need to see it for myself in case Clint made it up."

"That's impossible. We're on the top floor," I say as I follow her up the stairs.

"Nothing's impossible with these people, Pearl. One day, I'll be swimming in my very own heated pool on top of the world. Just you see." Suddenly she stops at the top of the stairs. "Whoa."

The first thing I notice is the floor-to-ceiling windows all around us showcasing a 360-degree view of the city. Still holding my hand, Stella slowly walks toward the closest window. "Have you ever seen anything as beautiful?"

I almost tell her that yes, I have, like the big blue skies of Taos and the Sangre de Cristo mountains but everything about home escapes me when I see the city below. New York at night from the ground can be exciting and scary but fifty stories up, the view of the city is breathtaking.

While Stella explored almost every nook and cranny of the city she could step into before she returned to her small town of Bisbee, Arizona, I stayed in the apartment and read books, choosing to live my life vicariously through the heroes and heroines on the page.

But I can't keep doing that, not when there's a world out there I can experience firsthand before I return home after I graduate in two months.

"Pearl, look." Stella tugs at my hand and I follow her gaze to the people in the pool, steam rising from the surface. Some are talking while some are kissing and then there's a couple at the far end of the pool. The woman sits on the edge of the pool, her legs wide open as the man buries his face between her thighs.

"Holy shit," Stella whispers. "Clint wasn't kidding when he told me Calista's parties are wild. She and Daniel used to host these things but they stopped when they broke up four months ago."

My chest tightens. "Daniel?"

Stella waves her hand toward the pool where the same couple has traded places with the man sitting on the edge of the pool and the woman going down on him. "Small ones although Clint said they were never this big. Guess she's back to hosting them again, with or without him."

"Did Clint ever say why they broke up?" Calista has everything, even a heated swimming pool overlooking the world.

"Who knows with these people, Pearl? But it wasn't another woman; at least, that's what stumped Clint. Guess Daniel tired of all this," she replies. "Can you believe he's quitting his job at her father's firm? It's where he got his start."

Suddenly I don't want to hear anymore. It's one thing to know Calista and Daniel were together for three years but it's another to learn that this was the life he had with her, one I cannot compete with at all. I'll never measure up to anything close to the type of women Daniel is used to. I'm probably a sideshow to him.

Besides, what do I have to offer him that she doesn't have?

"I have to go." I run down the stairs, not waiting for Stella to catch up. I need to find the front door, catch a cab and go home. But I'm turned around somehow, turning into a hallway that goes into another room with a sunken living room where men and women in various stages of undress fill the couches and the floor. Talking, smoking, drinking, and like the woman on her knees as a man eats her from behind, having sex.

"Wanna join us, baby?" asks a tall lanky man with curly hair before laughing as I leave the room as quickly as I can.

I'm not a prude. At least I don't think I am. As conservative as my family back home may be, I keep an open mind. But nothing can prepare me for the images that come to me of Daniel doing the things I've seen with Calista.

I need to go home. I need to return to my simple world where I can live vicariously through the heroes and heroines in my favorite books. At least, that's the world I know.

Not this.

Not Daniel's world.

Chapter Six

Daniel

"You've been avoiding my phone calls all week, Daniel," Calista asks, gripping my arm and forcing me to stop in the middle of the hallway. "Why? What'd I do?"

After Clint asked me about getting a drink, Stella had ferreted Pearl away to the pool area, but when I got there, guests told me they'd gone back down to the party. I managed to find Stella with Clint at the bar but Pearl was nowhere to be seen.

"I thought she was with you," Stella said. "She just... left."

And that's what I'm afraid of.

Calista's parties aren't for everyone and I had a feeling it would be too overwhelming for Pearl. Hell, it's overwhelming to me sometimes and that's saying a lot. She and I hosted these parties but they were never like this. It used to be just booze and music and a good time. Close friends hanging out, dancing, and jumping into the pool. The sex came a year later, and so did the drugs.

That's where I drew the line.

I've smoked pot recreationally with a few friends, but as the parties grew bigger, quaaludes, poppers, and cocaine were added to the mix. It was dangerous, but Calista didn't care. It transformed her penthouse into party central, placing her on a whole different level among our friends and she wanted to keep it that way.

"Daniel, did you hear what I said?" Calista's voice breaks through my thoughts and I turn to face her.

"You did nothing wrong," I say as I turn away, but her grip tightens.

"Dad told me you turned him down," she continues. "I thought you always wanted to have your own office."

"If that's the reason he offered it to me, then I didn't earn it on my merit."

"I did it for you," she says. "It's what you've always wanted, isn't it? Your very own firm, so why say no? Dad's hurt, you know. Why bite the hand that's fed you for the last three years? The same hand that put you where you are now?"

My jaw clenches. "Cal, stop."

"Fuck you, Daniel," she hisses. "You should be grateful to me for everything I did for you. For letting you into my circle of friends, for telling everyone what an amazing trader you are, and for getting you the clients that now pay your bills. But what do I get for all that?"

"I'm grateful for everything you and your father have done for me, Cal," I say slowly. "But this isn't the way to get me back."

"Who said I want you back? I just want a little acknowledgment, that's all." Calista's expression turns cold. "One word from my dad and no one will hire you, Daniel. Remember that."

As I study her face, I notice her pupils. She's high.

"What did you take this time?" When she doesn't answer, I add, "Does your dad know you're hosting these parties again?" While the penthouse is supposed to go to her eventually, it doesn't mean it's hers.

She shrugs. "He's visiting Gran in Albany this weekend. We'll get it cleaned up before he comes back. He'll never know."

"Do you even know who you invited over? I don't know half these people."

She shrugs. "I met some of them at the club last week. They're good." She lights a cigarette, blowing smoke in my face. "I can't believe you're going all righteous on me when you and I used to host these things. You didn't seem to have a problem then."

I spot Pearl emerging from the den, her face pale as she hurries toward the front door. "Look, I have to go. I'll talk to you later."

I catch up with Pearl as she steps into the foyer and stops in front of the elevator. "I've been looking all over for you. Where are you going?"

"I'm going home." She presses the elevator button. "You don't have to leave the party. I'll take a cab by myself."

"I meant it when I told Clint we weren't staying long," I say as the doors slide open and I follow her inside. "But if you want to go home, please let me take you. Please."

Pearl sighs. "Okay."

We don't speak on the cab ride to her apartment. Pearl despises me. I see it on her face. She's appalled by what she saw at the party, at what my friends do for fun. The booze, the drugs, the sex.

"I'm sorry about what happened back there," I finally say.

"Is that what you used to do when you and Calista were together?" she asks.

"Not to the extent you're seeing now," I reply. "Our parties used to be a lot smaller than what you just saw."

"How small?"

I shrug. "Eight... ten people, tops. Couples. Friends we all knew."

"Is that why you broke up with her?"

"It was a combination of things. But she began using," I reply, remembering the first time I caught Calista doing lines in the guest bathroom. A "quick pick-me-up," she called it but then other times followed and I realized she'd developed a habit.

"What about the..." she pauses, her brow furrowing.

"The sex? I did, but not with other people. Just her." When Pearl shoots me a disbelieving look, I chuckle dryly. "They're also my clients, Pearl. I need to look them in the eye when I do business with them."

As I gaze out the window, I realize we're one block from her apartment and the date is officially over. I take a deep breath. I didn't expect the evening to go downhill so fast, but it is what it is.

"I think we need a reset button somewhere, so can we pick up where we left off?" She rests her hand on mine. "Right when we walked out of the poetry reading?"

I grin. "Of course."

"Ask me again... about that nightcap?"

I clear my throat. "Would you like to come to my place for a nightcap?"

Pearl nods, a faint smile on her lips. "I'd love to."

We arrive at my building on the other side of town twenty minutes later. Pearl is quiet as we take the elevator to my apartment on the tenth floor.

"Whenever you want to go home, let me know," I say as I open the door to my two-bedroom apartment and she steps inside.

"I don't want to go home yet. I'd only return to my books and wish I could experience the things I read about instead of reading them," she whispers as I shut the door behind me and switch on the living room light. "But I have my limits," she adds, chuckling. "Like the party."

I smile, beckoning her to follow me into the living room. As she goes straight to the built-in wall of shelves, I make my way toward the bar. "What would you like to drink?"

"Surprise me." She turns her full attention to the books on the shelves. "I didn't realize you loved to read, maybe more than I do."

She scans the titles on the shelves, moving from the ones filled with finance and business books to autobiographies to the ones containing a few of my favorite novels. James A. Michener's *The Drifters* and *Centennial*, James Clavell's *Shogun*, Irwin Shaw's *Beggarman Thief*, and Terry Brooks' *The Sword of Shannara*.

"Whoa," she gasps as I set bottles of Scotch and Drambui in front of me before retrieving two old-fashioned glasses from the cupboard and filling them with ice.

"Anything wrong?"

"Since when did you read Harold Robbins?" She points to a stack of books at the end of the shelf closest to the couch. *The Pirate, The Carpetbaggers, The Betsy, The Adventurers,* and the book I'd bought a copy for her at the bookstore a week earlier, *Dreams Die First.*

I do my best to act nonchalant as I mix the drinks. "I told you I was going to expand my reading list so I bought his books and read them."

"Have you read them all?" she asks as I make my way toward her.

"I hope you like this. It's called a Rusty Nail." I hand her a glass and after a brief toast, she takes a sip. "I've read all of them."

Pearl stares at me in surprise. "You're lying."

I shake my head. "Nope. I'm a speed reader although I have to admit, there were parts in his books where I had to slow down and take my time. He's definitely a storyteller. He can write pretty wild storylines with lots of adventure, money, and sex." Actually, there was a lot of sex but I suspect Pearl already knows that.

"I just learned tonight that he didn't make up those scenes, did he?"

"No, he didn't," I say, my gaze drifting to her lips. How many times have I wanted to kiss her?

"You must think I'm so unrefined, to like the books I like," she says, setting her glass on the coffee table. "Unlike most of the books on your shelf, my tastes aren't exactly sophisticated."

I set my glass next to hers. "Your taste in books has no bearing on whether or not you're refined. And if you thought the books on these shelves make the man, you're wrong. They're not all mine."

"Whose are they?"

"My father's," I reply. "He was a financier."

"Was?"

"He died last year. Car accident."

Pearl gasps, her hand resting on my arm. "I'm so sorry."

"Thank you. He left me this apartment and everything in it, including his books. Or some of them. His collection of antique books remains with his wife upstate."

She frowns. "Not your mother? His second wife?"

I shake my head. "Neither. I'm the oldest son of his mistress."

Pearl's eyes widen. "Wow."

I chuckle. "Wow is an understatement but my mother did her best to give my siblings and me a normal life."

"How many siblings do you have?"

"Two twin brothers and a sister."

"Where do they live?"

"They live in Long Island," I reply. "That's where I grew up."

"I hope you don't mind me asking all these questions," she says as we sit on the couch.

"No. Ask away."

"Did you always know that you were a..." she pauses.

"A bastard? Not until I was about seven years old," I reply. "I thought he was a pilot, which is funny considering he never owned a pilot's uniform. But that's what our mother told us in the beginning."

"What happened?" Pearl asks. "How'd you find out?"

I lean back against the couch, doing my best to appear relaxed. I don't know why I'm sharing things about my past I never even told Calista or Clint, but there's something about Pearl's questions that tell me she's good at keeping secrets.

"We were at a party," I reply. "A birthday for some kid whose name I don't remember now. Out of nowhere, this woman comes at my mother calling her a whore and that we, the kids, were bastards. Before then, I didn't even know those words but that day, they became a brand—the bastard part. Dad—her husband—pulled her off my mother and we left through the back door."

I take a deep breath, my chest constricting at the memory of my mother's humiliation. But it's the look on my father's face I have never forgotten. The man who only came a few days a month, never staying long enough for breakfast, couldn't stand up for us at that party.

"How old were your siblings when it happened?" Pearl asks.

"My brothers were four and my sister was two, so they don't remember it at all." I finish my drink and set the empty glass on the table. I clear my throat.

"But they know what they are. His wife made sure that the entire city would know."

"That must have been difficult for you."

I shrug. "Nothing I couldn't handle."

"Is that how you got the apartment, after your father passed away?"

"His wife tried to stop it but he set everything up in various trusts," I reply. "This apartment went to me and one of his houses went to my mother. My siblings have their trust funds, only to be made available after they graduate from college which is proving to be a challenge." I grin. "If it's not my brothers getting into trouble, it's my sister who's crazy for whoever she's dating. She's nineteen."

"Do you see them often?"

"Not as often as I'd like, but I manage their money so at least once a month, they make it a point to call me. Sometimes they stay here for the weekend." I get up from the couch and hold out my hand. "Enough talking for now. Want to do something fun?"

She takes my hand and gets up from the couch. "You mean this isn't fun yet?"

"Not yet."

I take her to the den where a big screen TV sits on one side of the room. It's one of the latest models I'd seen in commercials and one my brothers love to play full blast whenever they stay for the weekend after they tire of playing pinball.

"Have you ever played one of these things before?" As I switch the Bally Evel Knievel pinball machine on, lights come on as the xylophone version of Trumpet fanfare fills the room followed by the sound of clacks and pops.

"My brother and his friends played them a lot when we were younger. But I thought they were banned in New York," she says as I bring a finger to my lips and laugh.

"They lifted the ban a few years ago," I feed two quarters into the slots and press Start. "Would you like me to show you how to play this one?"

She nods, her face lighting up. "Definitely."

For the next ten minutes, Pearl watches me play as I tell her the rules of the game, how to get the stainless-steel ball to hit the targets, and maneuver over ramps, bumps, and traps. I should end the game, let the ball slide between the paddles and let her play but I'm showing off. I want her to see the fun side of me.

I also want her—not the damn pinball machine—in my arms.

Enough showing off. I let the ball slide down the slot and step aside. "Your turn."

Chapter Seven

Pearl

I don't realize Daniel said something until he steps aside. I'd been so lost in my fantasies as he worked the pinball machine, his forearm muscles flexing, his hips moving with every press of the buttons that controlled the paddles.

One thing's for sure: the man can move.

"Want me to show you how to play?" he asks as he hands me two quarters that I feed into the machine and press Play.

"I'd love that." The scoreboard blinks, his high score replaced by a lone zero. "But I'm not sure if I can top your score, though."

He smiles. "What score? Just have fun."

A shiver of excitement runs down my spine when he stands behind me and rests his hands over mine. He doesn't have to show me how to press the paddle buttons but I let him, as if we're playing our parts in a secret dance. The knowledge that I hold some power over him makes me feel daring, willing to push things to the limit. I also want to see more of him like this, carefree and almost like the version of him I saw at the bookstore. I want to see him come out of his shell as I step out of mine.

"Pull the plunger," Daniel murmurs in my ear and I do as he says. As the stainless-steel ball flies across the playfield, I can't tell the sounds of the machine from the beating of my heart. It's as if a hundred horses are galloping inside my chest, the sound of their hooves on the ground rumbling in my ears.

Daniel's mouth brushes against my ear as he tells me when to push the flipper buttons, sending the ball to ricochet from corner to corner. With every move, his hips and thighs press against me. Soon, we get into a rhythm as the machine comes to life. I'm out of breath as the board lights up and the bells and pops go off against the rolling of the ball. Each thud against a mushroom bump, each ring of a bell or clang of a trap vibrates through me along with the feel of his body pressing and rubbing against mine.

When he slides his arm around my waist, I gasp at the firmness of his grip. When his mouth moves down my neck, no longer inches away but now kissing the skin between my neck and shoulder, I don't care that I'm about to lose the ball. All I want is the feel of his mouth against my lips, the possessive grip of his hand holding me to him.

"You're so fucking beautiful." He growls in my ear, his other hand wrapping around my waist as he squeezes my breast. When his mouth and tongue find a sensitive spot on my neck, I moan. My vision wavers, the playboard in front of us forgotten as my knees threaten to buckle beneath me. None of the books warned me it would feel like this, that it would leave me unhinged, unmoored, and wanting only one thing.

Daniel.

I want to know how it feels to be his, even for one night. I turn my head toward him, my mouth meeting his in a ravenous kiss. His hand leaves my breast and slides up to cup my jaw as our lips press together, tongues meeting, tasting, leaving me breathless.

I pull away, twisting my body around so I'm facing him. His eyes are dark, his gaze hungry. He wants to devour me and the realization that this is all real hits me low in my belly. This isn't anything like the books I've read, stories written by men and women who don't know Daniel or me. This time, the story is all mine. All notions of romance replaced by a carnal need that scares and excites me.

"Do you want to stop?" he asks, frowning.

"No!" I say, shaking my head as I bring my hand to his face, my fingers stroking his five o'clock shadow. "Don't ever stop."

And with that all words leave me as he presses his mouth to mine, his tongue sliding between my lips and sending an electric jolt through my body. As I kiss him back, heat builds inside me like a fire that's out of control.

But I'm not the only one. I can feel how hard he is when he presses into my belly. He's huge and for a moment panic seizes me. Can I take someone as huge as him?

Will it be just like in the books?

But my mind has drawn a blank, every word I've read about the act forgotten.

No, this time, there are no books to be remembered for no hero I've ever read can match Daniel's power over me. As his hands stroke my back, the feel of him pressing into my stomach sends another wave of warmth coursing through my belly, my nipples hardening against his chest. His hands move lower to cup my ass before lifting me on top of the pinball machine.

"What about the game?" I ask playfully as I circle my arms around his neck.

"Fuck the game. How about this instead?" Daniel's mouth covers mine, passion with not an ounce of hesitation in his kiss. It's overwhelming, tasting him, feeling him pressed against me, his arms wrapped around me. When he pulls away, I'm out of breath and dazed, but I want more. So much more.

"You have no idea how much I want you, how much I've been thinking of this moment when I finally get to hold you like this." He kisses my face as he speaks, my lower lip, my jaw, my cheek, my eyelids. "And kiss you like this."

I bring my hand to the back of his head and pull him to me, our mouths meeting hungrily. It's better than all the books I've read combined. Even better than my dreams.

"Can we go somewhere quieter?" I ask, giggling as the machine pings and the Trumpet Fanfare song begins again.

"Definitely."

Within seconds, we're on his bed, his body covering mine as we alternate between nibbling and kissing, tasting and savoring, our tongues tangling together, our hands exploring. For me, a new topography, hard and masculine and powerful.

I undo the tie of my dress, glad that I followed Stella's suggestion not to wear a bra. "Who wears them these days anyway?" she'd said. "You should try it, Pearl. It feels so liberating." And at this moment, it does. When Daniel's gaze moves down my body, there's a feral quality to his gaze, one that makes me feel triumphant, like I am the one with the power.

I can feel his hunger, his need. His ache.

"You're beautiful." The chesty rumble of his voice vibrates against my chest as he slides his hand down my body, sliding my skirt up to my thigh and finding me wet between my legs. That first contact catches me by surprise, the feel of his fingers so new to me yet one I've yearned for since I met him. Lifting his head so he can see my face, he slides my panties aside. I gasp as his fingers find me, so wet and so ready. For what? I have no clue. It's one thing to read about it. It's another to experience it. And right now, my mind is a blank canvas as my body awaits his touch.

I whimper when he slides his fingers up to the edge of my clit. "Fuck, you're so wet," he murmurs before lowering his head and burying his face in my neck, his tongue blazing a fiery trail of ache and need down my shoulders, my breasts, my nipples. He moves lower, planting kisses on my stomach and lower still as he tugs my panties down my legs and parts my thighs. Then his tongue dips between my legs and I stare at him.

"Daniel..."

"I'm tasting you. All of you." He lowers his head between my thighs again, his fingers parting me wide as his hot tongue licks long and deep. I lick my lips, shocked at the waves of pleasure that wash over me with every dip of his tongue, every circling movement over my clit, his five o'clock shadow rough against my sensitive skin.

As he sucks my clit between his teeth and his finger slides inside me, heat pools in the pit of my belly, growing like a fire that can't be stopped. I thrash on the bed, my body pinned against the covers by his mouth and his tongue, driving me to heights I've never been to.

I hear myself cry and whimper as he devours me with his mouth. I'm helpless against the onslaught of pleasure that grips me completely. None of the books told me it would feel this way. None of them told me I'd be laid bare, wide open.

Then it hits me, a wave of pleasure like nothing I've ever felt before, the flame that had been growing inside me finally consuming me and I come in a blinding rush, screaming his name.

When everything goes still, Daniel kisses me and I taste myself on his tongue. It should be wrong but it feels so right, my hands unbuttoning his shirt and pushing it off his shoulders. The sound of his belt unbuckling and his trousers getting kicked off to the edge of the bed before he pulls me to him. Being in his arms like this, his breath warm against my face, his body hard and lean. What else could be more perfect than this moment?

I hear the ripping of a wrapper and stare at the packet in his hand. My heart races, and I can almost hear the blood rushing through my temples. I want what comes next so badly but–

I grip his wrist, my eyes wide. "Daniel, I've never..." the words fade as his eyes narrow.

"You've never what?" When I don't answer, he sets the condom aside and weaves his fingers with mine. "You've never done this before."

It's not a question. Maybe he can see it in my eyes, the fear, the embarrassment. The shame of being the only 22-year-old virgin in all of Manhattan.

"We don't have to do this, Pearl," he says.

"But I want to. I just don't know how it's going to feel."

He brings my hand to his lips. "It's going to be beautiful."

"Are you sure?"

"I promise." Daniel guides my hand to his cock.

I gasp at how hard it feels yet so smooth, like velvet against my palm. He groans, closing his eyes as I squeeze his length, marveling at how huge he is. And beautiful.

I reach for the packet next to him. "Can I watch while you... put it on?"

He nods as he takes the opened wrapper from my hand and takes the condom out. There's a tight expression on his face as he rolls it over his cock, as if it's taking all his willpower to be as patient with me as he can be.

As I lie on my back, Daniel positions himself over me and slides his sheathed cock between my folds, coating himself with my wetness. "Look at me, Pearl," he says when I start to look away. "All you have to do is say stop and I'll stop."

I lower my hand between us and stroke his cock. "I want you inside me."

As if every ounce of his self-control abandons him, Daniel groans and covers my mouth with his in a hungry kiss. I'm dizzy with desire even as a sharp pain sears through me when he pushes inside me. But as quickly as it comes, it's gone, replaced by something else, something that builds, expands, a delicious ache that he fills with every thrust.

I dig my fingers into his back as he continues to spread me with every thrust, my walls taking him inch by delicious inch. This time, I don't look away in shame. For there's no shame in this at all, not when everything in this moment feels perfect.

Something blooms deep inside me, heat mingling with something I can't name. Something spiritual almost, building with every rocking of his hips, every clench of my walls around him, every breath from my lungs.

Daniel brings my arms up over my head, trapping my hands with his as he thrusts again. And again. As his mouth finds the sensitive skin behind my ear, his teeth raking against the skin, leaving his mark, the railing of sensations is more than I can bear. It sends pleasure to my clit, and whatever bloomed from the base of my belly—physical, spiritual, primal—explodes into a blinding sea of stars and I know then that tonight, I'm his.

Chapter Eight

Daniel

The constant ringing of the phone in the living room yanks me from a deep sleep. While there's a phone on the bedside table next to me with its ringer turned off, the last thing I want to do is answer the phone while Pearl is fast asleep next to me.

What happened last night was pure heaven. Her trusting me enough to be vulnerable. To gaze into her eyes as she came again and again and again.

I hate to wake her but she doesn't even stir when I ease my arm from under her and get out of bed. Padding naked to the living room, I pick up the phone, wondering who could be calling me at eight in the morning on a Sunday.

"Daniel, I need your help."

Calista.

I stifle a yawn and sit down on the couch. "What's going on?"

"Guess you haven't heard," she says, the sound of people talking and phones ringing in the background. "I need you to bail me out."

Suddenly I'm wide awake. Bail? "What happened?"

"The cops showed up last night at around three. Said they were there on a noise complaint. They found drugs and arrested everybody. Well, everyone who was stupid enough to stay long enough," she says, her voice trembling.

"Was Clint still there?"

"Yes, but his dad just bailed him and Stella out." She pauses. "You have to bail me out, Daniel. Please. At least come pick me up."

I remember her dilated pupils before I left the party. She'd had something right before I ran into her. "Did you have anything on you?"

"No, but they said I could be charged with possession anyway since it was my place," she replies. "Please, Daniel. I'm scared."

"Did you call Mr. Sullivan yet?" George Sullivan is their family lawyer and until this moment, Calista had no need of him. I've been part of the Gallo family ever since I started working for Tommaso three years ago and I know just about everyone in his circle. George is also one of my clients, one I'll lose when I leave Tommaso's firm.

"I called you."

"I'll call him and have him go to the precinct."

"Can you come, too?" she asks. "Please, Daniel. I need you."

From where I sit, I can see Pearl through the open bedroom door, still asleep. I'd planned on spending the rest of the day with her doing nothing but that's not going to happen now.

I take a deep breath. "Which precinct are you at?"

Twenty minutes later, I'm dressed and sitting on the bed. With her dark hair splayed on my pillows and the thick lashes resting on smooth dusky skin as she sleeps, Pearl is a vision I want to remember forever. I kiss her on the forehead as she stirs.

"You're dressed," she says, surprised as she tucks the sheets under her arms and sits up. "I'm sorry for staying–"

"I want you to stay," I say, pressing my finger to her lips. "Something came up, an emergency, and I have to leave, but I'll be back in an hour. Two hours tops."

She frowns. "Is everything okay?"

"The police responded to a noise complaint last night and found drugs," I begin. "I have to go to the precinct with the lawyer to bail them out."

Pearl sits up. "Stella!"

"She's with Clint and his father got them out this morning."

"So who are you going to the precinct for?" she asks, her eyes narrowing. "Calista?"

"Yes."

"Oh." Pearl's gaze lowers. "You need to go then."

"It's not how it looks like, Pearl. I'm meeting their lawyer at the precinct–"

She rests her hand on my arm. "No, you don't have to explain yourself. I understand."

"Pearl–"

"I said, you don't have to explain yourself," she says, her voice curt.

The phone rings in the living room but I answer the phone next to the bed. It's George, letting me know he's on his way.

"I'll meet you there in fifteen minutes." As I hang up the phone, I hate I have to leave Pearl, but I can't turn my back on Calista. She's right. I owe her and showing up for her right now is the least I can do.

I hang up the phone and sit back down on the bed, gathering Pearl in my arms and taking in her scent, rose and jasmine, and sex. I press my lips on hers, tasting her one more time before I pull myself away. Any more and I'll never leave.

"Two hours, max," I say as I get up from the bed. "There's lots of food in the fridge if you're hungry but we'll do take-out when I come back."

The corner of her mouth lifts in a smile that doesn't quite reach her eyes. "Okay."

Pearl is gone by the time I return two hours later. I didn't expect her to still be here but disappointment sets in anyway.

That and frustration.

I should have told Calista I couldn't be there. I should have let George handle everything even if, in the end, he needed me there to calm Calista down after some photographer hounded us all the way to the limo. That the news could get to her father isn't a good thing and that's why we're all at my apartment.

"You sure you can handle this, Daniel? I have to get back. It's my daughter's birthday and I've been gone long enough," George says as Calista closes the door to the guest bathroom. With some of Calista's clothes still in my apartment after I'd boxed them up for her to pick up, it means she can get herself cleaned up before I drop her off at her apartment. I can only imagine the state of her place at the moment but that's not my problem.

"Go," I say. "I'll take care of everything from here."

"I don't know what the hell she was thinking having all those drugs in the apartment," he says, shaking his head. "Tommaso's not going to be happy when he finds out."

"I'll have her call him herself."

"Good luck with that," George scoffs. "But then, if there was anyone who could get her to do anything, it was you."

"She'll have no choice in this," I say. "Whether or not she likes it, she'll need to tell him before he hears about it in the news."

George pats my shoulder. "You're a good man, Daniel. Tommaso always said you were the best thing to happen to Calista. Glad to see you guys are back together."

My jaw clenches. "We're not."

His eyebrows shoot up. "Oh. So that's why you weren't at the penthouse when the cops arrived."

"I was here." I don't give him any more details, not when I need to keep Pearl out of this whole affair. The sooner I take Calista to her mother's apartment in Midtown after she gets herself cleaned up, the better. I want to call Pearl and make sure she's okay. But who am I kidding? That's not the only reason I need to hear her voice. I miss her already.

I'm reading the Sunday paper on the couch when Calista walks out of the guest bedroom fifteen minutes later, leaning against the door with only a towel wrapped around her.

"Why aren't you dressed?" I ask. "Your clothes are in the box next to the–"

She drops the towel on a nearby chair and walks toward me, naked. "You used to like it when I did this," she says as I set the newspaper next to me, doing my best to act calm even as my anger builds.

"Put some clothes on," I say as she approaches, her blonde hair damp and falling over her shoulders. A necklace I'd given her for her birthday a year earlier hangs between her breasts. "Please, Cal."

"Remember when you used to love it when I did this?" She kneels between my knees and rests her hands on my thighs. I know where this is going and if it were a different time—one where I hadn't yet met Pearl—I'd totally go for it.

But that was then.

As she runs her hands up my thighs, I grip her hands halfway. "Stop this," I say, clasping her hands between mine. "There is no more us, Calista, okay? Right now, you need to call your dad and tell him what happened."

Her eyes glisten with tears. "She spent the night, didn't she? You fucked her."

"It doesn't matter."

"It does to me," she says as tears roll down her cheeks. "I just wish I knew why you stopped loving me, Daniel. What did I do wrong?"

"It's not you, Cal. It's us. We changed." I take a deep breath, wishing I could turn back time and find the love I used to have for her, but I can't. How can you retrieve something that isn't there anymore?

I've had four months to think about what I walked away from when I told Calista we were over, two months to think about what I'd be leaving behind when I finally give my notice to leave her father's firm. All I know is that it's time for me to strike out on my own and stop feeling like I owe my entire career to the Gallos. Yes, they helped me get my foot through the door to my father's world—the bastard son making good, vetted by one of their own and getting a chance to prove he was worthy—but after three years, I'd like to think I've earned it. I've done the hard work.

If I'd had any doubts, meeting Pearl that night crystallized the decision for me. I needed to move forward.

"I'm going to let go of your hands and you're going to get dressed," I say slowly. "And while you're getting ready, I'm calling your dad and you can tell him what happened."

She sniffs. "What if he already knows? I'm sure George called him already."

"He still needs to hear it from you. The important thing is that he'll know you're okay," I say, holding her gaze in mine. "Will you do that for me, Calista?"

She swallows nervously and nods.

I let go of her hands and get up from the couch. Retrieving the towel from the chair, I wrap it around her. "Now go, and I'll be right here."

An hour later, Tommaso arrives at the apartment, having flown from Albany as soon as he finished talking with Calista. Although he'd been angry on the phone, he calmed down during the flight and the drive from the airport.

"Where is she?" he asks as I close the door behind him.

"She's sleeping in the guest room," I reply. "I can wake her up and let her know you're here."

He shakes his head, waving for me to join him in front of the window overlooking the city. "Let her sleep. We need to talk."

"About what?"

"Your decision to leave the firm," he says, lighting a cigarette and taking a long drag. "You are leaving, right? There's no point pussyfooting around the issue."

"I was going to give you my notice this week."

"So you're joining the Becket brothers?" When I don't answer, he shrugs. "The Becketts, Lehman, Goodrich... it doesn't matter. You're going to kill it wherever you go."

I shove my hands in my pocket. "You okay with that?"

"What do you expect me to say, Daniel? I can't stop you from going after what you want. Besides, if you've outgrown the firm, then you've outgrown it," he says. "But there will be conditions in your exit contract. You understand that, right?"

"Yes, sir."

"You can't bring your clients with you," he says, waiting for my reaction but not seeing any. "Now if they want to follow you, I can't stop anyone but it will be our duty to remind them they may incur charges if they decide to transfer their investments to a new firm. Fees, taxes, and whatnot."

"Understood."

"You'll need to find yourself a new circle of friends," he continues, the burnt end of his cigarette falling on the carpet as he gazes out the window, "for my daughter's sake. That includes your access to the private club as my guest. I'll be rescinding your invitation so it's best you don't return. Maybe one day when you can afford to pay the fees yourself, but only the board approves your application although I wouldn't hold my breath."

My throat tightens. I'd grown fond of visiting the private club where I got to rub elbows with men who knew my father and being treated like one of them. Being invited by a member like Tommaso meant I didn't have to pay any dues which saved me quite a bit of money.

"I understand."

He turns to face me. "We could have achieved many great things, Daniel, but there's no point in dwelling on what could have been. Thank you for taking care of Calista. That woman will be the death of me yet just like her mother. Stubborn as ever." He cocks his head toward the guest bedroom. "I don't want to take any more of your time, Daniel. It's time to wake her so I can drop her off at her mother's."

As I head toward the guest room, Tommaso says my name and I stop, turning to face him. "Oh, and one more thing. I hope you understand if I don't give you a recommendation. After all, I do have to protect my business interests no matter what," he says with a practiced smile. "I hope you understand."

Chapter Nine

<hr>

Pearl

I'd love to stay and wait for Daniel but fifteen minutes after he leaves, I get out of bed and drag myself to the bathroom. He'd set aside a brand-new toothbrush for me on the counter along with a towel and a washcloth.

I shouldn't do it but just before I leave, I open all the drawers and closets looking for proof that he may still be seeing Calista, but all I find is a box in the guest room with her things. Stella would call it snooping and she'd be right. But I can't help it, for doubt lingers long after he left to go to Calista and a part of me can't understand why.

Doesn't she have anyone else who can help her? Is her hold on him that strong?

But I tell myself not to dwell. I need to go home and catch up on my sleep even if I'd rather sleep in Daniel's bed, bundle up under his covers, and inhale his smell on the pillows. None of the books I've read ever mentioned that little detail, about how intoxicating it is to wake up in a man's bed after a night spent making love. Making love. At least, that's how it felt to me even if Daniel probably wouldn't call it that. Maybe to him, it's just sex but to me, it was everything.

I splash water on my face, reminding myself to get myself cleaned up. I'm in New York where, according to Stella, fairy tales come to die and that's why you have to hustle hard. For money, for respect, for love.

Half an hour later, I climb up the stairs to my apartment and slip the key into the lock. I hope I don't run into any of our neighbors because there's no way I can hide the fact that I spent the night with someone, especially with the love bites Daniel left on my neck that my hair can barely hide.

"Pearl? Is that you?"

I whip around to see Jace getting up from the floor across the hall where he'd been sitting against the wall. As he stretches his legs, he looks like he'd been waiting a while.

"Wait, have you been waiting for me all this time?" I ask as he gives me an awkward hug.

"Me and Gael. He's home for a few weeks and he thought it would be a good idea to surprise you. We got in last night." He tilts his head toward the stairwell. "He went out to get something to eat. That should be him coming back."

As I push open the door and step inside, Gael appears at the top of the stairs carrying a McDonald's take-out bag and a drink carrier with two cups of coffee. With his hair cropped short at the ears and his skin tanned from being stationed in the Philippines, he looks so grown up. I want to run into his arms but one look at his face and I stop. He stares at me for a few moments, his mouth pressed in a straight line as his gaze drifts down to my dress and back up to my face.

"Where've you been?" he asks as he walks past me into the apartment. "We've been waiting for you since last night."

I look from him to Jace. "In the hallway?"

"No, we went back to the motel to sleep and came back an hour ago but you still weren't home," Gael says, the accusing tone in his voice and his gaze unmistakable as I brush my hair over my neck with my fingers. "Neither was your roommate."

While I was the bookworm who read about Mesoamerican pottery and romance books, Gael was the hothead who always got into trouble at school and almost joined a gang. For a while, it was my parents' greatest fear to see police officers at our door notifying them that something bad had happened. When he graduated high school, they worried about his lack of interest in attending college. Then one day, he announced he was enlisting in the Army. It would get him out of everyone's hair, he said and would allow him to see the world outside Taos.

"Is this what you've been doing instead of studying? Going out with guys and coming home in the morning? Do Mama and Papa know?"

"That's not fair," I say, sitting down across from him at the table. "For your information, I don't go out that much. I'm at school or the library or here at home."

"Which one of these places were you at last night?" he asks. "School? Library? Because you weren't here."

"I was out with friends."

"This friend," he leans forward and pushes my hair from my neck, "have a name? Because I can't read his calling cards."

"Gael," Jace says, his voice clipped. "*Déjala en paz*. Leave her alone."

"She's not your sister, man," Gael says with gritted teeth. "So stay out of this."

"So what do you plan to do?" Jace asks, folding his arms across his chest. "Pack her up and send her home? She's 22 years old and last I checked, the law says she's an adult. She can be with whoever she wants to be."

As Jace glances at me, there's a resigned look on his face that tells me he understands what's going on and he's okay with it. Or that's what I tell myself. But Jace was always calm and level-headed, the complete opposite of my brother. But it's also what has made us feel like friends more than anything else. There isn't any chemistry no matter how much our parents want there to be.

"Mama and Papa pay a lot of money for her to go to school, not sleep around," Gael snaps.

"Stop talking as if I'm not here. And no, I don't sleep around and you of all people should know that, Gael." I remove the coffee from the cardboard carrier and set them on the table. I'd been afraid to face him when I first saw him but now I'm angry. Indignant, even.

"So who is he?" he asks. "What does he do? And why didn't he take you home himself?"

I open my mouth to answer but stop myself. I'm not going to go into a question-and-answer routine with my brother like I'm a child. What happened last night between Daniel and me may be a one-time thing—a one-night stand, as Stella would say—but I will not let Gael make me feel bad about it. Or guilty.

I get up from my chair and head to the cupboard to retrieve two plates. "Why don't you two eat your breakfast before it gets cold? And maybe later, when you're calmer, we can talk like adults."

But as I set the plates and napkins in front of them and they dig in, my chest tightens at the reality of what could happen. What's to stop Daniel from going back to Calista?

Why else did he get up and leave me so quickly if he didn't still love her?

"Are you okay?" Jace asks as we sit across the table a few hours later. After breakfast and a change of clothes for me, I suggested we go for a walk around the neighborhood to lighten the mood. Get some fresh air while we were at it, too.

And it helped. We ended up at Central Park where watching the people and their pets around the Mall and the 72d Street Fountain proved to be a worthy distraction. Like the woman with her five tortoises, each one sporting a different bandana, and her three pugs. Or the man on a bicycle with two macaws, one on each handlebar. Soon, Gael and Jace were back to their relaxed selves, much to my relief. At least, for a little while, the spotlight wasn't on me.

After grabbing some sandwiches from the local deli on our way back, we're back at the apartment.

"I'm good. You?"

He smiles. "Better now. I was worried about you."

"Jace, I–"

"It's okay," he says, holding up his hands. "Really, it's okay. I'm good."

"I'm sorry."

He chuckles. "It's ironic, though."

"What is?"

"Growing up, Gael was all; she's off-limits, man. Don't you dare look at her or I'll beat the crap out of you," he says, mimicking Gael's deep voice as we laugh. "Then last year, he wondered what I was waiting for. That he was okay with us dating."

I frown. "What brought that on?"

"Selfish reasons, mainly, I'm sure," Jace replies, grinning. "So you wouldn't meet anyone out here and stay home with your parents. I mean, it was a given that you'd go back home." He pauses. "Or has it changed because of your mystery man?"

I shake my head. I haven't told them anything about Daniel because I didn't want to break into tears. "No, that's still the plan."

He smiles. "Good. Everyone misses you back home. Rosalie especially. She thinks you're having way too much fun out here without her."

I roll my eyes. "Only if you consider having a full load each semester fun."

He shrugs. "I wouldn't know. I've never been to college."

"You can always go after your contract ends."

"Maybe," he replies as the phone rings and I rush to answer it.

"Hi, it's me." As soon as I hear his voice, I feel it, my body letting go of the breath I didn't realize I'd been holding in since he left this morning.

"Daniel."

"How are you?" he asks, his voice tired.

"I'm good. How'd it go with Calista?"

Daniel doesn't answer right away. "It... went well. She's at her mother's."

"She made bail?"

"Yes," Daniel replies. "I tried calling you earlier but your machine picked up and I didn't feel like leaving a message."

On the couch, Gael sits up. "Is that him?" he asks and I nod. "I want to meet him."

"Who's that?" Daniel asks.

"My brother and his friend are in town. We were hanging out at Central Park when you called." I pause, clearing my throat. "He'd like to meet you."

"Of course. What about my place for dinner tonight?"

"His place. Tonight," I tell Gael as he and Jace exchange glances.

"We'll be there," Gael says as Jace chuckles.

"That was easy."

If I thought Gael would give Daniel any trouble, he proves me wrong the moment we step into the apartment. Maybe it's the sight of the jukebox or the view of the city from the windows. Or maybe it's Daniel's quiet confidence, the same one that caught my attention when I first met him. I could feel their anxiety dissipate the moment he opened the door and introduced himself.

But there's something about Daniel lingering under the surface that I can't put my finger on. It's the smile that doesn't reach his eyes even though he's enjoying himself. It's the way his jaw clenches when he studies me from across the table. The way he lets out a breath when he thinks I'm not looking.

It's the absence of the box of Calista's things in the guest bedroom.

"What's wrong?" I ask Daniel while Gael and Jace are playing at the pinball machine. "And don't lie to me. Just tell me."

"I like you very much, Pearl."

My breath stills. This is it. This is where he ends it between us and goes back to Calista. I look down at my hands, not wanting to look into his eyes.

"But if I have nothing to my name," he continues. "Not this place, or everything it represents... hell, not even a career, would you still want to be seen with me? Would you still want me?"

"Why wouldn't I?" When he doesn't say anything, I continue, "I liked you before I saw all this, Daniel, or knew what you do for a living. I liked you for you." I pause and study his face. "Did something happen this morning? I mean, I understand the thing with Calista but... did anything else happen?"

Daniel thinks for a moment, then shakes his head. "Nothing I didn't expect."

I frown. "Is that a good thing or a bad thing?"

"It's only bad if I didn't make any contingencies ahead of time, but I won't know until it happens. And it will. Until then, there's us. There's this moment, and I want to enjoy it with you." The butterflies in my stomach come to life as he studies my face, his hand stroking my arm as I settle against him. "I'm in love with you, Pearl. You know that, right?"

My throat tightens. "I know it now."

"Good."

I bring his other hand to my lips. "But I'm in love with you, too. You know that, right?"

"I do now." As Daniel smiles, whatever doubt that had been on his face earlier disappears. It's just us and only us.

"Don't you think we're rushing this though?"

"Do you want me to slow down?" he asks and I shake my head.

"Hell no."

"What are you two talking about there?" Gael asks as he leans next to the pinball machine as Jace plays his turn.

"Just the future," I say, blushing as Daniel leans closer, his mouth brushing against my ear.

"Our future."

Thank you so much for reading Always You, *the beginning of Pearl and Daniel's love story. I've wanted to tell their story for a long time and I'm so glad to be have the opportunity to do so as part of this romance anthology.*

If you'd like to learn more about me and my books, please join my newsletter at www.lizdurano.com/subscribe

Delayed

Evey Lyon

Delayed

Evey Lyon

It took one second for Tristan's night to change – the departures board flashed delayed. But that was only the start, because getting stuck by chance at a cheap airport bar next to his sister-in-law's sister Marisa is darn right unexpected. And as their conversation evolves, it takes only a second for little coincidences to show them that maybe fate has plans...

Chapter 1

Tristan

Staring up at the screen that lists destinations, departures, and ETAs, I curse to myself.

Delayed.

The word nobody wants to hear at an airport; not quite as bad as canceled but a solid second.

Pulling my phone out of my pocket, I see that I even made it on time for boarding too. I had to run through O'Hare airport due to security taking way too long, and now, it was all for nothing. The delay indicates at least an hour, and that's enough time to hit up the airport bar and send out a few work emails, because clients never seem to get the memo that Tristan Joseph actually takes nights off. Luckily, I was flying to Colorado the night before a big meeting, so there is room for error in terms of travel logistics.

My screen has a new notification from this app that I've been playing around with. Never in my thirty-two years of life would I imagine swiping left or right, but I don't have time for anything more. Then again, I still have yet to actually meet someone from the app, as my friend signed me up as a joke the other day when we were watching Monday Night Football at my apartment downtown.

Ignoring my phone, I head straight to the bar that is two gates down. It's crowded, but I spot two empty seats and grab one. Immediately, I ask for a beer, thinking a scotch on the rocks is my option B should this journey get another delay.

Reading the menu, I debate if a burger is a good choice since it is already 6pm.

"White wine and mozzarella sticks," a woman requests at the same time, and she rolls her carry-on bag to the chair. She sounds like she's been running or is simply overwhelmed—her voice is familiar, too.

When I glance to my side, my eyes do a double take because there is no way that my brother, Matt's sister-in-law is about to sit next to me. I haven't seen her in a few months, the last time being in a busy room filled with people for a family holiday party.

"Marisa?"

Her emerald eyes peer up, and her lips form a smirk of recognition. "Tristan."

Quickly, I stand and help her move the high stool so she can get settled. "Small world. What are you doing here?"

"A work trip. I'm supposed to be flying to Toronto, but it's delayed due to weather." She smiles at the bartender who seems to be doing his best to throw her a charming grin as he sets her cup and small wine bottle in front of her.

Marisa is a gorgeous woman. Long brown hair with waves, always in cute sweaters and jeans, plus she's easygoing. She is one of those people that when they smile, the world smiles with them. She's also a few years younger than me, and her sister Kelly would probably be none too pleased if I ever made a move.

"I'm delayed too. Supposed to be on my way to Colorado. Guess I'll just chill here until they say they'll depart."

She snickers as she twists the cap off her bottle. "We're in Chicago, that departure may be never. Literally. I swear it's always without fail a fifty-fifty chance that your flight ever makes it out of this city."

"It's because it's a good city; why would anyone want to leave? And I didn't realize you travel a lot for work." I take a sip from my beer bottle.

She finishes her sip of probably crappy wine, and her face even makes a funny look when she swallows. "Yikes, this is 100% airport wine."

"If you want, we can head to the business lounge. They have good alcohol, and I'm allowed to take a guest."

Her eyes narrow in on me. "Ooh, look at you, Mr. Fancy Pants. Then why wouldn't you just go there in the first place? Instead, you're out here with us peasants," she teases.

I lick my lips, enjoying her humor. "I don't know. I was kind of thinking that as soon as they announce boarding then I'm at a close distance to get on that plane."

"Fair enough. Anyway, yeah, I have a new job, so traveling a little bit for the role. It's marketing, social media, all that jazz. You're still making numbers look fancy and ordering around employees?"

I scratch my cheek as I take in her impression of me. "You mean successful, good-looking, and living the good life? Yep, I am."

"Wow, that's some image." Her eyes seem to be stuck on me, and I notice the way she traps her bottom lip between her teeth.

I'm a red-blooded man and I know that look when I see it. She's attracted to me, but I think maybe we've always kind of orbited around one another. Before I get a chance to think deeper into it, the bartender delivers a basket of fried mozzarella sticks.

"Good choice. I was debating a burger."

Her eyes focus on the food as she takes a piece. "I'll share if you're nice."

"I'm always nice." I grin.

Marisa tips her head to the side and squints an eye. "I guess that's true. In the, what, few years that you've known my sister, you haven't done anything questionable... or was it you who organized the strippers at your friend Royce's bachelor party a few months ago?" She throws me a fake inquisitive look as she points a stick of cheese at me.

I hold my hands up. "That was probably... maybe... me."

Her eyes grow large, surprised that I admitted it. "Well, well, well, at least he's honest." The sound of her phone vibrating against the bar top draws her attention to the device that she picks up to study the screen, then plants it back down on the bar. "Sorry, I thought maybe it would be the airlines with an update, but unfortunately not."

"I kind of feel like this journey may be doomed."

She quickly pulls my arm. "Shh, you can't say that in an airport. You never know who is sitting around us."

It causes me to grin.

Her phone vibrates again. "Will people just leave me alone, gah." She picks up her phone, then snorts out a laugh, rolling her eyes as she sets it back down. "It's even worse, it's a notification from some dating app."

Quickly, I touch her arm as I take in the news. "Why are you on an app?"

Marisa nearly blushes then smiles to herself. "My friends did it. They thought it would be fun to sign me up."

I don't like that thought, not for her.

"Must be a full moon somewhere, because a friend also did it to me. My guess is it wouldn't be the same app, though." Mine is for hookups and hers is hopefully for refined dining and getting to know a guy who she'll take to meet her grandma.

"Why is that?" She seems entertained.

Shaking my head, I debate how to phrase this. "Probably different goals, that's all."

Her giggle is fucking encouraging, cute, and I want to hear it again under different circumstances.

"Anyway, I'm probably going to delete the app as soon as I figure out how to," she mentions, which is a relief for some reason to me. I'm not sure I like the idea of some other guy getting a chance to impress her.

My own phones beeps, and the moment I see the screen, dread aggravates me. I rub my chin as I try to de-stress in a temporary moment. "My flight is delayed yet again."

It causes her to check her own phone, then she holds it up. "Joining you there, cowboy."

"Okay, maybe a burger is what I need now." I wave two fingers in the air to grab the bartender's attention, and I quickly give him my order and throw in a scotch too. I ask Marisa if she wants another drink, and she requests another wine.

We catch up over little things, her family, my family, the dog she wants to adopt since she volunteers at a shelter and fell in love with a Labrador mix. It's an easy conversation, enjoyable even. And when I see other men eyeing her and wondering if Marisa and I are two strangers who met at an airport bar, I make it clear that she's with me. I move my own stool closer, and I graze my hand along her lower back. The smell of jasmine hits my nose, and her lashes bat a few times in my direction.

When she excuses herself for the ladies' room, I take the opportunity to check flights on my phone. My slither of hope that I'm getting out tonight is rapidly getting smaller. Admittedly, I check out the dating app to see if there are any potentials for a hookup later, because I'm beginning to die from blue balls, and I know Marisa is off-limits.

Marisa returns and she seems a little chipper or refreshed. I can't help but circle back to our conversation earlier.

"So... any eager sharks circling?" I raise my brows but focus on my beer bottle to look casual.

She offers me a sheepish grin. "Actually, I haven't looked lately. I just keep getting notifications that a match has been found. Maybe I'll make you a deal. You show me your fish-in-the-sea option, and I'll show you mine."

I slide my phone off the bar. "Deal." My thumb scrolls the screen, and I see I actually have a recommended match too. "Uh-oh, apparently my future wife has been suggested to me."

She's busy looking at her own screen. "Oh, yeah? My future husband is apparently waiting for me when I click on the button."

"Okay then, let's swap phones and we can assess our options for each other."

Without hesitation, she offers me her phone and we swap. My eyes bug out when I see that we use the same app, which is slightly concerning.

I gently whistle a form of shock. "Wasn't expecting you on *this* app."

"I'm not surprised you use it too. Okay, on three we both click that little binocular button to see our recommendation."

"Deal."

"One, two, three."

My finger taps the screen, and as soon as her suggested match opens, I pause and wonder if the devil is playing with me. My eyes draw a line up from the screen to Marisa who seems to have an entertained look on her face as she studies the screen from multiple angles.

"Everything okay?" I stall.

"It's, uhm... well." She draws it out.

"Yikes, that bad of a match. Is she at least easy on the eyes?" I ask.

She shrugs a shoulder. "I would say so. I mean, she does work out."

"Oh yeah? What are her hobbies?"

"Saturday markets, frisbee, and puppies." She isn't looking at the screen as she lists those facts. I notice she swallows a breath. "What about for me? Am I going to gawk at his photo?"

"Probably."

"Hobbies?"

I don't look at the screen. "Monday Night Football, visiting breweries, and Saturdays in the park."

We both look at one another curiously for a few beats.

"On three we show one another?" she suggests.

I nod as something inside of me quickens, excitement maybe, or acknowledgment that fate may be playing a role. I feel it deep that this evening may just take a spectacular turn.

"One, two, three," she blankly says with a wry smile fixed on her mouth.

The moment we move our phones to display, we don't need to look.

Because I've been looking down already at a screen that flaunts my photo, just as she has been looking at a screen with her own photo, because the app suggested us.

She licks her lips and blushes. "Looks like we are a match."

Chapter 2

Marisa

Delayed flights are my new favorite occurrence if this is what happens. Tristan is my match, and I'm his.

It's not completely crazy, or it is. I'm not sure. How could a woman not enjoy looking at him? He's always well-dressed, and his hair forms a perfect wave across his forehead. The man may be in dark jeans and a button-down shirt, but he still oozes success.

In the corner of my head, an alarm rings that he is off-limits, as my sister would kill me. But for the most part, I don't think I care.

For months, he's floated in my head, and now external forces are clueing us in that we should perhaps explore something.

"The power of data, right? It must pick up that we're within the vicinity of one another." It's my attempt to give us an out.

But to my surprise, he leans in a little closer by moving his stool. "So, what are we going to do about this?" His tone has a hint of sinfulness, and I realize that maybe he too wants to test the waters.

"There are many things we could do, but we also face one another at Thanksgiving dinners, so..." I play with the rim of the wine cup to focus my attention away from his mouth or his spring-fresh scent.

"Do we have ourselves a situation? Is this going to be one of those things that will come up at family functions when we are stuck alone in the kitchen because someone asks us to find a cake knife?" His smirk is a weapon that's breaking down any normal logic.

"Are you saying if we ignore this that it will still come up? Or that if we do something it's going to go wrong?" I ask with a playful curiosity.

He scratches his five-o'clock-shadowed chin. "Who says it will go wrong?"

Now he's just flirting with me.

I down the remainder of my awful wine before my hand runs through my hair, as I'm at a loss for how this evening has taken such a turn, yet it excites me, and I'm not going to back out.

"Are you even attracted to me?" It's a bold question, but I'm not going to go down this route if some ridiculous app is the catalyst as to why we are having this conversation.

"Do you remember the wedding reception?" He gives me a cheeky look.

I roll my eyes, because how could I forget? We were pretty flirty when we got thrown together at the bride-and-groom's table. That was both before and after umpteen rounds of champagne.

My palm flies up to stop him. "Okay, you're right." I can't help it, and I feel a smile spreading from ear to ear. "We both acknowledge that maybe there is... something."

"Agreed."

"But any moment we are both getting on a flight to different destinations, and then what?"

"I don't know." I like his honesty as his eyes stay glued on me.

The sound of people groaning brings our attention to a group looking at the departures screen. People are shaking their heads before letting out an audible sigh.

Two seconds later, both of our phones go off with a notification. We both glance down, and the word every passenger fears comes up.

Canceled.

My mouth gapes open as I mentally digest what this means for my planning. Judging by the number of people with canceled flights, coupled with the fact that there was only one more flight out to Toronto tonight, then I know that I'll either have to cancel the trip altogether or try again tomorrow.

But when I look to Tristan, he seems to be focusing on me as his fingers tap the bar.

"Shouldn't you be more stressed right now?" I give him a peculiar look.

He finishes his drink quickly. "Nah. Sucks for my PA who will have to find me a new flight, but least this night isn't a total failure. You and I are stuck at an airport bar realizing the universe is trying to throw us together."

"So that's a good thing?" I feel my cheeks heat.

He shrugs a shoulder. "Yeah." His answer is spoken softly. "Anyways, we should get out of here. I would say let's get a ride back to my place in the suburbs, but my guess is we both want to stay close to the airport to try and get the red-eye in the morning."

"I think I might try, yes. What did you have in mind?" I play coy. However, I make no mistake the reputation that this man has, and I can only imagine his plan involves me, which I really like. "You know airports are technically like no-man's land, so what happens here can stay here because we're not really in Chicago. Just like what happens in Vegas stays in Vegas."

"I like that logic, and there is a hotel near the airport, just remodeled and with a decent bar."

"Decent rooms too?" I know my sultry look is thrown on my face.

He leans in, his finger brushing along my jawline to my hair to wipe away from my face. Tingles move in a wave down my spine to my toes. I want him to touch me again and everywhere.

"Let's get out of here, Marisa."

He doesn't even give me an opportunity to answer, as he is already throwing a few twenties onto the counter for the barman.

Then it's a blur as we leave the airport, grab a shuttle, and find ourselves in the hotel lobby of the type place that only business travelers seem to find themselves at.

I stand at the side as Tristan arranges a room. Internally, my entire body feels like it's on fire, and we haven't even kissed.

When he returns to me, holding up a key, it's a confirmation that we are about to do something unbelievably reckless, stupid, delicious, and possibly resulting in the best night of my life.

I ceremoniously take the key and we head to the elevator. The moment the elevator doors close, the tension between us rises, especially as he steps closer and closer to me until he has me trapped between the wall and his body. He sets his arm above me, and it would be so easy for him to tip his chin down and capture my mouth.

"Can we clarify one teeny tiny thing?" I squeak out, and my thumb and forefinger come together to show size.

"It's anything but small, thank you very much," he retorts.

I breathe out a breath because I wouldn't imagine anything less. "I'm sure, but what I mean is we are two different creatures. You hook up, and I, well, I'm not entirely sure what I do. Except I do want this, but I'm wondering, is this... a one-time thing?" I manage to get it all out and internally I pat my back.

A knowing grin cracks on his mouth. "I would joke that it depends on performance, but I respect you too much, considering our dynamics. However, I don't know. I mean, a hookup doesn't really feel right between us, and that's new to me."

"Oh, so we are going to a hotel room to play Go Fish or watch a movie?" I joke.

He shakes his head. "I just mean, don't worry. Can I say that?" I hear his words that are flooded with sincerity, and everything inside me tells me to go with this and follow his lead.

I nod in agreement, just as his mouth brushes against my own, causing excitement to swirl between my legs. His lips press down, and I kiss him back. Wow, he *is* a good kisser. Soft lips, right amount of pressure, and his arms encircling my waist pull me closer to him.

In the background I hear the sound of the elevator doors opening, and we both walk with our suitcases rolling but our mouths not parting. We have no clue where we're going, only that we do not want to untangle.

We both quickly glance to our side to see our hotel room number, and I fumble with the keycard against the knob to hear the click.

Next thing I know, we are tumbling into the hotel room. Our poor suitcases are dropped to the side as soon as the door closes, as he lifts me up, with my legs wrapping around Tristan's waist.

We both seem hungry for each other as our mouths devour one another. Even when he drops me onto the mattress, he is quick to hover over me.

"Clothes off," he demands.

"Ooh, bossy," I tease as I quickly discard my sweater, and the moment I begin to unzip my jeans and peel them down, his fingers grip the waistband to help speed the process up.

My eyes are stuck on the image of him before me, shirtless, with his defined muscles on display. I want to touch him, lick him, and do things that would make a grown man blush.

Next, my shirt is off which leaves me in a bra and panties, while he is now in boxers. We take a moment to survey one another, but then we are at it like wolves, both kneeling on the bed.

Our mouths run along necks; my head falls back to allow him access to my body as his mouth moves lower.

He pulls our bodies flush, and I feel the heat of his skin. This is exhilarating, and I'm getting lost in what is transpiring between us. My own hands explore his body, but my favorite part is feeling his length pressed against my belly.

It's true.

Nothing tiny there.

The feeling of his fingers unhooking my bra indicates we are taking this up a notch.

"Fucking beautiful," he whispers right before his mouth covers a nipple, and it feels like he is feasting on me.

Biting my bottom lip, I can't help it and my sound of approval escapes my lips.

Then he moves lower and lower. His lips brush down my body, circling around my navel, and then he teases me as he heads down. In one sudden move, he pulls me by my thighs, causing me to fall until I'm lying on my back.

"That was a super move," I quip.

His eyes peer up at me as his teeth trace the edges of my panties. "You have no clue what's coming," he warns.

Next thing I know, he whips off my panties too, and I'm completely naked and bare for him. Yet I'm not self-conscious or shy, it feels right for him to look at me this way.

Then his tongue is on me, between my legs, causing my body to arch up into him, offering myself to him. He doesn't relent, no, it only encourages him to press my belly down with his hand until he has me coming and writhing underneath him.

Even when I am shuddering from an orgasm, his mouth doesn't leave me. And he doesn't stop there. He opens me wide, hovers over my body, and enters me with his thick length, causing me to see stars.

Slow at first, but then we find a rhythm, and it's every bit as wonderful as I dreamed. And I think he feels that way too, because we go at it again and again.

Chapter 3

Tristan

My eyes scan the room as I leave the bathroom with a towel wrapped around my waist and see the plates of leftover room service on the side, before my sight lands on a beautiful woman lying in bed with the sheet half wrapped around her.

Marisa begins to stir in her sleep. It's near four in the morning, and I didn't want to wake her, but I guess she sensed me wake. Slowly she rolls up to sitting, groggy and well-fucked, with her hand rubbing against her face.

"What time is it?" she asks in a husky tone.

The mattress dips when I sit on the edge of the bed next to her. "Way too early, but I'm going to try and make the red-eye."

She leans over to turn on the side table light. "Oh yeah." She grabs her phone and sighs in relief. "I'm not rescheduled until 8am."

"You should sleep in, you need to recover."

A chortled laugh escapes her. "That may take me a few days."

Leaning down, I can't help it, I run my lips along her arm until I nip at the curve of her shoulder. I don't think I'll be able to be near her now and not touch her. That may be a problem.

"I should get dressed," I mention sadly.

Her lips part open, and she seems to want to say something, but the words don't come out. "Right." I hear the disappointment in her voice.

"I wish I could stay."

She begins to pull the sheet around her body, as she is now wide awake. "It is what it is."

"Give me your phone." My fingers curl and motion for her to hand it over. Reluctantly she agrees and even unlocks the screen without any protest. Finding the icon, I delete the app. "You won't be needing this anymore."

"Oh yeah? Why is that?"

My eyes widen at her as I hand the phone back. "You found your match."

She snickers this time, slightly taken aback. "Have I now?"

I get up off the bed and begin to search for my clothes from my carry-on. Jeans and dressy sweater will be the outfit of choice. "I'm not the dating type," I admit as I begin to pull on some boxers.

"This doesn't bode well for me." She watches me with bewilderment.

"But if I were going to try, then you are the winner."

"Still not great."

Throwing the towel to the side and pulling on a white t-shirt, I know I need to step it up. I playfully return to the bed and tackle her back down onto the mattress.

"Let's do this again. I'm back in three days, would that work? We can even meet at my place since we don't need to get up at the crack of dawn," I explain.

She pretends to think about it, humming out a sound, which causes me to tickle her. "Okay." She giggles. "In three days, we have a date."

"Good, and let's make it the kind where we don't skip to dessert. How about box seats at a hockey game, then dinner?"

Now she looks impressed. "Wow, really throwing in the big guns."

I lean down to peck her lips with a kiss. "Big is all I know." I wink.

"Will you delete your app?" she asks me.

I grin to myself. "Already did around ten pm last night." It causes her to smile.

Getting out of bed, I find my watch to latch it back on to my wrist. Christ, watching her in bed examining my every move is freaking hot. Will I make it three days? I've got to because there isn't any other option.

"Not to freak you out or anything, but we kind of forgot something." Her face squinches together.

"Whoa, whoa, whoa, we wrapped it up every time," I assure us both.

She ruefully shakes her head. "No, not that. I mean, someone is bound to see us together and report back to the siblings." Her eyes give me a knowing look.

"Who the fuck cares?" I admit.

"This is going to be fun," she mutters to herself.

She meets me halfway when I dip my head down, and she tilts her head up to meet me for a kiss.

"Thank God for delayed flights and bad airport bars." My thumb caresses her cheek.

"You know, if this thing between us turns into something, then one day we would have a hell of a story. One twist of fate after another and all in a night."

"Don't I know it."

A quick goodbye and a promise of seeing her soon, then I'm out of there.

Chapter 4

Marisa

"I'm delayed. No, not even that. My flight was canceled because of weather out west," Tristan tells me through the phone I have pressed to my ear.

I sigh, as I'm already standing in the hall outside his luxurious apartment at seven pm like we agreed earlier in the day. After our hotel tryst, we agreed to meet tonight. He was going to meet me at his place after his flight got in. I was so busy at the office, and the last message I saw, he was waiting on his flight. It wasn't going to leave on time, but it *was* going to leave.

"Oh? That's not great. I'm already here, but I'll just take the food home with me and ignore the fact that I have something red and lacy on underneath my clothes." I glance down to the bag of extravagant takeout from the deli around the corner.

"Red and lacy?" He nearly chokes on his words.

"Only covers the essential bits," I tease, and I feel my cheeks tighten from a smirk.

The sound of a door opening breaks my attention, and I look to my side to find a very handsome man leaning against the stairwell door pane, grinning at me.

"Good thing I get to see it live then." Tristian grins as he holds his phone up.

"W-wait, I thought you were stuck at an airport somewhere." Realizing the phone is now an obsolete accessory, I bring my hand down away from my ear.

Tristan strides a few steps, with his small carry-on in tow. Leave it to him and his muscular superpowers to walk up a few flights of stairs with a suitcase.

"I was going with our whole travel-mishaps thing we had going on and wanted to joke with you a little." He wraps his arms around me, leans down, and places a gentle yet intense kiss on my lips. "But here I am. In the real world and no longer in our travel bubble."

"Right," I draw it out. "We're now in the see-where-this-is-going phase."

Tristan unlocks his door and takes the bag of food hanging off my fingers. "Something like that. Although we may need to speed this up a little. My brother said he wants to set me up on a blind date, and I can only come up with so many excuses."

I follow him in. "That's funny. My sister said she has a doctor she wants to set me up with."

"That ain't happening." He sounds adamant, and it's almost protective, which is just all the more sexy.

"I told her that I'm seeing someone tonight." His head perks up, a little concerned to see if I'm being honest. I'm quick to clarify. "I made up a story about how I met some guy at a bar who plays minor league hockey. I think she bought it, and lucky for us, your brother and my sister are on their last night of their little trying-to-have-a-baby getaway, so she won't bother me, as she's occupied."

Tristan snorts a laugh while he rummages through his cupboards for wine glasses. "Thank fuck for baby-making then. A hockey player. Is that what does it for you?"

Perching my behind on the stool at his kitchen island, I hum a sound of pretend consideration. "Maybe. But unlucky for fictitious hockey guy, I kind of hooked up with someone maybe slightly forbidden and ten times hotter."

Tristan rumbles a sinister chuckle as he leans over the counter to capture my lips in a kiss that feels like he's staking a claim. "How about we just enjoy dinner, maybe skip the movie, and we head straight for other activities," he suggests.

"I could be on board with that."

The next few minutes, we gather plates and set the table for dinner. By the time we sit down with wine glasses in hand and delicious Italian food on our plates, everything feels like we have done this a thousand times, which feels far too right and makes me giddy inside.

"I didn't pick anything up for breakfast," I mention then take a sip of my wine.

"Someone is presumptuous," he jokes. "Don't worry, we can head to Count of Choc for coffee with chocolate-covered chilis." It's a small chocolate café here in Hollows, the suburb where Tristan lives. He's not far from me, as I live a few towns over, but my sister and her husband also live in this town, so I've been to the coffee spot a few times.

"I love that place. So, how was Colorado?"

Tristan circles the wine in his glass. "Good. I went to this brewery, Matchbox. I love their beer, and coincidentally, the owner is a former hockey player. Anyway, we had a business conference in Sage Creek where the brewery is. How was work?"

"Totally eventful. Apparently, one of the graphic designers is sleeping with one of our owners, as proven by the fact she's having his baby. Best part is that she is also the sister of our other co-owner. It was an exciting day at the office."

Tristan's eyes bug out before he laughs. "You win by far. Look at us being all domesticated about our daily happenings. Offer to do my laundry and I think we can confirm we have a real future."

I throw a piece of bread at him but admittedly can't stop smiling. The thing is, we've always had good banter between us. Now, we just upgraded our platonic relationship to more.

Setting my fork down, I stand up and walk around the table and land on Tristan's lap. I melt into him just the way I hoped. The thing with lust is it can be a fleeting moment, but it turns out that we are moments, plural.

"I think we might have a situation," I whisper as I loop my arms around his neck.

He runs his hands along my waist to find a home on my hips. "What might that be?"

"We enjoy one another. Some people need to build up to a relationship, but something feels like we get to skip that step, and with a click of the fingers, poof, here we are." Maybe I'm thinking crazy.

He nuzzles his nose into my hair, and it sends a sensitive flutter across my body. "You didn't leave my fucking mind at all the last few days. I said that I'm not the relationship type, but I hate the idea of you with anyone else. I also want you in my bed, walking around my house in my shirt, and to hear how your days are. That wasn't me, but here I am. I think you may be right."

The beat of my heart intensifies from the words flying off his tongue. I don't want to get too excited because we are so new, very new. But damn, it's as if I kissed him and it erased the possibility for any other man to sweep me off my feet.

That's worth celebrating.

"You have some great ideas, but you should probably give me a test run in your bed first, considering I have yet to be in it." My voice is sultry, and there is a little giggle because we're acting like two lovesick puppies.

But then I feel his fingers sneaking up and under my blouse, spreading heat across my skin, while his mouth covers my own in another kiss.

"I have every intention to lay you in my bed after I get you on your knees. I want to do dirty things to you, but also sweet things," he murmurs against my lips.

My body turns extra sensitive and every swipe of his fingers against my skin only intensifies it.

"We should probably get to work on that then," my voice rasps.

In a swift movement, he stands us up and throws me over his shoulder, and with his free hand, he spanks me once on my ass, causing me to shriek in pleasant surprise.

We quickly work our way through his place until he drops me onto his mattress.

"Undress until the only thing you are wearing is that little red number," he demands as he tugs his shirt up and over his head.

Obeying, I work fast until I'm kneeling in the middle of the bed, feeling confident and ready for whatever ideas this man has in his head. This bra-and-panties set is lethal; it boosts my sensual side, and judging by the growling sound from Tristan, I think it makes him feral with need.

The moment he crawls onto the bed to guide me to my back, I'm entranced.

"I intend to get you naked, but only if my teeth manage to rip this off of you."

I moan the moment I feel his length hit my middle.

"Lucky me." I grin before he rolls onto his back, taking me with him.

Staring up from my coffee, I feel like a zombie. I lost count of the rounds somewhere after midnight.

"Are you sure nobody will run into us here?" I need to double-check.

Tristan sits across from me, sipping from his espresso. We are in Count of Choc, and it's fairly quiet. There are a few spots to sit and enjoy a drink, but the smell of chocolate is overpowering, as this place is also a store, with mounded displays of chocolate for sale.

He sets his cup down. "Relax. My brother texted that their flight was delayed, so they won't be back until later today. There is no chance of running into them."

I look down at my phone and see that it's already pushing eleven in the morning, and it's thankfully the weekend too.

"Sorry, it's just, as confident as we are about our stellar compatibility on all fronts, we should probably wait to tell them."

"Agreed. Now eat your chocolate chili, it's an aphrodisiac."

I shake my head at him in amazement. "As if I need more of that!"

Tristan chuckles, but then his sight drifts in the direction of the door. He's frozen from something he sees. In fact, his grin fades.

I feel it in my bones that it's what we fear. Damn it, the sibling connection.

Glancing over my shoulder, I have confirmation. At the door, my sister and her husband are standing there with their attention fixed on us.

"I knew it!" my sister announces rather loudly before storming in our direction. Her brown hair bounces behind her.

Tristan and I are quick to stand, unsure of what our siblings' reactions will be.

"Oh, hey there, Kelly, look who I ran into." Tristan throws his thumb in my direction.

His brother, Matt, steps forward. "We're not idiots."

"I thought your flight was delayed," I say in an attempt to divert us onto a new topic.

My sister scoffs a laugh. "We actually got an earlier flight and decided to see if we could catch you two in the act."

"What do you mean? We're like two nights into this thing between us," Tristan lets that fact slip while he gapes in disbelief.

His brother shudders. "TMI. So, what, you two are just having fun? I mean, way to go for making family gatherings fucking awkward. Going after my sister-in-law, geez..." He rubs his hand across his forehead.

"What if we're not having fun?" I shoot out with a need to defend us.

"What if you all just quiet down, sit down, and let us old folk enjoy our coffee," an old man interjects, and we all turn our heads to see the man holding up his cup where he sits at a table by himself with a newspaper.

We all look at one another and nod in agreement before slowly sitting down.

"You sent me a photo of your new blouse, and you forgot to move the bag from the deli out of the photo, the deli *next* to Tristan's place." My sister crosses her arms with a proud smirk that she caught me out.

"Oh." I duck my head at my stupid move.

"Seriously, what the fuck?" Matt seems to be the one to keep us tense in this moment.

Tristan blows out a breath. "It's not really any of your business, considering we are all adults, and I'm sure your precious annual Thanksgiving dinner will go down without a hitch because we will be there... together."

I smile fondness at the man who just made a proclamation for me. "Exactly."

My sister brings her hands together and smiles before she nudges her husband's arm, telling him to behave. "This could be great. Slightly awkward, but totally great." Kelly pinches his arm now.

Matt straightens his shoulders. "Yeah, peachy." I don't hear any enthusiasm in his voice, but at least my sister is on board.

Tristan slides his chair closer to me so he can give me a side hug. "We'll prove you wrong."

And I've never believed in anything more.

Epilogue: One Year Later

With room service arrived and ready, I place it on the corner table in the same room of the same hotel where Marisa and I were exactly a year ago. We both arrived at different times, so she's been in the shower since I got to the room. Other than calling out to her that I'm here, I let her have her peace, as I know she has a special lacy piece she wants to surprise me with... Oops, I snooped into her shopping bag the other day.

It's perfect timing, as I can double-check my jeans pocket for a little square box, ready for its debut. Our siblings are finally onboard. But after tonight, I will just prove their theory wrong.

I work the foil off the champagne bottle, but then I hear the click of the bathroom door. Truthfully, I didn't notice that the shower had turned off.

Turning around, I expect to see my girlfriend in a hot black number. Instead, she's wrapped in a towel, still not a bad sight, and looks at me blankly. Shit, is she on to me?

"Champagne and food are here," I say.

"Oh... great." She seems odd, nervous, or maybe she doesn't know what to do because all the signs are here that our anniversary is the big night to pop a cork in celebration.

Maybe I should just get us to the celebration faster?

"You know tonight is one year for us. One year since every twist of fate the world could throw at us landed in our laps, then you sat in my lap literally," I quip.

"Fate hitting us all in one night is really our thing, isn't it?" She swallows and looks nearly gray.

"It is. But tonight perhaps isn't so spontaneous, no surprises. Well, I have one surprise—"

"Me too. Let's count to three, shall we do that?"

Wasn't what I had in mind, but tradition is tradition. "Sure."

"One, two, three," she counts.

"I'm pregnant."

"Marry me," we both say in unison as she brings a white stick up from behind her back and I pull out the black box from my jeans.

When I register what just happened, the wind is knocked out of me. Yet to my surprise, I still muster words. "Well... that is a surprise."

"I know." She blinks a few times. "Kind of fate? Like we get everything in one night. Right?" She seems to be testing me.

Blowing out a long breath, I think about it for a second. "I mean, not planned, but what the hell, right? A sign or something that we find out now." My mouth curls into a smile before I step to her and take her in my arms. "I love you. This is... wow."

"Okay, so that's a good answer." She seems relieved. "I love you too."

Kissing her, I know two facts.

First, she's the one.

And two, fate has a thing for us on this night every year.

Fuck, this hotel better give us a discount for next year...

The End

Evey is known for writing heartwarming romance with steamy moments, often in small town settings. Her characters bring the swoon with a lot of wit. An American from the Midwest, she now lives in Europe where she types away to cure her homesickness, often with country music on repeat and coffee nearby.

Discover her stories and grab a free novella at www.eveylyon.com/news letter or follow her on social media @eveylyonbooks.

Wine Cellar Rendezvous

D. Kelly

Introduction

The following story centers around Wyatt and Anna Smith, characters in The Illusion Series World. This series follows the band Bastards and Dangerous (aka BAD) on their farewell tour. These rockers are ready to show you all the highs and lows that come along with fame and fortune. Sex, drugs, and rock and roll are only the beginning, so strap in and get ready for an emotional ride with lots of twists and turns!

Meet our cast of characters:

Sawyer Weston – Lead Singer, guitarist, Noah's twin brother

Noah Weston – Singer, guitarist, Sawyer's twin brother

Wyatt Smith – Backup vocals, guitarist, keyboardist

Darren Miller – Backup vocals, drums

Amelia (Mel) Greyson – Romance author touring with the band.

Belle Dixson – Reporter for *Slammed Inc.*

Anna Smith – Wyatt's wife and Sawyer's best friend.

Mac – Head of BAD security

Warren – BAD's manager

Sam – Anna's boss and Warren's husband.

I hope you enjoy Wyatt and Anna's story! You can find more of their journey in Just an Illusion – Side A (Currently free on all participating retailers.) For more information on The Illusion Series and other books you can visit www. dkellyauthor.com.

Part One

Wyatt

"Why did you offer to drop me off? Mac was ready to go," I ask Sawyer as he punches in the gate code for the sprawling estate in front of us.

"It was either go for a drive and drop you off, go to a bar and find a rando to fuck, or stay on the bus and annoy Princess and Noah. Figured this was my best option."

Sawyer is trying to be sincere, I can tell, but he's got so many issues that taking a drive isn't going to solve them all. "Why do you push them? Especially her? You could try being nice for a change, Sawyer."

The house is lit up as we turn off the long entrance road to the circular drive in front of the estate. "I'm just trying to get to know her—see where her boundaries lie and what I can get away with. Don't let her sweet smile fool you. We've only known her a few weeks, and she has more access to our lives than we've ever given anyone. She could still screw us over."

Sometimes, Sawyer's skeptical nature gets the best of him. I wish he had more of an optimistic personality like his twin, Noah. "Tonight is a good night, and I'm not going to let you get me down. When you go back, try to be nice, if for no other reason, do it for Noah."

"We'll see... it's fun watching her blush," he replies with a smirk. "Don't forget you've only got three hours, Wyatt, so make them count. And hey," he says as I reach for the door handle, "tell Bethie Happy Anniversary from me."

"Will do, but don't forget while you're making her blush that she's off-limits. Mel works for us, remember?"

"Doesn't mean I can't have a little fun. Later, Wyatt."

I close the door and bound up the stairs to the entrance. My wife, Anna Beth, is Anna to everyone except Sawyer, who calls her Bethie. They've been best friends since we were in junior high, and I know it's killing him not to see her tonight. But I figure on today, of all days, husband trumps best friend status. He'll see her soon enough.

Our band Bastards and Dangerous, aka BAD, has only been back on the road for a few weeks. This is our last tour, and as much as I'll miss performing, I can't handle constantly being away from my wife. We agreed early on she would focus on her career and that means staying behind while I'm touring. I'm immensely proud of her for rising through the ranks of her publishing company, but only seeing each other once a month blows. For years, she's sacrificed for me, so now, it's my turn.

Today is our anniversary, not of our wedding but from when we first started dating. It's been fifteen years, and as much as I wish we could have more time, our bus leaves in a few hours, and this was all we could make work. This house belongs to an executive from our label, and he graciously offered it up to us while his family is out of the country. Really, he did it for Anna—they hit it off years ago, and he's had a soft spot for her ever since.

I pull out the key and open the door, locking it behind me. We can never know for sure when we've been followed by a fan, and since I managed to get our security team to let me come alone, the last thing we need is trouble.

"Anna, are you here yet?" My words echo as I walk through the empty house. All the lights are on, and as I enter the kitchen, I see her phone on the counter and her suitcase next to the island. I bet I know exactly where she is.

We've stayed here a few times over the years for networking events, and Stan isn't the least bit stingy with his wine collection. Anna was extremely excited when he said we could help ourselves because we've never actually seen the inside of his prized cellar. As I pass the library, I notice the door to the stairs leading down to the wine cellar is ajar.

After descending the stairs, I open the massive door to the cellar. The lights are on, but they're dim, and I don't see her right away. "Anna, are you down here?"

"Oh, Wyatt, thank God! Don't let the door–" The door slams shut behind me as she rounds the corner. "Close," she adds with a sigh.

"What's going on? I thought you'd look happier to see me."

She flashes me a soft smile, "Baby, I'm always happy to see you, but something is wrong with the door. I don't know how long I've been down here, but it's been a while."

I turn back to the door and try opening it, but it's no use. It's stuck. The door is solid oak, and the hinges are on the outside.

"No problem. I'll just call and tell Sawyer to turn back around."

"Oh good, you have your phone. I left mine upstairs in the kitchen."

The first thing I see when I pull my phone out of my pocket is the flashing no signal warning. Shit. I show Anna my phone, and her face falls slightly as she takes my hand and leads me deeper into the cellar.

"The impressive thing about this house is that Stan thought of everything. There's a small kitchen down here, and it's fully stocked with glasses, meats, cheeses, crackers, and there is even a bathroom. Don't be mad, but I started without you."

Stan is a foodie and a bit of a lush, so when we round the corner and come upon a plush extra bedroom with a nice sitting area, I'm not surprised. An uncorked bottle of wine and a nearly empty glass of Cabernet are on the table. Anna leads me through the bedroom and into the bathroom, which is equivalent to five-star hotel suite accommodations.

I wrap my arms around her and kiss the top of her head. "Well, we won't starve, and we won't be dirty. Everything else will work itself out."

She leans against my body and sighs. "What about your show?"

"I'll make it."

"How do you know?" she asks, turning in my arms to face me.

"Warren talks a good game, but we've never left anyone behind before. Mac will drive up here and find us when I don't show up. Even if the rest of them head out, Mac will have a backup plan."

Warren is our manager, and Mac is our head of security—they'll be more worried than anything. Disappearing is a Sawyer or a Darren thing. Noah and I are the reliable ones, and since they know I'm with Anna, once either of us don't answer our phones, they'll come straight here.

"I'm sorry, Wyatt. This isn't exactly how I thought this would go."

I take a few steps forward, backing her into a wall, and her eyes widen. "I'm not. There is no one I'd rather be locked up with than you."

She inhales audibly, and the connection between us zaps with electricity. I trace her lips with my finger. "It's been far too long since these lips were on mine."

"It has... but first any truths?"

Anna and I have a system. We've found that the key to a successful relationship is to have complete and total honesty. Between overzealous fans, meet and greets, hotel ambushes, and the way the media can take a photo completely out of context, we had to find something that worked for us. Before we lose ourselves in our desire, if something is bothering either of us, we pause and ask for the truth.

"Nothing, Anna. My heart, my love, and my body are only for you."

"Promise?" she asks softly, and I know she saw something that's put her on edge.

"Cross my heart. Do you want to talk about it?"

She shakes her head. "Not now."

That's not how this is supposed to work, but we have such little time together tonight that I let it go.

"Can I kiss you?"

"I hope you'll do more than that."

My lips graze hers, and she wraps her arms around my neck. Damn, I've missed the feeling of her body against mine. The scent of her perfume lights my senses on fire. It's times like these that I know I made the right decision to stop touring. Anna is my entire fucking world.

Our lips meet, and her mouth opens to me. As our tongues collide, I taste a hint of wine as she slides her leg against mine. I lower my hands to her ass and lift her. Anna wraps her legs around my waist and whimpers as my cock presses against her. I lower my mouth to her neck and bite down as I pull her hair, and she cries out.

"God, I've missed you. I want to feel you for days Wyatt."

"Is that so?"

"Mm-hmm."

Anna tosses her head back, allowing me to nip her neck and jaw with my teeth. She holds me tight and writhes against me. I slip my hand up her skirt and groan... "You're not wearing any panties."

"We have limited time, and they'd just get in the way. I love you, Wyatt."

"I love you, too."

"Good, now fuck me like you don't."

I love that my wife tells me exactly what she wants. I carry her over to the bathroom counter and set her down.

"You're feisty tonight." I step back and take off my shirt before kicking off my shoes and unzipping my pants.

"Maybe it's the wine... or maybe I'm just tired of getting myself off."

I try not to let that last part get to me.

"Whatever the case may be, I like it when you're riled up. It makes fucking you into submission all the more fun."

She bites her bottom lip and nods. "Take the boxers off, Wyatt. I want to watch you stroke yourself."

Anna scoots back on the counter, putting her feet up on the edge, and spreads her legs wide. As I reach for my dick, she slides her finger through her wetness and then holds it out to me. "Want to taste?"

My cock leaks, providing the added lubrication I need. She watches mesmerized at I step closer and lower my mouth to her outstretched finger. As my tongue circles her essence, she whimpers, never taking her eyes off me.

"You're sure you want to feel it for days?"

"Weeks." Her voice cracks. "But I figured that was too big of an ask."

Reaching for her legs, I slide her to the edge of the counter. "Good choice with the flowy skirt."

"I thought so, too," she whispers as I pull her from the counter and face her toward the mirror.

"Bend over."

She does as I tell her, and I flip her skirt up, giving me a perfect view of her ass. As I run soft circles over the globes of her ass, her eyes meet mine in the mirror. "Please, Wyatt."

When I lower my hand to her ass, the sound echoes through the room. Her eyes light up in the mirror, and she smiles. "Harder, babe. Make it bruise."

Anna has one big kink; she loves being spanked. Even more, she loves seeing the imprint of my hand on her ass. Turning my wife on is my number one goal. When she's turned on, I am too, but sometimes, I have a hard time with the idea of bruising her.

"Wyatt, look at me." Our gazes meet in the mirror. "Don't freak out on me. We're two consenting adults, and this makes me happy. You're visibly turned on, so stop overanalyzing and feel how wet I am for you already."

I lean over her and kiss her neck as I slip my finger inside her. She's extremely wet, and it's been way too long since we've had sex. As I slide my finger to her clit, I spank her again and again. Her pleasureful cries fill the room, and when her ass is bright red, I thrust into her.

"Yes, Wyatt, yes!" she screams as I fill her completely. Nothing feels as good as being inside my wife. Knowing I won't last long, I reach around and squeeze her clit, and she comes fast, bucking back against me as she screams my name. With one last thrust, I come inside her before gently lying on top of her.

Anna giggles, and I kiss her cheek before pulling out of her and standing up. "What's so funny?"

She moves over to the massive oversize bathtub and turns on the water. "Take a bath with me?" I nod, and she moves around the bathroom, opening cabinets until she finds towels and brings them back to the counter. "I was just thinking that most people locked in a room would be freaked the fuck out, but we just jump right into sex."

I step into the tub and hold out my hand to her. I'm so much taller than she is, so she waits until I'm settled and then tucks herself between my legs.

"Well, I'm perfectly happy to be locked up with you in our own private sex dungeon. We've got enough stuff down here to live happily for at least a week."

She giggles, "There's enough food for about six months. I think Stan hides from his wife down here for weeks at a time."

"Even better. We'll be well-fed, happily buzzed, and we can fuck like rabbits. What more could we want?"

Anna leans against my chest and sighs contentedly. "Nothing. It sounds nearly perfect."

We relax in a comfortable silence for a few minutes before Anna laces our fingers together. "Do you realize that's the first time we've had sex since I went off the pill?"

Recently, we decided we're ready to start the next phase in our lives. Since it can take a while to get pregnant, and we only see each other once a month, Anna went off the pill. I couldn't be happier—I'm so ready for this next step.

"I didn't even think about it, but that's cool. Are you okay with your choice still?"

"Totally. With how much we see each other, I'm sure it won't happen right away, anyway. Knowing that we're trying after all these years makes me undeniably happy."

I squeeze her hand and kiss her head, "It's incredible. Now, do you want to tell me what was bothering you earlier?"

"Nope, I want to enjoy my buzz and my post-orgasm high. We'll talk later. Right now, I just want to relax and relish our time together."

Sounds good to me.

Part Two

———————

Anna

After our bath, I found two big fluffy robes in the closet for Wyatt and me. While he looks for a couple of bottles of wine for us to try, I'm making us a tray of snacks. He's giving me space, but I know he's worried about what's bothering me. Hell, I'm worried too. We have debriefing rules in place for a reason. When you spend a lot of time away from your uber-famous spouse, things can fester quickly if you let them. We are not a couple who typically lets anything fester.

I'm honestly more angry with myself right now. Ever since I stopped taking the pill a little over a month ago, my hormones are all over the place. I know my husband is faithful, but for the first time, I can't shake the feeling something happened he isn't telling me about.

"Earth to Anna... you've got enough food there to feed an army."

I look down at the summer sausage I was slicing and chuckle. "Oops, I got lost in my thoughts. We'll pack up any leftovers once we're sprung from our jail, and you can take them on the bus."

"Jail? Hell, baby, this is paradise. I'm going to ask Stan if I can send him on vacation just so we can do this again for an entire weekend next time."

Wyatt grabs some wine glasses and a super fancy corkscrew while I put the finishing touches on our food before following him to the little sitting area in the bedroom.

"Just be sure you clear the destination with Stan's wife," I caution, Lydia is a force to be reckoned with, and no one wants to end up on her bad side.

Wyatt nods as he pours our wine. "Noted." He passes me a glass and lifts his in a toast. "I know we don't get much time together, but I love that we make the best of the time we have. You are my best friend and the love of my life. Happy Anniversary, Anna."

"Happy Anniversary, my love." As our glasses touch, I blink back my tears, and Wyatt sets down his glass.

"Okay, enough. You aren't an emotional person normally. What's going on?"

I shake my head and sniff. "Nothing big, I swear. I think it's birth control hormone withdrawal or something."

He looks at me, and his brow furrows. "The doctor said that could happen right?"

"Yes, she said some women have hormonal shifts as their bodies reset, and it should be temporary."

Wyatt leans back in his chair, and I gulp my wine. It's really good and meant to be savored, but I need some liquid courage and fast.

"Well, that's good, but if you keep feeling off, promise me you'll make an appointment."

"I promise."

We snack a little and sip our wine, but the whole time, he keeps glancing at me as if he doesn't know what to say.

"Oh, this is ridiculous!" I throw my hands in the air before blurting out what's been bothering me. "There was a photo in a tabloid of you hugging Eliza Waterstone." His eyes widen, and it's not a good look. My stomach lurches as more tears spring to my eyes.

"Anna, it's not what you think."

"Then tell me what I think, Wyatt, because we had an agreement that you'd *never* hang out with her again. I know pictures can be misleading, but your hands were around her waist and resting on her lower back. The two of you looked awfully cozy with smiles and all."

With an exaggerated sigh, I reach for my wine. I hate being this person, but the only time Wyatt and I have ever fought over other women has been when Eliza is around. She's one of the executive's daughters, and she gets whatever she wants. Eliza has the world's biggest crush on Wyatt and even went as far as getting him drunk before kissing him at a party. What hurts the most is that he kissed her back. It was early in their career, and she's the reason we tell each other everything now, even if it hurts. So the fact that he didn't even mention that he saw her screams betrayal.

"I'm sorry, Anna. I know I screwed up." Wyatt places his wine on the table and gets down on his knees in front of me.

"Why didn't you tell me you saw her?"

He pulls my hand to his mouth and kisses it. "Because I wanted to avoid arguing. I took care of it, and it will never happen again."

"You were hugging her, intimately!"

Wyatt releases an exhausted sigh. "No, I was hugging you. Fuck... just listen for a minute and believe in us, okay?"

"Okay," I answer wearily.

"Some executives showed up the second week of the tour. Eliza is working at the label now, so she was with them. She thought it would be a 'hoot'—her words, to make me think you were there. She told a brand new intern she was my wife, and she wanted to surprise me. Long story short, I closed my eyes, and when I opened them, I was hugging her, not you."

"You couldn't tell?"

He runs his hands through his hair. "Of course, I could., I knew I wasn't hugging you immediately, and that's when I opened my eyes. Rapid-fire flashes blinded me the second I did, and I instinctively smiled because that's the job. It lasted less than a minute, but that's all it took."

I believe him, but I'm also furious with him and with the guys. "God, she's such a bitch! Why didn't anyone tell me?"

"They didn't tell you because I asked them not to. I handled it. We were in a meeting, and the intern pulled me out—said there was something important I needed to take care of and then filled me in on my surprise. As soon as I could, I pulled Eliza from the room, back into the meeting, and threatened to leave the label. They fired Eliza, security got the reporters to delete the images in exchange for interviews, and that was it."

Wyatt stands and pulls me from my chair. "I planned on telling you. I just wanted to find the right time. I didn't want to hurt you or piss you off, and it was important to me I do it in person. Baby, I couldn't stand knowing I disappointed you again, but I promise you, it was nothing but a nightmare. You're my world, Anna, and I will quit the band right now if it makes you feel better. Nothing is more important to me than you."

He pulls me into his arms, and my worries melt away. "You had to know the photo leaked."

Wyatt sighs. "Yeah, but you don't read tabloids, and everyone knows you don't enjoy hearing tour gossip. I thought if you saw it before I could tell you, you'd talk to me about it. Sawyer told me I was being stupid, but he's not exactly a relationship expert, you know?"

"He's my best friend. He should've told me."

Wyatt tips my chin up so our eyes meet, "No, I'm your husband, so I should have told you. He respected that boundary, even if he didn't like it. He also wanted me to tell you Happy Anniversary."

"You should've asked Mel for her advice."

He cracks a half-smile, and I melt a little more because Wyatt has the best smile. "I barely know Mel, but since she's a romance author, I'm supposed to assume her advice would be good?"

I reach up on my tiptoes and kiss him briefly. "No, you're supposed to ask her advice because she'd give you a woman's point of view."

"And let me guess, women are always right?"

Wyatt pulls me close and spins me around before tossing me on the bed. I can't help but laugh as he lands on top of me. "Not all women, but Mel's a smart cookie. I trust her. Hopefully, we'll become friends."

"That would be nice," he murmurs against my neck as he peppers a trail of kisses along my skin. "Forgive me, Anna?"

"Always, as long as you never break my heart."

He unties my robe and sits up on his knees and takes his off. Naked Wyatt has always been my favorite view. He doesn't give me long to enjoy it before he lies down next to me.

"Take your robe off, Anna," he says before stroking his cock.

I follow his instructions while watching him play with himself.

"Are you just going to stare?"

"What would you like me to do?" I'm torn between sucking him off and riding him until we both come.

"Ride me, baby. Give me something to think about when I'm alone on the bus."

I climb on top and position him at my entrance before slowly sliding down his length. When he's fully seated inside me, I gasp. I'll never tire of the way it feels when Wyatt fills me.

His hands move to my hips, and he squeezes me tightly, just the way I like. We find our rhythm easily, and when I lean down to kiss him, he moves his hands up my back, pulling me flush to him.

Losing myself in Wyatt's love is what I was made for. As we kiss, our bodies move in a seductive dance. We make love until we're breathless, and just when I feel like I'm about to levitate out of my body, he brings me back to earth with a soul-shattering orgasm. My screams are loud enough to rival one of his shows, but thankfully, no one is around to hear me. Wyatt comes with me, and when we're both spent, I collapse on his chest.

"I miss this so much." I gasp, heart still racing from our sexcapades.

He runs his fingers through my hair and kisses the top of my head. "One more year, Anna, and then we're going to have so much sex you'll wish you could send me back out on tour."

"Hm, never, the sex is far too good. Besides, your new job as a stay-at-home dad will probably tire you out."

I'm having a hard time keeping my eyes open. The sex, the wine, all the emotional turmoil—I'm ready for a nap.

"Oh, I remember, and I can't wait."

Bam, bam, bam!

I jump up, still half asleep. "What was that?"

Wyatt is off the bed in a flash and grabs his robe off the floor as the banging starts again. Scurrying out of bed, I toss on my robe so I can follow him. When I reach the outer room, I'm not surprised to see our friends.

"What's with all the banging?" I ask through a yawn, and notice that the door is now propped open with a cinderblock. I vaguely remember seeing it out in the entryway, guess I know why now.

Sawyer smirks and motions toward me, clutching my robe. "Thought we'd give you a chance to get decent. You're welcome, Bethie."

Darren, the band's drummer and our other best friend, laughs. "Personally, I think we deserved a show since we had to come all the way out here to rescue you two."

"Sorry, guys, I got excited about the wine and got locked in. Then Wyatt came looking for me, and I didn't catch him in time, so the door closed before I could warn him. I feel awful."

"Likely story." Sawyer smiles and shrugs at the same time. "Well, get dressed. Noah and Mel went ahead to the next venue on our bus. The four of us and Mac are flying, which means you two lovebirds get your own room tonight after all."

"Uh, not me. I'm supposed to stay here and fly out in the morning." I'm tired, but I'm not delusional.

Darren snorts. "It's funny she thinks she has any say about this. Anna, you know us well enough by now to know that this is already a done deal."

"Don't be a dick," Sawyer snaps back. "Look, Stan feels bad. Mac called to see if he had camera access to the house, and that's when he remembered he didn't fix the cellar door. Stan said he'd prefer if you wouldn't stay here alone since the wine lures people in or some shit like that. Warren called Sam, told him what happened, and Sam said you deserve an extended trip, and he'll pick you up at the airport when your flight lands tomorrow night."

My boss, Sam, is married to the band's manager, Warren. Sam is a hopeless romantic and would do anything in the name of love.

"Okay, well, not to burst your bubble but chop-chop. I have a Skype sex session set up, and the two of you are seriously cock blocking me. The sooner we're on the plane, the sooner I'm in my hotel room and can get rid of my blue balls. I'll be in the car with Mac." Darren takes off, and we all burst out laughing.

I head toward the bathroom to get dressed, but curiosity gets the best of me, and I turn around. "Who is he Skyping?"

"Belle," Wyatt and Sawyer answer in unison.

"That's still going on?" I'm shocked. Darren is usually a one and done, fuck 'em and leave 'em kind of guy.

"Yup, I think our boy is whipped," Wyatt replies.

"That's two tonight," I warn him. "Better not make it three."

"Two?" Sawyer asks curiously.

"I told her about Eliza. She saw the photo."

Sawyer whacks Wyatt on the shoulder. "Told you, dumbass. Bethie, it was no big deal. She's a bitch, but if you want to figure out if Wyatt forgot to fill you in on anything else, you can sit by me on the plane."

"Not happening," Wyatt growls.

"Whatever offer stands if she wants it. Seriously, though, you two need to get dressed. The jet is waiting for us."

Sawyer leaves, and Wyatt and I quickly get dressed. I find some Ziploc bags in the kitchen and bag up the snacks while Wyatt washes the glasses. The least we can do is leave the place almost as clean as we found it.

I take one last look around, and Wyatt wraps his arms around me from behind. "This was fun," he says. "But I am sorry for keeping that secret. I know I broke our rules, and I will never do it again."

"I know you won't, and you're right. This was fun. If we hurry and get on the plane, we can have some more fun before I go home tomorrow. Happy Anniversary, Wyatt."

He spins me around and kisses me deeply. "Happy Anniversary, Anna."

The End

Thanks for reading! If you loved Anna and Wyatt and want more Illusion Series fun – you can start at the beginning with Just an Illusion – Side A.

Broken

Dakota Willink

Chapter One

Harper

The crowd applauded as I stepped away from the microphone on the stage at the Women Rise fundraiser. I ducked my head in an attempt to hide my blush. Their praise was unexpected, and I was moved by their reaction to my speech.

They were giving me too much credit. All I did was recap stories of the women helped by Women Rise, a branch of The Stoneworks Foundation, the non-profit organization where I worked. Their focus was on gender equality, and they'd hired me to be the Director of Advocacy four years ago. In my short tenure, I'd watched many struggling women break through the social norms by fighting to achieve income security, decent work, and economic autonomy. Their stories were inspiring. This night was about them and all the women we would help after them.

"You killed it, Harper!" Justine Andrews, my boss and friend, said as I approached where she stood near the bar. She wrapped her arms around my shoulders in a congratulatory hug. "If donors don't open up their wallets after that, I'll be surprised."

I glanced over at the large projector screen on the wall. A computerized graphic of a woman's fist pushing up toward the sky filled the screen. The image was partially lit, the pink neon color rising just past the wrist. The goal was to raise enough money throughout the night to light up the fist completely, making it shatter the digital glass ceiling hovering at the top of the screen.

"Londyn from the Center for Reproductive Rights is supposed to speak next. Hopefully, she'll get us halfway up the hand. The sooner that big fist turns all pink, the sooner I can relax."

"The hard part is over. At least now you can grab a drink and mingle," Justine said, holding up her pear martini. "You've got catching up to do! Let me grab a drink for you."

I contemplated my options and decided I wanted a classy drink to match the sophistication of my black evening gown. The rhinestone spaghetti strap dress had been a rare splurge—one from which my bank account would take months to recover.

"I'll have what you're having," I told her.

"One pear martini coming right up!"

Angling her body toward the bar, she motioned to the bartender and then pointed at her drink. Within two minutes, he had another pear martini served.

"Thanks," I said to Justine as she handed me the glass.

"No problem. So, do you see that guy over there?" she asked, pointing over my shoulder. "Navy suit, red tie."

I turned my head and followed the direction of her finger.

"Yeah, I see him."

"That's Noah Jackson from the Smith and Jackson Law Firm. And before you ask—yes. It is *the* Noah Jackson, the firm's founder."

"Okay, so what about him?"

"He's the number two reason I came here tonight."

"And the number one?"

"I'm the Head of Relations and Fundraising for The Stonework's Foundation. It wouldn't look good if I didn't show support for one of our divisions. Plus, I believe in the good work happening at Women Rise. But Noah Jackson? Mm, mmm," she said with a smack of her lips. "I've been single for long enough. My sister-in-law, Krystina, told me I should start dating again, and I think she's right. It's been four years since my divorce. I think I'm going to try talking to Noah later on and see if he wants to grab a bite to eat with me later this week."

Noah Jackson was attractive. I couldn't deny that. But he also had money, and if I knew Justine, she wouldn't be just cozying up to him for a date. She'd also be looking for a donation to tonight's fundraiser. I glanced around the ballroom and thought about the guest list. Everyone here was rich. Very rich. And everyone was a potential donor with whom I needed to connect throughout the night.

While I took in all the faces, I couldn't help noticing the elegance of the crowd and the room. Chandeliers sparkled in the dim lighting of the room. Round tables spread across the floor, with pink tablecloths and centerpieces made of glittering lilies. As I scanned the large space, the hired band began warming up, preparing to entertain guests between the multiple speeches scheduled for the evening. A few members of Congress were in attendance. That made me happy to see. We needed federal support now more than ever. I made a mental note to thank them at some point during the night.

My eyes continued to roam until I was suddenly overcome with the feeling of being watched. I could feel it blazing from somewhere on the other side of the room like pulsing energy. The sensation was all too familiar. I should have known better than to look, but there was nothing I could have done to stop myself. I knew who I'd discover standing there. Only one person could make me feel that sort of blistering heat.

I slowly turned, and my eyes landed on Greyson Hughes. All that invisible energy crashed like the sun's flares, searing as the flames licked my skin. My legs seemed to wobble on my four-inch heels.

My hand shot out to clutch Justine's arm, bracing myself so I didn't fall. Justine grabbed my hand, and I sensed her searching my face.

"Honey, what's wrong?" she asked.

The answer seemed to lodge in my throat, and I felt starved for oxygen as my gaze stayed fixed on the gorgeous man across the room. He was the man who broke my heart, only to return ten years later to tell me it was all a big mistake. I'd run into him at the Stoneworks Foundation after he'd taken a lofty position at Stone Enterprise working security. Since then, Greyson had spent the better part of the past two months trying to convince me he still wanted me, but I'd rebuffed his advances.

But oh, how I wanted him—desperately.

My body ached for him, but my heart had a long memory. Allowing Greyson back into my life again would only bring more heartache.

I cleared my throat and turned back to Justine.

"He's here," I whispered.

"Who?" she asked with a frown.

"Greyson Hughes."

"Greyson? As in *the* Greyson? You've got to be kidding me," she hissed.

Justine knew about Greyson because I'd confided in her about him shortly after she'd hired me to work for Women Rise. She'd also been present at the office for one of his many attempts to win me back over. She still laughed about how easily he managed to charm a group of staunch feminists to do his bidding. The way the entire office staff scrambled to find vases and a place for

Greyson's personal delivery of ten dozen long-stemmed red roses wasn't something easily forgotten.

"Considering who his family is, he certainly has the means to be here," I mused. "I just hadn't expected him to come."

"That man can't take a hint. Where is he?" She pushed away a lock of sleek black hair that had fallen free from her updo as she searched the room.

I pointed blindly in a general direction over my right shoulder. She looked behind me for a few moments before recognition flashed across her face.

I thought about what his being here could mean. I didn't have the luxury of entertaining his wiles today. Not here. I had a job to do. Networking with donors needed to be my focus, and I knew his presence would be a distraction I might not be able to keep at bay.

"God, Justine. I can't have this right now. Not tonight."

"Do you want me to tell him to leave?"

"No. It's fine. I'll figure something out."

"Good. But whatever you decide to do, I think this cat and mouse game you're playing isn't doing you any good. I know you worry, but I've seen how you look at him. Maybe it's time you stop avoiding him. Ten years can change a person, Harper. Just think about how much you've changed."

"I don't know. Maybe you're right."

"I'm always right, sweetie. You know that," she added with a wink. "Now, if you'll excuse me, there's a sexy lawyer I need to cozy up to."

Justine gracefully walked off in search of a date with Noah Jackson, leaving me to collect my thoughts. I looked back to where I'd seen Greyson, wondering if Justine was right. Perhaps I'd avoided him long enough. Deciding to confront the situation head-on, I moved in his direction.

I knew Greyson had already spotted me but he was making a good show of pretending otherwise. He didn't appear to be with anyone and looked like he was trying to find someone. A younger version of myself wanted to believe he was looking for me, but the grown woman who remembered how he'd once crushed me knew better than to get my hopes up.

As I approached him, I took in his fitted, expensive black tuxedo over a crisp white shirt and platinum tie. It made him look even more broad-shouldered than usual. His hair was cropped short, leaving nothing to obstruct the view of his gorgeous face. If anything, it accentuated his strong jaw and prominent cheekbones. A shiver ran down my spine at the sight of him.

When he turned his head, his eyes locked on mine. I felt pinned beneath them and had to remember to put one foot in front of the other. His lips curved into a gorgeous, plush smile made for kissing. I suddenly found it hard to swallow.

A flash of the young love I once felt for him ricocheted in the depths of my heart. It was a love I'd convinced myself I had given up on, knowing that waiting for him to come back to me would cause me to lose myself entirely during a time when I'd already lost so much. Yet here he stood, appearing taller, broader, older. He watched me as if he knew what I was thinking, his expression full of something dangerous, possessive, and alive. He still made my heart flutter.

All those things, combined with the memory of a young girl's emotions, only made him that much more appealing. I wondered if that appeal was messing with my brain or if what was building between us was bigger than I wanted to admit.

Chapter Two

Greyson

Since the moment I met Harper, she had the power to drop me to my knees. Time hadn't altered that. She was so stunning that I couldn't think straight, a reaction I seemed to have whenever she was around.

Tonight, her auburn hair was styled in loose curls cascading down her back in silky waves. Even from where I stood, I swore I could feel the warmth emitting from her very essence. She moved with devastating grace, her body wrapped in a black satin dress meant for sin. Those tempting curves had been my sin once upon a time. Taking her, then leaving her, had been the biggest mistake of my life. Nevertheless, here I was again, feeling that same intense lust overtake me. It was so forceful that it made me dizzy.

I sucked down a breath and took a few steps toward her, closing the remaining distance between us.

"Small world," I remarked with a playful smile. I took her hand and brought it up to tenderly brush my lips over her delicate fingers.

"Small world indeed. It's funny. I didn't see your name on the guest list," she noted, eyeing me suspiciously.

My hand migrated to her wrist, giving it a subtle squeeze before releasing her. "That's because I wanted to surprise you. Did it work?"

"Oh, it worked alright." Then, turning her head, she surveyed the room. "I didn't think this was your kind of crowd."

"Maybe it is, maybe it isn't. God knows, I'm going to be in a world of trouble for being here tonight," I admitted with a light laugh.

She cocked her head to the side, her blue eyes sparkling with curiosity. "Why is that?"

"My father is tired of being the Minority Whip, so he's pushing to become the New York State Republican Senate Majority Leader after the next election—assuming they win the majority, which I think is doubtful in a blue state. I don't think his party will look kindly on his son coming to a fundraising event for reproductive rights."

The scowl on her face was fierce when she said, "So, why come?"

"I wanted to see you," I answered matter-of-factly, acting as if I didn't notice her cynical tone.

"Is that so?"

I suppressed a sigh, second-guessing my decision to be honest with my answer. My father and I were the complete opposite. He was a staunch conservative, while I leaned left of center. His votes never strayed from the party line—including the most recent State Senate vote on a package of bills aimed at protecting abortion seekers and providers. My father voted against it, and Harper knew this. I would be wise not to bring attention to my connection to him—especially here. I needed to distract her.

Glancing up at the stage, I noticed the band had finished their warmup and was about to strike up their first song. Taking the glass Harper was holding, I placed it on the bar.

"Please allow me the honor of the first dance, my lady," I said with an exaggerated bow and a teasing wink.

Her irritated expression melted away to a smile. Then she laughed softly, and the sound reminded me of a time when we'd been young, carefree, and innocent—when she'd been mine.

However, instead of taking my offered hand, she stepped back.

"I'm sorry, Greyson. I can't. While the band is playing, I need to be on the floor talking to donors. They'll play for thirty minutes, and then we'll break for our next speaker. Do you see that partially lit neon pink fist over there?" she asked, pointing to a wall of large panels placed together to make one large, wall-sized flat-screen. "I need to make the fist shatter the glass ceiling. I can't do that if I spend all night dancing with you."

"Just one dance," I insisted, wrapping my arm around her waist and leading her to the dance floor.

"Greyson..." she warned.

I chuckled and pulled her against me just as the band's female vocalist began to sing a cover of Annie Lennox's "I Put A Spell On You." Splaying my palm firmly against her lower back, I guided her into a slow dance.

"You look beautiful tonight."

She blushed but tried to conceal it with a roll of her eyes.

"Stop that," she scolded.

"You never could take a compliment. But, I guess some things never change."

"Yet a lot of other things *did* change, Greyson."

"Very true, but what truly matters remains the same," I said with utmost sincerity, hoping she would actually hear me this time.

I felt a shiver run down her body, and I grinned in satisfaction. I knew I was getting to her, slowly breaking down those walls she tried so hard to hold up. I'd spent the past two months trying to tell her that my feelings for her never died—that she'd been the one who I foolishly allowed to get away.

But so far, she'd refused to listen to anything I said.

"That's what you've been saying, but..." she trailed off, confusion evident in her eyes. She started to say something but seemed to hesitate.

"But, what?" I prodded.

Her body moved with mine to the music as I led her around the dance floor. Our feet shuffled in time effortlessly as if she were made to be dancing in my arms.

"Nothing," she insisted. "This isn't the time nor the place for serious discussions."

"So when is the right time? I mean, you've been going to great lengths to avoid me. I'm here now with you in my arms. It's only you and me, baby. Nobody is listening. If you have something to say, say it."

She pressed her lips together in a tight line as a civil war waged in her eyes.

"Fine, Greyson. If you want to know, I'll tell you. I just ask that you don't overcomplicate what you're about to hear. Tonight is too important, and I can't allow my past to collide with the present, potentially screwing up everything I'm trying to do here."

"I understand how important tonight is for you, Harper. I won't do anything to mess it up."

She still seemed cautious, and when she finally spoke, she sounded resigned.

"Things happened after you left. We were so young, and I..." She let the sentence linger as if she were collecting her thoughts. "I was only seventeen when you enlisted. You were gone, and I was alone. And I was pregnant."

I froze, but not before I saw her flinch at the last word.

"I'm sorry, but did you just say you were pregnant?" I asked incredulously.

"Yes. I didn't find out until after you left for basic training. My parents pushed me to get an abortion. I refused. In my young naiveté, I somehow thought a baby would be like having a piece of you. I also thought maybe it would mean you'd come back to me, even though I knew deep down that wasn't possible. You were going away to be a soldier—to a life I wasn't old enough to be a part of."

I thought back to the day I'd left her ten years ago. I'd been reckless in my youth, living it up more than I should. My conservative father thought the Army was the answer—especially after I'd come home high as a kite in the middle of a Wednesday afternoon. He'd marched me straight down to the recruitment office, not caring one iota that I reeked of pot smoke, forcing me to enlist.

One week later, I left for Fort Benning to begin basic training. I didn't know where I'd be after that, so I broke it off with Harper. I didn't think it was fair to make her wait for me. Even if I wanted her to come with me, she couldn't. She was a year younger and still in high school. She had her whole life in front of her, free to do as she wanted—or so I'd thought.

Pregnant. I'd left her alone and pregnant.

"You said you'd refused an abortion. Does that mean..." I couldn't finish the question. Shock rendered me speechless as the idea that I might be a father slowly sank in.

"No, it's not what you think. You—we—don't have a child. I would have told you if that were the case, but I ended up having nothing to tell. Regardless of what my parents or I wanted, I had no choice but to terminate. The pregnancy was ectopic. I could have died if I didn't abort."

I stared almost disbelievingly, unable to comprehend what she'd endured while I'd been completely unaware. As I processed her words, I began moving our bodies into a slow dance once again.

"Harper..." I pulled her tighter against me, not caring about who was watching. Every pro-life politician in the country could be here and reporting back to my father for all I cared. Harper was all that mattered at that moment. I leaned in close to whisper in her ear. "I'm sorry I wasn't there for you. I wouldn't have been able to leave basic, but I would have figured out some way to help you through everything. You shouldn't have had to go through it alone."

"It's fine, Greyson. It was a long time ago. Everything happens for a reason, right?"

"I came back after basic training. Did your father ever tell you?"

She sucked in a sharp breath, and a look of shock came over her face, but I continued, needing her to know exactly how much I thought of her over the years.

"I went to your house after I completed my ten weeks. I only had three days' leave before stationing in Fort Bliss, but I had to see you. Your father answered the front door but refused to let me talk to you or tell me anything about you. He said you'd moved on and that I should too. Still, even after all the discipline taught in basic training, I was never one to follow directions. At least not back then. So, I called your house, but the phone number was disconnected."

"You said it was right after you finished basic?"

"Yes."

"That would have been around the time I had the abortion. It was a rough time for my parents and me. I was devastated about so many things and not speaking to them much—if at all. My parents also dumped the landline around that time, and we all switched to cell phones. Based on what you're telling me, I wonder if that was a coincidence or by design. I didn't know that..." she trailed off, her eyes becoming glassy. "I didn't know you came back for me."

"After the Army, life went on, but I could never forget you. There were women, but nobody serious. Something about them just never felt right."

"I know what you mean," she murmured.

"When I ran into you at The Stoneworks Foundation, I instantly knew why the other women didn't seem to fit. It was because they weren't you. I wanted you, Harper. Always. It was just you."

I watched her as we moved ever so slowly across the dance floor, the beat of the music somehow matching the beat of my heart. Her expression went from astonishment to hopeful to sadness in a split second, but I also saw regret.

As if on a cue, the band changed songs. I instantly recognized the acoustic guitar rhythm as it rippled across the room. Soon, the lyrics to "Broken" by Seether began to sound.

I looked down at Harper, studying her face. Her eyes were wide. She blinked rapidly, almost as if she were fighting back tears, and I understood why.

Every teenage couple had a song. This had been ours. It became our song because it was playing on the radio when we had sex for the first time. We were an awkward, twisting mass of limbs in the backseat of my father's Buick, but she'd been so trusting, giving me her virginity without an ounce of hesitation. She knew I loved her. In hindsight, I'm embarrassed about how I'd first taken her. She deserved so much better than the backseat of a car in Corona Park.

"That was one dance, Greyson. Thank you, but I have to go now," Harper whispered and pulled away.

"Wait," I said, reaching out to her.

She didn't pull away again but let me guide her slowly back into my arms.

"Just one more," she whispered the warning like she didn't really mean it. But she knew what I was feeling—she felt it too.

I could barely breathe as the female vocalist sang. Her range was uncannily similar to Amy Lee's, making the moment all too real. It brought me back to another time and another place. Even the smell of Harper was the same— that jasmine scent I'd never forget. While the song lyrics were sad and certainly unfitting for two teenagers in love, it was fitting for who we were today. For ten years, I'd been broken.

I just hadn't known it.

A lump formed in my throat, and I swallowed, wanting to beat myself for wasting so much time. I should have tried harder to get in touch with her. Now, I worried that too many years had gone by.

"Harper, I know you don't want to believe me, but I truly have spent the past decade regretting my choice to end our relationship. A part of me wishes I'd asked you to wait for me, but I also know how I was back then. I had no direction, and when I see how accomplished you are now, I think staying with me would have held you back. But you must know I'm not the same person I was then. I was eighteen years old with no future in sight. I—"

She silenced me by placing a finger on my lips.

"Shhh...don't ruin this moment by talking about the past."

We fell silent and moved to the music, her body moving with ease against mine. The song ended all too soon, and I didn't want to let her go. When she began to pull away a second time, I didn't hold her back. She had a job to do, and it was wrong of me to get in her way.

"Duty calls," I said lightly, trying to break the intensity in the air.

"Yes, it does. I need to go work on lighting up the fist."

"Can I get another dance later?"

"Maybe." She said it so quietly that I barely heard her over the final guitar riff. She stared at me for a beat, her expression impenetrable. Then, without another word, she turned and walked away.

I must have stood there like a fool for another three minutes at least, stunned by the connection I still had to this woman. I shouldn't have been surprised. It had always been there, but now it was burning brighter than the sun. I shook my head, forced myself to leave the dance floor, and headed to the bar.

"I need a fucking drink after that," I muttered under my breath.

After ordering a Henry McKenna Single Barrel neat, I scanned the crowd until I spotted Harper. I watched her work the group for a while, completely in awe of her ability to move efficiently around the expansive ballroom, never lingering too long with one guest before moving on to the next.

She was beautiful—the whole package—and not just in appearance. It was her entire persona and the way she presented herself. There was so much goodness in her, and I wondered if she even knew it. I always knew she was destined for greatness, and tonight was proof.

The music stopped, and another speaker took the stage, but I barely heard a word of the speech. I was too focused on Harper. I never wanted her more than I did right then, to feel her pressed against me in another dance. I recalled the feeling of her tight little body, the way she moved with me in time to the music, and I began to envision more. Being with her again. Inside her. Hearing her scream my name. I could almost picture her just as she was in the back of my father's Buick, eyes wide with desire. I wanted to see that look on her face now, but this time as a grown woman.

I looked up at the pink fist on the flat screen. It was more than three-quarters of the way lit, the lights barely grazing the curved knuckles. The sooner that fist shattered the glass ceiling, the sooner I could have Harper all to myself.

On impulse, I headed to the area where workers were accepting donations.

"How much more do you need to make that thing light up?" I asked the young girl behind the table.

She looked down at her computer screen, then back up at me.

"We are hoping to hit one hundred thousand tonight, and there's about nineteen more to go!" she announced cheerfully.

"Oh, nineteen hundred isn't too bad."

"Oh no, sir. There's nineteen *thousand* more to go. Not nineteen hundred."

Nineteen thousand.

I nearly cringed. That amount would take a sizable chunk from the deposit I planned to make on a late model Sea Ray boat I'd been eyeing up at Montauk Marina.

"Would you like to donate, sir?" the girl prompted, eyeing the line of people standing behind me. "You can do it right here, or we have a website where you can donate anonymously through your smartphone."

Fuck it.

Harper was more important than a boat. Without further hesitation, I pulled out my wallet.

"Does the website take credit cards?"

Chapter Three

Harper

The entire ballroom erupted into cheers, causing me to pause the conversation I was having with Alexander Stone, the CEO of Stone Enterprise and founder of The Stoneworks Foundation. I turned around to see what the commotion was all about and saw the shattered glass ceiling. Bright pink lit up the flat screen, illuminating the entire room.

"Well done, Harper," Alexander said.

I looked back at him, my mouth curving in an ear-splitting grin.

"Thank you!"

"I guess you don't need a donation from Stone Enterprise after all."

"It's funny you should say that. I was just speaking with your wife," I said knowingly, thinking about the conversation I'd just had with Krystina Stone about adoption rights for the LGBTQ. "She'd like The Stoneworks Foundation to help fund programs at Women Rise that offer guidance and legal counsel to LGBTQ couples looking to adopt. So anything we raise above our goal tonight could go to that."

He offered me a wry smile.

"My wife always has an agenda," he said with a chuckle. "I'll head over to the donation table right now. If I don't, Krystina will never let me hear the end of it."

I laughed as he walked away and scanned the room for the heads of my partner organizations in this endeavor. They were gathered with their staff in celebration as well. I smiled to myself. Today was a good day.

The band took the stage for another set, starting with an upbeat tune to match the crowd's excitement.

"Now that your work is complete, I believe you have more time for dancing," said a low voice from behind me.

I slowly turned to see Greyson behind me. I smiled, feeling overcome with excitement from the jubilation that emitted throughout the room. Not waiting for me to respond, he grabbed me by the arm and twirled me onto the floor with the other dancers.

Another hour passed in what only seemed like five minutes. We danced and talked, our conversation jumping from one topic to the next. Some dances were fast while others were slow, but the slow dances differed from the first two we shared. There was this buzz in the air that made it seem like everything had a sexual undertone. The awkwardness from earlier was gone. Greyson's flirtations were deliberate, as were his hands, which shamelessly roamed over my back and hips. He made all the little hairs on my body stand on end, and my nipples went painfully hard every time I pressed against him. My body seemed to hum to life with only a single look from him.

After a while, we both needed a break and headed to the bar. Once our drinks came, Greyson turned to me and leaned in close to my ear.

"Room twelve-ten. Fifteen minutes," he whispered. Then he pressed a plastic card to my palm before leaving me alone and slack-jawed with a keycard to a hotel room in my hand.

As I stared down at the black plastic, my heart thudded loudly in my ears. I wasn't naïve. I knew what the invitation meant without him even saying it.

I can't go to his room. Or can I?

I managed to bury the past for a while tonight, but I wasn't sure if I could take the next step with Greyson. Overwhelming panic consumed me. I searched the room for Justine. I needed a friendly ear—a sounding board to help me work through this—but she was nowhere to be found.

Dammit!

I took a long swig of pear martini number two. I wasn't a big drinker, so having already consumed a martini and a couple of glasses of champagne, this one was going straight to my head. I set the glass down on the bar, knowing I needed a clear head. I still had strong feelings for Greyson that had never died with time. Tonight had been fun with him, but I was flirting with danger.

After ten minutes of indecision, I knew what I had to do. I couldn't bury my feelings for him any longer. Justine was right. Greyson and I had left too much unfinished.

My hands trembled as I fumbled to insert the keycard into the slot of the hotel room door. When I entered, I found more than just the average hotel room. Greyson had reserved a suite, complete with a sitting area and separate bedroom. Music played softly in the background.

Greyson stood near the couch, and the entire space seemed consumed by his presence. He'd removed his tuxedo jacket, leaving it tossed haphazardly on the back of a settee. His tie was loosened at the neck, and one hand rested in his pants pocket while the other ran anxiously over the top of his head. His presence pummeled me, so powerful and raw, and energy seemed to crawl up the walls.

His eyes showed hesitations as he took me in, but there was also desire.

"I'm glad you came," he said huskily.

Memories—flashes of another time—ricocheted through the depths of my being, causing a shiver to race down my spine. I saw us as we once were, a fumbling ball of passionate limbs.

"I'm glad, too," I breathed.

"Strawberry?" he asked, pointing toward the coffee table.

My gaze followed his finger toward a platter of strawberries, each artfully arranged to surround a bowl of whipped cream. Champagne had been poured, the little bubbles slowly rising to the surface of two crystal glasses.

I hadn't expected this. It was seduction in every sense of the word and so different from the Greyson I once knew. It was what he'd been saying all along —that he was different now.

"I, um..." I faltered, words just seeming to ramble from my mouth. "Sure."

I felt rooted to the spot, undecided on my next move. But, as it turned out, I didn't have to decide because Greyson did it for me. He was already moving closer, possession in each measured stride. He leaned in and pressed the gentlest kiss to the curve of my neck. His spicy and masculine scent clouded my senses. I trembled when he reached up, his fingers softly brushing along the side of my cheek. I dared to look into his eyes; gray pools swirled with something fierce.

"Let's sit down."

He led me over to the couch, and we sat. I stared at the plate of strawberries, my mind in a daze. I blinked once, then twice, trying unsuccessfully to break free from the spell he seemed to have me under.

"Greyson," I began, attempting to find some sense of balance. But anything I might have said was silenced by the strawberry he brought to my lips.

"Taste," he demanded.

Oh, God...

So much more was laced in that one little command. My already pounding heart began to race faster and faster. Every single dirty fantasy I'd ever had about Greyson over the years wanted to come to life right here in this room. I thought I might combust just from the images conjuring in my head. I needed to rein it in—to try harder. My heart demanded it or risked being shattered all over again.

Except this time, I wasn't feeling schoolgirl emotions. I was a woman with complex ideologies and sentiments. If I lost him again, I wasn't sure I'd be able to recover.

"Greyson, I know you said things would be different, but—"

"It killed me to walk away from you," he interrupted. Stark vulnerability oozed from his truth. My throat tightened with an onslaught of emotions. "If nothing happens here tonight, I need you to know that much, at least."

"You took a piece of my heart when you left."

"And I left my whole heart with you," he confessed, grief written in his expression. I nearly broke from his words as his head dropped to rub his nose against the side of my face.

"You say you've changed, but I've changed too," I began again, ready to lay it all out on the table. There were parts of me I'd tucked away, hid from, and ignored, but they would always belong to him. He needed to know how badly he could hurt me if he walked away again.

My mouth felt dry. I unconsciously ran my tongue over my lips to moisten them so I could speak. Greyson's eyes dropped and followed the path of my tongue before finally making their way back up to mine. As I was about to speak, his lips crashed down on mine.

I didn't even attempt to protest, surrendering to his hot, merciless kiss. Our tongues quickly found each other, his more aggressive than mine. This was not the kiss of a high school boy I once knew. This was so much more. It had the ferocity of a hot-blooded male taking complete and utter control.

"I never meant to hurt you. I'm so sorry," he murmured feverishly against my lips.

Tears sprang to my eyes, confusion winding through the very depths of my soul. Layer by layer, he was stripping me bare, peeling away the hurt to expose the love I'd kept buried for far too long.

"I would have waited for you," I whispered between kisses.

"I couldn't let that happen, Harper. You deserved more. So much more."

His hard contours pressed against the softness of my body, and I found myself reaching up to thread my hands through his cropped hair. Greyson groaned when I tugged on the short ends, pulling me tighter against him. I'm not sure when or how it happened so quickly, but we went from kissing to fervently groping each other in a matter of minutes.

My fingers found the buttons of his shirt, and I worked my way down, the desperate need to feel his bare flesh under my palms becoming all-consuming. He caressed a hand down my back, along the zipper of my dress, and settled at my waist. Shivers raced down my spine, wishing he'd tug the zipper down. He made me want things that I'd never wanted with anyone else. Every time he was near, I felt an unexplainable connection between us, like an invisible line that remained unchanged over time.

Greyson pulled back slightly, leaving us both panting. He was a disheveled mess, his hair sticking up wildly. His shirt was twisted, only having been partially removed. His chiseled abdomen rippled as he shrugged impatiently out of the rest. Once it was off, he reached for me again, but I froze when I caught sight of a tattoo. It was high on his right arm, a thick line with jagged edges wrapping around his bicep up to his shoulder like a snake. In the center near his shoulder, the word Broken was scripted in a tribal font.

My eyes widened in shock. I felt like I'd been punched in the gut. I shifted my gaze to meet his, terrified of what I'd find but still desperate to see his expression. He pressed his forehead to mine. I almost couldn't breathe.

"When did you get that?" I whispered, fearful of what his answer might be but needing an explanation, nonetheless.

"Seven years ago. It was after I completed my three-year commitment to the Army and before I started working security at Stone Enterprise. I told you, Harper. I've never stopped thinking about you. I've never stopped loving you," he said in a voice low and throaty with emotion.

Loving me.

Greyson just admitted that he still loved me after all this time.

I clutched a hand over my drumming heart. All the oxygen seemed to vacuum from the room. I would have accused him of lying if he'd said that to me a few weeks ago. I would have assumed it was some fairytale designed to dupe me into dropping my panties. I pulled back a few inches to study his face. I saw the torment in his eyes, but there was also devotion and love. I couldn't doubt his words. He was speaking the truth.

I choked back a sob.

"Greyson, I..."

"I don't want to live in the past anymore, Harper. I want what I have here. Right now. I want to be with you."

Elation raced through my veins like a potent drug. He was all around me, his presence thick and consuming in a way only he could be. It had been so long since I'd wanted—and I mean, really wanted—anyone. I'd fantasized so many times about what it would be like to make love to Greyson again, but never in my wildest dreams did I think I'd have the opportunity.

I closed my eyes as he pressed soft kisses down my neck. He exuded testosterone, drugging my senses until I was high on him. I soared, my blood heating, my flesh on fire.

When he brought his lips to mine, he hovered over them, barely touching. My lips parted, and we breathed together, slowly inhaling each other's need. I'd never loved anyone the way I had loved him, and at that moment, I realized I never stopped. It was still as potent as it had been ten years ago. My body, the shell that had lain dormant for ten years, had finally awakened because of Greyson. My Greyson. Only he could make me feel this alive.

I gave in and felt my body melt into him, burying all fears of a broken heart and letting go of every ounce of resistance.

Chapter Four

Greyson

I sensed the moment she surrendered. Her cheeks flushed, and her eyes darkened, the color turning a deep blue and brimming with possibilities. I knew I should take my time despite the electric heat burning through my system. I had planned to take her to dinner first, then maybe to see a show on Broadway. I had wanted to give her romance like I never did all those years ago.

But then tonight happened. After feeling her warm body pressed against mine and her hips gyrating against me on the dance floor, I threw any thought of taking things slow right out the window.

Now, I could barely believe she was here in my arms. What Harper and I had was nothing but pure and good. It was real. I'd missed her, and I had missed this.

"It's been too long. Just too damn long," I whispered against her mouth before running my tongue over her perfect lips, demanding she open to me. I kissed her. Tenderly. Passionately. Desperately. I wanted her to feel everything I felt—to feel the relief from finally having something we'd denied ourselves for so long and to bridge the distance time had left between us.

My arms banded tightly around her, and I hauled her to my chest, carrying her tight body to the bedroom. I never took my lips from hers, guiding her as I plundered her mouth. Once there, I carefully set her back on her feet, turning her around to press her back against my chest. I held her close, palm splayed across her firm abdomen as I leaned in to graze her ear. My breath was hot on her neck as she tilted her head so I could nibble down to her shoulder. A shiver rocked her body, and she moaned.

"Greyson..." she sighed and tried to turn to face me. I stopped her, keeping her back firmly against me. I wasn't in a hurry. I wanted to savor every moment with her.

"I don't want to be rushed. I want to take my time and make you feel good."

"I need to touch you," she persisted.

"We'll get there. But, first, let me relearn your body. I want to feel every curve, to memorize you with my hands. With my tongue. I want to taste every inch of you."

She shuttered again as I moved my hand up her back to the zipper of her dress. Slowly, I tugged it down to expose the delicate curve of her spine. Then, looping a finger under each strap at her shoulder, I slid them down until the silk pooled at her feet.

I pressed my lips to her shoulder, trailing soft kisses along the hollow at the side of her throat as I reached around to cup her breasts through the black strapless bra. The material was rough yet soft against my palms, feeling nothing like the basic cotton she had worn all those years ago. What she wore now was lace. It was sexy. Intimate. And all woman.

I groaned my approval as my cock strained in my pants. I thought I might come on the spot. I restrained the mad desire I felt for her, forcing myself to do exactly as I'd promised, and went through the motions of memorizing every delicious inch of her body. My mouth moved across her shoulders, working my way down her back and over her hips.

More lace. And a thong, no less.

"You're unbelievable. You don't know what you do to me," I uttered as I cupped her ass and raked my tongue over the curve of one cheek, then the other, before moving down and up each of her legs. "Your taste. Your scent."

Working back up her body, I finally turned her to face me. Pure lust thrummed through my veins, and I felt my jaw tighten, desperate to see everything underneath the few scraps of black, sexy lace. I reached around to her back with slow, purposeful grace and unclasped her bra. Perfect mounds and pink nipples spilled free.

"Oh, God," she gasped.

I cupped her neck and ran my tongue down the base of her throat, over her clavicle, until I captured one hardened peak in my teeth. I relished her startled cry as I rolled the other nipple between my thumb and finger. I lured her back toward the bed until the backs of her knees hit the mattress. Legs buckling beneath her, she sat down.

"It's just you and me, baby. That's all it was ever supposed to be. I'm sorry for leaving you. Now, lie back. I'm going to take care of you," I told her.

She hesitated, her eyes fraught with an emotion I couldn't identify, and my stomach sank. I nearly swore, hoping like hell she wasn't having second thoughts now.

"Harper, don't look at me like that. Don't tell me to stop."

"Then stop apologizing. I don't want to be confused about the past. I want this, Greyson. I need it—I need you. No more talking. Just touch me, please."

"No talking? I'm sure I can think of something to keep my mouth occupied," I teased as I coaxed her back, eager to remove that final barrier of clothing so I could taste her. If she didn't want to remember the past, that was okay. I didn't want the chains of history to hold us down any more than she did.

Sliding down the lace thong, inch by beautiful inch, I tossed it aside and dropped to my knees between her legs. Grabbing her ankles, I pushed her legs apart, carefully assessing her expression as I did. Desire pooled deep in her ocean blue eyes, the delicate blush moving from her cheeks to her breasts.

Tearing my gaze from her face, I allowed myself finally to look down at her now exposed sex.

So fucking gorgeous.

I slid the pad of one finger gently over her clit. Her back immediately arched, and a gasp wrenched from her throat.

"Oh!"

I parted her folds and slowly sank one finger inside her heated well, a sharp hiss escaping me.

"God, you're exquisite. So wet. So ready. So damned tight." I slid another finger in, stroking her inner walls while my thumb traced slow, leisurely circles over that pulsing bundle of nerves.

She gasped again, and I sank low, unable to go another minute without tasting her.

"Tell me you want me, baby. Tell me you want this."

"Yes, yes! I want it," she unashamedly begged.

Wedging my shoulders between her legs, I rested my face against her inner thigh and inhaled her sweet scent. Dipping down, I swiped my tongue over her entrance in one long lick. She tasted as good as she smelled.

Her hands reached down and grasped the ends of my hair, searching for something to hang onto as I explored every nook and crevice of her most intimate parts. I dipped into her core before laving her oh-so-sweet spot, making her writhe beneath me. I pressed my tongue flat against her, rolling until that beautiful nub began to pulse. It was only a matter of time before she came apart.

"That's it. Let go, baby. Let me taste you on my tongue. I want you to feel it. I want you to feel everything I was meant to make you feel."

"Oh, God. Please!"

She pushed up against my mouth. I glanced up to find her head lolling from side to side, auburn hair splayed out on the bed, desperate for the release that was so near. Harper, without inhibition, was intoxicating. I could drown in her. Her hips bucked, but I held her still, bringing her to new heights.

Her body stiffened, and she inhaled sharply. When she came, she screamed out my name, and it was the most glorious thing I'd ever heard.

I toed off my shoes and shed my pants, leaving only my boxer briefs in place. I eased her body up the bed and blanketed her with my weight, sinking us deeper into the mattress. My throbbing cock pressed against her abdomen as I worked my hand up her thigh, peppering light kisses along her collarbone.

"Do you feel how hard you make me?" I whispered.

She looked into my eyes, and I saw something shift.

"I feel you, Greyson. And I want you to know that I'm yours, just as I was ten years ago. I'm trusting you with my heart again. Promise you'll be careful with it."

I had the power to crush her. I knew this, yet I wasn't concerned about it because I knew it would never happen. Not again. There was something about the way she curved into me, the way she smelled like jasmine and sunshine, that made everything else in life fall away. She was the only woman I could ever remember wanting to hold on to for more than a fleeting moment, and I knew, without a shadow of a doubt, that I still loved her. We belonged together. She might not realize it now, but I trusted her with my heart just as much as she trusted me with hers.

"Harper, I love you. I always have—I promise you that. I'll stop now if you want to slow things down, but baby, I've never wanted anything more than I want you right now."

She reached up to cup my face.

"Then what are you waiting for?" she asked.

Not wanting to spend another moment hesitating, I got up from the bed and opened the nightstand drawer to remove the box of condoms I had placed there earlier.

"Were you planning this all along, Mr. Hughes?" she teased, but there was a hint of suspicion in her question as well.

I chuckled.

"I know how it looks, but no. I shot over to the corner store while you were schmoozing donors. After dancing with you, I figured I should grab them just in case."

I shed my boxers and made quick work of the condom. Before climbing back onto the bed, I took a moment to appreciate her nude body spread out before me. Harper was like a feast I couldn't wait to devour. She was always beautiful, but a naked, luminous Harper was something poets could write sonnets about.

I crawled up her body, and she bent her legs, cradling me. Positioning myself at her entrance, I pushed forward, barely sliding through the arousal between her lips. Her slender arms clung to my neck encouragingly, and I drove all the way in. I sucked in a gasp so hard it made my lungs hurt. The effect she had on me hit me like an earthquake. Lacing my fingers through her hair, I captured her mouth with mine.

"Greyson," she whimpered as my forehead rocked against hers.

"Do you remember what I told you the first time you gave yourself to me?"

When she responded, her voice was thick with emotion.

"You said I was beautiful, and you loved me."

"I meant what I said then, just as much as I mean it now. I love you, Harper."

"I love you too, Greyson. I've always known. I was just afraid to admit it."

I continued to push into her, our words hushed as our bodies moved together.

"Nobody has ever fit me the way you do. Night after night for ten long years, you crept into my dreams. I dreamed about touching you. Kissing you. Fucking you. I let go of you once. I promise I won't ever do it again," I declared, the words a breath of a whisper against her lips.

She moved her hips, matching my thrusts as she gripped my shoulders. It was as if she couldn't get close enough, and it was a feeling I understood all too well. I felt it too. I had to remind myself to go slow when every fiber of my being wanted to fuck her hard and claim her as mine once and for all.

Her nails raked down my back to my ass. I felt their bite against my skin as she made those little gasping noises that made me impossibly hard. Nothing had ever felt or sounded so damn good. She was perfect. There was just the right amount of give-and-take as I drove into her deep and hard. The air in the room seemed to come alive—the energy and the connection the most genuine thing I'd ever felt. I could worship her all night long.

I tried to keep some modicum of control, but it was to no avail. I could feel her desire building as she moaned my name. Our bodies were slick with sweat, pleasure bound, and full of need. When I felt her start to fall apart again, I pinned her arms above her head. I plunged into her, possessing her, the tightening of her perfect body making me feel like I could live forever.

My body raced, my dick pulsing with need, hard and desperate. Hunger ravaged my veins, and every muscle in my body tightened, rippling with an unbearable force. I slammed home, and my world flashed white. So bright. A blinding light that left me quaking in her arms.

We lay there panting for what seemed like hours, but it was probably only minutes. After a time, I rolled off her, and she snuggled into the crook of my arm. Her arm draped across my torso, so warm and familiar. It was where she was meant to be.

She looked up at me, her eyes searching for something. What it was, I didn't know. I reached out and brushed my thumb across the bottom of her swollen lip. Old hopes mingled with new ones filled my mind. They were thoughts of what once was and what could be.

When she reached out and pinched my arm, I jolted. It wasn't a hard pinch, but it surprised me nonetheless.

"What was that for?"

"Just making sure you're really here. Is this real, Greyson? Are you really with me?"

"I was a fool to walk away ten years ago, but I'm here now. This is as real as it gets."

Afterword

I hope you enjoyed BROKEN, a short spin-off of THE STONE SERIES, my *USA Today* bestselling billionaire romance. Greyson is a side character in this steamy five-book series that follows the epic and unforgettable saga of Krystina Cole and Alexander Stone.
Start the series: https://dakotawillink.com/the-stone-series

Dakota Willink is a *USA Today* Bestselling Author from New York. She loves writing about damaged heroes who fall in love with sassy and independent females. Her books are character-driven, emotional, and sexy, yet written with a flare that keeps them real.
Dakota often says she survived her first publishing with coffee and wine. She's an unabashed Star Wars fanatic and still dreams of getting her letter from Hogwarts one day. Her daily routines usually include rocking Lululemon yoga pants, putting on lipstick, and obsessing over Excel spreadsheets. Two spoiled Cavaliers are her furry writing companions who bring her regular smiles. She enjoys traveling with her husband and debating social and economic issues with her politically savvy Generation Z son and daughter. Dakota's favorite book genres include contemporary or dark romance, political & psychological thrillers, and autobiographies.

A Defiant Beauty

Jocelyne Soto

Chapter One

Alana

It was just supposed to be a summer class. Something to help me get ahead in my undergrad degree. One summer where I was going to go to school, get ahead, but also enjoy my life as any nineteen-year-old would.

It was going to be just one summer where I would not get boy crazy. No relationships, because fuck that, I am not made for them, and maybe have a one-night stand or two.

That was my train of thought.

That was my damn mindset at the beginning of summer. And I was going to stick by it.

Until...I saw *him.*

The second that my eyes landed on him, all the plans that I had made for myself for the summer, both personal and scholarly, disappeared.

Me not going boy crazy and concentrating on my summer class was no longer in my head space.

From that point forward, I had one goal for the summer, my old plan had gone out the window, and everything shifted to the new man that had just walked into my life.

Now it was a new plan.

A new goal.

Get him to notice me.

It was that simple.

Get this gorgeous man with the specks of gray in his beard and hair long enough to run your fingers through, to notice *me*.

It sounded easy.

But every part of me knew it wasn't going to be.

Nothing is ever easy. Especially when it comes to men.

Ever.

But it didn't hurt to try.

And now, now, I'm paying for my decisions.

Every one of them.

Chapter Two

Alana

I can feel him.

He is holding me down, and all his body weight is on me, and I'm loving every second of it.

Everything about what he is doing to me feels earth-shattering, even though it shouldn't, not with him. Not with Sawyer Jacobs, the man that I just met and have not said a single word to.

But it feels right.

It feels right when his cock slides into the wet folds of my pussy. It feels right when we shift, and I slide down to my knees and take him into my mouth, tasting both of us, until I can no longer breathe.

Everything feels right. *He* feels right.

I arch my body more, so I can get as much pressure as possible. And within seconds, I'm panting, exploding, and silently crying out in pleasure.

I would be screaming at the top of my lungs, but since I'm in my school library, I can't.

You may be asking, Alana, why the hell are you having sex at school?

Well, the answer would be that I'm not having sex, per se. I'm playing with myself with a pocket-size vibrator. All that hot sex was just a fantasy that would never play out in real life.

Now that I think about it, though, saying that I was playing with myself doesn't sound all that much better.

And as to why I'm doing it at school, instead of in the comfort of my own bedroom, is because about twenty minutes ago, the star of all my fantasies as of late, walked by me looking all hot and sexy.

It did things to me.

So, I found a very secluded corner in my university's library, took out the vibrator that always travels with me, and got to work.

Having a vibrator in my backpack is not normal.

I'm not normal.

I never have been.

Ever since I turned sixteen, I grew into my sexuality and used sex to not only express myself but also to let myself forget about my early childhood years.

I don't want to say that I've had a hard life. There are others in the world that have had it even harder. It was an interesting life, to say the least. At the age of ten, I was taken in by my grandparents because Mommy and Daddy decided that drinking and partying in Vegas was more important than raising a kid.

Yay me.

I went from a household of party animals to a household of overly religious grandparents. Church had gone from nonexistent to being a focal five times a week.

Don't get me wrong. I love my grandma and grandpa. They're amazing. But it got to a point where it became a little too much. They pushed me in all aspects of life. Because of them, I was able to graduate high school with honors and get accepted into one of the most well-respected colleges in the Pacific Northwest.

But even though my grandparents were strict with me and held me to a higher standard than most kids, my parents fucked me up.

Even at a young age, I was exposed to their party ways. Every day our house was filled with strangers, alcohol, and seeing and experiencing things that no child should be subjected to.

I thought that was the norm.

So when I reached my teen years and felt like going against my grandparents' rules, I did what my parents did. What they taught me.

Party. Drink. Kissing boys I shouldn't.

But as I got older, the more my ways of rebelling evolved.

I was almost sixteen when I realized that boys at my school saw me a certain way. In a sexy way. Puberty had hit a few years before, and it was then that guys started realizing that I had a chest and curves that shouldn't belong on a teenager. It was enticing to them. So, I started using sex, what my body had to offer, to have a little fun.

It was, it is, my way of expression, and I love every single second of it.

And the guys that I hook up with, do too.

One hundred percent of the time, the guys that I would hook up with were my age or a year above me.

Never has an older man caught my eye, nor did I find one sexy.

Until this week.

Until I laid eyes on *him*.

The second I saw him, everything I ever looked for in a sexual partner was thrown out of the window.

All it took was one look, and I wanted everything to do with this man.

He had broad shoulders and a tapered waist that had my eyes going wide. A jawline and golden eyes that made me want to stare at him all day. And long hair with small specks of gray that made me want to reach out and see if it was silky smooth.

I was a goner after just one look.

Even more so when he spoke and said his name.

Sawyer Jacobs.

I was in the clouds after that.

So much so that I went back to my apartment that day and played with myself for hours with him at the forefront of all my fantasies.

The marathon continued into the next day, and of course, into today while here in the library.

Did I go into today thinking that I was going to be an exhibitionist? No. But when the man that has overtaken my mind for the last few days walked by in black slacks and a white button-down with the sleeves rolled up, I had to relieve the ache I was feeling deep in my belly.

But the thing is, as much as looking at him does something to me, I'm not able to fulfill whatever fantasies I may have about the guy.

Why do you ask?

Well, for one, he's forty-one and I'm nineteen.

Second, he's my professor.

Chapter Three

Alana

Fresh off my forbidden thought-filled orgasm, I walk into my creative writing course, my only course of the summer. It's also the same course that is taught by the professor that I shouldn't be thinking sexual things about.

As soon as I step into the classroom, my eyes find Sawyer already at the front of the room. He's looking as yummy as he did not even an hour ago, getting ready for class to start.

A small smile forms on my lips at the sight of him. With my smile still in place, I square my shoulders and walk down to the first row of the auditorium-style room.

I walk down as if I'm on a mission.

And I might as well be.

I may not be able to get him to fulfill all my filthy fantasies, but that doesn't mean I don't want him to notice me.

Our first day of class was a few days ago, and during our two hours together, I didn't get a chance to get him to look at me. Today, though, I'm pulling all the stops.

I am wearing my plaid skirt, one that happens to be a little too short, and a top that brings out my best assets, my breasts. I'm blessed to have full C's, and at times they have come to my advantage.

Hopefully today is one of those days.

I don't know why I'm so adamant about getting this man's attention. Given his looks, he is probably used to women throwing themselves at him. He probably knows how to swat away all the advances coming his way.

But Sawyer Jacobs intrigues me. There is something about the guy that has me wanting to know more and who he really is as a person.

I may be intrigued by him a little too much, though.

After leaving class a few days ago, may have done some research. Research that consisted of finding out his age and his relationship status.

That's how I found out that he was forty-one. And as for his relationship, Sawyer Jacobs is a bonafide bachelor.

I should definitely go into private investigation instead of creative writing if I can find that information with just a name and place of work.

When I say how old he was, I didn't balk, which was surprising. I thought for sure I wouldn't find someone his age attractive, but once I saw the number, I didn't care.

I liked that he was that much older than me. In my head, I saw it as him knowing what he wanted in life and possibly had experience on how to please a woman.

The last part really shouldn't have mattered, but for some reason, I liked that thought very much.

Me looking into the man and wanting him to pay me some regard is asking for trouble.

I know that.

But that still doesn't deter me from going through with the plan I've come up with.

As I reach an available seat in my desired row, I decide to make a show of it.

A big show that the individual at the front of the room can only see.

Dropping my bag on the floor on purpose, I turn and angle myself so that my back is facing the front of the room, and I bend to grab it.

This is where I leave all the work to my short skirt. A skirt so short that as I bend at the waist, I can feel it ride up my butt. I don't need to turn around to see that not only is my skirt riding up but also my panties are showing.

Well, they are not so much panties as they are a piece of material that has no crotch or butt coverage. Everything is on display with these.

These were definitely a bold decision, especially with the shortness of the skirt. But if I was going to shoot my shot, might as well go all out.

Like I said, I'm not a normal person.

Without thinking about it, I wiggle my butt a little, just a bit, before I stand back up again. Standing back to full height, I act like I did nothing wrong and turn to take a seat.

When I look up, I'm met with a set of golden eyes staring back at me.

I stare right back, and the golden eyes don't look away. Not until I send a smirk in their direction and finally take a seat that the golden eyes divert.

The smirk stays on my lips as I take a notebook out of my book back.

There is no denying it. Sawyer Jacobs saw what I was doing, and for a minute or two, I'm able to grasp his attention.

His lust-filled attention, if I had to guess by the way his stare burned into me.

As I get situated for class to start, I can't help but wonder.

Maybe my fantasies have a chance of becoming a reality.

Or maybe I just found a way to get myself kicked out of school on the second day.

Chapter Four

Sawyer

Motherfucker.

I shouldn't have looked. I should have kept my eyes on the computer in front of me and shouldn't have looked at what was happening right in front of me.

But it was too hard to resist.

I first noticed her during our Monday class. I saw how she started licking and biting her bottom lip the second she walked in. I saw how her eyes never left me. I saw the lust in them. But I let it be. It was just a schoolgirl crush, and she wouldn't have been the first. There were countless students that have come into my classrooms through the years and have looked at me that same way. I never acted on it. I wasn't that man. I'm still not that man.

But then I saw her walk in today. A part of me had wished I was that man.

The short skirt that she had on barely reached her thighs. It looked like it belonged in a strip club and not in a classroom. Then her fucking top that brought out her luscious chest. A chest that I wanted to get my hands on, a chest that I wanted to mark as mine. From where I was standing, I could tell that she wasn't wearing a bra. I wanted to do things to those tits that would have women run away.

I was getting hard just watching her come down the stairs.

Then she bent down, and the skirt rode up and I went from getting hard to rock solid. Her ass was there for me to look at. She had pieces of fabric on the sides and nothing covering her cheeks. As she stayed bent down, my eyes traveled down her ass and caught a glimpse of her pussy. It was just a quick glance, but I was able to see that she was bare.

When she turned and caught me staring, she smirked. The look she gave me told me that she had gotten what she wanted. She wanted me to look and just gave it to her.

For a split second, I thought that maybe someone was setting me up. That they planted this girl in my class and dressed her up as sexy as possible to see if I would do anything that would get me fired.

It was plausible, but the thought only lasted a second. Nobody is that conniving.

Now as the class goes on, I keep finding any excuse to look at her as discreetly as possible, never for longer than a second.

Her eyes never leave me. I can feel her watching me. Whenever I look at her, she either bites down on her pen or her lip, and it's becoming increasingly hard to concentrate.

Since it's a creative writing course, I decided to change some things for today's lesson plan as time goes on. I need a break from talking to the class so that I can calm myself down. More like calm down a certain body part.

Once I assign a writing task, everyone starts typing away at their computers or putting their pens to their papers. I go sit behind the small desk in front of the room with my computer, trying to keep my eyes off the girl in the front row. Which is still hard, given that her legs are visible under the table.

Keeping myself distracted, I go through the attendance sheet. Since our school includes pictures next to each student's name, I'm able to see who's here without calling out names. It's helpful until I reach a certain young lady sitting in front of me.

Alana Perry.

A pretty name for a pretty girl.

The name Alana suits her. From the picture, I can see that her brown hair frames her face perfectly in waves. I can also see that her brown eyes look as if they have no end to them.

God, what is wrong with me?

I shouldn't be thinking about a student like this.

I shake my head and turn my attention back to my computer and exit out of the attendance sheet. No need to stare at her picture when the real thing is in front of me.

Time goes by, and the end of class is quickly approaching. One by one, each of the twenty-two students in the class, finishes their assignments and brings them up to me before heading out.

As student after student comes up, I notice Alana. I notice that she is still writing, but that her legs are open a little wider than they were before.

I can see that her skirt has ridden up, and her panties are showing.

Panties that happen to be crotchless from what I can tell, and her pussy is out for me to see. I continued watching her, keeping my head turned toward the computer, so no one could see where my eyes really are. I see her hand on her thigh, slowly caressing her skin. I see her fingers inching up until they reach her glistening lips.

Alana then slides her finger up and down her slit before inserting it into her pussy.

She's fucking herself in the middle of class, and all I can do is watch her.

I should stop her. I should stand up from my chair and walk over to her and demand that she stops what she's doing. I should kick her out of my classroom and walk her straight to admissions and have her kicked out. I should do all that, but I don't. It's as if I'm transfixed by what she's doing and can't move.

I am finally able to take my eyes off her hand movements and look up to see that she has stopped writing. Her pen is still in her hand, but her eyes are on me as she continues to finger fuck herself.

She's doing it for me.

She knows I've been watching her, and she is pulling this little stunt so that I would watch.

My line of sight gets diverted slightly when the two other students left in the room come up and turn in their assignments. They are so preoccupied they don't see what is happening at the table behind them.

They leave and that only leaves Alana and me. All by ourselves.

My eyes turn back to her, and she smiles at me.

"Do you like what you see?" she asks in a breathy tone. I look back down and see that she now has two fingers inside herself.

I don't respond. I just keep watching.

"I think you do," she says before she takes her fingers out and pushes her chair back.

Instead of leaving, she climbs up on the table. I watch as she situates herself, pulls her skirt over her waist, and opens her legs wide before going back to fingering herself.

I have a direct view of her pussy.

"What are you doing?" I ask. My voice is raspy and lined with lust. My cock is itching to come out and play.

"Giving you a better look."

There's a chance I'm going to hell for this.

Chapter Five

Alana

I'll be the first to admit that I probably went about this the wrong way.

I've always been open about my sexuality, but never this open. I have never gone as far as to finger fuck myself in a classroom in front of my teacher. While there were people still in the room.

The library was different. I was alone, and no one was able to see me. I could have gotten caught, but the chances were very low.

Now, doing it in front of Sawyer, I'm throwing everything out the window.

I should have thought this through. Maybe Sawyer doesn't want anything to do with me, no matter how much I tell myself he did when I caught him looking at me. Maybe it was just all in my mind.

But if it was, he would have stopped me by now. He wouldn't be enjoying the show that I'm giving him.

He likes what he sees. The way he's looking at me is telling me just that.

I continue fingering myself, and he stands up. My eyes travel straight to his crotch, and I see it tenting, his cock trying to break free from behind his zipper.

He's as turned on by this as I am.

I take my fingers out and hold them up.

"Do you want a taste?" I ask him in a seductive tone. He continues to look at me without saying anything. I wiggle my fingers at him, and he surprises me by coming toward me.

God, I want to get my hands on that bulge that he has growing in his jeans.

And I mean bulge. From just what I see, he's huge. What I wouldn't give to have his cock stretching out my pussy.

He comes to stand in front of me, keeping his eyes on me, but he doesn't touch me. He comes closer, and then he takes me by surprise again and puts his mouth around my fingers.

His tongue circles around my fingers, sucking my juices off. He leans back my fingers falling from his lips.

"Finish," he says.

God, his voice alone makes me as wet as a waterfall. His raspy and deep and so fucking delicious.

I do what he tells me.

I slide my hand back to my pussy and insert them into my tight little hole. Sawyer's eyes follow every moment I make. I start panting, and the only sound that fills the room is my juices slapping against my pussy.

His eyes stay concentrated on my pussy.

He doesn't move closer to me or say anything. He just stands there watching as I continue to fuck myself.

My eyes travel to his bulge and I can't help but lick my lips, thinking about what I might look like, feel like.

Sawyer standing here, watching me, watching me fuck myself, picturing what he would do to me, is what brings me over the edge.

Unlike in the library, I cry out loudly enough for it to echo through the room. With my fingers covered in my cum, I hold them out to him like I did before.

This time, he grabs my hands and brings my hand closer to his mouth. He sucks my fingers clean without taking his eyes off me. The look alone is going to make me come again.

Once he's done, he throws my hand forcefully away from him like it has insulted him.

"Get up and fix your skirt," He orders, backing away from me and heading back behind his desk.

I guess our time is over, and here I was going to offer to help relieve the pain he's experiencing behind his zipper. I guess he doesn't want that.

Whatever, I do what he says.

I swing my legs to my chair and fix my skirt. When I bend down to grab my bag, I give him another show. I just don't look at him.

There's a smile on my face as I leave the room. What I did just now was stupid, one that could get him fired and expelled, but I wouldn't take it back. I saw that Sawyer Jacobs was as affected by me as I am by him.

I just hope that he won't tell anyone about what happened here. I won't. But he doesn't know that.

Before I reach the door, Sawyer calls out to me, "How old are you?" he asks.

I turn and give a small smirk before answering him. "Nineteen."

Without a second glance, I leave the room, already planning all the orgasms I will be having tonight.

Chapter Six

Sawyer

Nineteen.

She's nineteen.

I let a nineteen-year-old not only show me her pussy, and masturbate in front of me but then I went one step further and taste her not once but twice off her fingers.

A forty-one-year-old man should have nothing to do with a girl her age, especially not sexually.

But I still see her.

I still have her taste in my mouth, even days later. My cock has been in my hand more times than I can count these past two days. I can't get Alana out of my mind.

Today isn't going to help either since we have yet another class together. I have to hope that what happened on Wednesday will not happen again today or ever.

I also have to hope that Alana didn't tell anyone about her little show. I sucked off her fingers. I saw her pussy and her ass. Those are all grounds for me to be fired, and if she was seventeen, those things could get me thrown in jail.

If she does something today, I have to put a stop to it. Whatever happened on Wednesday cannot happen again. Ever.

I may only be a fantasy for her or a way to get over some daddy issues, but this is my life. I can't have her ruining it.

Before walking into the classroom, I take a deep breath. I try not to look at her as I walk in farther. I planned my arrival so I will be getting here right at twelve and wouldn't have time to stare at her before class begins.

Walking down the steps, I notice that the seat she was in last class was occupied by a male student. I look through the row to see if I can see the head of brown curls, but I come up empty.

Why am I even looking for her?

I shake my head and head to the table in the front.

"Good morning, everyone," I say to the room. I face them, and they all greet me back. "Let's change things up a little bit today. Instead of learning about a writing process and only actually writing at the end of class, let's just write today."

I completely changed my lesson plan again, and yet again, it has to do with the fact that I can't get Alana out of my mind.

"Today, let's write something that we have always wanted to write. Let's open our minds to the endless possibilities and not worry about it being properly written or spelling errors. I don't even want to put your name on it. This will be completely anonymous, and I will give you points for just being here today. I will even join you. What does everyone say?"

Head nods and a bunch of "yes" roll out, and that is when I finally see her. She is sitting in the last row, keeping her eyes down, not looking at me.

Huh, for the last two classes, she couldn't keep her eyes off me, and now she is fighting to not look at me.

I don't know if that's a good thing or bad, and truthfully, I don't know what I want it to be.

The room shuffles around, and everyone gets situated with a pen and paper, and I do the same.

Usually when it comes to these types of assignments, I would grade papers or catch up on some reading. But since I can't get my mind off a certain subject, I decided it would be better to write. It soothes the soul and all that.

As I start writing, my mind drifts from where I want the pen to go. I start writing about a short skirt and a bare pussy staring back at me. I write about watching her fuck her fingers and her taste.

Half an hour into the class is when I finally realize what I'm doing. Jesus fucking Christ.

Reading it back, this is some erotica-type shit that has no place in a classroom. Especially when the topic is a student in said classroom.

I shake the thoughts in my head and begin writing again, but it's no use. The next line I write is an imagery of my cock sliding into her tight little hole.

The more I write, the harder I'm getting.

What the actual fuck is wrong with me?

Never has a student affected me like this. Yes, I have had attractive students but never has one made me hard as stone and had me thinking about their pussy on a regular basis. What did this girl have that she is turning me into a crazed animal?

I need to clear my head, and writing isn't doing it. I get up and walk out of the classroom as the students write, trying to hide my hard-on as best as I can, and head to the bathroom.

Walking into the bathroom, I head straight to the sink and splash water on my face. The coldness of it takes my head out of whatever cloud it's in. I'm trying to distract my mind so much, that I don't even hear when someone walks in until they are right behind me and I make eye contact in the mirror.

Staring back at me are big brown eyes with pieces of dark hair framing them.

"What are you doing in here?" I ask her through the mirror.

"I wanted to apologize for what happened last class. This seemed like the only time I could do it," she says in a small voice that lacks any confidence. A big difference from the voice that asked me if I wanted a taste a few days ago.

"Apologize?" I ask like I'm stupid.

"Yes, it shouldn't have happened. I not only put myself at risk of expulsion, but I also put your job on the line as well as everything else, I wasn't thinking. For that, I'm sorry."

She was apologizing for putting my career at risk and the possibility of me serving jail time. What I didn't hear is her apology for touching her pussy for me to see.

"You're not apologizing for the finger fucking," I state, not ask. And yes, my comment may be a little harsh, but there are a lot of things on the line right now.

She sighs and shakes her head. "I'm a sexual person, I won't apologize for that, and I never will. I'm very open about who I am in that retrospect, and when I'm attracted to someone, I'm vocal about it. So no, I'm not apologizing for what I did, just the way I went about it. For that, I'm sorry."

A sexual person that is attracted to me.

I'm not going to lie, but knowing that turns me on, and my eyes start looking at her in a different light.

She's right. She shouldn't be apologizing for being the sexual person she is.

"I accept your apology," I tell her. She nods. And then turns to walk out the door.

"Alana," I say, stopping her.

She turns to me and raises her eyebrow. "I am attracted to you too. If you want to act on it, do it. Just don't do it where you can get caught."

Alana smirks and comes closer to me.

"Are you telling me that you would like to watch me play with myself again?"

"Baby, I would do a lot more than just watch you," I say, and I lean in, my lips almost touching her ear. "I would fuck you so hard I would ruin you for all those little boys that don't know how to play with their dicks."

I lean back and don't look at her as I walk out of the bathroom.

Chapter Seven

Alana

I apologized.

After I left the classroom on Wednesday, I started thinking about all things that could have gone wrong. Like if he didn't have interest in me, then he might go to the admissions office and get me kicked out. So many scenarios worked their way into my mind that it became more than just getting off.

So, I convinced myself to apologize.

I was trying to not watch him during class. I tried to keep my eyes off him, and for the most part, I did. That is until he walked out of the room and I saw his hard cock had tented up in his jeans.

My mouth watered at the sight.

So, I followed. I was going to leave my apology for after class, but I decided that getting him alone sooner was better.

I apologized, and I was going to walk out and throw my plan to pursue him out the window. Then he stopped me and told me that he found me attractive and explained what he would do to me. To say I didn't get wet at his words would be a lie.

My plan was back on.

I just needed to be smarter about my approach.

An approach I will have to leave for another day because right now I'm trying not to go crazy with all my orders.

I got lucky by getting a job as a waitress at a bar close to campus. Usually places like this only hire people that are over the age of twenty, but since I'm only a few weeks shy of my birthday, the owner let me come on. It also helped that she was a woman and let me work only when she did to keep an eye on me.

It's Saturday night, and the bar is packed. I'm trying to get all my orders right and on time, and thinking about my professor isn't going to help.

And for most of the night, I'm able to keep my mind off him. That is, until around eleven, when a group of guys come in and sits at one of my tables.

"How's it going, guys?" I say, laying down napkins in front of them not looking at what they look like. "What can I get started for you?" I ask, finally looking up, and I meet his eyes.

Jesus.

Even with the darkness of the bar, I can still see his golden eyes sparkle.

I swallow down the lump and divert my eyes from him, but it's no use, I can still feel his stare.

"We'll have four of whatever you have on tap," the guy to Sawyer's right says to me. I give him a nod.

"I'll get that right away," I say before I scurry off from the table and submit the drinks. When I go back to the table to deliver their beer, I do it as quickly as possible and don't look at Sawyer.

I don't know why I'm being affected like this. Maybe because this isn't a classroom, and no one here knows he's my teacher.

"Alana," Grace, my boss, calls out. "Take a break. I'll handle your tables," she tells me.

Instead of going to the breakroom in the back, I head to the employee only bathroom. I need to freshen up, especially with how I've been running around all night. Never did I think working at a bar would be this hard, but the tips are great especially when you show a little cleavage.

I push open the door to the bathroom and I'm about to lock it when someone pushes it open behind me.

I'm about to tell them that employees only, but the words die down when Sawyer walks in and closes the door behind him.

"You shouldn't be working in a bar," he tells me, looking me straight in the eye. His voice is stern, like what a father would sound like.

"Why? Because I'm a girl?" I ask, crossing my arms.

His eyes go directly to my chest. He swallows.

"Because you're too young, and men are pigs and don't know how to keep their hands to themselves," he says.

"What if I don't want them to keep their hands to themselves?" I walk toward him, making sure that my chest touches his. "What if I want to feel their hands on my body? What are you going to do about it? You don't control me."

His hands go to my waist, and for a second, I think he's going to push me back for invading his personal space, but he doesn't. No, his fingers dig into my waist and bring me closer to him.

Close enough to feel his hard cock against my stomach.

"You're too young," he says again, and then he leans closer, his lips barely a whisper against mine. "But if someone's hands are on this body, then they better be fucking mine."

Before I can register anything, his lips land on mine, and my tongue is making its way into his mouth. My hands move around his neck while his moves down to my ass, and he grips tightly.

We somehow make our way to the small vanity that holds the sink, and he is hoisting me up. The second my ass hits the sink, he's between my legs as they wrap around his waist.

His lips travel from my mouth down my neck to the tops of my tits.

"Is this what you want? To have the hands of a man like me on this tight little body of yours?" he asks in between kisses on my skin. He starts nibbling and then through my shirt and bra he bites my nipple, hard.

"Yes," I pant, holding his head tight to my body.

"A little girl like you wouldn't know what to do with a man like me. Or even with a cock like mine."

"Why don't you show me?"

He stands back up. His hands move to my hair and pulls me toward him. "I'll show you. All show you what it takes to be with a man. I'll show you exactly what I wanted to do to you after the little stunt you pulled on Wednesday."

He releases me and steps back fully.

"Show me that tight little pussy."

Don't mind if I fucking do.

Chapter Eight

Sawyer

It's wrong. I'm forty-one and she's nineteen. I might not go to jail for this, but I can lose my job.

Yet, I'm still doing it. I hadn't planned on it, but the second I saw her tonight, it felt like I needed it. I needed to touch her. I needed my lips on her, my hands on her body. She was wearing little shorts and a tank top that barely covered her tits.

Every pair of male eyes were on her, including my buddies. Including me. When she dropped off our drinks earlier, we got the perfect view of her chest and the hard-on I've been rocking since I saw her turned into stone.

My eyes stayed on her, so when she went down the hall, I followed.

I shouldn't have, but she entices me. She has this power over her that pulls me in.

The second my lips touched hers, I was a goner. She tasted sweet and something I would never forget. Now I stand in front of her, telling her to show me her pussy.

She looks me straight in the eye as she lowers her shorts, and I see that she is wearing a black lacy thong that doesn't cover anything.

Through the lace, I can see her bare pussy. Before she can slide her thong down, I replace my hands with hers. But instead of sliding the piece of fabric down her legs, I tear the lace off.

"Those were expensive," she tells me with a smirk.

"I'll buy you new ones," I offer before I take her lips again and slide my hand to her center. "You're wet."

"That's what you do to me."

I take her bottom lip between my teeth and shove my finger into her tight little hole.

"You're so tight. I think you need an old man like me to stretch this little pussy out."

She whimpers against my mouth, and I swallow it down as I continue to work my fingers.

"I need you," she pants as her walls tighten around my finger.

"Is this what you were picturing, baby? When you were finger fucking yourself in my classroom? My fingers instead of yours?" I say as I insert another finger.

She whimpers again, "Answer me."

"Yes," she breathes.

"Good," I say, bringing my fingers out and inserting a third finger. I curl my fingers inside her, and her hands curl around my biceps, holding herself up. "You have no idea how much I wanted to touch you that day. How I wanted to take your hand and replace it with mine, how much I wanted to eat this little pussy until the whole school knew who was making you come."

Her nails dig deeper into my shirt, I can feel them in my skin, marking me.

"I wanted to make you come so hard, that your juices would squirt all over my fingers and the only way to clean them off would be with my mouth." My other hand moved to her ass and squeezed her, pushing her closer to me as she rides my fingers. "I've had your taste on my tongue since then, and I can't make it go away."

"More," she pants out, her eyes rolling to the back of her head in pleasure.

"You think you can squirt for me, baby? You think you can come so hard that everyone in this bar will know that you're mine?"

"Yes," she pants, and I can feel it. I can feel her pussy tighten around my fingers. "Don't stop."

"Come for me, baby. Squirt for me," I demand, and she explodes. Her pussy pushes out my fingers as she comes. I slap her pussy, and her juices cover my hand. I give her one more slap before I bend down and lick her clean.

"Oh, god." Alana lets out as her hand comes to my head and grabs onto my hair tight.

I lick her clean, biting her clit a few times before I stand back up and suck my fingers clean. She stares at me the whole time, catching her breath and her eyes full of lust.

She comes closer, her hands land on my chest, and she gives me a lazy smile before her lips land back on mine. Her tongue swipes mine, and I know she tastes herself.

If I thought that she was a little slut before, I definitely believe that now.

"Let me repay you," she says with a seductive smile when she pulls back.

I don't say anything. I just lean in and give her one final kiss. I need to get my mind straight. If she touches my dick, I will fuck her right here, and I can't do that. If I'm going to do this with her, then I need to control myself. Especially in public. "We'll talk about it more once you get off work."

She nods, and because I can't resist, I lean in one more time to give her a kiss before I walk out of the bathroom with the most painful blue balls.

Chapter Nine

Alana

Orgasmic bliss is how I would explain the state of mind I was in for the rest of my shift. It was like I was in my own little world, and nobody could ruin it.

I cannot begin to describe how it felt to have his hands on me, his fingers in my pussy. It was like a dream come true. Well, more like a fantasy. Never did I think that I would come to this, but I'm happy it did.

The only thing that threw me off was when he told me that we would talk after my shift. I thought that meant that he would stick around until closing, but he left with his buddies about an hour ago.

I was a little disappointed, but I was still in my little orgasm bubble. I wasn't even missing my panties he destroyed.

"Grace, I'm out!" I yell toward the kitchen.

She comes out to the bar area and nods. "You have your phone on you?"

I nod.

"The pepper spray and the blade I gave you?"

I nod again. When I first started here, she handed me a "pervert kit" that consisted of brass knuckles, pepper spray, and a switchblade that could make someone bleed with the smallest cut. She told me to always carry it with me, especially since I was leaving late.

"Good. Now call me as soon as you get to your place." I nod again and give her a smile.

"I will. Good night!" I say as I walk out the door.

Walking home at two o'clock in the morning isn't the best idea, but my apartment is three blocks over, and I don't have a car. Grace didn't like it, but I told her I was fine with my kit.

I walk out of the bar, and I walk into a hard wall of a man right away.

Before I even think about reaching for my pepper spray, I look up and see that it's Sawyer.

"What are you still doing here?" I ask, taking a step back.

"I said we would talk after your shift," he says. The way he says the words, throws me off. They're soft, but they still hold dominance and strength, but they aren't as hard as they were earlier.

"I thought that you had changed your mind since you left with your friends and all."

He nods. "I took them home and then came back."

He gives me a small smile. Oh, god. I have only seen him smile a few times in class. He's so handsome when he smiles. "Is your car in the back?"

I shake my head. "I don't have a car. I'm walking home since my apartment is three blocks over."

"You're going to walk at two o'clock in the morning?" He looks at me like I'm talking gibberish.

"I've been doing it for the last three weeks," I tell him.

He shakes his head and instead of saying anything, he sighs. "Let me walk you home then."

He cares.

If he didn't then he would have offered to walk me home. He could have just left me for my own regard, but he's not. That should say something, right?

I nod and turn in the direction of my apartment. For a few storefronts, we don't say anything. His hands are in his pockets, his eyes at his feet. I'm trying to keep myself from shivering. I didn't really think when I grabbed a sweater earlier. The one I'm wearing is very thin and doesn't help with the cold breeze at two in the morning. You would think it being June in Washington, it would be at least warm.

I don't have much time to think about my sweater choices because before I knew it, a warm jacket is being wrapped around my shoulders. I look up, and Sawyer gives me a sexy smile without saying a word.

"Thank you." I say and I just get a nod in return.

We get down a full block before he says anything.

"Alana, I have to ask," He breaks the silence.

God, hearing him say my name does something to me. It did it when he said it in the bathroom at school, and it happened again just now.

"Do you have daddy issues?"

I snort, not what I expected for him to ask. "What?"

He runs his hand through his hair, that has specks of white, and stops walking. "Never mind, I shouldn't even have asked you that."

"No, I get it. A nineteen-year-old going after a man of your age is out of the ordinary. 'Something must not be right with her,' is that where your mind was?"

Sawyer sighs, "I'm sorry, but yes. I can't help but wonder why you would be attracted to someone who is forty-one when there are plenty of guys your age that would be happy to be with you. Maybe you are looking for a father figure or something along those lines."

I want to laugh. I do, but I hold it in. I take a deep breath before I tell him my history. No one really knows about my parents, not even some of the friends I have back home.

"I guess you are kind of right about the daddy issues. My parents decided that it was more important to party and do drugs than to raise a kid. So, I was sent to live with my grandparents, who, by the way, are overly religious. But I'm not looking for a father figure. Up until now, I have never found an older man attractive. I have always steered clear of guys that were older than twenty. I guess you can say that you would be the first." I give him a sly smile.

"Your first," he says. Not a question, a statement.

"Yes," I say moving closer to him and sliding my hand up his chest. "What if we did this?"

"Did what?"

"This. You and me. I won't tell anyone, and I know that you wouldn't either. We can see where this goes, keep it to ourselves, and at the same time have some fun."

"I could get fired," he states. His hand comes up to stop mine from moving higher up his chest, but doesn't take it off him.

"I know. That's why we would come up with some ground rules. The first being that we don't do anything anywhere where we might get caught."

"It could be a lot worse than just losing my job."

"We're in Washington, where the age of consent is sixteen. Did you know that?" I can tell by the look on his face that he did not.

"No, I didn't." He gives me a sly smile in return. I want to see that smile all the time.

"I looked it up just in case Washington state had a weird law about the age of consent being twenty-one or something, but we are safe in that regard. Nobody would get arrested."

He lets go of my hand and I inch it up until my fingers are wrapping around his short hair.

"So, how do we do this?" he asks. I can feel his hand coming to my waist and bringing me closer to him. I can feel his hard cock against my stomach again. The things I can do to him. He's not dealing with no virgin after all.

"How about you come to my place, and I can show you?"

Chapter Ten

Sawyer

I should have said no.

But there is something about Alana Perry that captivates me, and I can't seem to turn it off.

The rest of the walk to her apartment was done in silence. A silence that didn't need to be filled because for some reason it was a comfortable one. I've known this girl a week, I've talked to her a total of three times, and I'm already comfortable with her.

Well, I did have my fingers inside her a few hours ago, and I licked her clean, so maybe that has something to do with that. I also still have her ripped panties in my pocket.

I play with the lace as we walk up to her apartment. Looking around, I notice that it's not a bad neighborhood, but like any place here in the city, it could be safer.

Alana puts her keys in the lock and then leads me up to the third floor. I don't even get to see her apartment because as soon as the door closes behind me, she jumps into my arms and starts kissing me.

God, her body feels amazing against mine, and I bet it would feel even better when we're naked.

"Someone is eager." I chuckle against her lips. My hands find their way down to her ass, and I lift her up so that she could wrap her legs around my waist.

"I've been thinking about your cock inside of me all week. I don't want to wait any longer," Alana says as her lips travel down my neck.

"Such a dirty mouth on such a pretty girl. Maybe I should show you one of my fantasies," I say before smacking her ass hard.

Alana groans before she leans back, abandoning her exploration of my neck. I see her eyes full of lust.

"Please do."

I let go of her ass, and she slides down my body. I take her face in between my hands and kiss her hard, leaving her breathless.

"Get on your knees," I say as I pull away from her delicious mouth.

"Gladly." She kneels in front of me. She doesn't waste any time by undoing my belt and then my slacks before she slides her hand into my briefs and takes my cock out. Her tongue comes out before she takes the head in between those luscious lips that are swollen from our kiss.

"Fuck," My head tips back the second she starts taking me deeper.

Fuck, how is this girl only nineteen and knows how to give head so good.

She takes me in deeper, and my hand flies to her hair, holding her there, hearing her gag on my cock as it hits the back of her throat.

"That's it, baby. Swallow my cock." I hold her head as I fuck her mouth. "You like having a big cock in that pretty mouth, don't you? I bet the little boys that you have been with have never fucked your mouth like this."

She shakes her head and sucks on my dick even harder.

The only sound I hear is her gagging and my heavy breathing. I tighten the hold I have on her hair.

"You going to swallow, baby? Because I'm about to come. Better move that pretty mouth out of the way," I warn, but she shakes her head and takes me in deep. The second the tip hits the back of her throat, I explode.

Fucking fuck.

I hold her head to my cock for a few seconds longer than necessary before I let her go.

"So fucking good," I pant out, looking down at her. She wipes some of my cum off her bottom lip before she licks it off.

That's when I lose it. I lift her up in my arms again and kiss her. I taste myself on her tongue, and I start getting hard again.

"It's a good thing today is Sunday," I say as I make my way down her neck to her chest.

"Why is that?" she pants.

"Because now it's my turn, and there's no way I'm going to stop once I've started."

My lips meet hers again, and I walk deeper into the apartment to where I think the bedroom is.

I told her I wasn't going to stop, and I was telling the truth.

No way in hell that I will give up the chance to be with her now.

Especially after that fucking blow job.

Chapter Eleven

Alana

I can't believe his dick fit in my mouth. It was so big, veiny, and had so much girth, I have no idea how it held together, but I did. And god, how I want to do it again and again.

But right now, I want to feel him inside of me. I want him to pound so deep inside of me that I feel him for days.

Sawyer walks down the hall and surprisingly opens the correct door that leads to the bedroom. My apartment isn't that big. There is only one bedroom and an adjoining bathroom. The living room barely fits the couch, and the kitchen doesn't hold more than two people at a time. But I like it, it's me.

Once in the bedroom, Sawyer tosses me on the bed. He stays by the foot of it, and I look at what his eyes are expressing.

They are filled with lust and as if he can't wait to devour me. Even more than what he has already done tonight.

My eyes travel to his torso as he works the buttons on his button-up shirt. The second that all the buttons are free, I can't help but drool.

For being forty-one, his body is perfect. He has abs that I just want to lick day in and day out and that V that most men dream about having.

God, this man is so sexy.

Before I can get to my knees and take his cock in my mouth again, Sawyer grabs me by the ankles and drags me to the end of the bed. He works off my shorts, and since he ripped off my panties earlier, my pussy lays bare to him.

I lean up slightly to rid myself of my tank top and swiftly take off my bra, and I lie back for all his glory.

He smirks and licks his lips before he falls to his knees, throwing my legs over his shoulders. The second his mouth meets my pussy, I let out a moan so loud that the people on the top floor could probably hear me.

"Holy," I moan out, my mind turning into putty.

This is more than just a lick; this feels like he's eating me alive and no way in hell am I going to stop him.

"So wet. So delicious," Sawyer says, and his voice sends vibrations into my body that brings my orgasm closer.

I let out another groan, and I can feel him chuckle against me. "I get the feeling that you like the dirty talk."

"I do," I pant and grab on to his hair. I just realized that having his head between my legs earlier was not enough. I needed more of him, and that is what I'm getting right now.

Sawyer inserts his fingers inside me, and I hear him groan when I tighten around them.

"You have a tight cunt," he says before he takes my clit in between his teeth. He pumps his fingers into me, and it starts becoming too much. I rub my pussy against his face to get myself closer to the edge.

"That's it, little girl, ride my face. I want to taste your cum for days," he tells me, and with his words, I explode.

As I pant, trying to catch my breath, Sawyer cleans me up with his tongue. Making his way up my body, he kisses every inch he can. By the time he reaches my lips and I taste myself on his tongue, I'm already set for the next round.

"Are you ready for my cock?" he whispers in my ear, and I swear I have an orgasm right there.

Chapter Twelve

Sawyer

When it comes to Alana Perry, I am not a strong man. Just one taste of her pussy, and I'm already looking for more.

The way her body looks right now is insane. Her dark hair is spread out over the comforter, her bare pussy uncovered and her tits are just begging to be sucked on.

She's gorgeous.

She's so beautiful that I want to make her mine in every way that I can.

I'm not a relationship type of guy. Never have been. Even at forty-one, I always have been one to run from commitment, but for some reason, I'm looking at this differently.

This makes me want a relationship. I don't know why, but I feel like trying. That's why I need to stop.

"I've been wanting your cock inside me all week," Alana says, wrapping her arms around my neck and kissing me. I slide my hands all over her body and roll us over so that I'm lying on my back and she's on top of me.

"Not tonight," I say in between kisses.

Alana leans back and gives me a look that says, "what the hell?"

"Why not?" She sounds like I just insulted her.

"Because I want to take you to dinner before I fuck you to the point you forget your own name," I tell her, tucking a few hair strands behind her ear.

"You want to take me to dinner?" she asks like it's the most ridiculous thing that she has ever heard.

"I do." I cup her cheek with my hand, trying to show her that I'm being serious.

"Why? Don't get me wrong, I would love to go to dinner with you, but I didn't peg you for a wine-and-dine type of guy."

Boy, was she right. I'm not that guy. I'm the fuck and walk out type of guy. Never have I been the guy that begs women to take let take to dinner.

"You're right. I'm not that guy. But for some reason, I want to be that guy with you." It's the truth. She doesn't seem to be the kind of girl that would be okay with just a fuck and be able to walk away.

One side of my brain is saying to do just that. Just fuck her and walk away but the other is telling me to figure out why this girl has captivated everything in such a short time. Why am I willing to throw my career away for this girl when others have wanted to do the same, but I didn't let them.

"You know, when I suggested that we did this, I didn't mean a relationship. Not that a relationship wouldn't be great, but I thought that we would fuck, and that would be it." Her eyes downcast, as if she were ashamed that she thought that. She may have said that she would be fine with just the sex, but her face is saying otherwise.

"I know, but there's something about you that I can't wrap my head around. I want to get to know you, spend time with you. Do we call it a relationship? I don't know, I don't really care what it's labeled. I just want to spend time with you. In and outside of the bedroom." I throw a smirk at her.

I thought that she would at least give me an eye roll, but she just keeps looking at me. For what feels like an eternity she stares at me until a smile finally grows on her face.

"Okay," she says.

"Okay?"

"Okay, take me to dinner."

Chapter Thirteen

Alana

What do you wear when your creative writing professor invites you to dinner?

Do you know the answer to that one? Because I have no clue. I've been staring at the contents of my closet for the past forty minutes, and I have yet to find anything to wear.

"Uh!" I throw some lacy top back into the pile.

Why is this so hard? I didn't have a hard time picking what to wear for class. Why does this have to be?

Well, because for class I have to dress somewhat conservatively, I can't walk in there half naked begging him to fuck me.

I can't help but laugh a little.

After our night last weekend, he stayed for breakfast, and he told me that he didn't want me wearing short skirts or shorts to class. He said something about it being hard for him to teach with me in the room. It's even harder when I'm dressed like I'm going to the club.

I agreed. Besides, the only reason I dressed a little slutty the first week of school was to get his attention. Now I got it. I don't need to use that dress code.

But this is dinner, not school, and I want his attention. I want him to have a hard time concentrating so he can only think of fucking me.

This week, class has been like this foreplay thing going on between us.

There has been no touching since last Saturday, but there have been a lot of sly smiles and very, *very* dirty messages exchanged.

Before he left my apartment after our night between the sheets, I set him up with a Snapchat account. I gave him my number, but if we wanted to exchange pictures, this was the safest way.

He looked at me like I had a second head, but he got over it. I did tease him a little about it though.

I look at the time on my phone. It's seven forty-five, and Sawyer will be here in about fifteen minutes. It' a good thing that my hair and makeup are already done.

Shaking my head, I grab the first skirt that I tried on and then the silky red top with spaghetti straps that's at the bottom of the pile. I pair the outfit with some black heels, and by the time the intercom goes off, I'm ready.

I open the door, and I have to cross my legs because standing before me, in black slacks and a black button-down that has the sleeves rolled up, Sawyer looks like a guy from a magazine. One that I want to lick from head to toe over and over again.

"Hi there, handsome," I say, leaning against the door, not hiding the fact that I'm checking him out. I can't believe that he's forty-one. He has a better body than most twenty-year-olds.

"Hey yourself," he says in the smooth sexy voice of his. He walks in and instantly takes me in his arms and kisses me.

I melt against him and when my tongue touches his, he lets out a groan that makes me want to skip dinner and stay in all night.

"Let's stay in," I mumble against his lips and instead of him agreeing, he just chuckles.

"As much as I would like to eat your pussy for dinner, I really want to take you out," he says, his hands running along my body like he can keep me from shivering at his touch.

"You're no fun." I pout at him, which only makes him laugh more.

He comes closer, his lips almost touching my ear. "I'll show just how fun I can be when we come back." Then he slaps my ass hard.

"Fuck." Usually, ass slapping doesn't turn me on, but fuck, this man is changing a lot of things, and it's making me want more.

"Let's go." He waves for me to go first. I grab my clutch and phone from the counter and head out. I may or may not have a little more swing to my step. I can hear him chuckle behind me, so I know he is keeping an eye on my ass.

Good.

When we step out of the building, I see a sleek black SUV parked in the front. I hold in my snort because this is exactly the type of vehicle that I pictured Sawyer in.

He walks me to the passenger door and holds the door for me. When I'm safely in the car, I watch as Sawyer walks around to the driver's side. There's a confidence to him that not a lot of guys hold. He's so sexy that he belongs on the cover of magazines.

I can see why some girls only go for older men. Sawyer is definitely a daddy. Oh god, I can't believe I just thought that.

When he gets in the car, I notice something, and I can't help but smile at him.

"What?" he asks as he pulls away from the curb.

"The windows are tinted," I state.

"Yes, they are," he says in a cautious tone.

"I like tinted windows," I say before I take my seat belt off and lean my body over the center console. My hand goes straight to his belt and I undo it.

"Is that so?" he asks, a small chuckle coming out.

I nod. I undo his slacks and slide down the zipper before I reach into his brief and take his cock out.

"Yes, let me show you," I say before I circle my lips around his head and take him all the way down until I hear him groan.

Chapter Fourteen

Sawyer

Fucking hell.

I have no idea how we made it to the restaurant in one piece. Her mouth on my cock was like a dream. I think the saving grace was the fact that we were stuck at a red light when I exploded in her mouth, and like the good girl she is, she swallowed my cum down.

When Alana got out of the car, she had a devilish little smirk on her face. One I wanted to kiss off her completely.

Now we are waiting for our food, and I'm trying to keep myself from spitting out my wine since Alana thought it would be a good idea to play footsies with my dick.

I felt her foot crawling up my leg when the waitress started taking our order, and it has been there ever since.

"You're a defiant one, are you?" I say, placing a hand over her foot and holding it to my crotch.

She laughs. "I've never called myself that, but yes. I am. There is no fun doing things that are expected of you. The fun comes with the unexpected."

Her smile as she explains this to me is so bright that I wish I could see it for the rest of my life.

Where did that come from? She's nineteen. No way in hell should I be thinking about the rest of my life with her.

One, she is still my student, and two no way this will last more than a few weeks.

But god, that smile.

"What?" Alana asks, taking me out of my thoughts.

I shake my head and give her a grin "Nothing, just thinking about something."

"And what is that?" she asks in a curious tone.

I lean closer to the table so that only she would hear. "Just how fucking sexy you will look with my cock sliding in and out of your tight pussy."

Alana leans back and swallows loud enough that I can hear, and a pink tint fills her cheeks.

She shifts in her seat, and in the process, shifts her foot to press it harder into my crotch.

"Well then, maybe we should see where that food is and head somewhere where you can see for yourself just how that would look," she tells me, and since luck is on our side, the waitress arrives with our meals.

We ate the rest of our dinner with some comfortable silence and more sly grins and glances. We decide to skip dessert, and when the check is paid, we make our way out. My hand on Alana's lower back.

Before we make it to the front door of the restaurant, I get stopped by an older woman.

"It's really great that you take your daughter out to dinners, just the two of you," the woman tells me with a warm smile.

"Um." Daughter, she thinks Alana is my daughter. And I wouldn't blame her because there is a twenty-two-year age difference between us. What else would she think? I clear my throat to answer the woman. "Yeah, it's great. Have a good night," I tell her and guide Alana out of the restaurant.

We don't say anything on the way to the car, and when I open the door for her to climb in, she holds off and crosses her arms.

"You could have corrected her," she says. She looks annoyed, and frankly, a little pissed.

"And tell her what? That 'no, she's not my daughter, she's my student that I am kind of dating?'" I ask her.

"Anything would be better than her thinking I'm your daughter." The look on her face tells me she's hurt by this.

"Alana, it just came out. She asked, and I said yes. It doesn't mean anything. This is new territory for me. So, can you please get in the car so that I can take you home?"

She sighs and gets into the car without saying a word.

Maybe this is a bad idea.

Maybe taking her to dinner was a bad idea and now it's coming to bite me back in the ass.

I shake my head and get into the car. As we pull away from the restaurant and head to her place, Alana is silent. She keeps her eyes staring out the window and her arms crossed over her chest.

She may be acting like a disgruntled teenager, but she still looks just as gorgeous. She leaves all the women that I have been with in the dust.

I haven't even had her yet, and she was already destroying every other woman for me.

I pull up to her apartment building, and I'm able to find parking right in front. I turn off the car and just sit there, listening to our breathing, staring out the windshield.

It's Alana who breaks the silence.

"Are we?" she asks.

I look at her and she is looking at her hands in her lap. I wait for her to continue.

"Are we sort of dating?" she clarifies, throwing the words I said earlier back at me.

I reach across the console and tug at her chin so I could look into her brown eyes.

"I would think so," I tell her. I have fingered her, eaten her pussy, she's had my cock in her mouth and has swallowed my cum. That would constitute as 'kind of dating,' wouldn't it? Or is it considered just fucking your student? "Do you want it to be different?"

I ask the question.

But all I get is silence and uncertainty in her big brown eyes.

Chapter Fifteen

Alana

I look at Sawyer and don't say a word.

I just look at him.

I don't answer his question. I just stare into his eyes.

Do I want more?

If I'm being honest with myself, yes, yes, I do. But I just met the guy last week, and yet I've already had sexual encounters with him. Usually when it comes to guys, I don\'t think about what I want. I just think about the sex. So why did Sawyer telling that lady that I was his daughter hurt me? Why do I care that she thought I was his daughter?

Because I do want more. I want more with Sawyer. I want to see what it's like to wake up to him. What it's like to sleep in his arms at night. I want it all.

Fuck.

I don't do relationships. I'm the girl that just uses men for sex and nothing else. I fuck, not fall for the guy.

Fucking hell, I can't believe I'm saying the next few words.

"I want more. You're the only one I ever have wanted more from." I tell him.

It's the truth. Every guy that I have been with hasn't taken me to dinner and haven't made me feel like Sawyer does. This, with him, is different.

"Then I'll try and give you more," he tells me, tightening the grip on my chin.

"Are you going to come upstairs?" I ask, leaning in so that my face is mere inches from his. His grip on my chin drops, and it lands on my hip.

"Why do you want me to come upstairs?" he asks, his eyes filling with lust.

I'm done with this whole back-and-forth thing. I'm telling him exactly what I want, and I'm going to get it.

"I want you to come upstairs, because I want you to fuck my pussy with your big cock until I black out," I whisper against his lips, "I want you to make me forget my name," are the words I say before I press my lips to his.

I give him a slow kiss before I pull back again and say the final words that will for sure make him know what I really want.

"I want you to come upstairs so that you can make me yours. Because that's what I want. I want to be yours. Make me yours, Sawyer. Please," I say to him.

He doesn't speak.

He continues to stare at me, and after a long minute of silence, he leans in and kisses me hard.

Please let this be him agreeing.

If he doesn't agree, I don't know what I will do.

Chapter Sixteen

Alana

He agrees with what I want.

How do I know? Well, he showed me. After he kissed me in the car, he took charge. Sawyer got out of the car, opened my door, and guided me into my building. He kept a hold on me the whole way to my apartment. He didn't even let go of me when I had to reach for my keys.

Once we were behind closed doors, he didn't hesitate lifting me up and attacking me with his mouth. I let out a groan the second my tongue meets his and I can't help but loop my arms around his neck to bring him closer to me.

The height difference between us is a good thing. I'm short enough that when he lifts me up, his cock aligns perfectly with my core.

And god, does he have a glorious cock. One that I can't wait to have inside of me.

I whimper against his mouth, and he takes that as a sign to move toward the bedroom. One second I'm in his arms, and the next I'm being thrown onto my bed.

"Strip."

Don't mind if I do.

I get to my knees while he stands at the foot of the bed, stroking his cock through his pants. So hot.

I unzip my skirt first and slide the material down my waist until it's at my feet and the only thing covering my pussy is a small piece of cloth. Next, I peel off the silky red top that doesn't go well with a bra. To make it more fun for him, I give him a titty drop before I throw the top at his face.

By the tent in his pants, I would say he likes what he sees very much.

"Such a gorgeous little slut," he says, and I can't help but smile. I crawl to him, my hand making its way straight to his cock, and I lean up and take his earlobe between my teeth.

"Are you finally going to use me like the little fuck toy that you've been dreaming of?" I press my tits against his chest to show my point.

I'm not into talking dirty like this, but something about being with an older man like Sawyer makes me want to be.

"I'm going to use you however the I want," he growls, and before I know it, I'm on my stomach with my ass in the air and his tongue in my tight hole.

"Fuck."

"Gotta get you all nice and wet for me, baby. You're going to take this big fat cock, in that little cunt of yours and I'm going to make you scream."

"Yes, yes," I pant into my comforter. The things this man can do with his tongue. It will be my undoing.

His mouth moves from my puckered hole to my pussy and he tongue fucks me until I scream, begging him to let me come.

Magically, he inserts two fingers in me, while another plays with my hole and I explode.

I see stars when he flips me over. I didn't even realize when he undressed, but he did, and he has the body of a god. I want to lick every single inch. But he doesn't let me, because now he's on top of me, licking every inch of *me*.

"Do I need a condom?" he asks, his lips making their way up my neck.

"No." I pant.

"Good," he says before he leans up, puts my leg over his shoulder and slams his cock into me with no warning.

No pain, all pleasure.

"Is this what you wanted, baby? My cock?"

"Fuck," I yell as he pulls out and then slams into me again. "Fuck, yes! Harder. Please go harder."

"Such a good little fuck toy." He pounds into me again and again.

And it's in this very moment, I realize Sawyer Jacobs has ruined me for any other man out there, and I'm not going to complain.

This man knows how to fuck.

Chapter Seventeen

Sawyer

Her pussy is so tight around my cock that I may come any second, but I hold off.

Alana has already come on my cock once already tonight. I'm going to need her to come one more time before I fill this tight cunt of hers.

God, she feels better than any other woman that I have been with.

So wet, so hot and so tight.

Without a doubt, just being inside her this one time has ruined me for other women. I won't be able to go back.

"More," she moans and I smirk. She wants more, I can give her that.

I pull out of her and I swear I hear her whimper because she misses my cock.

"Don't worry, baby, my cock isn't going anywhere." I kiss her lips before I grab her by the hips and flip her over.

A hand slaps against her ass cheek and she lets out another moan into her comforter, so I slap her ass again.

"Such a beautiful little ass," I say, caressing her pink skin. "I can't wait to defile it with my cock."

"Hmmm, do whatever you'd like."

"I do like the sound of that," I say before I jam my cock back into her pussy. "So. Fucking. Good," I pant.

"God, Sawyer. Yes! Yes!" Alana screams, and I feel her tightening around me even more.

"Come on my cock, baby. Cover it with everything you got," I pant out, and that's all it takes before she is screaming my name and spiraling into her orgasm.

As she is coming down, I slap her ass a few more times and tell her the dirty things that I want to do to it.

I pound into her once, twice, and a third time before I'm the one that's exploding.

"Fuck," I yell out as my seed fills her cunt. I fall on top of her, and for a few seconds, my whole body weight is on her.

Moving, I push myself to the side, and by doing that, my cock is out of the warmest place it has ever been in. I can see all my cum spilling out of her, and all I want to do is pound it into her so that she would be dripping it for days.

"That was fucking amazing," Alana pants next to me. I look over to her and her eyes are hooded, and she has sweat all over her body. She looks stunning and sexy.

"Yeah, it was," I agree, reaching over and bringing her closer to me so that her body is molded into mine.

She feels good. As if her body was made just for me. She is soft and smooth, and she fits perfectly into my side.

Like the perfect puzzle piece.

My defiant little puzzle piece.

We fall into silence, both of us trying to catch our breaths and falling into a slumber that may be too heavy to come out of.

"I want you to be mine," I whisper.

The words come out without even me thinking, but now that they are out there, I don't want to take them back.

I really want her to be mine.

Just as much as I want to be hers.

Even if people judge us for our age or for how we met. I still want to be with her. Fuck everyone's judgment.

I'm starting to think that she didn't hear me, that she might have fallen asleep. That my declaration went unheard, but she moves so that she is lying on top of me. Her chin on my chest.

"Then, I'm yours," she answers, her eyes so bright that you would think that she had stars in them, lighting up the world.

"Just that easy, huh?" I ask, giving her a sly smile, and she rewards me with a dazzling one that if I wasn't lying down, it would make me fall to my knees.

"Yup. That easy," she says before planting a kiss on my chest.

"Okay, then. You're mine, and I'm yours, and fuck everyone that says otherwise." My hands hold her a little tighter.

"Yes, fuck everyone."

God, I'm a goner for this girl.

Chapter Eighteen

Sawyer

Eight weeks.

That's how long summer courses are at this college.

For eight weeks, I stood in front of this classroom and taught a room full of students about creative writing. I can't forget that I also spent those eight weeks trying my hardest to not make my feelings for one of my students known.

And six weeks falling in love with that student.

The said student that is currently looking at me like she has seen me naked more times than she can count. She has, but we are in our last week of classes. It's not the time for her to look at me that way.

Even though I fucking love it when she looks at me that way.

I move my glance away from her like I have learned to do and continue with the class.

"So, for your final, it will consist of two things," I say to the class, "One, your attendance, and the other would be a completed short story. Please do not finish that before you come to class. You can start it, but you must finish it here and turn it in at the end of class on Friday."

Everyone nods.

I can't help but smile. In a few short days, Alana and I won't have to hide as much as we have been in this last month and a half. With summer courses coming to an end and her not being in any of my classes next semester, our relationship won't be as forbidden.

These last six weeks, we have spent almost every moment outside of class together. We have gotten to know each other in a way that I have never known a woman. She even told me about how she masturbated to me in the library the first week of school.

That was so hot that I had her recreate that very scene in my living room. I didn't touch her, and she came so hard that when I started to lick her clean, she came with the first stroke.

Then I fucked her until we were both seeing dark spots.

To say these last six weeks haven't been a sex-filled marathon would be a lie.

And now I can't wait to have even more time with my little minx.

God, just thinking about her makes my cock hard.

I'm about to dismiss the class, so that I can have Alana take care of the situation in my pants when the room door opens.

I don't remember seeing anyone getting up to use the bathroom.

I look up and see the head of my department walking in. It catches me off guard.

Given that it's summer, there aren't a whole lot of faculty here on campus just yet. The fall semester doesn't start for another month. So, for him to be here, it has to be a reason. A really big reason.

I shake my head and continue addressing the class.

"Okay, I think that is all for the final and for today. If you have any questions at all, email me. I want all of you to do well on this final, and I will do anything to help you with that," I say to the students.

They all nod and start gathering their things.

I catch sight of Alana as she does the same, except her eyes are starting to fill with worry. I guess she noticed the department head walk in too.

Giving her a slight nod, I turn to gather my own things before I turn to my colleague.

"Adam, I didn't know you were here early," I say to him with a smile, and I extend my hand to him, which he shakes.

"There were some pressing matters that couldn't wait until the beginning of the school year," he tells me.

"Oh, anything I could help with?" I ask, secretly hoping that he's not here because of me. But what would the odds be if he were?

I catch sight of Alana and she leaves the room, but not before she turns to face me and gives me a sad smile. I've gotten to know her well enough to know that she wants to stay, but she won't. Not when Adam is here.

"I think that you can," Adam says, and I take my eyes off the closing door and look at him. He walks over to the nearest row of tables and leans against them, looking me straight in the eye. "I got an interesting email the other day, one containing a picture."

"Okay?" I ask, confused.

"This email was sent by someone on this campus, and they thought that I should see it and do something about it before they send it to the dean."

"Okay, why are you here telling me about this then?" I ask, crossing my arms. I might look defensive, and that's because I am.

"Well, because in said picture, there are two people that look very cozy with each other. They almost look like a couple, at least to me. To the naked eye, it could just be a father enjoying a nice day out with his daughter."

Oh. Fuck.

I don't say anything. If the picture he is describing is really of Alana and me, then everything is fucked.

"The man in the picture looks oddly like you, and the girl looks so much like the young girl that was just in this class. And since I know for a fact that you don't have a daughter, then maybe she is a niece. But you wouldn't put a hand on your niece's ass now, would you?"

Fuck.

Fuck.

Fucking hell.

I have no words. I have nothing to say. What do you say?

The question that leaves my mouth, is so stupid that if I could slap myself in the face and kick myself in the balls, I would.

"Can I see this picture that you are talking about?" I don't move. I just stare at him. The ball is in his court.

He smirks and pulls out his phone. Turning it to me, I see it clear as day.

Alana and I at the Space Needle in Seattle. We wanted to get out of Tacoma. We wanted to be able to go out in public. So, I booked us a weekend in Seattle, and we were able to act like a normal couple for once. Instead of staying cooped up in one of our apartments.

We went with the mindset that no one from school would see us. We were wrong. Someone saw us, and now a picture of us at the Space Needle with my hand on her ass is in the hands of the head of the English department.

Our secret is out.

And we are going to lose everything.

Chapter Nineteen

Alana

I'm not stupid.

I know who the head of the department is. Do you really think that I would jump into a relationship with my professor without doing a little research as to who I have to look out for? I memorized each department head, every single professor, and every single person that reports to the Dean of Admissions and the head of the school. I know who everyone is.

So, I knew who the man was the second he walked into Sawyer's class. I knew why he was there.

I wanted to hang back and see what they were going to be talking about, but I couldn't. So, I left, and went straight to my apartment, and started to pace.

My phone is in my hand, my mind willing it to ring. I'm fighting with myself to call Sawyer, to know what is going on, but I hold back every time.

He'll call me when he is done talking to his colleague. I know he will.

I'm mid-pace, about an hour after I left class, when my phone rings. A sigh of relief is released when I see that it's Sawyer.

"Hey, is everything alright?" I ask, getting straight to the point.

Sawyer sighs, and I know that he's shaking his head. "Adam has a picture of us at the Space Needle and reported us to the Dean of Admissions."

"What?!" How is that possible? We were careful. We went all the way to Seattle, for fuck's sake. How did he get a picture to of us?

"He told me that someone emailed it to him, and he put two and two together. He saw you when you were leaving class. I was going to talk to him, convince him to not go to the dean but he had already gone before coming to me."

Fuck.

Everything was going so well.

I was so happy when I woke up this morning, because in a few days' time, Sawyer was no longer going to be my professor. A few weeks ago, after our first night, I made changes to my schedule so that we wouldn't even be in the same building. We were going to try to make this work, but now everything is going to get thrown away.

"What happens now?"

"Now," he says before he pauses for a second.

I can picture him. He is running a hand through his hair or pinching the bridge between his eyes. He is frustrated, and he doesn't know what to do, and I'm not there with him to comfort him.

"Now, I'm going to talk to the Dean of Admissions. He called me in a few minutes after Adam left. The picture doesn't look good. I'm going to try to see what I can do so that you won't get kicked out and I won't get fired."

"Let me come with you," I say. I make my way to the front door, and I'm putting on my shoes when Sawyer speaks.

"No, that would only make it worse. Stay there. You're probably next on the call list anyway." His voice is stern. I've never heard him talk like that. It scares me a little bit if I'm being honest.

"Okay," I say in a small voice, one that I don't even recognize.

"I have to go."

"Sawyer, wait!" I say before he hangs up on me. I know he hasn't because I can hear him breathing. "What does this mean for us?"

It's a stupid question to ask, but I have to know. I have to know if in the process of losing my education, am I going to lose him too? He might not know this, but I have fallen for him, and it will break me if I have to walk away.

"I don't know, Alana. I don't know what this means for us. Right now, I'm just thinking about saving you from getting kicked out of school, and losing your scholarship, and saving my job. I can't think about us," He answers me sternly.

I hate stern Sawyer.

I want to cry, I do, but I hold the tears in.

"Okay," is all I say. I hear him sigh.

"I'll call you later," he says before he hangs up.

I feel everything is in a tailspin, and I don't know how to stop it.

I guess this is what I get for being defiant and going after my teacher.

I feel the tears falling, and before I can wipe them away, my phone rings again. This time, it's not Sawyer.

It's the admissions office.

That's when I realize that I fucked myself over for fucking my professor.

Chapter Twenty

Sawyer

An hour is how long I have been waiting for the Dean of Admissions and the head of the faculty board in this stupid conference room.

Apparently, Adam the scumbag, forwarded the email to the heads of the school yesterday. They were going to call me in today and discuss this like adults, but the douchebag ruined their plans. At least, that's what the admissions assistant told me.

It has also been more than an hour since I have talked to Alana. I talked to her in a way that I have never talked to her before. I talked to her like a father instead of a lover, but I almost lost it.

At the moment, I didn't want to even think about us. I just wanted to save our futures. But it wasn't until the call was over that I figured out that my future includes her in it.

I haven't told her, but she owns my heart. My nineteen-year-old student owns my heart, and I don't want her to give it back.

I just have to hope that I don't lose my career and her all in the same day.

Fifteen minutes past the hour, the conference room door opens, and in walks the Dean of Admissions, the head of faculty, and to my surprise Alana Perry.

What the hell is she doing here?

I asked her to stay out of this.

"Miss Perry, why don't you have a seat, and then we can get started," the Dean of Admissions, whose name is Preston, tells her.

Alana gives him a small, closed-mouth smile before taking the seat next to me. She doesn't meet my glances, which I'm fine with. I don't need any more suspicion coming our way.

"Thank you both for coming on such short notice," Preston says while he does something on the tablet he is holding. He sits in one of the chairs in front of us and the head of faculty sits next to him.

"You didn't give us much choice," I grumble like the teenager that is sitting next to me. Actually, not like the teenager next to me. She has more maturity than I do acting like this.

My comment doesn't sit well with them by their expression. Pretty sure if Alana could, she would elbow me in the ribs for even speaking.

Preston clears his throat before taking his stare from me and directing it to the both of us. "We called you both here today because we have received some serious allegations concerning a relationship that you are partaking in," he says before he slides the tablet in front of us.

Right there is the same picture that Adam showed me earlier. If it were just Alana and me, I would say that the picture is hot and that we should get a copy for ourselves, but it isn't.

"As you can see, we have proof of these serious allegations, and we are here to discuss how we are going to handle it," Preston tells us.

He has a stern voice and given that he is a good three decades older than me, I would say that this isn't the first time he's had to have this conversation.

I need to come up with something to get us out of this mess. But what do I say? That picture clearly shows my hand on my student's ass.

"It's my fault," Alana says out of nowhere.

What? What the hell is she doing?

I turn to look at her, but she is looking forward, staring at the two individuals in front of us.

"I was the one that came on to Professor Jacobs in a sexual manner. He turned me down on numerous occasions, but I kept persisting. It was me that initiated the sexual advances, not him."

"Alana," I start to say, but she is shaking her head.

"It's my fault that we are here. If I hadn't flirted with you, if I hadn't approached you, we wouldn't be here. You wouldn't be risking your job," she tells me and then turns back to the two gentlemen. "I take full responsibility for this relationship."

She is taking all the blame.

She is making herself be labeled as something that she is not. Yes, she approached me first, but I'm not clean here. I flirted back. She tried to stop what she was doing, and I kept going.

I should be the one that should be taking all the blame, not her.

"We are both to blame here. And we both take full responsibility," I tell them.

The two gentlemen are silent for a few minutes, having a silent conversation with each other of sorts.

I am about to yell for them to say something when Preston decides it's time for him to speak.

"Relationships of this stature are taken very seriously at this university." Fuck. "But," Preston says looking at me and then to Alana. "Because the both of you are taking responsibility, I feel that the punishment should be as follows."

I hear the words suspension.

Deferment.

But I don't hear anything about being fired or kicked out or loss of scholarship.

Oh, shit.

Chapter Twenty-One

Alana

Deferment.

That's my punishment for being in a relationship with my professor.

Deferment for two semesters.

According to the Dean of Admissions, I can come back to school full time at the start of spring semester.

I also have to retake the creative writing course because my grade might have been influenced by what was going on outside of the classroom walls.

To be honest, I'm okay with that.

That's it.

I really thought that I was going to have to say bye to my scholarship and go back home, where I had to explain to my grandparents what had happened.

After I heard what I had to do, I was able to breathe in a big breath of fresh air. That is until I heard Sawyer's punishment.

He didn't get as lucky.

He was suspended from teaching at the university for a full year without pay. I almost cried.

How is he supposed to live, pay his rent, buy food, pay for his car, if he didn't have a wage?

I wanted to say something, but I didn't. I kept my mouth shut.

Before we left the room, Sawyer and I were told that we were strongly encouraged to end our relationship. Even if Sawyer and I can be together if he doesn't teach any of my classes, it is extremely looked down upon.

I just nodded.

I don't know where Sawyer and I stand right now, but I really hope we are not going to take the advice of these two dickwads.

We are excused, and Sawyer offers me a ride back to my place. A ride that is filled with silence the whole way. He doesn't even reach over and touch my thigh like he has done these last six weeks.

It's interesting how something so great can turn to shit in just a few short hours.

When we get to my place, we sit in the idling car, letting the silence wrap around us.

I'm the one to break the silence.

"I don't want to lose you," I whisper, looking down at my hands on my lap.

Sawyer reaches over, and I feel his fingers tug at my chin so that I could look at him. His eyes are staring back at me with every emotion of love known to man.

"You're not going to." he says in the sincerest tone I have ever heard come from him.

"You heard the dean; relationships are extremely looked down upon."

Sawyer nods. "They are, but I'm not walking away from you." He leans in and gives me a chaste kiss on my lips.

"So, what are we going to do?" I ask when he pulls back.

"Well, I think we should just finish the week. You take the final. And then we move on as best as we can. I have to find a job for the next couple of months, and then maybe when spring semester starts, we can put this behind us. We just have to make sure that we don't cross paths on campus, and we should be good," he says with a stern nod.

God, this man is something else.

He could have told me that he was going to walk away from me and go back to the school to get him his job back, but he didn't. He wants to be with me. Even after all of this.

"And what are we going to do now?" I ask since we are still sitting in his car outside of my apartment.

"Now." He tugs at my chin again. "Now, we are going to go up to your apartment and you're going to sit on my face, and my cock is going to make its way into your mouth, and we are not going to come up for air until we are both sated. How does that sound?"

"Sounds fucking perfect," I tell him. My clit is already throbbing just thinking about it.

"Fuck, yeah, it does." Sawyer gives me one more kiss before he jumps out of the car, rounds it, and then is at my side, opening the door.

Sometimes I forget that he is forty-one years old when he acts like this. It's a breath of fresh air.

When he opens my door and extends his hand, I can't help but tell him the one thing that I wished I had earlier.

"I love you."

The smile on his face is one that I wish I could see for the rest of my life.

"I love you too, baby," he says before his lips land on mine.

I guess I accomplished more than my goal this summer.

Epilogue

Three and a half years later

Sawyer

I never thought that I would be here.

Well actually, that is a total lie. I knew I was going to be here, but never did I think I would be here in this capacity.

I'm not here as a professor. No, today, I'm here as a boyfriend. The boyfriend of Alana Perry.

Today, she is graduating and getting her bachelor's degree and I couldn't be any prouder.

Even with a two-semester suspension, she was able to graduate on time and walk across the stage.

I sit in the stands with her grandparents. I look at them, and they both have tears in their eyes when they see her receive her folder. They are proud of her; you can tell from their expression. Alana has defined the odds against her. Her parents abandoned her, and her grandparents gave her what they could. She is strong and independent and beautiful, and she is lucky to have both of them in her life.

They have been accepting of our relationship. Alana introduced us during our suspension and even though they thought I was a little old for their granddaughter, they welcomed me with open arms. Which I'm extremely grateful for. Given that they were the two most important people in her life, I wanted them to accept me.

These last three years have been amazing.

Alana and I have come up with a system that has not only helped our relationship but also made it better. Ever since we got caught, we haven't gotten any other attention, which is good.

If we go out in public, we aren't very touchy, but we still act like a couple.

After her second year, she officially moved in with me. She was already spending all her time at my place, so it only made sense. We are living a happy life. We have even talked about marriage and kids, but that is further down the line. For right now we are just going to work and enjoy ourselves and maybe do some traveling in between.

And let's not forget the sex. The mind-blowing sex.

The feeling of her cunt wrapped around my cock is still the best thing I have ever felt. But hopefully that will change tonight. Since she agreed that tonight was the night that my cock might be able to slide into that other tight hole of hers.

Can't wait.

Maybe I shouldn't be thinking about this when I'm sitting next to her grandparents.

After the ceremony, the four of us, head for a quiet dinner before her grandparents head back to their hotel for the night.

The second we step foot into our apartment, I tear at her dress and push her against the door and fall to my knees.

"The prettiest cunt that I have ever seen," I say before I lick her slit from her asshole to her clit.

"Sawyer. More," she moans and I lick her again before I lift her up and rest her legs on my shoulders and eat her out like it's my last meal.

"Who does this pussy belong to, baby?" I lap at her again and again until I feel her start to shake.

"You. My pussy belongs to you," she pants out, and as a reward, I insert my fingers and start fucking her with my tongue and my fingers until she is screaming out my name.

"Such a good little slut." I clean up her cum before I set her back on her feet and walk her to the bedroom.

I rid myself of my clothes and position her on the bed on all fours. That delicious ass of hers is up in the air waiting for me to claim it.

Up until now, we have done some anal play. Whether it be a toy, my tongue, or my finger, but never my cock. Tonight that changes.

I spread her cheeks and fuck her tight hole with my tongue. She lets out a loud moan.

"I think you might be ready for me, baby," I say into her ass, and I think she says yes. I stand back up and run my fingers along her wet folds, covering my fingers with her juices before I stroke my cock. Making sure that I'm covered in her arousal.

"Are you ready for me, baby?" I ask, lining up my tip with her hole.

"Yes," she breathes.

"Spread your cheeks for me, baby," I say, and she does as she is told.

I slide my cock along her crack, moving my precum along the edges of her hole.

I look down at her, and I can't help but think that she looks beautiful. All spread open, and it's just for me.

She's mine, and I'm hers.

"I love you, Alana," I say, my tip at her entrance.

"I love you too, Sawyer Jacobs. So, fucking much," she says, and with that, I slowly slide into her tightness.

I fell in love with a student.

I fell in love with a young woman that has become my everything.

And now I have claimed every inch of her.

Just like she claimed every inch of my heart.

If I were to go back in time and change the past, would I?

Not a chance in fucking hell.

The
End.

About the Author

Jocelyne Soto is an independent author living in California. She loves reading romance and discovering new authors. She comes from a big Mexican family, and with it comes a love for all things family and food.
Jocelyne has a love for her mom's coffee and writing. In her free time, romance novel on her reader while writing heartwarming and chaotic romance stories in between.
Check out her website.
www.jocelynesoto.com

Follow her on social media.
instagram.com/authorjocelynesoto
facebook.com/authorjocelynesoto
tiktok.com/@authorjocelynesoto

Flirt Like a Player

Imani Jay

Chapter 1

Lallah

I look up when I hear a deep, masculine voice tinted with the slightest Eastern European accent call my name. No other than Ethan Antonov, international playboy, and the object of my filthiest fantasies stands before me. All casual and drop-dead gorgeous. He's wearing a battered denim shirt with the sleeves rolled up his strong, corded forearms. His loosely fitted beat-up jeans hug him in all the right places, making my mouth water. *Yeah, not happening.*

Ethan and I are both students in the prestigious Wharton MBA program on the San Francisco campus. He's in the Executives class, a part-time, intensive course for those like him who already have high professional responsibilities. And I'm in the full-time, regular program. We've barely ever met in the nineteen months since the program started.

There are a few like Ethan, tycoons, attending Wharton. It never gets old, seeing someone on the cover of Fortune magazine, or watching them on TV getting interviewed in the stock market section of the news, then crossing their path on campus. But it's more than that for me when it comes to Ethan Antonov. The sexy, twenty-seven-year-old, born from a Bulgarian father and an American mother, Ethan spent most of his life in Europe, but he's been living in the States for a good decade now. He came here after high-school and has attended the best universities since. Now he works with his dad. I may or may not have memorized every single news article I was able to find on the Antonov family and business. Not to mention the pictures of this heir to a multi-billion dollar business empire. Jet-setter, playboy, and business genius. I can't keep count of the number of his brilliant deals, or conquests. Mr. Antonov, son, is often spotted on the red carpet or at some charity event, always with a different gorgeous woman on his arm. Why he thought he needed Wharton is beyond me. Some say he's here for networking, others that his father wants him to get more grind under his belt before passing over leadership.

Me, I'm twenty-eight, single and one month away from graduating. Almost two years ago now, I split with my good-for-nothing ex and decided to give my life a boost. That's how I ended up at Wharton, leaving behind my accounting manager job and investing my savings in the program tuition. So, imagine my utter shock when classes started and I spotted this tall, lean, built, gorgeous piece of eye-candy on campus. I swear, I stood frozen in place, blinking my surprise away. Just that very morning, I'd made myself come imagining it was his long fingers between my legs, his sexy voice whispering naughty things in my ear... He's my celebrity crush. I've been lusting after this man for as long as I've known about him. He's occupied the number one spot in my spank-bank for years. So I made sure to avoid Ethan Antonov like the plague. I asked around to find out which program he was attending and kept myself away from all shared activities between our classes as much as I could. And if it wasn't possible, I made sure to not be found anywhere near his vicinity.

In a few weeks, I'll be out of here. I still have to decide which one of the great job offers made to me I'll accept. All thanks to the MBA and my more than decent performance. I did not allow myself to let my harmless crush develop into an obsession. And I'm certainly not taking a chance now.

I'm in the study room I booked at the library, where I was waiting for my end-of-year project partner. I didn't know who my partner was. Just that he or she had been assigned and would meet me when and where I indicated.

I've avoided having any direct interactions with this man for almost two years. And he's the one coming to meet me for a work session? *Come on, Universe!* I'm not getting myself tangled in whatever mess is sure to come with dealing with *The Tsar,* as the media have incorrectly labeled Ethan.

"Nope," I deadpan.

I gather my textbook, notebook, pencil pouch and stuff everything in my backpack, zip it, throw it over my shoulder, and look the personification of my wet dreams straight in the eye. His beautiful gray eyes. I hold strong and don't allow my gaze to waver even an inch over his stupid, perfectly chiseled features. Or down his strong, broad shoulders, wide chest and powerful runner's legs. *Fuck.*

"I didn't know it was you. Find yourself another partner."

Ethan Antonov, intercontinental womanizer and the most gorgeous man I've ever laid eyes on, rests a large hand over his heart. His fingers are long and elegant. *Is there anything unattractive about this guy?* His pretty face twists into a grimace.

"Ouch."

I scrunch my nose. I might have been a bit harsh but I don't have the time, energy or mental space to deal with spending one-on-one time with the billionaire I'm already infatuated with. And then what? In one month we go our separate ways and I'm stuck with images of him in my head for the rest of my life. No thanks. I already know this brief encounter will feed my daydreams for ages. I don't need to experience for myself how smart, funny and hot he is in person. I've seen enough of that in interviews and magazines. The way he's always relevant, witty and a bit flirty. I can't imagine how I could be able to handle weeks of direct interaction. Just having his gray eyes on me right now is making my nipples stand to attention. *Oh Lord.*

"Sorry, but your company is listed in freaking Forbes. I doubt you have enough time to dedicate to this project. And I need a partner, not someone who's expecting me to do all the work."

As the words escape my mouth, the hurt expression on Ethan's face morphs into a sexy smirk. His full lips hooking up on one side of his mouth. A twinkle of mischief sparkling in his gun-metal eyes. *Lord.*

"You seem to know a lot about me, Partner," he replies in his low, rumbly voice, rubbing the stubble on his square jaw.

Fuck, he's handsome. All golden skin, high cheekbones, straight, masculine nose and sculpted lips... I need this conversation to end very quickly before I lose all sense and climb him like a tree.

"Everyone knows who you are, and I'm not your partner. We need to request a different pairing. End of story."

Ethan's strong white upper teeth nibble on his bottom lip. A hint of a smile lingering on his tempting mouth. His eyes watching me with keen interest and a definite spark of desire. *Uh-oh.* Abort operation sassy mouth!

"Okay, bye," I throw over my shoulder, hurrying in the direction of the library exit.

But before I can make my escape, a warm, manly hand wraps itself around my wrist. The second our skins come into contact, it's as if a blanket of warmth and comfort envelops me. I raise my gaze to his and get lost in the flecks of green I hadn't noticed before. I've never stood this close to Ethan. Never had the luxury of studying him like this. We're locked in the moment. Him, all tall and looming over me. His expensive cologne saturating the surrounding air, making my mouth water with the need to taste his honey skin. *Fuck.*

"Wait," he rumbles, leaning closer. "Give me a chance to explain."

This motherfucker just sent my heart into overdrive. No, uh-huh.

We stand unmoving for a few seconds. Eyes hooked, Ethan's long fingers still wrapped around my wrist. The simple contact spreading all over my body like he's touching me EVERYWHERE. Like his big hands are exploring every inch of me. *Good Lord, what's happening to me?*

My face is hot, my heart beats fast, and I feel completely overpowered by Ethan's presence. He's so tall, so big, so handsome. The woodsy scent of his aftershave, and that undertone I can tell, is all him, intoxicating me.

I clear my throat before finding the strength to hook my fingers into his to remove his hand. But he doesn't let go, and takes advantage of my gesture to interlace our fingers.

I warn, "Ethan..."

The pussy-drenching smile hits me in full force. *This is not good.*

"Come on, let's get coffee. I'll explain."

And of course, I follow.

Chapter 2

Ethan

So this is what my father has been talking about. All his speeches about *The One*. About how he knew right away when he met Mama.

Fuck, I never believed in any of that shit. I was just focused on business and hopping from one woman to the other. Entirely dedicated to my family's business conglomerate. My time and energy focused on *Antonov Global*.

And now I meet her. Lallah, *fucking*, Aidara. She's perfect. And abso-fuck-ing-lutely, without a goddamn doubt, MINE. From the tips of her big, curly hair, to the points of her sneakers. Thick ass and thighs, tiny waist I could circle with my hands, full, round tits, big brown eyes, dark skin, juicy lips, and all in between. Mine. Period. For fucking keeps.

I've played the field, had way more than my fair share of pussy. So I know without a doubt this isn't just lust. A crush. An infatuation. I'm fucking gone for this woman. Her gorgeous face, sassy mouth, curvy body, attitude for fucking days. *God, how did I not notice her before?* I've been on this campus for more than a year and a half. Part time, yes but still. I cant believe Lallah's shine didn't reach me before today.

I wanna thread my fingers through her curls and pull her close. Take off her glasses and taste that fucking sexy mouth. Feel her full curves melt into my hard body. *Easy, Antonov. Don't scare her off.*

I clear my throat. My large hand still wrapped around her smaller, delicate one. I lower my gaze to hers, and *fuck, she's beautiful.* Eyes throwing daggers and all. I give her my most charming grin, the one that's never failed me. It's gotten me ice cream for breakfast when I was a kid, pacifies business partners and brings women to my bed without even a conversation.

"What's your poison?" I ask, while we're standing in the short line at the library's café.

Lallah huffs before pulling her hand out of mine. I let her. She crosses her arms over her generous chest, and it takes everything in me to not stare at the way her tits stretch the fabric of her thin cotton t-shirt.

"White chocolate mocha. And I'm only here because I totally deserve a fancy coffee, and you definitely should be the one paying for it after wasting my time and messing up my study schedule."

I just keep smiling. We'll talk when we're seated.

"What?"

Lallah studies me with widened eyes. Her walnut-colored gaze traveling over my features and body.

"Hey, don't look so surprised. I'm really gonna end up feeling insulted."

She clears her throat.

"Well, I thought I'd have to do all the work."

I shake my head.

"Nope."

She's still adorably squinting at me with suspicion.

"You have the top grades in your program?"

I nod but she still doesn't sound convinced.

"And the school is pairing us up because we're the two best in our respective classes?"

"Yup."

"Why didn't they just tell me all that?"

I give her a pointed look.

"They don't really explain themselves," Lallah answers her own question. "Now, what?" she adds after a bit, chewing on her plump bottom lip and making my cock twitch in my pants.

I stare for a second, using all my willpower to detach my eyes from her bee-stung lips.

"Now, we follow the project prep schedule. "

I wink, at the same time Lallah's gaze goes wide.

"You wanna meet everyday?" she almost screeches.

"Fuck, you're doing wonders for my self-esteem."

Another eye roll.

"Please, you don't need any help keeping that ego of yours inflated."

"Hey, you don't even know me."

"Sorry. This whole thing is just throwing me off."

I nod, eyes hooked to hers. Taking advantage of her contrite expression to stare to my heart's content. *This is gonna be fun.*

Chapter 3

Lallah

"You're shitting me?!" my best friend, Katusha yells through the screen of my phone.

This girl is so extra. We're on video-chat and I just told her about Ethan. All of it...

"You're telling me you've been paired with a sexy-ass classmate, who's also a billionaire, for your year-end project?"

"Crazy, right?" I ask, shaking my head. Barely able to believe my current circumstances myself.

"What's crazy is your ass only now telling me about this boy," Kat retorts.

"There was nothing to tell, I..."

She interrupts me with a stretched out, "excuuuuse me? You said there were rich people in your cohort. I thought you meant normal rich. Couple of houses, luxury cars, million dollars... not freaking *Fortune 500*! And you also said 'cute', not shortlisted for the sexiest man alive."

The volume of her voice, already high, gradually increases. Her eyes bugging like crazy. And I stare at my screen, waiting for Katusha to calm down, and questioning my decision to come clean to my bestie. Because let's face it, I've been holding back on her. I knew her loony ass would react just like this so I didn't tell her about the insane parallel dimension I've been living in, brushing elbows with the likes of Ethan Antonov.

"You have a crush on him," Kat deadpans.

"No, I don't. I'm just..."

She raises her eyebrows.

"It's not a crush, I just find him... attractive," I hurry to add.

"I bet you do," she mumbles. "You, me and most of the world population."

"See? That's why this is bad. I can't be into the guy I'm supposed to work with for the next month. Even worse, the guy EVERYONE is into. You should see him on campus. It's impossible. Girls throw themselves at him left and right. And when we had coffee together? The amount of attention he gets is just ridiculous. And the dirty looks I got? You'd think some of those women hated me."

"Huh...," Katusha hums pensive.

"Huh, what?" I ask her.

"How into him are you?"

"Very! That's the problem. I'm afraid I'm not gonna be able to focus on our work."

She waves a dismissive hand.

"You'll be plenty focused. You're not built to do a poor job. But, I think this is an opportunity for something else..."

She wags her eyebrows.

I shake my head, frowning.

"Like what?"

"You like him, you're gonna be seeing each other everyday, he's a known player... you guys should fuck."

"Kat!" I exclaim.

She rolls her eyes.

"Girl, please. You have the opportunity to get yourself some fine ass rich, European boy, don't waste it."

"What opportunity? What are you talking about? All I said is we'll be working together. Work. At the library or some other public place. With our clothes on. How did you come to the conclusion of us fucking?"

"You said he's a fuck-boy."

"Yeah, with other women. Not me."

"Well, I'm saying why not you."

I stare at the screen but have nothing to reply to that. *Why not, indeed?*

Chapter 4

Ethan

There's something different about Lallah today. She's not acting all tough and snappy. She's staring at me with her big, brown eyes, batting her long lashes, touching me every chance she gets, laughing her sexy, throaty laugh at my dumbest jokes.

I wonder what's happened since we were last together. When she looked at me like she didn't trust a word I said and avoided my touch.

When she lays a hand on my forearm for the tenth time, I put mine on top and ask, "what's going on?"

Lallah blinks several times before a smile that's too wide to be authentic takes over her gorgeous features.

"L... like what?" she asks, hesitantly.

I shake my head.

"Like you being all over me today, when the last time we met you made it clear you didn't want anything to do with me."

She sits back abruptly.

"You think I'm all over you?"

"Babe..."

I tilt my head to the side in a meaningful gesture.

Lallah buries her face in her hands and lets out a muffled, "oh my God..."

"Hey, it's okay," I reassure her. "I like you being all over me. Just wondering what's with the three-sixty."

She mumbles something but I can't understand her words through her hands over her mouth.

I gently pry her fingers and ask in a soft voice, "what was that?"

"I'm trying to flirt with you," she blurts out without meeting my gaze.

Making my eyes grow wide with surprise. But it only takes me a second to comprehend the magnitude of what Lallah just admitted and feel a smile stretch my lips. My girl is flirting with me. Not very skillfully, but the enthusiasm is there. Now what about her motive?

"Why?" I push gently.

Her eyes finally come to me.

"Why what?"

"Why are you flirting with me?"

"Hum.. because I'm attracted to you," she answers in a tone that implies, *duh.*

Ah, there she is. Is it wrong how much I find her sass sexy?

"I'm sorry if I've made you feel uncomfortable or something," Lallah rushes to add.

I bring her hand to my lips, pressing a kiss inside her wrist. And watch her beautiful eyes widen in surprise at my gesture.

"I've never been more comfortable. I just didn't know you were there with me. I'm all for flirting. I was trying to impress you with my big brain."

I wag my eyebrows and she giggles. The sound light and honest.

"I'm very impressed," Lallah says softly, looking at me from under her lashes.

And the natural gesture seduces me a thousand times more than her earlier forced sultry gazes.

"Would you feel comfortable taking a break till tomorrow? I think we made good progress."

Her assessing eyes go from her computer screen to the notes in front of her. And she must be satisfied because she nods.

"We did." Her expression is serene and satisfied. "Great job, Mr. Antonov."

I chuckle.

"Why, thank you, Ms. Aidara."

Her smile is measured. Gorgeous. It wraps itself around my heart and warms my insides. I'd do anything to be the one who keeps bringing this expression on her face.

I gather my stuff and Lallah follows my lead. Then I stand and stretch a hand for her to take.

"Let's go."

Chapter 5

Lallah

Breathe. *Don't hyperventilate. Don't you dare pass out and miss even a second of this, Lallah Aisha Aidara!*

I'm holding hands with, *fucking*, Ethan Antonov, leaving the study room we booked for our work session, on our way to some unknown destination. And I don't even care where we end up.

I glance up at Ethan. *Fuck, he's handsome.* He has the profile of a Greek statue. All sharp, angular lines. A bone structure to fucking die for. *And that full, pink mouth? Just fucking kill me now.*

Ethan lowers his gaze to me, giving me a smile. I blink up in a daze, completely under his spell.

"Uh... where are we going?"

"Would you clock me if I said your place or mine?" he offers with a naughty grin.

"What do you think?" I reply with a question of my own.

Ethan chuckles, the sound low and rumbly, feeling like a warm caress all over my skin.

"How about a late lunch, early dinner, then?"

"You mean l-inner," I tease with a wide smile.

He shakes his head.

"You, Americans."

I giggle.

"Anything you feel like?"

I scrunch my face.

"Not really."

"Any food allergies? Dislikes?"

"No and no."

Ethan watches me attentively.

"Are you sure? I know how women are."

I shake my head, rolling my eyes.

"Just feed me. You should know by now I'd tell you if I had any reservations."

His deep rumble of laughter is music to my ears.

"True. Okay, I know just the place."

"Should I follow you in my car?" I ask.

"Would you mind driving together?"

"No, I can leave my car in the parking lot and it later."

He nods, pulls his cellphone out of his back pocket and types for a few seconds before placing it back.

"So?" I ask when he doesn't volunteer any information.

"Shouldn't be long."

Ethan winks, making my stomach flutter.

I push through my butterflies, "what shouldn't be long?"

He smiles reassuringly, "my driver."

"Oh... what are we riding in?" I ask, images of my fantasies of Ethan and I doing naughty things at the back of a limo flashing through my mind.

"Uh... limo, I guess."

I feel my eyes widen and watch Ethan's face grimace in response.

"Too much?"

I shake my head.

"Nope. Perfectly fine. It's just..."

I look away, feeling my face heat. Unable to hold his gaze.

"It's just what, Lallah?"

I clear my throat.

"You know how I told you I was flirting and you said you didn't think I was there with you?" Ethan nods, a cocky grin stretching his deliciously lips. "Well... uh... actually, I've liked you for a while.'

It's his turn to raise his eyebrows in surprise.

"How long is a while?"

I scrunch my face. Not exactly embarrassed, but also not the most comfortable sharing this. But, *to hell with it*, I won't be seeing this guy anymore after graduation. Might as well, there's no harm in living our time together in full honesty.

"Since I was in high school, maybe."

Ethan's glorious smile shines even brighter, making my pussy spasm and my heart skip a beat.

"Really?" He scrubs his chin before adding, "but what does that have to do with the limo?"

Shoot. I peer at Ethan from under my lashes before quickly blurting, "I might have had a fantasy or two about you and me at the back of a limo."

Chapter 6

Ethan

Fuck. Could my woman be any more perfect? I want to take her out to eat in a limo because I'm trying to show her a good time. And she brings up back of limo sex... I couldn't have made her more perfect.

I let go of her hand and pull her close with one arm. Noticing in passing how perfectly she fits into my side.

I press a kiss to her temple before whispering in her ear, "it doesn't have to stay a fantasy. "

We stay like that, pressed close, till the car pulls up in front of us. My driver, Paul, and I exchange greetings and he gets the door for Lallah. I climb behind her and watch with pleasure as she takes in the luxurious interior. Dark woods and soft leather, a mini bar, a wide, comfortable booth that could fit at least four people.

"This is niiice," Lallah exclaims, her eyes jumping around.

She's so cute, like a child in a candy store.

"Glad you approve." I wrap an arm around her waist, pulling her close to sit next to me. "Now about those fantasies..."

I press a button, closing the partition between Paul and us.

"What about them?" Lallah asks, sounding a bit breathy.

"You tell me," I retort, wrapping a lock of her soft hair around a finger.

"There were a lot," she replies, her gaze darkening with heat.

"What's your favorite one?" I whisper, brushing over the swell of her full lips with the pad of my thumb.

We're both breathing hard, eyes hooked. My dick harder than it's ever been. My heart pounding in my chest. All I want to do is peel off Lallah's short, flowy dress and feast on her body.

"Prom," she breathes out. "You come pick me up for prom and we make out at the back of the limo."

"Fuck, baby," I growl. "Come here," I order, helping her straddle my lap.

Lallah comes willingly. Her full, soft tits pressed to my hard chest. Fucking gorgeous with all that big, curly hair. Her full lips parted, eyes glazed with desire. Pulse beating erratically at the hollow of her throat. She frames my face with her soft hands and I cup her ass, filling each of my big hands with a soft, round cheek. I squeeze then pull, making her gasp. I lean back into the booth, widening my legs, positioning my erection on her pussy. Only thin layers of clothes between us. I push my hips up, letting her feel how much I want her. Need her. And she moans, pressing a kiss to my mouth.

I let her kiss and taste me. Reveling in the softness of her lips, how good she feels all over my body. How I'm already intoxicated with the scent and savor of her.

Deepen the kiss and, without detaching our lips, I pull down the top of her dress and bra to reveal her breasts. *Fuck, utter perfection.*

I pull back, meeting her dazed gaze and gruff out, "if I was your boyfriend in high-school, taking you to prom in this car, we wouldn't have made it to the dance."

Lallah lets out a short laugh and I smile before resuming our kiss. This time, there are no hold backs. No soft presses of our lips. We've tasted each other and loved what we tried. Now, we're hungry, famished. It's a battle of tongues and teeth. Sucking, licking, not so gently biting. Making each other moan and groan. Our hands roaming over each other. My thumbs and forefingers pinching her erect nipples. Her full hips swiveling over me, pressing and rolling into my hard as rock cock.

I move my mouth to the side of her neck, kissing, licking and grazing over the tender skin, making her shake and whimper.

I rasp out at her throat, "what do we do in that fantasy?"

"Th... this," she stutters.

"That's all? We kiss, hump and I play with your tits?"

Lallah shakes her head, her curls caressing my face.

"No... you... you also... you touch me," she breathes out.

I bite her soft flesh and she moans long.

"Already touching you, *lyubov*," I say, calling her *love*. I thread my fingers into her hair at the back of her head and pull, holding her in place, exposing her beautiful breasts to my famished eyes. "How did I touch you, Lallah?" I nip at the swell of one breast and she cries in pleasure. I add in a growl, "where?"

"Your... your fingers... in my fantasy you fuck me with your fingers," she pants.

And I'm so hard it feels like my fly is about to burst open. Still holding her by her hair, I pull Lallah's face to mine and take her mouth in a deep, wet tongue-fucking. Then I let go, eyes fixated to hers. I run my palms over her delicious tits, cup them, squeeze the full flesh, before leaning to take one nipple after the other in my mouth. I suck, lick, nip and worship the soft globes till Lallah is trembling in my arms.

"You like that, dirty girl?" I ask, raising my gaze to hers.

She nods frantically, lips kiss-swollen, eyes glassy. *Fucking beautiful.*

Still lapping at her tits, I push her dress up her thick thighs, squeezing in passing. Letting the fabric pool around her waist, I pull the fabric of her underwear to the side and slide a finger down her slit. *Fuck!* She's swollen, warm and wet. *So fucking wet.*

Lallah moans, grinding herself even harder on me, meeting the movements of my hand.

"Yeah, you fucking like that... you're so fucking dirty... so fucking wet for me... fuck, baby."

I add a finger and glide lower, till the heel of my hand is on her clit and the tips of my fingers at her entrance. Then I gather her hair with my other hand and hold her in place again. *Yeah, I have a thing for dominance and restraint.* And this woman, *MY woman,* with her sassy mouth, attitude and openness about her desire for me... This woman presses all my buttons in the best possible way.

"I want you to fuck yourself on my hand," I growl, watching her pupils dilate with need.

Lallah lays her hands on my shoulders and uses me as leverage to push herself up... and down. Her tight, wet cunt engulfing my fingers. Grinding on the heel of my hand, rubbing her clit.

She closes her eyes and I firm my grip on her hair.

"Look at me," I command, my gaze eating her up.

My cock pulses with want. My balls so tight, they hurt. *Fuck, I need inside her.*

Chapter 7

Lallah

We're a tangle of limbs and lips, right there on my couch. Lunch never happened and since my place was the closest, that's where the limo took us.

Ethan pulls me onto his lap, and I straddle him, never breaking our kiss. Flashback from our drive here. I can feel his heart racing against my chest, and I'm sure he feels mine as well. His hands are firmly placed on my ass, and I'm scratching his neck with my fingernails, making him moan against my lips. He's hard everywhere, and when I feel him grow even bigger under me, I grind down, making us both pant and moan in want. Ethan kisses my jaw, then my neck, his hands travel underneath the skirt of my dress. I feel his fingers Lallah the edge of my panties, pulling on the delicate fabric. I rake my hands over his wide shoulders, his strong chest, and my body moves on its own accord over his hard length. Ethan curses under his breath, and I smile. We've been here before, I'm starting to learn his cues. I know what makes him writhe, and I cant wait to learn what makes him come apart.

"I need you out of these clothes," he breathes against my neck. "I need you under me, Lallah. I need you..."

He doesn't finish his sentence. With his strong arms firmly holding me, Ethan gets up from the couch, carrying me as he goes. I wrap my legs around him, anticipation buzzing through my body. He lays me down on the bed, just looking down on me for a minute. I'm breathing heavily, looking right back up at him through hooded eyes.

"Take your clothes off," I say, and a chuckle escapes him.

"So bossy."

He's still smiling, but his hands are moving over the buttons on his shirt, and more of his body becomes visible to me. A smattering of chest hair, darker than the chestnut on his head, it continues down his sculpted belly, only to disappear down his jeans. Ethan throws his shirt to the side, and unbuckles his belt before stepping out of his jeans. His boxers are working hard to contain his erection, and I rub my thighs together at the sight of his arousal. I can't wait to find out what it feels like to be filled by him.

Ethan climbs into bed, covering me with his body. He drags the fabric of my dress up my thighs, and I help him pull it over my head. He leans down, pressing kisses to my collarbone, teasing one nipple through my bra with one hand, making me needy for more. "God, that feels good," I say, my words barely audible over the sound of our breathing.

Ethan reaches behind me and unclasps my bra, kissing and nipping at my breasts.

"So beautiful," he whispers, swirling his tongue around my hardened nipple. He moves down my stomach, pulling my panties off in one fluid motion. "I've wanted to taste you all day," he says, his face just above my wet pussy. "Wanted to hear what noises you'll make when you come for me."

I smile, shaking my head at him. Ethan pushes me down fully on my back, his hand firm but gentle on my stomach. I moan as he moves down, as I feel his tongue on my most sensitive parts. He is licking and sucking on my swollen clit, making me buck up against his mouth. Damn, he's good at that. Increasing his speed, Ethan reaches up to touch my breasts, never letting up with his eager tongue. I feel my orgasm start to build, already so close to falling over the edge. I can't even remember I orgasmed by anything other than my own hand, and having him there, giving me all that pleasure, is an image I could get used to. I come not even three seconds later, moaning his name as pleasure shoots through me. Ethan looks up, a pleased grin on his face.

"You're looking entirely too cocky right now," I say, breathing hard.

He climbs up from the edge of the bed, covering me with his body. I feel just how hard he is as he drags his erection between my legs, and I really need him to get inside me. Ethan kisses me, holding me close. I wrap my legs around him, wanting him even closer still.

"I have condoms in my nightstand," I say, and he reaches over and grabs a square packet. He puts it on quickly, just as eager as I am to finally sink into my heat. He's not smiling anymore, his brows set in a serious look of concentration as he positions himself over me. I pull him down for a kiss as he thrusts into me, and both of us hiss as the sensation of us joining takes over. Ethan holds my arms up over my head, kissing me deeply as he moves. He is dragging in and out, slow motions that send small sparks over my skin, even my scalp is tingling. He's practically panting over me, and I move with him, enjoying the weight of him nestled between my thighs.

"You feel amazing," he says as he's picking up speed. "So good, Lallah. So fucking good."

I smile against his shoulder, kiss the skin there before I throw my head back when Ethan slams into me, harder and harder. There's nothing gentle about what we're doing anymore, every movement as desperate and hungry as the last. Ethan keeps hitting me just right, and a second orgasm rips through me, and I cry out as my release takes over. I feel him stiffen over me, feel him shake and pulse as he falls over the edge. He's kissing me, tethering himself to me as we come down together. He pushes himself up, taking some of the weight off of me. I almost protest, wanting him right there, but it's getting hard to breathe with his body covering mine. He pulls away, falling on his back next to me on the bed. He looks at me then, his beautiful eyes full of affection. I know that look. I've seen it before. In my wildest dreams. And I'm sure it's mirrored in my own eyes.

Ethan is grinning, and props himself up on his elbow. His other hand stroking my stomach, his fingers drawing circles around my belly button. He leans down and kisses me slowly.

"It was incredible."

I nod.

"Yes, it was."

"Good," he says. "Because I plan on doing it again."

I laugh, a pleased feeling swelling in my chest. He wants to do this again.

"I'd like that." I ignore the nagging sensation at the back of my head. The words that spill through the cracks of my mind, I refuse to let them ruin the moment. And yet, they're there. You only get him for a little while.

Then Ethan Antonov proceeds to blow my mind.

"Wipe that look off your face, love. You're fucking mine. I'm not letting go. Not today. Not ever."

I stutter, "w... what?"

"That look, as if this was a short term thing and you were already bracing for the end. Not happening."

"Ethan, we just met."

He raises a cocky eyebrow.

"You've been into me for a decade and I might have some catching up to do, but I'm all in, babe."

He kisses me long and hard, making my pussy contract.

"I... I think I'd like that."

The rueful grin returns.

"Good, cause I already texted my folks to expect a visit from us in Sofia."

"What?" I squeal.

"Not wasting anytime," he whispers against my lips.

Before pulling me on top of his amazing body and imprinting himself even deeper into my soul.

THE END.

Thank you for reading *FLIRT LIKE A PLAYER*! I really hope you liked Lallah & Ethan's story!!

About the Author

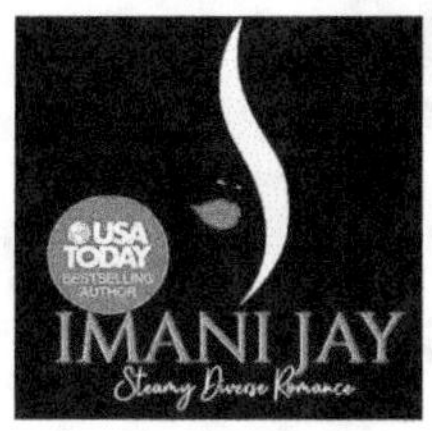

If you like bite-sized, steamy romances with hunky alphas and their sassy curvy girls, you've found the right gal for your needs!

    Follow me everywhere!

    Subscribe to my newsletter & get a FREE story!!

Check Out ALL My Books!

https://linktr.ee/ImaniJayBOOKS

Close to You

S.M. West

Chapter 1

Wren

An embarrassing shudder rushes down my spine and knocks my stomach into my knees. "Goodness gracious, what on earth was I wearing?"

Nose nearly mashed against the glass of the display cabinet, I try to get a better look at the cringe-worthy photo. Among team trophies and other club pictures, the offending image hangs on the far right. As one of eight students in my high school's yearbook club, I'm in the middle of the back row, flanked by the only boys in the group.

For as long as I can remember, I was always one of the taller girls in school. Come to think of it, at five feet ten, I still stand out among the women in town.

I stare at the picture a little longer. My long, red pigtails, a white button-down shirt stuffed into overalls, and my red Chucks. I suppose I was going for cute back then, though truth be told, I had no fashion sense. It was high school after all.

Thank goodness, the same can't be said today, and I should hope I've learned a thing or two by the age of twenty-five.

A contented smile pulls at the corners of my mouth as I glance down at my flowy plaid dress and comfy, yet stylish, lace-up black booties.

A thumping sound causes me to look to my left, then right. I thought I was alone. Principal Crandall let me in on her way out and said as much.

In either direction, the hallways are desolate. Of course I'm alone. It's almost seven on a weeknight. Winslow Grove High School is a ghost town. All the teachers and students are gone, even the custodians.

Besides, most people in our little Montana town should be home by now, seeing as a storm is headed our way. I should get home too. I don't want to be caught out when the bad weather hits. And as if I need any more reasons to get home, I have homemade pot pie and the latest Mhairi McFarlane novel waiting for me.

Thud, thud, thud.

Warily, I trek in the direction of the persistent sound that gets louder the closer I get to the gymnasium. Outside the double doors, a mini orange pylon—the cones Coach uses for training drills—props open one of them. In addition to the thumping, the squeaky scrub of rubber along the wooden floor hits my ears. I pop my head through the open door.

My pulse quickens.

Oliver Winslow.

He's the only one in the gym, dribbling a basketball, and he hasn't noticed me. I take this rare moment to study him. My teenage crush.

Crush? It doesn't seem fitting when he's the only man I've ever loved.

At six-three, he's the perfect mash-up of superhero—hello, Thor—and NFL star athlete JJ Watt. Oliver's always had that all-American, boy-next-door vibe.

With his back to me, in a slate-gray Henley and faded blue jeans, he lopes toward the net on the far side of the gym.

Posture relaxed, his broad back muscles ripple and flex as he gracefully guides the ball over the court. I'd forgotten just how wide and defined his shoulders are. Well, one thing is for sure, he's no longer a boy.

All man now.

Chiseled arms, narrow waist, and what a great ass, so firm...

He spins around, maybe sensing my presence, and stops short. Shoot, did he catch me ogling him?

I force my eyes all the way up to his handsome face, and my cheeks grow hot at his big smile.

"Wren." He grips the ball to his hip and wrinkles a brow. "What are you doing here?"

I try to ignore the little lurch in my stomach at the warm rasp of my name. He runs a hand through his light-brown hair, short on the sides, a little longer and wavy on top.

"Is that anyway to say hello?" I smile and, on shaky legs, step over the pylon.

I can only hope my teasing tone and confident strides belie the butterflies unleashing chaos on my insides.

"Sorry, that came out all wrong." He hangs his head for a beat. "It's nice to see you."

"You too. I was just dropping off some books from the library. We're donating them to the high school. We do it every few years when we need to make space for new books."

Shut up.

I'm rambling, and he doesn't care about what my job at the Winslow Grove Library entails. "What are you doing here?"

"Came to see Coach Bell." He starts bouncing the ball again, almost as if needing something to do.

Enthralled by his sinewy forearms, my knees shake, and I wipe at the corner of my mouth, worried I'm drooling. I'm not.

Good God, it has been far too long since I've seen Oliver. Usually, I go out of my way to avoid him, and despite any proof, I'm pretty sure if I were to be lacking in this effort, his fiancée would step in to pick up my slack.

He stares at me, curious and maybe a little concerned. Shoot, did I blank out while getting an eyeful? What was he saying? Oh, yes, Coach.

"Um, sorry. Is Coach Bell here?" I tear my eyes away from him to the far corner where the office is.

"Nah, he left but said I could stick around." Again, he drops his chin to his chest, and when he looks back at me, his cheeks are now flushed.

Is he blushing? Why?

"Okay." Although it's all I say, he must hear the curiosity in my voice or maybe he wants to talk to me some more.

"I got a bit nostalgic and felt like playing some ball."

"Me too." I titter at our similar sentiment. "Nostalgic, I mean. I was wandering the halls when I heard the basketball and wound up here."

He effortlessly dribbles the ball, feet dancing left to right, then pauses once more to glance at me.

Something sexy yet daring flashes in his inquisitive gaze. "Wanna play horse?"

My nerves spark, and an electric current shoots through my veins at the idea of playing ball with him again. "What? Now?"

Real smart, Wren, of course now.

Nodding, he bites his bottom lip, clearly waiting for me to respond. Strangely, a yes springs to the tip of my tongue, clamoring to burst free. Flattered and hopeful— though I can't say why—I want to play with him and shouldn't. He's getting married.

But it's only basketball; it isn't like we're going to have sex.

Shit, why did I just go there?

Clearly, it's been far too long since I've had sex, and truthfully, I don't see anything happening in the near future to change that.

He arches a brow. "Wren, what do you say?"

"Sure, but I'm not exactly dressed for it." Nervously, I look down at my outfit. "Coach Bell and Principal Crandall will have my hide if I play on this floor in these."

I lift up a leg to show off my booties, and his gaze lingers a little longer than expected on my bare skin. His usually light hazel eyes smolder as he stares at my leg for what feels like far too long and not nearly long enough.

My core clenches and my cheeks burn.

He steps closer and bends to look at my shoes. "The soles look like they're rubber. They should be fine. I'm not dressed for it either." He stands to his full height, and there's a playful glint in his eye. "Or is there some other reason why you're looking for an excuse not to play?"

Hands on my hips, I narrow my gaze. "I never said I wouldn't play."

"And you never said you would. I mean, you were one of the best athletes in high school, but maybe you no longer have what it takes?"

I gape and a few seconds pass as my mind digests his challenge—or is it an insult? I was one of the best. I loved basketball and volleyball, but our school didn't have enough girls to form an official team in either sport. It sucked though we made do, and sometimes the guys let me practice with them.

Oliver, on the other hand, was an all-around great athlete. Not only was he starting fullback position for the varsity team but also on the basketball team and ran track.

"Listen, Twist." I close the distance until we're only a foot apart, and his eyes widen at my use of his nickname.

Back in elementary, we both had parts in the school production of Oliver Twist. He was one of Fagan's boys, and I played the infamous Fagan. It was quite the coup for a girl to take the part, and I killed it.

During rehearsals one day, I called him Twist. I don't remember why, but it stuck, and soon after everyone was calling him by that moniker.

Now, while it sounds foreign on my tongue—it's been years since I've used it—I'm glad I did. Keeping him on his toes boosts my confidence.

He widens his stance and inches closer still. "I'm listening, Tyler."

A tingling warmth spreads from the center of my chest at the use of my last name. Oliver wasn't the only one to call me Tyler—it's common in sports—but for some reason, he was the only one to make me feel special or more of every-thing when he did.

Flustered, I raise my hands toward my head, and the rub of my dress against my nipples causes them to harden, suddenly tight and achy. I hurriedly weave my long hair into a messy bun on the top of my head, and he watches intently, eyes never wavering from my hands.

Now's my chance to get one up on him.

I snatch the ball from him. "I still have what it takes, and I'll prove it."

Chapter 2

Wren

At first, Oliver's rooted to the spot, probably stunned, and I dribble the basketball away from him. His trance-like state doesn't last for long and soon he's on my heels, laughing.

"That's what I'm talking about. Yes." His deep voice and the warm melodic rumble of his laughter cause my insides to heat and legs to wobble.

Focus, Wren, focus.

I peer at him over my shoulder. "Do you want to flip a coin or take a shot to see who goes first?"

"Shot." He juts his chin toward the basket. "You first."

Gratitude and annoyance compete for top spot, as I'm unsure how I should react since he's letting me go first. Does he think I need the help?

Horse is like Simon Says, and if I go first, I can make the shots as hard or as outlandish as I want, and contrary to what he might think, I'm not that rusty. I volunteer with the town's elementary sports club and I'm an assistant coach to the Winslow Grove boys' basketball team.

Oliver ties his shoelace as if he isn't in the least bit concerned. "Remember, first person to horse loses."

The ball flies through the air and sinks into the net without touching any of the rim. He tips his head back to watch the swish, while a confidence I only get when playing overcomes me.

"I know the rules, Twist. Let's play." I can't help my smug smile.

His eyes glitter with sheer amusement. "Game on, baby."

Damn, I usually don't like those kinds of terms of endearment, but I can't deny how his calling me "baby" does something strange and fluttery to my insides.

It shouldn't. Especially since he can't mean it that way. He's engaged, and it was most probably a slip of the tongue. And if I don't get a grip and focus on the game, he's going to clean the floor with me.

Channeling all my creativity, I make the shots crazy and difficult, and he matches me every time, both of us good-humoredly trash-talking the other, until I goof and he gets the ball.

Now it's his turn to call the shots, and he follows my lead, challenging both of us, until he flubs. I now have the ball, and we're neck and neck with only one letter to go. The next person to get the "e" of Horse loses.

"Opposite hand," I call, not sure if it's the right move, but I've made shots with my left hand before.

He groans but quickly covers with a neutral expression like it's no big deal. His cool and unwavering mettle gives me pause, and because using the opposite hand isn't hard enough, or I'm plain stubborn, I back up from the net to make it long range and shoot.

Every muscle in my body tenses. The ball soars toward the basket, bounces off the backboard, and circles the rim before dropping into the net. Air rushes from my lungs, body loosening as I jump up and down, giggling.

A wicked grin flashes across his face, making him look boyish, so much like the teenager I so wanted to notice me.

He points at me, face alight like a candle. "Tyler, you're on fire."

"Your turn, Twist. This could be it." I wink, not sure where this flirty me is coming from.

He follows my moves and shoots with his left hand, not bothering to take his time or at least that's how it seems. Did he even try to make the shot or did he throw the shootout?

The basketball hits the backboard and still airborne, arcs past the net onto the court with a whack. We both watch the ball bounce a few more times, neither of us going after it.

Game over.

Standing several feet behind him, I watch his shoulders round and body slump, as he grunts in defeat. I jog toward him, battling the urge to gloat. Maybe I will just a little. He'd do the same if he won.

Oliver doesn't notice me and twirls in my direction. We nearly collide, but I quickly dodge to one side and end up tripping over his ankle. Everything that comes after happens so fast.

Strong, confident hands latch onto my waist and stop me from falling flat on my face. Goose bumps break out on my arms. He spins me to face him, and at his touch, my yelp lodges in my throat.

Now I really am on fire.

With one arm sliding around my back and the other grasping me by the waist, he draws my body into his until we are chest to chest.

Every solid inch of him heaves against me. "You okay?"

Being this close to him scrambles my brain, and I struggle to breathe let alone comprehend the question. He smells of pine and soap and a salty masculinity I've never experienced before.

I like it.

A lot.

His knuckles graze my cheek, and I shiver at his gentle touch. "Wren, talk to me. You sure you're okay?"

Captivated by the gold-and-emerald flecks in his tender eyes, at first, I'm mute and bemused. Then I blink and push away the thundering of my heart.

"Uh-huh. I'm good."

My response erases the worry from his attentive gaze. "That was a close call."

I'm not sure if he means my near face plant or the game.

"Yes." I swallow with difficulty.

This moment, our connection, seems so intense. It would be so easy, so natural, to reach up and kiss him.

No. This is wrong. Oliver is with Dot. Like it's always been, this strange and overwhelming connection, as if he's knitted into my very being just like DNA, is one-sided. All in *my* head.

Oliver's two years older than I am, to the day, and yet, we've known each other most of our lives, have had many shared birthdays. We're childhood friends, met through sports, and while we somewhat drifted apart in high school, we still hung out. But we were never anything more.

My skin heats, now tight and prickly with embarrassment, but before I can pull away or apologize, a deafening crack of thunder tears through the air.

Startled, I wriggle a little in his grasp. "Wow. Sounds like it's getting nasty out there. Thanks for catching me. Sorry."

He pulls back, my movement probably giving him the impression that I want out of his arms. I should, but in reality, it's the last thing I desire.

Carefully, he releases me. "You still got it, Tyler."

A blush at his appreciation spreads from my chest upward, and just the thought of my reddening complexion causes mortification and likely more of the crimson tide.

"You sound surprised. Of course, I still have it." My hands smooth down my dress and then release the knot in my hair. "I should get going before the torrential downpour that they're predicting gets here."

"Ah, yeah." He rubs at the back of his neck. "Let me walk you out."

He saunters toward his jacket on the floor, and already moving toward the door, I wave off his offer.

"No. No. You stay." I push the door open wider and spin to face him with my back against the wood. "Twist, this was fun. Maybe I'll even agree to a rematch." I wink again. *Who am I?* "See you around."

He hesitates. "Yeah, it was, but I'm afraid I'll have to say no to a rematch."

My stomach knots, dipping and speeding toward my toes. Yeah, this attraction—or whatever—is clearly all in my head.

Diverting his gaze, he looks off into the middle distance as if something weighs heavy on his mind. Did my flirting take things too far? Does he think he has to set me straight? Let me down easy?

Oh, God, I'm going to be sick, and yet I can't move, get the hell out of here, even if I want to. I need to hear what he has to say.

Eventually his gaze finds mine once more, but only long enough to get the words out. "Tonight's my last night in Winslow Grove."

A shock wave ripples through me. That isn't what I expected him to say.

"What?" I push off the door, suddenly perturbed and wanting answers. "No."

He can't leave.

All thoughts of going home before the storm vanish, and I stride purposefully toward him.

Oliver's head swings to look at me, expression surprised, as if he can't believe I'm reacting this way, that I care. Why would he think that? Of course I care that he's leaving.

Then he looks beyond me, and his features morph into a deep concern or maybe even...alarm.

"Wren. No." He sprints past me. "No. No. No," he chants as if by saying it enough, whatever he doesn't want to happen, won't.

Confused, I awkwardly spin in the same direction. The door I was just leaning against swings toward the frame, and the force of it causes the pylon used to keep the door open to shift. The small orange cone sails into the hallway and the door closes.

"Fuck." His hands slam onto the long metal bar of the door.

Nothing happens.

"What's wrong? Oliver, why won't the door open?" Suddenly my heart beats double time, yet I'm still not sure what exactly the problem is.

Turning to face me, he rakes a hand through his light-brown waves, expression grim. "The door sticks. Coach Bell warned me not to shut it because he wasn't sure it would open again."

"What?" Tight bands of metal weave through my voice as I try to block out how parts of my body reel from what I fear this means.

I'm lightheaded and faintly nauseous.

Something disquieting lurks in the depths of his usually serene gaze. "Wren, we're stuck in here."

Chapter 3

Oliver

The gleam of victory that was in Wren's bright brown eyes after our shootout—intoxicating and phenomenal to witness—is now gone. Completely erased by our reality. We're locked in the gym.

"What do you mean stuck?" She shoves on the metal bar running along the door with all her might, but it doesn't budge. "I don't understand."

"Coach said it started yesterday. The door wouldn't open. They had to use a drill or something to get it open, and ended up removing the handle. A locksmith's coming tomorrow to look at it."

"I don't understand. The bar's on the door." She bites her lip, and I can't help but stare at her, not fully believing she's here.

Stunning.

I always thought Wren was beautiful.

Still is.

And now, in that dress, how it clings to her chest and then flares at her slender waist, and her flaming red hair. The long natural waves accentuate her high cheekbones and those cupid's-bow lips.

Damn.

"Oliver?"

I look away, needing to break her spell. "Uh, yeah. Remember Wade?" I pause until she nods, recalling the school handyman. "Well, he didn't know about the problem, and when he saw the door dismantled..."

I can't help but smile and let out a long sigh. Wade Jeffers means well, always wants to help where he can.

"Let me guess. He put the door back together thinking he was fixing things."

"Yeah. Coach figured it was still jammed and didn't want to risk finding out with classes already underway. So he kept the doors wide open, only placing the cone there for me before he left."

"Sorry." Still chewing on her plump bottom lip, her gaze searches the gym. "Where's your phone? You could call Dot to come get us out."

I stiffen at the mention of my would-be wife, or at least that's how Wren knows things to be.

As if sensing my apprehension, the ever-present rosy color in her cheeks fades. "Or maybe that isn't a good idea."

She isn't wrong, and the implication hangs between us awkward and thorny. My ex-fiancée would lose her shit if she found me alone with any woman, but most of all Wren.

Dot and I started dating early in the fall of the year Wren returned from college. I'd been waiting for Wren, missed her, and was determined, once we were both back in Winslow Grove, to find out if we could be more than friends.

But Wren came back with a boyfriend. I was upset, jealous even, and not long after that, Dot asked me out. Foolishly, I said yes, figuring it wouldn't be anything serious. I'd wait Wren out.

In hindsight, I should've stayed single and steered clear of Dot. She wasn't easy to shake, and though Wren broke up with the guy she was seeing, not even six months later, she was with Lane. In my mind, there wasn't any doubt—Lane was the one.

My chest tightens just thinking about it. I wouldn't be surprised if they're engaged. If not now, soon, for sure. By then, Dot was pressuring me for more, her claws deep into me, and things unraveled from there.

Wren's voice slices through the gnawing in my gut. "I could call Percy or Pop."

Yes, her younger sister or father are much better choices to call for help.

"Sure." I grab my jacket and fish out my phone from the inside pocket. "Shit. I've got less than ten percent battery."

"That might be enough." She takes the phone and punches in a number.

"I'm impressed you know the number. I'd be screwed without my phone."

"Pop drilled it into our heads." She smiles and taps her temple. "It's ringing." Her smile gets a little bigger, and I try not to think about the meaning.

Is she eager to get away from me? Was that our problem? I wanted something that was never there?

Nah, we had chemistry. Shit, we still have it, this much I know.

Timing was always at the heart of it, and even now, timing will screw us over. She's with Lane, and of all the nights I could run into Wren Tyler, have a chance to really talk to her, tell her how I feel, it's the night I'm leaving town.

This woman. She still sparkles. She's lit from within and makes any room, along with those in it, glow. People are drawn to her much like when you gather around a fire to bask in the warmth. Happy and comforted.

When was the last time I felt this way? This strange and vibrant buzzing under my skin—I've only ever experienced it when Wren was near.

I suppose it was the last time I really talked to her. How long has it been since we've been alone like this? Five years? Maybe longer?

Winslow Grove is a small town, and most people know of or about you, but weeks can go by before you see the same person twice. While Wren and I run in similar circles and frequent the same places, we usually only see each other a few times a year. And never alone. Even then, it's only a wave, a smile, or a head nod. No conversation.

Her brow furrows. "It's not working. The phone rings, but only once and then the connection cuts out." She glances at my phone. "Less than three percent battery now."

"All right. Where's your phone?" I shove mine into my jacket pocket again.

Useless. I'd planned on charging it on the drive out of town.

"Oh no. My phone, jacket, and purse are in the school library. I left them there when I decided to take a stroll down memory lane."

"Okay." I rock on my heels, stalling but knowing I have to mention him. "What about Lane? Surely he'll go out to look for you when you don't come home. Did he know you were stopping at the high school on the way home?"

Now it's her turn to tense and grimace. "Lane? Uh, we split eighteen months ago."

"Seriously?" My heart flips.

"Yes. He now lives in Prospect. He might even be engaged." She sounds almost chirpy like she's glad to be rid of him.

I get it. I'll be glad to be rid of Dot. I just need to get out of town first.

Wren's revelation sinks in. Lane's gone to Prospect, a larger town forty minutes away, and the closest one to us. Doesn't seem far enough, but good riddance. I never did like him. Pompous jerk. Especially for Wren.

Shit. Does this mean she's single?

Timing. Even now it's getting in our way.

"Who ended it?" A small part of me immediately regrets asking the second the question is out of my mouth.

She tilts her head to one side in challenge. "Why does it matter?"

Deep down it does. I'm tongue-tied and unsure how to respond without sounding like someone drowning under the impossible weight of an unrequited crush.

Crush.

Was that all Wren ever was? And if so, why is this feeling so fierce and all-consuming? My heart palpitates in a way that makes me both giddy and distressed as if I'm not in control. Fuck if I know.

But...

I still yearn to know if she walked away or if Lane broke her heart. Like it matters. I won't be here to have a chance with Wren Tyler.

If only.

Putting me out of my misery, she says, "I ended things. Lane and I were never right for each other. What about Dot?"

My stomach roils painfully, not anticipating the same question. I don't want to get into the mess of my relationship with Dot.

"What about her?"

"Won't she worry or try to find you when you don't come home?"

Time to come clean or at least give her the bare minimum.

"Dot and I are over."

"Since when? Isn't the wedding only a few months away?" She flushes and averts her gaze as if caught with her hand in the cookie jar.

A bitterness lodges at the base of my throat. "Yeah, this latest date change made it January. You know what I find very interesting?" I arch a brow at her with a strong need to get off the topic of Dot. "How you know what's going on in my life. You keeping tabs on me, Tyler?"

"Hardly. All of Winslow Grove knows about your upcoming nuptials and how the date keeps changing. What is this now, the fourth or fifth time?" She must see me bristle, as worry spreads across her features. "God, sorry, Oliver. Me and my big mouth."

"It's fine. Nothing you said isn't true. Can we talk about something else? Like how we're going to get out of here." My words are abrupt, more so than I intend, and she flinches, visibly taken aback by my harsh tone.

"What about Coach Bell's office?" She ambles that way, not waiting for me as if seeking space. "He must have a phone."

"Wren, shit, I'm sorry. I didn't mean—"

"It's okay. Your relationship with Dot isn't any of my business."

Not knowing what else to say, I quicken my pace and get back to the matter at hand. "Good thinking about the office. Coach might have a landline in there."

Sure enough, an ancient phone sits on the desk, and I lift the receiver to my ear. Nothing. My finger presses the button a few times. Still nothing.

"The phone lines must be down. There's no dial tone."

Wren takes the phone from me, and I drop to my haunches to check that it's plugged in and connected to the jack. Yes to both.

"It isn't working." She puts the receiver down and blows out a frustrated breath. "What about the windows?"

She points to four thin rectangular windows at the top of one wall, each no more than one foot high and maybe three feet wide. It's black as tar outside with not much of a moon to light the night, and while she's slim, Wren might have a hard time getting through that opening.

"I don't know, and even if you could get through, then what? How will you get down safely?" I scan the office, looking for another option.

Not much has changed since my high school days. Coach still has the sofa, vending machine, bookcase, two hardback chairs, his desk, and an office chair.

"If these windows are the ones I think they are, the shop garage is there." She points to the right of the office. "I can jump down onto the garage roof. It isn't as high."

"Then what?" A flash of blinding white light streaks across the coal sky. "Jesus. You can't go out there. You'll be struck by lightning."

She rolls her eyes, though I don't miss the flicker of apprehension. "I'll be fine."

"Say you do this and don't get fried in the process, how do you get down from there?"

She chews on her lip. "I don't know. Maybe there's a dumpster to break my fall or the bleachers. They aren't too far."

"They might be farther than you think. And what if you can't?" I shake my head, rejecting this crazy idea.

"We have to try. We're stuck in here."

"Is that really so bad? They'll find us in the morning. We're indoors, and we've got restrooms." I hook a thumb toward the locker rooms. "We're here together."

Brown eyes settle on me, and I wonder if maybe that's what scares her the most.

"Can we give it a try?" She tips her head toward the windows. "And if it works, you come to my house for chicken pot pie. Made from scratch."

I groan at the thought of food. Wren's homemade cooking at that. Dinner was another thing I'd planned to do on my way out of town.

The twinkle in her eyes tells me she knows exactly what she's doing. Bartering to get her way. "If I can't get down, I promise I'll come back in." Her hand latches on to my arm for a quick squeeze.

I sigh heavily, and despite being against this idea, there's no way I'll say no to her, this smart, brave, resilient woman. And once she realizes she can't get through that opening, she'll give up and settle in until they find us.

"Fine. But promise me, if you can't get through the window or the second you realize there's no *safe* way of getting down, you get back in here."

My arms stretch outward, hands ready to grab her, and she stills. "Wait. Maybe this won't work. I'm too heavy."

Now I roll my eyes. "Wren, no. Come here." And I pull her to me.

At my touch, she quakes, sucks in a soft breath, and her eyes darken, pupils slightly dilating. Then on a jerky laugh, words tumble from her mouth, "Please don't drop me."

A strange tenderness erupts in my chest, and a steady thrum of arousal—the very one that sprang to life the second Wren showed her face at the gym door—charges through my body, pulsating just under my skin.

"Tyler, I'd never let you go." I confidently grip her waist, trying to infuse in her the strength and conviction of my words. "Do you trust me?"

A quick, breathy yes skates past her lips followed by a timid and no less sweet smile.

"Okay. I'll lift you onto the desk." It's perfect as a launching point. "Then I'll make a foothold with my fingers and help you get higher."

She bends one leg. "Okay, I'll get onto—"

"Uh-huh. I got you." My fingers dig into her slender waist, and her fingers curl into my shoulders.

My balls tighten at the feel of her hands on me.

Fuck. Concentrate, Oliver. Not on how good she feels in your arms, or how much you'd like to kiss her. Taste her. Have her. Concentrate on steadily hoisting her up, making her believe she's safe and secure.

With a deep inhale, I lift her until she's firmly standing on the desk. Her legs are at my eye level, and damn, I need to stop staring at her porcelain skin and lean muscles. My fingers itch to trace a line down her silky smooth calf.

Jaw clenched, I knit my fingers together and place the makeshift foothold in front of her.

"My boots..." She hesitates. "I don't want to hurt you."

"You won't."

Tightening her grip on my shoulder, she rests one foot on my interlocked fingers, and I push her upward.

"You all right?" I make the mistake of glancing up and get an eyeful under her dress.

Bare, toned thighs and her magnificent heart-shaped ass in a pair of lime-green form-fitting boy shorts.

Fuck me.

"Yes. What about you? Are you okay?" Her voice carves through my lust-filled thoughts.

"Yeah." My tone has more of an edge as I grit my teeth so as to keep it together. "Don't worry about me."

Her upper body leans against the wall, and her arms reach for the window. "There's a latch but it won't budge. It's been painted over and..." She huffs out a strained breath, swaying with the effort, and I tighten my grip on her boot, the other going for her legs.

The instant my fingers wind around her firm calf, she utters a half gasp, half hiss. "Shit, Oliver."

"You all right?"

"Yeah. It's just that it's glued shut. I can't get the latch to move."

Not bothering to hide it, I'm a bit too eager to get her down and onto firm footing. "Okay. You tried." My urgency is as much for her safety as my sanity. "Down you come."

Holding her like this for any longer and I'll be more than full-on gawking at all that's beautiful and sinful under her dress. I'll want to touch and savor, consequences be damned.

Carefully, using my body for leverage, I lower Wren. Her soft curves glide along my torso, and it takes everything in me not to release a long, drawn-out hum of appreciation.

Her feet hit the floor, but I don't let go. She tilts her neck to look up at me, and her lips, lush and rosy like the natural hue of her cheeks, are only inches away. I've stared at those lips so many times, remembering the one and only time I kissed her.

Does she taste the same? Sweet like honey. And I can only imagine the sounds she'd make. If I got to kiss her again, once wouldn't be enough.

A searing, quivering heat sweeps through me, from the top of my head all the way to the tip of my toes. I'm shaken with an impulse, out of my control. She's a flower and I'm a steadfast bee, drawn to her nectar.

I couldn't stop even if I wanted to. I'm in so much trouble.

My mouth skates over hers, at first soft and tentative, but when she moans and tips her head back for a better angle, I take her lower lip between mine and suck with deliberate intention of making her moan.

Her chest thrusts into mine, her back arches, and when she whimpers my name, I'm almost undone by the possibility that she may have hungered for this as much as I have.

The lights flicker and we break apart, both glancing up at the ceiling as we're plunged into darkness.

Chapter 4

Wren

The inky darkness eats at me. I gasp and lean into Oliver, struggling to focus on how sturdy and warm his body is against mine. Every one of his measured breaths helps me to do the same. Yet still, my burgeoning fear has a mind of its own.

"Wren." The calming sound of my name on his lips further settles the caged animal inside me.

Only for a blink.

I can't get past our predicament.

We're stuck in a box with no light...and no exit.

The dark.

We could be here for the entire night in absolute blackness. I can't see Oliver's face even though he's only inches from me.

Lightning flashes and Coach's office beams for the briefest of seconds, both of us illuminated. Strangely, it's as if time stops.

Oliver stares down at me, features twisted in concern, such care and compassion etched in his ruggedly handsome face, his lips red and still glistening from our kiss.

Once more, darkness steals the moment. An alarmed whimper pops from my mouth.

"Wren." His fingers trail a soft path along my cheek, the other hand firmly holding me close. "Are you still afraid of the dark?"

I'm a mixture of both stunned that he remembered and comforted by the attentive tone in his voice. There's no teasing or admonishment in the fact that I'm a grown woman and the dark still makes me want to cry.

"You remember?" The question is a croaky whisper as if the loss of electricity also caused my voice to fade.

"Of course, I do. The best seven minutes of my life."

There's a hint of a smile to his tone, and unpredictably, I'm grateful for the conversation. His teasing.

Playfully, I slap at his hard chest. Once more, his unwavering firm body helps to ease my rattling nerves.

"Shut up. It was seventh grade." Or at least it was for me. By then, Oliver was a freshman at Winslow Grove High. "I'm sure you've had more memorable experiences since then."

His long fingers gently wrap around my wrist and hold my hand to his chest. The beating of his heart, constant and precise under my palm, does wonders to soothe me.

"No, seriously, Wren, I remember every single second."

My stomach churns, not quite trusting his words, and almost immediately, I'm taken back to that night. It was a birthday party for his best friend, Kellen, and we were at the age when some of us were dating, crushes ran rampant, and almost every girl I knew wanted Oliver Winslow.

He was a great catch. No, *the catch.*

Athletic, gorgeous, funny, smart, liked by all, and above all else, Oliver was kind to everyone. So when Kellen declared we were playing seven minutes in heaven, my heart sank, convinced Dot—she'd wanted him for as long as I had—or any other girl but me would get him.

Weirdly bolstered by the dark, I say, "You know, it's strange, but I both wanted and didn't want to be paired with you."

"What?" There's so much wariness in his one word, he sounds even a little hurt, and I so wish I could see his face clearly, get a better read on what he might be feeling.

Murky moonlight slinks in through the tiny windows high above but only casts shades and angles, nothing sure or concrete.

"I can't explain it any better than I was nervous. I only liked you, and one thing was for sure, I didn't want to be paired with anyone else."

"Me neither."

"Really?" It seems silly that I care how he felt after all these years and yet, I do.

His head nods, a dark shadow bobbing up and down. Ironically, my greatest fear—the dark—somehow feeds me the courage to do this, to share my feelings even if I'm questioning if I can trust his.

"I was flying high after that party." My bubbly jubilance from back then is a welcomed memory. "You had an away game, and I couldn't wait for you to get back."

"I remember. I was counting the minutes until I saw you again."

Tensing at his words, I don't completely believe his account of things. How can I when everything after that proved otherwise?

"Well, Kellen found me first when the team got back. He told me he'd goofed at the party." My nerves get the better of me, and I clamp my mouth shut to stop from spewing any more. This is harder than I thought, baring my soul, scars and all, even after all these years.

Feeling exposed, I squirm and mentally pick through all the ways to continue this conversation, looking for a path least likely to break my heart. But it's futile; each option makes me no less raw or vulnerable.

As if sensing this and knowing what I need, he rubs a reassuring hand along my back. "Go on."

"He, um, said you wanted him to put you in the closet with Zoe." Even after all these years, saying my then best friend's name causes tears to prick at the corners of my eyes. Dammit. "Kellen said he messed up, and it should have been her and not me with you."

When Kellen dropped that bomb, I was devastated, all hope lost. The hope that our seven minutes was the start of something more. My humiliation, the way Kellen's dark eyes bore into mine, willing me to understand that Oliver never wanted me, still hurts to this day.

"He didn't." Oliver vibrates with an unnamed force, as jarring and sharp as his clipped tone. "Fuck him. Now I get it."

"Get what?"

"Why you never showed up as planned. Why you'd changed. I tried to tell myself you were busy with school, basketball, but when we'd worked together at Pop's that summer, you were different."

I nod and sniff, unable to form the words for fear of crying. Why is this so difficult?

Because that party changed everything. It was both the best and worst night of my young teen life, and to now hear the version I was handed wasn't the truth...

"Yes. I put distance between us. Oliver, I don't know if we should talk about this." My forehead presses into the solid warmth of his chest, and I'm afraid I'm getting it all wrong. Again. And nothing's changed.

He clasps the back of my neck, fingers sliding through my hair. "Hey, we should clear the air."

I lift my head, and he keeps his hand where it is, cradling my skull. How do

I explain that I did it out of self-preservation without putting all of me out there?

Oliver made the most of our seven minutes together—talking me through my fear, kissing me—and even after I found out he'd wanted to be with someone else, while it hurt like a son of a bitch, the truth didn't change my heart.

The stupid organ wouldn't move on. I still longed for him despite knowing the feelings weren't reciprocated. Call it my competitive streak or plain old stubbornness, but I knew, if given the chance, I might try to change his mind.

The ache was too much, and I couldn't risk hurting like that again. There and then, I vowed I would be no one's consolation prize. I deserved someone who wanted me.

"Okay, I'll go first." His curt tone sends a shiver of dread racing down my spine. "Kellen lied. He wanted you for himself."

"What?" My heart batters against my ribs.

"I'd asked to be paired with you, not Zoe. He knew how much I liked you, and while he'd never said anything to me, I sensed he felt the same way. I figured he was being a good friend by keeping quiet. Not making a move. Until that night. There was something in his eyes." His body stiffens, matching his brittle tone. "I had a feeling and checked the names he'd paired together. Sure enough, he'd screwed me over, so I switched his name for mine. There was no way I was letting him near you, not even for a second."

A silly giggle bursts from me, hardly believing him but refusing to let this rush of excitement go. "Really? I wish I could see your face."

He guides my hand to the firm line of his stubbled jaw and bids my fingers to roam freely. It's an innocent invitation, but as I trace the ridge of his nose, the soft dip just above the center of his upper lip, and the smooth rise and fall of his mouth, this moment, these feelings are so poignant, so intimate.

Hands shaking, I cup his face and draw him nearer. His closed mouth presses into my hairline, and like a drizzle of warm honey, his lips skim over my forehead, linger at the crest of my brow, rest gently at the arch of my cheek-bone, and finally press firmly against my mouth.

My breath flutters faintly in my chest like the beat of butterfly wings. He breaks our kiss but not the connection of our mouths.

"Wren, pretend we're in that closet one more time. We'll block out the darkness, the storm, everything."

Chapter 5

Wren

Oliver's fingers slide deeper into my hair, massaging my scalp, and the fingers of his other hand dig into my hip. His lips are on mine, and as effortlessly and gratifying as breathing, we make out.

Forgotten are all the years since that fateful night, the lie that pulled us apart, and my misguided need to protect myself with indifference and space.

No one kisses me like he does.

Even young and inexperienced, when we'd first kissed in that closet, I never could match that feeling with anyone else.

With every one of his kisses, each stroke of his tongue, and his guttural moans sliding down my throat, Oliver seeps back into my pores, my blood, deep into my bones, and my very soul.

My insides simmer, my clothes too confining, my skin too sensitive, and the thrumming low in my core heightens the reawakening of a long since buried desire.

With my underwear now near soaked, I slide my hands down to grab his backside and pull him into me. The long, hard outline of his erection pushes into my stomach.

He leans his forehead against mine. "Fuck, Wren."

"That's me." I kiss the tip of his chin, smiling, and the muscles in his face pull upward to do the same.

My hands release his ass, and I playfully push him backward, testing that the desk is where it should be. Oliver backs up until he can't anymore, and I press into him again.

Wordlessly, he understands and bends his large body to sit on the edge of the desk. He spreads his rock-hard thighs and drags me between them.

The salty-fresh scent of him burrows into my senses, and I take his mouth again while tugging his shirt from his waistband. My hands slip under the material and glide wild and free over his incredible abdomen.

He wrenches his mouth from mine. "Jesus, what are you doing to me?"

His fingers throb and flex in my hair, and before he has a chance to stop this, my mouth covers his once more. My hands resume their wandering, over his hard plains and corded muscles as they tighten and jerk beneath my fingertips.

Finally he relents, and his hands drop from my face to pull up my dress until my thighs, ass, and panties hit cool air. He explores the backs of my legs, up, up, and up. Wherever he touches me, my skin burns.

His mouth skates over my collarbone, and I groan softly at the scrape of his teeth as he finds my panties. I shamelessly rub against the palm of his hand, now cupping my sex through my soaking-wet underwear.

"You're drenched." He sounds both awed and pained, and it makes me laugh. Duh, of course I'm wet and oh, so ready.

He hooks a finger in the crotch of my panties and pushes them aside as he continues to grind the heel of his hand against my clit.

My knees buckle at the pressure, and fingers curl into his hot flesh. "Oliver."

He kisses me again, long and hard, and his finger slips inside me, then he rubs my arousal over my clit in slow, deliberate strokes. I bite his bottom lip, and he chuckles while switching to his thumb and increasing the tempo to fast, mind-blowing circles.

One finger slips inside me, pumping, then two, harder and faster as he twists and crooks his fingers in a way that brilliantly hits my G-spot, making the stars light up behind my eyelids.

"Yes. There. Just like that." I hardly recognize my voice, breathless and needy.

Holy hell, this…no one else has ever made me feel like this. And the sounds I make, unfettered, almost feral, reverberate around us.

"Oliver, I'm going to—"

His mouth seals mine, tongue probing, as he drinks in my gasp of pleasure. "I got you, Wren."

I spasm around his fingers, legs trembling, muscles tightening, and I cling to him. He mutters something indecipherable as my climax surges and sends my world spinning. Both electrifying and shocking. I muffle my whimper against the scruff of his neck.

My stomach growls like a dragon storming the room, and he chuckles. The shake of his body is like a sweet aftershock to my sex, then he withdraws his fingers and rights my panties.

Unable to make out what he's doing, I busy myself with straightening my dress. We're still touching. His breathing is heavy, heat radiating off him, and a long slurp or sucking causes me to freeze, then a loud pop.

I stare up at Oliver, all dark angles and shadows, so wishing I could see him. Did he just do what I think he did?

"Wren, it sounds like you're hungry. You should taste yourself." His slick fingers tap on my mouth to open and he feeds me my arousal. "You're fucking phenomenal."

I suck on his long, thick fingers, and heat sparks in my core, wanting him, all of him. He moans at the flick and twirl of my tongue around his digits.

"Fuck, if you weren't hungry..." He doesn't finish his thought and removes his fingers. His other hand brushes my hair. "Let me feed you."

At the idea of food, I reluctantly park my arousal and wipe at the corners of my mouth. "You have something to eat?"

We both chuckle at the innuendo, and this time, his laughter is deep and generous. The vibrations of his joy course through my body, thrilling me further.

"Ah, I wasn't referring to that, but maybe later. I wish I had a meal to give you. I was thinking the vending machine."

"Okay. And you can find it in this dark hell?"

He gets to his feet and crowds me, as if reminding me that he's here—that I'm not alone. I melt into him.

"I promise to go slow, and I won't let you go."

"Okay, lead the way, Twist."

True to his word, Oliver clutches me close to his body, our steps slow and measured as we hobble across the shadowy office.

"What we need is a flashlight," he says.

"And you wouldn't happen to have one, would you?"

"No, but Coach does. If only we can make it to the—fuck." He jerks back from whatever it is he's bumped into and curses again under his breath.

"Are you okay?"

"Yeah. I found one of the chairs." He shifts me so I'm almost behind him. "Hang on. If we are where I think we are, it's close, but I don't want you crashing into things."

I slide one hand into the back pocket of his jeans to grasp his ass, and he lets out a throaty groan. "Tyler, I've never known you to not play fair. Hands in a safe place."

"Safe place?" I slide my hand from his pocket to the front of him.

My nails graze his hard abdomen through his shirt, and he tenses under my touch. "Fuck, Tyler, you're dangerous."

He spins so fast, a whoosh of air washes over me for only a beat before his hands are on me. Everywhere. In my hair, skating down my cheeks, skimming the sides of my breasts, squeezing my waist until they settle on my backside.

"Now how does it feel?"

"Pretty amazing actually." My lips dance along the underside of his jaw, and he tips his head back to give me better access.

This time his stomach gurgles, and he belts out a deep belly laugh. His Adam's apple bobs and reverberates under my teeth. With a nip at his flesh, I push onto my toes and plant a kiss at the corner of his lopsided grin.

"Okay. Both of us need food first, then more of this."

Within minutes, he has the flashlight, and while I wish it was bigger and brighter, the pointed beacon does the trick and helps us get around the office.

No surprise, Oliver knows how to get food out of the vending machine without money or power. He tips the large box to one side while I aim the flashlight in his direction, and with a few whacks of his fist, we have our pick of chocolate bars, candy, and bags of chips.

We sit side by side on the sofa eating, and when I come to the last of my peanut M&Ms, satiated if not a little thirsty, I am ready to brave one of the two topics I so desperately want answers about.

My hands rub along my skirt while I mull over how best to broach the subject of Dorothy Malone, his longtime girlfriend turned fiancée. The fact that she snagged Oliver aside, I never much cared for her.

She has always been a mean girl, always talking down to everyone like she was better than they were. Pretty in that *won't leave the house without her hair and makeup done like she's going to the Oscars* kind of way.

We were never friends, but I didn't consider her an enemy. She and Oliver became an item several months after I returned from college, and while I was with someone at the time, something shifted between us. Dot suddenly didn't have a kind word or look for me.

I never fully understood it nor did I lose sleep over it. Oliver and I had never dated and yet, she acted as if I was his mistress. And when I was with someone—even the years I was with Lane—it never placated her. If Dot could have erased me or kicked me out of town, she would have.

He taps my knee. "You full?"

"Yes, but junk food never satisfies for long."

"True."

He shifts and I glance over at him, only able to make out his vague profile. Although we now have a flashlight, we agreed to conserve the battery and only use it when necessary.

"Oliver, will you tell me what happened between you and Dot?"

Chapter 6

Oliver

"You don't give up, do you?" I hook an arm around Wren's shoulders and bring her head to lean against me.

"Yep. But honestly, you wouldn't want me any other way." She turns her face into my chest, and I swear she breathes me in.

Fuck, does this mean I can have her? I'll take her any way I can get her. *Thank you, Coach Bell and the faulty gym door.*

My lips lightly brush the top of her head and her scent—the one I first inhaled earlier when she tripped over my shoe, fresh and subtly floral, the one I can't name but want more of—fills my nostrils.

"What do you want to know?" I ask into her glossy hair.

"Everything. Anything."

Something loosens in my chest at how blunt and honest she is with me. Finally. I'd missed this easy and open Wren.

When she told me about Kellen, I wanted to beat the shit out of him. Back then, in high school, it had taken me a while to figure out he was bad news. A liar and a cheat. We parted ways before college, but if I'd known what he'd done, how he'd sabotaged my chances with Wren... Fuck, it makes my blood boil.

I can't think about that. That's the past, and she's here with me now.

Though I can only make out her silhouette, I sense she's waiting for me to go on. It isn't easy to think clearly, especially about something so messed up as Dot, and when exasperation and longing are all tangled together in my mind.

"I called off the wedding two years ago."

Her head snaps up, and she pushes away from me. Still I don't release my hold on her. She has been too far from me for far too long. Not going to let it happen tonight.

"Two years? But...I-I don't..." Clearly puzzled, she flounders for the words. "But you live together. Your wedding date was set. Why?"

"You know Dot." I lightly bang my head against the wall and groan, if only to punish myself for all the things I wish I could change.

When I look back on those years we'd faked it for everyone, half of the entire time we'd been together, I question why I stayed so long. Why we got engaged in the first place. Dot picked out the ring, even set the date and time for the proposal—all I had to do was show up. She was even the one to ask.

By then, Lane was a permanent fixture in Wren's life. People were talking like they'd be soon walking down the aisle. I'd lost all hope and didn't see any kind of future with Wren. That realization made me careless. Stupid.

Wren rubs at the center of my chest and brings me back to Coach's dark office.

"Let me start by saying, I wish I could have a do-over. I would've made a clean break. She cried and begged me for another chance, and at first, I agreed."

Deliberately, I don't elaborate on how she lashed out, nearly had me arrested for stealing my own car, and how staying seemed easier.

The only woman I'd ever wanted was with someone else, and all I had or cared about was tied up in being with Dot. I had a lot to lose if I took Dot on by leaving her.

Wren's question cuts through the haze of those disturbing days. "So this was going on for more than two years?"

"Yeah. More than I care to remember. We should never have been together. I wouldn't say this to just anyone, but it's you." I find her hand and interlace our fingers. "She's manipulative and conniving and used to getting her way."

Wren snorts. "That's an understatement. I still remember what Pop said when..." Her breath hitches and the pause, to catch her breath or rethink what she's going to say, takes way longer than it should. "You know what? Forget it. You don't need that."

My throat tightens. Pop is important to me. I never hid my feelings for his daughter from him. And now, I see him around town, say a few words here or there, but I miss our long talks, hanging out with him.

When I was younger, he'd take me fishing at the crack of dawn on Sundays with his girls, Wren and Percy. He included me in a lot of their family gatherings, including Wren's birthdays since we shared the day, and I worked at his diner all through high school.

At times, I felt closer to him than my own father. Pop never came with any of the unrealistic expectations my dad had of me.

I wrap my fingers around her hand resting on my chest. "Please tell me. No matter how harsh or critical, I respect Pop and care what he thinks."

"I shouldn't have said anything. I'll feel like shit saying it."

"Come on, it's me and I'm asking."

She relaxes further, sinking into me. "Pop said you were in for a world of pain with a woman like Dot." She rests her head on my shoulder. "I'm sorry. I know at one time you and Pop were close."

She trails off briefly, maybe lost in thoughts of her father, then says, "Gah, I almost went by the Grill tonight for a burger. If only I had, he'd have a search party out looking for me by now."

Her hollow laughter and all her talk about her family restaurant makes me wish for a simpler time. Pop's Grill is a popular place in Winslow Grove and dare I say, the heartbeat of the town.

I groan and close my eyes. "What I'd give for one of his burgers."

She huffs and I can almost imagine her rolling her eyes. "Liar."

"What? Why do you say that? I'm not lying."

"It's been years since you stepped foot in Pop's, and don't tell me otherwise because you and I both know the truth."

My stomach churns at how things used to be, and I can't refute anything she says. Instead of doing so, I try to make her laugh. "Well now, you seem to know a lot about my whereabouts. Are you stalking me, Tyler?"

A *pfft* sound comes from her but nothing more, and the joke falls flat. She wants honesty. Now more on edge than before and no one to blame but myself, I root for the words.

Without getting into all of it, none of the responses I come up with make sense or even come close to a logical reason for staying away.

"Shit. I-I, Wren, you know Dot. She never wanted to eat there. Her figure and all that shit, and..."

"Don't sweat it. Like you said, Dot always gets her way, and she wanted you. I figured she was the reason you didn't come around." She pauses again, almost as long as the time before.

What is going through her head?

When she finally speaks, her first few words break on a stifled sob. "I still remember the day I heard the two of you were dating. The first thing I thought was, well, Oliver Winslow's taken for good. There was no way Dot was gonna let you go. And that's when my final, tiny scrap of stupid hope, the one I'd hung on to for so long, died."

A fist tightens in my gut. "Hope?"

"Yeah." She lets out a shaky chuckle. "Hope of a chance with you. It's stupid."

My heart physically aches at the pain in her voice, although a small part of me can't help but rejoice in hearing how she yearned for me.

I wasn't the only one.

My teeth clench just considering how different things might have been, if only...

"Shit, Wren." I squeeze her tight, needing to know this is real. She's in my arms. "If I'd known I had a chance to be with you, I'd have left Dot so fast..."

Regret pinches at my chest, and I grind my teeth once more. Regrets are mean bastards, pointless and punishing.

I clear my throat. "It seemed to me that you weren't interested and even at that, you were always dating someone when I wasn't and vice versa. I remember when you came back from college, you were with that cocky guy."

I know his name but never much liked him. Come to think of it, I didn't like any of the guys Wren dated. Or more truthfully, I never liked any of them for her.

"What? Jett Kincaide?" There's laughter in her tone while her hand drifts down my abdomen to rest just above my waistband.

She's trying to torture me.

"Yeah. I heard you'd met him at a rodeo or something, and every time I turned around, there he was, always with you." I fail to curb my biting tone, but she doesn't seem to notice or, more likely, care.

Wren chortles and curls her nails into my abs. "No way. Now look at who seems to know an awful lot about my business. Were you keeping tabs on me, Twist?"

I tense, not at her teasing tone, but at the stab of arousal shooting straight to my crotch. I try to ignore my dick straining against the front of my jeans.

"So what if I was?"

"Well, you need to brush up on your detective skills, or maybe I should say, stalking skills." She pokes at my side, and I flinch. "I went on like two or three dates with Jett. He's a wonderful guy, but we're better friends than anything else."

I grunt, not wanting to encourage any more conversation about the cocky, flirty Jett Kincaide. "Do you want to hear more about Dot, or can we be done with it?"

"Nuh-uh. Nice try." While the words are playful, her tone is gentle and more somber, as if letting me know she'll take whatever I have to give. And this is Wren. I can't hold back any of this even if it isn't pretty.

"At first, I agreed to keep our breakup quiet, and she moved the wedding date out. She said she needed time to tell her family and friends, and I understood. I even told her she could say she broke up with me, but that wasn't enough to bait her into action."

"So you two lived together in that house for more than two years, but you weren't together and no one knew." She sounds incredulous, and I can't blame her.

All told from the outside looking in, Dot and I were together for four years. No one knew, well only one, maybe two people, that our relationship was rotten to the core. Had been from the beginning and instead of getting loose early on, I stayed. At first, out of resignation, since I'd lost any chance of being with Wren, then indifference settled in and things got complicated.

"It's a big house. She had her space and I had mine. I thought by going along with it, I was avoiding Dot's drama and whatever lies she'd spread about the breakup. It wasn't ideal, and at times, when things got to be too much, I stayed with Eddie. He knows the truth."

"What does he think of all this?"

I shake my head, recalling how my older brother called me a fool for going along with anything Dot wanted. He never liked her and warned me to lose her from day one.

"He said I should cut my losses and take whatever shit she was gonna throw my way. I should've listened to him."

"To save you the misery of rehashing this, I think I get the gist and can guess how things went down. Dot kept changing the wedding date, buying more time, but never showed signs of telling anyone you two were over."

"Yup. I now see that she was hoping I'd change my mind or just give up and stay put."

"What finally caused you to make the break?"

"I didn't want this to be my life, and she was threatening me with the house and the business, and I realized this was always going to be the way with her. Whether I stayed with her or not, she was going to make my life a living hell."

Not only did I date the woman and get engaged, but I also built a house for her and went into business with her.

What a fucking fool.

And why? I didn't love her. I cared for her, and at some point, I thought it was love, but if so, why didn't it hurt to end things? The breakup felt right.

Relief swept through me, clearing away the shackles and heartache, and in its wake, leaving a tremendous sense of freedom.

Whereas Wren and I were only ever a promise of something, and yet, when that went nowhere, I hurt like a son of a bitch. Some days it was hard to breathe. Some days it was like the very essence of me was crushed under losing her. I get what she means about hope.

Most of my life I've been hoping for Wren Tyler, and now that she's here, in my arms, I can't say it changes anything, no matter how I wish it could. Dot and her family are a threat—they'll ruin me and anyone I care about.

I can't stay in Winslow Grove.

Chapter 7

Oliver

In the dark, Wren's voice jerks me from my chilling thoughts. "Is Dot the reason you're leaving?"

"You're brutal, Tyler." I huff out a bitter laugh. "One tough topic after another."

"I just don't get it. Forget that you stayed with her for way too long. This is your hometown. Your ancestors founded Winslow Grove. If anyone has to leave, it should be her. Why are you leaving?"

She squeezes my thigh to urge me to answer, and a pointy, tickling sensation settles at the nape of my neck.

"I feel like a coward for saying it out loud." Something thick and weighty lodges in my throat, and I attempt to get off the couch, hoping maybe the movement will kill this difficult conversation.

Wren's faster, most probably sensing both my literal and figurative retreat, and crawls onto my lap. Straddling me, her legs bracket mine and she glides her splayed palms up my chest to clasp her fingers at the back of my neck.

"Look, while I don't know your reasons, I do know that you aren't a coward. Talk to me."

"I feel like leaving is the only way to force Dot's hand and not be around for the blowback."

"What do you mean?" Her fingers play with stubble-like hair at the nape of my neck, and I lean into her touch.

"If I stay, I'll never be free of her. She isn't going to tell anyone we're over."

I can already imagine what Dot would say if Wren and I started seeing each other. Wren would be the homewrecker or worse, and I'd be a cheater. The truth would never see the light of day.

"Then you tell them. She doesn't call the shots. Are you just going to walk away from the house you built? Your business?" Her voice rises with each question, clearly on a roll.

It's funny how little we've said to each other over the years, but through the gossip mill, we know a fair bit about the other. And even with the years and distance, we're as close as ever.

"Wren, she can keep the house. I don't want it." My hands run along her back, needing to touch her. "Too many bad memories. But the business..."

She waits a beat, then two, and on the third, tries again. "Why were you really here tonight?"

Like a stealth bomber, she sneaks up on me and never misses her mark. How she knows there was more to my visit here tonight is uncanny, but I've got nothing to hide from her. Never from Wren.

"Coach called me. I figured it was good timing since I was leaving and I wanted to say goodbye."

"What did he want?"

"It hasn't been announced yet, but he's retiring at the end of December. He thought I'd be a good replacement."

"Wow, that's great news." She bounces on my lap, and my dick twitches as I emit a low growl. "Coach is right. You'd be a great PE teacher."

I shrug. I do have the degree, and teaching was always the plan after graduation. "I don't know. I kind of shelved that dream a long time ago."

"Why?"

"Winslow Nest. I really enjoy what I do."

I make custom furniture for a living and kind of fell into it through my love of woodwork. After college, a friend of mine couldn't find the crib they'd envisioned for their first child, and I helped them out by building them a custom one.

Things grew from there, and now I'm known for building one-of-a-kind pieces with orders from as far as New York City and Canada.

Her tits rub against my chest, and she lightly kisses my mouth. "But you're going to walk away from it. Why let Dot keep it? What is she going to do with the Nest without you?" Her voice is tinged with a mixture of indignation and determination. "You're the talent. The one who makes the designs, oversees the builds. What does Dot do? Run the office. Answer the phones?"

She pushes away from me, and I immediately resent the loss of her but can now breathe again. I'm barely keeping it together as it is.

Every time she touches me, kisses me, my brain short circuits, switching to only one track.

Wren.

I want her.

I want to be so deep inside her that she'll never be able to get me—the awareness of me, the impression of me—out of her mind, body, and soul.

"I'm not belittling what Dot does, but you can train anyone to do those things. Replacing you isn't as easy, and it sounds like you don't really want to give up the Nest."

"Wren." My sharp tone equals the meaningful squeeze to her waist. "Drop this."

"You could buy her out."

I'm grateful for the darkness so she can't see my scowl. Not at her persistence, but at how frustrating and futile all of this is. And I've no one to blame but myself.

Her warm breath washes over me, and I can't complain. I want her here. Sure, she isn't backing down, not until I answer her, but she only wants to help, even if she doesn't fully understand what I'm up against.

"I could try to buy her out, but her parents helped me get the Nest off the ground. They gave money."

"Okay. Can you get a loan to give them back what you owe?"

"I've already paid them back."

"Then what's the problem?" There's a slight tone of irritation in her voice, and I wonder if she's disappointed in me that I'm not the man she thought I was.

"Dot isn't the way she is just because. The apple doesn't fall far from the tree. Mr. Malone's a hard-ass, and when he finds out I've broken his baby girl's heart,"—even I almost bristle at my sarcastic tone—"he's gonna make me pay. There's no way he's going to let me take the Nest even if I buy out Dot fair and square."

I haven't told Eddie, the only family I have left, but he's also why I'm leaving town. He's got a thriving garage business, but it wouldn't take much for Mr. Malone to shut him down.

My hands frame her face, and I press my mouth to hers in the most tender of kisses. "I appreciate you wanting to talk this through with me, to find a solution."

I kiss her again. "If I'm being honest with myself, Wren, I'm exhausted. The past several years with Dot haven't been fun, and stupidly, I stuck around, not because I wanted to work things out with her, but because I didn't know what to do. Our lives are so entangled. I've been stuck for far too long, and the path forward looks brightest if I leave Winslow Grove."

A sharp twinge of regret or anger stabs at my chest every time I think about leaving.

"You already know this and the decision is yours, but I say you stay and fight. Without you,"—she presses a finger into my chest—"Winslow, the creator and artist, there's no Winslow Nest. And I promise to be right by your side."

A rush of arousal races through me at how vehemently she has my back.

"We're done talking." I kiss her, wandering from her mouth to leave a trail of hot kisses along her jaw, behind her ear, and down her neck.

Her fingers dive into my hair, kneading and scraping my scalp, as she presses her damp panties against my hard length.

I bend my head and suck her nipple through her dress, gently biting down on the hard tip poking through the material. She tugs at my shirt, urging me to take it off, as her legs tighten around my waist and she rocks into me.

"Holy hell, Oliver. God, you feel amazing."

"You're the one who's amazing." I brush hair off her cheek, and the heat of her makes me wish we had electricity.

I want to see just how far down her rosy glow, the one I'm sure colors her cheeks right now, travels when she's aroused. Her hands grasp my head and she kisses me. It's the purest, most blistering kiss. The kind that burrows deep into your soul and makes you feel irrationally and irrevocably adored.

She breaks the kiss but only long enough to say, "Oliver, I want you to fuck me."

Mouth back on mine, she eats at my lips as if starving and I'm the only one, my taste, to ever satisfy her.

Her words slice through me, circling my mind but not quite sitting right. I've dreamed she'd utter that very sentiment—"fuck me"—too many times to count, yet there's also something flawed and mistaken about them. What I want to do to her is more than fuck.

Her mouth pulls away from mine again. "Oliver, don't you want to?" Unease dwells in her voice.

My silent ponderings—I took too long to respond—causes her to doubt this. Doubt us.

"God, no, I want to. More than anything." My kiss is passionate and frenetic. "But are you sure?"

"Yes." Her teeth bite at my bottom lip.

I chuckle, trying hard to focus and not get carried away. "Uh, I don't have a condom. Didn't think I'd need it to visit with Coach."

She lets out a breathy laugh but abruptly cuts her amusement short. "I've got the patch, and I haven't been with anyone since…" She pauses, clearly not wanting to say her ex's name, and I'm grateful for that. "Well, you know who, and I've been tested recently. I'm all good."

"Same here. I haven't been with anyone in two and a half years."

"What? Not even—" She stops herself.

Neither of us wants to think of our exes or anyone but each other.

"No. No one." With my hand cradling the side of her face, I sense her features tighten, her brow furrow, and I release a quiet laugh. "Hey, it may seem strange but I never wanted anyone. Didn't miss it." While that isn't entirely true, my hand did fine at fulfilling the need. "I'd made a million and one mistakes with you know who, and I didn't want to do it again. If I was going to be with someone, it was going to be for the right reasons."

I sense her smile before I hear it in her voice. "And being with me is the right reason?"

"The only reason." I kiss her tenderly. "If not you, then no one."

Until now, I hadn't imagined this, long since believing Wren Tyler would never be mine. And while staying celibate hadn't started out as a conscious choice, I meant what I said. I didn't want to find myself mixed up with another woman who I couldn't see a future with.

And to be honest, Wren Tyler is the only woman I can truly say ever fit me.

Clearly done with conversation, her hands slide lower on my stomach, fingers grabbing at my button and zipper. While gripping her hip, I lift myself from the couch and help her ease off my pants.

Now in only my boxer briefs, I trail my hand up the sides of her dress, desperately wanting it off her.

She twists her back to me. "Unzip me."

In a flash, the dress is gone. Now in just her bra and panties, she sits in my lap, and I feel every inch of her heat with only the thin fabric of our underwear between us.

Hard as a rock, my dick aches for her, and as if reading my mind, her fingers palm me through the cotton. Like being struck by a bolt of lightning, my body sparks, muscles shudder, and cock swells even more, if possible.

"You first." With a trace of anguish in my voice, I tug her hand away from my boxers.

That yields a low whimper from her as she stands and then straddles me again in no time flat.

Holy damn, her panties are gone.

Heat flares low in my stomach, and my balls twitch.

"I'm ready." Legs spread wide, she slides up and down my shaft. Her drenched pussy dampens my boxers and her arousal seeps onto my dick.

The burn of desire tears through me. "Fuck me."

"That's the point." She pulls at the waistband of my boxers, and my cock springs to life, slapping against my belly, and once more, I help her get rid of my last remaining piece of clothing.

Now we're both gloriously naked.

This is happening.

Grabbing her by the waist, I stand and flip her back onto the sofa. I hover above her, and as much as I like the idea of her riding me, I want to control the pace. My fingers glide through her slick folds and stop to circle around her sensitive bundle of nerves. She utters my name, back arching as she slides her legs farther apart.

My legs shake with need as I settle between her thighs, fisting my cock and then thrusting into her.

Chapter 8

Wren

The tip of Oliver's long, thick cock breaches my entrance, and he makes a rough and ragged sound. He is massive, and I gasp his name at his first thrust, almost painful in the way he stretches me. So attuned to me, he leans forward, mouth capturing mine, and swallows the sound.

Slowly, he slides in deeper, and the pressure is enormous. More expanding and burning, inevitable and exquisite, and my eyes flutter closed, savoring every glorious inch of him.

I whimper when he hits my sweet spot, and he pauses, breaths heavy and choppy. "You okay?"

Squirming to adjust to him settling deeper inside me, I nod but quickly remember the dark. I so wish the lights worked, if only to see if his hazel eyes are as black as night, or how wide his pupils are blown. To see his desire for me. The thought is heady, and it's only the sound of my name that makes me snap out of this trance.

"Wren." He strokes inside me, and my sex pulses around him.

"Don't stop." I squirm once more, seeking movement and friction. More of it, more of him.

"You're so tight." Strain traces his voice and he presses a soft languid kiss against my parted lips. "So fucking beautiful."

I can't believe I'm having sex with Oliver Winslow. The situation isn't ideal, and he hasn't changed his mind about leaving, but I can't second-guess this. If this is my only chance to be with him, I'm grabbing the proverbial bull by the balls.

He pounds into me, his hands fisting my hair and arms shaking. My nails dig into his back, and I propel my hips forward to meet his and increase the waves of pleasure washing over me.

His rough, stubbled jaw rubs along the side of my face, and my tongue licks his fevered flesh, relishing the masculine taste of him. And his scent—he smells divine. Part salty and part clean.

"Fuck." He pauses as I clench around him.

"Oliver, I'm close."

"Hang on. Wait for me." He quickens the pace and deepens the angle.

I latch onto his shoulder blades, his skin hot and damp beneath my fingers, and it isn't long before almost every muscle in his body tightens. Hard as granite.

My head spins, my breath stutters, and a sharp jab of pleasure rushes up my spine. Oliver jerks and mutters something indistinct, and I cling to him, press my head into the seat cushion, and cry out his name again and again.

He collapses on top of me, though I can sense he's holding back, not all of his weight on me. His forehead presses into mine as each of us try to catch our breaths.

"You good?" His lips lightly brush me.

I smile against his mouth. "Better than good. You?"

He holds me tight and twists our bodies so we're lying on our sides, facing each other on the narrow couch.

"Incredible." His arms hug me tighter to him. "You're fucking perfect. Always knew you were."

I snicker, loving the compliment no matter how ludicrous it is. "You're darn near perfect yourself, Twist."

"What? Only near? Ouch." His cock twitches inside of me and though we've only just climaxed, both of us spent, he's semi-hard.

I like this nearness. This intimacy. We're chest to chest. He's buried deep inside of me. I'll never tire of how close we are. The closest two people can ever be.

His wandering fingers poke at my sides to get my attention, and I laugh, recalling his mock injury.

"Oh, please, Twist. Like you need me to tell you you're fucking hot. Anyone with a vagina in Winslow Grove fawns all over you. No, make that all of Montana." I exaggerate though I doubt by much.

He doesn't care for my teasing and proceeds to mercilessly tickle me. I yelp, wriggle, and writhe, and somewhere through all this jostling and fooling around, he slips from me.

The loss of him is like a thunderbolt to my heart, and I'm immediately filled with a strange melancholy. It's an irrational sensation and yet, I can't stop the crushing pall of dread dampening my spirits.

We lie there, close and silent, and slowly a sticky wetness gathers between my legs, another reminder of my loss. Attentive even in the dark and instinctively sensing what I need, Oliver springs to his feet.

His strong hand curls around my shoulder, warm and reassuring. "Stay put, let me get something. Then we'll go to the restrooms and clean up."

I roll onto my back and stare in the direction I think he is. He didn't take the flashlight, and what I'd give to see Oliver Winslow prancing around Coach Bell's office right now.

Naked.

Now more than ever, I mentally plead for the lights to miraculously flicker on, even if only for mere seconds. Alas, my prayer goes unanswered.

Then he's back and I clean up enough to make it to the locker rooms. With the beam of the flashlight to lead the way, our scattered clothes in hand, we stumble to the bathroom joking and laughing, all limbs, always touching.

At the entrance to the locker rooms, he hands me the flashlight. "I don't need it. I'll wait for you out here. Are you going to be okay in there?"

He's sweet enough to not complete the thought, leaving out the part where I'll be alone in the dark.

"I'll be fine." As I turn, he grabs my hand and stops me.

"Hey, Wren, don't get dressed." His clothes drop to our feet.

I shiver at his request, both excited and a little stressed at the idea. "What? It's chilly."

His arms engulf me, and he draws me into the heat of him. "I'll keep you warm."

Readily, I relinquish my clothes to the floor and snuggle into his embrace. He kisses me, and while it's brief and for the most part chaste, his tongue swipes at my lips before he pulls away.

"And I'm not saying we have to be naked all night, although I'm not against that." The soft vibrations of his laugh shoot straight to my still throbbing core. "But we're not done."

"Oh, really?" I challenge.

He grips my ass and squeezes. In turn, my hips push into him and his hard length prods my stomach. I want to drown in the warmth of him, eager for more of him, and with that thought, I'll do just about anything he asks of me.

"Okay." I slap his butt cheek before we separate.

Alone in the bathroom and once properly cleaned up, a twinge of panic seizes me. Unexpectedly, this time, it isn't the dark freaking me out. It's what I've done.

I had sex with Oliver.

That in itself isn't bad. Not at all. In fact, I just had the best sex of my life. I can't explain it, not even to myself, but for as long as I've known Oliver, anything I've ever felt for him has been more. More powerful, more consuming. Just more everything.

Naturally, sex would be too.

But he's leaving town.

No matter how I tried to convince him earlier to stay, he didn't budge. He's still set on leaving. And while I didn't have to say it, I live in Winslow Grove and would be here. That fact didn't seem to sway him one bit.

I'll have to act like this is no big deal. But what exactly was this? A one-night stand? I've never done that before, and since this is Oliver, it didn't feel like a one-time thing. Or maybe that's my stupid heart talking.

What am I going to do?

I'm not so sure I can pull off easy breezy.

While he's looking for a way out, leaving town, I'm looking for a way into his heart.

Chapter 9

Oliver

For a second time that night, we have sex, and then I raid the vending machine. In the dark, I count my steps back to where Wren should be and lay a stash of food in her lap.

"Thanks. I wish we had real food." The crinkling of a chip bag opening follows her lament.

"Me too." I drop beside her on the couch and want to promise to take her out for breakfast tomorrow morning but don't.

How can I assume she'll want to or have the time? She'll probably have to go home to shower and change before work, and I'm leaving town.

Nothing has changed, and everything has changed.

She leans her head on my shoulder, and the soft fabric of my flannel jacket, the one I convinced her to sleep in instead of her dress, brushes my bare arm.

We eat in silence, and once the food is done, we share the unopened bottle of water I found in one of the desk drawers.

An awkward silence settles between us for the first time tonight, and I wonder if she's thinking the same thing I am. Do we talk about what happened? What comes next or more like, what doesn't? Does she expect anything from me? And can I make promises when I've got an uphill battle where Dot's concerned?

Leaving Winslow Grove is the smart move.

But Wren's here.

We only have a few more hours left together.

My lips graze her temple. "Tell me something I don't know, something that no one knows about you."

"Like what? There's plenty you don't know."

Anxiety kicks at my gut. I want to know everything about her, but we don't have enough time.

"Anything, but it has to be something you've never told anyone. If you want, I'll go first."

She hums her approval, and I tilt my head back and tighten an arm around her. "I love that you're a librarian. You don't want to know how many times I've fantasized about you."

"What? You have?"

"Yeah. When I first saw you at the library." My heart pounds, imitating the beat of a heavy metal song. Loud and thrashing.

"When?" With that one word, it's clear how much she wants me to tell all.

"I don't know. It was early days. I was returning some books for my mom and you were helping Mr. Cooper with something on one of the computers. You didn't see me." My voice carries a wistful quality as I'm taken back to that day. "You were in a tight black skirt, what do you call it? Something like a crayon skirt? Or is it marker?"

She curls into my chest and laughs. "It's a pencil skirt."

The lilting vibration sets off a chain reaction within me. Warmth spreads from the center of my chest outward, lungs constricting, muscles coiling, and all my nerve endings tingling to life.

"Yeah. That's it. You in a pencil skirt, your fucking long legs in high heels and those black-rimmed glasses you sometimes wear..."

I lose myself in the vision of her, only prompted back to the here and now by the sound of her voice. "And?"

"And... Wren, you were fucking sexy as hell. My fantasy come to life." I bend my head and search for her mouth.

I plant kisses on her eyelashes, then the tip of her nose, before my tongue pries open her mouth. All the while, blood pounds in my ears, drowning out any doubts or worries about what comes after tonight.

Because I don't know where we go from here. If I stay, be with Wren—what I want more than anything else in this world—I might as well hand her father, her sister, and Wren over to the Malones for them to do with them as they wish.

Winslow Grove is a small town, and while the Tylers are well-respected and much loved, the Malones have money. I don't even want to think about what they might do. I can't do that to Wren and her family. I won't do that to them—I love them all too much—and if I did, that would make me one selfish bastard.

Wren digs her fingers into my scalp and pulls her mouth away, maybe sensing my mind has wandered into dark territory. "You okay?"

"More than okay."

"Tell me then, what exactly did you fantasize about?"

My lips ghost over hers. "I wanted to bend you over the long front desk of the library and haul your skirt up to bare your ass and fuck you senseless. Not giving a fuck who sees. I'd want everyone to know you're with me."

Her breath hitches and thighs rub together. I love how responsive she is and sense she's on the verge of losing control.

I'm more than happy to join her, but she straightens and clears her throat. "The glasses are fake. Just for fashion."

"I don't fucking care. You're hot as fuck in them. Now it's your turn."

"Um, I don't know."

The silence between us churns with tension, and I can't tell if it's because she's searching for something to say or if we're both very aware that our time together is quickly coming to an end.

"Come on, Wren, what have you got for me?"

"Okay. I didn't tell you the whole story about why I'm afraid of the dark." She lowers her voice and seems to shrink a little beside me, then burrows still closer.

"Okay. What's the whole story?"

"Remember how I told you I got lost in the woods?"

"Yeah. You were out there in the dark, and it took hours for Pop to find you. Even the police were looking for you, right?"

"Uh-huh. What I didn't tell you...what I haven't been able to tell anyone is I took off on my own. I was running away."

"What?"

"It's silly really. Percy and I were arguing, about what I couldn't tell you now, and Pop took her side or at least that's how I saw things. I was so mad at them, and Mom had died a little over a year before, so I felt like I had no reason to stay. She was gone, and Pop and my sister didn't want me around."

"So you took off?"

"Yeah. It was stupid, and when night fell, here I was, barely eight, in the woods alone. I didn't even have a coat or a flashlight."

"And you never told Pop?"

"Not the real reason I was out there. I didn't want him to get mad at me. I was to blame for the chief, deputy, several police officers, and volunteers being out there looking for me. Pop was just so happy to have found me. Percy too. I couldn't tell them. And now..." She shrugs. "It no longer matters. It's been so long."

"I think you could tell him, and he'd understand. You were just a kid."

She shakes her head into my neck as if she doesn't want to hear any reason.

I brush back her hair. "It's okay. I promise, I won't tell anyone."

Her chin rests on my chest. "Your secret was better."

"I wouldn't say that. Maybe more fun, but thank you for telling me yours."

I gently kiss her and we lie down on the sofa, Wren more on top of me than beside me. My body's tired, wrung out and sated, yet I don't want to sleep. I should let her sleep—she must be tired—but I want to spend every minute with her awake, catching up, being with her.

"How's work?" The question sounds exactly like what it is—chitchat, filler.

"Good. I'm running things now at the library. Mrs. Thatcher retired."

"I heard. Is it everything you hoped it would be?"

"Yes. It's more than a place with books, you know. I've introduced game nights, Sally holds yoga classes three times a week in the rec room, and I've rolled out several book clubs for different genres and ages from kids to adults."

She yawns and I squeeze her tight. "Sounds like the library's the place to be." She growls and I chuckle. "We should get some sleep."

"Okay." Her lips press to mine then she lays her head on my chest. "Night, Oliver."

"Night, Wren."

Sleep doesn't take too long, but sometime during the early hours of the morning, the power comes back on, and the glaring white light pricks at my closed eyelids.

Wren's still asleep, face hidden in the crook of my neck, and my arm, the one she's sleeping on, tingles with my slight movement. Numb.

I could get up and turn off the office light, but I don't want to move. Not only because I don't want to risk waking Wren, but more because I'm a greedy son of a bitch, and finally, I can get my fill of her.

For all those hours in the dark, it was torture to not be able to capture the subtle shifts when she reacted to something I said, when she was turned on, when she came, when she uttered my name.

In some ways, the lack of sight heightened my senses and made her every noise and every twitch more intense, more compelling, but I also craved her every expression. Not wanting to miss any bit of herself she had to give.

While she sleeps, I shift to get a more unobstructed view of her face and wish I could have this all the time, without any concern for how Dot or her family might retaliate.

At some point, I must fall asleep, only to be awakened by a banging on the gym doors.

This is followed by a faint call from the other side of the door. "Hey, anyone in there?" Another close-fisted bang. "Hello?"

Wren stirs, and I scramble to my feet. "Wait here." Rubbing at my eyes, I jog to the door.

"Coach. It's Oliver." I lightly knock back on the wood. "The door's closed." I pause, contemplating if I should mention Wren but figure he'll see for himself. "I couldn't get out."

"Oliver. You've been stuck in there all night?" Concern and astonishment lace his words.

"Yeah." I chuckle. "But it's okay. I figured someone would be back in the morning."

I glance over my shoulder at movement, and Wren's now at my side.

"Hang on, Oliver," Coach hollers. "We'll get you out."

His heavy footfalls retreat, and she springs into action, whispering as if Coach or someone else might hear us. "We better change."

Her hand sways down the length of my jacket, draping her bare body, and I look to my boxers. Nodding, I take her hand and we amble to the entrance to the locker rooms where, left from last night, our clothes lie in a heap on the floor.

We start to dress, both of us stealing glimpses at the other. I slide on my Henley and stall when my jacket falls to the floor.

Wren's snow-white skin, the flare of her hips, her pert tits, and the way her pink nipples, once exposed to the cool air, immediately harden into two sharp points completely distract me.

Fuck, my cock throbs, and pre-cum wets the cotton of my boxers. Damn.

With her bra now in one hand, she must sense me staring and snaps her fingers several times to get my attention. My body jolts and eyes drift to hers.

"Focus, Twist." She purses her lips and narrows her gaze. "Now isn't the time for any of that."

"But we could." I tilt my head to one side, gift her my most endearing smile, and grab for her gorgeous body. "I'm guessing we've got five minutes, maybe even ten before coach gets that door open." Then I lean in and whisper, my lips grazing the shell of her ear. "How about a quickie?"

She drops her bra and trembles in my arms, body pressing into my growing arousal even as she groans, "Oliver, we can't."

Despite her protest, she allows me to guide her backward until I'm pinning her to the wall. She's so close to giving in, it's there in the flickering flame in her eyes, in the way her hands clutch me like she never wants to let go. Patiently, she waits for me to go on, teeth chewing on her bottom lip, and eyes wide and willing.

"Wren." I pause more for effect than anything else. "I've got a better idea. Let me go down on you."

Slack-jawed, her lips crack a huge grin, and she slaps her hands over her face. Through her fingers, she mumbles, "Oliver, this is cruel." Then she drops her hands to her sides, cheeks a bright red and eyes sparkling. "How can I say no to that?"

I laugh, pretty sure my eyes shine with all the naughty ways I want to pleasure her.

"Exactly. You'd be surprised at how fast I can make you come." I nip at her collarbone and she moans. "Fuck, Wren, I really want to go down on you."

She shudders, on the brink of caving, but something shifts in her and suddenly, she nudges me backward by my shoulders, putting distance between us.

"Oliver, you could...I mean, we could do this later...tonight at my—"Another shift in her demeanor and she shakes her head. "Forget about it."

I don't push or encourage her line of thinking though I want to. She's suggesting more of this, more of us at her place.

Tonight.

But we can't.

That would mean I stay or postpone my departure. But I'm not so sure delaying the inevitable is the right thing to do. It'll only make things harder.

Now by our clothes, she fastens her bra and waves her hand in the general direction of my still very hard dick. She bends to snatch my jeans from the floor and the mood is gone, or so it seems.

Until in her haste, with my crotch in her eyeline, she stares at the hard ridge of my erection straining against my boxers. There's no mistaking how much I want her.

"Shit. Oliver." My name comes out sharp and curse-like, and I can't help but chuckle.

"Sorry, Tyler." I plant my hands on my hips and unabashedly thrust them out, making sure she gets a good look. "This is what you do to me."

She snaps up and whirls around to give me her back. "Oliver, get dressed. Now."

Even admonished, I laugh while throwing on the last of my clothes before slipping in front of her so I can see her face.

Both now fully clothed, she combs her fingers through her tousled hair, giving off strong "I don't have time for you" vibes, but that isn't true. I curl one hand around her hip and slide her body close to me.

She comes willingly. We're still on the same page. My flattened palm advances up her back to curl around her nape where I subtly angle her head just so.

"You look fucking fantastic." Our noses are only an inch or so apart.

"Well, you've got that freshly fucked glow." She quirks an auburn brow.

I raise the pitch of my voice and flutter my lashes. "Do I? That's the look I was going for."

She twitters into my chest. An electrifying and also comforting warmth curls around me. This right here is all I want. Her.

A clatter on the other side of the door followed by a solid heave on the wood causes us to spring apart like teenagers caught making out. Two more pushes and the door swings open.

Coach strides in. "Ah, there we go. Sorry about that Ol—" He stalls at the sight of the woman at my side. "Wren Tyler?"

"Hi Coach." She offers a little wave.

His silvery brows furrow and he scratches at his bald head. "How'd you wind up here? Does Pop know you're okay?"

She smiles sheepishly. "He doesn't know I'm here, but he isn't worried. I was dropping books off for the school library, we had to make room for new ones and—"

To save her from herself since she's talking fast and throwing a lot at him, all clear signs that she's on the verge of rambling, I cut in. "It's a long story."

"It's my fault we got locked in." She blushes.

"It's no one's fault." I take her hand and at the same time, Coach says, "If anyone's to blame, it's me. I should have had Wade dismantle the door again." He shakes his head as if chastising himself.

"Nah, Coach. It's fine. We survived." I share a knowing look with Wren.

"Yes, we're fine, but I should get going." She pulls her hand from mine. "I've got to get home, change, get to work." She strolls toward the doorway. "Thanks, Coach."

He nods and offers a tight smile, still clearly blaming himself. "All right, Wren. Be sure to call Pop and tell him you're okay. And if he wants to be upset with anyone, tell him to come see me."

She laughs. "All right, but I doubt that'll be necessary." Pausing at the door, she waits for Coach to amble toward his office before looking at me. "Bye, Twist."

Coach takes his time and isn't too far from us when he stops in the middle of the gym to busy himself with his phone. It's plain to see, he's curious and listening.

Her hair falls over one shoulder, and she licks her lips in that tentative way of hers. The way she looks at me, with tenderness and desire in her gaze and with glistening pink lips, causes a moan of longing that I've been trying to suppress to claw its way up my throat. What I'd do to kiss her once more.

Eyes flaring, she inches closer and lowers her voice. "Oliver, will I see you soon? My offer about after work tonight still stands. I make a mean chicken pot pie, and it's untouched at my place. "

There's a vulnerability to her, in her voice and body language, that I've never seen before and it nearly undoes me.

"I don't know." I drop my gaze and scratch at the scruff on my jaw.

I wish I had a better answer, but I won't lie. I've got to do the right thing.

A soft sigh escapes her lips, and the light dims in her eyes. Before I can say any more, she turns and sprints from the gym.

My heart twists and stops for a beat before kicking into hyperdrive, lungs spasming and palms suddenly clammy.

What the hell am I doing? I can't let her walk away like that.

Hands down, last night was the best of my life. If I let Wren walk away, it'll be my biggest regret. I sprint toward the gym exit, confident I can catch her.

"Oliver, wait a second." Coach's commanding voice brings me to a complete stop.

Shit, no.

I peer at him over my shoulder. "What's up, Coach?"

"I'd like a word with you." He marches toward his office and waves for me to follow.

This time is like every instance throughout high school. Coach doesn't ask, he tells. But this time, I have to protest.

"Coach, I need to talk to Wren."

"That can wait, Oliver." He spins around, eyes sharpening on me. "This can't."

Want to find out if Oliver stays and what happens with Wren?
Grab All of You, the first book in the Winslow Grove series, to see what happens
next.

USA TODAY bestselling author, S.M. West writes sexy, angsty stories about brave hearts and wild love, including, more times than not, heart-pumping twists and turns. For new releases, exclusive excerpts, giveaways, and more, sign up for her newsletter.
www.smwestauthor.com

Her Cocky Neighbor

Carrie Lomax

Chapter 1

Evan

The new owner of the apartment across the hall had moved in less than forty-eight hours ago, and already, Evan wanted her gone.

More specifically, her dog.

The woman's pet howled pathetically for hours on end, the sound echoing up and down the public hallways of the condo building for hours on end. At noon, a dog-walker brought a half-hour of peace, after which the incessant wailing resumed until evening, when the owner returned.

He liked dogs as well as the next person, but this forlorn furball was turning his home office from a sanctuary into a prison.

Evan shoved back his chair and stomped to the new neighbor's door. His finger hovered above the bell, lit a menacing shade of orange, while his eyes focused in the dim light to read the sign taped to the door.

My name is Rusty. I don't mean to be a pain. I lost my mom recently, and I get confused in my new home. I have cataracts and can't see well. My new dog-mom says I'll calm down soon once I figure things out. Thanks for your patience with me!

Below the message was a photocopied picture of a cocker spaniel with long ears and a beseeching expression.

"Dog-mom," Evan scoffed.

The name beside her mailbox read Sara Wilson, but he never saw his mysterious new neighbor. Clearly, she didn't work from home, like he did.

Some "dog mom" she was, leaving her pet home alone all day. He'd never call himself a dog dad, even if he did own one, which he didn't. Nor was he

445

looking for canine companionship—but something had to be done about Sara's furry friend.

"I can't work with you howling like this, Rust-bucket!"

He tried to manage. Evan stuffed his ears with cotton balls. He listened to music to drown out the poor animal's sad yips and lonely whines. When that didn't work, he tried using headphones.

By evening on the third day, Evan was done. He yanked the cans off his head and dug the cotton out of his ear canals, ready to explode. Not at the dog —the poor thing was clearly suffering—at its heartless, horrible owner.

Clearly, this Sara Wilson person was neglecting her pet. It was time someone intervened—and since the condo board didn't usually like to get involved with noise complaints, he was the someone.

The instant he heard the door open across the hall, he flicked the locks on his door open, determined to give Sara a piece of his mind. If it wasn't her, then her dog-walker should know when the owner was getting back.

He wasn't quick enough. Evan caught a glimpse of a short, dark-haired woman in gray jeans leading a caramel-colored canine with a stubby tail as they disappeared into the elevator.

Huh. The dog walker was hot, at least from the rearview. The impulse to yell at her instantly faded into curiosity.

Evan darted to the stairwell and ran down three flights, taking the steps two at a time. He burst out onto the sidewalk and saw them striding to the corner, in the direction of the park.

Rusty didn't appear particularly unhappy. He trotted along, sniffing trees and hydrants, barking only when a large truck rumbled past. It was the woman in jeans who held his interest. She didn't look like a dog-walker. He usually saw them in workout gear, leading packs of varying-sized canines around the park.

"Hey!"

She crossed the street without hearing him, or possibly ignoring him. Evan jaywalked to catch up, nearly getting run over by a cab for his efforts. He finally got her attention when the spaniel stopped to do some business against a fire hydrant. Classic.

Up close, he saw the woman was prettier than he'd dared to hope. The clear plastic frames of her glasses couldn't conceal her large hazel eyes and thick lashes. Her white blouse was unbuttoned just far enough to show a hint of cleavage. Evan smoothed his rumpled Henley self-consciously. He did not need to dress for work. Ever.

"Excuse me, did you just move into the building?" he demanded.

"Is it about the dog?" she asked, frowning.

"Yeah. Can you tell his owner to keep it down? I work from home, and it's hard to concentrate with him howling. I feel bad for this little guy. No real dog-mom would leave her pet to suffer alone all day."

There was a beat of startled silence, as if Evan had missed something obvious. Beneath the big eyes were a straight nose dotted with freckles. Her lush mouth was unsmiling. If anything, it turned downward at the corners before forming the words, "Sure. I'll let the owner know."

"Thanks." Rusty came over to sniff his leg. Evan bent to stroke his head. The animal's eyes were strangely milky. "Nice to meet ya, furball."

She tugged the leash. "Come on, Rusty."

"Hey, can I ask you something?"

"Yes?" she said with expectant, wary patience.

"Can I get your number? My friend has a dog he might need walked," Evan lied, loath to end the conversation. The city was full of pretty girls, but he didn't like dating apps and preferred to meet women the old-school way. This one made his pulse quicken. He probably should've waited until he saw her around again, but considering how hard she'd been to find this time, he didn't want to pass up the opportunity.

"My number?" Her mouth curved upward in a bemused grin. "Are you for real?"

"Yeah. It's a bitchin' fries or some weird name like that?"

"You mean a Bichon Frise. Looks like an Ewok?"

"Right. Exactly like an Ewok. What's your name?"

"Um. I don't know if should tell you. Do you live in the building?"

"I'm across the hall from the new owner. Name's Evan Santander." He started to offer his hand, but she stared at him instead of shaking it, so he ruffled his hair and tried to play it off like he'd meant to do that.

"Nice to meet you. I'm Sara. I'll have to check my dog-walking schedule." Mirth glimmered in her pretty eyes. "I'll let you know if there's an opening."

Crap. Way to make an impression on his hot new neighbor.

Chapter 2

Sara

The caveman across the hall was awfully cute, for a guy who'd insulted her by way of greeting. She was half-inclined to give him her number just in case he really did have a friend with a Bichon Frise. Somehow, she doubted it.

Regardless of whether Evan Santander wanted a dog-walker or a date, it was clear that her current arrangement wasn't working. Sara sighed. She'd hoped to have a little more time to find a better solution. It had been a dicey two months since she'd taken in Rusty after her grandmother died. Her old apartment didn't permit pets, and it was a rental anyway—she couldn't pretend the dog was "only visiting" indefinitely. Sneaking him in and out of the building in a stroller worked for a few weeks, but it wasn't a permanent solution. A move had been inevitable. The inheritance she'd received made it possible to buy an apartment, and Sara lucked into a warehouse conversion that allowed dogs.

She was not giving up Rusty for anything or anyone. He was her Nana's baby, and there was no one else in the family who could take him in. On the other hand, she couldn't give up her job to keep him company, and with his cataracts, she couldn't send him to day care, either. He was too scared, and spent the day cowering instead of playing.

They made it to the park, where Rusty inspected the underbelly of a picnic table and rolled in a patch of grass. With company, he was fine. In her old building, Sara had been able to rely on the neighbor to watch him part of the day.

Which gave her an idea. Evan must have some form of employment that allowed him to work from home, if he was around to hear her dog whining complaint.

"Come on, Rusty," she said sweetly. His ears pricked, as much as they could. "Let's go home."

They didn't meet Evan in the hallway. She peered curiously at his door, from which emanated the sound of rock and roll. Apparently, he didn't work in the evenings, either. She liked the spaciousness and charm of the warehouse conversion, but the soundproofing was subpar at best.

If she could get Rusty adapted to his new surroundings before her neighbors grabbed pitchforks and drove her out of the building, life would be downright sweet. Settled. Appropriately adult, something she'd never thought she'd be able to achieve living in an expensive city.

A note was taped to her door. Sara scanned it. Her shoulders sagged. There had been more complaints, and the board was now involved, idiosyncratic capitalization and all.

Your pet was approved conditionally. The Board has received numerous complaints about Rusty, the Cocker Spaniel residing in 4C. Please make alternate arrangements for your dog during daytime hours, or we may revoke approval if he continues to be a nuisance.

Well, fuck.

"Great," she grumbled. She couldn't exactly afford to move again.

Inside her apartment, she poured kibble into Rusty's bowl and changed his water before staring at her refrigerator willing dinner to magically appear. It didn't—but a possible solution, did.

She might give Evan Santander her number, after all.

When he answered the door, Sara was pleased to discover he'd undergone a transformation from scruffy nerd to hipster hottie. His dark hair was damp from a shower, he wore fresh jeans without holes, and a black T-shirt clung to his pecs. The man cleaned up nicely.

"Hi," she said. "Am I interrupting?"

"No, not at all." He leaned against the jamb. "Listen, I'm sorry I insulted you earlier. I didn't know you were his owner."

Sara let a little smile play on her lips. She was counting on a bit of guilt to get him to go along with her plan.

"It's alright. I know he's been noisy. I appreciate that you took the time to chase me down in person instead of calling in anonymous complaints to the board." She licked her lips, wondering how best to present her idea. "You said you work from home, right?"

"Yeah."

"What do you do?"

"I'm an illustrator."

Sara blinked. "You can make a living doing that?"

He laughed. A dimple popped in his left cheek. She was a sucker for guys with nice eyes and broad shoulders and dimples. Add in a couple of tattoos and she'd give him *all* her phone numbers. Work, mobile, email, *all* the contacts. Heck, she'd even give him the office fax machine number if he had a tattoo.

She peered around him into the apartment. His was larger than hers was, almost cavernous, with a stairway leading to a loft and a large drafting table, tilted at an angle, near the huge wall of windows. An upside-down bike sat in the center of the living room, propped on its handlebars and seat. Sara bit back a smile. Classic.

"It's possible. I got a lucky break early on, got an agent, worked in comics for a time. I still get residuals from that project." He shrugged. "Means I don't need a day job. You want to come in?"

"If I'm not intruding." Across the hall, Rusty whined. Sara winced. Even with the door closed, she could see how Rusty's whining was a distraction. "I'll keep it short."

"Does this mean you'll give me your number?" he asked with a wink.

"Maybe." She grinned and accepted the beer he offered her. "Why do you need it? For real, I mean."

Evan gave her an adorable little smirk, like a little boy who'd been caught fibbing.

"So I can call you. When your dog feels lonely," he answered with a sly grin.

Sara bit the inside of her cheek. A tattoo peeked out from the short sleeves of his T-shirt. Check that box on her personal checklist of hot-guy attributes. His eyes were deep brown with a lighter center that reminded her of crackling fires and crisp autumn leaves. Sara shivered. Evan was dreamy. But did he like dogs enough to be boyfriend material?

If not, that was an automatic disqualifier. Rusty was family.

"Sure," she said agreeably, then inhaled. "You can have my number if you're willing to try letting Rusty hang out with you during the day."

Evan gave her a look that said, *No fucking way.*

Sloan's stomach sank. Not only had her gambit failed, she'd pissed off her cute new neighbor in the process.

Damn.

Chapter 3

Evan

He didn't see that coming. Evan's new neighbor was full of surprises.

"Rusty likes you," Sara said in a rush, clearly wanting him to say yes.

"I've never had a dog. I don't know how to take care of one."

"It's easy. I'll show you. Rusty just wants to know someone's there for him. He's blind, so if he doesn't hear someone moving around, he thinks he's alone and gets scared."

"I work, though."

"I know. I promise he doesn't do anything but sleep all day as long as he isn't alone. He lived with my grandmother until a couple of months ago, so he's used to having someone around all the time."

"What happened to your grandma?"

"She died."

Well, fuck. That was the second time he'd tasted shoe leather by putting his foot in his mouth around her.

"Maybe he could spend the day with you tomorrow? As an experiment?"

Sara tipped her head, pleading. She was still wearing the gray jeans which hugged her gorgeous ass. They'd look amazing crumpled in a pile next to his bed.

"I'll even throw in my work number," she wheedled.

"Yeah," he found himself saying. "That might work."

She beamed. "Wonderful. I'll drop him off with you tomorrow before I leave. I'll get everything together and leave detailed instructions. I'll even pay you." A bark from across the hall made her wince. "I'm so sorry. And thanks. It's been great to meet you."

"Hey."

Sara glanced back over her shoulder.

"You don't have to pay me. Rusty and I are gonna be great friends. Right?"

Evan's first clue he was in over his head came at the ungodly hour of eight-fifteen the next morning. Who was awake at that time of day? The best part of being self-employed was never having to get out of bed until mid-morning.

"Hold on a sec." Evan splashed water on his face and pulled on yesterday's jeans. He answered the door shirtless. Sara peered up at him sideways, a chunk of her thick, dark hair falling over her eyes and getting tangled in her glasses.

"Hi," Sara said as she stood up slowly. Evan's bare skin pulsed with embarrassed pride as her gaze lingered on his chest, checking out his tattoos.

"Hi, yourself. I guess we should've discussed details last night?"

"Yes, although I need to get to the office. How about I have you over for dinner tonight, and we can discuss how things go today?"

He shot Rusty a stern glare. Things had better go well today, because Evan was not passing up dinner with Sara. The animal began sniffing Evan's couch. "Is he going to...?"

"Oh! Over here, Rusty. Atta boy. Wow. This place is huge. Were you one of the original buyers?" Sara scanned the room, barely keeping an eye on the dog until he lifted his leg. She intervened just in time to prevent the dog from spraying his entertainment center.

"Yeah, about ten years ago." Buying this apartment had been the decisive investment that let him continue working as an illustrator.

"Oh, wow. You even have a balcony. I'm so jealous!" Sara's wide eyes went even wider. It made her even cuter, a little naughty counterpoint to her smart, playful sexiness.

The dog scampered out onto the glass-walled balcony and whizzed on a potted plant. Fortunately, it had been dead for months.

"Oops. Sorry. I took him outside already, but he can't see so he thinks he's where it's okay to do that. He won't pee in your house, I promise."

Evan squinted at the contraption strapped around the critter's chest. "How does this work?"

"You clip the leash onto the metal ring on his back. Be careful when you're walking him—Rusty loves to chase squirrels."

"I thought he was blind."

"Mostly. His nose is in perfect working order, though. Once he gets wind of a critter, he pulls like a tow truck. Whatever you do, don't let go. The duck pond in the park is especially infested with fuzzy-tailed vermin." Sara's expression darkened.

Evan bit his lip to keep from laughing. She really didn't like squirrels.

Sara handed him the leash. Evan swallowed as the light scent of honey and soap from her skin touched his nose. "Here you go. Bags to pick up the poop are here."

"What? You never said anything about picking up dog shit, Sara." Evan's complaint softened as she placed the palm of her small hand on his arm and stood on tiptoe to kiss his cheek.

"Thanks for helping us out, Evan."

He had the resistance of a wet paper towel. "Okay. Have a good day at work, honey. I'm sure we'll be fine. I'll call you if I have questions."

Sara waved goodbye to the dog and kissed him on the lips. Evan grunted, bringing his arm around her waist, his pulse racing. Moving fast. That was fine by him. He watched her butt all the way to the elevator, then heard a scuffle from his kitchen.

"No! Rusty, damn it."

Trash was spilled all over his floor. The dog ran guiltily over to his couch and hopped onto it, scarfing a hard pizza crust so fast Evan was worried he'd choke. Grumpily, Evan pulled the masticated crust out of Rusty's mouth, cleaned up the mess, shoved the garbage can under the sink to keep the dog out of it, and got to work.

By nine-thirty that morning—the time when he was usually rolling out of bed—Evan was cranking on his latest passion project, a kid's book in comic form.

True to Sara's word, Rusty slept on his couch all morning without a single whine. Unless you included the funny way he kicked and huffed when he was dreaming—probably about squirrels. The sound was quiet, though, not plaintive and carrying.

At noon, he clipped the leash on and took Rusty out for his midday stroll.

"Your dog is so cute!" a blonde woman in running shorts squealed, crouching to pet Rusty. His stumpy tail wagged.

Hell, if he'd known a canine companion was the key to meeting women without technical intervention, Evan would have gotten one years ago. Not that he needed dating assistance now. Not after that kiss. They'd fallen into it so easily. He couldn't wait until Sara got done with work and they could take things further.

Her brunette friend held out a manicured hand. "May we pet him?"

"Sure. He's a cocker spaniel." Evan informed them, as if he knew shit about breeds.

"I see that. Oh, look at you, you're so sweet!" squealed Brunette. With a final pat, the two happy joggers grinned their thanks and went on their way.

"Hell of a superpower, doggo," Evan mumbled, an idea for a new comic-book hero and villain taking form in his mind. The heroine would look like Sara, with big eyes and a mask. She'd wear a black bustier, bondage style, and towering high heels. She'd be so fucking hot...

"Hey! You can't leave that." A stranger shouted and pointed at Rusty, who was squatting to make a deposit on the ground.

"Sorry. Forgot the bags." Evan tried to slink away.

"There's a dispenser right over there." The man's eyes narrowed.

Evan forgot all about his imagined Sexy Badass Sara character as he yanked out a thick plastic bag and did as he was told. The charm of dog-sitting had worn off. "C'mon, mutt. I gotta get back to work."

Rusty dawdled on the return trip, sniffing every trash can and lamp post on the way home. It took twice as long to walk back as it should have. By the time he half-dragged, half-led the animal into his apartment, he was sweaty and irritable. Creativity: destroyed. Evan was sold on Sara—just not her pet.

He wondered what she did for a living. The card she gave him with her number read *Sara Wilson, MLIS, Archives & Preservation.*

A librarian?

Chapter 4

Sara

No pink message slips were on her desk when she arrived at her office —itself a win. She'd been ignoring calls from the board since moving in.

She updated a finding aid with new entries, helped a researcher locate images related to historic houses in the neighborhood, and tried not to fall asleep during the mandatory budget meeting at eleven. It ended early, and she spent the rest of the afternoon working on reference questions that had come in. For the first time in months, she didn't worry about Rusty.

Sara practically skipped down the sidewalk to her home.

Maybe Evan worked shirtless. Sara hoped so.

He's your neighbor, and he's doing you a favor. Not your fuck buddy.

Yet. Things were off to a good start, though.

To her profound disappointment, Evan was wearing a clean T-shirt and jeans when he let Sara into his apartment that evening. She bit back a grin. He'd made an effort again, and she liked to think it was for her.

"How'd it go with Rusty?" she asked anxiously. She needed this arrangement to work.

"Um. Okay." Evan ran his hand through his hair until it stood up on end. "He slept with his head on my foot all afternoon. Now it's all pins and needles."

Sara's laugh echoed from the high ceiling. There was a scuffling sound, and Rusty appeared from a stairway to the lofted area above the kitchen, where she assumed his bedroom was. She patted her knees. The old dog sat and put his front paws in her hands.

"Hey, boy. Sounds as if you've made a friend." She cast Evan a sly grin. "You know you can move your foot, right, Evan? Once he's asleep, Rusty doesn't care what he's napping on."

"Yeah, but he was cute there."

Sara's heart melted. With a final pat, she rose. "Can I pay you with dinner?"

"No. But I'd love some company if you wanted to stay here."

"Yeah? Are you asking me out?" Sara's face warmed. She shrugged out of the blazer she'd chosen to look extra professional for the budget meeting that morning. Her place wasn't exactly ready for prime time. There were still boxes piled in her living room.

"No. I'm asking you in."

"I wouldn't say no to that. Give me a few minutes to change?"

He moved closer. Sara couldn't help but notice the breadth of his chest and the sinewy cords on his forearms. How did a guy who drew cartoons for a living get arms like that, anyway?

Yesterday, she'd thought he was a random awkward nerd trying to hit on her. She'd been right about the flirting, wrong about the first impression.

Gently, he removed her glasses and said, "If you want to take off your clothes, you can do it right here."

She giggled, her face burning. "Smooth, Santander."

He laughed and leaned in. "Did I mention I have a thing for sexy librarians?" His hands went immediately to her waist and ran up the arc of her back. Warm. Smooth. Gentle. The glide of his hands matched the rhythm of their tongues as they explored one another.

A whine and a cold nose against her calf interrupted them.

"Not. Now. Rusty," Sara muttered through gritted teeth.

"He's just lonely, aren't ya, boy?"

Evan broke their kiss to pat the dog's head.

After all I've done for you, you're cock-blocking me? Sara glared at her pet.

"Hang on. I'm just going to put him in my apartment for a little bit. He can spend twenty minutes alone, right, big boy?"

Rusty whined when she clipped on the lead. What a traitor, gazing up at Evan with adoration in his milky eyes as if their neighbor across the hall had been the one to take him in, who fought to give him a home, who filled his food dish twice a day. Sara couldn't help but smile. Maybe Rusty still hadn't forgiven her for making him go to the vet for an eye evaluation. Or maybe he could sense, even though he couldn't see well, that Evan was a sexy sweetheart.

"If you think we're only going to need twenty minutes, Sara, you're out of your mind."

He caged her against the door and kissed her hard, his thumb brushing the underside of her breast.

"Hold that thought," she said, tugging a recalcitrant Rusty out into the hallway. "I'll be two minutes. Not even." She fumbled to get her key into the lock. Inside her own apartment, Sara bent to unclip his harness, dropped a scoop of kibble into his dish, and quickly checked her appearance in the bathroom mirror. No point in adding makeup; it was just going to get messed up anyway.

She toed off her heels and kicked the shoes under the entryway chair, then hustled across the hall, barefoot. Nervously, she knocked on Evan's door.

For several agonizing seconds, she heard nothing. No music. No movement. Had he changed his mind?

A click and the grate of metal rocked Sara back on her heels.

"Hi."

"Miss me?" she asked, pushing forward without waiting for an invitation. He caught her around the waist, palming her ass. Sara breathed him in, enjoying the rasp of his five o'clock shadow on her tender skin.

"I was counting the seconds. For the record, you took more than two minutes."

She laughed. "Pedant."

"Ooh, the sexy librarian uses fifty-cent words. Hot." He grinned in between kisses.

"With inflation, certain words are up to seventy-five cents," she deadpanned. Evan scooped her up and set her ass on his kitchen counter, going straight for the buttons on her blouse. She hadn't taken the time to change, so she was still dressed in her work clothes, a white shirt and navy pants.

"Keep it up. I have a whole jar of those dollar coins the Metro gives you as change. I'd spend them all on your fancy words." He parted the placket of her shirt, baring her breasts. At least her bra was lacy, if plain in color. "Let's get you out of that boob prison."

Sara laughed. He was so easy. A little ridiculous, teasing and fun. The last thing she'd been looking for was a hookup. It occurred to her that sleeping with her neighbor a day after she'd met him was potentially setting herself up for trouble down the line, but Evan got her bra unhooked with one expert flick of his wrist and then he was sucking one stiff nipple into his hot mouth, and she decided that was a problem for Future Sara to solve.

She tugged the back of his shirt up, until he broke contact long enough to take it off. Then they were skin to hot, slick skin, chest to chest when she scooted down from the counter and worked one hand between them to find the hard ridge of his erection.

Nice, was her last coherent thought. She was wet enough to let him take her right there.

"Shall we relocate, or do you have a thing for doing this in kitchens?" he asked.

"Never know when a sharp object will come in handy."

"Should I be afraid?"

"Very afraid." She grinned up at him with her arms twined around his neck. "I'm kidding. Where's your bedroom?"

And then, just as things were getting good, a distinct yip followed by a pathetic whine came from the hallway.

Chapter 5

Evan

He's only a sad little dog, Evan reminded himself, trying to tamp down the burst of annoyance. He knew they wouldn't have long. But Rusty was going to have to learn how to be alone for more than a few minutes at a time, for everyone's sanity.

Right now, with Sara naked from the waist up, willing in his arms, he did not want to think about a needy little furball. Even if Rusty was cute and was sad over losing his owner recently, and confused because he'd been moved twice and could hardly see.

He understood. Evan got it. He really did. But. *Come on, Rusty, buck up; you're not being abandoned! We're just having sex.*

In theory.

"Where's your bedroom?" Sara asked.

"You're going to ignore him?"

She made a face. "Make me sound cruel, why don't you. He's had company all day long. He'll survive a few minutes."

"Might be more than a few minutes," Evan said, scooping her up.

"I sure as heck hope so."

Sara wrapped her legs around his waist. She wasn't very heavy. Round in the right places, but slight enough for him to carry to the stairs. There, he set her down to let her climb up to the loft, ogling her ass greedily the whole way. The plain navy trousers didn't hug her hips as lovingly as the gray jeans did yesterday. No matter. What was inside counted, not the packaging.

At the top, Sara covered her bare breasts with crossed arms.

"Oh, no, I can still hear him." She frowned.

"His voice really carries," Evan agreed, flinging himself across the bed and fiddling with the stereo. Miles Davis came on just loud enough to drown out Rusty's yips of despair. Whatever Sara thought of his taste in music, she didn't protest.

He tugged her hand, bringing her down onto the bed, half on top of him. Her hair fell in a curtain of bronze and umber, shadows sharpening her delicate features.

"I'm really glad you moved across the hall," he said, stroking the curve of her cheek with his thumb.

"Aww." She bent to kiss him, soft lips pressing along his jaw. A flick of her tongue along his throat. Sara kept working down, licking his nipple, squeezing his rock-hard cock through his jeans. Down to his belly button. Unfastening his pants. Evan knew he should push her away, that this was too much, too soon, and unlikely to last. He didn't. Couldn't. His blood was thick in his veins and her lips felt so good as she licked up the underside of his cock and sucked him into her mouth.

He glanced down. Only the scrap of her underpants shielded her from his hungry gaze. He couldn't reach her from this angle, and with her working his cock with her tongue like that, Evan doubted he was coordinated enough to give a commensurate performance. Instead, he reached down, nudged the hem wide, and ran the tip of his finger over the wet nest he found there. Tracing the shape of her.

Sara made a feminine little grunt and shifted wider, giving him better access. He found the source of her dampness and marveled at her tight passage. Then stroked upward to the sensitive bud at the peak of her sex. If he angled just so, he could hit both places at once...

She gasped and sat back, back arched, breasts peaked with tight beads, stroking him haphazardly as she came. Gorgeous, with her lips parted and a flush turning her skin rosy.

"I need you inside me right now," she demanded in a breathless growl.

"The words every man longs to hear."

Evan chuckled when she swatted him. He rolled her to her back but didn't give her what she wanted. Not yet. He didn't bother with preliminaries, simply shouldered his way between her thighs so she was laid out like his personal feast. Her sex glistened with need. He bent his head and started with a lick up her center. Sara fisted the bedcovers.

Good.

He kept going. Her knees fell open, then tensed and came up again. A crescendo of moans and music echoed in his ears as he laid into her with the flat of his tongue. Sara grabbed his hair and bucked against his face. Satisfied, he crawled up her body on his elbows. She dragged him in for a kiss.

"Now I can be inside you."

She managed a brief nod. Evan couldn't think, couldn't stop. He simply fitted himself to her and bucked forward—

Bliss.

Sara moaned and sank her teeth into his shoulder. He tried to be gentle. His size meant he couldn't carelessly pound into her without hurting her. But Sara seemed to like it on the rough side, so gradually he let go, chasing his pleasure, feeling hers rise around him. Feeling the rhythmic clenching of her around him before giving in and diving over the edge, taking what he needed.

Surfacing, breathless and sweaty, breathing in the scent of her skin. Sara's hands ran up and down his back. Soothing. Evan let her take his weight. Slowly, her eyes drooped and then closed. Her breathing turned rhythmic. With a kiss to her temple, he rolled off her, pulled her into his arms, and dozed off.

Sara

Rusty wasn't happy.

Sara rubbed her eyes and sat up, disoriented. There had been music. What happened to the music? Where was she? Why was her dog crying—

Evan.

He'd pulled on his briefs and was sitting cross-legged at the end of the bed. Seeing her stir, he bent forward to kiss her on the lips, then sat back.

"I made a drawing for you." He held up a large sheet of paper against his chest. "You can keep it."

"This is beautiful."

She'd never had a man draw her a picture before. While she usually rolled her eyes at the sexy librarian thing, she loved the way he'd depicted her: confident, in a tight skirt with a white blouse and sky-high heels. Like a pin-up girl.

Whatever part of her that was still clinging to the idea that this was a mistake, that it would backfire, and nothing good came of diving into sex with the neighbor she hardly knew.

But it was Rusty's bark that had her leaping out of bed and reaching for her pants.

"Damn it!" Sara pulled on her clothes haphazardly, grabbing his shirt when she couldn't find her own. "I forgot about the dog. Thanks for watching him today. He likes you." She kissed his cheek. "He's not the only one."

"So, we're doing this again tomorrow?"

"I'm counting on it!" she called over her shoulder as she raced down the stairs.

"Good, because you're not getting away with stealing my favorite T-shirt.

Sara chuckled, a gleeful grin on her face. "Watch me."

"See you in the morning," Evan called after her.

Chapter 6

Sara

"Archives and special collections, Sara speaking."

"Ms. Wilson?"

"Yes."

"This is the building manager at the condo building. The board had an emergency meeting last night. Your pet isn't working out. I'm sorry, but your conditional approval has been revoked. You have 48 hours to find it a new home."

Sara burst into tears. She wasn't a crier, but this was Rusty and he was her last living connection to her beloved grandmother, and she adored the troublesome furball. She also didn't want to move out of her new home. She hadn't even fully unpacked yet.

I guess that'll save on moving fees, she thought despondently. It shouldn't be so difficult to find a place to live with a dog, but in their city, single-family homes were out of her price range. Maybe, if she'd stretched, she could have gotten a townhouse with a small yard, but she'd have been house-poor for the next twenty years. Besides, that ship had sailed. She'd made the best choice she could at the time. Now there was no way she could afford to sell her condo and buy a new home.

There was no help for it. She was going to have to sublet the apartment, if the board would approve it, and find a rental that accepted dogs. Really accepted them, not just on the condition that they were perfectly silent at all times.

And things had been going so well with Evan. Sara sighed.

When she stopped across the hall that evening, Evan took one look at her face and pulled her into his arms. Even Rusty seemed worried, his stumpy tail wagging uncertainly.

"The condo board says I have to find a new home for him."

"For real? They'll make you do that?"

"Apparently so." She sniffled. "I thought he would adjust, but he hasn't. Maybe I was overly optimistic. He's old. He can't see well."

"We can't be with him 24/7."

"I know." They still had to grocery shop and run errands or go to doctor's appointments. Places you couldn't take a dog with you. Even two people couldn't be with Rusty at all times.

"It's not your fault. You were a great dog-sitter." Kissing him, she added, "And an even better...um, fuck buddy doesn't seem to cover it."

He recoiled as though she'd slapped him.

"We're not fuck buddies," he insisted. But they'd never defined what they were. They'd been living in limbo since they got together, and now the stick had lowered so far that they couldn't back-bend under it anymore.

Now she'd inadvertently offended him. As distraught as she was, Sara tried to be an adult about the situation.

"Whatever we are, I have to find a new place to live. I've decided to rent out my apartment until Rusty passes. I'll be back in maybe five or six years."

"Five or six *years*?" He gaped at her. "There's got to be a better solution. Besides, I'm not sure you can do that until you've lived in the building for a year, under the condo bylaws."

"Then what *can* I do? Go into foreclosure? Be homeless? I'm at my wits' end, Evan."

"Give me a day to think of something," he said. "I don't want to see either of you go."

Sara patted Rusty's head.

"We don't really have a choice."

Sara tried to bargain for time, to no avail.

You were given 48 hours, Miss Wilson, came the curt reply. The building manager was apologetic. The board was firm. They wanted Rusty gone. Now.

She read the condo documents on subletting only to discover that Evan was right. Renting out her apartment wasn't permitted until she'd lived there for a year. She was going to lose either the precious inheritance her grandmother had bequeathed her, or her grandmother's dog. Her dog, now. Sara had become very attached to Rusty in the months since she'd become his owner.

But where would they live? She couldn't afford to pay for two apartments.

On the second day of Rusty's eviction notice, with no solutions and fading hope, Sara's phone beeped with a message from Evan. He was the one bright spot in this whole mess. Although she'd been too afraid to leave Rusty alone since the notice came through—she'd called out sick from work just to stay with Rusty and explore her options—he hadn't stopped checking in. He let her leave Rusty with him whenever she needed to step out, too.

Sara flat-out didn't want to move. She loved her new life, except for this one hiccup.

When Evan texted, **Can you come over? There's someone I want you to meet**, Sara let herself feel the tiniest crumb of hope.

I'm bringing Rusty.

Yeah, he texted back. **I expected you to.**

"Come on, little guy." Sara picked him up and tucked him under one arm. It was a lot of dog to carry, but the distance wasn't far.

When Evan let them in, Rusty began kicking and scrambling to get down. She deposited him on the floor and bussed a hello kiss on Evan's cheek. Growling came from the next room.

"What's going on?" she asked.

"I got Rusty a friend."

Sara stared.

"Come and see." He took her hand with a nervous grin. In the open living room was a small black-and-white dog with fluffy fur and bright eyes. "This is Flora. She's a Boston Terrier-bichon fries mix."

Sara howled with laughter. "Bichon Frise."

"Yeah, that." Evan gave her the sexiest half-grin ever leveled at a woman. Still ridiculous. Teasing.

"You did not get a dog just to keep mine company."

Flora looked at her askance while Rusty sniffed her butt.

"Maybe. It might not work. If it doesn't, I'll adopt him. I'm home most of the day. If they make me get rid of him, you can adopt him back. We'll play football with the furball, metaphorically speaking, until the board gives in. He's not so bad. Is he, Flora?"

Flora's tail wagged. She took her turn investigating Rusty's hindquarters.

Sara wrapped her arms around Evan's middle. "I love you. I have never met anyone like you."

Evan held her close and stroked her back. "I wasn't going to let you get away as easily as you came into my life. I didn't know I was looking for you, Sara, but the instant I found you, I knew you were the one for me."

Within minutes, the two dogs were curled up on the couch together, like old friends.

Evan and Sara were married later that year. The board never received a complaint about Rusty again.

About the Author

Carrie Lomax is the bestselling author of historical & contemporary romance. She also writes angsty new adult fantasy romance under the pen name Joline Pearce. Get a free historical romance prequel when you subscribe to her newsletter.
Follow Carrie on TikTok, Instagram, Facebook, or Bookbub. Check her GoodReads page for book reviews.

One Halloween Night

DL Gallie

Prologue

It's Halloween and once again, I'm dressed as a witch. Witch rhymes with bitch, therefore, it's perfect for me and this year, I'm bitchy witchy.

Being a witch has been my go-to costume for as long as I can remember...it was also the costume I was wearing when my life changed. I was on a path of self-destruction, and the night I switched it up and became a slutty, sexy bitchy witchy, it could have ended so badly for me but my knight—literally—in zombie scrubs, swooped in and saved me.

It was the night I fell for *him*, and this is the start of our story.

Chapter 1

Lily

"Gah, Mom, you are such a, gah...you really do live up to your bitchy moniker."

"Do not sass me, young lady," Mom snaps, resting her hands on her hips, meaning business.

"Mom, I'm eighteen," I angrily retort. "I'm an adult now." Slamming my clutch onto the table by the door in anger, I glare at my Mom.

"And when you act like one, I'll treat you like one. Now, go and change from that slutty, skanky costume. You will not be leaving this house looking like a whore."

"I hate you," I snarl and send daggers her way.

Lately, she and I fight like cats and dogs; guess that's bound to happen when we're two peas in a pod. Not only do I have my mom's fiery temperament, but we look so much alike that we can pass as sisters and not mother and daughter.

Turning on my heel, I storm back to my bedroom, slamming the door behind me in anger. Taking a deep breath, I lean my head back against the wood and close my eyes, I can hear Mom's heffalump footsteps storming down the hallway. Coming toward me for round two.

With my eyes still closed, I count to ten to try and calm myself down when through the door, I hear Dad talking to Mom. "Kitten, you need to calm down," he tries to placate her; he's always playing peacemaker between us.

"Fuck you, Core," Mom snaps at him.

And in three. Two. One. "Watch your mouth, Kitten." Daddy hates when

Mom swears and, each and every time, he'll tell her to watch her mouth and, each and every time, she'll tell him where to go. They are total opposites but at the same time, they are freakin' perfect for each other.

"Not now with the 'watch your mouth, Kitten' bullshit. Your daughter is dressing like a skank."

"Our daughter is not a skank, besides it's Halloween. Let her have some fun before she runs off to college next year."

They quietly talk among themselves. I can't hear what they're saying, but I know if I don't open this door soon, they'll be making out before long. You'd think with the number of times they get it on, I'd have a gazillion brothers and sisters, but there was a complication when Mom had me and she was unable to conceive after that. I often wonder if the reason we butt heads so much is because she hates me for not allowing her to have more kids.

"When did our baby grow up, Core?" Mom sniffles and hearing her upset, upsets me. "Why can't she keep dressing as a cute witch? Don't get me wrong, she looks amazing as a sexy witch, but my baby can't dress like that."

"Isn't it meant to be *me* worrying about our daughter's virtue?"

Swinging the door open, I startle them. "My virtue is fine Mom, Dad. You raised me better than that. Besides, I know how to kick ass just like you, Dad. You taught this grasshopper well." I press my hands together and bow down to Father Master.

"See," he says to Mom, "she'll be fine. Plus I know how to cover up a murder, so it's all good."

"I'd pay to see that," Mom responds through a laugh. "Strait laced Agent Corey Cox covering up the murder of his daughter's boyfriend."

"I'd do anything to protect my girls, anything."

"Yeah, you would." I roll my eyes, and Mom swoons. Her eyes glaze over, all dreamy like, and I know as soon as I walk out this door, they'll be getting it on—*gag*.

"And on that note, this sexy witch is heading out." I kiss each of them on the cheek and walk down the hallway, adding an extra sway to my hips to piss Mom off some more. Before I reach the living room, I look over my shoulder. "Don't wait up," I singsong and throw a wink at them.

I hear Dad growl, "Down, Kitten" and then smooches...and that's my cue to get out of here.

Grabbing my clutch from where I placed it when Mom attacked me earlier, I head outside. When I look up, I smile as I see my best friend, Madison MacDonald, waiting in the driveway in her dad's bright white BMW convertible.

"Duuuuude, you look totally fuckable," Mads says in way of a hello, as I climb into the front passenger seat.

"Says the totally fuckable one."

Leaning over, I place a kiss on her cheek. "Now, let's go get our drink on,"—thank you, fake ID—"dance up a storm, and then find someone who is as equally as fuckable as us to keep us warm. Allllll. Night. Long."

"You had me at let's get our drink on."

Madison turns up the stereo and as she backs out of the driveway, we sing along to "Poker Face" by Lady Gaga. Little did I know, my night wasn't going to go quite as planned.

Chapter 2

Cj

"Make sure you keep an eye on Pepper, I'm entrusting you with her safety tonight," Mom tells me as she messes with my hair, getting it just perfect to complete my zombie doctor look.

"Mom, Pepper is three years older than me, I think she needs to be watching out for young impressionable me."

"You are far from young and impressionable, dear son of mine."

I look at her with a 'really' expression. I'm what you'd call a chic nerd—black-rimmed glasses, facial scruff, dark brown hair, and athletic. I can thank my dad for my build; he and I run each morning he's home. But seriously, if anyone's to get into trouble tonight, it will be me. The nerd in me ALWAYS finds the bullies, and the bullies love to hulk out on my inner nerd...that is until I turn around and whip their ass—thanks, Dad.

"Ready to rock, Baby Bro?" my sister Pepper asks. She's dressed as a Woodstock hippie. Pepper is obsessed with everything related to Woodstock, with her favourite artist of all time being Jimi Hendrix.

"Sis, you look awesome," I tell her, taking in the multi-coloured pink, green, purple, and orange dress in a psychedelic print, with matching headscarf, and a peace sign medallion. She finishes off her outfit with pink plastic knee-high boots and her blonde locks hang down her back in waves.

"As do you," she looks to Mom, "and, Mom, you did an amazing job on his makeup."

"Excuse me," I interrupt her. "I did my makeup. Mom just played with my hair...like she always does."

"Such a mommy's boy," she teases me.

"Says daddy's girl," I throw back at her.

"You fucking bet I am."

"Language, missy," Dad scolds her as he walks in the front door.

"Looking good, CJ, and Pepper, you look beautiful."

"Thanks, Daddy," she coos like the total suck-up she is.

"Thanks, Daddy," I mimic. She sticks out her tongue at me. "And on that note, let's head out."

"Where exactly are you two off to tonight?"

"Chili's. They're having a Halloween Spectacular tonight."

"Sounds fun, but remember b—"

"Behave and look out for one another," Pepper and I singsong in unison.

"And no drinking, Clay," Mom adds. "You're not old enough to drink in public."

"Yes, Mom," I deadpan. I had already decided to be DD tonight anyway so she doesn't need to worry about that.

Linking arms with my sister, we walk down to her Mini. "You be all right to drive this home since you're the DD?"

Nodding my head, I climb into the front passenger seat. Pepper climbs in and when she starts the car "Foxy Lady" by Jimi Hendrix blares through the speakers.

"Wow, how can you concentrate and drive with the music blaring like that?"

"I don't," she snaps. "I had a mini concert when I got home earlier."

"You are such a nerd."

"Says the nerd."

Sticking out my tongue at her, I roll my eyes. "Shut up and drive."

"Ohh, I love that song." She picks up her phone and scrolls through Spotify and a few seconds later, "Shut Up and Drive" by Rhianna begins playing.

Sitting back in my seat, I stare out the window as my crazy sister weaves in and out of traffic through Chicago. Finally, she pulls into the parking lot at Chili's and when I look to the car next to us, I smile. Lily Cox and her friend, Madison, are here too.

I've had a crush on Lily for as long as I can remember, but I'm me and she's, well, she's Lily-fucking-Cox, the girl of my dreams who is sooooo far out of my league that I don't stand a chance in hell with her.

"Lily!" Pepper shouts, but she can't hear since the windows are up. She quickly climbs out and shouts Lily's name again.

"Pepper!" Lily screeches, and the two of them embrace as I climb out and join them.

"You look amazing," Lily says to my sister.

"As do you. I see you're still a witch but this year you're rocking the sexy, bitchy witchy, I love it."

"You know it." She links arms with my sister and Madison, and they start walking in. She doesn't acknowledge me and that hurts, but then she looks over her shoulder, and our gazes meet. "Looking good, Knight."

She winks and then turns her attention back to Pepper and Madison. I stand on the curb and watch the three of them walk, no strut, into Chili's. All eyes are on the three of them when we enter the bar. They are the center of everyone's attention and who can blame them, they all look hot, and yes, I realize I just referred to my sister as hot, but it's not in the skeezy creep, incestuous way, it's in a blanket 'she looks pretty' way.

The three of them make a beeline for the bar but are stopped by Bryson-freaking-Anderson. "You look totally fuckable tonight, Cox."

I watch as Lily slows down and pulls away from Pepper and Madison, they continue onto the bar and she, cocks her hip to the side and stares up at the jock. "I always look fuckable, Bryson." She steps in closer and runs the tip of her finger down his exposed chest on his toga. "Play your cards right and—"

"The fuck you looking at, nerd boy?" he snarls at me as I'm walking past.

Lily looks over her shoulder. "If you're referring to the sexy nerd, zombie boy behind me, then you need to cool your jets. Knight and I are just friends."

I went from a high from her referring to me as a sexy nerd zombie to the lowest of lows at being referred to as 'just her friend'. Those two words cut me deep. Not wanting to get kicked in the guts anymore, I walk over to Pepper and Madison.

"He's so fucking hot," Madison swoons and I roll my eyes. This night has turned to shit and we've only been here for five minutes—fucking Halloween.

Chapter 3

Lily

"**Y**ou are mine tonight, Cox!" Bryson shouts as I walk backward to my friends. Throwing him a wink, I turn around just as he yells out, "Mine." *Slutty witch for the win,* I think to myself as I shake my ass at him and make my way over to Pepper and Mads.

Looking up, I almost trip midstep. Standing next to my girls is CJ and in the dim lighting of the bar, he looks fucking hot. Sure, he looked good outside, but now that I have the chance to check him out, wow. *When did he get hot?* It's like he grew into those glasses all of a sudden...and I wouldn't mind getting a peek at what's under the scrubs. I wonder if he's as ripped as his dad? Dr. Knight is fucking hot for an old guy.

When I reach Pepper and Mads, they're both gushing over Bryson and his hotness and how it's not fair that I've snagged him, again.

"Oh my fucking God," Mads coos, "Bryson is staking his claim...in front of everyone."

"Can you blame him?" I cheekily say. "I look fucking amazing."

From behind I hear someone say, "You always look amazing," but when I turn my head, I only see CJ and a creepy as fuck skeleton. Skeleton guy is eye-fucking me and not in a good way. He gives me the heebie-jeebies, my skin breaking out in goosebumps at his stare. I shudder at the lewdness in his expression and turn back to the girls. The hairs on the back of my neck are prickling and when I look back, creepy guy and CJ are both gone, as is the prickly feeling.

Shaking it off, I look to my friends and grin. I love Halloween. For one night a year, you get to dress up and let your hair down. Dress and do things; things that on any other day, you wouldn't.

"Lil, you really look hot tonight. I'd kill to have legs like yours," Mads says, handing me a lemon drop. Sure, I'm underage but that's what fake IDs are for, just don't tell my dad or Uncle Dominic. Besides, I'm sure they did stuff like this when they were my age.

"Umm, hello, have you seen your pins? Yours go on and on and on until we reach your sexy AF Kylie hot pants."

"She's right," Pepper agrees, "But she's also right when it comes to you, tonight, Lily. If I batted for the same team, I'd totally do you."

"It's the killer Cox genes," I nonchalantly reply, taking a sip of my cocktail.

From the corner of my eye, I see Bryson is still staring intently at me and I grin. I know he's waiting for me but patience is a virtue, so I ignore him. Spinning around, I lean against the bar and with my eyes on his, I seductively wrap my lips around the straw in my drink and sway to the beat of the music.

Pepper's head nods toward him. "You totally have that boy under a spell," she teases.

If only you knew, I think to myself. "I am a witch after all." Finishing my drink, I place it down on the bar. "Now, watch me work my magic." Throwing her a wink, I saunter over to Bryson and pull him out onto the dance floor just as "Don't Cha" by The Pussy Cat Dolls begins to play.

Wrapping my arms around his neck, he slides his around my waist. Our bodies grinding against one another. The song changes to "Touch It!!" by Monifa and we really bump and grind now. Spinning around, I rub my ass against his crotch and slide my hand up into his hair. Leaning down, he whispers into my ear, "You ready for this, baby girl?"

Looking over my shoulder, I stare into his bluer than blue eyes, and wink. "Baby, I was born for this." Turning around to face him, I slide my hand around to his ass, grip it in my palm, and squeeze. He stares at me, shocked. "Shall we?"

He nods and swallows deeply. He grabs my hand off his ass, laces our fingers together, and we weave through the guests, heading toward the back of Chili's. Pushing open the door to the outdoor area, which is closed for tonight, we step out into the cool and frigid night air.

"Shit, it's cold," I voice, as the door slams shut behind us.

"I can warm you up," a deep voice says from behind me. Spinning around I come face-to-face with Hook aka Tyson. "But I'd much rather warm him up."

Tyson steps around me and pulls Bryson into his arms. He kisses the ever-loving shit out of him. Bryson grips his cheeks and kisses him back.

"Fuck, that's hot," I breathlessly say and I continue to watch the two of them tongue wrestle one another. They break their hello-I-wanna-fuck-you-now kiss and stare intently at one another. Those two have a love like no other and I hate that they hide it, but I'm happy I can play interference, so they can be together.

Who knew I was such a softie when it comes to love? I'll admit, the first time Bryson knocked me back, I was shocked. No on turns me down but then, I found him with Tyson and it all made sense. I can't remember exactly how our arrangement came about but I'm happy to play along.

It seems like they've forgotten that I'm still here as they begin to kiss again, grinding up on one another. It's like I'm watching a live action porno. "Sooooo, I'm gonna slip out and leave you two to warm each other up."

"Shit," Bryson says, pulling himself away from Tyson. "I totally forgot you were here."

"So I saw, but it's okay, I love me some live-action gay porn, but it's fucking freezing out here so I'm going to go hide in the car. Come get me when you two are finished and then we can head back in."

"You really are the best," he says, placing a kiss on my cheek.

"I know," I reply. "And remember, boys, if it's not on, it's not on." Saluting them both, I sneak out the back gate and when I round the corner toward the parking lot, I'm grabbed and shoved into the building face-first.

My face is pressed against the brick wall and whoever has me is squeezing my upper arms tightly, pressing their erection into my ass.

My heart begins to race.

My eyes well with tears and for the first time ever, I wish I'd listened to Mom. I'm going to be raped because I dressed like a slut.

It's all my fault.

He circles himself on me, grinding his length into my ass. He breathes heavily into my ear, grunting as he slides his hand around and cups my breast. "You like that, slut?" he snarls.

Gripping my hair, he pulls my head back and licks up my neck. Closing my eyes tightly, I shudder in disgust but he takes it as a pleasurable move. "Yeah, you love that, don't you, whore?"

"Please," I beg and again, he takes it as I'm into this. "Don't do this," I cry.

He pauses and spins me around, slamming me back into the wall, the wind knocked out of me from the force. He leans in and presses his lips to mine. I clamp them closed, not allowing him access. He presses his tongue against the seam of my mouth but I refuse to open for him.

Pulling back, he glares at me. Reaching over, he places his hand around my neck and begins to squeeze. Anger reflects back at me and then I realize, it's the creepy skeleton guy from before.

"You," I whisper.

"Yeah, slut, it's me."

"Please don't do this," I cry. "I won't tell anyone, just let me go. Please."

"I love it when whores beg."

"Please don't do this," I cry again, but he ignores me. He leans back in to kiss me again. Closing my eyes, I wait but it never comes because someone snarls, "Get your filthy fucking hands off her."

Both our heads snap in the voice's direction.

They argue and then, in the blink of an eye, the pressure on my neck is gone. Skeleton guy is on the ground and someone in a white coat is straddling him, then there's a crack. My eyes widen when I finally realize who my rescuer is because he was the last person I expected to save me.

Chapter 4

Cj

Watching the woman you're lusting over grind against a douchehole on the dance floor is the last thing I want to do, but my eyes are locked on Lily as she rubs herself up against him. *I wish it was me,* I think to myself but that's never going to happen. Girls like Lily don't fall for guys like me.

"What's up, Baby Bro?" Pepper asks, throwing her arm around me. "You look like your puppy just died."

"Nothing," I say with a sigh, but my uber observant sister doesn't believe me, hell, I don't even believe me. She follows my line of sight and she too sighs.

"Dude, just go for it."

"No fucking way," I snarl at her. "Girls like Lily don't fall for guys like me."

"Never say never. Look at Lil's mom and dad. They are complete opposites but the two of them go together like corn and carrots."

"The saying is peas and carrots," I correct her.

"Yeah, but peas are gross so corn and carrots it is."

"Veggies aside, it's not gonna happen, Sis. Look at him and then look at me, we are nothing alike."

"Dude, you need to give yourself more credit. Yes, he has more muscles than you and can probably bench press you twice over BUUUUT he's not you, therefore, straight up, you win." She pauses. "Just think about it. Now, I'm going to hook up with Thor over there so I do—"

"I thought you were more of an Aquaman-type of girl."

"I'll take whoever gets the clit buzzing."

"Eeeeew," I protest. "I do NOT need to know that about my sister."

"You love me." She nonchalantly shrugs. "Now, I'm going to go ride Thor's hammer, therefore I don't need a ride home." She looks to where Lily and Bryson are walking toward the back of Chili's and nods toward them. "Use tonight to make your move, I think you might be surprised."

She kisses my cheek and walks over to Thor, and three-point-five seconds later, the two of them are making out. It won't be long before...nope, not gonna finish that sentence. I wish I could be confident like her but that's just not me.

Sighing, I head to the bathroom. After taking a piss, I decide to head outside for some fresh air. Everyone is starting to pair off and I don't feel like being the only loser without someone to suck face with.

Stepping in the back courtyard, I'm thankful to be alone and then I hear a noise coming from around the side. My curiosity spikes and I walk toward the sound. Peeking around the corner, I see Bryson from the back, he has someone —Lily—pressed against the wall and they're kissing.

"Fuck, I love your hand on my dick," he groans and then I hear them kissing again. His head drops back and I duck back out of sight. Leaning against the wall, I close my eyes and listen to them get it on. Wishing that I could be getting it on with Lily...or anyone, for that matter. At this rate, I'll be going off to college a virgin. How freaking sad is that? Eighteen years old and still a virgin.

Feeling like shit, I decide to head home and since Pepper has other arrangements now, I don't need to worry about her. Walking back inside, I make my way through the bar, toward the exit.

Heading to the parking lot, I dig in my pocket for the key to Pepper's car when from somewhere in the lot, I hear someone snarl, "I love it when whores beg."

Wow, someone has a dirty mouth and then I hear a pained, "Please. Don't do this." And I realize, someone's in trouble. A force overtakes my body and I walk farther into the lot, spotting them a few feet down. I sneak closer and that's when I realize, it's Lily.

Lily is being assaulted. Knowing it's her, my fuse is lit and I storm toward them. "Get your filthy fucking hands off her," I snarl.

Both of them turn their heads toward me. He keeps his hand around her throat and I see red. "Fuck off, nerd boy, you can have the whore when I'm done."

Hearing him refer to Lil like that causes something inside of me to snap. I launch myself at him, taking him, and myself, by surprise. The dick and I fall to the pavement and Lily screams.

Landing on my back with a thud, the wind is knocked out of me, but seeing the fear on Lily's face snaps something inside of me. Jumping up, I push the douche back down and straddle him. I rear my hand back, and slam my fist into his face, my knuckles colliding with his nose. A crunch echoes through the air and I growl, "Ouch." Wincing in pain, I shake my hand back and forth, trying to ease the pain. I've never hit someone before and it really fucking hurts. "Fuck me," I groan in pain.

"Did you just swear, CJ Knight?" Lily asks, breaking the silence, well silence, except for the douche holding his nose and groaning.

Looking up, I see her still standing, pressed against the wall.

Jumping to my feet, I walk over to her, the pain forgotten as I focus on Lily. "Are you okay?" I ask and lift my hand to cup her cheek in my palm.

Staring into her eyes, I wait for her answer. Fear festers within my body, fear that the asshole hurt her worse than what I can see right now.

"I'm...I'm okay," she whispers.

She lifts her hand and covers mine. A spark jolts between us when our skin touches. She gently runs her fingers over my knuckles, I wince because it's the hand I used to hit the guy.

We stand here, staring at one another.

Everything around us fades away. I'm about to lean in and kiss her when the asshole who attacked her growls, "You fucking hit me."

"And you had your filthy hands on a woman who is waaaaay out of your league."

"And you think you have a chance?" he throws back at me.

"I...I.."

"Yeah, that's what I thought. You can have the whore; no snatch is worth this."

He stands up and I turn, covering Lily with my body, he'll have to go through me if he wants to get her again. Without uttering anything else, he spins on his heel and walks away. Leaving Lily and me alone.

Turning back to her, she's starting to shake; she's going into shock. I want to wrap her in my arms and protect her, but I don't want to scare her any more than she already is. Thankful that I have Pepper's keys, I ask, "Do you want to get out of here?"

Chapter 5

Lily

"Do you want to get out of here?"

Staring at CJ, I try and process all that just happened but I know that yes, I do want to get out of here, and I need to get out of here now. Words elude me so I just nod my head.

CJ nods back at me. He gently takes my hand in his and leads me over to his sister's mini. As soon as his hand touches mine, I immediately feel safe, knowing that I'm in good hands. He clicks the button on the fob. The car beeps and unlocks, causing me to jump. My nerves are frayed right now, causing me to be jumpy and on edge.

"I've got you," he reassures me. He opens the front passenger door and I climb in without saying a word.

Collapsing into the seat, I stare out the windshield. I'm in shock right now. CJ climbs in next to me and starts the car. "Lil, I need you to put your seat belt on." Turning my head, I stare at him but I don't move to put my belt on. "Do you want me to?"

Mutely, I nod.

CJ leans across me and I take in a deep breath. All I can smell is him and a calmness washes over me. He clicks the belt in and I keep staring at him.

"Are you okay?" he asks me.

Looking at him, I shrug and nod, then shake my head. "I...I don't know." I stammer because I really don't know how I feel right now.

"I'll take you home."

"No," I shout, shaking my head. I cover his hand with mine. "Not home. I...

I can't go home just yet, I need to...to... I don't know what I need." The first tear falls. "I just..."

He reaches over and wipes the tear away. He stares at me and I feel at ease, less afraid now. "I know the perfect place." He utters before putting the car in reverse and taking me away from Chili's, and *him*.

The trip passes by in a blur and when the car stops, I notice we're at the Knights' house. Turning my head, I look quizzically at him.

"Our treehouse is the perfect hideout."

Nodding, I smile because he's right, it's the perfect hideout. I spent a lot of my childhood years up in that treehouse; it's the best freakin' treehouse in the history of treehouses. CJ's dad, Preston, built it and his mom, Cress, decked it out on the inside. Even though we're all grown-up now, we still hang out in there when it's called for and this is definitely one of those moments.

CJ and I exit the car, quietly closing the doors, and we sneak around the side of the house. Tiptoeing across the lawn, we head toward the treehouse. CJ tugs on my hand and whispers, "I'll be up in a sec." Before I can protest, he heads toward the house. Watching him go inside, I stand here and think over everything that happened tonight and I can say, it did not go as planned. Well, the helping Bryson part did, but afterward, that was NOT on the agenda for tonight...or ever.

Not wanting to think about it, I turn around and climb up into the sanctuary of the treehouse. It's been years since I've been up here and when I finally make it to the platform, I sit on my knees and look inside. I drift back to a time when this was the ultimate kids' treehouse. In the corner was Pepper's little kitchen, by the window was CJ's Nerf guns and other boy toys, and in the middle was a small table and three chairs. We all used to fight over who'd get to sit at the table—it was always us girls who did—but every time, the boys would argue for a spot at the table.

Now, instead of kid things and toys, it's more of a teenagers' retreat— blankets and pillows are along one wall and a little shelf to the left houses comic books and still the Nerf guns. Cress has worked her mom magic again and turned this into the ultimate teenagers retreat. It really is a magical oasis here now, and the perfect location to hide out and process the events of tonight.

Standing up on the deck, I duck my head and walk inside. Dropping to my butt, I shake my head as I look around. "This is..." I drift off as I have no words.

"It's pretty awesome up here now, hey?" CJ says, startling me. "Shit, I didn't mean to scare you."

"You didn't scare me," I refute. "I just wasn't expecting you to come back so quickly and I jumped a little."

"The definition of scared," he teases as he enters the treehouse and drops down next to me. He hands me a bottle of water.

"Thanks," I tell him as I accept it. Our fingers brush and a spark ignites between us. That's never happened before and I don't know what to make of it.

Twisting off the cap, I take a sip. The cool liquid slides down my throat and for the first time since the incident with skeleton guy, I feel calm and less jumpy. But then the memories of him pressing me against the wall and his breath on my face causes my eyes to well with tears.

"Come here," CJ softly says, and without any hesitation, or thought, I shuffle over to him and fall into his open arms. Resting my head on his chest, I let all the tears and apprehension out. Now that the floodgates have opened, I can't stop the tears.

He wraps his arms around me, pulling me sideways onto this lap. The sincerity in his hug makes me cry harder. "Shhhh," he coos, rubbing my back in that soothing way. "You're safe now. I've got you and I won't let anyone hurt you." He places a kiss on my head. My body tingles. It's an odd feeling to have when you're falling apart, but if I'm honest, I like it. I really really like this feeling. I'm safe and cherished in his embrace, like nothing can hurt me.

Holding on to him, the tears subside but I make no move to hop off his lap. Letting out a sigh, I open my eyes and realize that music is playing. Lifting my head, I look out the window and concentrate on the song. It's "Not in Love" by Olin and the Moon.

Smiling, I turn my gaze to CJ and notice that he's watching me intently. As I stare up into his hazel eyes, that tingly feeling washes over me, and again I shiver.

"Are you cold?" he asks me.

Shaking my head, "No," I whisper. Lifting my hand, I cup his cheek. "Thank you, CJ."

His face scrunches up in confusion. "For what?"

"For saving me. For holding me. For everything tonight."

"I'd do anything to protect you, Lil."

"You only have to because your mom and my mom are frenemies."

"Frenemies is a mild way of putting it, but that's not why." My mom and his mom, Cress, have a love/hate relationship. Apparently it's better than it was, but you can still cut the tension between the two of them. From memory, it was Cress who gave my mom her 'Bitchy Baylor' nickname.

"Then why?"

"Because, it's you, Lil. You are..."

"Are what?" I ask, my heart racing and not in the scared way like earlier this evening. It's racing in that romantic movie kind of way when the hero is about to make his move, and even though I've never thought of CJ in this way before, I'm seeing him in a whole new and exciting, yet scary, light. Because it's Clay Knight, I've known him my whole life. I've never seen him as anything other than Mom's frenemy's son but right now, he's everything.

"You are perfect, Lily Cox. Absolutely perfect."

My eyes widen, he just voiced what I was thinking but in a different and more poetically perfect way.

Leaning forward, I press my lips to his. Never have I wanted to kiss anyone more in my life. As soon as my lips press against his, everything around me fades away. He's frozen and I start to think that I've made a mistake, but he covers my hand still cupping his cheek and finally, he kisses me back.

Breaking the kiss, I lean my forehead against his, and breathe him in, taking a few seconds to process what just happened. He places his finger under my chin and lifts my gaze back to his. "I want to kiss you again," he whispers.

My lips lift in a smile and I nod. "I want you to kiss me again too," I reply.

We lean forward and begin kissing again. With our lips fused, I wriggle around and straddle his thighs. Wrapping my arms around his neck, I deepen the kiss. Our tongues slip and slide in an erotic dance. Who knew CJ could kiss like this?

This is the best moment of my life and for the first time in forever, I feel free and happy.

Chapter 6

Cj

Holy fuck, Lily Cox is kissing me and I don't want to ever stop. I've imagined this moment many times over the years, but I never thought it would happen. And I can say, kissing Lil real life is sooooooo much better than imaginary kissing Lil ever was.

When she straddles me and presses herself against me, deepening the kiss and our connection, my cock likes it. He likes it very much and stands to attention.

Lil pushes on my chest, breaking our kiss. Both of us are breathing heavy. We stare intently at one another. My cock twitches again and presses into her stomach. Her eyes widen and she swallows deeply. Dropping her gaze between us, she stares down at my protruding dick. Since my costume consisted of scrubs and a lab coat, it's not doing anything to hide my hard-on. I'm not one to brag but my cock is of a decent size and going by Lily's wide-eyed expression right now, she's impressed...or in shock...or scared...or all of the above.

"Holy shit, Knight, who knew you were packing that all this time?" she says, licking her lips as she continues to stare at my cock.

A smirk forms on my face but I quickly school it, no one likes a show-off.

She lifts her gaze back to mine, her eyes hooded with lust. Her cheeks pink with arousal. Her nipples, poking through the black material of her dress. She bites her bottom lip and I want to bite it too. Lifting my hand, with the pad of my thumb, I pull her lip free. Running my thumb over the skin.

Our eyes are locked on one another. The air around us thick with desire.

Want. Need and everything in between those emotions. I'm confused because a few hours ago, she was nearly raped and now...now she wants me. "Make me forget, CJ."

"I'll do anything for you, Lil. Anything."

We silently stare at one another. The air around us beginning to crackle again. She leans into me and whispers, "Make love to me, CJ."

Blinking rapidly, I stare at the woman of my dreams and process her words. She wants me. Lily Cox wants *me*, Clay Knight. "Please, CJ, make me forget his touch. Just make me forget." She nuzzles along my jawline and up to my ear. She bites the lobe and it causes my body to come alive. Pressing her lips to mine, we begin to kiss slowly. My hand lifts and I cup her breast, she moans into the kiss, indicating that she wants this.

Pulling back, I stare at her. She's flushed and ohh so beautiful. "Are you sure, Lil?"

She nods, "Yes, I'm sure." She cups my cheek in her palm, her touch gentle yet firm. "Please make love to me, CJ. Replace his touch with yours."

My heart stops once again at those words. My throat dries up. I've never had sex before, I know Lil has and I'm scared I'll mess up but at the same time, I want to help her. "It's...it's my first time," I croakily mumble.

She leans back, rests on her heels and stares at me. Lifting her hand, she cups my cheek and whispers two words that shock the ever-loving shit out of me. "Mine too."

Blinking rapidly, I continue to stare at her. My mouth opens and closes. "But..."

"Things aren't always as they seem, CJ. I'm not the whore everyone thinks I am."

Shaking my head, I cover her hand on my cheek. "I don't think that at all, I just thought...well, I presumed that you weren't like me."

"Surprise," she teases, "I'm just like you, CJ, and...and I want my first time to be with you. This," she waves her hand around the treehouse, "and you, are perfect in every way." She swallows deeply. "Please, CJ, pop my cherry."

A laugh breaks free. "Trust you to make light of this."

"It's only something scary if we make it. Sure, it's been a scary night but I feel safe and cherished with you. Therefore, it's perfect."

"We can pop each other's cherry."

"Yep." She lets the 'p' pop.

Leaning forward, I press my lips to hers for a quick and searing kiss.

"Is that a yes?" she asks, her voice wavering.

Nodding my head, I confirm, "Yes, it's a yes."

Threading my fingers into her hair, I pull her to me and press my lips against hers. With our lips locked, I lower her to her back and cover her body with mine. Thankfully, Pepper and I transformed this into a comfy retreat. I don't want my first time to be on a sand-covered wooden floor with an Easy-Bake Oven and G.I. Joes scattered around me.

Lily slides her hands around to my back and down to my ass; she squeezes my cheeks and I smile into our kiss. Shimmying myself between her legs, she opens and allows me in. She lifts her hips, pressing herself into my growing erection.

A groan forms in the back of my throat and a similar sound slips through her lips.

She runs her hands under my scrub top and when her skin touches mine, every inch of me comes alive. She slides her hands up and around, lifting my shirt up. Pushing myself up, I rip it over my head one-handed.

"That's hot," she murmurs, her eyes locked on mine.

"What's hot?" I question, confused as all I did was remove my shirt.

"When guys grab their shirt and remove it like you just did."

"I'll keep that in mind. Now how about you lose yours too?"

She licks her bottom lip. "Can you help me?"

Nodding, she smiles and offers me her hand. Pulling her into a sitting position, she begins undoing the bow on her top. With nimble fingers she unlaces her corset. Her hands are shaking; it's nice to know I'm not the only nervous one.

Her top falls open, exposing her lace-covered breasts. My hand lifts on its own and I trace my fingertip along the top of her bra, before cupping her plump mound in my hand and gently squeezing. Goosebumps appear on her skin.

Lifting my gaze from her chest, I lock on to her eyes. We stare at one another as she slides her top off, and then she lowers the zipper on her skirt and awkwardly removes it. Leaving her before me in just her panties and bra.

"Fuck, Lil, you're gorgeous."

"You swore again."

"You bring out a different side of me." Her face falters and I don't like it. I quickly shake my head. "Lil, it's not a bad thing. You bring out a side I didn't know existed and tonight, right now, I feel like I can take on the world and YOU did that."

"You bring out a different side of me too."

"How so?" She shrugs. "Tell me, I won't judge you."

"You must be the only person who doesn't judge me. Most people look at me and see a skanky, slutty bitch, even my mom thinks that."

"She doesn't think that."

"She said as much tonight," she spits at me.

"Well, Baylor and everyone are all wrong. I see a beautiful, confident, amazing woman."

"You're just saying that because I'm half naked."

"Nope, I mean it. Lil, you're amazing. I wish you could see what I see."

She cups my cheek, and I'm starting to really like her doing that. "You are something else, Clay Knight."

We stare at one another. She licks her bottom lip and it's the sexiest action ever. My cock agrees because it hardens and pokes out the top of my scrub pants. She notices and drops her gaze.

Biting her bottom lip, she reaches her hand out and slides underneath the waistband of my pants and grips my cock. "Fuck, your dick is huge." She pushes my pants and briefs down, freeing my dick. Standing up, I remove my pants and shove them to the side, leaving me naked before her.

She licks her lips. She's at dick height so she leans forward and swipes her tongue over the head. I hiss, it's the most amazing sensation ever. That is, until she sucks me into her mouth. "Liiiiiil," I moan in delight. She bobs her head up and down, my dick sliding in and out of her mouth. This is so much better than my hand.

Looking down, I watch Lily suck on my cock. It's mesmerizing watching her swallow me. "Lil, I'm gonna come if you keep that up."

My cock pops out of her mouth. "I don't mind."

"But I do, I want my first time with you to be in you."

She nods in understanding. She stands up and slides her panties down her legs. Reaching behind her back, she unclasps her bra, dropping it to the pile of clothes next to us.

Staring at her, my eyes roam over her body. "You are exquisite, Lily Cox."

Dropping to my knees, I press a kiss to her stomach and slide my hand up her leg. She trembles at my touch. She widens her stance, allowing me to slip my hand between her thighs. With my eyes locked on her, I run my finger between her lips, it easily slides between her folds.

"Claaaay," she moans when I push my finger inside her. I normally hate my name but hearing Lily breathlessly whisper it, I don't mind at all. "I'm...I'm gonna come," she pants. Her walls clench around my finger and she lets out a guttural sound that has my cock hardening further.

She collapses into me. Pulling my finger from between her lips, I wrap my arm around her thighs, holding her up. Her breathing is hurried. She runs her fingers through my hair. "Holy shit," she pants, "that was amazing. It's sooooo much better when someone else does it."

A laugh escapes me. "I thought the same thing. Your mouth on me was so much better than my hand. Imagine what the real thing is going to be like?"

She drops to her knees before me.

We stare at one another.

My heart is racing.

This is the moment. This is the moment I become a man and she becomes a woman.

Lily leans over and grabs her clutch, she removes a condom and hands it to me. Thank God she had sense to think about this, my brain is not focused on that at all. I'm focused on the naked angel before me.

While I sheath my cock, Lily lies down, her eyes locked on my hands as I slide the rubber down my shaft. Lowering myself, I hover over her. Sliding between her legs, I stare at her and can't believe that I'm about to lose my virginity. With Lily Cox. Who is also going to lose her V card.

This moment could not be more perfect. Gently easing my hips forward, I press the head of my shaft between her lips and gently push in.

"Earned It" by The Weekend comes on and the music, combined with the moment, is perfect. The song is slow. Sensual.

Perfect song.

Perfect girl.

Perfect moment.

Everything is just perfect.

Chapter 7

Lily

He gently eases himself inside me. It hurts but at the same time, it's the most amazing feeling ever. Closing my eyes, I wince in pain as he pushes further in. I'd heard it will hurt the first time, but I have to say, it isn't as horrendous as I thought. But that could be because CJ is taking his time.

"Are you okay?" he asks, his voice laced with fear.

Nodding my head, I open my eyes. "Yeah, it just hurts." He tries to pull out but I shake my head. "No, just push in."

"Are you sure?"

"Yes, just push your cock inside of me."

He looks uneasy but does as I ask. He thrusts his hips forward and pushes his monster cock all the way in. My eyes widen at the intrusion and pain but just as quickly, it subsides and is replaced with an amazing euphoric feeling.

We fall into a steady thrusting rhythm.

Back and forth.

In and out.

Over and over.

I've never been fuller and never have I felt pleasure like this before.

"Claaaaaaaaaaay," I moan, adding a million extra a's to his name as I shatter around his cock. Never have I orgasmed that quickly, but then again, never has a dick been in my va-jay-jay before either.

My eruption sets him off and he grunts through his release.

"Sorry, I was so quick," he breathlessly pants.

"I was quick too." I pause. "But it was perfect." I whisper the last word.

"Yep," he agrees.

Rolling off, he collapses to the floor next to me. Removing the condom, he throws it to the side and slides his arm under his head, staring up at the tree-house roof that I now notice is littered with tiny little fairy lights.

We lie here naked. Not saying a word, but no words are needed because words would ruin what just happened between us. And as if the world is mocking us, "4 Minutes" by Madonna and JT begins to play.

We both laugh at the song playing. A force pulls me toward him and I burrow into his side. There's a chill in the air but his body warmth is all I need. Resting my hand on his abs, I throw my leg over his thigh. He wraps his arm around me and we snuggle. The song changes to a Coldplay one. We lie in each other's arms, neither of us makes a move to re-dress. We just enjoy the moment.

"Lil," he says, breaking the silence.

"Yeah," I reply, lifting my head to look up at him.

"Are you really okay?"

"I am now...thanks to you." I place a kiss on his chest.

"Thanks to me? How?"

"You saved me and made me forget." Shit! That came out like I just used him to forget how the night started. Rolling so I'm half on top of him, I look down into this gorgeous eyes. "What I'm trying to say, is that I'm perfectly perfect. You make me feel safe and I cannot thank you enough for what you did for me tonight. Both rescuing me and popping my cherry."

"You popped mine too...and I'm glad we popped each other's. Maybe..."

"Maybe what?" I push him.

He slides his arm from under his head and brushes a loose strand of hair behind my ear. "Maybe we can do it again?"

"Have I created a sex monster?" I tease with a laugh but at the same time, I roll farther on top of him and straddle his thighs. Staring down at him, a feeling of awe washes over me. Leaning forward, I press my lips to his chest. Kissing and nibbling my way up, I cover his mouth with mine and kiss him deeply.

Sliding my hand between us, I grip his shaft and it immediately starts to grow in my hand. He moans into my mouth, "Liiiil." The extra five i's in my name is awesome to hear.

Breaking the connection, I push myself up into a sitting position and shuffle forward. Letting go of his shaft, I lift up onto my knees and line his cock up at my entrance. With our eyes locked on one another, I lower myself down his erection.

Last time it hurt when he pushed in, but this time, this time it's amazing from the get-go. Rocking my hips back and forth, the pleasure within builds much quicker from this angle. And this time, I can feel it everywhere, from head to toe.

The first time was great but this, this time around it's so much more.

CJ sits up and wraps his arms around me. Wrapping my legs around his waist, we thrust back and forth. He presses his face into my breasts, my head drops back and I mewl like a cat in heat. The stubble on his face scratches my skin, but I love it. Holding on to him tighter, I push him into the girls and he doesn't disappoint.

He cups one breast and squeezes, the sensation sending a jolt directly between my thighs. I'm finally experiencing those sensations that are described in the novels I read and I can unequivocally say, it's a million times better in the flesh than imagining them.

When he twists my nipple, I cry out in ecstasy. He lowers his head and sucks the taut peak into his mouth. The combination of the sucking and his cock sliding in and out of me, is the most amazing feeling in the world.

"Suck harder," I pant like a hussy.

He does that, and more. He gently bites the tip, and holy hell, that feels incredible. "Again," I unabashedly moan.

He sucks harder and then kisses up my neck, nibbling along my jawline and up to my mouth. Our lips meet. Our tongues slip and slide in rhythm to his cock thrusting back and forth.

"I'm close," I whimper.

"Me too," he pants.

"Together," he demands.

"Now," he growls and somehow, we climax at the same time. Moaning each other's name as we tumble over the orgasmic cliff edge. My first sex-derived orgasm was out of this world but the second time around, it was so much more.

My whole body is buzzing and I never want this feeling to end.

Our bodies still and we gaze at one another. Panting heavily.

"Wow," he whispers.

Words elude me right now, but I manage to nod my head. Lifting off his lap, I lie down next to him and then I sit bolt upright.

"What's wrong?" he asks, his voice high pitched with worry.

"We didn't use protection." We look between my legs and see his seed dribbling out of me.

"Shit," he curses. "Are you on the pill?"

Nodding, I swallow. "Yeah, I am. I'll um, ahh, get the morning after thingy later today."

"I'm so sorry, Lil."

"It's okay, it takes two to tango. We just got caught up in the moment."

"In a fantastic moment."

Looking up at him, I smile and nod. "Yeah, it was pretty great. One of the best, actually."

He lies back down and stretches out his arm and nods to it. "Lie with me."

Not needing him to ask twice, I lie down and snuggle into his side. Throwing my leg over him, I scrunch my face up.

"What's with the face scrunch?"

"I think I just dribbled cum all over you."

"It'll wash off," he nonchalantly replies.

Tracing my finger over his chest, I process the events of tonight and can't believe how it turned out. I went from the lowest of lows to the highest of highs and now, in the light of day, I don't know what to do next.

Even though everything tonight, after we arrived at the treehouse, has been perfect, I'm scared about what's going to happen next between us. I don't know how to proceed....or even what I want.

On one hand, Clay is perfect boyfriend material and I know Mom and Dad would accept him, but I'm not the relationship type. Well, I don't think I am. I've never been in one before, what if I'm a shit girlfriend? What if CJ and I ruin the relationship between our families? I mean, our moms already love to hate one another, what if us being an "us" ruins that further? My mom can be an unreasonable bitch at times—hello, her nickname is Bitchy Baylor—but I can see his mom, Cress, being #TeamUs. However, I think the biggest red flag is that we're total opposites. He's a nerd, albeit a sexy one—how did I not notice how good-looking he was prior to tonight—and he follows the rules to a T; whereas me, I'm a wild child—you've met my mom so we know where I get THAT from. I march to the beat of my own drum. I'm a rule breaker, line pusher. I'm no good for him. I'm no good for anyone.

Looking over at CJ, he has his eyes closed and his breathing has evened out; he's asleep. I take the time to appreciate him. I'm totally seeing him in a whole new light now, and I have to say, I like it. Who knew underneath those nerdy glasses was a sexy as hell alpha man, with an amazingly huge dick and a heart of gold?

He really is a great guy, and to keep him a great guy, I need to let him go. I need to pop tonight into my memory box and move on.

If only things could be different. If only I could be different for him. Running my fingertip gently down his face, I whisper, "Why can't I be with a guy like you?"

Chapter 8

Cj

With my eyes closed, I lie here sated and content. I'm close to falling asleep when I feel Lily's fingertip graze my cheek and hear her whisper, "Why can't I be with a guy like you?"

"Why can't you?" I whisper back.

Opening my eyes, I turn my head toward her. She's in shock that I heard her. I stare over at my dream girl, waiting for an answer to my question. Her silence is unnerving and I have a feeling I'm not going to like what comes next. Seems that our perfect night has come to an end.

After what we just shared together, I was hoping it would be the turning point, the starting point, for us. The start of something amazing, but I should have known better; Lily Cox would never want a guy like me outside of this treehouse.

We silently stare at one another as we lie here in the treehouse in my backyard. Her mouth opens and closes, she's at a loss for words and doesn't know what to say so I voice it for her. "It's because I'm a nerd and you're you, the dream girl of all dream girls." And it's true, Lily fucking Cox is the ultimate girl but because I'm me, in the light of day, we can never be.

"CJ," she pleads, "I'm—"

Cutting her off, I press my finger to her lips. "Lily." I reach up and cup her cheek, taking a deep breath. "Lily Cox, you are a beautiful, amazing, strong woman who is going to make someone very, very happy one day." *I just wish you'd give me a chance.* "I will always remember our night together and I'm glad you were my first."

"I'm glad you were mine too, CJ," she quietly adds.

Leaning forward, I place a kiss on her cheek. Closing my eyes, I lock the memories of this night away. When I open them again, Lily is staring blankly at her hands and that hurts.

Lowering my gaze, I dejectedly sigh. Lifting my head, I look over to Lil. She looks confused—like me—but she also looks ohh so beautiful in the bright morning light.

She lifts her head and our gaze connects. Her eyes well with tears, "I'm sorry, CJ," she whispers. "I wish…"

"I know," I interrupt her, "I know."

Silence envelops us as we sadly stare at one another.

"Get dressed, Lil, and I'll take you home." It comes out harsher than I intended but I don't want to hear, 'It's not you, it's me.' I don't want that from her. What I need to do is save tonight in the 'it was fantastic' folder and the possibility of an us into the 'never gonna happen' tab. I need to remember tonight as a good time and move on.

She nods her head and smiles at me. Like always, when she smiles it lights up her face, but this time, it's marred with sadness, giving me hope that one day I might get my chance with her. As I gaze over at her, I make a promise to myself, even though I haven't won her over, I know that with time, I can. But then doubt creeps in, and I begin to wonder if this is all I'll ever have with her. I'll always treasure tonight forever because for once, I was the hero. I was the hero who got the girl—if only for one night.

Silently, we re-dress and climb down from the treehouse. The sun is starting to rise and the sky looks magical right now. Sneaking back out to the street, we climb into Pepper's car and I drive Lily back to her house. Pulling up at the curb, I climb out and walk around the hood and open her door.

"Thanks," she timidly says, as she climbs out. She brushes a tendril of hair behind her ear and silently we walk toward the front door. It's awkward and therefore feels like our old relationship. At least I still have that.

Placing a kiss on her cheek, I turn and walk back to Pepper's car, looking back over my shoulder. "Night, Lily."

"Night, CJ," she whisper-shouts and waves at me.

Waving back, I continue down the path back to the car. I climb into the driver's seat and pull my belt on. I wait for her to go inside and once she's safe behind the front door, I start the engine and head home.

Tonight wasn't what I expected, but this Halloween was the best one ever…and I vow that one day, Lily Cox will be mine.

Chapter 9

Lily

Closing the door behind me, I lean against the wood and let out a sigh. I have a feeling I just made the biggest mistake of my life by pushing CJ away.

"Are you just getting home now?" The sound of Mom's voice startles me and I jump.

"Yeah, I fell asleep at..." I can't tell her I was with CJ, that will open a whole nother can of worms and I don't even want to face the current can, so I lie. "Mad's house."

"You expect me to believe that?" Mom snaps at me.

"It's the truth," I throw back at her.

"Then why were you leaning against the door as if you were sneaking in and glad that you weren't busted."

"I wasn't sneaking in," I snarl. "I'm just tired. It was an eventful night."

"How so?"

Shit. Shit. Shit. "It was Halloween at Chili's."

"That doesn't explain anything."

"Mom, I'm tired. I'm heading to bed for a few more hours." Pushing off the door, I walk toward her. "I'll see you when I wake up." I kiss her on the cheek and when I pull back, her eyes widen.

"Is that stubble rash on your neck and chest?"

Glancing down, I see what Mom's referring to and suddenly get an image of CJ's head pressed up against the girls. My clit begins to throb as I remember the sensation of his face in my breasts and my nipples in his mouth. A smile appears on my face but I quickly school it when I see the look that Mom's giving me.

"Lily Anne Cox, what did you do last night?"

"I went to a Halloween party," I sassily reply and step around her. She reaches out and grabs my arm. I flinch as the memory of skeleton guy doing exactly that flashes before my eyes. Wrenching my arm free, I turn and race to my bedroom. Mom is yelling and I can't deal with her crazy right now.

Reaching my room, I slam the door shut and flip the lock. Sliding down the door, I rest my head on my knees. My eyes well with tears as I continue to remember being pushed against the building...and then CJ rescued me.

My knight—pun intended—swooped in in his zombie scrubs and saved me...and then gave me the best few hours of my life.

Leaning my head back, I sigh in frustration. "Why did I walk away from him?" I mumble. "Stupid. Stupid. Stupid," I berate myself, banging my head on the door. Just as Mom knocks and jiggles the handle.

"Open this door, Lily."

"Leave me alone," I shout, but my voice lacks the conviction I usually have when I yell at her. I know my mom; her momma bear instinct is going to kick in and I know she won't give up until she gets answers. I have three choices: 1. I shut her out and we get into a huge fight.

2. I tell her CJ and I had sex and we get into a huge fight. Or 3. I tell her about skeleton guy and that CJ saved me, avoiding a huge fight.

That seems like the easiest option, so I stand up, take a deep breath, and disengage the lock. Opening the door, I stare at Mom. "I'll tell you but you need to promise not to kill anyone...or tell Dad."

"I don't keep secrets from him, Lil, you know that."

"I," I place a massive emphasis on that word, "need you to do this for me. Otherwise, I won't tell you anything...ever again."

We stare intently at one another; I learned all my sass from her, so she only has herself to blame. "Fine," she relents.

Stepping aside, I let her in. Closing the door, I relock it and walk over to my bed. Sitting on the end, I cross my legs. Mom mimics my pose and when I look over at her, I realize this is what I will look like one day when I have a teenager of my own—but I won't be as bitchy or as much of a pain in the ass as her.

"Okay, Lil, what's the big secret?"

Taking a deep breath, I begin. "Last night I was attacked by a skeleton but CJ, the zombie doctor, saved me."

"What the ever-loving fuck?" she growls. She grabs my arms and I flinch at the contact. She immediately drops her hands and takes mine in hers, squeezing in the mom-like way. "Are you okay, Lily Pad?"

"Thanks to CJ, I am."

"As in Clay Knight, CJ?"

"Yep...Mom, he was a total badass. It was amazing to watch him like that." Silently I add, *and you should have seen him in the treehouse. All alpha, sexy as hell. And his cock, holy hell, I've never seen one more beautiful.*

"Geeky CJ Knight saved you?"

"Yep," I confirm, letting the 'p' pop.

"Is that how the stubble rash happened?" Mom points to my chest.

Nodding, I don't say anything because that's not how the rash occurred, but it's better she thinks that than know the truth.

"And you're okay now?"

Shrugging, I purse my lips. "Yes. No. I don't know. I'm pretty overwhelmed, to tell you the truth."

"That's understandable." Mom reaches over and cups my cheeks. "I'm glad you told me. I was worried that you were out sleeping around all night."

"It's nice to know what you really think of me," I snap, grabbing her hand and pulling it off my cheek, even if there is an ounce of truth to her statement. I know I shouldn't be angry with her because she's right, I *was* sleeping with someone. It's just, I hate that my own mom thinks so little of me. "I need to shower and sleep," I dismissively tell her. Our happy mom/daughter moment is over and we are back to snappy mom and Lily.

For once, Mom doesn't argue with me. She stands up, places a kiss on my forehead, and leaves me with my thoughts. Which, once again, are of CJ and what we did last night.

Falling onto my mattress, I pull my pillow over my head and scream into it in frustration. Why can't I stop thinking about him? When I close my eyes, I feel him sliding into me. I feel the bite of his teeth sinking into my breast. "Damn it," I whine into my pillow.

Letting out a sigh, I throw my pillow to the side and climb out of bed. Glancing at my reflection in the dresser mirror, my eyes home in on the bruises starting to appear on my upper arms. I have to keep what happened between Mom and me, just Mom and me. Dad cannot find out.

Picking up my brush, I run it through my hair and a laugh escapes me. I think this, just now, somehow brought Mom and me closer together, but I know her, she'll still be a controlling bitch, and I'll be a witchy bitchy back to her.

Dropping back to the bed, I trace the fingerprints as memories of that moment come flooding back to me. My eyes well with tears. What would I have done had CJ not found me when he did? I'd certainly have more than just bruises on my upper arms, that's for sure.

I hate myself for allowing that to happen but more so, I hate that in the heat of the moment, I wasn't tough Lily; I was frail, frightened, and timid. I was weak. That's not who I am. My dad raised me better than that, but when my attacker had his hands on my arms and my back pressed against the brick wall, I couldn't move. I was frozen.

Letting out a frustrated sigh, I cross my legs, wondering what next weekend at the monthly barbecue will be like when I see CJ again. For as long as I can remember, once a month, someone hosts a barbecue and the attendees are the Kelly, Knight, Cox, and Cruz families. We're like this weird-ass Brady bunch of sorts, and now that Mason and Carter have hooked up, it's really weird-ass.

Once again, I think about CJ. I'm pretty sure I broke his heart earlier this morning, but nothing good can come from us being together. But what if I'm making a mistake? What if he's 'the one' and I just blew my chance at happiness?

Chapter 10

Cj

One week later

... Tonight it's our turn to host the monthly barbecue and at the moment, Mom is running around like a mad woman. "Cress, babe, you need to calm down," Dad tells her as she nearly trips and face-plants while setting the table.

"Preston, don't tell me to calm down. I'm all in a fluster because I'm running late and you know I hate running late."

"It's a barbecue, it's not like the Queen is coming."

"Bay's coming."

"Bay is not the Queen."

"No, she's a bitch."

A laugh escapes me from my spot on the sofa, both of them turn to me. "Whaaat?" I defensively ask.

"Go and get ready, Clay," Mom snaps at me. It's on the tip of my tongue to also tell her to chill, but I look down at myself. Normally, I'm not concerned about what I wear, but tonight I want to make an impression on one of the attendees, so I hop up and head to my room to change. I'm excited because Lily will be here, it will be the first time I've seen her since last weekend. But there's also a part of me that's apprehensive because she shut me out the next morning.

All week, our night together in the treehouse has been at the forefront of my mind. Every time I step into the backyard, my eyes drift there—and in vivid Technicolor, I'm assaulted with memories of what occurred up there.

I walk over to Mom and Dad. "Mom, it will all be fine. Have a glass of wine and then when the others get here, you can all do it together...like you always usually do."

"When did you get to be so wise?"

"I've always been wise, Mom."

She taps my cheek and smiles. Turning on my heel, I head to my room to change.

Once I'm dressed, I head outside since it's a nice afternoon. Taking a seat near the unlit firepit, I chillax back. My eyes drift to the treehouse and I smile, once again memories of last weekend assault me.

"What's got you grinning like a carnival clown?" my older half-sister, Lexi, asks as she takes a seat next to me. Lexi is home visiting for the weekend since the NY Crushers are playing Chicago this week. She's a physical therapist for them. She landed her dream job straight out of college. She moved halfway across the country to New York and hasn't looked back since.

"Nothing."

"I call bullshit on that."

"Seriously, it's nothing."

"Is it a girl?" she teases.

"No," I snappily refute.

"Ohh, it totally is. Is my wee lil brother in loooooove?" She adds a million extra o's to the word love and I laugh.

"No," I snarl.

"You're protesting too much, dude." I go to interrupt her but she raises her hand. "Whoever she is, she better look after you."

"Isn't it generally the guy who gets the 'you better look after her' chat? Not the other way around."

She shrugs at me. "I'm not a parent so I don't know the ins and outs but as the big sister, I'm on your side."

"And I'm on yours, too. Speaking of, how's what's-his-face?"

"He's an ass."

"Do I need to kick his ass?"

Lexi bursts out laughing. "I'd pay to see you kick anyone's ass. You are the least ass-kicking person I know."

"You know nothing, Lexi Knight."

"Did you just Jon Snow me?"

"Yep, I sure did. You'd be surprised at what I can do," I inform my sister, as memories of punching that skeleton jerk last weekend flash before me.

"You constantly surprise me, Clay, and one day, you will meet Mrs. Clay and she'll be a lucky, lucky gal."

I've already met her, I think to myself.

"And you'll meet Mr. Lexi and he, too, will be lucky."

All afternoon Lily has been avoiding me. It's like she doesn't want to be alone with me, but whenever we aren't together, her eyes always drift toward me... much like mine.

Grabbing a root beer from the cooler, I take a seat next to Mason near the firepit. He, his brother, Marshall, their dad, and my dad are talking about some race car driver, Marshall somebody, who is finally retiring. Apparently, Flynn treated him back in the day after a horrific accident.

"Nobody" by Dylan Scott begins to play. Focusing on the flames, I let the words sink in. I feel each and every one of them. The words of the song really resonate with me. Looking across the firepit, I see Lil sitting next to my sisters and I watch her. At this very moment, I realize that nobody will ever love her like I could. This song is literally meant for me. For us. I can see myself falling for her. Loving her. Growing old with her. I just need to convince her; I have to change her mind and there's no time like the present.

Challenge accepted, Lily Cox, challenge accepted.

Our eyes lock and I notice her breath hitches. I flick my head toward the treehouse and plead with my eyes for her to meet me up there. I feel like I'm waiting forever for her to reply and then finally, she subtly nods in agreement.

Covertly, I slink away and make my way to the treehouse. It feels like an eternity before I see her head pop over the edge and she climbs in. Like last weekend, we sit across from one another. Silently staring into each other's eyes.

"Hey," she greets me, breaking the silence.

"Hey," I reply, taking in her beauty. "How's your week been?"

"Good, yours?"

"Good."

This is awkward and not what I was hoping would occur.

Silence surrounds us once again, until we both say each other's names. We both laugh and finally the awkwardness has passed.

"You go first," I quickly say, eager to hear what she has to say.

"I've been thinking about you a lot this week." A grin appears on my face hearing this. "Last weekend started off pretty shitty, thanks to that skeleton fucker, but I also thank him because it led here." She waves her hand around the treehouse. "Had that not happened, I don't know that we would have, you know."

Nodding my head, I shuffle closer to her. "I've been thinking about you too...and what happened here...and I too, thank that skeleton fucker."

"You swore again, CJ. I think I'm a bad influence on you."

Feeling brave, I reach out and cup her cheek. "You are perfect for me, Lily Cox."

She leans into my palm and covers my hand with hers. She lifts her gaze to mine. "Where do we go from here?"

"Where do you want to go from here?"

We silently stare at one another. "CJ, I wish I could be what you want me to be, but I'm not the person you think I am."

Shaking my head, I envelop her hand that still covers mine on her cheek. "I see you, Lil. I see the real Lily Cox and one of these days, you'll see what I see."

"Isn't the girl meant to be all sappy like that?"

"You call it sappy, I call it manly."

"You really are something, Clay Knight."

"A good something, right?"

"A very good something." She bites her bottom lip. "I...I think I want to see where this goes, but I'm scared about what will happen when they," she nods outside, "all find out. My mom and your mom barely tolerate each other as it is."

"Don't worry about them. At the end of the day, they want us happy and you, Lily, are what I want to be happy."

"I want you, too," she quietly whispers. "Can we keep it between us? For now at least."

"As long as there's an us, we can be secret or we can sing it from this treehouse. I just want you."

"You really are sweet. Now come here and kiss me."

"Yes, ma'am."

"Call me ma'am again and we will be over before we begin."

"I'm pretty sure your mom said the exact same thing to me one day when I called her ma'am."

"You were getting it on with my mom?"

"No. No. No. Not what I meant. All I meant—"

She presses her finger against my lips. "I know what you meant, now shut up and kiss me."

"Yes maa—I mean, hell yes."

Sliding my hand around the back of her head, I pull her to me and press my lips to hers. Her tongue pushes into my mouth, slipping and sliding with mine in an erotic tongue dance.

Our kisses last week were awkward and new but this, this kiss feels right in every way that a kiss should.

She pushes me backward and I fall to the floor, letting out an 'ooof,' as I wasn't expecting it. "Sorry," she murmurs against my lips.

"It's fine," I reply, keeping my lips pressed to her.

Rolling her to her back, I cocoon her underneath me. Our lips never part. Sliding my hand up her side, I cup her breast in my palm.

"More," she begs.

"More what?" I question.

"Just more," she replies, covering my hand on her breast and gently pushing.

"As much as I want more, a hell of a lot more, our families are downstairs and I don't want to get us in trouble."

"Ever the good boy," she teases, "but I agree. I've only just found you and I don't want my dad to kill you."

My eyes widen at her words because she's right, Corey would kill me if he knew I was up here doing un-PG-like things to his only daughter.

"We better head back before people become suspicious."

"Yeah, I guess we should."

At the same time, in unison we say, "When can I see you again?"

We both laugh. "I don't know," I honestly tell her. "But just know, I'll be thinking of you until I get to."

"Me too, Knight, me too."

She places a quick kiss on my lips and climbs down.

Standing up, I look out the window and watch her walk across the yard. She really is the most beautiful person in the world. She takes a seat back next to my sister's and I watch the two of them interact. Lil laughs at something Pepper says and it lights her face up, and the sound of her laughter is music to my ears.

Before I climb down, I sit on the treehouse veranda and stare out at the night sky. I feel like I've crossed over to the *Twilight Zone* or something because I, Clay Joseph Knight, am secretly dating Lily Cox. How is that possible?

My gaze gravitates toward Lil's again, and this time she looks up. We stare at one another across the yard and I whisper to myself, "Mark my word, Lily Cox, one day you and I will officially be Mr. and Mrs. Knight, but for now I can accept us as Clay and Lily, dating in secret."

Chapter 11

Lily

For the last week, the events of the treehouse, and now yesterday, have played on a loop over and over in my mind. My body still buzzes when I think about it. Who knew CJ could kiss, or fuck, like that? But with a cock like that, it's no freakin wonder. I've totally been missing out all these years...and even though I pushed him away, he's managed to worm his way into my life. Sure, it's going to be in secret but for now, that's all I can do.

A knock on my door startles me and I quickly jump back into bed. Pulling the comforter up to my chin, I yell, "Come in."

My dad steps into my room and he looks questioningly at me because it's almost lunchtime and I'm still in bed. Again, that's not me, I'm up at 5:30 every morning.

"You okay, Lily Pad?" Dad voices, walking into my room and sitting on the edge of my mattress. He touches my forehead, checking for a temperature and stares down at me. "It's almost twelve and you're still in bed."

"I'm fine."

"Fine," he scoffs, "you and I both know that when you or your mother say fine, you are anything but." He pauses. "Wanna talk about it?"

Do I wanna talk about it? Yes. No. I don't know. Maybe I need his perspective on the CJ thing, so I nod my head. I go to sit up and then I remember I'm in a tank and I still have a few bruises on my upper arms. I've managed to hide them all week and I will keep hiding my upper arms until they're gone. Dad would lose his shit and murder the fuckwit skeleton if he sees the marks he left on me. He's too pretty for orange...and I really don't want to be left with mom on my own. She and I would definitely kill one another and I, too, do not look good in orange. "You make coffee and I'll meet you out back after I use the bathroom."

"It's a date." He leans down and presses a kiss to my temple. "Love you, Lily Pad."

"Love you too, Dad."

He exits my room and as soon as the door closes behind him, I jump up and pull on my NY Crushers jersey, covering myself up. I slip my feet into my Uggs and head into my bathroom. After using the toilet and brushing my teeth, I head out to meet Dad.

He's sitting on the top step on the back deck, two coffees sitting next to him. He and I used to do this when I was little, but instead of coffee I had chocolate milk or juice.

Taking a seat next to him, I lean my head on his shoulder and he hands me one of the mugs. I take a sip of the liquid gold in my mug and sigh. An image of sitting here like this with CJ flashes before me and I smile.

"Dad," I ask, breaking the silence, "how did you know Mom was the one?"

"I knew from the first moment she told me to go fuck myself when she was in the interrogation room that she'd be mine."

A laugh breaks free. "I still can't believe you two met while she was under arrest."

"Not all happily ever afters start off in the traditional way, and you know what?"

"What?"

"I wouldn't change a thing. Your mom is my everything and I'm a lucky, lucky man because I have you both in my life. Lily Pad, you both are so much alike. I don't know whether to be scared or proud that there's another tenacious Cox woman out there."

"Please," I scoff at him, "I'm nothing like her. I'm not a controlling psycho bitch who's obsessed with purple."

"Watch your mouth, Lily Pad." I roll my eyes at him. "And that eye roll there, proves how much you two are alike."

I guess he's right, Mom and I are very similar in a lot of ways, but I'm also like him too. "I think I'm more like you, but yes, I can see Mom in me too."

"You're the perfect mix." He places his mug down and pulls me in for a side hug. "You know," he says with a laugh. "I'm gonna be gray before you finish college, if you don't start acting like the responsible, beautiful, amazing young woman I know you can be."

I stare at up Dad in shock, because someone else recently said that I was a beautiful, amazing woman but when they said it, I felt their words deep in my soul and it left me feeling all warm and fuzzy.

"One day, Lily Pad, you will meet the one and fall for him without even knowing it. You're gonna make some man very happy one day...but not until you're at least forty."

I laugh at his words because I think already have met him and we're currently secretly dating. Taking a sip of coffee, my eyes widen and when it hits me, ohh fuckballs, I'm falling for him. I'm falling for Clay Knight.

The End!!!!!

Want to find out what happens next with CJ and Lily? Keep your eye out for *Falling for Him*, a full length Falling Next Gen novel, coming in 2024.

In the meantime, you can see how CJ's mom, Cress, and dad, Preston, got together in *Falling for Dr. Knight*. You can also meet Bitchy Baylor aka Lily's mom, and her dad, Corey Cox in *Falling for Agent Cox*.

About the Author

DL Gallie is from Queensland, Australia, but she's lived in many different places all over the world, including the UK and Canada. She currently resides in Central Queensland with her husband and two munchkins. She and her husband have been together since she was sixteen, and although they drive each other crazy at times, she couldn't imagine her life without him.

Shortly after her son was born, DL began reading again. With encouragement from her husband, she picked up the pen and started writing, and now the voices in her head won't shut up.

DL enjoys listening to music, drinking white wine in the summer, red wine in the winter, and beer all year round. She's also never been known to turn down a cocktail, especially a margarita.

FACEBOOK ~ INSTAGRAM ~ BOOKBUB ~ GOODREADS
Sign up to my newsletter.

www.dlgallieauthor.com
dlgallieauthor@outlook.com

Forbidden

S.L. Sterling

Chapter One

B^ree

The rain pelted down on the windshield, my wipers struggling to clear away the rain. I had wanted to get back to New York this afternoon, but Mom insisted on me staying for a reheated Thanksgiving dinner after the funeral. My brother Fletcher had offered to drive me back home or at least follow me, but I wouldn't hear of it. Instead, I took off like the stubborn-minded individual I was only to come to a mess of construction. I was forced to take a detour, and now I had gotten myself turned around and was in a part of New York I didn't recognize.

I slowed down and stopped at a red light and fiddled with my phone, trying to pull up a map of the area. The poorly lit streets and boarded-up businesses made me feel as if I had entered some sort of an alternate universe, instead of New York City. I was trying not to panic and felt a little better when, finally, the map loaded. I was about to zoom in on the area when the screen dimmed and went blank. I hit the power button and then realized it must have gone dead. I fiddled with my old broken charging cord. I had been meaning to buy a new one and was suddenly angry with myself for not making it a priority before I left home.

. . .

The sound of a blaring horn behind me caused me to look up to see the light had turned green. I looked both ways and slowly proceeded into the intersection to have the guy behind me squeal his wheels and drive around me, spraying my windshield with water.

I struggled to see as I continued down the dark road. I just really wanted to find my way back to a familiar area and get back to my dorm room. I gripped the wheel, driving as slowly as I could, and glanced around the empty, rundown area. There was nothing here.

Another red light caused me to stop, and I pulled my hoodie around me a little tighter as a chill ran through my body. I turned up the radio to help distract me from the silence when my car started to make a funny sound.

"Oh no. No you don't. Not now," I muttered to myself as panic filled me. "Don't you dare crap out on me. I need to get home."

I knew I should have let Fletcher check it over before I left home, but I had been in a rush to get back before dark.

The stoplight turned green, and I pressed on the gas, the engine now knocking and sputtering. I had just gotten through the intersection when the car sputtered again, a loud bang sounded, and my car died. I slammed my hands on the wheel and rested my head, praying that I was really only in a bad dream.

"What am I going to do?" I muttered as I sat debating my plan of action. I couldn't even call my roommate to come and pick me up, I thought. I sat there on the verge of tears, praying that the rain would stop. I had no idea where I was, no idea what was around here, but I couldn't sit here praying for some knight in shining armor to drive by either.

I waited until the rain stopped and gathered my purse and phone and climbed out of the car. The air was cold and damp, and I zipped my hoodie. I locked the doors and looked both ways before crossing the street. I knew there was nothing but empty buildings from the way I had come, so I decided to continue walking in the direction I had been heading. Surely, there must be something up ahead—a business, a store, a late-night restaurant, somewhere I could use a phone and wait for someone to come and pick me up.

I had gone about four blocks when I heard loud music nearby. I picked up the pace, rounded a corner, and looked up to see a dimly lit sign: The Velvet Growler.

There were motorcycles lined out front of the building and a few rather rough-looking men stood outside. I'd heard my brother talk about this place and had been warned by him and others to stay away, but I was desperate.

I inhaled deeply. With that warning standing out in my mind, I stood there trying to decide if I should go in or not. I had been walking for what had to be at least thirty minutes. I was cold and tired and just wanted my bed. However, it was also the only place I had seen in the past hour, and I had no idea how much farther I would have to go to find another one.

I watched the men out front. They stood there talking, smoking, and drinking, and then a loud rumble caught my attention. I watched as a couple of bikers pulled in. One got off his bike and removed his helmet, and the men who had been out front stopped drinking as he exchanged some words with a couple of them and continued into the bar.

I let out a breath and began walking across the road towards the front door. I was just going to pay them no mind and walk inside as if I belonged there. I was just about at the first step when one of the guys in front of me punched another one in the shoulder and shoved him out of the way.

"Lookie what we have here," he purred, looking me over. My eyes fell to the name on his jacket: Snake.

The other guy turned and looked at me. "Well, well." He approached the edge of the step, his eyes scanning my body.

. . .

It took every bit of courage I had to climb the steps and walk by the two men, ignoring them, but I did it. I walked to the door and pulled it open, stepping into the stale smelling bar. The second the door shut behind me, it was pulled open by the two men who had been trying to block my way in. The place grew quiet and all eyes turned on me.

I glanced around the room, locking eyes with each and every man in there before I gathered up every ounce of courage I had and walked over to the bar. I could feel their eyes on me the entire time.

"What do you need, little lady?" the man behind the bar asked while wiping his hands on a dirty towel.

"I um...need to use your phone."

"She needs to use the phone." A roar of laughter burst out from behind me, and I turned to see the guy who had been outside standing there.

I looked at the bartender, pleading with my eyes. "My car broke down. I need to call for a ride," I muttered.

"We can take you wherever you need to go, little lady," the man from the parking lot gritted into my ear. "A sweet little thing like you can ride on the back of my bike any day," he said licking his lips as his eyes ran over my body like I were a piece of meat. He stepped closer behind me and ran his finger over my cheek.

A chill ran through me as I looked at the bartender, once again giving him a pleading look. "Hey, Mack, how about that beer." Apparently, Mack was the bartender, and instead of handing me the phone, he turned and began pouring another glass of beer.

. . .

"Take a seat there, angel. We don't bite."

"Speak for yourself," a couple of the other men said, laughing. "I love to bite into nice ripe juicy peaches."

I felt myself heat up at the comment. I looked around the bar at all these men, mad at myself for taking that detour, angry that I hadn't stopped and purchased a cable or let my brother look over my car, and slowly made my way to a seat at the bar. Even if I had wanted to walk out the door, I doubted they would let me. So with all eyes on me, I took a seat as most of the men went back to talking amongst themselves.

I continued looking around, praying there may be a pay phone on the wall that I could use. This place did look older than any bar I'd been in. Perhaps the phone company was too afraid to come in here.

That was when I saw him. The man who had ridden up on his bike when I was checking the place out. He stood off in the darkness, not saying a word, just watching me.

Chapter Two

S ebastian

She'd seen me as I watched from above as every one of my crew surrounded that twenty-five-year-old princess down below. *Fucking animals, all of them.* When I saw Snake lay his fingers on her again, I wanted to tear him apart. She looked familiar to me, and since I was feeling highly protective over her, I walked to the stairs. She had walked into my bar, swinging her perfect, tight little ass, practically begging to use the phone. Mack knew better. He avoided the plea altogether as he was supposed to. He knew I didn't want any trouble with the law, and if she had called the police, they would be down here all over this place. It wasn't me who would have been in trouble, but most of these guys broke the law repeatedly.

As I descended the stairs and got a good look at her, I stopped in my tracks. I'd know that face anywhere. What the hell was Bree Walker doing here in this area of town at this time of night?

The more Snake touched her, the more irritated I became. He had been all over her since she had walked in here. I couldn't blame him. That long dark hair, small waist, tight ass, perfect breasts... I'd be all over her as well if given the chance. Over the past couple of years, I had dreamed of it myself.

She gave him a scolding look and turned her back to him. He persisted until, finally, she said something that made him back up with his hands in the air. The second she turned her back, he was right on her again.

As much as I was enjoying watching her try to take control, I could sense she was beginning to feel uncomfortable. When he reached out and placed his hands on her hips and she squirmed under his touch, I lunged forward.

"Get your hands off of me," she gritted.

Snake did nothing but laugh. "I love it when they get all feisty."

She tried to pull away, but I could tell he wasn't going to give up. Gripping her tighter, he pulled her into him and held her against him. "You smell good there, gorgeous," he said, trying to nuzzle her neck.

"Let go of me," she said, trying to fight him.

I was growing tired of Snake's actions. I had just put my foot onto the concrete floor when I watched this pretty thing in Snake's arms turn and smack him across the face. Immediately, Snake gripped her, a look of utter anger pouring across his face.

"Snake, let her go. You've had your fun," I bit out.

Snake turned and looked in my direction and removed his hands from her body, backing up. He knew better than to mess with me. I stepped forward and gave her a reassuring look.

. . .

"You say you're car broke down?" I questioned.

The second she turned those pretty pleading blue eyes on me, I knew I had to have her, regardless of my friendship with her brother, regardless of the fact I had promised myself I would never touch her. She didn't respond. She squinted those eyes at me, trying to see who was calling to her. I stepped forward into the light.

"That's enough bullshit. Can't behave yourself, you'll need to leave. This is no way to treat a guest. Make yourself scarce, Snake," I bit out. Snake and I hadn't been seeing eye to eye on a lot of things, and lately, I tolerated him at best.

"It's okay, princess, you can talk. They won't hurt you," I said, walking over to her and pulling a barstool between my legs and straddling it.

She just glared at me. I could tell it was a façade. She wanted to be tough when, in fact, she was scared shitless. The guys all stood around waiting for her to say something, staring at her, taking her in, making her feel even more uncomfortable.

"Why don't you guys fuck off," I barked to all of them, glaring at Snake.

It didn't take long for my glares to work, and soon they had all backed off. I turned and looked at this sweet, scared little princess sitting before me and reached forward to brush a strand of hair out of her face. I knew her first instinct would be to pull away, but as soon as my fingers touched her, she surprised me by almost leaned into my hand.

"I'm Sebastian. I own this place. You're Fletcher's sister, Bree, right? What are you doing out here, princess?"

. . .

She glanced over at the table full of men and then over to Snake who stood staring at us, before looking back to me, a look of relief coming over her face. "Could I get a glass of water," she mumbled.

I snapped my fingers at Mack, who practically jumped to get the water and set it on the bar. I picked it up and held it out for her to take.

"Thank you," she muttered as she took the glass from me and averted her eyes to the ground.

I watched as she drank the water down and set the glass on the bar. "My car broke down." Her eyes met mine and she studied them. "I just wanted to call my friend to come and pick me up."

"How about, instead of calling your friend, I take a look at your car?"

Chapter Three

Bree

Perhaps it was the fact that Sebastian new my brother, but even before I knew that, something told me I was safe with him. I nodded. "Would you mind?"

"No, princess, I don't mind." He stood and held out his strong hand. I glanced down and saw the words "Full Throttle" tattooed between his thumb and index finger. I was hesitant, but I slid my tiny hand into his and followed him out of the bar.

With my hand in his, I followed him down the stairs and over to what must have been his bike. "We're getting on that?" I asked, my voice shaking.

He chuckled to himself. "Never been on a motorcycle before?"

I shook my head. He held out a helmet for me and waited until I reached out and took it from him. I slid it over my head, and he walked around and secured it. "Got to make sure you are safe," he said, tweaking my chin.

He turned and straddled the bike, holding it up with his legs as he waited for me to get on. I just stood there not really knowing what to do. "I would rather walk," I muttered.

"Come on, princess, let's go," he said, tapping the seat behind him. "It's perfectly safe."

I took a step forward and swung my leg over the back of the bike.

"You may wanna hold onto me, princess," he said as the bike roared to life. "Don't want you falling off."

The second the bike rolled, my arms were wrapped tightly around his waist and I had my face buried into the back of his leather jacket.

We were barely on the bike for five minutes when I felt the bike slow down and come to a stop. I opened my eyes and looked up to see my car sitting in the dark. He cut the engine and silence was all around us.

"This it, princess?" he asked, propping the kickstand up.

"Yes." I got off the bike and walked over to the driver's side door. I pressed the lock button on my remote and opened it so I could pop the hood for him.

Sebastian walked over and lifted the hood of the car and immediately started checking things over. He pulled out a dipstick and looked at it.

"When was the last time you had an oil change in this thing, princess?"

I shrugged my shoulders. "I don't know. My brother normally takes care of those things for me. Why?"

"Looks like it's been a while. It's bone dry. Did the car make any noise?"

"A sputtering or maybe a knocking, then a bang, then it died. Is it bad?"

"Looks like it could be a blown engine, princess."

I ran my hand over my face. "That can't be good," I muttered just as a loud clap of thunder rang out and I felt a few drops of cold rain hit the top of my head.

I leaned up against the car door and placed my hands on my face. I had no idea what I was going to do, and now it was going to start pouring.

"Where do you live?" Sebastian asked, shutting the hood of my car and walking around to stand beside me.

"The other side of the city. I was on my way back to school from my grandmother's funeral when I took a wrong exit, then had to take a detour to get around due to construction. I'm new here. I seriously have no idea where I even am. Fletcher wanted to drive me back, and I was adamant I was fine. He also wanted to check over the car before I left, but I refused."

I could feel the tears starting to build. I was beyond frustrated with myself, and within seconds, I felt a tear slide down my cheek. I squeezed my eyes shut, trying to fight them off, when I felt a large, calloused hand on my cheek, and I opened my eyes and looked up to meet his.

"No tears, Bree. I'll take you home. I look after my own." His eyes locked on mine and we stood staring at one another. "Where you living?" he asked in a lower voice.

"I'm in the dorms at Columbia University. I just transferred and have my first class in a week."

"No problem."

I watched as he walked over to his bike and held out the helmet I had been wearing for me to take. I reached for it and then watched him as he straddled the bike and put his own on. This time I didn't hesitate. I wanted to get home, so I hopped onto the back of his bike and held on for dear life as he started it up.

We had just gotten onto the highway when the rain started pelting down so hard I had no idea how Sebastian could even see. I was cold and wet, and I did the best I could to shelter myself behind him. He didn't drive very far, pulling off the highway and onto a side street in a residential neighborhood.

A couple more turns and he pulled into a driveway of a large home and parked his bike just in the garage behind the house.

"Where are we?" I asked as I looked around.

"My house. Well, my clubhouse. It's too hard to see. The roads are getting slick. You'll stay here with me until the rain stops."

He didn't give me any other options. He just headed for the back door of the dark house. He had opened the back door and then turned around to look at me. "You coming, princess, or you going to stay out in the rain all night?"

I was already soaked to the core and couldn't feel my fingers as I glanced around the area. Then, without any other arguments, I climbed up the back steps and entered the house behind him.

I watched as he peeled off his wet leather jacket and flung it on the back of a chair before turning the light on over the sink. I glanced around at the pile of dirty dishes that sat on the counter. He walked through the kitchen into another room. I heard a couple things drop, then he came out of the room in nothing but black sweats. My eyes trailed over his muscular, bare chest. He had two full sleeves and numerous other tattoos covering his built chest and back.

"Here," he said, holding out what looked to be a shirt.

"What's this for?"

"You're soaked. Let me dry those for you."

"I'm good, thanks," I said, shoving the shirt back at him.

"You are soaked to the skin. You aren't good. You were shivering so hard you were making me cold. Besides, you're not getting into my bed with wet clothes on."

I looked around the room and down to the shirt in my hand. "If you think for a second I am going to get changed right here in front of you, you are wrong. I'm also not the type of girl who crawls into bed with some stranger."

He looked at me, a wry smile on his lips. "Bathroom is just through that door." He nodded in its direction. "I'm not a stranger."

I couldn't help the smile that fell onto my lips. I walked past him and was just about to close the bathroom door when he cleared his throat. "You will sleep with me, unless you wish to sleep with Snake. His bed is the only one that has room."

I turned abruptly and glared at him. "You mean he is coming back here?"

"Yep, most of those guys are. They live here as well, princess."

"Well, what about the couch? Surely, you have one of those."

"Yep, there is a couch, but I will warm you the girls who sleep on the couch are pretty much fair game. So, it's up to you. Safe with me or fair game. Your choice," he said, shrugging.

A chill ran through me, and not from the fact that I was soaked to the skin. I didn't know what to say, so I just stood there.

"You know, you should go get changed before the others get back here," he said, flipping on the kettle and pulling two mugs from the cupboard.

Chapter Four

Bree

I walked hesitantly by him and shut the bathroom door. I flipped the light on and leaned up against the door and took a deep breath.

I fished through my purse and found my charging cord and plugged it into the bathroom plug. I needed just enough power to call my brother. I wanted him to know where I was, I figured he had probably tried to call me by now and would be worried.

I stripped out of my wet clothes, leaving them in a pile on the bathroom floor. I opened the door just a crack and saw Sebastian standing at the counter, his phone in hand, typing furiously. I cleared my throat, "Is it possible to get a towel, and could I use the shower?" I asked, my voice weak.

"Yep." He walked back into the room he had gotten changed in and handed me a black plush towel.

Not wanting him to hear my call, I shut the door and started the shower – I would warm up after. I dialed my brother's number and waited for him to answer. Two rings later, I heard his voice on the other end of the phone.

"What the hell happened to you?" he questioned, sounding rather worried.

"My car broke down."

"And you are just calling now? Where the hell are you? I'll be there as soon as I can be."

I could imagine my brother running through the house, throwing on a pair of pants and grabbing his keys in a rush to come and save me.

"I followed a detour, and then my phone died, and then my car died. I had no idea where I was."

"You had? Or you have?"

"Had. I started walking..."

"What? At night, in a part of New York that you didn't know?"

"Yeah, but it's okay. I came across the Velvet Growler and..."

"Jesus, Bree, what the hell. That part of New York is dangerous. Did you go in there?"

"Yeah, I met Sebastian. He took me and checked out my car. He's pretty sure the engine blew."

"Dammit, I told you to let me check it out before you left."

"Fletcher..."

"Where are you now?"

"I'm at Sebastian's. It was raining too hard for him to take me home."

Fletcher didn't say anything in response. I was pretty sure he was pissed, but I didn't know why. I would have thought he would be happy to know that I was safe.

"Fletcher, is there a problem? Something that I should know?"

"Bree, I'm going to say this, and I pray to god you listen to me. As soon as it's possible, you have Sebastian take you home. You hear me?"

"Why?"

"Bree, just listen to me for once."

"But why? Am I in danger?"

"No, not with Sebastian, but the others...Just promise me you will listen to me."

"No problem, I promise."

"Do I need to call Sebastian myself?"

"Please don't. He doesn't know that I called you."

"Just call me when you get home okay? No matter what time."

After reassuring my brother I would call, I hung up the phone and powered it down, leaving it to charge while I quickly showered. I had just gotten in when I heard a knock on the door.

"Bree, you just about finished?" Sebastian asked through the door.

"Yep," I called back, shutting the water off. I'd probably spent a good ten minutes on the phone with Fletcher, and I prayed that Sebastian hadn't heard a word, especially since he had been right outside the door the entire time.

Chapter Five

Sebastian

I couldn't take my eyes off her as she stepped out of the bathroom. The T-shirt I had given her covered her just enough that I couldn't see anything. She sat down at the table, and I placed a mug of hot tea in front of her.

She sat there with her head down, quiet as a mouse, while I poured myself a cup and sat down across from her. I knew the guys would be here soon, and I wanted her tucked away safe with me before they arrived.

"So, how do you know my brother?" she questioned as she took a sip of her tea.

"Your brother and I used to club together. You would have only been thirteen then, and I didn't always look like this, either." I gestured to my tattooed-covered body.

"But I don't remember you being around the house either," she said, taking a sip of her tea.

"We didn't hang around the house. Fletcher was so much older than you, so we often met up at clubs, especially after your parents forbid me from coming around."

"Why would they have done that?"

"It's a long story, but my father passed away when I was sixteen. I went through a troubled phase I guess you could say. I got myself mixed up with an outlaw biker gang. One night, I was brought home by the police. As if I wasn't in enough trouble, that was when she spotted my first tattoo," I said, pointing to a tattoo of a bike with the words "Live to Ride" over it. "My stepmother kicked me out. I'd been in and out of trouble with the law a few times prior, and I guess she'd had enough this time."

"What did you do? Where did you go?"

"Your brother wanted me to talk to your parents. He was sure that they would let me move in, but when I'd asked if I could stay, they felt it was a bad idea."

"That doesn't sound like my parents."

"They felt that I would be a bad influence on your brother and you. Your brother told me it was more to protect you from me than anything. I had come by a few more times, and then they kindly asked me not to come back."

"But they were and always are wanting to help people."

"Well, it wasn't the case with me, so I did as they wished. I moved into The Scorpions clubhouse. I was with them for a while, until I got myself into some more trouble with the law. This time I had to call my aunt and uncle. I ended up moving in with them after that, and with their guidance, I cleaned up my act pretty quick. My dad's brother ran a tight ship. They enrolled me into school with your brother, and I graduated with honors."

"So what are you doing here?" she questioned, running her finger around the rim of her mug, looking around the room.

I shrugged. "After a bad breakup, I just gravitated right back towards this life. I started The Spades and a couple years ago opened The Velvet Growler. Even though on the exterior it looks like I'm trouble, I can assure you that I stay on the right side of the tracks now."

She nodded and took another sip of her tea. "You're still friends with my brother?"

"Yep, he frequents the Velvet Growler quite often. Mostly on weekends, but he told me about your grandmother. I'm sorry."

She nodded again. I could tell she was wondering if her brother was involved with us. I wanted badly to calm her mind. "Don't worry your pretty little head. He isn't involved with us. He just comes and hangs out with the guys."

"It doesn't matter to me if he is or not. I just can't figure out why he has never mentioned you."

"I can't speak for Fletcher, Bree. He must have his reasons, and whatever they are, you should respect that."

"How did you know who I was?" she questioned, taking another sip of her tea.

"What do you mean?"

"You recognized me. I mean, if it's been years since you saw me, I just wonder how you knew who I was."

I thought it over. How was I supposed to answer this question? Fletcher had come to me last year and asked me for help. Bree had gotten herself mixed up with this guy who was absolute bad news. He had asked that I keep an eye on her and protect her should the guy get out of hand. I had watched her days and nights for a couple of weeks, and when I saw things I didn't like, I had threatened him. He broke it off with her, and she knew nothing about it. However, I had continued to watch her after that without Fletcher knowing.

I shrugged. "Fletcher showed me a picture the last time I saw him. I have a good memory."

She looked at me with questions in her eyes. A loud clap of thunder followed by a strike of lightning that lit up the kitchen causing her to jump. I could hear the roar of bikes in the far distance.

"You just about done your tea? We should get to bed. It's late."

"Is Snake really coming back here? I don't really want to see him again," she said, drinking down the remains of her tea.

"He is, but don't worry, you're safe with me. Are you ready?"

Her eyes widened at the sound of bikes. They were getting louder, and I figured they were just around the corner. Another clap of thunder rang out, and she looked at me with fear in her eyes.

I didn't want her to be afraid. I wouldn't let anything happen to her. I held out my hand for her to take, and once her small hand was tight in mine, I led her through the dark house and up a set of stairs and down the hall. I opened a set of double doors that opened to the large master bedroom. A small side table light was on, giving off just enough light that we could make our way over to the bed. I left her standing there and went to shut and lock the doors.

Chapter Six

Bree
I'd seen the way he'd been looking at me downstairs. The way his eyes had run the length of my body when I had stepped from the bathroom. The way he had studied me as I sat drinking the tea he had made. I was as mysterious to him as he was to me, and the fact that my brother had so sternly warned me to stay away from him made him all that much more mysterious.

I watched as he shut the door to his bedroom, and then he turned the lock.

"Why are you locking the door?" I asked as another loud crash of thunder sounded, almost drowning out my voice.

"I always sleep with my door locked, but it's more to keep you safe," he said, walking back to me.

I couldn't help but allow my eyes to fall down to where his sweat pants hung off his hips. His solid eight-pack flexing as he walked, the outline of his semi-hard cock present behind the grey material. I licked my lips and bit my bottom lip.

My look didn't go unnoticed, a half-cocked smile sat on his lips as he placed his hands on my upper arms and leaned into me. "Like what you see, princess?"

The room started to get hot as his eyes connected with mine. I swallowed hard as we stood staring at one another, until voices below caused us to break our concentration.

"The guys are back? Does that mean Snake is here?" I asked. I could feel the terror building in me and could hear it in my voice as I looked to the bedroom's double doors.

I could feel him watching me. A loud clap of thunder and flash of lightning and the room was bathed in darkness. I could hear footsteps climbing the stairs and the rowdy laughter of the other men coming closer. I swallowed hard, praying that they couldn't get in the room. I could feel myself start to shake when I felt his warm touch on my cheek.

"Relax. You're safe."

I felt his breath across my cheek, and his lips grazed mine. At first, I didn't move, and then his lips grazed mine again, nipping my bottom lip. All my senses were heightened, and a surge of want ran through me, and this time I kissed him back. The sudden urge to get lost in him and forget about the other men outside the door was overwhelming. My hands found his and our hands clasped together. I felt him let go and wrap his arm around me, pulling me in closer for a deeper kiss. All it had taken was one touch...one kiss...and I was hooked.

When I felt his other hand let go of mine, I wrapped both arms around his neck. As we kissed, I felt his hands travel down my back, one hand gripping my ass as he pulled me against him. I could feel his hardness through his pants as he ground into me. I couldn't help the soft moan that escaped my lips at the feel of him.

He backed me up until the backs of my knees hit the edge of the bed. "Lay down," he whispered.

I did as I was told. In another clap of thunder and flash of lightning I caught sight of him. He had dropped his sweats, and I felt him kneel on the bed. He pushed my legs open and crawled up between them, leaning down to kiss me.

His fingers laced with mine, and he brought my hand to his cock, wrapping my hand around him. He met my lips as I started to stroke him, a gasp coming from him as I ran my hand up and over the head of his cock, where I concentrated on the bead of precum that sat there.

He kissed me deeply, his hands roaming my body, running over my breasts, teasing my nipples through my shirt. I let go of his cock as he sat back and opened my legs, first kissing each knee, and then his strong hands grasping the insides of my thighs. I hadn't put my panties back on after my shower and could already feel how soaked I was. The thought of him touching me was almost more than I could bear.

His hands traveled down closer to my center, around to the outsides of my thighs, then around to my ass.

"No panties?" he whispered.

Even though he couldn't see me, I shook my head no.

"Maybe you have a naughty side after all, princess," he whispered as his strong hands grasped my ass and squeezed. He pushed the T-shirt I was wearing up, and before I knew it, the shirt was on the floor.

He kissed my neck and slowly began moving down my body. Kissing and biting the top of each breast gently, running nothing but the tip of his tongue around both my nipples, sending chills through my body. He continued kissing down my belly, running his tongue around my belly button, and then kissed the top of each hip. As I bucked off the bed, I felt his one hand move between my legs, and two fingers slid inside of me, causing me to let out a loud moan at his intrusion.

A couple of pumps and he slid a third finger in, stretching me. "So fucking wet," he whispered as he nipped the side of my hip with his teeth.

He pulled his fingers out, and I instantly felt the void. He reached over on the nightstand and opened the drawer, feeling around in the dark. When he had grabbed what he wanted, he gripped my hips and rolled onto his back, pulling me with him.

I straddled his hips, unsure what he wanted, and then I heard the rip of the foil packet. Another clap of thunder and flash of lightning gave me enough light to see him rolling a condom on. He held onto my hips and guided me on top of him. He positioned himself at my entrance and, gripping my hips, he lowered me onto him, a low moan escaping me as he filled me.

"Don't move. Just relax," he whispered as he held my hips tightly. He started to move, guiding my hips to match his movement. I rested my hands on his chest. He was buried so deep inside of me, I could feel every inch of his movements.

I could feel the pleasure building inside of me, and I started to squeeze him tighter. His breathing grew more ragged with every matched stroke.

I kept fighting my moans, wanting to keep quiet so the other guys didn't hear, but as he picked up the pace, I couldn't hold them back any longer.

My head fell back, and I let out a loud moan as his thumb connected with my clit. A couple more pumps, his thumb stroking my clit, and I was a quivering mess, coming all over him. As I collapsed on him, he gripped me tight, pumping hard and fast and allowing his release to escape.

Chapter Seven

Bree

A loud bang and a roar of bike engines woke me from a deep sleep. I glanced around the strange room. I'd slept so soundly I'd almost forgotten where I was. I looked to the other side of the bed for Sebastian but it was empty.

I thought back to last night. I'd fallen asleep with his arms wrapped around me. Sometime in the middle of the night, I'd felt someone roll me over, and when I opened my eyes, I'd found Sebastian with his face firmly planted between my legs. I'd run my fingers into his hair, gripping as he licked and sucked at my center, until I was panting and calling his name. A surge of excitement ran through me at the memory.

I sat up, holding the blanket around me. I had no idea why. I was the only one in the room, and the doors were still shut tight. I glanced to a chair in the corner to see my clothes waiting for me in a neatly folded pile.

I slipped from beneath the covers and slid into my panties and bra, and then I walked over to the bathroom. I quickly ran some water, splashed my face, and glanced in the mirror.

I walked over to my clothes and slipped into my jeans and T-shirt and picked up my sweater. There underneath sat my purse and phone. I powered it up and noticed that it was almost ten. My first thought was my brother, who had probably been waiting for me to call him most of the night.

I needed to get home.

I slipped into my hoodie, shoved my phone into my back pocket, and grabbed my purse. I walked to the bedroom door and prayed that all the guys were gone already. I wandered down the hall and down the stairs, trying to remember the way to the kitchen.

The second my foot hit the top step, the smell of bacon hit my nose and my stomach let out a loud growl. I was just about to the bottom step when Sebastian appeared carrying a plate with pancakes and bacon on it.

"There you are. I was just bringing you breakfast."

He didn't appear as frightening as he had last night when I first met him. He wore a pair of loose-fitting jeans and a white T-shirt that stretched over his muscles.

"Thanks, but I need to get going." I didn't want to appear rude, but I knew if my brother had decided to come looking for me and found me here there would be a huge fight.

"Oh..."

"It's just my brother is probably worried sick," I murmured.

"He already called. I told him I put you up for the night because of the storm and all. He knows you're safe. I will take you home after you eat," he said, and guided me into the empty kitchen.

Chapter Eight

Sebastian

I sipped on a coffee, while she sat there eating every drop of food on her plate. She picked up her mug and washed down the last mouthful with coffee and looked up at me. The innocent look she gave me went straight to my cock as she licked her fingers.

"How am I going to get my car?"

"It's already taken care of. I had a couple of guys go and take it to a local garage. I will have it repaired and returned to you."

Her eyes widened at my words. She set her mug down on the table and looked at me. "Let me know what that will cost please."

"Why?" I sat there with a cocky smirk on my face.

"Well, because I would like to repay you."

"No need. It's being taken care of."

"No, I won't hear of it. Please just let me know."

"Your brother said you'd probably put up a fight. It's taken care of, end of story."

"But..."

"No buts," I said, getting up and removing the dirty plate from in front of her. "We should probably get you home."

She nodded and grabbed her purse, throwing it across her body. I reached for my leather jacket and slipped into it.

Once she was secured on the back of my bike, her arms wrapped around my waist, where I silently prayed they might stay for a while, I started the bike and took off.

Forty minutes later, we pulled up outside of her dorm. I parked the bike and walked her to the door where she leaned up against the brick building and looked into my eyes.

"Thank you," she whispered.

"No, thank you," I said, tweaking her chin with my thumb and forefinger.

She looked as if she wanted to say something but no words came out. Instead, I leaned into her and met her lips. I felt her arms wrap around me, as she deepened the kiss. I could feel myself growing harder and wished that I had taken her for one last spin before dropping her off.

"Can I come up?" I asked.

She shook her head, kissing me again. "My roommate will be home."

I felt the surge of disappointment hit as I sucked her bottom lip into my mouth. The sound of voices around the corner forced me to break off our kiss. She looked up at me with pleading eyes, but I needed to go. I couldn't risk getting caught here.

"I'll let you know when your car is ready," I said as I made my way over to my bike. She nodded. "Go inside."

I watched as she pulled the door open and made her way inside, soon disappearing from my sight. I got on the bike, revved the engine, and took off in the direction of home.

Chapter Nine

B ree Kendall and I walked down the hall towards the library. We had talked most of the weekend and had stayed up almost all night last night while I had filled her in on everything that had happened and why I hadn't come home. I wasn't going to lie; Sebastian was the only thing on my mind. The vivid memory of the night before was still at the forefront of my mind.

"I still can't believe that you were brave enough to walk into that bar."

"Well, I was desperate. What was I going to do?"

"Apparently Sebastian." Kendall laughed out loud.

"Shut up," I said, elbowing her in the side.

"I'm just glad you are safe, and I can't wait to meet him. Perhaps you could hook me up with one of his hot friends."

"Perhaps, that is if I ever do see him again. I mean, I have to get my car back, but other than that, I haven't heard from him at all."

We entered the library and sat down at one of the tables and cracked open our books. We had an hour until our next class and figured we would get some work done, but soon we were back to talking about Sebastian.

The hour passed quickly, and we made our way to our next lecture. The room was full, and the voices were loud as we walked in. The professor didn't appear to be in the room yet, and there were only two seats available side by side in the second row which we grabbed.

We had just sat down and were trying to hear one another over the loud chorus of voices behind us when we heard a door open and slam shut. I looked to the left and right and couldn't see anyone, which meant the door must have opened from the back of the room.

I opened my book to a blank page as the voices began to quiet. A loud bang sounded as the professor with his back to us dropped his briefcase on the desk at the front of the room and proceeded to the board. He quickly scribbled something on it and began making his rounds through the first row.

My phone vibrated and I quickly grabbed it, reading the message. I was just about to send a response when a hand gripped my phone. I looked down to see a tattoo I'd recognize anywhere. The words "Full Throttle" sat between his thumb and index finger. With my heart in my throat, I slowly glanced up to see Sebastian looking down at me. What the hell was he doing here? There was no way he was my professor for this class. I could feel my face heating and quickly put my phone down as his eyes washed over me.

"And you are...?" his deep voice asked.

"Bree Walker." I swallowed hard again, almost choking on my own name.

"Well, Bree, there will be no cell phone use when you are in my lecture hall, understand." He used the same authoritative voice he had used on me when he demanded I spend the night in his room or suffer the consequences.

I could barely move. I simply nodded. Less than seventy-two hours ago I'd woken in the middle of the night with his face buried between my legs, and now he stood before me as my professor. He looked amazing dressed in a suit and tie, and I felt the familiar ache building between my legs as he stared into my eyes.

One touch, one kiss, and I was hooked. He should have been *forbidden*.

About the Author

USA Today Bestselling Author S.L. Sterling was born and raised in southern Ontario. She now lives in Northern Ontario Canada and is married to her best friend and soul mate and their two dogs.

An avid reader all her life, S.L. Sterling dreamt of becoming an author. She decided to give writing a try after one of her favorite authors launched a course on how to write your novel. This course gave her the push she needed to put pen to paper and her debut novel "It Was Always You" was born.

When S.L. Sterling isn't writing or plotting her next novel she can be found curled up with a cup of coffee, blanket and the newest romance novel from one of her favorite authors.

In her spare time, she enjoys camping, hiking, sunny destinations, spending quality time with family and friends and of course reading.

Facebook: http://bit.ly/SLSterlingFB
Goodreads: http://bit.ly/SLSterlingGoodreads
Instagram: http://bit.ly/SLSterlingInstagram
Bookbub: http://bit.ly/SLSterlingBB
Sterlings Silver Sapphires: http://bit.ly/SterlingsSapphires
Newsletter Signup: http://bit.ly/GetmyNewsletter
Website http://www.authorslsterling.com

Our Final Takedown

Vi Summers

Chapter One

Cameron

His larger-than-life portrait took my breath away. The last time I saw Raidan Kaspar in the flesh was almost ten years ago, and being confronted by his oversized, glossy image each time I disembarked the train in the subway was a kick to my heart. We'd been nothing but naïve teenagers thinking we were in love, but that didn't stop me from wanting to pull him from the photo and bury his face between my legs. He didn't do much of that when we were younger, but now I was older and knew what I liked, I indulged in the daydream of Raidan falling to his knees between mine.

I cleared my throat and forced the fantasy away, then hoisted my handbag higher on my shoulder. We'd been in love once—innocently head over heels until I broke it off, breaking our hearts in the process. Until that day, we'd spent every hour we could together. Laughing, studying, fooling around, and getting lost in each other's bodies.

A scared part of me still yearned for him. Still loved him.

With the number of women Raidan Kaspar was photographed with, he no doubt spared no thought to little ol' Cameron Pearce from Rock Hill. And just because he was in town didn't mean we would ever cross paths—not in a city of over three million.

With only three days before the ultimate fight night, he was caught up in a whirlwind of pre-fight chaos. "Killer Kaspar" they called him, which contrasted with every single thing I knew about Raidan. When we'd dated in high school, he'd been the perfect mix of sweet, attentive, assertive, and driven. And when he started winning state-wide championships in wrestling, we both knew he was going places. Places I wouldn't be able to follow.

By the time we'd hit eighteen, he'd been winning most, if not all, wrestling matches in his weight division. He wanted more. To push himself further. To be the best of the best, so he shifted divisions to MMA and set his sights on UFC training in Las Vegas.

I knew he had both the passion and skills to go all the way, and it was at that moment I knew he'd outgrown me. So, I broke things off before my heart could shatter further. Ultimately, Raidan's MMA plans didn't include me, and I couldn't bear to hold him back from his dreams. I did what I thought was best at the time. And fuck it still hurt.

Dumping him was my biggest regret. The woman I'd grown into would have tried harder. Fought to make it work until the bitter end. Instead, I'd been left wondering if we could have ever made it through the high-profile life he led.

I cautiously picked my way up the subway steps in my stilettos and emerged into the early morning Miami daylight.

I'd moved to Miami to chase a career in modeling. While my portfolio wasn't one to be scoffed at, I was still looking for my *big* break. The break everyone in the industry craved: the one that propels a model into stardom and big contracts.

Weaving in and out of the sea of people emerging from the Metro, I began the two-block walk to the agency. I had a photoshoot today, hence the early start, and used the journey to Downtown to get my head in the game.

I remained zoned out and focused while waiting for the pedestrian light to turn green, then stepped onto the crossing with purpose. Halfway across the street, a sharp impact to my shoulder had me stumbling and cursing at whoever slammed into me.

"Ah fuck. Watch it!" I yelled, despite chiseled arms encircling my waist to stop me from toppling in my stilettos. As fast as his touch stabilized me, it was gone.

I turned toward the tall, muscle-backed stranger striding away. "And thanks," I called snarkily. "Asshole!"

His prowl-like swagger slowed, and he twisted at the waist. The icy glare bounced off my hardened exterior, and I sent him a grin that was sure to have me haunting his memory all day. It got a reaction, but not the one intended. His expression morphed from agitation to shock.

Then it hit me all at once. Memories rushed back with alarming force, and I faltered, open-mouthed and lost for words.

The busy Miami street snapped back into focus with a loud, continuous honk. I gasped and turned on my stiletto, hurrying off the crosswalk as quickly as possible. But the chorus of honking didn't stop. It continued, then multiplied as more impatient drivers added to the disturbance.

Once safely on the sidewalk, I pressed a hand to my chest.

"Cammi!" was yelled, causing me to turn.

My pulse kicked harder as Raidan strode toward me, not giving a fuck that he still held up traffic.

"Cameron!"

Pedestrians parted like the Red Sea for him. Dazzling blue eyes pinned me to the spot. They burned with a heat that far surpassed the anger when I broke up with him. His heated glare took my breath away, and it satisfied me to no end that I could still bring his world to a halt.

An audience gathered; their attention drawn by Raidan calling my name.

He stepped intimately close and used his muscled shoulders to shield me from the spectators. My body grew heavy with longing and regret. Despite me thinking about him for the last almost-decade, I wasn't ready for this confrontation, and absolutely *not* in public.

"Raidan," I breathed out. The single word was nothing but a ghost of an exhale as it left my mouth.

"Fuck, it really *is* you," he whispered as his eyes followed the path his thumb traced over my jaw.

"It's me." I forced a smile, but it came out shaky.

Suppressed feelings came flooding back as his penetrating gaze scrutinized me at close range. And I wasn't surprised when his attention narrowed on my nose.

I thought he'd say something about it, but as soon as his eyes flicked to mine again, the words on the tip of his tongue vanished.

Indecision swam in his expression for a beat, then after a short pause, he dipped his head and captured my lips with his. His thumb sought access at the corner of my mouth while his tongue flicked and teased mine.

The street, the spectators, hissed murmurs about the great Raidan Kaspar, the need to get to work... it all fell away and became muted. Kissing him after so many years sent thrill after thrill through me. We'd both outgrown who we once were—two loved-up high school kids—yet the spark between us still burned as hot, if not hotter, as it ever did.

Gentle pressure forced me back until I hit the brick wall of the building behind me. He broke the kiss and studied me. Dilated pupils and the unbridled desire in his gaze made my breath snag, then a hint of amusement tugged at the corner of his mouth.

"You're taller," he murmured.

"That's what happens when I live in stilettos."

Raidan released me and stepped back a pace. I stood still while he undressed me with his eyes—I even struck a natural pose like I was taught to under pressure. The leisurely roll of Raidan's tongue over his lower lip accompanied an appreciative nod as his focus returned to my legs.

"It's rude to ogle, Raidan. I know your mamma taught you that."

His eyes cut to my face again, and the ghosts of yesteryear passed within the blue depths. The good and the bad, the happy and the sad, the memories of what we once were... all written in his expression. While I expected to see humor winning out, sorrow and regret shone through. Seeing it etched so clearly on his handsome face made my heart drop.

"Cammi—" He cut off when my cell phone started ringing.

I dug it out of my handbag and cursed at Destiny's name on the screen. "Sorry, Raidan, I need to take this really quick."

He waved a hand, then folded his arms across his chest. My eyes remained locked on his as I answered, "Hey."

"Hey, where the fuck are you? We're supposed to be here early."

I pulled the phone away to check the time. "Shit!"

"Yeah, shit," came Destiny's sass. *"Get your ass here before Bree. I do not want to be part of the fallout."*

With her warning ringing loud, she disconnected, leaving me staring at Raidan with the phone still pressed to my ear.

He arched a brow in question.

I swallowed down the disappointment over having to rush off while shoving my phone away. "Sorry, Raidan, I need to go. It was, uh, nice to see you again. You look... good."

His smirk widened into the boy-next-door grin I first fell in love with. "You look good too, Cammi."

"Good luck with the upcoming fight," I said over my shoulder, already angling away in my need to hurry.

One hand whipped out and snagged my inner elbow. The force spun me one-eighty and my chest collided with Raidan's. Breathless from the impact, the last of the air in my lungs was stolen from the searing kiss he had laid on me. He gripped both sides of my face and tilted it to the side, creating heat between my legs that amplified when a deep hum rumbled within Raidan's chest. I gathered his tank in my fists and held tight.

The palpable energy radiating off his torso sent my temperature soaring, and I swayed on my feet. A surge of reckless need had my chest thrusting higher and my back arching.

Raidan pulled away without warning, panting as if he'd just done a round in the cage.

"Shit," he hissed, and ran a hand down his chin.

The edge of torture bunching his brow had me blinking hard. Seeing him again hurt so much, let alone kissing him, and stirred up the old feelings I thought I'd outgrown.

"I'm sorry," I stammered. "I really need to go."

Spinning on my heel again, I blinked rapidly to clear the sheen of heartbroken tears clouding my eyes. I power walked with my chin held high around the block corner and rushed through the agency door. While riding the elevator to the loft, I checked my makeup and applied a hasty layer of gloss, hoping it would take the focus off the reddening kiss-rash forming around my mouth.

The instant I entered the loft, Destiny was on me. "Girl, you okay?" Her perfectly dark penciled eyebrows angled with concern. "You look m'fucking flustered."

"I *am* flustered." I flapped at my cheeks, hoping to erase the blush. "I just bumped into Raidan..."

She snapped up a hand. "Raidan who?"

I bit down on my grin. "Kaspar."

"Girl, now I know you're trippin'."

"I swear I'm not tripping. Like, legit Raidan Kaspar."

She at least humored me. "*Well!* What happened?"

"He *kissed* me."

Her large brown eyes flared impossibly wider, then her attention dropped to my mouth. "That explains that mess but doesn't explain why he came out of nowhere and kissed you."

I laughed breathlessly and pressed a hand to my chest. "No, he called my name, chased me down, and caged me against a wall, then..."

Her eyes narrowed in suspicion. "How the fuck did he know your name?"

I ran my tongue over my bottom lip, tasting my cherry gloss. "We dated in high school."

Destiny's lips pouted and her brows lifted with attitude. "Mmhmm?"

"Des, I swear. You know the R tattooed close to my hoohaa?"

A devilish smile broke through her sassy expression. "R marks the spot?"

"Yeah, that one. R is for *Raidan*."

Her jaw dropped. "No fucking way."

"And the rest is history. It's been nine years, so..." I shrugged.

"Girl, you don't get a guy's initial tattooed on your hoohaa then shrug it off as if it's nothing." When her eyes snapped from my lower abdomen to my face, she smirked. "He's gonna be comin' for you."

I scoffed and breezed past her. "Don't be ridiculous. He's got all the women he needs, and I'm the girl he doesn't anymore."

The bitter edge to my voice was distinguishable. In fact, it tasted as acidic as it sounded.

"But not the one he *wants* by the sounds of things," Destiny called after me.

I waved her off and headed to the dressing room to properly assess the damage. We had a branding shoot today for a massive corporation, and the last thing I needed was for my mouth to be red with a rash when Bree arrived to set us up. She'd pitch one hell of a bitch fit.

My fingers trembled as I lifted them to my lips. I could lie to myself and say his kiss meant nothing, but my reflection didn't lie. The emotion in my eyes held all the truth: I still loved Raidan as much as I did the day I left him.

Chapter Two

Raidan

Rooted to the spot, I stared after Cameron's pert little ass snapping from side-to-side as she walked away from me.

Cameron Pearce was the one that got away. When she dumped my ass in high school, I naïvely thought I'd been set free. Despite loving her, I couldn't fucking deny I'd been a little relieved that I could selfishly pursue my quest for turning pro without the guilt over being expected to tow her with me.

As I rose to fame, a niggling part of me always wondered what Cammi and I would have become. Our friends from high school were now getting married and having kids, and here I was, fucking most things with two legs, all while trying to take my mind off the one pair I could never forget.

Said pair of legs though... I grunted under my breath when they disappeared around the block corner.

While everything was bone-achingly familiar, Cammi was vastly different. She held herself with power and assertion now. Even when I prowled toward her, she met me head-on and without fear. She walked on those stilettos with fierce strides that were new to me.

Her body was thin and lithe, which wasn't like her; the Cammi from high school had healthy curves and an ass I could use as a pillow. She'd barely be light flyweight now, at best. And her nose... It cut me deeper than expected to see she'd had the little hump removed. The one I used to glide my finger up and down while she lay with her head resting on my stomach.

"Raidan, who's the girl?" someone called, accompanied with running footfall.

"Fuck," I hissed, turning to see the first set of paps showing up to get the fucking scoop.

Without giving him time to accost me, I strode to the edge of the footpath, then picked a gap in the traffic. Running across the crosswalk where my past had crossed with the present, I simply couldn't force Cammi from my head.

I jogged back to the downtown gym and barged through the doors, gunning for the battle ropes to start the gym portion of my workout. Pumping my arms until they burned failed to shift the focus from the first love of my life. In my dreams she'd been the same, and my teeth ground together thinking about how much she'd physically changed.

Ironic, since I'd shed my former self, both physically and mentally. I'd hardened to the cutthroat world of making it in the UFC. For Cammi, though, I already let my guard down to reveal my old softer side, and on a street in downtown no less.

I growled and dug in harder, working my arms relentlessly to combat the realization of how stupid I'd been. Not that my publicist would care—as she said, all publicity is good publicity, especially in the lead-up to a fight.

Aki, my coach, appeared and closely scrutinized my form. Over his expansive career as a world-renowned coach, he'd trained many UFC champions before me. I'd switched to him a few years back when I started to stagnate under my former coach. The fresh start with Aki had been the fucking wake-up call I needed to get the fire back in my belly. He had a way of pushing me past previous boundaries and elevating my skills to the next level. Everything he'd taught me so far had served me well in the cage, even if I hated him at times during the grueling training.

Aki clapped once, and I immediately dumped the ropes on the floor and sucked in lungfuls of air.

"Death jumps," he stated, still eyeing me with his arms crossed over his chest.

I moved to the end of the row of boxes and began jumping up and down from each.

Aki's sharp-toned voice cut through the concentration. "Where's your head at, Raidan?"

"Never fucking mind," I bit back.

He strolled alongside me as I jumped. "I do fucking mind, especially this close to match night."

When I ignored him, he sniffed, then yelled, "Bag rack, now!"

Throwing a pissed off glare over my shoulder, I jogged to the bag rack where fifty one-hundred-pound boxing bags hung in wait.

Shoving my way through the first row, I then kicked, kneed, and punched my way through hundreds of calories until Aki finally called the training to a halt forty minutes later.

He clapped three times, thus concluding the session. "Cooldown stretches, then ice it up."

I snatched up my discarded tank and scrubbed it over my face and torso, mopping up the sweat that streamed in salty rivers. After sucking back a bellyful of water, I gently lowered into the first of a series of yoga poses Aki had taught me. The first time he'd led me through the new cooldown routine, I'd looked at him like he was fucked in the head, though now I welcomed the stretch for my coiled muscles and joints.

Fifteen minutes later, I'd just lowered myself into the ice bath when Aki's squeaking footsteps came in my direction.

"Finley is singing your praises," he announced with amusement in his voice despite it not showing in his face. The Korean was a master of his expressions, and I'd learned to listen for his tone instead of seeing it on his face.

"And why's that?" I drawled, suspicious. If Finley didn't have a rod stuck up her ass, she might actually be fun to have around.

"For the free publicity." Aki flipped his tablet around and showed me a brand-new news article.

"The fuck!" I exclaimed, launching forward, and sending a torrent of iced water onto the concrete floor.

The article was published in the Miami DT news less than an hour ago, featuring me and Cammi.

"Who took these?" I demanded.

"Dunno. But seems that you and this woman are the fresh talk of the rumor mill. Everyone wants to know who she is, especially being spotted with you. The headline is fucking unoriginal, though; Beauty and the Beast," Aki snorted.

While scrubbing both hands over my face, my frustration grew. I had kept Cammi in my memories for years, and I wasn't okay with sharing her with the world. Especially not under the circumstances of misconstrued gossip.

"Who is she?" Aki pressed.

"Just some girl I dated in high school," I lied.

My coach saw through the bullshit. "You don't look at a woman like that, then kiss her like *that* when she's just some girl."

"Fuck off with your wisdom," I grumbled.

He chuckled softly, then tutted while looking at the pictures again. "No wonder your head was off this morning." He scrolled using his gnarled middle finger and pursed his lips. Then piercing dark brown eyes lifted to meet mine. "After you're iced, we meditate. I need to be sure this is gone from your head. We can't afford *any* distractions."

"She won't be a distraction. If anything, seeing her gives me a reason to fight harder. We broke up when I wanted to pursue my UFC career."

What I thought was understanding entered Aki's gaze, and he nodded swiftly. "Two more minutes, then we meditate."

I reclined again, panting slightly against the icy cold that clamped my lungs and made it hard to draw a proper breath. As I let my head tip backward, memories of Cammi came rushing back.

She stole my heart, then broke it. And because of the loss, I vowed our breakup wouldn't be in vain. I vowed to make her proud and make up for losing her.

When the timer went off, I slowly climbed from the tub and stripped off my underwear. With a towel wrapped around my hips, I then made my way to the adjoining changing rooms where I quickly showered under tepid water.

By the time I emerged wearing sweats, socks, and a hoodie, Finley was in Juan's office pacing back and forth. They spotted me through the window and Finley gestured for me to get my ass into the office ASAP. I took my sweet fucking time strolling to the closed door, then compiling her impatience by knocking.

"Oh, hurry up, Raidan; you know we're waiting for you!" she snarled.

I emphasized my grin as I opened the door. "Ah, Finley. What a pleasure."

"Don't be a smart-ass." She thrust the tablet at me. "Who is she?"

"A friend," I deadpanned.

Finley's eyes narrowed. "Not buying it."

I leaned around her and widened my eyes at Juan—my manager. "Aki's waiting for me for meditation."

"After this, Raidan. I haven't heard what Finley wants to say yet."

More than a little pissed, I sat in the chair in front of his desk, set my elbows on the arms, and steepled my fingers in front of my chest.

"If you're going to hound me about who she is, then you're wasting your breath. She's a friend; one I don't want dragged into my world."

"Dragged, huh?" Finley scoffed. "So, the name Cameron Pearce doesn't mean anything to you?"

I was on my feet in an instant. "How—"

"It didn't take long to make the connection. Social media is a wondrous thing when you need to dig for information." Her eyes then dropped to an article I hadn't yet seen, and she read aloud: "Cameron Pearce, up-and-coming model in downtown Miami currently modeling for *Wave Babes* swimwear, was seen in a passionate lip-lock with UFC's champion Killer Kaspar early this morning."

Her striking hazel eyes hit mine again. "We'd be foolish not to jump on this opportunity."

"Opportunity?" I waited for her to elaborate.

"The modeling world is an untapped market, one we haven't ventured into. We can use the hype surrounding you and this 'mystery girl'—" Finley air quoted, "—to our advantage. Not only will that push publicity into unexplored avenues, but it garners extra attention in the lead-up to your fight. And extra attention equals more revenue." Her eyes danced and shone from simply *thinking* about the potential.

I, however, shook my head. "No. I won't use her to further my career."

Finley's expression turned sly. "The way I see it, it's mutually beneficial. There's money to be gained by teaming up with her agency for an exclusive photoshoot. And for Cameron, this is an opportunity to propel her modeling career to new heights. After all, that's what all models want, right? Their lucky break. You'd be hers... Which is so fitting since she let you go so you could chase yours."

I rounded on her. "You prying bitch!"

Not intimidated, she smirked. "It's called doing my job."

"It's called overstepping boundaries, Finley!" I shouted.

"Oh, come on, Raidan! Since when do you care about boundaries? Cameron dumped your ass in high school, so why not use her for all we can get?"

"I'm fucking done here," I hissed, turning to Juan. "She'd better be fucking *gone* by the time I get back."

Storming from his office and heading out the back door of the gym, having no idea where I was going or what I would do once I got there, I headed onto the street.

All I knew was if I had my way, Finley's ass would be fired for merely *suggesting* I used Cameron for personal gain.

Unable to let sleeping dogs lie, I headed for the beach and pulled out my phone. Cameron's image appeared as soon as I searched her name—the first time I'd looked her up in years.

Her modeling profile took my breath away. The confidence she exuded in front of the camera created a wash of pride. My heart then dropped when I saw a contact number at the bottom of the page. Surely it wasn't hers.

Only one way to find out.

Chapter Three

Cameron

The shoot for *Wave Babes* swimwear finally wrapped up at midday, and I hadn't eaten since yesterday afternoon. We were all on a strictly no-food-before-a-shoot contract, and my stomach had been in knots for the last hour.

"Oh, thank God! I'm about to pass out," I hissed, accepting the skim iced coffee from Maleke, my close friend and non-binary model.

They raised a brow and pointed at me. "And, bitch, as light as your ass is, I am not picking it up off the floor unless I'm dead drunk and need lifting too."

Their pout made me laugh. "Which, speaking from experience, isn't as easy as it sounds."

Maleke's lips pursed harder as they tried to suppress a grin. A wicked glint then entered their eyes, and they waved a flamboyant hand around. "Okay, we're all wondering about this, so I'm just gonna come out and say it; are you fucking Raidan Kaspar and how do I get in on that action?"

The sip of iced coffee hit the back of my throat as I inhaled. Maleke slapped my back halfheartedly while I coughed and spluttered.

When I finally came up for air, red-faced and teary-eyed, they handed me a napkin and deadpanned, "Dramatic much."

I continued to shallow cough while dabbing my under-eyes. "That was so mean, Maleke. Why did you wait until I was drinking?"

They flicked their fingers again. "It's not my fault you were an eager beaver. Speaking of—spill the tea already, honey."

"There is no tea to spill," I replied hoarsely.

"Uh, huh; that's not what the rumor mill is saying."

I aimed a glacial glare at Destiny. She held up her hands and shook her head.

"Girl, I did *not* breathe a word. Besides, I've been shooting with you all morning. Unless Mal can read minds, that did *not* come from me."

"I know, Des, I'm just... shocked that this got around so fast."

Maleke scoffed. "Bitch, this is Miami. What did you expect?"

"What have you heard?"

I was ready for their reply this time as I took another sip of iced coffee.

"More like what I've seen. You're blowing up social media with your little show on the street this morning. Oof..." They shivered. "...The photos still get me a little heated."

"Gross, Mal! And what photos?"

They pulled out their phone, made a show of tapping the screen with a nail-polished forefinger, then flipped it with a raised eyebrow.

Images of me and Raidan crossing the street appeared first, then one with his hand wrapped around my inner elbow, then another of him pressing me against the wall and kissing me like we were in private.

"Shit," I breathed out.

"Yeah, *shit*," Maleke snipped.

Destiny rushed over. "Babes, let me see."

"Oh, sure thing, babes," Maleke agreed, as if they were doing us both a favor. While Des hummed and zoomed in on the photos, Maleke lifted their eyebrows again.

"You're blushing, honey. C'mon, out with it!"

I let out a heavy sigh. "We dated in high school."

They scoffed. "Is that it?"

"Pretty much. We thought we would be together forever, but it didn't work out."

Out of nowhere, Maleke sucked in an exaggerated, noisy gasp. "That ghastly tattoo by your cock holster—R is for *Raidan,* isn't it?"

"It's not *ghastly*!" I exclaimed, crossing my arms. "And yes, it's for Raidan."

Maleke let out a giggle that outshone both mine and Destiny's, then made a show of pulling up a new contact listing on their phone.

"Yeah, so I'm gonna need his phone number, you know, for best friend purposes of checking him out and making sure he ain't gonna hurt you."

I playfully knocked away their phone and rolled my eyes. "The only purpose you want his number for is so you can hit on him. Besides, I don't even know his number."

Maleke's eyes narrowed. "So, you didn't intend to meet this morning?"

"No." I shook my head. "That was a complete accident." One I was both grateful for, and still a little broken over.

Those thoughts must have shown on my face. Maleke wrapped their arms around me and swayed us from side to side.

"Don't be sad, Cam Cam. Be happy—you were obviously destined to meet again."

"Maybe."

"Maybe yes. And by the look of those photos, he never got over you, honey."

I pulled away and forced a smile. "Thanks for the pep talk, Mal, and the iced coffee. I'm going to get changed and grab some fresh air."

They and Destiny exchanged a look but gave me a reassuring smile. "Sure thing. Drinks later?"

"I'll be there."

I hurried to the dressing room and sat on the wooden chair closest to my locker. The entire encounter with Raidan had tipped my world off-kilter. Just when I finally felt as if I had a handle on my life, his reappearance shook the foundations I'd worked so hard to build.

I took another sip of iced coffee, then set it down while I went to change my outfit and check my phone. A missed call from an unknown number immediately caught my attention. My lungs squeezed as I pressed the phone to my ear and waited for the new voice message to play, hoping it was from someone wanting modeling services.

The elation quickly turned to confusion when the message seemed to be blank. I pulled the phone away from my ear and frowned until a low, murmured voice began to speak.

"Cammi, it's Raidan. I uh... fuck, I dunno. Seeing you today just got me thinking about you and... I just wanted to let you know the media is speculating, and I'm sorry to get you caught up in it. If you wanna chat, vent, or whatever, call me back sometime."

The line went dead, and I couldn't draw a breath for an entire minute. He sounded just like the old Raidan, *my* Raids, complete with the hint of shyness in his voice.

With my pulse still elevated and the phone shaking in my grip, I lowered onto the chair and took a long sip of iced coffee.

I deliberated whether or not to call him back. I feared that fantasies and memories were setting me up for a hard fall back to reality. The Raidan of today was a far cry from the boy he used to be, and I had to remind myself of that fact.

On a deep sigh, I set my phone aside and stripped from my robe to re-dress. Destiny breezed in with her robe billowing behind her just as I fastened the last stiletto strap.

"All peachy again, girl?"

"All peachy." I smiled and tugged at the high hemline of my dress. "We're done for the day, right?"

"Done 'n' dusted."

"Thank God. Wanna grab Keto Bowl with me?"

"Nah, girl, I gotta bounce. I start work at three," she mumbled, stripping without a care before stepping into a lacy thong.

I shouldered my handbag and closed my locker. "I'll see ya tomorrow, then."

"That's the plan."

I emerged from the changing room into a hive of activity. Camera equipment was being packed and swimsuits were being tossed into various suitcases.

Bree stood with the shoot director, looking over his shoulder as they scrutinized the images of me and Destiny. From their body language and hand gestures, it appeared to be good feedback.

She glanced over her shoulder, then straightened when she saw me. "Before you go, Cameron. I had a last-minute call from a publicist wanting to do an unusual shoot."

Unease unfurled in my stomach. There were straight up dubious contracts, and I didn't want to get involved with one.

"Unusual, how?"

"With Raidan Kaspar of all people. Apparently, there are some images of you two floating around and his publicist wanted to enter into a mutually beneficial promotion opportunity."

Ignoring the kick within my chest and how my lungs refused to inflate, I forced my voice to be steady. "How is that meant to be mutually beneficial? Swimwear and MMA literally have nothing to do with each other."

Bree had the sense to look a little uncomfortable. "His publicist said, and I quote, 'Take advantage of the gossip to expand your modeling base.'"

"And what's the benefit for Raidan?"

She shrugged. "Publicity. He wouldn't have been circulated in modeling circles before, so I guess that's their angle."

Dejection cut across my stomach, and I forced my shoulders back to prevent them from slumping. "No, sorry. I'm not interested."

Bree's jaw dropped. "Are you serious? You're a fool for passing this up."

If only she knew the real story. "I don't need to be piggybacked to where I want to get to, especially in modeling. You can tell his *publicist* that I won't do it."

Vexation hardened the lines on her face. "That, my dear, is a mistake you'll regret."

"I don't think so. Can I go now?"

She gave me a frosty look and sniffed. "Yes."

With a wave of dismissal, she returned to pouring over the images from today's shoot.

I'd become breathless and on the verge of tears by the time I entered the elevator. The suggestion that a shoot with Raidan would help propel my modeling career forward had me vibrating with anger. It was an insult. And the phone message from Raidan himself only added salt to the wound. I felt used; he'd taken advantage of the feelings he'd rekindled by kissing me.

When the elevator opened on the ground floor, I pushed through the exit and onto the busy sidewalk, falling into step with the current of pedestrians. Gaining more strength as each foot hit the ground, I dug through my handbag for my phone; Raidan was going to get a piece of my mind.

He picked up with a cautious, "Hello?"

"Raidan?"

"Cammi?"

"Yes."

An audible puff of air came through the phone. "I have to admit, I wasn't sure if you'd call back or not."

"This isn't a social call, Raidan. Where the fuck do you get off by playing me?"

A hardened edge entered his voice. "Excuse me?"

I scoffed. "Don't play dumb. I know you got your publicist to set up a photo shoot. One that is utterly belittling and nothing but an insult."

"You fucking *what*? I told Finley I didn't want to do it. You need to believe me, Cammi; I did *not* condone this," he urged.

"Either way, I declined the *opportunity*. You can both stick it up your asses. I don't need to ride off your name just to make it in this world, Raidan. And I'm fucking pissed it was insinuated that's what I need."

"Jesus, Cammi, calm down—"

My voice pitched, drawing attention from the surrounding people. "I will *not* calm down!"

"Okay, fuck. Seems that this morning has been taken out of context and every man and their dog are trying to make a dime off it."

"There are pictures of us," I hissed.

Raidan growled. "I know. And I'm furious that Finley is fanning the flames. I'm so sorry, Cam."

The softness returning to his voice thawed some of my temper.

"I thought you were trying to capitalize off it, and that fucking *hurt*."

A rude scoff came through. "Trust me, babe, I don't need the money."

"Nice for some. And don't call me babe," I snapped, slowing my strides as I neared *The Keto Bowl*. "Look, I have to go, but thanks for setting the record straight."

"Are you busy this afternoon?"

Maleke's suggestion of drinks flashed in my mind. "Yeah, I'm going out with a friend later."

"A friend, or... more?"

"Goodbye, Raidan."

"Ca—"

I jabbed the disconnect button. It didn't matter if I was going out with a friend or on a date, what me and Raidan had was in our history, not our future.

Chapter Four

Raidan

I pulled my cap lower as I strode along the corridor. I was much too old to be sneaking out, yet here I was, practically tiptoeing past my coach's suite so he didn't fucking catch me. It was after 11 p.m., and I couldn't settle, let alone begin to think about sleeping after texting Cammi and getting a bunch of convoluted texts back about being out with some guy called Maleke.

Our messages played over in my head.

Me: Hey, you still out?

Cammi: Yeah, we are.

Me: Where?

Cammi: Downtown.

Me: No shit. Where?

Cammi: Why?

Me: Might wanna come say hi.

Cammi: Maleke says yes, I say no.

Me: Who's Maleke?

Cammi: My friend.

Me: Boyfriend?

Cammi: Nope.

Me: Fiancé?

Cammi: Nope.

Me: Fuck buddy.

Cammi: LOL definitely not.
Me: I like Maleke.
Cammi: You'll regret saying that.
Me: Why?
Cammi: You'll see.
Me: So, where are you?
Cammi: At Ombre.
Me: I'll wait for you outside.
Cammi: We're not leaving yet.
Me: I'll text you when I'm outside.
Cammi: Suit yourself.
Me: I will.

I checked my phone one last time to find no new messages, then stepped from the elevator into the empty hotel lobby.

Downtown Miami at night was electrified with flamboyance and flare as people from all walks of life mixed together. I matched the flow of the surrounding crowd while searching for the bar *Ombre*. My steps faltered a little when I came across the well-known gay bar, and gay bars meant *a lot* of attention. Thank fuck I told Cammi I'd meet her outside.

Putting two and two together, I deduced that her friend was gay, and that sat pretty fucking well with me; he wouldn't be dipping his cock into my girl.

The bar came into view on the opposite side of the street, and much to my dismay, Cameron, and who I assumed was Maleke, emerged from the entrance.

Cammi's laugh reached me on the breeze and kicked my pulse into over-drive. I waited for a gap in traffic, all while keeping an eye on them both. Cammi pulled out her phone, and I received a message seconds later.

Cammi: No show, huh?
Me: I can see you and your friend. Don't move.

I smirked when she craned her neck this way and that, searching for me. Picking my way across the street, the instant her eyes fell upon me, I swear time slowed. A brilliant smile formed and illuminated her entire face, shrouding her in a blinding light only I could see.

Her mouth opened to call my name but closed again after I quickly held my forefinger to mine, urging silence. The last thing I needed was a swarm of attention. Tonight, I wanted to fly under the radar, and that meant cautioning Cammi to keep quiet.

"Raids," she breathed out and sent her arms wide. They slung around my neck and hugged tight as I wrapped her in my arms and lifted her from her feet.

"Hi, beautiful. Keeping out of trouble?"

She giggled. "Always."

Setting her back on her high heels, I gave her a once-over, appreciating the view while growling under my breath at how much skin she was showing.

My focus cut to her friend when he stepped between me and Cam, much too fucking close for comfort.

"Maleke, I assume?" I drawled.

"For you, I'll be anyone you want me to be, honey." A wicked smirk accompanied the suggestion and had me feeling violated through my clothes.

Cammi scoffed and slapped Maleke's shoulder. "Oh, *stop*, you big flirt. Raidan's as straight as they come."

Her friend pouted as his eyes dropped down my body. "They always are."

"Riiight," I drawled, then looked at Cammi. "Where to?"

"Home," Maleke cut in.

I raised my brows and gave him an *"in your dreams"* look. Cam laughed and linked arms with him.

"Actually, Maleke's not joking. We're on our way home."

"Together?" I asked, unable to keep the jealousy from my tone.

Maleke snorted. "She wishes. Unless we keep this party cranking as a threesome, we're going home alone."

"We ain't having a threesome," I stated through a chuckle. "C'mon, I'll walk with you. Where are you heading?"

"Mal is getting an Uber just down here, and I'm heading to the subway," Cammi explained, falling into step between me and her friend.

I claimed her hand and linked our fingers, just like old times. Her fingers flexed against the back of my hand, and she looked up at me as if I'd hung the goddamn moon.

"How much have you had to drink, babe?" I murmured.

"Only a couple; calories and all that shit."

I couldn't help the disdain from showing on my face. "You shouldn't be dieting; it's not good for your body."

"Says the one who earns a living beating people up for entertainment."

A chuckle left my chest. "Touché. You've got me there." I was in the midst of dehydrating for weigh-in and the process was brutal, not to mention extremely unhealthy.

"Oh, here's my ride," Maleke called and waved his hand above his head, hailing the Uber to the curb.

He kissed Cammi on the lips, then pressed a hand to my chest, copping a feel as he said his goodbyes. Once sitting in the back seat, he wound down the window and looked Cammi square in the eye.

"Tomorrow, this bitch—" he pointed to himself, "—wants *all* the details. And that includes measurements," he yelled as the car pulled away.

Despite my dick size being the topic of Maleke's demands, I chuckled and shook my head. Cammi's laughter pulled me further into her orbit, and I found myself staring, utterly captivated, and thrown back to a time when other moments like this had also caught me off guard. I still remembered the time, much like this one, when I realized I'd fallen for her.

Her laughter trailed off and her tongue darted across her plump lower lip. Nostalgia swamped her expression and tugged on my heart strings.

Reaching for her, I cupped her face and set my mouth upon hers. Unhurried and light, I stole another kiss that wasn't mine to claim. I groaned while savoring her lips and sweet tongue moving against mine.

I immediately lost myself in her taste and in each little hum of pleasure. Her fingertips grazed over my short hair, then anchored at the back of my head. My hands dropped down her arched spine and smoothed over the curve of her ass, pulling her to me.

I shouldn't have been kissing her at midnight in the middle of Downtown, but I had absolutely no control when it came to Cammi. Her body had always been the autopilot switch for mine, and nine years apart hadn't changed that.

Cammi eased the kiss to an end, then rested her forehead against my lips. I breathed in her scent, noticing how it had changed over the years. Once fruity and sweet, the fragrance she now wore was sexier; more floral with a hint of something heavier I couldn't put my finger on.

Inhaling one last time, I released my hold on her hips and linked our hands again. Fuck, I'd missed her. "I don't want to let you go."

Conflicting emotions played out across her face. I remained unblinking as her eyes flicked between mine.

"If you're searching for answers, let me know when you find them because I'm at a complete loss over what to do," I murmured.

Her lips arched downward at the corners. "I wish I'd never let you go, but I'm glad I didn't hold you back from your dreams, Raidan."

My thumb brushed along her lower lip. "In a way you did; you were once the biggest part of my dream."

Her eyes immediately dropped, taking my heart with them. She and I had plans. Dreams of growing old together, before her path and my aspirations started to misalign.

"I should go," she whispered.

"Let me walk with you. You're not going in the subway alone at this time of night."

"It'll be fine, just like every other time."

I frowned—unreasonably possessive, despite having absolutely no right to her. "Maybe I should ride all the way back to your place just so I *know* you got home safely."

"I don't think so," she stated, this time with strength. "We both know how that will end, and it's not wise. We can't become too attached, Raids."

"I'd be a gentleman, just like old times."

Her little giggle coaxed my smile to form, and we walked side by side with my arm slung around her shoulders toward the subway.

"You were always so attentive during sex—always worried you'd hurt me."

I ran a hand down my face to hide the mild stain of embarrassment. "Christ, don't remind me, babe. It makes me cringe now because how we fucked in high school is nothing like I—" I cut off, already too fucking deep in the confession to back out or patch things over. "*Shit!*"

Cammi scoffed. "It's fine, Raidan. It's no secret that you've slept around. Besides, I've definitely had my share of men."

That summoned a low, rumbling growl from deep within my chest. The thought of someone else between her legs had me seeing red. "And yet I'm not okay with that."

"Oh, come on. We were never going to wait for each other, so don't get snippy with me for living my life."

"I know we weren't, but that doesn't mean I like the thought of another man touching you. You were mine first."

We paused at the top of the subway steps to make sure Cammi had her footing, then descended in-step. I almost missed the bottom one when her question caught me off guard.

"Do you still love me?" she asked quietly. "Because now that I've seen you again, in person, I still get the same feeling in my chest as I did in high school."

I swallowed while staring straight ahead at the concrete wall on the other side of the subway rails. Do I admit it? To myself, as well as Cammi?

The pause lengthened until she dropped her arm from around my waist. "Forget I asked. It was just me stupidly getting all sentimental."

I snagged her inner elbow as she went to walk away. "Being with you tonight still hurts as much as the day you broke up with me," I hissed with an edge of anger in my voice. "It hurts because I want you so fucking badly, but I know I can't keep you."

Green eyes held mine without blinking. They saw directly into my soul, then claimed it a little more when she whispered, "I know."

Frozen in a pivotal moment where everything until now seemed inconsequential and what came next revolved around our next series of breaths, wave after wave of longing swamped my chest. I wasn't ready to let her go again.

I captured her face in my palms and urged her gaze to meet mine. "I'll be in town for a couple of days after the fight. Meet up with me, properly this time. For the weekend."

She nodded without pausing to consider the offer. "Okay."

Lowering my mouth to hers, intending to send her home with my taste on her tongue, movement behind her caught my attention. I halted with Cammi's face still poised in my hands, then shoved her behind me as a man drew out a switchblade.

"Raidan, behind us," Cammi whispered with a terrified tremble to her voice.

"Fuck," I hissed, seeing another guy approaching from the opposite direction wielding a larger knife.

I shoved Cammi against the dirty subway wall and backed against her. They'd have to get through me to get to her, and there was no fucking way I'd let that happen. Dividing my attention between the two attackers, I issued a warning despite already knowing it wouldn't deter them.

"I wouldn't fuck with me. I'll lay both your asses flat in two moves."

The fat guy laughed. "Sure you will."

Other guy chimed in. "Chumps like you always say that but are always the first to run and leave their missus screaming after them."

"Give us your fucking wallet and phones," fat guy demanded.

With Cammi trembling behind me and clutching my shirt, I laughed and shifted my weight from foot to foot. "Ain't happening. Cammi, babe, let go," I murmured.

A whimper came as she reluctantly released me, giving me the freedom to move without being hindered and dragging her with me.

Skinny guy made the mistake of lunging first. The blade glinted off the ceiling light as it headed straight for my torso. I blocked his forearm and threw him off-balance enough to turn my attention to fatty, who'd made his move during the distraction. Shifting my weight, bending backward while rolling my hip, I roundhouse kicked that fucker into the wall. While he stumbled from the impact, I set the skinny guy in my sights again.

It only took two punches to the face to knock him out cold, lying face up with blood streaming from his nose. Within the same inhale, I turned back to the fat bastard who was riled worse than a bear disturbed during hibernation.

He lunged at Cammi with his arm extended and blade flashing. She let out an ear-piercing shriek that echoed off the subway tiles, then a gasp when I booted his arm against the wall. The knife dropped from his hand with a cry of pain, but there was no fucking way I was letting him walk. He was big, but slow. I stunned him with an elbow blow to the jaw, then grabbed the back of his head and repeatedly forced his face down into my knee until he fell limp at my feet.

On high alert with a violent surge of adrenaline burning in my veins, I backed into Cammi again while making sure others weren't lurking nearby waiting to strike.

"You okay?" I panted.

Her fingers re-gripped my shirt. "Yes, but I can't wait to get out of here. That was so scary. I'm so glad you were with me."

I turned and caged her with my body; one forearm pressed to the wall above her head and the other hand anchored to her hip.

"You've now got two options: one, I escort you all the way home and leave after you're locked within your house, or two, you come back to my suite for the night. No games, but at least I know you'll be safe."

She blinked rapidly to clear a sheen of tears from her eyes. "Is yours closer?"

"Presumably. It's a few blocks away in downtown."

The decision immediately set in her expression. "Yours."

"C'mon." I propelled her up the steps with a firm hand on her lower back, then tucked her against my body when we reached the street.

"Normally I'd walk, but you're shaking so much I'm getting us an Uber."

Much to my surprise, Cammi didn't argue, let alone speak. She hastily nodded and hugged both arms around my waist.

Holding her and kissing the top of her head went some way to settle her, yet the Uber ride back to my hotel was still filled with silence. As was the elevator ascent to my floor. And the walk to my suite.

Once I'd sealed Cammi inside and flipped the lock, I scrutinized her from a safe distance, knowing that I'd made both the right and worst decision by bringing her back here.

Chapter Five

Raidan

Cammi blinked once, twice, and her green eyes never left mine. I swallowed thickly and forced myself to remain rooted to the spot, ignoring every cell in my body screaming to touch her. My limbs thrummed with the pent-up adrenaline from the attempted mugging, and Cammi's energy radiated across the room in all-consuming waves.

Somewhere between an inhale and an exhale, the air changed from lingering shock to sexually charged.

We moved simultaneously and collided with a force that pushed the wind from our lungs. Without stopping to find a breath, our lips met, and I devoured her with blind need as I shed my shirt.

Cammi's tits bounced free when I tugged her little top over her head. With a tortured growl, I took one nipple into my mouth and sucked. She arched, thrusting her chest higher as I gently bit on the pebbled peak.

Keeping one hand splayed wide on her back, the other dropped to fumble with my pants' button and zipper. I kicked them free and hissed when her fingers wrapped around my dick and started pumping.

My head fell back, and my hips bucked forward. "Fuck, Cammi! You still know what I like." I groaned when her grip tightened.

"I never forgot."

Pistoning my hips, I fucked her hand while my fingers tucked under her skirt and grazed up her inner thigh. Widening her stance, she welcomed my fingers sliding through her arousal before pushing two-deep.

"And you still know what I like," she breathed out.

Pleasure-laden praise fell from her parted mouth while I finger-fucked her, hooking and rubbing the sensitive walls of her holy land.

"That feels so fucking good," she panted.

With a gritty hum of agreement, I reluctantly removed her hand from my dick before she pushed me past the point of no return.

She took that hand and set it on her throat. My eyes connected with hers, seeking confirmation. Hers remained unblinking, dark, and swimming with desire as one whispered word set my soul on fire.

"Squeeze."

My cock hardened impossibly further. I adjusted my grip, then squeezed either side of her throat. "This is new for you, Cammi."

Her hooded eyelids fell closed. "I come harder this way," she replied hoarsely.

I cursed and worked the spot inside her to set her off. Finger-fucking her was like walking down a lane I hadn't visited for decades and realizing just how much I'd missed it. The thought had me squeezing a little harder on her throat, and much to my wicked pleasure, she bit down on her lower lip as her face reddened.

"Oh fuck," she managed to cry out before her orgasm hit.

Her body shook violently under my hold, and I kept flicking the sensitive spot in her pussy until her thighs clamped around my wrist.

I released her throat yet kept a hold of her jaw. "That was torture to watch. I need to know what else you like."

"There's lots of new stuff, Raidan," she panted.

"Take your skirt off."

The millisecond it was gone, I dropped to my knees and froze in shock. My eyes lifted to find hers.

"You still have it?"

"Have what?"

I ran my fingers over the inked R. *My* R. "My initial," I breathed out in disbelief.

I'd assumed she'd had it removed to help erase me from her life. For years that thought had bothered me, and now, seeing my mark under her skin filled me with possession like no other.

I dove between her legs, first kissing the inked memory, then running my tongue through her arousal.

With a half-smothered inhale, I licked and sucked like only a starved man would, only to halt when Cameron took my face between her hands.

"I want you on the bed, lying on your back," she commanded.

I rose on shaky legs while eyeing her. "Gonna ride my cock already, babe?"

She snickered and straddled me. My hands grazed her thighs as she climbed further up my body, stopping with her knees planted on either side of my head.

A sexy little smirk quirked one edge of her mouth as she looked down at me. "I don't settle for just one orgasm anymore, Raidan. You gave me one on the inside, so now you're going to give me one on the outside."

"Well then, make sure you ride my face hard, Cams; do it good and proper."

She widened her stance and rocked against my waiting tongue. "It's the *only* way I ride face now."

Groaning because I couldn't fucking wait to sink into her, I lapped at her arousal and ran my tongue through her slit a couple times before gripping her ass and forcing her closer. With her pussy covering my mouth and my nose brushing against her clit, she rocked her pelvis, angling to hit the spot she needed.

The build-up to her second orgasm was slower, but it was just as explosive. When she finished grinding out the last of her pleasure on my face, I flipped her sated body over, spread her legs, and moved between them.

"You're two up on me now, so tell me how you want to be fucked first: from the front, or back?"

"I don't care," she breathed out.

Fisting my cock, I smoothed the head through her slick heat, then nudged into her opening. I slid in with one smooth thrust, and fuck me, it felt like home.

Filling her pulled a throaty curse off her tongue while a sharp hiss made its way through my clenched teeth.

"You've got rumors and expectations to live up to," she teased.

"About?"

"About how hard you fuck nowadays compared to high school." A devilish glint of a challenge entered her eyes; one that had me pushing in harder and grinning wickedly when she gasped.

"Still want it hard?"

"Go big or go home, Raids."

I chuckled at the reference to our teenage mantra, then let my overwhelming craving for her take control. Flipping her, I lifted her up onto her knees, then feet.

"Hold on to the headboard and lower your ass like you're going to sit. Pop your booty for me, Cam."

Grinning and lightly spanking her ass once she had a firm grip on the headboard, I ran my fingers up and down her slit again. "So wet for me."

"And *waiting*."

Her expectant gaze watched as I positioned myself behind her and gripped her hips. Without giving her time to brace, I slammed into her and kept on pounding. Fucking her recklessly in a way I'd never done before. When her pleasure-laden curses filled the air, heightened with the demand for more, I fisted her hair and forced her head back.

Sounds of flesh meeting flesh echoed throughout my suite. Cammi's sweet voice chanted curses and begged for more.

Crazed lust had me thrusting in with wild, reckless abandon, not caring that her grip on the headboard began to falter. Looking down at her ass bouncing and rippling with each thrust was my undoing. The uncontrollable spike of lust had my balls tightening and my cock swelling.

I came with a breathless roar and didn't stop fucking until a violent, satisfied shudder interrupted my rhythm.

Spent and gasping for breath, I fell backward onto the bed, pulling Cammi with me. Both fighting to catch our breath, we lay side by side for a minute before I dared to turn my head her way. She stared at the ceiling, unblinking and unmoving.

"Are you okay?"

"No," she whispered.

Concerned, I rolled up onto an elbow and smoothed my hand across her abdomen. "Did I hurt you?"

A gorgeous smile broke out across her face and her eyes met mine. "And there it is: the sweetness."

I ducked my head and smiled to myself, then looked at her from under my brows. "It's still in there, but only for you. Did I hurt you?" I asked again, low-toned and worried.

"You didn't."

My gaze searched hers. "Then why the *not okay*?"

A ghost of a laugh left her mouth, and she shook her head. "Because now I know you fuck like *that,* and I feel like I'm missing out."

I chuckled and gathered her against me. Lying on our sides facing each other with her leg slung over my hip, my mind became consumed by Cammi when it should have been focused on the upcoming title bout. It was, after all, only two days away. The same conflicting emotions from nine years ago flooded back and left a hollow void in my chest. It felt like the end all over again. Only this time, I didn't want there to be an ultimatum. I wanted my career and Cammi too, but if I couldn't have both, I'd make a choice before she made it for me again.

"I'd quit for you, Cam."

Her eyes sprang wide. "Don't you dare! Not after working so hard to get where you are. And most definitely not at the height of your career."

"Going out on top is the *only* way to go out."

"And I'd never forgive myself if you quit because of me."

My eyes burned yet wouldn't release her from the unblinking stare. "I guess that would make us even, then?"

A confused little pucker appeared between her eyebrows. "What do you mean?"

"I never forgave myself for letting you walk away. I was selfish, and I've regretted it every damn day since. Now that you're back in my life, I'm not okay with you being out of it again." I toyed with a lock of her hair, rolling in between my fingers as I clarified, "You're *mine*."

Cammi's eyes narrowed. "Are you just saying that because we almost got mugged? Events like that have people making all sorts of rash declarations."

I *tsked*. "The wannabe mugging is nothing. If you were hurt though..." I tilted my head from side to side, thinking of the wrath I'd inflict if one of those motherfuckers had managed to lay a hand or blade on her. "I would have killed them," I whispered, sending a shiver down her bare spine.

I trailed my fingertips along the dip of her waist and smirked when goose-bumps rippled along her skin. "I mean it, though. I told you earlier this evening that I still loved you, and I think I always have."

"Raidan..." Cammi sighed. "But what do we do with that? We lead separate lives now."

I grunted, frustrated over having nothing to counter the argument.

"Tonight was scary," she added, breaking my thoughts.

I gazed into her green eyes and ran the back of my knuckles down her cheek. "I'm so fucking thankful I was there to protect you. It makes me enraged thinking about you using the subway alone at night. Please tell me you don't usually do it."

Cammi grimaced. "I kinda do. It's normally fine."

I bit the inside of my cheek to stop an angered retort; I wasn't her keeper.

When her expression grew troubled, I tightened my hold on her. "It's still bothering you, huh?"

"Yeah," came her quiet reply. "I'll be okay tomorrow, but I'm glad I didn't have to go home tonight."

My lips brushed her temple as I peppered kisses along her skin. "Would you have come here with me if the attack hadn't happened?"

Cammi snorted. "I'd like to think not. I was trying to stay strong and not give in to temptation."

I chuckled under my breath and traced circles on her hip. "That didn't go according to plan, did it?"

"No, it didn't. But I'm kinda glad it didn't."

"Yeah? Why's that?"

Her eyebrows rose. "You know why."

"The fucking?"

She laughed lightly, though there was a hint of sadness. "Yeah... the fucking."

With gentle pressure to her waist, I rolled her onto her back, then hovered above her. Pinning her in place with my hips, and my hands planted either side of her head, I smirked. "There needs to be more, but this time I'm going to take my time with you, Cameron Pearce."

"Starting where?"

"Right here." I walked my fingers up her lower stomach. She sucked in a breath as I kissed my way from her belly button to her breasts. I welcomed her legs wrapping around my hips as arousal began to rekindle once more.

I took my time with her this time. Sucking, licking, fingering, familiarizing myself with her body that had changed so much since high school. Above all, I found myself appreciating having her taste on my tongue and her lithe body beneath mine as I eased into her for the second time tonight.

I savored her satisfied sighs and kissed her with the same leisurely rhythm my hips rolled to. When she came around my cock, I gritted my teeth to ride the crest as long as I could before groaning through my orgasm.

Allowing my weight to relax onto her, I pressed my nose into the juncture of her neck and breathed her in. The scent—a mix of perfume, sweat, and arousal—called to my soul.

After minutes of stillness, I climbed off the bed and held out my hand. Cammi followed me into the bathroom to clean up, then I gave her a moment of privacy.

When she emerged, I offered her a T-shirt. "Found you something to wear to bed, if you want it."

A sly little smirk tugged her mouth. "No thanks; I sleep naked."

I cursed, ran a hand down my face, and tossed the tee aside. "Of course you do. Make yourself at home," I deadpanned as she pulled back the blankets and climbed into my bed as if she belonged there.

I stared for a beat, blown away by how perfect she looked while fussing with the white pillows until they were just right.

Her gaze then found mine and her eyebrows pinched at the center. "What are you staring at?"

I chuckled and flipped off the main light before climbing in naked beside her. "Just admiring the view."

She rolled away, then twisted to speak over her shoulder. "Spoon?"

Snorting, because I hadn't fucking spooned in years, I moved up behind her. Having her body slotted against mine was pure fucking heaven, and I fell asleep hoping that Cammi being in my arms wasn't just a fleeting dream.

Chapter Six

Raidan

"**C**ammi, wake up, babe."

"No," she mumbled.

A sleep-husked chuckle caught in my throat, and I pressed my lips to her exposed shoulder. "It's early, but we need to get you up and home."

Arms stretched above her head, and she emitted a squeak as she reluctantly roused. "What time is it?"

"Just before seven."

"*Fuck!*" she exclaimed, bolting upright. "I'm never going to get home and back to the agency in an hour!"

I set a hand on her warm thigh, hoping to ground her. "Shower here. Wear your outfit again and one of my shirts. That's fashion, isn't it?"

She scoffed and gave me a condescending look. "I don't think so."

I rolled from bed and ripped back the blankets, revealing Cammi's long legs and manicured toes. "It's the best we've got so late in the game."

Pausing with my hand out waiting for hers, I flapped at her when she didn't move. "Babe, c'mon; shower."

Her soft voice created ice in my chest. "We're not together, Raids, so please drop the act."

My hand dropped from the air like a lead weight. "It's not an act. I care about you, Cam. A lot. More than I care about anyone."

She rounded the bed with no shame of being naked and pressed one palm to my chest. The innocent touch seared as if molten, and it resonated deep in my heart. My fingers instinctively clamped on her waist, and I physically braced against her softened tone.

"Thank you for protecting me last night; and thank you for letting me stay. It was nice to... reconnect."

I rolled my eyes. "That's putting it mildly."

When she went to move away, my fingertips bit harder. "Cammi."

Green eyes met mine and swam with a thousand questions.

"You're not just a one-night stand."

She smirked. "I kinda am."

I shook my head and pulled her closer. "You're not; you're the one that got away."

"Raidan," she sighed, flicking her eyes back and forth between mine.

"Yeah?" The air electrified as I ran my tongue over my lower lip. My body tensed and my cock hardened. The exhale forcefully expelled from my lungs when she wrapped her hand around my erection and squeezed.

"I made the right decision at the time to let you go."

"And I hated you for it, at the time," I whispered as arousal took hold.

"I hated myself," she admitted.

I trailed an invisible line from her neck to her nipple, and tweaked the semi-alert peak, rolling it between my thumb and forefinger.

I wanted to tell her that I worked hard to prove myself–to prove that our breakup hadn't been in vain. The years had eventually diluted my need for Cammi's validation, and after I shed the last of the guilt over selfishly losing her, my thirst for championship belts intensified.

Cammi's breathy inhale drew my eyes back up to hers, and I saw the blatant hunger burning in them. Her hand jerked on my dick as she returned my suggestive smirk. Fuck me, it hit square in my chest.

In one swift move, I gripped her by the ass cheeks and lifted her into my arms. Long legs wrapped around my waist and her tits bounced in front of my face.

"You 'n me are gonna shower, and I'm going to put a smile on your face that'll last all day."

With each step toward the bathroom, my cock grazed the line of her pussy and had me rushing for the nearest wall. Cammi's back hit it with a thud and my chest met hers with force. The impact punched the air from our lungs, but I gave us no time to recover.

Gripping my cock, I lined myself up with her entrance and worked my way inside. Once seated as deep as I could go, I ground hard as raw need overrode every cell in my body. I pulled her into me as I thrust upward. Her tits bounced in my face with each push, and I welcomed the sting of her nails gouging into my shoulders. Cammi's hips opened further, taking me deeper. Sealing my lips over hers, I consumed her with desperation, scared out of my goddamn mind that this would be the last time, and I wasn't okay with that.

I came too fucking fast for my liking, and with her still sheathed around my dick, I strode to the shower. While it heated, I set her on her feet and turned her back to my chest.

"Legs open," I growled against the shell of her ear, my breath still coming hard and fast.

Her head fell against my shoulder as I pushed my fingers through her slit, then plunged two inside. Drawing them in and out, I circled around her clit while nipping at her ear.

"I may have finished, but this ain't over until you do too. Tell me where."

I massaged tiny circles until her breath hitched. "*There.* Right there."

Toying with her breast with my free hand, I focused on heightening her pleasure, only breaking the rhythm to push into her pussy to re-lubricate my fingers with my cum.

Signs of a building orgasm began to vibrate through her body. She trembled against my chest, and I splayed my hand across her breasts to lock her in place.

Her body convulsed without warning, and an unbridled moan broke free. It echoed around the tiled bathroom and danced upon the rising steam from the shower. I kept rubbing her clit until she snagged my wrist. There, we both paused.

I studied her body through the half-misted mirror, my hand still wedged between her legs and her fingers restraining my movements. Fuck, she was perfect. An ache knotted in my throat at the thought of this potentially being our last time together.

An audible drip of moisture hitting the tiled floor had her eyes opening. They found mine as she giggled. "I just pushed out your cum."

I snickered and kissed the back of her head. "You definitely did." As if she needed evidence, I lifted my cupped hand and showed her. "Jump in the shower, Cam. While I love coming, I'm not a fan of holding it in my hand for longer than necessary."

One eyebrow arched. "You hold it often?"

"Only if I need to... you know."

Her attention dropped to my dick, then back to my face. "Thought you wouldn't need to jerk off with all the women lining up to keep you company."

I motioned for her to enter the shower before me and shook my head.

"There's no line, babe, and sometimes a guy just wants to pump one out without the strings."

"Same as women."

"You're joking!" I exclaimed, my voice rising.

She snickered while easing under the hot water. "Nope, not joking."

I pulled her into my arms, encasing us both under the shower spray. "Do you do it often?"

She schooled a tugging smile and tried for a look of complete innocence. "Do what?"

"You know..." I thrust my pelvis against hers, "...satisfy the itch."

"Now that is something you don't get to know."

"Oh, c'mon; we're friends from way back."

"Friends don't need to know everything. Unless you're Maleke," she added with a cheeky grin.

Possession tore through my veins. "You mean *he* knows how often you masturbate?"

Her laugh grew louder as she dispensed body wash into her palm. "*They* like to think they do, but they really have no idea."

"Fucking better not," I grumbled, ignoring Cammi's scoff. "And why are you calling him *they*?"

"Maleke is non-binary," she explained nonchalantly.

"Oh..." I rubbed my chin and thought back to last night when I'd met Maleke. "Kind of makes sense now."

Cammi giggled but didn't add further explanation. We fell silent while washing, alone with our thoughts. Once Cammi finished rinsing out her hair and shut off the shower, I handed her a towel before wrapping one around my waist. I glanced at her and paused as she dried her hair.

I swear that time stuttered. It halted, then lurched when her eyes met mine and a shy smile formed on her naturally plump lips. I searched for something to say, only to come up blank. And I didn't miss the fleeting disappointment cutting across her face when I snapped my mouth closed.

"I'll meet you out there," I mumbled.

I paced the bedroom after pulling on a pair of sweats. Scrubbing my hands over my face failed to ease the weight in my chest. What the fuck was I thinking? Our paths had veered down two different tracks many years ago, and I had to stop wanting them to gravitate back together.

The bathroom door quietly opened, and Cammi padded into the bedroom wrapped in a plush white towel.

She saw my expression and halted. "Are you okay, Raidan?"

My heart ached from her always putting me above herself. In high school, she'd always done it, and it seemed that part of her hadn't changed.

I drew her close and kissed her forehead. "Yeah, babe, I'm okay."

"You've grown distant all of a sudden."

"Just getting my head back in the fight."

She acknowledged that with a nod, then started collecting her tangled clothing. "I *have* distracted you over the last twenty-four hours."

I chuckled. "Just a little. Don't tell my coach; he'll fucking lose his shit. Not even lying about that."

"I'll be sure to sneak out," came her muffled voice as she worked her head through her top.

I sat on the edge of the bed and sighed. "Sneaking out sounds like I'm ashamed of you staying. I'm not."

Her green gaze found mine when her head popped through. "I meant sneaking out so your coach will be none the wiser about me staying. Wouldn't want you to get in trouble."

After tugging up her skirt, Cammi sauntered over and dropped a kiss on my mouth.

"Thank you again, Raids. And good luck with the bout."

"You'll watch?" I asked, hopeful. When hesitancy created a little crease between her eyebrows, I shrugged. "Or not."

Cammi shook her head and placed her palm on the center of my chest again—a gesture I was rapidly growing to love. "It's not that I'm not interested; I just haven't watched a match since we split up. I found it too hard…"

"I get it. I wanted to look you up for years but was both too stubborn and a little scared about what I'd find." Lifting her hand from my skin, I pressed my mouth to her palm.

She smiled and reluctantly tugged free. "Good luck, Raidan."

"I don't need luck when I have mad skills, babe."

Her snicker eased while she slipped her high heels on. "And Killer Kaspar is back with the confidence and arrogance we've grown to expect. Goodbye, Raids."

Rushing after her, I met her at the suite door and caged her against it with my body—her back to my front. "You weaken me," I whispered against her neck, welcoming the shiver racking through her body. "But don't you dare tell anyone."

"That Killer Kaspar is a big softie at heart? Never." She teased.

"That's a good girl. Now, get out of my room and out of my head, then I'll see you on the weekend, yeah?"

"Yeah," she breathed out and craned her head to meet my kiss.

It was hot and heavy, and over far too soon. As quickly as it started, Cammi broke away and tugged the door open. She threw a, "See ya 'round," over her shoulder as she stepped from my hold, leaving me breathless and pressing a balled fist to the doorframe above my head.

Fuck. That was the one woman I didn't like watching walk away. I gave myself a minute—just one—to acknowledge history repeating, then shook free of the memories.

I had a title bout to focus on.

Chapter Seven

Cameron

After rushing from Raidan's suite, I headed straight for the agency. I needed to change into a fresh outfit, plus do my hair and makeup before everyone else arrived for the day.

That plan was blown out of the water as soon as I rounded the block corner. A swarm of media was outside the agency doors, hovering impatiently and jostling for a prime position. They spotted me and immediately moved as one. I could have turned and run, but I pulled my shoulders back, sealed my lips and strode toward them without giving them the satisfaction of showing fear.

Microphones, phones, and voice recorders were thrust into my face as reporters shouted question upon question.

"Cameron, how long have you been dating Raidan Kaspar?"

"Did you stay with him last night?"

"Can you confirm that you were once engaged?"

"Is this a publicity stunt?"

"Are the pregnancy rumors true?"

"There's footage of him attacking two knife-wielding men in the subway. What's your side of the story?"

I clenched my teeth and pushed through the mob until I reached the agency entrance. Shielding the pin code as best I could, I hurried through the door, then slammed it closed behind me. Panting hard, I took a moment to catch my breath.

As per usual, the media was trying to make something out of nothing. I sure as hell wasn't going to feed their hunger for fake news. The pregnancy rumors were preposterous and made me snort. However, them digging into our history created deep unease.

I rode the elevator to the loft floor with Raidan consuming my thoughts and the media compounding my worries. The doors pinged open, and I strode out minding my own business, only to stop short when Bree stood at her desk and set her hands on her hips.

"You're early." Her focus dropped down my body, then returned to my makeup-free face and unkempt hair. "And you look like you've rolled straight out of bed."

I bit back a snort. "That's why I'm here early—to get sorted before everyone arrives. Well, that was the plan." I gestured outside. "Were all the reporters here when you arrived?"

A sly smile slid across her face. "They were. And I've been fielding calls and emails since late yesterday evening. Seems that your little scoop with Raidan Kaspar has caused quite the stir and everyone wants in on the action."

Dread balled in my stomach. "What do you mean?"

"You're booked up for months, Cameron; that's what I mean."

My jaw hung slack, and I coughed and sputtered for words. "I am?"

"Seems that you finally slept with the right person to get noticed."

Indignation flooded my chest and my fists balled, immediately angry all my hard work had been instantaneously discredited.

"I didn't sleep with anyone to get bookings, Bree. I've worked my fucking ass off to get to where I am."

Her penciled eyebrows lifted. "Uh huh. So, tell me, whose bed did you just roll out of?"

"That's none of your fucking business."

"It is, since I'm your agent."

"Who I sleep with is *none* of your business." I turned on my stiletto and headed for the changing room.

She scoffed, determined to get the last word. "I hope he was worth it, honey, because he's eventually gonna drop you like a hot stone. This wave of popularity won't last."

My steps faltered ever so slightly, and I resisted the urge to march over and slap her face from her body. Instead, I paused with my hand on the door handle and smirked over my shoulder.

"Considering I was the one to dump his ass nine years ago, and he couldn't get enough of me again last night, I'd say that hot stone you refer to is full of shit. I'll be out in forty minutes, then we can go over my new schedule."

Leaving her gawking and spluttering for a comeback, I stepped into the dressing room and quietly clicked the door closed behind me. Everything shook. My hands, my legs, hell, even each breath. Not only had I disrespected my agent, but—if what she said was true—I had bookings for the foreseeable future. Despite the excitement, I refused to believe it until I saw it. There was nothing worse than hopes being struck down after receiving the wrong memo.

Forty minutes later and not a minute sooner, I emerged from the dressing room in a designer peach dress, heels to match, my hair straightened and makeup impeccable, and I meant business as I strode for Bree's desk.

"Okay, what do you have for me?"

She spun in her seat and indicated for me to sit in the chair beside her desk. She opened the online diary to my page, and I gasped. Booking after booking filled the screen. The more Bree scrolled, the harder my hand pressed to my chest in utter shock. So many inquiries and appointments from industry names that made my eyes water.

When she stopped at the end of the list, I swallowed before finding my voice. "All that overnight?"

Bree nodded. "That's correct. Welcome to your big break, doll. Ride it while you have it."

Chapter Eight

Raidan

I stood at Aki's desk with Juan at my flank, both unmoving, while I watched the leaked security footage of me giving the two would-be muggers a beat down. When it was done, I straightened and shrugged.

Aki sighed and dragged a hand down his face. "I know Finley says all publicity is good publicity, but this can be taken one of two ways, Raidan."

"It was a fine line," I agreed. "But those assholes came at us with knives. You'd do the same, especially if Eun-Ju was in danger."

Acknowledging me using his wife as an example to emphasize my point, Aki nodded in his ever-wise manner. "I would." His expression then hardened. "The problem I have is you were *supposed* to be on curfew. We're one night out from the bout, Raidan. What if you'd been stabbed, or set upon by a group?"

I shrugged again. "I would have laid them all flat."

Juan pushed off the nearby wall. "The media is going to be all over this at weigh-in. Don't engage on the matter and keep the interview strictly to the bout. Now go get your shit. We need to head out."

Ezzine Mansouri. AKA The Marrakesh Devil; my opponent. Born in Morocco and having a black belt in jiujitsu, Ezzine had a reputation for coming out swinging and taking down his opponents in record time. He was known for his aggressive striking and was the one expected to take me down.

I sized him up while he weighed in. While I had an inch on him, he was slightly wider. Our weight, attitude, and thirst to fuck the other up was comparable. I anticipated this fight was going to be hard and dirty.

Coming in a hair under one hundred and fifty-four pounds, just as I had, he stepped from the scales and came at me in an attempt to intimidate. I surged forward and Aki made a show of holding me back while Mansouri and I faced off.

Nose to nose, we glared and leered, trying to fuck with the other's head. His almost-black eyes bore into mine, then crinkled at the corner when he smirked.

"Once I claim your title, I'll then claim that tight-piece-of-ass model."

The taunt bounced off my shuttered exterior. "And I'll be stopping by your momma's house again. Might send you a little snap this time."

His eyes twitched. He could try to fuck with me all he wanted, but I had something he didn't: time in this profession and the mental fortitude that came with it.

"She won't be as sweet as Cameron's pussy," he spat back.

I tilted my head to the side and smirked. "I'd know. I have, after all, had *both*."

The barb hit and landed, despite him trying to school the reaction. I chuckled and lifted my eyebrows as the umpire pushed us apart.

"I'll see you tomorrow, Mansouri. Sleep tight knowing I'll be fucking your mom come the weekend."

"Fuck you," he boomed, throwing a fist at me.

I laughed to rile him further.

"Back down, both of you!" the umpire shouted.

Turning my back on Mansouri's irate cussing, I calmly went back to Aki and Juan, still chuckling my ass off.

"Shaken, not stirred?" Juan drawled.

I scoffed. "Shaken *and* stirred, and ready for blood, just the way I like 'em."

"You'll have that soon enough," Juan mumbled, tossing me a water bottle.

I snatched it from mid-air and drank half of it in one go. The re-hydration process had begun. Aki would have me doing a very light session today, plus a meditation/yoga mix, then nothing tomorrow before the fight. Being in top physical condition, and with the weigh-in done and fluid passing my lips again, I was as prepared as I could be for tomorrow night.

"Don't let him get too close and watch for his kick. He's gonna want to keep you on your feet, so go for the takedown and use your grappling to your advantage. *Position before submission*," Aki emphasized, slapping his hands down on my shoulders.

I nodded while taking in the last snippets of hasty advice. I was a natural when it came to grappling thanks to the wrestling I did in high school. If I got Mansouri to the mat, I'd have the advantage.

Aki slapped me on the shoulder one last time, then shoved me at the cage door. After prowling back and forth a couple of times sizing up Mansouri, the announcer officially started the match. Best of five rounds, or less if I got the fucker into submission before then.

We bumped gloves, then it was on. Mansouri came at me with a double jab. I anticipated his kick, blocked that, and immediately took him to the mat. I pushed him into the cage, landing jab after jab to his torso while his legs linked around my waist and squeezed.

He pulled my head into his neck and locked it in place, slamming forearm shots onto my head before I got a hold of the offending arm. With my range of motion restricted and him trying to find a weakness in my grapple, I held onto him while working myself into a better position.

I landed a couple of punches to his ribcage, then inched my way up his body. His grip loosened on my head, but the moment I lifted it, his elbow collided with my eye socket, sending me into the stars for a moment.

I ducked to regain focus, leaving blood smears on his shoulder, then worked my legs higher up his torso. I bided my time, taking two punches to the ribs before spurring into action.

Rearing up with my forearms raised to block any elbow shots, I then used my weight to rain down punch after punch on Mansouri's face. His forearms came up to block, which partially exposed his chest.

I landed blow after blow, occasionally getting lucky when my fist found its way through. The sounds of my fight gloves meeting his flesh sang to my fight-tarnished soul.

Mansouri's hips thrust up without warning, setting me off-balance enough to turn the tables. I ended up in the position I didn't want to be in: leg locked and unable to maneuver out to land a punch or kick.

Pushing up on my hands, I managed to tug my leg free, but received a brutal heel to the kidney. I grunted against the impact and kicked out just as the bell went off, calling an end to the first round.

Sitting in my corner, Aki iced my neck while Filipe—the team physician— wiped the blood off my split brow.

"Don't get complacent. Watch out for that leg lock," Aki bellowed. "Position, Raidan. Awareness! Now go fucking get 'em."

Bouncing from foot to foot, round two commenced. As expected, Mansouri came at me with fists. I backed up and blocked, then got a kick to his ribs. He landed one on my calf, then grabbed my head and thrust it down to meet his rising knee.

I came up swinging and landed a fist to his nose. The millisecond reprieve allowed me to take his ass to the mat again where I held his arms above his head while getting into position. Bucking again, the prick managed to roll from my grapple and spring to his feet.

We hit the cage and bounced; fists, elbows, and knees flying at every opportunity. He had me pinned and on the defensive against his punches. I went to the ground and dragged him with me, only to end up pinned under his weight when he maneuvered out of my hold.

Blow after blow to my sides knocked the air from my lungs. Knowing I'd been caught in the wrong position had me pushing to my feet and kicking out Mansouri's knee. He crumpled against me and landed a couple more body shots until I grabbed hold of his head and connected it to my upthrusting knee.

The crowd thrived off each and every hit—consuming them and hissing them down like shots of tequila.

Pushing away from the cage, we faced off in a series of blows that ended in a standing grapple. I managed a few jabs to his torso, but not enough to allow me the momentum to end the fight before the round bell went off again.

Round three felt different. We both tired quicker, and I knew I needed to get strategic. Mansouri lunged and tried to take me to the mat. The position gifted me room to land elbow after elbow on the back of his head.

Realizing I'd caught him in a weak position, he fought to get upright again. That was my chance. I elbowed and punched the back of his head until his knees faltered. We broke apart. He took three paces back and reset.

Setting him in my sights, he expected a kick, but not the flip beforehand. The heel of my foot landed on the side of his head while I was in the air, and the impact sent him crumpling to the mat. He went down with a thud. I seized my chance while he remained dazed; getting him in an arm lock that would have broken the bone of anyone not conditioned to harsh UFC fighting. I added pressure and clenched my teeth, waiting for the tap out.

I welcomed the three taps Mansouri landed on my leg, and I immediately released. We broke apart as the umpire rushed in to declare the fight over.

My hand was thrust high, and my team surged into the cage to congratulate me. I accepted it with grace and waited until Mansouri was back on his feet.

After shaking his hand, I ignored everything hurting like a motherfucker and stood in the center of the ring to receive the title belt for the fourth championship running.

Bleeding, bruised, swollen, and fighting the urge to limp as I exited the cage, I barely had enough focus to comprehend what Aki screamed in my face. He tapped my cheek as his lips moved, but the buzzing in my head overrode all other noise. I rode the wave of my team hustling me to the after-match room where Filipe would fix me up.

I'd poured everything into that match, and fuck, I was spent. But one thought—one *person*—played on a loop in my head as Filipe assessed my injuries.

I looked for Juan. When he came to my side with concern etched deep into his features, his expression warped into surprise when I pointed to my gear.

"Cammi. Ring her and get her here."

Chapter Nine

Cameron

My entire day was filled with meetings to sign contracts for everything from more swimsuit modeling to TV commercials. By the time I got seated on the subway later that evening, exhaustion took hold over my body. However, my head refused to quieten, especially once Raidan came to mind.

Only an hour until the fight. I still hadn't decided if I would watch it; the thought of witnessing him get hurt was enough to turn my stomach. But for the first time since high school, I felt like I should. It seemed fitting somehow. Like closure to our latest chapter.

Despite the ache in my heart, I had to be realistic about where we were heading; him in his direction, and me in mine.

On a dejected sigh, I relaxed into the seat and gently rocked with the motion of the train. Stop after stop, it took me closer to home, until finally arriving at my station.

The balls of my feet were killing me by the time I'd walked the few blocks home. I pushed through my front door with a wave of relief and immediately kicked off my heels. Locking the door and throwing my keys and handbag on the kitchen counter, I walked to my room, peeling off my dress as I went. Changing into a cute pair of beige linen pants and a pink tank was the perfect end to a crazy, life-changing day.

I dragged my ass back into the kitchen, grabbed a bottle of water from the fridge, plus a low-carb muesli bar, then sat cross-legged on the couch.

Maleke was next. I took a sip of water while waiting for them to answer the promised video call.

Their pretty face appeared as I recapped the water bottle.

"What the fuck took you so long?" they exclaimed.

"Uh, walking home. Calm down, I'm here now."

"The fight is about to start!"

I gulped. "Is it?" A part of me hoped I'd miraculously missed it.

"Yes, bitch. Turn the TV on already."

"I'm scared, Maleke. I don't know if I can do this."

Their expression softened. "I know you are, honey, but I'm right here. We'll watch it together."

I sighed and reached for the remote. "You suck."

We were both quiet as I clicked on the TV, and I glanced at Maleke to see their attention already focused on the live stream at their place. Their eyes lit with blatant lust when Raidan entered the stadium to the rap song "X Gon' Give It To Ya" by *DMX*.

"His eyes are different," I murmured. All softness was gone. This Raidan was focused and set to kill, and the sight took my breath away.

Maleke's inhale also hitched, and their words matched what was running through my head. "Sweet baby Jesus, he's hot. Doesn't it make you just want to lie back and watch him fuck you?"

"Uh, yeah, it actually does," I admitted in a shaky whisper. "He never used to listen to this kind of music."

Maleke shifted in their seat as I clenched my thighs together. Gone was the kind-hearted guy that existed under the cocky exterior. Gone was the shining light in his eyes, replaced with a darkness that I found pretty fucking appealing.

The crowd roared and cheered as he stepped into the cage, and I had to acknowledge the pang of jealousy that speared through my chest when the cage bunny gave him a little smirk.

"Skank," Maleke spat, echoing my thoughts again.

My leg jiggled with nervous anticipation. Maleke shifted again and leaned forward, seemingly as anxious as I was to get the fight underway.

The air stilled in my lungs the instant the umpire called bout on. The nausea climbed higher in my throat each time Raidan bore the brunt of a fist, kick, or elbow, and I couldn't help but flinch during the most brutal parts.

My heart ached when Raidan's blood fell. The belt around my ribs tightened further when he rained down punch after punch while straddling Mansouri's torso. I lurched off the couch when Mansouri got the upper hand.

By the time the first round finished, I was panting as if I'd done one round in the cage myself. Maleke looked at me with wild eyes and now-disheveled hair.

"I'm going to need a cold shower after this!" they hissed.

I pressed a hand to my chest. "My heart is racing so hard! I want him to win so badly."

"Same, honey, but shit, that Moroccan is built like a god!" Maleke flapped a hand at the screen, then turned their sole attention back to TV. "Bitch, hush. We're ready to rumble again."

The snicker dried on my tongue the instant Mansouri came at Raidan and landed multiple shots, including a sickening knee to the face.

Maleke gasped dramatically while I grimaced around the ever-rising bile burning in my esophagus. This was the first, and *last*, time I would watch a UFC fight.

The break between rounds two and three didn't seem long enough. As soon as the umpire called "fight," this round seemed destined to be the most brutal so far. I could see the anger, the frustration, the *thirst* from them both.

"I'm going to need a Xanax after this," Maleke exclaimed, right before a scream of shock when Raidan flipped and kicked his opponent on the back of the head.

I was on my feet without thinking, yelling at the TV, urging Raidan to lock him down.

The moment Mansouri tapped out, a surge of adrenaline sent my arms high. I pumped them and jumped up and down, screaming, "He did it, he did it," at the top of my lungs.

On the other end of the video call, Maleke was losing their shit just as hard as I was. I snatched up my phone and blinked back the unexpected surge of tears.

"Maleke!"

Their wild expression filled the screen. "Oh my god! That was so fucking intense!"

"I know!" I cried, swiping a finger beneath each eye, then holding my hand up. "I'm shaking so hard right now."

"Bitch, I can't even!"

"I know right!"

Maleke fell backward on their couch and pressed a hand to their forehead. We spent the next few minutes rehashing snippets of Raidan's win. I was taking another sip of chilled water when a phone call interrupted our conversation.

"Oh, shit, hold up, babe. I'm getting a call."

"From whom?"

My wide eyes locked on theirs. "Raidan."

Maleke flapped a frantic hand. "Fucking answer it, bitch!"

So I did, breathlessly. "Hello?"

"Cameron?"

My eyes narrowed. "You're not Raidan, so why are you calling from his number?"

"I'm Juan, his manager. He asked me to call you... He wants you to come and meet him."

"When?"

"Now," he emphasized. *"Give me your address, and I'll pick you up."*

"Na-uh. Not until I know this isn't a prank."

An impatient exhale sounded, then he called out, *"Raidan!"*

"What?" came Raidan's snap.

"Tell me something about Cameron only she would know. She's suspicious about the call, man."

I gulped and pressed the phone harder against my ear.

Raidan's curse then a murmured apology sounded in the background. His pain-strained voice came stronger after a brief pause.

"I dunno, Juan. She fucking rode my face on Wednesday night. Happy?"

I gasped and my cheeks immediately burned. Juan coughed and cleared his throat, then spoke with amusement.

"Does that confirm—"

"Brownsville, 56th Street, and don't ever speak of this conversation again." Mortified and dying from embarrassment, I disconnected on Juan's laughter and pressed a shaking hand to my face.

Maleke's high-pitched, manic laugh came through the speaker.

"Oh my god, I forgot to disconnect you!" I exclaimed.

Their laughter grew until they gasped and wheezed and made a fucking spectacle of themself. "Of all the things he could have said... the riding his face has got to be the best—" Mal cut off again and rolled with hilarity.

"And his entire fucking team heard!" I cried, then hissed. "For fuck's sake. Maleke, I'm disconnecting this video call now."

They hiccupped through their laughter and dashed away tears. "Sure, bitch. I'll see you Monday. Happy face-ri—"

I cut the call short and sat shaking my head. Un-fucking-believable. The moment I saw Raidan, I'd be giving him a piece of my mind.

Chapter Ten

Cameron

My bone to pick with Raidan evaporated the instant I entered the rear entrance of the arena. Nerves hollowed out my stomach and had my hands fidgeting as Juan led me to Raidan's dressing room. I forced a deep breath before following him inside and held it as I searched for Raidan.

When I saw him, my heart dropped so hard it took my lungs with it.

Despite the eye puffed closed, red bruises marring his torso, and the tape holding his cut eyebrow together, he rose to his feet with a visible wince and rushed toward me.

"Oh my god," I exclaimed. "Are you okay?"

My arms carefully laced around his waist as he gathered me close. "I am now. I won, baby."

Relief washed through me. "I know, I saw it."

Raidan reared back with utter disbelief in his dazzling blue eyes. "You watched?"

A hint of heat flooded my cheeks. "I did. Maleke and I watched it together. They overheard the conversation with Juan too. In fact, your entire team did, so thanks for that," I admonished.

Raidan chuckled and rocked us from side to side. "Hey, if you ask questions straight after a fight, you get the uncensored version. I've settled now."

"I couldn't even look Juan in the eye when he picked me up."

Another laugh vibrated within Raidan's chest, followed by a quiet groan.

"So now what?" I asked.

His head lifted to look around the room. "Now we head back to the suite before I can no longer walk."

Clasping my hand in his, he hobbled to his seat and gathered his belongings. His fingers never released mine. Even when I slid into the backseat of the car his coach drove, he held firm.

The walk from the hotel parking to Raidan's suite was a long, arduous process. Shrouded by security guards and team members, we made our way to the suite I'd stayed in two nights prior. Once inside and alone, a lull settled where neither of us spoke, though the void was filled with a grunt of pain as Raidan lowered himself onto the couch.

"Aki, Juan, and Filipe will be up soon," he explained.

"So, coach, manager, and...?"

"Team physician. He's already checked me over but likes to keep a close eye on things for the few hours after a bout. Especially one that's been so physical."

I tenderly sat beside him and touched his knee. "How are you *really* feeling, Raidan?"

He re-linked our fingers and smiled. "Getting sore now that the adrenaline's faded. It's a little hard to breathe and my head is pounding, so you'll need to go easy on me later."

I looked him over from head to toe. "Yeah, we're not doing *anything* later other than sleeping."

"We'll see."

"Yeah, we will."

Raidan's low chuckle had my heart tripping. I'd seen a different side of him tonight. A ruthless and savage one he hadn't had when wrestling in high school.

His thumb smoothed rhythmically over the back of my hand. "As much as I want to keep holding your hand, I need you to move across, babe. My feet are swelling, and I need to put them up."

Worry had my eyebrows pulling low as I shuffled to the far end of the couch. "Have you iced?"

He hummed and kicked off his loosely laced shoes. "Somewhat. The guys will bring some up to add to the bathtub."

My instinct to care for him kicked in. "I'll start running it."

I moved before he could protest and hurried to the bathroom. While the other night I thought the size of the bathtub was a huge fucking overkill, tonight I understood the need for it. Raidan's body would be able to be fully submerged to soothe the post-fight bruising.

Leaving the cold tap running, I returned to Raidan and carefully lifted his legs as I sat on the couch, then lowered his feet onto my lap.

He grunted and pressed a hand to his ribcage with the movement.

"Sorry," I murmured.

"Don't be, babe. Moving is going to be sore regardless."

I studied his tortured shins and bruised feet. The punishment they'd received tonight made my heart pang.

"Cammi?"

I glanced up to see Raidan staring at me intently. "Yeah?"

"Don't be alarmed if I can't walk or even tie my shoes tomorrow morning. My hands and feet will be swollen. It's normal."

Lifting the hand laying on his torso, I carefully touched each of his fingers, then gently kissed each knuckle.

His smile pulled a little wider. "You're too damn sweet, Cam."

"It sounds like you just wanted me here to tie your shoes for you," I teased.

He chuckled and amusement danced in his blue irises. "Nah... I actually wanted you here so I could ask you to marry me."

I burst out laughing until the intensity of his gaze didn't ease.

"Wanna hear a crazy idea?" he asked.

My voice shook right along with my head. "No."

I steeled my heart. Wanting to fall head over heels yet unable to completely let my guard down just in case I jumped to the wrong assumption. I loved Raidan, and my chest clamped with uncertainty.

His hand twisted and captured mine. "Let's head home and see our parents tomorrow."

Shock lifted my eyebrows. "Are you serious?"

"I am. I thought we could give them a little surprise."

"What kind of surprise?" I managed to whisper around the wedge of emotion in my throat.

Raidan's eyes heated further. "Cameron Pearce, will you..."

- 24 hours later -

Raidan

"You should be resting, not ringing me," Aki answered without pleasantries.

I laughed, really not giving a fuck. "I *am* resting. I'm calling because I need Finley to drop a press release for me, but I wanted you to hear the news from me first."

His voice swam with suspicion. "Hear what first? You better not be retiring, Raidan."

"I'm not. I'll send it through by email." I tapped send and I waited.

A hiss of shock sounded, accompanied by, "Jesus Christ, is this true?"

"Yes. It happened today."

"Well, that's a blindside. Congrats, kid. She's the one, huh?"

"Always has been. I would have been a fucking fool to let her go again." I winked at Cammi, who was soaking in the bathtub surrounded by bubbles and holding up a glass of champagne.

"I'll be damned," Aki drawled. "Now get off the fucking phone and go woo your wife. I'll see you in a week."

I chuckled and hung up, then sat on the side of the bath staring at Cammi like a lovesick dope.

She lifted her leg from the water. Seductive bubbles ran down her leg, luring me closer. "Coming in?"

"Yeah, babe, in a second."

I just needed a few moments to absorb the surreal moment. To actually fucking pinch myself that I'd won more than just the title bout this weekend. I'd achieved something I'd deemed impossible—claiming Cammi back while still having my UFC career, and at the height of it to boot. Second chances like Cammi didn't come around often, so I'd seized it while she was still within my grasp.

"What's that look for?" she whispered.

"Cameron Kaspar..." I shook my head and grinned. "It sounds pretty fucking good, doesn't it?"

A beauty queen smile pulled her mouth wide and the love in her eyes took my fucking breath away. "More perfect than you know."

"Well, *shit*." I ducked my head as my heart swelled. Her smitten smile was still in place when I met her green gaze again.

I gingerly stood and tugged the towel from my waist. "Move over, babe. I'm coming in. Be gentle with me."

Chapter Eleven

PRESS RELEASE

Raidan 'Killer' Kaspar married his high school sweetheart, Cameron Pearce, in a surprise private ceremony in their hometown of Rock Hill, North Carolina, on Saturday night. The loved-up couple is back in Miami after their shotgun nuptials, where they will be living during Kaspar's post-fight recovery. The UFC Lightweight Champion has confirmed he intends to defend his title next year and has quashed the pregnancy rumors. In a personal statement, he wrote, [quote] "Cammi was the one that got away nine years ago, and I sure as [censored] wasn't going to let it happen again" [unquote].

It seems that Kaspar is living proof that the Beast really can claim his Beauty.

- The End -

Acknowledgments

Acknowledgments

Gywn McNamee for organizing this anthology and having me be a part of it. It's an absolute honor! xx

A massive thank you to my epic **beta readers: Nicole, Marnie, and Kellie.** You all did so awesome, and I appreciate the hell out of you guys! xx

Thank you so much to **Jenny from Owl Eyes Proofs and Edits** for doing such an amazing job of editing my words, again. xx

Thank you to **Emma** for proofreading for me, especially around your crazy work schedule! I appreciate the hell out of it and, as always, I'm so happy with your attention to detail! xx

To my **readers:** THANK YOU for reading Raidan and Cammi's story! I love a steamy MMA romance, and I hope you loved this one! xx

Until next time, Vi xx

About the Author

Vi Summers hails from New Zealand.
She is a confetti queen, cheese fiend, tea addict, beard lover, and hot-mess
Mumma, all rolled into one International Bestselling Romance Author.

When you read Vi's books, you can expect heat, heart and suspense.
In these gritty romances, Vi loves breaking her characters before piecing them
back together.

Connect with her on BookBub, Facebook, Goodreads, Instagram, TikTok, and
her website https://authorvisummers.com/

Walking on Sunshine

Claire Hastings

Chapter One

Carlos Rivera could not imagine loving anyone other than Leona Filipe.

Although, at this point, maybe he needed to start calling her Leona Cruz. They might not be married yet, but the massive diamond on her left hand that was currently sparkling in the Caribbean sun as she spoke to a guest certainly made it as official as it needed to be.

It had been almost a year since she'd shattered his heart, following hers right into the arms of legendary football star Cullen Cruz. Carlos wanted nothing more than for her to be happy; he just also wished he didn't have to witness it all day every day. But unless he found another job, it was just the lot he was stuck with.

Turning back toward the beach, he tried to focus on the reason he was out here, rather than replacing the showerheads on the eighth floor of Barracuda tower. As the head of maintenance of the Indigo Royal Resort in St. Thomas, there was always something for him to be working on.

Yet, here he was, standing on the beach, because Leona needed his help.

"Drea said someone from the local vet is on their way," Leona said, after the guest walked away. "Now we just have to find the dog again."

"Lee, this is ridiculous."

At least, he felt ridiculous. Playing dog catcher was not part of his job description. Then again, "keeping guests happy" was part of everyone's job around here, and when Drea Miller, Leona's best friend and part owner of the Indigo Royal, sent him a text asking for his help in looking for the stray that had been running up and down the beach for the last few days, he knew he couldn't refuse. Even if there were rooms needing a new showerhead.

"It's not how I want to spend my day either. And before you say it, it's also not my job. I'm the head of housekeeping, not a pet sitter. But Drea needs our help. Guests are complaining. And we're a team, so here we are."

Carlos let out a grumble. Leona was right though. They were a team. Looking around him, he inhaled deeply, letting the salt air fill his lungs. The beach was mostly empty, which was typical for this late in the day, making it easy to see that the dog in question was not down here.

"Look!" Leona exclaimed, pointing to something behind him.

Groaning again, he spun around, expecting to see nothing but the long stretch of shoreline that led to the marina. Instead, he saw a black-and-white blur rushing across the wet sand. He blinked hard, trying to wrap his head around it. There really was a dog on the beach.

A few seconds later, the pup turned, making its way up the sand, headed right for them. Leona made a little noise, stepping backward, like she was trying to get away from it. He had no interest in Leona though, heading straight for Carlos, circling him, jumping up and nudging his hands.

"Aww, he's friendly," Carlos said, kneeling down to love on the dog. He was wet from the ocean, and smelled like it, but it wasn't anything a bath couldn't fix.

"You're sure it's a he?"

"He's got the required parts." Carlos pointed to the dog's undercarriage, laughing.

Leona huffed, and it was all Carlos could do not to laugh. Reaching forward, Leona held out her hand, trying to pet the little guy. The dog wasn't having it though, cowering back, a low growl rumbling from his throat.

"Oh, good puppy," Carlos said, scratching behind his ears.

"Hey!"

Carlos laughed, not stopping himself this time. He couldn't help but tease her. Thankfully, she took it in stride, still committed to being friends. His heart ached over how long he'd waited to share his feelings, but it didn't matter now. It was over and done with. He needed to move on.

"You found him! Or her!" Drea called out.

"*He*...found us," Leona shared.

Looking up, Carlos continued to scratch the dog's ear, not wanting to lose contact with him, afraid that if he did, the little guy would take off again. He'd already lost a portion of his afternoon to this; he didn't need to waste any more of his day.

"Aww, looks like he likes you."

The voice was new to him. Bubbly and sweet, it sent a shiver down his spine. Who was that? Glancing over his shoulder, it took him a minute to fully register what he saw. A tall, curvy blonde stood next to Drea, a medical bag slung over her shoulder. The bright smile on her face was giving the sun a run for its money, sunglasses hiding away eyes that he just knew sparkled like glitter. His heart skipped a beat, his eyes dragging along her body, taking in each one of her luscious curves. Full-figured women weren't his normal type, but there was something about this beauty that took his breath away. He couldn't take his eyes off her, every part of him dying to know what her body felt like against his.

"Hi, I'm Dr. Ashby Carver. I'm a vet with Paw It in Neutral, currently working with the local clinic in Charlotte Amalie. This guy is a stray?"

"I guess?" Carlos choked out, still caught off guard by just how beautiful this woman was.

Out of the corner of his eye, he saw Drea and Leona head back to the main part of the resort. He was happier to see them go than he probably should have been, but he really liked the idea of being alone with Ashby.

"He's been wandering up and down the beach all week."

"Well, let's get him scanned and see if he has a chip." Ashby reached into her bag, pulling out a collar attached to a leash, slipping it over the dog's head. "Here, hold this."

Taking the leash from her, he watched as she ran a handheld device over the dog's back. Her smile never faded, radiating joy like he'd never seen. What was it about this woman? There wasn't just one thing—everything about her called to him in a way he couldn't explain.

"No chip. And he isn't neutered. So, my guess is that he's not someone's pet."

"So then, what now?"

"That depends. Like I said, I'm with Paw It in Neutral, a nonprofit that works with municipalities on spaying and neutering strays to help curb the population growth, but also on educating the public on why getting your pet fixed is so important. So, my first recommendation is for him to see Dr. Snip."

She made a scissor motion with her fingers to illustrate her point, making him laugh again. One joke in and he already loved her sense of humor. The sound of her laugh wasn't bad either. In fact, it was intoxicating, and he was already trying to work out a way to make her do it again.

"And then?"

"Again, it depends. I don't know much about the local adoption programs on the island. I'm a rotating vet, only here for six weeks for this campaign."

A rotating vet, only here for six weeks. That would explain why he hadn't seen her before. He might have spent most of his time on-site at the resort, but the island of St. Thomas was small. He would have noticed her. It would have been impossible to not—she was absolutely stunning.

"I can take him."

The words were out of his mouth before he even had time to think about it. But now that they were out there, he knew he didn't want to give him up. Ten minutes in, and he was already attached. Just like he was to the woman in front of him. He didn't really have time for a dog, although having the company would be nice. The bosses probably wouldn't object too much to bringing him to work. With the right training, Carlos was sure the little guy would be a great addition to the resort.

"You sure?"

"Yeah, why not? Can you tell how old he is? And what kind of dog he is?"

"Based on his looks, he's pure Heinz fifty-seven mutt," she said with a laugh. "Age is harder, especially since he's underweight, but I'd say a year or two?"

Carlos nodded, trying to think of something else to say. He wanted to keep her talking. Keep her here with him. But his mind went blank.

"He's gonna need a name. Preferably before I take him in to be fixed. So we know what to call him."

"How about Mickey?" Carlos offered.

"As in Mouse?" Ashby asked, her brow furrowed in confusion.

"As in *you're so fine*," Carlos corrected her, hoping she got it and that he wouldn't actually have to sing. "We have a thing for eighties music around here."

"Oh, gotcha. Well, then Mickey it is."

Ashby stood, holding out her hand to take the leash from him. Carlos reluctantly handed it over, more upset than he thought he would be about letting the pup go. Not just the pup—Ashby too. He needed to see her again.

"Here's my card," she said, handing it to him. "Text me so I have your number and can call you when this guy is done with surgery. Might be a couple of days before we can fit him in."

"And if I want to text you about non-dog-related things?"

"Such as?"

Even behind her sunglasses Carlos could tell her eyes went wide, her cheeks pinkening slightly. She hadn't been prepared for the question.

"Like dinner? Or a night out of some kind?"

"Sure, you could text me about those too."

With another bright smile, Ashby spun around, tugging on the leash lightly, and walked away. Mickey followed her, his tongue hanging out the side of his mouth, turning around to look at Carlos every few seconds. Watching them walk away, his heart beat faster, sad to see them go. Although, he couldn't deny he enjoyed the view of Ashby from this angle.

Laughing to himself, Carlos started back toward the resort. Just an hour ago he was having a pity party over Leona. Now, he was trying to figure out how soon was too soon to text Ashby. He didn't want to scare her away, but one conversation wasn't enough. Not even close. What was it the girls had joked about? Best way to get over someone is to get under someone else? He wasn't sure that applied to men the same way, but right now, he was more than willing to find out.

Chapter Two

Carlos: He looks drunk
    Ashby: Sedation will do that to anyone. Canine, feline, human…

Carlos chuckled at Ashby's response, hearing her sweet voice in his head as he read the words. They may have only talked for a moment in person the other day on the beach, but that was all he needed for such a pretty sound to stick with him.

Clicking on the photo to enlarge it, he couldn't help but smile at the image of Mickey, staring back at him, eyes glazed over, looking like he'd just stumbled out of a frat party.

Carlos: It's the lip, all curled up and stuck on his gum like that. Like he knows that he knows something we don't
    Ashby: He's smirking
    Carlos: It's cute
    Ashby: There, I fixed it

Another photo popped up, this one of the pup, lips back in place, shit-eating grin on his face.

. . .

Carlos: Now he looks like he stole the last Magic Muffin from the kitchen

    Ashby: Magic Muffin? Just what goes on at that resort?

Carlos: Not that kind of Magic Muffin lol

Carlos: Miller, our head chef and one of the owners, makes these amazing muffins every morning. They are part of what the resort is known for. It's coconut flour, mangos, blueberries, coconut, this sugary stuff on top...and they're, well...magic

    Ashby: Sounds delish

Carlos: You should stop by for breakfast sometime

    Ashby: The Indigo Royal is a little out of my way just for breakfast

Staring at his screen, Carlos had to stop himself from replying that the Indigo Royal wouldn't be out of the way if she spent the night here. With him. In his bed. He was dying to know what she felt like against him—under him—and his mind ran wild with ideas of all the things he could do to her. The sound of her sweet voice calling his name as she came made his dick twitch. Maybe it was time he changed the subject from Mickey. She had said he could text her about *other things*. So far all their texting had been about Mickey. It was time to kick it up a notch.

Carlos: Not if you're already here

    Ashby: And why would I already be there?

Carlos: I can think of a few reasons... ;)

    Ashby: Only a few? ;)

Carlos let out a groan. Never in his life would he have thought something as simple as a winky emoji would give him a boner. But here he was, pitching a tent, all from a semicolon and close parentheses.

Carlos: Maybe more than a few

    Carlos: Not that I've counted

    Ashby: I'm not sure if I'm disappointed by that or not

Carlos: I could just start listing them if you'd like

. . .

A long moment passed without a response, making Carlos start to worry he'd crossed a line. He wanted Ashby—there was no doubt about that. But what he didn't want was to scare her away.

Carlos: But seriously, I do want to see you again

    Ashby: Well, I do have to bring your dog back

    Carlos: True. But that's not why I want to see you

    Ashby: Oh?

    Carlos: I did mention dinner the other day, didn't I? Or was that just in my head?

    Ashby: No, you said it out loud

    Ashby: Either that, or we can communicate telepathically

    Carlos If that's the case, then you know just how badly I want to see you again

    Carlos: And not just because you have my dog...

    Ashby: OK

Those two little letters made his insides jump. He wanted whatever time she was going to give him. Wanted to find out more about the woman behind that smile that had put the Caribbean sun to shame. And she had just agreed.

Carlos: How about Tuesday? Every week the resort hosts this bonfire, it's a whole thing. Come

    Ashby: Tuesday? As in four days from now?

Blinking, Carlos read her text again. Was that...disappointment in her response? Fuck, he hoped it was.

Carlos: You're right. Too far away. Come now.

    Ashby: lol

    Ashby: Tuesday works. We don't currently have any surgeries scheduled for that afternoon, so I can block it off. And I can bring Mickey to you then. He should be mostly healed by that point.

Carlos: A pretty girl and a dog? Does life get any better?

Ashby: lol

Carlos put his phone down, his heart squeezing at the thought of seeing her again soon. Problem was, as Ashby had pointed out, Tuesday was still four days away. He wasn't going to last that long. Grabbing his phone again, he snapped a quick selfie, the sunset in the background, hitting send immediately.

Ashby: Pretty

Carlos: Most dudes prefer handsome, but I'll take pretty

Ashby: I meant the sun setting over the beach. But I guess you're not bad lol

Carlos: Ouch!

Ashby: lol

Carlos: Same sunset I see every day, so...

Ashby: Jealous. It's much better than the ones we have back home

Carlos: Where's home?

Ashby: PNW

Carlos: ummmm, should I know where that is?

Ashby: Pacific Northwest.

Carlos: Tell me about it. Tell me about you.

Ashby: Me?

Carlos: Yes, you...

Ashby: Not much to tell... born and raised in Independence, Oregon...

Settling into the slingback beach chair, Carlos watched as a series of texts popped up, one after the other, rapid fire in their chat. For someone who thought she was boring, Ashby certainly had plenty to say.

And he loved it.

Chapter Three

"Ready to head to your new home, Mickey?" Ashby asked, helping the dog out of the back of the vet clinic's van.

The black-and-white pup smiled back at her, tongue hanging out the side of his mouth. His incisions were almost fully healed, and his energy had returned over the last few days, allowing him to show off his personality. Fun and playful, but a good listener, Mickey seemed like the perfect kind of dog to hang out at a resort, helping out the maintenance staff. Ashby had been more than a little worried when Carlos had volunteered so quickly to keep him, but was relieved when he had told her that his bosses agreed when they were texting this past week.

Leading Mickey into the Indigo Royal's open-air lobby, a sadness washed over her as she wondered if the return of Mickey meant no more texting with Carlos. Their back and forth had become a daily thing—no, that wasn't quite right. It had become an *all day* thing, ever since that first puppy face emoji appeared on her screen. She'd come to really enjoy their back and forth, hoping it could continue.

"OMG, look at this little guy!" a cute brunette with corkscrew curls cooed from across the lobby, rushing toward them. It was the same gal who had greeted Ashby when she arrived the other day, but for the life of her she couldn't remember the woman's name. "Hi, I'm Drea, we met last week."

Drea, that's right...

"Hi, I'm Ashby," she returned, thankful for this woman's manners. "And this guy has officially been named Mickey."

"Now I just need not to sing that song, because I will never get it out of my head. I've gotten pretty good over the years at not singing things with all the song titles we have around here, but this one might be too much."

"Yeah, Carlos clued me in to the eighties theme. Surely, not every building is named after a song."

"Oh, it is. As is every department in my spa," Drea said, a bright smile on her face. "Did he not give you a tour?"

Ashby shook her head, trying to figure out how much to reveal. Carlos had mentioned that Drea was one of the owners of the resort, along with her three uncles, making her his boss. She couldn't think of a reason that their texting would be against the rules, but for some reason it felt like it. Maybe it was just because there had been a flirty undertone to them. Or at least, there was what she had hoped was a flirty undertone to them. Either way, the last thing she wanted was to get him in trouble with the boss.

"Carlos! Give the girl a tour!" Drea called out, her eyes looking behind Ashby.

Spinning around, Ashby had to catch her breath, the sight of Carlos walking toward her sending a jolt through her. Tall, dark, and oh-so-fucking-sexy, Carlos smiled at her, his perfect grin melting her panties right off her. He looked too good for words in his fitted white T-shirt and khaki shorts, like he was walking straight out of a magazine ad. Ashby's mind flashed straight to what was under the shirt, sure that every inch of him was well defined.

"Hey you," he greeted, his eyes dancing up and down her body.

"Hi."

Her pulse sped up, enjoying the feel of his eyes on her. There was something in his expression she couldn't quite read, but whatever it was, she liked it. No one had ever looked at her quite like Carlos was in this moment. And it felt good—damn good. Ashby was comfortable in her body and proud of who she was. That said, she knew that there were plenty of people who had no problem shaming her for being a bigger girl. Especially men. But not Carlos. He seemed to like what he saw, leaving her feeling all giddy inside.

"Boss lady says I should give you a tour, so, what do you say?"

"Sure."

"I'll take Mickey over to the bonfire, so take your time!" Drea said, starting to walk away. "And make sure you show her the spa. Ashby, I owe you a spa day as a thank you for helping with this guy."

Ashby started to reply, but Drea waved her off, leaving them alone. Sucking in a breath, Ashby reminded herself to stay calm. The bass from a pop song thrummed through her, the flicker of flames from the bonfire off in the distance catching her eye.

"Cherish Spa is through those doors," Carlos pointed out. "And we'll get you a menu so you know what they offer and can pick out treatments. Then, over that way," he continued, twisting to point in the opposite direction, "are Barracuda, Purple Rain, and Black Velvet, the guest room buildings. Past that are the Villas."

"Those are the beach bungalows named after Madonna songs, yes?" she asked, following him out of the lobby.

"Someone was paying attention."

"Of course I was. It's not every day you meet someone who grew up in the Caribbean. I think there is something unique and fun about it. And that you've worked here so long. Where I'm from, you'd be hard-pressed to find someone who is still at a job they started at as a teenager."

"I'm sure there are a lot of things about Oregon that are different from our island."

"Oh, so I'm not the only one who was paying attention."

Slipping his hand in hers, he led her out to the beach, closer to the bonfire, but still far enough away from the crowd that they could have some privacy. Butterflies filled her tummy, liking it way too much that he seemed to want alone time with her. She was only here for a few more weeks; she didn't need to be getting involved with someone. Although a fling never hurt anyone.

"Dr. Ashby Carver, born and raised in Independence, Oregon," he started, continuing to ramble off all the random facts she'd told him about herself. Ashby was amazed at his memory, the butterflies going wild with each new thing he remembered.

"Holy wow."

"Sorry, I don't mean to come off as weird, I just…"

"No, not at all. I…"

Ashby let herself trail off, not knowing how to continue. Why was she suddenly so awkward? This was not who she was. She was loud, proud, and everyone who thought she was too much could go fuck themselves. Yet, for some reason, she really wanted Carlos to like her. The real her. She just didn't know how to let that shine and not overwhelm him.

"How about a dance?"

"What?"

His question caught her off guard. A moment ago it seemed like he was about to get serious, picking up on the get-to-know-you game they'd been playing over text messages. But now he wanted to dance?

"Dance with me."

Carlos wasted no time, slipping an arm around her, tugging her into his hard body. The soft cotton of her blue sundress felt like it could incinerate any second from all the heat between them, making Ashby's heart skip. His body against her was magical, making her feel like the only woman along the beach. Despite her better judgment, she was starting to really like Carlos. As in *like* like him.

The heavy beat surrounding them faded into something softer, more sensual, as the DJ merged two songs together. The shift didn't faze Carlos though, slowing his movements, pulling her closer. Ashby's mind raced with all the things she wanted to say in this moment, but couldn't bring herself to speak. Carlos's eyes were locked on her, the corner of his mouth upturned into a sinfully delicious smile. One she couldn't help but reciprocate.

"Do you know how *intoxicating* you are?" he asked, his head dipping down slightly.

"Intoxicating, huh?" she teased. She couldn't tell if it was a line or not, but either way, she liked it. The idea of being intoxicating to someone like Carlos made her heat up even more.

"I am aware of how cheesy that sounds, but right now, I don't really care. I'm much more concerned with whether it'd be too forward to kiss you right now."

"Not at all."

Her response was out before she even thought about it. Not that she would have answered differently, but at least for appearance's sake maybe she should have at least pretended to think about it. Carlos's arm tightening around her waist pushed all thoughts of appearance's sake straight out of her brain, however. His head dipped lower, until his lips were a whisper away from hers. The space between them was almost imperceptible but felt like a million miles. He paused for a moment there, letting the anticipation building within start to bubble over. If he didn't kiss her now, she might just burst into flames.

A second later his mouth captured hers, soft and light at first, growing more powerful by the second. Fireworks lit up inside her at the feel of his strong lips against hers. Her mind went blank, the whole world seeming to fall away as he continued to kiss her like he had all the time in the world.

"Woof! Woof!"

The sound of Mickey's bark startled her. The pup jumped up against them, his front paws hitting Carlos's hip, breaking the kiss. Part of her wanted to curse the dog for interrupting, but her head was still too swimmy to find the words.

"Hey boy," Carlos said, reaching down to scratch him. "We're gonna have to have a talk about not cock blocking me, 'kay?"

Ashby laughed, her heart soaring at the hottie in front of her talking to his dog like he was his wingman.

Looking up at her, Carlos gave her the same devilish smile he had earlier. "Whatcha doing tomorrow?"

"Ummmm, working?"

"Skip it. It's my day off. Come hang out at the beach with Mickey and me."

Ashby knew she should object. But she couldn't bring herself to. She hadn't had a day off since she'd arrived on St. Thomas, and she knew her boss wouldn't care. Plus, she really wanted to spend more time with Carlos.

"It's a date."

Chapter Four

Mickey whimpered, growing restless at Carlos's feet as they stood in the lobby waiting on Ashby. The sun was bright in the sky, without a cloud to be seen and get in its way, warming the two of them. Turning around to see what he was whimpering at, Carlos couldn't help but smile, drinking in Ashby's beauty as she approached.

"I feel the exact same way, dude," Carlos muttered to the dog.

Kissing her last night had not been his plan. Neither had dancing with her. But as they stood there on the beach, every part of him had ached to hold her. Then once she was in his arms, well, he was done for at that point. Ever since, kissing her again was all he could think about.

"Hi boys," Ashby greeted, adjusting the large tote bag slung over her shoulder.

Waiting until she was a few steps closer, Carlos placed his hand on her hip, kissing her gently. She tasted just as sweet as she had last night, exciting him all over again.

"Are you ready for the best day at the beach ever?"

"Ever? That's a tall order, sir. Are you sure you can deliver?"

Oh, I can fucking deliver...

"Only one way to find out," he replied, giving her a wink.

Slipping his hand into hers, he led her out of the lobby, down the little path referred to as Electric Avenue, heading toward the large grouping of trees that separated the guest area from the staff section.

"Isn't the beach that way?" Ashby asked, looking behind her.

"The guest beach is, but the staff beach is just past these trees."

They rounded the corner, the staff dorms on the left, Kyle and Drea's cottage to their right, just adjacent to the Big House, where Drea's three uncles lived. Carlos felt like he was walking on sunshine as they arrived at the vacant beach, walking a little past the houses so they had more privacy. Not that anyone was home, since they were all working, but still. He wanted to make sure that they were totally alone.

"This is beautiful," Ashby commented, taking a deep breath of salt air.

Carlos laid out a large blanket, tugging her down onto it and into his arms. She crumpled into him with a laugh, Mickey settling at their feet.

"You're beautiful."

"You're just full of all kinds of lines today, aren't you?"

"What makes you think that's a line?"

"Isn't it?"

"Not at all."

Ashby gave him a skeptical look, making him sit up. What on earth would make her think that was a line?

"I don't mean to doubt you, it's just..." she paused, biting her lip, looking like she was trying to choose her words carefully. "Look, I know I'm beautiful. I'm comfortable in my own skin, and frankly, I don't give a fuck what anyone thinks about my size. That said, I know what guys like you think when you see a girl like me."

"Guys like me? What kind of guy am I?"

"A hot one."

"And what kind of girl are you?"

"You know...plus-sized."

Carlos blinked, trying to make it all add up in his head. He really had no idea what the term "plus-sized" was supposed to mean. Sure, Ashby was bigger than some other girls, but everything about her was gorgeous. Her full, lush curves were what dreams were made of, and his hands ached to be able to explore them.

"So, if I looked on the tag of that dress you're wearing there would be a plus sign?"

"What? No! That's just the stupid term that marketers use to—"

Carlos cut her off with a kiss, hauling her into him. Relaxing into his arms, she returned his efforts, ramping up his excitement. His hands found her sides, wandering down to her hips, loving how she seemed to fit perfectly in his grasp.

A cold nose nudged them apart, and Carlos let out a groan. Apparently he and Mickey needed another chat about how to be a proper wingman.

"Mickey, we talked about this, dude."

Ashby giggled, placing a kiss on the pup's nose. Her smile was bright, even in the Caribbean sun, and it made his heart squeeze.

"Ash, I don't give a damn what size you are. I think you're stunning. And—"

"Carlos," she interrupted.

"No, let me finish. Please," he said. Taking a deep breath, he tried to find the words to express this properly. He didn't want to scare her off. "Can I be honest with you about something?"

"No, I'd prefer that you lied to me."

"What?"

"Kidding. Be as honest as you like."

"This is all kinda new to me. I recently had my heart stomped on."

"Someone dared to dump you? You're like, a walking, talking desperate housewife fantasy!"

Carlos threw his head back with a laugh. He loved how open and real Ashby was. This girl said what she thought, no holds barred. If he were to ever say he had a type—that was it. A woman who knew her own mind and wasn't afraid to speak it.

"I'm going to take that as a compliment. But yes. We weren't together, exactly. We were friends with benefits, or whatever you want to call it. But I'd had feelings for her since we were teenagers and was just waiting for her to change her mind about only wanting sex."

"What happened?"

"She changed her mind. I just wasn't the guy she wanted more than sex with."

Saying it out loud made him feel pathetic. This wasn't the vibe he wanted for their beach day. He'd intended today to be all about fun and relaxing. Instead he was pouring out his soul.

"I'm telling you this not so you'll pity me, but because you are the first girl I've met since Leona that has made me feel anything at all. And even though we haven't spent that much time together, I do feel quite a few things when it comes to you."

Ashby's eyes went wide, her mouth opening slightly. His heart raced, hoping that he hadn't said too much. All he wanted was for her to know that he meant it when he said she was beautiful. It wasn't just a line. Everything about her sent him reeling—in all the right ways.

"I don't date much either. It's hard when you're only ever in a place for a couple of months max. Doesn't provide much time for guys to get past the exterior and see just how fucking awesome I am," she laughed.

He returned her laugh, kissing her again. Pretty sure he was already addicted to her kisses, he tried to push the reminder that she was only here for a short time from his brain. Just because he knew all this could ever be was a fling didn't mean he had to dwell on it.

"I'm rather fond of the exterior. Although, I do agree, you are pretty fucking awesome."

Another giggle rang out into the air, this one getting Mickey all excited. The pup howled, as if he were trying to join in on their laughter. It only made them laugh harder, adding some lightness to the moment.

"While we're being honest," he continued, "I think it's time you took that cover-up off and showed me that *exterior* of yours. Because I'm dying to see you in a swimsuit."

"I'll show you mine if you show me yours," she challenged.

Carlos was sure he'd never moved that fast in his life, whipping off his T-shirt. Pushing to his feet, he gestured at his chest, before slowly turning around, as if he were on stage showing off. Ashby sucked her lips into her mouth, trying to bite back a laugh as her eyes scanned him up and down. He could tell that she liked what she saw, sending a jolt straight to his dick.

Behave...behave...

Holding out a hand, he helped her to her feet. Everything inside him came alive, anticipation swirling around him. He couldn't wait any longer. Bending his knees just enough to grab the hem of her dress, he pulled it up, revealing her body inch by inch. Ashby raised her arms above her head, letting him peel the garment off her. Carlos's eyes danced up and down her body, appreciating her beauty. His cock ached at the sight of her, the black-and-white swimsuit she was wearing hugging her in all the right places. He needed to behave, or else she was going to think that he only wanted one thing. A distraction—that's what he really needed.

Stepping in closer, he smiled, looking her straight in the eye.

"Last one in is a rotten egg."

Chapter Five

Ashby couldn't remember a day when she had laughed so hard. From the moment he'd issued a rotten egg challenge—she hadn't heard that since childhood—her smile had never faded. Even in moments throughout the day as they'd gotten more serious, talking about family, hopes, dreams, and all the kinds of things you share with someone as you get to know them, she'd smiled. Just being around him did that to her. Of course all the flirting, touching, and kissing didn't hurt either.

Carlos made her feel...adored. That was the only word she could come up with. She knew it had only been a week, but there was something about him that was different—special. Maybe it was because they both knew that they had limited time. But whatever it was, he didn't waste a moment, always making sure she was fully aware that he was into her.

Which is why she had agreed to go back to his place in the staff dorms. The suite-style room felt like a small apartment, complete with a kitchenette and en suite bathroom. She couldn't help but be impressed, even as nerves started to chip away at her cool exterior.

"He's made himself right at home," Ashby said, nodding at Mickey who had promptly curled up on the couch when they'd walked in.

"He claimed that spot last night, so I'm pretty sure I'm never getting it back."

Ashby laughed, hearing her own nerves in the sound. Why was she suddenly so edgy? Taking a deep breath, she admitted what she already knew. She wanted him. Bad. So much so she was willing to toss all her rules about not sleeping with a guy for at least a month right out the window. No one had ever looked at her like he did. Like he wanted to devour her. And fuck, did she want to let him.

"I want you," she blurted out, her hands flying to her face the second the words left her mouth.

Well done, Ash. Way to be cool about that...

The corner of Carlos's mouth quirked upward, sending a wave of lust crashing through her. That smile was dangerous, and she was pretty sure he knew it.

"I want you too," he returned, closing the gap between them. Carlos's hand found her hip, giving it a squeeze, making her heart leap. "Even more so now that you said it. I like a woman who speaks her mind."

"Oh, well, that's good, because my filter is broken."

Carlos laughed, the deep rumble of it making her skin vibrate. The air around them seemed to sizzle. Or maybe that was just her—so turned on that everything had a new feel to it. Whatever it was though, she wanted more. So, so much. His hand squeezed her hip again, his other one tucking a stray hair behind her ear.

"You have no idea just how much I want you, Ashby. How much I want to get lost in your body— exploring, teasing, worshipping."

A shiver ran through her body, just as a wave of heat crawled up her skin. She hadn't even realized such a thing was possible. Nonetheless, here she was, panties melting right off of her, her whole body raring to go. If he would only kiss her.

"Then what are you waiting for?"

A slight shrug of his shoulder and a wicked smirk was all the warning she got. Next thing she knew his hands were on her ass, lifting her in the air, his mouth capturing hers in a hot, hard kiss. She kissed him back, matching his intensity, getting lost in his taste. It was like rich, dark chocolate, with none of the bitterness, melting on her tongue. A taste she knew she'd never forget.

Carlos laid her down on the bed, never breaking their kiss. His hands were everywhere all at once, ridding her of her clothing. The cool air of the room hit her skin, making her nipples harden, stealing her attention away from him briefly. She was naked. In front of Carlos.

"Oh, fuuuuuuck," he muttered, stepping back, letting his eyes wander up and down her body. "I think you lied to me earlier, Ash. You said you know you're beautiful, but I don't think you really have any idea just how magnificent you are."

The heat returned, leaving her feeling like she could combust. Carlos licked his lips, his eyes dark and hungry, looking like a man possessed.

"Only problem is, I just don't know where to start..." he muttered, licking his lips again. Kissing her, he quickly moved to her jawline, traveling down her neck. "I guess I'll just have to start at the top and work my way down."

Doing just that, he continued to move south, his hot, wet, open-mouthed kisses sending sparks through her. Each one felt better than the last. When he reached her breasts, he wasted no time, taking one in his mouth, his tongue circling her nipple, his fingers mimicking the movements on the other side. Ashby gasped. It all felt so good, she could barely think about anything else. It was like he'd been given a map to her body and knew exactly how she liked her nipples to be played with.

That didn't last long though. He released the taut peak with a pop, the cool air hitting it, sending a new sensation coursing through her. She missed the attention from his oral assault and wanted to object. But the soft touch of his lips on her belly distracted her. Was he really loving up on her there? He answered her unspoken question by nipping at her skin, the sharpness of it making her lady bits sing.

"Carlos..." she moaned.

"I've been waiting to get my hands on these curves since the second I saw you, and let me tell you, they do not disappoint," he growled. His voice was deep and feral-sounding, like he wasn't able to control himself. "So I know that your pussy is going to be even better than I imagined."

Oh, fuck...

The next thing Ashby knew, Carlos's tongue found her pussy. Licking, sucking, nibbling in all the right spots. Now she was convinced he'd been given a map, or at least some kind of decoder ring. How was it possible that this man knew all the exact right places to touch her? Was he a magician? He had to be, because her climax was building in her faster than she could ever remember, and he still hadn't touched her clit. Once he double-clicked that button, she knew it would be all over.

He moaned into her, sending vibrations through her, slipping two fingers inside her. Ashby gasped, gripping onto the bedspread, his tongue finding her clit a second later. The world came to a standstill, the pleasure rushing through her making it hard to breathe. Carlos didn't let up on his efforts though, circling her clit faster and faster, until she was bucking wildly, her orgasm taking over her whole body.

"Oh my...I...what...I mean..." she said, trying to find her words in between heavy breaths. That was easily the best orgasm she'd ever had. In fact, she was pretty sure that was the orgasm to ruin all orgasms, because nothing was ever going to live up to the talent of that man's tongue.

He cut off her ramblings with a kiss, letting her taste herself on his lips.

Her body relaxed completely, the weight of him on top of her comforting in a way she couldn't describe.

"You taste like raspberries and red wine," he told her between kisses. "Two things I happen to love."

Oh, swooooooooon...

Ashby's heart squeezed, his sentiment overwhelming her. She was already feeling so much for him. Much more than she should. But that was tomorrow Ashby's problem. Right now Ashby only wanted one thing.

"Fuck me," she whispered.

"Happily."

In a flash, he was naked, his beautiful, tan body on full display. Ashby bit her lip, her eyes settling on his cock—long and thick, already hard and ready for action. Part of her wanted to reach out, take it in her hand, and play. But a bigger part of her wanted him inside her. Carlos apparently wanted that as well, making quick work of rolling the condom down his shaft and settling between her legs.

As he was sinking slowly into her, they both let out a moan. Every inch of him was glorious, filling her like she'd never experienced before. He didn't wait for her to adjust, finding an easy, steady rhythm, moving in and out of her. Her hands flew to his back, tugging him in close, her nails digging into his skin. She needed him closer to her. Needed his skin against hers, their bodies coming together as the world around them melted away. She could feel him all the way in her toes, loving every second of his touch.

Another climax started to build in her, and she knew she wasn't going to last long. Not with the way he was grinding his hips against her, finding her clit with each new movement. This guy was a fucking god. Like, a literal god of fucking. Picking up the pace, she tried to match him thrust for thrust, wanting everything he had to give her. Out of nowhere her orgasm hit her, a crescendo of pleasure that made her see stars. Ashby screamed out, unable to hold back. Carlos didn't seem to mind though, her screams all the permission he needed to let himself go, finding his own release.

"Stay with me tonight," he whispered a moment later when they caught their breath.

Ashby smiled, unable to hide the giddiness.

"I'd love to."

"Good. Because I'm nowhere close to being done with those sexy curves of yours."

Chapter Six

Carlos glanced down at his watch, hurrying across the resort toward the bonfire. He was running late, thanks to a clogged garbage disposal in the kitchen that had exploded all over him, requiring a shower before meeting up with Ashby. Being late made him anxious anyway, but the idea that he was missing precious minutes with her, when they were already on borrowed time, made it even worse.

Ashby came into view as he turned the corner, the sight of her hitting him like a wrecking ball. She looked gorgeous in her denim shorts and a square neck, cropped blouse, letting just enough midriff peek out to drive him wild. His dick twitched, making him wish he could haul her back to his suite and have his way with her. She'd spent every night of this last week with him—curled up in his sheets, talking, laughing, getting handsy. She was beautiful, inside and out, and he hated that she was only here for the summer.

"Sorry I was late," he said, placing a kiss on her cheek. "I lost a fight with a garbage disposal this afternoon."

"That sounds...intense."

"It was. Where's Mickey?" he asked, looking around. Ashby had taken him with her this morning, and he had missed having him by his side all day.

"Drea made off with him. Something about introducing him to a Jonas brother?"

"A Jonas brother?"

"At least I assume that's what she meant. She said a Jo-bro was coming."

Carlos laughed. "Jo-bro is what they call her best friend's younger brother. Josef is fourteen. Drea and Lee were big fans, and the nickname stuck."

"That makes a lot more sense," she commented, stepping in closer to him. "And makes me really glad I didn't ask her to take me instead of the dog."

Carlos laughed again, pulling her in for a long, drawn-out kiss. He loved her sense of humor. It was just one of the many things that made her so damn sexy. Ashby deepened the kiss, her fingers looping through his belt buckles, her curves against him making his head spin. The bonfire always had a romantic undertone to him, and he'd longed for the day that he could spend it with someone that he cared for. Now, here he was, and he wasn't going to waste one second.

"There you are!" Leona called out, rushing toward him.

So much for enjoying this moment...

"Sorry to interrupt, but an entire panel of lights went out in the laundry and well...the bulbs need replacing."

Carlos froze, Leona's words catching him off guard. "Replacing light bulbs" had been their code for hooking up while they were friends with benefits. Before she'd broken his heart. In the year since they'd ended things, she hadn't once come to him with the request. He didn't know if that had been luck or carefully planned on her part, but here they were.

"And that's a legit request, not a..." she trailed off.

"I would expect nothing less," he replied, eyes flying to her hand. Yup, engagement ring was still there.

The moment didn't sting as much as he thought it would. Or really at all. He'd figured the first time that she asked this question it would hurt like a gunshot wound. But it didn't. And he knew exactly why.

Ashby.

"Why would it be anything other than a legit request?" Ashby asked, her brow knitted in confusion.

"Ashby, this is Leona, our head of housekeeping."

He kept the introduction simple, hoping that she followed. He'd told her all about Leona, their "relationship," and just how heartbroken he'd been. Ashby had listened intently, letting him word vomit all about it, never once judging him. Of course, when he'd told her everything he had, no part of him had planned on this meeting ever taking place.

"Leona...which is long for Lee. You're the one who..."

Leona nodded. "That's me! I'm the villain in the story."

"You're not a villain," Carlos said, slipping his hand into Ashby's. It was warm and comforting, right where his belonged. "And we can go replace the light bulbs."

"Would it be too awkward if I reminded you to *be safe* in the process?"

Ashby spit out a laugh, her hand covering her mouth like she hadn't meant to do that. Still, the light in her eyes told him that she saw nothing but humor in Leona's comment. Carlos's heart squeezed, all his emotions hitting him at once. How was this his life?

Giving Leona a nod, he tightened his hand around Ashby's, leading the way to the laundry room. Missing out on the bonfire was not how he had seen the night going, but being on call meant he had little choice in the matter. And truthfully, there were worse places to be alone with the girl you liked than the laundry room.

"So that was Lee," Ashby finally said as he worked on the overhead light fixture. Twisting on the ladder, he handed her the burned-out bulb, taking a new one from her.

"That was Lee."

"It's impressive that you two are still friends. Even if that was a little awkward."

"Believe it or not, it was a lot less awkward than I expected. In my head, the first time she asked me to change out bulbs was going to be—I dunno—a lot worse." Closing up the light, he worked his way down the ladder. Ashby smiled at him, his insides turning to goo from how bright it was. "We've been close since high school, so it was important to us that our friendship didn't go away, but we both knew it would change. Like I told you before, she might not have realized I had feelings for her until too late, but she was fully aware she stomped on my heart. She's been pretty respectful of that."

"Do you think we can stay friends after I leave next week?"

Her question caught him off guard. *Next week?* That wasn't possible. He knew her time was limited, and that she would be going back to the States at the end of the summer, but they still had weeks together. As in plural.

"Next week? You said you were here for six, and it's only been two."

"Since I met you. But I'd been on St. Thomas for almost a month when Drea called about Mickey."

Carlos's head was spinning, and not in the good way this time. Why he assumed she had only just arrived when they met was beyond him, but he'd never thought to ask. Damn, that was dumb.

Tugging her into him, he spun her around so her back was to the large metal folding table, lifting her onto it. He wrapped her legs around his waist, resting his hands on her luscious hips. He loved having her wrapped around him, and now that he knew their timeline was even more accelerated, he wanted to remain like this as long as they could.

"There's no chance of you staying, huh?"

"No," she answered, resting her forehead against his. "I'm a traveling vet; I go where needed. Both the agency I work for and Paw It in Neutral are based out of Portland. I'm headed back there, unless they call to tell me they have another project for me to go work on right away."

The raw ache Carlos felt in his chest was starting to spread. It might have only been two weeks, but he'd gotten used to having Ashby here with him. The idea of not having her around every night made him want to puke. Portland was on the other side of the US, which meant a four-hour time difference. That didn't mean staying in touch was impossible, but certainly made it harder. He hated this. But he wasn't going to stand in her way either. Ashby was a shining star, with a huge career ahead of her. He couldn't be a roadblock to that.

"Of course we can stay friends. Just know that Mickey and I are going to miss you."

"I'm going to want regular photos of our little guy. And his owner too."

"For you, Ash, anything."

Chapter Seven

The Cherish Spa was unlike anything Ashby had ever seen. Posh and extravagant, but still comfy and cozy, the spa seemed to ooze relaxing vibes, putting everyone instantly at ease. With each distinct area named after an eighties song, there was also a lightheartedness to it that made Ashby smile.

Walking out of the main part of the spa, she slowly wandered through the courtyard. Passing the thalassotherapy cool pool and the one-of-a-kind three-tiered whirlpool spas, Ashby tightened the cinch on her robe. No need to give anyone in the whirlpools a show. She'd been intrigued by them when Drea had given her the tour that morning—three hot tubs built into the ground that flow into each other and get progressively cooler—and part of her was still dying to try it out. But she had somewhere to be.

Every part of was relaxed, her whole body feeling a bit like jelly after the almost two-hour massage she'd just received. When she'd arrived this morning and had been given her itinerary for all her spa treatments, she'd been more than a little taken aback. Her entire afternoon was filled with fancy treatments —some of which she'd never heard of before—including the most intense and luxurious massage. One that had easily ruined her for all other massages ever.

"This is too much," she'd insisted at check-in.

"I have strict instructions to make sure that you enjoy every last second that you're here," the tall, willowy brunette behind the counter responded. Her name tag read Maeve, and Ashby couldn't help but think that the name seemed fitting for a gal with such a sweet smile. "Also, these are for you."

Reaching below the counter, Maeve pulled out a small box with a clear top, passing it over the counter to Ashby. Three chocolate-covered strawberries sat on ocean-blue tissue paper. They looked both gorgeous and delicious, making her mouth water. Flipping open the little card taped to the corner, Ashby couldn't hide the grin taking over her face.

JUST A TASTE OF WHAT'S TO COME...
-Carlos

Ashby's heart squeezed, her eyes glued to Carlos's all caps handwriting on the card. She should have known when he said he wanted to make her last night on the island memorable that he'd pull out all the stops.

"I...I..." she started, unable to find her words.

"It's called Cherish for a reason," Maeve answered with a wink.

It sure was...

Inhaling deeply, the salty ocean air filling her nostrils, she continued on to *Almost Paradise*, the open-air relaxation room that was listed as her last stop. She had no idea what waited for her there, since the treatment column next to the location was blank. But based on how her afternoon had gone, her mind was running wild with possibilities.

"Hey there, beautiful," Carlos greeted her.

The deep rumble of his voice gave her goosebumps, her body coming alive at the sound. It had quickly become one of her favorite things, like hearing the opening notes to your favorite song. Familiar, comforting, and exciting all at the same time. His smile was much the same. It made her feel all sorts of things she wasn't aware a person could feel. All sorts of things she was going to miss desperately after tomorrow.

"Hey there yourself," she returned, stepping up into the room.

The beautiful free-standing room had floor to ceiling windows facing toward the ocean, overlooking the beach. The late afternoon sun had started to set, sending a glow inside that seemed magical, like candles flickering in the glittery light. Carlos wasted no time in wrapping his arms around her, pulling her into his hard body and kissing her as if he hadn't seen her in months, rather than just a day. She kissed him back, returning his efforts with her own, so happy to see him she felt like she could burst. Maybe it was because she knew these were their last moments together, or maybe it was because she had started to fall more than she was letting on, but either way, there was an intensity to the moment she hadn't been expecting.

One that she wasn't entirely prepared for.

"Thoroughly relaxed?" he asked, pulling back from the kiss.

"I don't know that I have ever been this relaxed in my life. I kinda feel like I could just melt into a puddle right now."

"If you're going to melt, the only place it's going to be is into my arms."

"Is that so?"

Carlos nodded, taking her hand and guiding her over to a pair of loungers pushed together, covered in rose petals. In one swift move he sat down, pulling her into his lap. His arms surrounded her, the heat radiating off him making her want to snuggle into him and never let go.

"I know there is a lot going on in your world right now, and that things are...well...busy," he whispered, placing a kiss just below her earlobe. It sent a shiver through her, goose bumps appearing once more. "So I figured that the best thing to do tonight was just be. You and me, the sunset, and the sound of the waves. Nothing else. One last night to remember for all our lives." He paused, placing another soft kiss on her neck, this one right on the slope that met her shoulder. "And maybe a chocolate-covered strawberry or two."

"Those were delicious, thank you."

"Anything for you, Ash."

"And I like the idea of just being."

Of spending tonight forgetting this is the last time we'll be like this...

Settling in, Ashby leaned back against Carlos's chest, enjoying the feel of him. It was easy to be comfortable in his presence. Easier than with anyone else, even her best friend.

"Do you have any idea what's next?" he asked after a long silence.

"Nope. Which isn't unusual. Unless I'm going directly there, rather than stopping back in Portland, I generally don't. I'll spend a couple of weeks at home, doing laundry, catching up with friends, all that. And then it's off to the next adventure."

"And you love it?"

"I do," she answered, her stomach flipping slightly at her answer. She did love it. She always had. She'd wanted to be a traveling vet ever since she'd heard about the idea in high school. But suddenly, the idea was sounding less fun, ripping her away from something new she had come to love. "It's been great to see so many new places, meet some amazing people. What about you?"

"What about me?"

"You love what you do?"

Carlos laughed. "I do. I always knew I would never be a sit at a desk type of guy. I love working with my hands, and there is always something to do around here. I might not get to visit lots of places, but thanks to our guests, I get to hear about cities all over the world. I've met quite a few characters over the years, and as crazy as it might sound to some, I'm not sure I ever see myself doing anything different. I'm happy here, and I'll gladly be here, fixing whatever breaks, for as long as Drea and her uncles will have me."

Sucking in a deep breath, Ashby slowly exhaled, letting his words sink in. She loved that he was as passionate about his job as she was hers. It was part of what made him so damn special. Part of why she was falling for him.

"I already know the answer, but I'm going to ask anyway," he said, twisting her so he could see her face.

Ashby's heart skipped a beat, his deep, soulful brown eyes full of so much emotion. She wanted to kiss him so badly, take away some of the hurt she saw there. But she knew she couldn't.

"There's no way for you to stay, huh?"

"No," she whispered, shaking her head. "My job, my life, is back in Portland."

It was the truth. Didn't matter how much fun the idea of staying was—how much she wanted it. Nothing about it made sense. She had a life—family, friends, a career—back in Oregon. The only thing she had here was Carlos. And while she knew they had something special, something that was once in a lifetime, that wasn't enough to give up everything else, was it? To throw away everything she had worked for? Her head told her that it wasn't a reason to stay. That it was perfectly obvious. But her heart was torn.

"As much as I want to, I can't ask you to give that up. But I hope all those pets know just how lucky they are to have your hands all over them."

"Kinda like how I want your hands all over me right now?"

The corner of her lips lifted into a smirk, a rush of excitement washing over her. He'd said he wanted a night to remember. She wanted that too. And that meant one last time together.

"Do you now?" Carlos wagged his eyebrows, returning her impish look.

Ashby nodded, afraid to say anything, not wanting to ruin the moment. She was sure there must be some cute, coy comeback—one that would rev his engines, driving him wild. For the life of her, she just couldn't think of what it would be.

"Tell me, gorgeous...are you wearing anything under that robe?"

Chapter Eight

Ashby's eyes flared wide, her pretty pink lips separated just enough, forming a small O. Carlos felt all the blood start rushing straight to his dick, the thought of those lips wrapped around him taking over his thoughts. He could hear the audible gasp that escaped her, her breath heavy, her gaze locked with his.

Shaking her head slowly, almost imperceptibly, Ashby licked her lips. Carlos had no idea if it was an unconscious move on her part, or if she was trying to be sexy—but it didn't matter. The move was more than enough to ignite the already growing fire within him. He shifted her in his lap, returning her to the position she had been in, with her back against this chest. The softness of the spa robe she was in almost tickled his skin, fueling his desire to get her out of it. His hands worked at the knot at Ashby's waist, loosening it, letting the lapels drape open.

"Carlos..." Ashby muttered on a sigh.

His name sounded incredible in her low, breathy tone. The open robe still mostly covered her, but he could see she was naked underneath it, her breasts heaving with each breath she took. He loved the look of her like this, knowing just what beauty waited for him under that terry cloth. Leaning down, he nipped at her earlobe, earning him a moan, his hands toying with the silky hem of the lapel. His hands ached to rip the cloth from her body, flip her over and have his way with her. He wanted her so bad he could feel it deep in his bones. But he also wanted this to last. He got one last night with her, and it needed to be perfect.

Ashby squirmed in his lap, obviously still anxious for what she had requested earlier. His hands all over her. And that was what he intended to give her.

Slipping his fingers under the fabric, he drew it open, taking his time in revealing her body, drinking in every beautiful inch of skin. She was built like a goddess—one that deserved to be adored and worshipped at all times. Her soft skin felt like heaven, calling his name as he softly ran his fingers along her belly. Another moan escaped her, his touch moving up to her luscious breasts, lazily tracing the tips of his fingers around her nipples. He was careful to keep his touch light, teasing them until they were taut peaks, begging for his attention.

"You're killing me."

"You like that, huh?" he teased. Ashby inhaled deeply, pushing her chest up, trying desperately for more contact. Carlos laughed lightly, loving that she was needy for him. But he wasn't going to give it to her just yet. "So what if I did this?"

With the same featherlight touch, he walked the fingers of one hand down her body, heading for where he knew she really wanted to be touched. His other hand continued to trace a pattern around her nipple, his own urge to up the ante starting to fight back. His cock pulsed, getting harder by the second as he drew this out. When his hand slipped over her mound, her pussy already wet with anticipation, they both groaned, and Ashby shifted again, this time her ass rubbing against his dick.

Fuuuck...

Just as he had with her breasts, Carlos softly, slowly toyed with her folds, avoiding the little bundle of nerves calling his name. Ashby's breathing turned heavy, her hips rolling, seeking out his fingers. Every new whimper and coo that came from her turned him on more, loving just how responsive she was to him.

"You're so wet for me, Ash."

"Please...please..."

Her begging was music to his ears. Knowing that she was just as turned on as he was, lost in this moment and craving his touch, was everything. Ashby whimpered again, letting him know it was time. Teasing her, bringing her to the brink was a dream, but he also knew just how incredible she looked and felt as she came apart. That was what he wanted—no, *needed*—now. He needed to feel her lose control from his efforts.

Lightly brushing the pad of his thumb over her clit, Carlos leaned down, nibbling on her neck. Ashby cried out, lifting her hips in search of more. More that he was gladly going to give her. He returned his thumb to her clit, circling it in earnest now, his teasing done. He'd learned exactly how she liked to be touched over these last couple of weeks, and he was going to put that knowledge to good use. Slipping two fingers inside her, he quickly found the spot he knew would push her toward the edge, giving it the attention it needed.

A second later Ashby screamed his name, her hands gripping onto his thighs. Her whole body went rigid, pussy clamping down on his fingers. It didn't stop him though. If anything, he picked up the pace, wanting to make sure she felt every last bit of the orgasm that was taking over her. She continued to wiggle and writhe in his lap, her curves stroking his dick through the fabric. It felt incredible, yet not enough.

Nothing will ever be enough with her...

Ashby's head fell back against his chest, as she tried to catch her breath. Staring down at her, he couldn't help but be transfixed by her breasts, watching them move. Fuck, she was stunning. He took one in each hand, giving them a squeeze, rolling her taut nipples between his fingers.

"Mmmmmmm," she moaned. Her hands ran up and down his thighs, fingertips grasping at the hem of his shorts. "Why are you still wearing clothes?"

"Technically, we both are," he said, giving the robe she was still half wearing a tug.

"But you can't fuck me wearing pants."

"I could," he replied, slipping out from behind her. "But I don't want to. I want to feel your skin against mine. Be as close to you as possible."

"Same."

Pushing up from the lounger, he made quick work of ridding himself of his shorts and tee. Ashby's eyes ran up and down his body, committing his form to memory, licking her lips. His dick twitched, making her eyes widen with anticipation. She reached out to grab it, but Carlos slid his hand into hers instead, tugging her to her feet. Their bodies collided together with an oomph, and he wasted no time in capturing her mouth in a hot, hard kiss. She tasted sweet, just like those strawberries he'd sent her earlier. He was pretty sure he could kiss her for forever, never getting tired of the softness of her lips.

He spun them around so his knees backed up to the chaise, never letting up on the kiss. It was too good, too delicious. It was so easy to get drunk off her kiss, to get lost in the little noises she made each time his hand caressed her. Everything about her was just magical. Slowly pulling back from her, he lowered himself onto the lounger, his hands running down her arms, taking the robe with him.

With her body fully on display like this, Carlos was speechless. He'd never seen anything like her. His heart squeezed as he thought about how this was the most beautiful moment of his life. Someone as amazing as Ashby was standing in front of him, willing to give herself to him. All sorts of emotions swirled around inside him, but he couldn't say any of them out loud. Not without ruining the moment.

"You are magnificent," he murmured, letting his eyes roam over her body again.

"So are you," she said, stepping closer.

Placing one knee next to him, she wrapped her arms around his neck before sliding her other knee on his opposite side. His hands instantly found her hips, pulling her in for another kiss as she settled into his lap. Yup, it was official, her kisses were like a drug—one he was going to be in withdrawals over starting tomorrow.

"I need a condom."

Ashby shook her head, moving her core so that her pussy rubbed against his rock-hard dick. Fuck, that felt amazing. If she kept that up, he wasn't going to last very long, and he needed to be inside her.

"I want to be as close to you as possible," she said, using his words from earlier.

Carlos blinked. Did she just say...? They'd had the birth control and health test conversation last week, so he knew that everything was good there. But still, going bare was a big step. One he wanted to make sure that she wouldn't regret.

"Are you sure?"

Circling her hips again, Ashby nodded. "I trust you. I want this."

"Me too."

There was nothing left to say after that. Those few little words said every-thing they were feeling—and more. Carlos felt like he could explode, both from what his heart was screaming at him and from how hard his dick was. He needed inside her. Now.

Lining himself up with her entrance, he pulled Ashby close, capturing a nipple in his mouth. Ashby cried out, lowering herself onto him as he nibbled and sucked, giving her tits the love they deserved. It was all he could do to concentrate on them, her hot, wet pussy squeezing him as she rocked in his lap. Fuck, she was perfect.

Carlos let go of her nipple with a pop, looking up at the beautiful blonde in his arms. Bliss was written all over her face, her head tossed back as she rode him. She felt so good in his arms, on his dick, but he wanted to make her feel better. Picking up the pace with his thrusts, he reached in between them, toying with her clit, just as he had earlier. That earned him a deep, guttural moan, her grip on his shoulders tightening.

"You feel so good, Carlos," Ashby said, her head falling forward, forehead resting against his. "Yes...yes...right there..."

"Come for me, baby. Come for me."

As if his words were a magic command, Ashby let out a yell, her hips finding a new rhythm, meeting him thrust for thrust. Her pussy squeezed his dick, drawing his own climax from him. He pulled her in closer, not wanting there to be any space between them. He needed to feel her like he needed his next breath, the most intense pleasure he'd ever felt still rippling through him. She didn't let up either, her body writhing in his arms, her moans filling the space around them. He was sure he'd never come this hard before, and couldn't help but wonder if anything would ever top this moment.

After a long moment, Ashby pulled back, kissing him lightly. Her brow was sweaty and her hair a mess, but Carlos was positive he'd never seen anything more beautiful in his life.

"Carlos," she whispered, her breath still ragged.

"Ash."

"I...you...you have no idea what you make me feel."

"If it's anything like you make me feel, it's pretty fucking wonderful. Like walking on sunshine."

"Yes, like walking on sunshine."

Chapter Nine

The low, even purr of the cat curled up next to Ashby's laptop as she did paperwork in the vet's office should have been calming. Under normal circumstances the sound would help her focus, keeping her mind clear. Not today.

These reports were the last thing she had to do and then she was done with her project for Paw It in Neutral. Her bags were packed, and the flight back to Miami was in a few hours. She knew she should be excited about heading home and finding out her next assignment. That was why she'd become a traveling vet—for the chance to see new places and try new things. Now she was starting to rethink that.

Steeling herself, she put her fingers back on the keys, telling herself to start typing. But it was no use. Her thoughts were not on final numbers of procedures performed or on the status of supplies. They were back with Carlos, reliving the perfect goodbye he'd given her last night. That luxurious massage followed by an incredible dinner. Just the two of them in *Almost Paradise*, an open-air room in Cherish Spa that overlooked the beach as the sun was setting, was like something out of a movie. To say nothing of how perfect it felt every time he held her. She'd had to pinch herself a couple of times just to make sure it was real. But it had been. And now, it was just a memory.

"Dr. Carver!"

The knock on the door pulled her from her thoughts, the sweet, older veterinarian who ran the clinic calling her name. Ashby looked over to find him standing in the doorway, a gentle smile on his face.

"Dr. Metcalf, hi. I'm just finishing up on the last of the reports for Operation: Snip It, Snip It Good."

She giggled at the name that Carlos had come up with when she had told him all about her work and why she was here. The love of eighties music and the commitment to using song titles to name everything at the Indigo Royal was impressive, and just one more thing she was going to miss.

"Oh, wonderful," he said, coming in and sitting down in the chair next to the desk. He ran his thumb along the top of the sleeping cat's head, his gentle smile brightening. "I think your time here was very productive, and I hope you do too. You did a lot of good for the animals of St. Thomas, and I hope your heart is very full."

Too bad it's also breaking...

"It is, and I'm glad you think we made a difference."

Ashby sat back in her chair, trying to enjoy the praise she was being given. Making a difference is why she worked with Paw It in Neutral. She'd wanted to use her vet training to help educate pet owners and aid communities so that everyone—humans and animals—could have a better life. She just had to remember that was where her focus needed to be. Not on nursing her aching heart.

"I do, but that's not why I'm here in this particular moment."

"Oh?"

What on earth could he want? A quick glance at the clock on her laptop told her that she didn't really have time to help with another procedure, but maybe there was another client he wanted her to see? She'd loved helping out with his regular day-to-day patients on top of the spays and neuters that had been on the books over these last few weeks. It had been a long time since she'd worked as a primary care vet, and she hadn't realized that she missed it.

"We've really enjoyed having you here this summer. And by that I mean me, my staff, and Charlotte Amalie as a whole. I've had a number of clients mention to me that they thought you were wonderful, and that I should keep you."

"Keep me?" she squeaked. Dr. Metcalf was a kind man, somewhere in his early sixties if she had to guess. Not someone she could ever see doing anything nefarious. But after a comment like that, Ashby's mind couldn't help but wander to all sorts of places.

Dr. Metcalf laughed. "Sorry, when I word it like that, it seems rather ominous, doesn't it? That's not my intent. It's simply that I have been thinking a lot about retiring lately—I'm up to six grandchildren now, and I would like to spend more time with them. But I've had a hard time with the idea of handing this place over to just anyone. It's been my baby for almost forty years, after all.

But you, Dr. Carver, aren't *just anyone*. At least I don't think so. And my staff and patients seem to agree. So, I would like to ask you to consider staying."

Ashby's eyes went wide, her brain trying to process everything he'd just said. He wanted her to stay? To take over his practice? No, she was imagining this. She must have fallen asleep writing her reports and it was just her brain playing tricks on her. Pinching herself, she realized she wasn't. Dr. Metcalf was still sitting there, looking at her, the same kind smile on his face.

"You want me to run this place? Just like that?"

"There would need to be some transition involved, but I don't see it being too difficult. So, yes, just like that."

Sucking in a breath, Ashby blinked rapidly, letting it sink in. When Carlos had asked her last night if there was any way for her to stay, she hadn't hesitated in saying no. Because that had been the answer. Now...now there was a way. But did it make sense? Did he even really want her to stay, or was that just something he said in the moment? Could she really just give up the life she had built over a summer fling?

"When do you need an answer by?"

"Soon. But I don't want to rush you. I know you have a flight scheduled for this evening, so if you need to catch that and then call me in a couple of days, that's fine."

Ashby nodded, unable to do anything else. Her heart said one thing, but her head was questioning that answer.

Chapter Ten

Letting out a long breath, Carlos resigned himself to the fact that Big House Beach was never going to be the same. Actually, nothing was ever going to be the same. Not without Ashby.

She'd blown into his life, turning it upside down, making him feel things he didn't realize were possible. Especially after what happened with Leona. Ashby had made all that hurt disappear, replacing it with something even stronger. He'd considered telling her last night just how he felt—those three little words right on the tip of his tongue. But he couldn't do that. It wasn't fair to her. And he wasn't going to stand in her way. That's not what you did to someone you love.

Mickey dropped the slobbery tennis ball at Carlos's feet, nudging his hands with his damp head. Carlos scratched behind the pup's ears, thankful he still had his new companion to help fill the gap Ashby left.

"Someday it'll be our turn, dude. Someday."

WOOF!

"I'm glad you agree," Carlos laughed, the dog's timing impeccable.

Mickey let out another loud bark, his attention on something behind Carlos. Turning to see what was going on, he was stunned to see Ashby walking toward them in a blue-and-white sundress, looking like she stepped off a page in a magazine. His heart leaped at the sight of her, even as his head tried to make sense of it.

"Hi," she greeted him.

"What are you doing here?"

The question was out of his mouth before he could stop it. But he needed to know. He just also needed to kiss her, feel her curves in his hands, and about a million other things. But those were going to have to wait, since he'd spoken prior to thinking.

"Aren't you happy to see me?" she asked, her smile falling from her face.

WOOF!

"We both are," Carlos answered, wrapping his arms around her and pulling her close. Her heat engulfed him, her soft curves welcoming him. "But I thought you were supposed to be on a plane right now."

"I am. I was. I just...last night when you asked me about staying, did you mean it?"

He could hear the concern in her voice. Like at any moment he was going to burst into laughter and tell her this was all a cruel joke. There was only one way to fix that. Leaning down, he kissed her, softly at first, then deepening it as she kissed him back.

"Of course I meant it. How could you think I didn't?"

"We haven't known each other that long, and so I wasn't sure if maybe it was just something you said—"

He cut her off with another kiss, tightening his arms around her until he felt her relax into him.

"Ash, I don't care how long it's been, or hasn't been. When you know, you know. And I know. I love you."

Ashby's mouth fell open, her eyes widening and turning glassy, tears forming in the corners. Audibly sucking in a breath, she giggled, the sound going straight to his groin.

"I love you too. As crazy as it sounds."

"Doesn't sound crazy to me."

"So, what if I stayed?"

Stayed? She couldn't be serious. He wanted her to be—desperately. But she had a career, one that took her all over the place. He couldn't ask her to give that up.

"You'd have one happy maintenance man on your hands," he replied, just before Mickey barked again. "And a happy puppy too. But I can't ask you to give everything up for me. Loving you means wanting what's best for you, and as much as I want it to be, is that really a life here?"

"I think so."

Come again?

Carlos blinked rapidly, her words still echoing in his head.

"You're serious. But your job...Paw It in Neutral?"

"Dr. Metcalf is looking to retire and offered me his practice. I could still work with Paw It in Neutral, just only do one or two trips a year. We've been talking with the city of San Juan for years about helping spay and neuter all the stray cats over there, and it would be a lot easier with a vet who is semi-local. Staying and taking on the practice is a big risk. But one that's a lot easier to tackle if I know I have another reason to stay."

Ashby was staying. Carlos felt like he could shout his excitement from the rooftops. Or better yet, do a little dance.

"You have two. Me and Mickey," he told her, trying to keep his voice even. His heart felt like it could beat out of his chest at any moment, and he was sure Ashby could hear it thundering. "I can talk to the Quinlans about allowing you to stay in the dorms while we look for a place we can live with Mickey and... sorry, I'm getting ahead of myself."

"Don't be sorry. That's why I'm here, to make sure you're in this. If I stay, I want this. You. Us."

"I'm all yours."

Ashby threw her arms around his neck, a squeal escaping from her. He understood exactly how she felt. Tightening his arms around her again, he picked her up, twirling her around until she giggled.

"I'm all yours too," she said, trying to catch her breath as he returned her to her feet.

"Then here's to us, spending the rest of our lives walking on sunshine."

About the Author

Claire Hastings is a walking, talking awkward moment. She loves Diet Coke, gummi bears, the beach, and books (obvs). When not reading she can usually be found hanging with friends at a soccer match or grabbing food (although she probably still has a book in her purse). She and her husband live in Atlanta.

Links: https://www.clairehastingsauthor.com/links

Take a Chance on Love

Lyra Parish

Chapter 1

Izzy

"Y ou almost ready?" Luke, my brother's best friend, asks as I dig in the trunk of my Mustang.

"Yeah, just double-checking that I remembered to pack everything before we hit the trail. Because I know there will be no turning around," I explain, placing extra granola bars in my hiking backpack. Lucas, or Luke as he always corrects, has been my brother's bestie for as long as I can remember. I consider him a friend, too.

"You're right about that," he tells me, bending down to tighten the laces on his boots. We're supposed to meet at the base of the summit tomorrow to celebrate my older brother Joey's thirty-fifth birthday. We have to cover ten miles of trails today to catch up with everyone who's trying to surprise him before he makes it down from the mountain.

As I strap the thirty-pound bag to my back, I can't help but feel a twinge of excitement and nervousness. I haven't been on the trails since last year, but Luke has always been outdoorsy, and I trust him to guide us there safely. Otherwise, my brother would probably murder him. There is a reason why he has the maps and compass, and I'm just along for the hike and views. And I'm not just talking about the mountains views.

We make our way to the trailhead, our boots crunching on the gravel beneath us. It's a beautiful day, the sun is shining, and the birds are chirping. The path isn't too steep as it leads into the lush forest, and we find our rhythm easily. As we hike, I can't help but take in the beauty around us. The trees are tall, offering plenty of shade, and the trickling streams we cross over are crystal clear.

"Are you excited?" Luke asks from over his shoulder. He throws me one of his signature smirks that nearly singes me as long rays of sunshine cast through the branches above. I can feel the heat spreading through my body as my heart races. Luke's smirk has always had the power to make me weak in the knees, and I've crushed on him since I was nine. Here we are over twenty years later, and it's never once changed. But the timing has never worked out, or we were both in relationships. That is, until now.

"Yeah, I am actually," I manage to reply, trying to keep my voice steady. "This is amazing. I'm glad I decided to do this."

"I'm glad you did, too. It was worth all the begging." He chuckles.

While it's true that Luke did beg me to come along and promised to act as my tour guide, the reality is I couldn't resist spending time with him alone. I've always loved the outdoors, too, but spending time with him is one of the only reasons I said yes. The other was I genuinely wanted to celebrate my brother's birthday.

We continue on the trail, our conversation flowing easily as we catch up on each other's lives. Eventually, there is an opening in the clearing, and in the distance, I see the tall peak of the summit and smile. Lucas stands beside me, drinking cool water.

"It's beautiful," I say, admiring the pointy peak with snow that hasn't melted, considering the temperatures at the top are still around freezing.

"Yeah, and to think Joey is up there right now."

"Wow, really puts it into perspective," I admit.

My brother enjoys hiking backcountry trails alone, which I could never do.

Before I can say anything else, my stomach growls and Luke hears it.

"We should probably eat. Perfect place," he says, moving toward a small stream that flows into the meadow and sits.

"Good idea," I admit, setting down my bag and resting beside him. We use our big packs as support and kick our legs in front of us. We've only gone a few miles, but my muscles are already burning. I should've prepared a little better, considering this has been planned for over six months, but I was busy.

"I can't wait to send Mom these pictures," I tell him, snapping a few of the scenery with my phone.

"Let's send her some of us," he suggests.

My mother calls Luke her second son, so she'll get a kick out of it.

"Smile big," he tells me, pulling me into him. I'm close. The smell of his soap and sweat mixed with the earthy scent of the forest is intoxicating. His arm wraps around my shoulder, and I hold up my phone, taking pictures of us. They all look the same except for the slight tilt of my head.

"We're super cute," I say, and he nods in agreement, popping a few almonds in his mouth.

"Oh, Mom told me about the breakup," I add as I open one of the beef jerky packets I brought. I want him to know that I know he's single.

"Yeah? What'd she say?" he asks, looking my way.

"Just that you and Talia were over," I tell him.

He shrugs. "Talia shouldn't have been a cheater."

My heartstrings tug, and then the anger I feel toward her for doing that to him immediately appears. Luke is loyal to a T and has always treated his girlfriends like royalty. He's who I'd always compared my dates to, but it was useless. I always knew they'd never be Luke.

I feel the mood shift and know I shouldn't have mentioned it. "Sorry. No more talking about her."

"Thanks. Have you been on any more dates with Calvin?" he asks.

The last date I went on was two months ago, and I was unlucky enough to run into Luke and my brother at a bar. Then my overbearing brother basically threatened the poor guy.

"Clinton," I correct. They had drunk quite a few when they realized I was there, and I couldn't escape fast enough. "And no. Not after the last outing."

Luke chuckles, and he must remember the whole thing. "Sorry about that."

"Nah, you two acting like assholes didn't scare him away. There just wasn't a...*spark*," I admit when I meet his eyes, feeling the very thing that was missing from one of my random online dates.

"Attraction is important."

Heat swarms between us, and he continues. "I'm convinced I'm going to be single forever. Who wants a thirty-four-year-old male whose only hobby is hiking?"

Me, I wish I could say, but instead, I laugh.

"There's hope. I mean, look at me. Thirty. So single, I might join the convent. Don't even have a pet fish because I'd forget to feed it."

He stretches. "Well, if we're both single when you turn forty, we should just get married."

I nearly choke on the water I'm drinking. "Us?"

He shrugs. "Why not?"

"I don't really think I'm your type," I explain.

A grin meets his lips as my eyes meet his. "Please, entertain me, Isabella. What's my type?"

The way he doesn't use my nickname drives me crazy, but in a good way. "It just seems like all of your exes are the same type of girl. Blonde."

"You mean high maintenance?" he laughs.

"Yeah, that too." I tuck auburn hair behind my ear. The silence lingers for a brief moment. "I might try the dating app thing again, maybe next week. Dip my toe back into the dating scene."

"Just your toe?" he asks.

"Well, I'd give my whole body to Mr. Right," I admit, noticing something flash in his eyes. Want? Desire? "Don't start with the big brother, overprotectiveness thing again," I quickly add. Placing him in the same bucket as my brother usually removes the awkwardness when it grows between us. It grounds us because we realize—or at least I do—that my brother would never approve of this relationship.

"Can't help it. You date douchebags."

I gasp. "Joshua wasn't a douchebag. You liked him."

"He wore a pocket protector."

I pick up a pebble and toss it at him. "That just means he's responsible."

Lucas laughs and stands, grabbing his backpack, then reaches his hand out toward me. "Whatever you say, your highness. We should get going, though, if we're going to make it to the first base camp before the sun sets."

I take it. "Okay, okay."

He pulls me up with too much force, and I crash into his chest. I look up into his warm brown eyes, and when our gazes meet, the air around us grows thick with tension.

Is it possible he feels the same way, or am I projecting?

My breath hitches, and I think this is it. This, right now, in this very moment, is my chance. I try to work up the courage to press my lips against his, but I'm too damn shy. Feeling this way only happens when I'm around him. Deep down, I think I'm still his best friend's annoying little sister.

He clears his throat, bringing me back to reality.

"Sorry." His voice is low and husky.

"It's fine," I whisper, needing to break out of this trance as the light summer breeze whips across my skin.

"You've got goosebumps." Luke reaches out and brushes his fingers down my arm.

We're still too damn close.

"The wind," I explain, rubbing my hand over where he touched me, trying to put out the flames.

I swallow down the knot that quickly forms in my throat as my cell phone rings in my pocket. It pulls me away. I smile when I see it's my mom.

He snatches my phone and answers, and I can hear my mom's excitement on the other line. As I watch him walk, I realize he has no idea what he does to me, and I only wish I had enough courage to admit it and make a move.

Chapter 2

Luke

"I've missed you!" I tell the woman whom I've always considered my second mom. We continue down the trail, and I soak in the sunshine. Izzy walks beside me like she's trying to hear what her mother's saying.

"How's Izzy? Is she still trucking along?"

I chuckle. "She's keeping up."

Izzy glares at me.

"I'm so glad you could talk her into it. Joey will be so surprised when Izzy and his entire friend group shows up to tell him Happy Birthday."

"I know. I can't wait to see the look on his face," I admit.

"Yes. Now, let me talk to my stubborn daughter." She laughs.

"Okay, okay!" I hand over the phone with a grin, and we continue moving forward.

"Mom!" she snaps, pressing the volume key on the side so there's no way I can overhear anything that's said.

I want her to want me as much as I want her. The thought is too much, because I know Joey would cut off my balls if I even hinted about wanting to date his sister. He's always been so protective of her, and I'm honestly afraid of hurting her. Or not being enough or what she wants. But it doesn't stop me from dreaming about having more.

She ends the call, then glances over at me.

"I'm sorry, she's embarrassing," she says.

"I'm used to your mom moming me," I remind her.

I can feel the tension tightening between us. It's still easygoing, but the underlying current that surrounds us is undeniable.

Izzy is beautiful, with long brown hair that falls in soft waves down her back and bright blue eyes that sparkle even in the shade. Her smile? It's perfect. *She's perfect.* And off-limits, I remind myself.

Her presence is intoxicating, and I imagine what it would be like to run my hands through her hair, feel her lips against mine, and touch her in ways I've only dreamed of. But I would never risk ruining my relationship with Joey. I always promised myself I'd never make the first move with her. She's never been afraid to tell me or any man what she wants. Izzy is *fierce* like that.

If she wanted me, I'd be hers. It's that simple.

As we continue forward, the sun begins to set, casting a warm glow over everything around us. Even though it's summer, the air is cool and crisp.

"Did you bring a tent?" I ask her, setting up mine, that's only big enough for one.

"I did," she exclaims, pulling the two-person tent from her pack.

"How much did that weigh?" I ask her because on long hikes, every extra pound matters.

She shrugs. "Don't care. It could've weighed ten pounds, and I'd have brought it. I cannot sleep in those claustrophobic single-person tent coffins. I need more space."

"It's not that bad," I say, contemplating sleeping under the stars, but I don't want to be covered in dew. When she shivers, I pull out my small axe and cut a few logs, then start a fire.

Izzy and I huddle in, listening to the crickets chirp as the wood crackles in the fire. It's quiet out here, in the open, under the night sky that's full of sparking diamonds. Peaceful.

"Wow," she says, pointing up to the sky. "I just saw a shooting star."

"I think the Arietids meteor shower is this weekend. We're supposed to have up to sixty meteors per hour. Apparently, well, they say you can see them in the day, too."

"Seriously?"

I nod, loving her enthusiasm. "We'll have to keep an eye out tomorrow once we're closer to the summit base."

"Yeah, that sounds nice." Izzy reaches down, pulls a large glass bottle of something from her bag, and then smiles.

"I cannot believe you carried that, too. When we go on week-long hikes, I'm checking your pack before we leave the parking lot."

She takes a big swig as the fire crackles and pops. "You said *when.*"

I meet her eyes; the brightness of the flames licks the side of her face while the other is hidden in shadow. She offers me the bottle, and I take it.

"Why not? I'd hike with you on longer trips. You can actually keep my pace." I drink, taking a long pull from the bottle. It burns my throat going down but also soothes my nerves. I hand it back to her.

"Whoa," I say, grabbing her attention, my head feeling dizzy. "What is that? It's strong as fuck."

"Homemade moonshine," she says, with a lifted brow, then bringing the bottle back to her lips. I watch her throat as she sucks the liquid down, and the urge to lick her from top to bottom nearly takes over.

"What?" she asks, handing it back to me. We've drunk a lot of it already.

"Nothing," I shake my head. A meteor rips across the sky, leaving a trail of sparkling dust behind it. Izzy and I both yell, pointing upward. Our voices echo into the vastness.

"Make a wish," she tells me. "But first, you have to close your eyes."

I play along and do what she says. "Now, think hard about your deepest desire, anything you want, wish it, then count to ten to seal it in place. Ready?"

"Yeah." I close my eyes, knowing exactly what I'm wishing for—*her*.

Chapter 3

Izzy

I wonder if the liquid courage has me crossing the lines or if it's my undeniable desire to have Luke. Still, I move close to him, then brush my lips against his when he opens his eyes. Kissing him like that is something I always imagined and wished for.

I almost expect him to push me away, question me, but instead he reaches forward and threads his fingers through my hair.

His lips are warm and soft, moving with mine like we were made for each other. I run my tongue over his lips, asking for permission to gain entrance. Our tongues meet, waging war with one another, and my body feels like it's burning from the inside out. I groan, wanting more of this, wanting more of him.

I moan softly, not breaking the kiss as I straddle his lap. He's hard, *very hard*, and thick. I rock against him, my needy clit begging for more friction. Feeling his hard length rubbing against that bundle of nerves has me panting, and gasping for air.

I see the desire in his eyes, and I want him so goddamn badly that nothing else in the world matters. I want to feel his touch, his lips. I want to feel him deep inside me, in places only a few have ever been.

"Isabella," he whispers my full name again. "Are you sure this is what you want?"

"Yes, yes," I nearly beg breathlessly.

"Once I've had you, I don't think I'm ever going to let you go," he admits, his possessive side sparking alive.

"And what if Joey doesn't like it?" I ask.

"And what if he doesn't care?" he states, and I laugh, knowing better.

I want to ask more questions, but they can wait.

Leaning down, I whisper in his ear, "I want you."

He whispers. "Let me taste your sweet pussy."

I push away. "Okay. but..." I capture his mouth again, roaming my hands all over his chiseled body.

He breaks the kiss. "But, what?"

"No one I've ever been with has liked doing that."

He looks at me like he can't comprehend what I've just said and gently lays me on my back. "I can't wait to show you how fucking good it feels," he says, spreading my thighs and pressing his face against my joggers. Just the pressure of him there through the fabric drives me wild. "Fuck. Izzy. You smell *so* good."

I close my eyes, enjoying his hands on me.

Slowly, he peels my joggers and panties from my body. Then he opens my legs wide, admiring my freshly waxed pussy. When I feel his hot mouth and tongue against my clit, my entire body shudders. He laps me up, twirling his tongue in precise circles, and though he just started, I don't know how long I'm going to last. It's too intense.

When he places a finger in my pussy, my back arches. "Luke," I whisper.

"Fuck, you taste so goddamn good," he says. "You're so tight and wet."

He gives me another finger, and the pressure of his big hands as he flicks his tongue against my sensitive bud is too much. "Oh God," I huff, teetering on edge, and then, as if someone cut the thread that held back my orgasm, I fall into the abyss. I gasp for air, every muscle in my body tightens, and I'm coming like I've *never* come before.

Luke doesn't stop his assault on my pussy and laps up every drop of my cum. He crawls toward me onto the blanket and slides his lips across mine, allowing me to taste myself.

"You're so goddamn sweet," he whispers, twirling his tongue in my mouth, giving me more. I'm surprised by how much it turns me on to taste myself on him. Reaching down, I grab his cock, surprised by how hard he is. "That's what you do to me, what you've *always* done to me, Izzy."

I laugh. "Really?"

"Yes," he admits, as I pull down his joggers, allowing his beautiful thick-as-fuck cock to spring free. I reposition myself on all fours, then turn around so he'll have a good view of my dripping wet cunt. Happily, I open my mouth as wide as it will go and take him.

"Do you know what I wished for when I closed my eyes?"

"Tell me," I say, gazing over this python he's kept hidden in his pants.

"You," he whispers as I slide down him, wanting to have all of him in my mouth but finding it nearly impossible.

"I wished for you, too," I admit. He places his large palm on my ass, then his fingers slide back inside me.

"This cunt is perfection." He gently thumbs my clit. My body instantly responds, nearly begging to come again. While his movements are slow, the orgasm continues to build. Wanting to tease him as much as he's teasing me, I twirl my tongue against his tip, then trace down his large vein.

"Fuck," he pushes deeper into my throat, hitting the back, testing my gag reflex. "You're working me so good, sweetheart."

I grab him with my free hand and stroke while I suck. If our first time together is also the last, at least I'll leave him with an experience. He pants, and I can tell his orgasm is building, but so is mine. We race to our prospective finish lines, and I rock my hips against him, creating more friction with his fingers. When he realizes I'm much closer than him, he adds a bit more pressure to my clit and catapults me into oblivion. I throw my head back and come under the stars again.

He sits up, kissing my ass, then when he begins to devour me again, I turn around and meet his eyes.

"Fuck me," I demand, needing him inside me, filling me full.

He smirks, reaching forward and smacking my ass before repositioning himself behind me. "You're such a bad girl. So fucking demanding."

His cock throbs at my entrance and I'm tempted to fall back on him, but I don't think I've ever been with someone this size. His cock is definitely not the kind you *fall* onto.

"Please go slow," I say, my ass upright as he enters me from behind. I relax my body and widen my hips as he takes his time, allowing me to adjust to him.

I suck in air and moan with pleasure. "Luke," I hiss. "Your cock should be illegal."

He chuckles. "Your pussy should be, too. You're so fucking tight."

Though I've had sex plenty of times before, it's been nothing like this.

This is...mind-blowing. Pussy-shattering. This is a wish come true.

Once he's settled inside me, he picks up the pace, and I'm so wet he easily slides in and out.

With each thrust, I feel another orgasm build. I close my eyes, grabbing the blanket with my fist, and then it happens—Luke comes, then I come again and again.

Chapter 4

Luke

The next morning, we are more relaxed than I'd expected. There's not a tinge of awkwardness.

The only difference is that I now have this burning desire to touch and kiss her now that the lines have been crossed.

"Coffee?" I ask when she comes from her tent, wearing a sleepy face. I'm boiling water in my camping pot over the fire.

"Instant?" She gives me a look, and I nod. "No thanks. I'd rather eat dirt."

I chuckle. "It's not that bad in a pinch."

"My head already hurts enough. I'm good."

I think about last night and how we fucked under the stars after drinking half a bottle of moonshine. She sits next to me, holding her hands out to warm up. Then we both open our mouths to speak and then close them at the same time.

"You go first," I tell her.

A blush hits her cheeks. "I don't even know what to say, honestly."

"Do you regret it?" I ask, unsure if I want the answer, but I need to know.

"No, absolutely not," she tells me. "I was hoping you didn't."

"Hell no," I admit. "I've been dreaming of that for as long as I can remember."

A smile touches her lips. "Really?"

"No bullshit." I mix the powdered caffeine into the hot water. I blow on the top, looking at her over the mug, taking in the warmth of the fire. We'll have to break down camp soon and then have a couple miles until we meet everyone to surprise Joey.

She swallows hard, tucking messy hair behind her ear as I wrap my free arm around her. She leans into me, and I sip my coffee, trying to wake up.

"Mm," she hums. "This is nice."

"It is," I admit, leaning in and kissing her forehead. Her long eyelashes flutter closed, and she smiles before kissing me.

When we break away, I meet her blue eyes. "We're gonna have to get that out of our systems before we meet up with your brother."

She lifts a brow. "Are you embarrassed by me?"

"Fuck all that," I say, wishing she knew how goddamn beautiful she is. "I don't want Joey trying to fight me after hiking eighteen miles downhill. I'd really hate to kick his ass on his birthday."

She snickers. "That makes total sense."

We each eat a banana and some cheese. Afterward, we pack up camp and begin the rest of our hike. Today we can move slower and enjoy the fresh air and view.

When the path widens, I walk beside her and randomly hook my pinkie with hers. It's a simple but sexy gesture, and I can't help but feel a rush of excitement stream through my body when we touch.

After we cross a wooden bridge, we have the perfect view of a large waterfall. The sound of the water crashing onto the rocks is so loud I can barely hear her speaking, but when she turns to me, Izzy places her hand on my cheek and slides her tongue into my mouth. Her hands roam over my body, and I grow harder with each touch.

Without breaking the kiss, I lift her, and she instinctively wraps her legs around my waist. She drops her backpack on the ground, and I pin her against the tree, pressing myself into her, feeling her warmth against me. She moans as I trail kisses along her jawline, down her neck, until we're both lost in the sensation of freely touching one another. I'm ready to take her right here, right now, but before we can go any further, I hear voices in the distance.

Based on how wide Izzy's eyes are, she heard it too. We're both on high alert.

She laughs as I set her down on the ground.

"Whoever that is, they're not far behind us," I explain. "Thirty minutes."

"I need more time than that." She smirks. "Rain check."

"Deal," I say, looking forward to being with her again. I nod, thinking about how tonight we'll be with my friends, celebrating Joey's birthday around the campfire. I doubt we'll be able to break away without it being too suspicious. But hell, it's worth trying.

I interlock my fingers with hers, and we continue forward. The trails begin twisting and turning, the scenery changing from dense forest to open fields, and I know we're getting close. The sun shines brightly overhead, casting a warm glow on Izzy's bronze skin. Her hair is messy from being whipped around by the wind, and she looks like a goddamn goddess when she smiles at me.

One thought races and repeats in my mind: I want to make Izzy mine... forever. Every cell in my body screams to never let her go. She's the real deal, the kind of woman that once you have, you keep.

My heart thumps faster the closer we get, and I remind myself that Joey won't like this one bit. He's threatened all her boyfriends since the beginning of time, and I don't think he'd go as easy on me.

Somehow, I'll need to work up the courage to admit to him how I feel about his sister.

But only when the timing is right.

Chapter 5

Izzy

When we round the bend, I see the group of people set up in a base camp at the bottom of the summit. At least eight or nine people are standing around several tents, and someone is building a fire. They're loud, and their chatter travels in the summer breeze.

"Who all is here?" I ask Luke, honestly not expecting this many people. But then again, I wasn't told who was invited, only that Luke wanted me to join him.

He squints. "I honestly don't remember who said they'd make it. And I told everyone to invite anyone who's a friend of Joey's. It will be a surprise to us both."

I grow nervous when I realize how many of my brother's crew are here. They're all older than me, and I've always been known as the little sister. Knowing the lines are blurred between Luke and me makes being here a little more complicated. I'm not ready to publicly admit my feelings for him until my brother knows. The thought of telling him I've always had a major crush on his best friend makes me nervous. Luke is right. We should probably wait until after his birthday.

Luke's hand brushes against mine. It's a small gesture but enough to make my heart flutter. I know I should pull away but I can't bring myself to do it. Instead, I lean closer, yearning for his touch because we won't be able to do that much longer.

We approach the camp, and I can feel everyone staring at us. I try to ignore them, but their eyes linger for a moment too long. I can sense their questioning looks, but I'm sure they're just surprised. I've skipped a lot of the parties my brother has thrown over the years.

"Hey, guys!" Luke calls out. "Can't believe you're all here."

I give everyone a shy wave. Their greetings are warm and friendly, but I can't help feeling out of place. I'm not used to being around people much older than me, let alone in the middle of the wilderness.

"Izzy," Zane says. He's tall and muscular; I haven't seen him in years.

"Oh my God, Zane!" I give him a hug. "Didn't recognize you with that beard."

"Going for the mountain man look these days," he tells me, introducing me to his girlfriend, Charlotte.

"It's nice to meet you," I tell her, and she gives me a kind nod. By how she's acting, she must feel out of place, too.

Zane points out everyone as Luke chats with another group. "That's Fallon, Jessica, Brandon, Jacob, Kyle, Chase, and Noah."

"I think I've met a few of them before," I explain. "But it's been a long time."

"Yeah, it has been a while. The last time I saw you..." He thinks about it. "Your high school graduation?"

I laugh. "Oh wow. Yeah. Over a decade ago. Do you know when my brother is supposed to make it down the mountain?"

He wraps his arm around his girlfriend and checks his watch. "In about an hour."

"Great," I say.

"Honestly, I can't believe Luke got you to come." He smirks, and I wonder if he can tell the lines between Luke and me are blurred. I push it away, knowing there's no way.

"You can blame my mom for that one. You know how her guilt trips are."

"Don't I." Zane chuckles. "Anyway, I'll let you go set up your gear and get comfy. Many of us packed some booze in our bags."

"Same." I make my way over to Luke as he laughs with a few of the guys.

"You guys remember Joey's little sister, Isabella, right?"

"Izzy," I correct with a smile.

"Yeah!" many of them say, and we make small talk.

Luke and I set up our tents and eat a few snacks. Fifteen minutes later, everyone starts singing Happy Birthday. I turn around and see my brother descending the single track toward us. His smile is contagious, and I can tell he's shocked that so many are here.

As Joey approaches the campsite, the whole group rushes to greet him. I can't help but grin wide as I watch my brother embrace each of his friends. It's hard for me to remember the last time I saw him this happy, and I'm so damn grateful that Luke organized this trip.

Joey's eyes light up when he sees me. "Izzy!" he exclaims, pulling me into a tight hug. "I can't believe you're actually here."

He pinches himself, and I playfully smack him.

"Wouldn't miss your birthday for anything," I reply, beaming up at him. He's always been my hero.

Before the sun sets, we gather around the campfire, roasting marshmallows and sharing stories. I listen intently, soaking up every word. We toast to Joey, and everyone shares stories of their past adventures and all the trouble they got into in their early twenties. I've been smiling so much that my face hurts, and I find myself laughing with the group, enjoying their company.

Luke and I steal glances, and my heart flutters. I wish we could sneak away. I almost suggest it until I realize he's looking in the distance.

"Fuck," I hear Luke whisper. "What's she doing here?"

Several heads turn, and that's when I notice two girls hiking down the path, heading straight toward us.

One of them is Talia.

Luke's ex.

Chapter 6

Luke

"What the fuck?" I hiss only loud enough for Izzy to hear. Zane and Charlotte spotted them, too.

Joey cups his hands over his mouth. "Who's there?"

The two women laugh. "Breanna and Talia."

A knot forms in my stomach. What is she doing here? The last time I saw her was when we broke up. I thought I'd made it pretty fucking clear that I never wanted to see her again after cheating on me.

Izzy nudges me. "Are you okay?" she whispers.

I nod, not trusting my voice.

Breanna and Talia walk over to us, their hips swaying in unison, and drop their packs on the ground.

"Hey, boys," Talia says, winking at me, and I turn my head from her gaze. Even Joey tenses because he knows exactly what she did. Actually, every person here does. Awkward is an understatement.

"Talia, can't believe you're here," Joey says, and I can hear the sarcasm dripping in his tone. He's been drinking, so his tongue is looser than usual.

"I was invited," she says, and that's not a lie, but a lot has changed since we made plans for this surprise party. She has no respect for me or my boundaries. I try to swallow down the surge of anger that rises within me. Izzy pats my leg, bringing me back to reality.

"Guess we should set up our tents," Breanna says, and Talia follows her.

The air grows thick.

"Tell me more embarrassing stories about my brother," Izzy says, bringing everyone's attention to her. I'm thankful for the change of subject.

Kyle grins, clearly enjoying Izzy's request. "Oh man, where do we begin?" he says, taking a long swig from the whiskey bottle. And we're right back to chatting like Talia and Breanna didn't just waltz up like they're welcome here. However, it's too late in the evening to send them away.

As Kyle launches into a story about how they left Joey naked at a friend's house, I let out a sigh of relief. I can feel the tension subsiding, replaced by a sense of nostalgia. I replay some of the good times I've had with my best friend over the years.

Kyle continues to chat about stories from our past, and my mind slowly drifts back to Talia when she joins the group. I can feel her eyes on me and know she's wearing a smug smirk on her lips. I try to push the thought of her out of my mind and keep my eyes focused on the fire.

We eventually decide to break to eat. As Izzy and I devour several packs of tuna, she looks at me with concern.

"You're not okay," she says. It's not a question.

I hesitate for a moment, then shake my head. "No, I'm not."

"After we eat, let's call it a night. Wake up early and get out of here," she suggests, and I can tell that she's uncomfortable about the situation, too. Everyone is.

"That's a great idea." I pause for a brief moment. "I'm really sorry. I didn't realize she'd be he—"

"No one did." She smiles, reaching for my hand and squeezing it, then lets it go. There are too many people around.

After we finish eating, Joey and Jacob add more logs to the fire, and Izzy hugs her brother good night.

"I'm heading in, too," I say with a smile. Joey seems to want to say something more, but when Talia walks up, he doesn't. I don't give her the attention she's craving and make my way into my one-person tent, hoping I'll fall asleep sooner rather than later. It's barely after dark, but Izzy and I were up late last night, so I'm not complaining about the extra rest. However, I wish I were in Izzy's tent, lying next to her.

The following morning, I wake up before Izzy and pack my things. All the guys are already awake, but they're trying to be as quiet as possible so no one is disturbed.

"We're going down to the lake. It's about a mile away. Wanna join us?" Kyle asks.

"Nah, I'm good," I tell him. "I'll keep the fire going."

He grins. "Thanks, man."

I add some more wood, pull out my small coffee pot, and boil water for my instant coffee. As I mix it up in my mug, I look up and see Talia walking toward me.

"Can we talk?" she asks when she's close.

"No." It's a complete sentence. I have nothing to say.

"Please? Just hear me out," she begs. "In private."

I glance around at the tents, and I agree when I see tears well in her eyes. I've always been weak when it comes to seeing anyone cry, so I give in. "Five minutes."

"Okay," she says.

Talia leads me away from the still erect tents, away from everything, so there is no way we'll be seen or heard. I look at the time on my watch and then back at her. I will walk away once her five minutes are up.

Talia meets my gaze with a mix of regret and defiance. "I came to apologize. You blocked my number and I had no other way of getting in contact with you," she says, her voice barely above a whisper. "I know I messed up and want to make it right."

I scoff, barely able to control my anger. "Make it right? You can't just waltz back into my life and expect everything to be okay. You cheated on me, Talia. You destroyed our relationship. You threw it all away. And I'm just supposed to forgive you and take you back?"

She steps forward, her eyes filled with regret, or what looks like it. "I know what I did was wrong, but I hoped you'd give me another chance. I love you, Luke."

Chapter 7

Izzy

I crawl out of my tent and realize Luke has already packed his things. His backpack is on the ground, but he's nowhere to be found. The sun is just rising, casting a golden light over the mountains.

Quickly, I stuff everything in my bag. Charlotte crawls out of her tent and smiles. "Good morning."

"Morning," I tell her. "Have you seen Luke?"

"I think I heard him chatting with Talia."

It takes every bit of strength I have not to make a face and to keep my expression flat. Somehow I accomplish it.

"Oh, awesome. Thanks," I tell her, keeping my tone straight. "I think I'm gonna look for my brother real quick."

She yawns and nods, moving closer to the fire.

I follow the sound of voices and find Talia looking up at Luke. She takes a step forward and slides her lips across his. Immediately, I feel sick. I try to stay calm, but my heart is racing. I quickly turn around, hoping they didn't see me, and try to steady my breathing as I rush back to camp.

How could Luke do this?

I thought we shared something special, but now I realize I was just fooling myself. Maybe I will always be the annoying little sister in his eyes. I want to confront them, but it's not my business.

"You heading out?" Charlotte asks when I pick up my backpack and slide it on.

"Yeah, I think so. I couldn't find my brother, but if you see him, let him know I'm leaving. If I get going now, I can make it back to my car by dark."

"Okay. I will." She smiles. "It was nice meeting you."

"You too," I tell her, returning the kind gesture, then I leave.

The trail was pretty easy to navigate, and as long as I stay on the main path, it will lead me back to the parking lot. Fifteen miles in a day is a long way, but I'll let my emotions fuel me. I feel betrayed, but I have no right. What happened between us was nothing more than a hookup. I realize that now.

As I hike, I can't help but think about Luke and Talia. I thought I knew him so well, but now I feel like I don't know him at all. I try to focus on the beautiful scenery around me but my mind constantly wanders.

After a few hours of hiking, I come across a beautiful lily pad pond. I decide to take a break to quickly eat, and find a seat on a log by the shore. As I sit there, I hear twigs snapping behind me and turn around, only to see Luke.

My brow furrows, and I return my attention to the sun reflecting off the water.

He sits next to me.

"Wow, can't believe you're here after I saw you kissing Talia."

"She kissed me. I'm sorry you saw that," he says quietly.

I let out a deep breath and shake my head. "You don't have to apologize. You're single."

"Izzy," he says.

I sigh and turn and meet his eyes. "If you want to get back with Talia, go for it. I don't care."

He shakes his head, finally understanding the gravity of the situation. "What? Hell no. That's not happening."

My expression softens. "It made me sick seeing her lips on yours."

"Did you see me push her away? Or wait around for her meltdown?"

I glance over at him. "No."

"After I walked away, she made a huge scene," he explains. "Be glad you didn't witness it."

We sit silently for a moment, and Luke leans closer to me. "There is only one woman I want in my life, Izzy. *You.*"

I feel that familiar flutter return in my stomach.

He takes my hand and looks at me sincerely. "I only want you. I've always ever wanted you. The timing was never right until now, and I'm not giving up a chance to be with you."

My heart races as I look into his eyes. "I don't want to be one of your weekend hookups, Luke."

He nods. "I understand. But I can promise you that it would never just be a hookup with you. I want forever."

I can feel his breath on my skin and my heart races. I want to believe there's something deeper between us, but I'm scared to take the risk.

"Seriously?" I whisper.

He nods, closing the distance between us, and presses his lips to mine.

That spark between us reignites, and I'm tired of ignoring how I feel about him. I've always known deep down inside that we were meant to be together.

We sit in silence for a few more moments, taking in the pond's serene beauty.

I can feel his eyes on me, and I turn to look at him.

"Before I left camp, I found your brother and told him I was in love with you."

My eyes go wide. "*What?*"

"I couldn't hold it in anymore."

I study him and don't see any black eyes or bloody lips. "And you're alive and unscathed?"

He chuckles. "Yeah, he told me it was about time I woke the fuck up, and if I didn't find you on the trail, I was pretty much dead."

I shake my head, a smile forming on my lips. "You're insane, you know that?"

He shrugs. "I'm just crazy about you, Izzy."

I turn to him, feeling the warmth of his body as he wraps his arm around me. "I like the thought of that," I admit.

He grins, his lips brushing against mine. "Good. Because I don't plan on letting you go anytime soon. You're mine, sweetheart."

"So, we're official?" I ask, needing to hear him say it.

"Yes. And then, eventually, I will put a ring on that finger and make you my wife."

I feel a shiver run down my spine as I look at him in disbelief. "You're not just saying that, are you? I mean, you're not just caught up in the moment?"

He takes my hand and brings it to his lips for a soft kiss. "I mean it. I want to spend the rest of my life with you. Hike. Make love under the stars. Maybe adopt a dog?"

I can't help but feel overwhelmed with emotion. All the doubts and insecurities I had earlier simply vanish.

"I don't know what to say," I whisper, so relieved and happy I'm nearly speechless.

"Say you're mine," he mutters with fire in his eyes.

"Of course, I'm yours." I lean in and kiss him again, ready to take a chance on love.

THE END

Did you enjoy Luke & Izzy's story?

**If so, sign up for Lyra Parish's newsletter to keep up with all of
her future releases.
lyraparish.com/newsletter
You can also follow her on social media:
Tiktok: tiktok.com/@lyraparish
Instagram: instagram.com/lyraparish
Facebook: facebook.com/lyraparishauthor**

Her Nemesis Until 5pm

Eve Pendle

Chapter One

First day of her new job, in a new city. That required caffeine, a positive attitude, and a lucky dress. Emily had two of those, but she'd only moved into her flat yesterday and the coffee had been nowhere to be seen. She wanted to be at work early, when her new boss had said her hugely talented colleague would be in, so hadn't had time to pick up a caffeine fix.

No pressure.

Outside the office she took a deep breath. She would show her new colleagues she was great to work with, make her parents proud, and build a new life away from London.

The lights were on and she peeked into the estate agency just past seven thirty in the morning. Behind a computer monitor sat a gorgeous man with a sulky mouth sipping from a grey travel cup. Her colleague and rival. Pauline had said Luke Weston was unconventional and sharp enough to cut yourself on.

She was going to charm his pants off.

"Hi! I'm Emily Tumbler, the new sales negotiator," she said in her trademark chirpy tone as she walked into the office. "You must be Luke. You were doing a viewing when I interviewed. I'm really happy to meet you."

He glanced up and his eyes widened in shock as his hand lowered his cup slowly to the desk.

"Hi." He looked back at his computer screen.

The scent of artisan coffee wafted from his desk.

"That smells good. Where do I get coffee around here?" She dropped her handbag onto the desk Pauline had told would be hers. Opposite Luke's.

"Backroom," he said without looking up.

"Do you want another cup?"

He shook his head once.

Huh. Friendly.

In the tiny kitchenette she flipped on the kettle and searched the cupboards. A dodgy-looking plastic container labelled coffee contained depressing sticky black granules. But if this unprepossessing start produced coffee as tasty as what she'd smelled from Luke's cup, she'd take it. The only mug she could find was brown and chipped and she washed it thoroughly. She'd need to get her own.

Nevertheless, she hummed as she re-entered the office with a cup of coffee. First day, back on track. She invariably felt better with a good coffee and a day of work ahead of her.

"Are you always here at this time?" she asked Luke. She'd be collegial, get this taciturn man on her side by pointing out what they had in common. "I like to get some work done early, maybe you're the same? It's great to tick things off your list before nine A.M."

"Mm." He kept his eyes trained on his computer screen.

Excellent conversationalist. How on earth did he sell anything? She sat at her desk and opened her computer, taking a sip of coffee as the digital gerbil spun its wheel.

Bitter stale-tasting water burned her tongue.

"Eugh!" She slammed the mug down. "That is undrinkable."

A smile tugged at Luke's mouth.

"Are you laughing at me?" She tried for light-heartedness, but offence sneaked in. Being sniggered at on her first day, and he couldn't even be bothered to look her in the eye or say a full sentence. "Do you drink this?"

"No."

She gave a forced smile. "Is it an office prank?"

"No."

"How long has that coffee been there?"

"A while."

She hesitated. Maybe he'd go for the damsel in distress routine.

"Just can you please tell me where to get a nice caffeine fix?" she begged. "I'm hanging here. I had nothing in the flat because I haven't had time to unpack yet. Please, help me out." She smiled ingratiatingly. "One caffeine addict to another."

A long pause. He looked up and stared right into her eyes. Her stomach did a little flip, which she ignored.

"There's no decent coffee around here."

Fuck. Irritation clawed at her skull. *He* clearly had delicious coffee. Why wouldn't he tell her where he'd bought it? Was he being proprietorial about a coffee shop?

"Yours smells great." She indicated his reusable grey glass and cork travel cup. "Where's it from?"

"You want my coffee? Take it," he deadpanned.

"You're too kind, but I couldn't," she said even as she internally rolled her eyes. How was he so obnoxious? Her lack of caffeine probably wasn't helping her reactions, which would usually be more controlled, but was it really so much to ask him to help out a new colleague?

She sighed, turned back to her computer and took another sip of the terrible black water. "I could murder a decent latte."

Or maybe just murder him.

Luke would have braced himself if he'd known. Instead he'd been checking his calendar when she walked into Hapthorpe Estate Agency like a breath of mountain air and sunlight on his face. Then she'd smiled and his heart had stopped. Or it might as well have. Her smile was incandescent.

He risked a covert glance at her. Short, with creamy skin and dark hair in loose curls, she wore a pale bluey-green shift dress in a soft-looking fabric and a tailored navy blazer. Her brown eyes were the sort of lipid darkness he could lose himself in.

She was exceptionally pretty. He'd never thought he had a type, but apparently he did, and it was her.

Perhaps he ought to have warned her about the coffee, but he hadn't been sure she would notice. Lots of people drank floor scrapings and judged it as fine. He definitely hadn't been about to follow her into the tiny kitchenette, warn her what she might think was perfectly adequate coffee was crap, and stand over her as she poured the kettle. He'd been told following women into small spaces was intimidating because he was tall and muscled, and he didn't want Emily thinking that about him.

"Hey Luke, could you help me? Where are the logins for the sales sites, please?"

She was chatty and though usually he wasn't a fan of that, her sweet lilting voice made him want to listen.

"Shared folder."

She let out a frustrated huff. "I don't know where that is. Could you explain in full sentences, please?"

He struggled to find the right words, because he couldn't say, *I don't think I can. I'm a bit afraid to talk with you because you're a dream incarnate, and I really don't want to fuck this up, and by trying not to fuck it up, I might be fucking it up.*

"There's a shortcut on your desktop." That was true. AND it was a full sentence. It had a verb and nouns and everything. Did it? Fuck. Whatever.

"No," she said with exaggerated patience, "there isn't."

This was a terrible idea, he knew it as he made his way to stand behind her and look at her computer. She smelled like roses and caramel and his mouth watered as he leaned over her desk to see her screen.

He allowed himself a glance at her, and her mouth was right there. Red lipstick. A vibrant deep red that made him think of ripe strawberries, roses, and ruby engagement rings. She licked her lips and the sight of her wet lips made his cock thicken.

He swallowed hard and focused on her computer screen.

She was right, no shortcut. He could talk her through it, but that would take ages and he wasn't at all sure he wouldn't have a raging hard-on by the time they'd finished. Better to leave that for after five P.M. and just quickly fix this for her. He took her mouse, made a series of rapid clicks, and reinstated it.

"Thank you," she said sweetly, "but please don't take over my computer again without asking me. This is *my* computer."

He free-fell in the chasm of her brown eyes flashing orange with anger. Slowly, he nodded.

"Sorry."

"Apology accepted."

Back at his desk he snuck another look at her. He now knew three things about Emily. She had good taste in coffee and drank it with lots of milk; she wore a pale bluey-green colour; and she took no shit.

He could work with that. He already had an idea of how to win her around with just those facts. He'd stop at the shop on the way home tonight and at seven-thirty tomorrow he'd be ready.

"Emily!" Pauline strode into the office and Luke looked down at his computer screen, thankful for the reprieve.

Their boss was obviously delighted with her new hire. And no wonder. She came with impeccable sales credentials from London, having moved down to the West country to be near her ageing parents.

Watching Pauline and Emily from the corner of his eye, he typed meaningless nonsense into an email. Emily had a surfeit of thin gold rings on her fingers, each different, and her hair curled in tousled waves that would look amazing spread on his pillow.

He was going to have to ask Emily out. There was no way he'd be able to play a long game with her. The attraction was too immediate, too visceral.

He managed to get a token bit of work done while expending all his energy not looking at Emily. Tumbler was such a ridiculous surname. He googled it. Turned out one of her ancestors would have been an acrobat. It suited her perfectly. She was bright and effervescent, but also smooth. Whereas he presented houses in near silence and gave people the space to make their minds up, and occasionally weaponised a three-second pause to bring out a higher offer, he'd bet she charmed everyone with friendly chatter.

A trill rang out across the office, and they all looked up. It was Pauline's rule that all phones must be on silent or vibrate. No tones.

"I'm so sorry!" Emily called, snatching up her phone, silencing the noise and making for the door. "I keep my husband's calls audible because he works as a cruise ship officer, and can't get the phone. He's on his way home after four months away." There was no mistaking the pride in her tone and the light in her eyes as she scurried out to take the call.

Husband. His heart... Tumbled.

Married. Fuck's sake. He finally met the woman of his dreams, she just walked into the office and sent him head over heels.

And she was *married.*

He wasn't going to ask her out, after all. Luke stewed for the ten minutes she was gone, rearranging photos on a webpage randomly until he could no longer sit still and went to the filing cabinet to pick out printed brochures for viewings scheduled for later in the day.

"Everything alright?" Pauline asked as Emily returned.

"Absolutely fine," Emily replied, but her eyes said, no. She hesitated in the middle of the room, seemingly unsure where to go. "He's decided..." She swallowed. "To take a holiday out in Bali while he's there. Completely understandable. It would be silly to waste the chance."

Oh great. Not only was she married, she was married to a fuckwit. Her evident distress made his hands itch to reach for her, so he stuffed them into his pockets.

"Instead of coming straight home to you," he couldn't help saying.

"He works really hard," she snarled, spinning around to stare at him. "I don't begrudge him a well-earned holiday." But her eyes were too shiny.

He held her gaze, steady. So loyal to a husband who clearly had hurt her by not coming home when she expected. She'd been waiting for him, and he decided to go off and vacation on his own.

Luke tried to tell her via telepathy that if she was his, she would be his first priority. Not a holiday. Not a job. *Her*.

She wasn't just casually seeing this doorknob of a man; she was married to him. 'Til death do us part. He couldn't even hope she was crap at her job and would be fired. He'd seen her CV. In fact, he'd advised Pauline to hire her because she looked like she'd give him someone to compete with on sales targets, and be good for the agency overall.

"Right." He sat down at his desk and opened his calendar.

"He works four hours on, eight hours off, constantly. He's responsible for a whole ship of people when he's on watch. It's very stressful, not like just showing people around houses."

Is that what her husband told her? That his job was more important and stressful than hers because she *just* sold houses. Luke's dislike for the man increased.

He had to leave this office before he said or did something he regretted.

"Where are you off to so early?" Pauline asked as he dragged on his suit jacket.

"Viewing."

Pauline raised one eyebrow but let it slide.

As he passed Emily's desk, he stuffed his hands in his pockets to stop himself from reaching for her.

"Is he always so quiet?" He heard Emily ask as he left the office.

He didn't hear Pauline's answer, but he knew the slightly confused tone she'd use. Because no, he wasn't always abrupt. Just when a tiny seedling of attraction had all its leaves snipped off. Efficient, yes, grumpy, often. But he could put on a decent show of being professional for prospective buyers. Why couldn't he do that with Emily?

He had a horrible feeling that little shoot of attraction might continue growing anyway.

He couldn't allow her to know how he felt about her. He had to keep her at arm's length at all times and if that meant she thought he was silent, grumpy, a bastard, or even that he hated her. Well, so be it. Better that than her knowing he'd developed an instant and embarrassing crush.

The only way to cope with his attraction to her was denial. Absolute denial.

Chapter Two

The next day Emily was determined to do better. As she walked to work, she listed her aims.

First, she would not let Luke Weston get to her.

Second, she would not become all teary when Eric revealed, yet again, he wouldn't be coming home straight after his stint at sea. Four freaking months away, and he missed her so much he wanted to spend half his time off without her. A whole month he was going to be in Bali. Parroting his excuses to her new colleagues had been like turning up to work naked and claiming she wore the latest Prada pantsuit. She wasn't fooling anyone. But she still felt the need to defend—if not Eric exactly—then her decision to stay with her childhood sweetheart.

Third, she would prove herself to be a great sales negotiator, and well worth her generous salary. Not as high as Eric's, or what she'd earned in London, naturally, but decent, and rent was a bit lower.

Fourth, she would not think about the aeons of time before she'd be able to start a family, or the wrinkles in her parents' brows when they asked if they were going to have grandchildren soon. Her priority was her career, as was Eric's, and that meant sacrificing her longing for a baby, for now.

As yesterday, only Luke was in the office, diligently tapping at his computer. He nodded in response to her bright, "Good morning!"

On her otherwise clear desk, there was one of those reusable coffee cups in seafoam green. Steam wafted from the sip hole in the top and it smelled like caffeine heaven. Far better than the cafetière stuff she'd gulped at home, and ten times better than anything she'd passed in the fifteen-minute walk to work.

"Is this..." She stared at the coffee cup. It took all her effort not to grasp it up. "For me?"

"No, it's to lure in the lesser spotted coffee bear."

She stifled a laugh.

"I'll take that as, yes. Thanks." She sank into her seat and examined the cup. It was a pretty, girly colour. Surprising choice for Luke Weston, in his sharp grey suit and crisp dark green tie. The cup on his desk was the same manufacturer, but smoky grey. Probably he'd just had it in the cupboard, spare. But why the colour when his was grey? She couldn't imagine him using this, and indeed, there were no signs of wear. Perhaps he'd bought it for a girlfriend and she hadn't used it much. That was like fur brushed the wrong way. Which was a totally inappropriate thought to be having about a colleague, and when she was married.

"You don't want the coffee?" he muttered.

Ah. Drink the coffee like a normal person rather than inspecting the cup like it was a bomb. She took a sip. Oh man, this was really great coffee. "If this has laxatives added, I can't taste them. You have to tell me where you bought it."

"No." He didn't even look up.

"At least allow me to pay you for it." It must have been expensive. It was so rich and smooth; it was practically orgasmic. And it was a latte. Her favourite morning drink.

"No," he snapped, staring intently at his computer screen, refusing to meet her eyes.

He was good-looking, but not in the film star way. He had a square jaw, straight nose, and hair that if you wanted to be disparaging you'd call ginger, but honestly she'd probably say auburn. Dark brown with a hint of red. His eyes were green. Despite not being conventionally attractive because of his red hair, he was nothing less than stunning.

She could notice that even if she was a married woman, right? Just so long as she didn't act on it. It wasn't a betrayal of Eric to notice a man was handsome. Eric was always worried about her cheating on him and sending a "Dear John" letter splitting up with him when he was away at sea. But noticing that antagonistic, silent Luke Weston was handsome was no sort of cheating.

The one way Luke was conventionally attractive was he was tall. Practically a giant. And although she couldn't be certain, it looked as though he was muscled underneath his suit. His shoulders were broad and she thought if she raised her arms she would have to—

"Can I help you?"

Luke speared her with his gaze.

She'd been caught staring.

"You can tell me where you bought this coffee." That was the matter at hand, not his muscles.

"Nowhere you can buy it."

"What's your problem?"

He opened his mouth and his eyes went dark green as a bottle of wine.

"There's a viewing for the Newhouse Lane house this afternoon. Been on for a while. Want to do it?"

"Yes—"

"I'll send details." He reached for his mouse and looked away.

"But I can't."

His gaze snapped back to hers and he scowled. Where she thought his auburn hair might make him sweet looking if he smiled, he now looked downright scary. Like a Scotsman from a Shakespeare play who would murder you and your family.

"Why not?"

"My car has a worn clutch. It's in the garage."

"Clutch? How old is your car?" He leaned back in his chair, feet planted on the floor, hands loosely folded across his flat stomach.

Old enough to drink and drive. "None of your business."

"You should have a reliable car for this job. Why didn't you get a hire car? If the garage didn't have one available, you should rent one."

"Because I can't afford it." He annoyed her into spitting out the truth.

That only deepened his scowl. "How much are you paid?" He named a salary the same as hers. "Plus commission on top. If you're paid less than that, we need to talk with Pauline." His eyes were fierce. "You're as experienced as I am; you should have the same salary. And basic commission for a few months until your first sales complete. No reason for you to be out of pocket."

"It's fine. The issue isn't salary," she ground out.

"Have you got a gambling problem?"

She almost choked.

His brow was creased with concern. *No,* it was puckered with disapproval.

"Debt? Asking for help is—"

"Stop it, alright!" she burst out. "I'm not in debt, and I don't gamble. Neither am I an alcoholic, drug addict, or any other unsavoury thing your low opinion of me is imagining."

"Then why can't you afford a decent car?" He was like a dog with a bone.

"My finances are nothing to do with you." Conversation closed. She pretended to look at her email.

"They are if it interferes with your ability to do your job. I'm your mentor."

"As you just pointed out, I'm an experienced sales negotiator. I don't need your 'mentoring'." She definitely didn't need his bossy, high-handed arrogance.

"Not without a car, or understanding of the local area. Why don't you have a functioning car?"

He was relentless. And damn him, he was right.

"If you must know, it's because the cost of running a two-bed flat in a nice neighbourhood on my own is ridiculous."

"You're married and running a household solo?"

"Because why should my husband pay for a house he doesn't live in most of the time?" She'd fought with Eric about exactly this, and lost. It was frustrating, but once the precedent had been set years ago, she hadn't been able to make him budge. "He pays his half when he's back."

"He can afford to holiday in Bali," Luke drawled. "But you can't afford a reliable car."

"Indonesia is very cheap." But that wasn't his point, and they both knew it.

"Move to a less expensive area."

"Eric wants me to be safe." They'd had a bit of a disagreement about it. Eric had vague ideas about the areas that they—she—ought to live in. Those concepts were incompatible with her being able to afford to live.

That earned her a blink. "Like if you had a partner living with you, sort of safe. Or the racist sort of safe of an entirely white neighbourhood?"

She resented that he was now repeating to her not her words to Eric, but her innermost thoughts. The uncharitable, mean thoughts about her husband that she didn't like to admit, even to herself.

"Not everyone is meant for a mortgage and two kids kind of life. It's okay to rent and be footloose."

A strange look shifted across his face, there and gone before she could identify it. "You rent?"

"Sure." Her tummy did an uncomfortable twist.

"You're an estate agent, and you don't own a house. With a mortgage," he clarified.

"No." Wow, that sounded like the defiance of a seven-year-old having broken a plate. She wanted a house of her own and Luke's surprise was warranted. Estate agents not only liked property, as a rule, they also got the first scoop on all the best places. A career estate agent without a house was like a vet who owned no animals. An oddity at best, suspicious at worst. "Do you?"

"Own a house? Yeah," he replied casually, like she'd asked him if he wore trousers. *Obviously*, yes.

"What is it?" The question was out of her mouth before she could think better of it.

"Three-bed end terrace Victorian. Big garden."

Her heart throbbed. She could see it. A classic redbrick house that echoed his hair with Farrow and Ball colours and...

Nope. That was what *she* wanted.

With his sharp suit she'd bet his home was tidy and clinical. An absence of colour and all the character stripped out. He'd probably concrete paved the whole garden and put in cheap white PVC double glazing.

"Visit sometime," he said, voice dripping with sarcasm. "When you have a functioning car."

Was there a ruder man this side of the Atlantic? "Where do you keep it?"

They were staring at each other across the gulf of the gap between their desks.

"What?" he asked impatiently.

"Your Oscar for outstanding rudeness. Can you not be civil to me? I am supposed to be your colleague."

There were five whole seconds where he held her gaze and she was sure he was going to break and laugh or snap and throw something.

"Drink your coffee." He returned his gaze to his computer screen, but although she could see his hands were moving, the cadence of the keystrokes told her he wasn't actually doing real work.

"We're the two sales negotiators. We should work together," she insisted. "Agree on targets and duties, and ensure we don't mess up each other's leads."

He stood abruptly and walked to the backroom, pausing at the door, he nodded meaningfully, and she remembered there was a massive whiteboard in there.

Following him into the small, poorly lit room, she stopped beside him, looking at the board. Very old school. Her previous agency had used an online system, but Pauline seemed as though she liked the personal touch.

"These we need to shift." Luke grabbed a board pen and shoved his hand closest to her into his trouser pocket. He wrote an x with a casual flick next to several property names. "Think you can do it?"

"I'll sell them this month." Once she had her car back.

He nodded as though this was precisely what he expected. "We'll see. Your target for the quarter?"

He caught her eye and she could have sworn the air vibrated with tension between them. He was the one to look away, moving to another smaller board which had names and tallies.

"To restrain myself from murdering you."

"Sales," he clarified in a dry voice.

"One more than your target." There was no way she'd let him get ahead of her.

He wrote her name in careful lines then scrawled the same number under his name and hers.

"I said, one more."

He recapped the pen, put his other hand into his pocket too, and leaned against the wall.

Had she said he wasn't male-model handsome? She'd been wrong. He absolutely was. That square jawline, the straight nose. Even his eyelashes were excessively long, and his green eyes had darkened to almost black. Probably because of the poor light. Although it wasn't particularly dark.

"You going to beat me?"

"I am going to trounce you so thoroughly you will be crying into your pyjamas at night and begging me for mercy. I will be so effective at selling houses you will crawl to me for tips. I will be a house-selling goddess. There will be no houses left to sell and the sales will go through to completion in record time."

His eyes gleamed. "Good."

She stared him down. Her nemesis.

Chapter Three

Six months later

Every morning he woke with a hard-on, an image of Emily in his mind, and the intention of quitting and taking up one of the half-dozen head-hunting offers in his inbox. And three days out of seven, instead, he made her coffee.

Three days were perfect torture. Two days were Emily's days off, when her empty desk mocked him. The remaining two days were his days off. They passed reasonably enough, with longer trips to the gym, trail running, and tweaking the decor of his house, wondering if she'd prefer that lamp shade or this towel, before shaking himself out of it and buying whatever he liked. That pale green had still turned up everywhere. Cushions, her mug, a new toaster.

He tried to limit his spurious planning of where he'd take Emily on their days off together to one morning. Admittedly, sometimes it bled into a bit of googling at the office while he waited for something to print. A few minutes when he browsed boutique hotels and envisaged Emily leaning on a balcony rail, enjoying the view while he stood behind her, his arm around her waist. Or he'd hear on the radio about a restaurant and imagine booking a table for two, just for the pleasure of seeing her eyes widen as she ate a delicious morsel.

But those three days they worked together were what he looked forward to. An hour each morning was just the two of them in the office. He ensured he was there just before Emily to place coffee on her desk so it was ready when she arrived.

There was no snarky comment when she picked up her coffee that morning, just a quiet, "Thanks".

He glanced up to see if Emily would begin a staring competition, his favourite part of the mornings they spent together. But her gaze was trained on her computer screen and her expression was devastated. Broken. Her eyes were shiny, like she might cry.

"What are you doing?" he asked, then wanted to kick himself.

She straightened and her brows shot together, blinking hard. "You're not my boss."

"I'm..." He searched for a spurious reason. "About to chase that flat I did your second viewing on. I don't want to duplicate."

"No, you take it." Her gaze was back on her computer, her voice dead. "It's only a one-bed, and I don't think they're going to buy it, anyway. I'm doing the particulars for the house on Castledine road. It's really nice."

She didn't look like she thought it was really nice. She looked like it was breaking her heart.

He was on his feet and at the filing cabinet before he could overthink it. Grabbing out a set of particulars at random, he approached her desk silently, and looked over her shoulder.

The screen was open on a photo of a nursery. A pretty room painted in creamy yellow, a white crib with a pink blanket and a wooden mobile, and soft toy animals lined up on a shelf.

Was this what had made her sad?

"You should move the picture of the garden forward in the sequence of photos. It's a major selling point for a family house." He didn't want to embarrass her by letting her know he suspected why she was down.

"Thanks for your input," she replied sarcastically, wiping her eyes aggressively. "I have done this before. I can probably manage."

Did she want a child, and her husband didn't? Or maybe they were trying for a baby and it wasn't going well. Both thoughts made him want to throw things. Preferably sharp objects at her husband's head.

"It's overpriced. And not that great."

Her eyes flashed as she looked up at him, all trace of tears gone. "That is a fair price for a desirable property."

"An average house dressed with nice furniture. You're on a hiding to nothing." Animosity would get her out of this funk.

"Good thing it's my sale. It'll be gone within a week."

He made a sceptical sound. "Not possible. If you can sell it within a week you can have my commission this month as well as yours."

Her pretty red lips fell open. "That's like taking money from a ba... Bastard."

"If you're so confident, take the bet."

"What do you get if you win?"

He hesitated. It was tempting to say nothing, or a kiss, or one night in her bed. But then it might feel sleazy, or risky for her. And since he had no intention of winning, he could keep it within the parameters of their professional rivalry.

"Same. Double commission or nothing," he replied with the utter confidence that he was going to win this game. She just didn't know the real game was ensuring she forgot whatever had made her sad.

Watching her think always entranced him. He could almost see as she plotted out the possible risks and benefits. She grinned and it was so unexpected and bright, it was like flicking on a floodlight.

"This is going to be a fun week, planning what to spend my windfall on."

"I suggest a deposit on a new car. Yours is shit." Now when she thought of that pretty nursery she'd remember her triumph in beating him and taking his month's commission.

"I'm thinking a manicure and a new pair of shoes." She winked saucily. "I saw this amazing cat eye nail varnish the other day in a perfect seafoam green."

He thought he couldn't fall any further for her, but he'd been wrong. That naughty smile, an indulgent suggestion of what she'd do with his money, and it had been him that pulled her out of the low mood. He was in even deeper trouble than ever.

"Car," he said, just to annoy her.

He wasn't going to quit. He would continue to be here as long as she needed him, whatever she needed him for.

But he still desperately wanted to know why she'd been sad today.

Chapter Four

F ive (more) months later

As usual when Emily arrived at work there was a cup of coffee on her desk. It appeared every morning as if by magic, and the cup was scooped up silently by Luke at the end of the day.

"Good morning, nemesis. Still trying to poison me?"

She had tried literally every coffee shop in the area, and none were half as good as the coffee Luke provided. He must have a coffee machine at home, but infuriatingly, he wouldn't tell her anything about it. Not the brand, not the coffee beans, not anything. He ignored her when she offered to pay him. He rolled his eyes when she said she'd buy the beans, and shook his head wearily when she suggested she clean their mugs.

He speared her with those green eyes that set her heart racing like he was a monster—a dragon maybe—and she was a trapped princess. Trapped was true, at least. In the almost-year since she'd started at Hapthorpe Estate Agency she'd been stuck sitting opposite her awful, silent colleague.

"It's formaldehyde."

"Really? You want to preserve me? That's so sweet." It was her mission to incite him into a full sentence. Maybe even a paragraph.

He didn't reply.

He made her so cross, constantly leaving her hanging. Not so much as a "mmm" or "huh", or a polite nod of the head. Just silence and scowls were all she got from Luke Weston.

Since the first morning they'd stared across the gulf of the office, him frowning like her presence offended him, their daily staring competitions punctuating her day. Not punctuated with normal things like commas and full stops. Punctuated with semicolons. The sort of punctuation no one except weirdos used, nobody understood, and everyone thought was pretentious.

Pauline arrived like clockwork an hour after Emily. She'd given up trying to persuade Emily that Luke wasn't that bad, and had embraced the rivalry between her two sales negotiators. In her first month Emily had sold every house Luke had labelled with an x, and one more property overall than he had. Six months later, she'd sold a house within a week and won their bet. That manicure had been *the best*.

They egged each other on. Goading Luke was almost as much a part of her day as staring at him before Pauline and the others arrived.

"Luke, I wanted to talk with you about your grandmother's house in Devon," Pauline said when she walked in.

"I'm going to do the valuation tomorrow," Luke replied, looking up with an open expression he never directed at Emily.

"That's what I wanted to discuss. I think it's a conflict of interest, since you're a beneficiary of the will."

"I'm professional," he growled. "It won't be a problem."

"It won't," Pauline agreed. "Because Emily is going."

"No!" they said at almost the same time.

"She doesn't know the area," Luke said implacably.

"I have other appointments tomorrow," Emily protested.

"I'll cover your appointments, they're already moved to my diary." Pauline nodded as though that settled the matter.

"I have to do it." Luke rose with stilted movements, flicking his gaze between Pauline and her. He thrust his hands into his pockets. "The house is a wreck; it's dangerous unless you know your way around."

"Dangerous?" Pauline enquired.

"It's a farm. Rusting bits of equipment, trip hazards galore, half the farm buildings and part of the house are falling down. There's no electric or heating, and I'll need to check where the nearest supply could come from, because every potential purchaser will ask. The water is from a well that, if you're not used to it, gives you a stomach upset like no other. And that's just the beginning."

Pauline tapped her pen on her lips thoughtfully. "Still, I don't think it's appropriate for you to do it alone, Luke." She paused. "You can both go."

"Are you sure that's necessary?" Emily tried to salvage the situation. "Luke sounds like he's in a better position to judge the value of the house."

"Conflict. Of. Interest," Pauline enunciated carefully. "You will both go, and that's final. It's only a few days until Christmas and it's quiet. I can spare you. How is the sale in North Street progressing? Have they exchanged contracts?"

And that was the matter settled.

"About going to Wildbrook tomorrow," Luke said, planting himself in the space between their desks, hands in pockets as usual, and forcing her to look up at him. A long way up when she sat, even though he wasn't close. "I'm driving."

"Fine." She stopped typing and saw his gaze move to her hands. He went very still. There was a paler line of skin revealed, but she doubted that was what he had noticed.

"No defence of your death-trap car?" he said eventually.

"I would like to kill you." He would barely fit in her car, and besides, she had no desire for him to criticise her driving for three hours. "But I want to live. A car accident wouldn't serve my purpose. And one death in your family is enough for now."

"Is that what passes for condolences from you?"

"I'll bring you tissues."

As she looked back to her computer, her gaze caught on his trousers, slightly tented at the crotch by his hands in his pockets. Two full seconds and she looked back at the unimpressed expression on his face, she knew they'd both had the exact same thought.

"I won't need tissues."

"For tears!" Oh God this was terrible. She'd just accidentally implied... "I meant for tears, not... In case you need to cry, which would be absolutely A-okay. You can be upset about your grandmother. I'm really sorry. About your grandmother. And any misunderstanding." She needed to stop digging this hole. "Sorry."

"That's okay."

Then they were staring at each other again, and there was... Something. Not antagonism, not sympathy. Not even the attraction she thought she sometimes felt spiralling through her. Another feeling between them, like a thread that vibrated.

Understanding, and yet... Not.

She understood almost nothing about this man. One thing in particular.

"Why do you always put your hands in your pockets when you speak with me?"

He quirked an eyebrow. "Everyone has a stupid habit they ought to lose. Ditch your husband and I'll take my hands out of my pockets."

"Does it please you to be such an arsehole?" And right. Fucker. How did he know she'd divorced Eric?

"Yes." He turned away.

Luke didn't know today, just like he hadn't known five months ago when she'd finally told Eric she wanted a divorce. But somehow he'd known she needed a distraction then, and given her that ridiculous wager that she couldn't sell a perfectly good house. The house with a nursery that had made her well-up with acknowledgement of what she'd lost. The potential for a family.

He didn't have telepathy about her divorce, since he still had his hands in his pockets and she'd kept it quiet in the office. She'd only taken off her wedding ring today, previously disguised amongst her other rings. Phone calls from Eric had always forced her to make her life more public than she'd have liked. For the last five months she had instigated a strict personal and professional divide.

Admittedly, staying with Eric for so long was about as bone-headed as Luke's habit of putting his hands in his pockets all the time. A bad habit run out of control.

She should have left Eric years ago, when he'd made it clear he didn't much care about seeing her. But Eric had been so damn charming, she'd forgiven him at every turn. He'd always had the right words to talk her down and she had been desperate not to face the reality that their marriage was over.

The final paperwork for their divorce had come through that morning. She was officially no longer married.

Marriage. She almost snorted at the thought. Two-minute phone calls every few days and one month together in every six was hardly a marriage. It felt like a failure to admit she'd been totally wrong about Eric; her parents were unbearable. They'd always said he was smarmy and untrustworthy, and they'd been right.

"Be ready at seven tomorrow," Luke said a few minutes later.

"Seven? We don't need to leave here at seven. That's absurdly early."

"Weather forecast," he said, spearing her with his poison-green gaze.

Shooting him dagger eyes, she checked. And damn him, Luke was right. Unless they were back by five, they'd be caught in the snow forecast for late afternoon in Wildbrook.

"Fine, but you better bring coffee." Bastard he might be, but Luke had a source of coffee that was nothing less than life-giving nectar.

"I will." Had those two words ever sounded sharper? Luke Weston somehow managed to clip half the letters out of every sentence.

Suddenly his stance, hands in his pockets, head tilted to the side watching her with those green eyes, annoyed her more than anything else in the world. It was sexy as all get out, and for almost a year she'd been blocking out noticing that he was devastatingly gorgeous and her body responded to him. It was like a self-closing door she'd kept propped open with the words, *I'm married*, and now the marriage was gone and she needed him to stop looking so hot or she'd do something she'd regret.

And unlike almost everything else in her life, she had the magic key to stop him. "Take your hands out of your pockets."

"Not until—"

"The divorce final order is in my inbox. I've stopped doing the stupid thing, you should too."

She didn't think she'd ever seen him look shocked. His expressions usually varied from scornful, through smug, to grumpy and bored.

He opened his mouth and she couldn't bear it.

"Save it. You're not sorry; you don't give a shit. No one died. It was amicable, or as amicable as it could be given he had been cheating on me for over a year." She'd blown her no personal information rule, but it was only Luke. He hated her anyway.

He removed his hands slowly, like a bear waking from hibernation. And without that cocky hands-in-pockets stance, he looked... even more attractive. Damnit.

"What's your address?"

"So you can firebomb my letterbox?"

"Pick you up tomorrow morning," he said flatly.

"We can meet here."

"A waste of time and effort on a long day." He chucked a pad of post-its and pen onto her desk and retired to his own.

She scribbled her address and phone number on a post-it and sauntered over to his desk. Luke's gaze dropped to her calves, paused, then returned to her face, steady as if he'd never checked out her legs.

She stuck the post-it on his screen. "Don't be late, nemesis."

Chapter Five

He was waiting outside her building, leaning against a spotless teal blue SUV in a woollen overcoat, typing on his phone.

"It's before seven, I'm not late," she grumbled as she approached. She'd expected to be the one waiting for him.

"Good morning to you too." He turned and opened the passenger door he'd been leaning against.

Emily couldn't avoid this chivalrous gesture and accepted him closing the door with suspicion. The car was already warm and was perfectly clean and tidy.

Not like most estate agents, she reflected as she took off her coat, in which she was instantly too hot. Mostly estate agents lived out of their slum-like cars. Hers needed a health warning. She still hadn't replaced it. After her argument with Luke it had become a point of pride not to.

When he slid into the driver's seat, he'd taken off his suit jacket and tie and rolled up his sleeves, exposing forearms that had muscles she didn't know the names of but her pulse shot up anyway. The sight of him casually dressed did strange things to her body. Between her legs went hot and loose and tight at the same time, her breath constricted, and her heartbeat felt a million times louder than before.

"Is that really professional?" she said primly. Or as primly as her breathy voice allowed. He looked like he was going home after a long day at work.

"I didn't think the client would care, even if she was still alive." He pulled out of the excruciatingly tight parallel parking space with zero effort.

He fell silent and she permitted herself to snuggle into the leather seat and really look at him for almost the first time since they'd met. Sure, they had their conflict-ridden staring competitions in the mornings, but she didn't allow herself to feel anything. She catalogued his expressions, his blinks, when he looked away. The focus on brinkmanship allowed her to hide from all the other things that simmered beneath the surface.

There was no hiding from it now as he glanced across to her, only the rumble of road noise between them. Sexual tension.

The sort that screamed, *rebound*.

And *mistake*.

In the centre console sat two matched coffee cups. His and hers. She picked up the seafoam green one. "Are you contractually obliged to bring me coffee?"

"No."

"Why do you buy me coffee every day when you hate me?"

"You're not normally so wrong." He navigated the morning traffic without any of the swearing or irritation she would have shown.

"What am I wrong about?"

"Everything in that last sentence."

She examined the words. "I guess it's not every day, only the days we're both in. I wish you'd tell me where I could buy it. I really need a decent caffeine fix the rest of the week and it's driving me a bit nuts that I look forward to the days you're in because I have good coffee."

Not just that, if she was honest with herself. She'd begun to enjoy their rivalry. He was sharp and insightful and she admired his style. He weaponised silence and used words so sparingly they took on a new weight of significance. It was different to her approach, and suited the customers who found her too talkative.

"I'd provide you coffee every day if you just asked."

"In your dreams, nemesis. You want me to grovel? I'm not going to beg you." Except, obviously she might.

His eyebrow quirked but he kept an unnecessarily diligent focus on the car in front.

"Did Pauline ask you to do it to make up for you being so grumpy that first day? And all the other days."

"For a smart woman, you are very dense."

"I hate you and your coffee."

"No, you don't."

Was her lusting for him that transparent? "I don't hate your coffee.'

They stopped at a red light and he leaned his elbow on the armrest, looking at her finally.

His eyes were dark, as they often were when they argued, and his whole infuriating face was so beautiful she bit her lip. Close to, she could see his day-old stubble was slightly auburn rather than the brown-black it seemed from a distance. What would it feel like on her skin? What would his lips taste like?

"I don't mind being your nemesis, but do you really hate me?"

The darkness of longing in his eyes called to a creature in her chest. A dark, fanged thing that saw him and growled, *yes, mine, now.*

He'd taste like coffee. She didn't even know how he took his coffee and suddenly it was critical she knew and there was only one way to find out.

Her hand shot out, but instead of going for his coffee cup, it went to the back of his neck and dragged his mouth to hers.

They met in the middle and he let out a surprised grunt. His lips were soft though, like he'd been expecting this, and opened to her. It took him all of a second to take control of the kiss. She'd thought of an angry clash, but he angled his head to make the kiss sweeter, hotter, and much deeper.

She was hanging onto him, not dragging him to her. She was the one being spun around on the waltzers, hair flying out, screaming, *faster, more, please.* When his tongue teased at her lips she opened for him and he languorously stroked her, sending skitters of need down her spine.

A horn sounded.

Emily ran her hand down his neck to his open collar, and Luke groaned and touched her hair, pushing in his fingers.

Horns blasted in a cacophony and both their eyes flew open.

They sprang apart.

Luke accelerated the car forwards, knuckles white on the steering wheel.

"That was a mistake; it shouldn't have happened; I'm so sorry." She tried to shut up but her mouth didn't get it. "I don't know what came over me. Getting molested by your colleague. I wouldn't blame you if you complained to Pauline."

"I'm not going to complain to Pauline." He looked entirely unaffected, until he ran a hand through his usually tidy hair and left it all askew.

"Tell me about this property," she blurted desperately.

"We're not going to discuss that kiss, huh?"

"No. We're never speaking of it ever again. We're never thinking of it again. It didn't happen. It was momentary caffeine-induced madness." She wanted another kiss with him. Immediately.

"Right."

She could have sworn he looked... disappointed. But the expression cleared instantly.

"The house belonged to my grandmother. She died a few months ago and left it to her grandchildren. That's me, my elder sister, Trish, and my younger sister, Ros."

"I'm sorry for your loss."

"Thanks. She was eighty-seven. We were mostly surprised her terrifying pre-war farm machinery didn't kill her decades ago. Heart attack in her sleep, the coroner said. The way she'd have wanted to go. She never went to a hospital in her life and I'm glad she didn't end up in one. Never had an ailment she didn't think she could cure with something from the garden or Vaseline. She really liked Vaseline."

"Were you close to her? Your grandma, I mean. And what are your sisters' thoughts about the property?" She had to get this back onto a professional footing, after she had fucked up so spectacularly. And looking at him, all she really wanted to do was fuck up more. With him. In the car. Against a wall. Across his desk in the office. Literally anywhere.

"Yeah. We were all close. Ros wants out of the property, would rather just not deal with it. Can't manage the ghosts. Trish is usually to be found hanging off a mountain somewhere, but the house is partly hanging off a mountain, and I think that's why she's interested. She's been talking about living there, which Ros and I think is a terrible idea." He slanted a look at her, as though trying to understand what she was doing.

"And you?"

"It's a house. I'm always interested in property, but I like where I am."

She kept up a steady stream of questions, some of which were a little more personal than she would use as just background for a client. Luke knew that, glancing at her each time a question was out of the ordinary, but still answering. He didn't call her on it.

They turned onto smaller and smaller roads until eventually they were on an overgrown unsurfaced track up a hillside. Good thing they'd brought Luke's SUV. She wasn't sure her car would have enjoyed the ride.

"Is that it?" She glimpsed a roof amongst trees.

"Yep."

"OMG." They rounded the corner into a cobbled farmyard, stone barns on each side. A three-storey farmhouse rose in the middle with even sage green framed sash windows either side of the rose-covered porch. Made of grey stone with a rough texture and with a slate roof, it looked like a postcard of a farmhouse. Perfect. Apart from all the repairs needed.

"You spent summers here?"

"Most of them."

It would have been an idyllic place for kids. The fields sprawled out on each side of the farm, sloping up the hill on one side and flat on the other, looking over the valley. There were little groups of trees, and intriguing dips and rocky outcrops. Places to explore and build dens and hide.

She'd love her kids to visit somewhere like this and run wild. The image was vivid. A spring day, the trees coming into leaf. A girl with long auburn hair and brown eyes and a little boy with a straight nose and serious green eyes playing in the fields.

Shit. Where had that come from?

"This place is amazing on a cloudy winter day," she said, pulling herself forcibly from the inappropriate daydream. "How much better is it in the summer?"

A smile tugged at Luke's mouth. "Pretty good."

Luke pulled up and shrugged into his jacket. The cold was biting as soon as Emily opened the door and she huddled into her coat. Luke looked at her, stuffed his hands into his pockets and jerked his head towards the farmhouse.

"Come on."

She wasn't married anymore. She was free to date anyone she wanted. She could date *him*. The thought was a drumbeat that shook his whole body, and it hadn't stopped since he'd noticed the lack of ring on the fourth finger of her left hand.

And then she'd kissed him, and the drumbeat had become like hail on a tin roof, so loud and incessant, it was all he could do to think.

Inside the house was equally cold, and Emily shivered. He rolled an offer around in his mouth. *I'll keep you warm.* But that was nonsense. The only warm place was the car.

"Don't wander off," he warned. This house was barely habitable by any normal person. Grandma had not been normal.

"Don't talk to me like I'm a child," she replied, peering through into the front room.

"I'm not. I'm talking to you like you're an insatiably curious estate agent. Let's start downstairs." Quicker they were done, quicker he'd get her back in the snug car and ask if she wanted to kiss him again.

He was halfway to the kitchen when he realised she wasn't following him. He almost sprinted back to the hallway and his heart slammed into his throat at the sight of her on the third step. She screamed as he yanked her backwards by the waist. A heartbeat later she was held safe against his chest.

"What the fuck?" she exclaimed.

"I told you not to wander off!"

His pulse beat like he'd done a hundred burpees. *Shit.* She'd nearly been hurt. For a second he took in the feel of the front of his body pressed against her back. She was soft and curved against him. He imagined turning her in his arms, pushing her against the wall, shoving aside their clothes and taking her. Holding her bracketed by his body, safe, cherished, loved, wanted, as he pleasured them both.

She pulled from his grasp and rounded on him. "What do you think you were doing? I wasn't wandering off, I was going upstairs to take photos, since you were starting downstairs. What is so dangerous about going upstairs?"

"See the pattern?" He pointed at the odd snaking line of wear on the threadbare carpet.

"So?" she said mulishly.

His arm brushed hers as he stepped past her to the stairs, taking the left-hand side. On the third riser he paused and stepped with his foot onto the right-hand side of the next step.

The whole board flicked up on the left side with a squeak. It would have been easily enough to send her tumbling down, off balance and in shock.

"This is a family trait, then? Setting people up to fail?"

He'd prevented her from being seriously hurt. Hardly the same fucking thing, and they both knew it.

"An old lady lived here, and no one thought to fix the stairs?"

"She liked it this way. Said it defended against burglars." Stealing what exactly, Luke had never ascertained. "I said the house was dangerous."

"You need to fix the stairs before viewings."

As if he didn't know that. Ros was being sentimental about any changes to the house.

"Follow the path," he snapped as he mounted the stairs, Emily just behind him.

On the landing a thud stopped him dead.

"What was that?" Emily's voice was high and faint with fear. His hand went to the small of her back. Whether to comfort or support her, or bring her close to protect her, he didn't know. Both, probably. His adrenaline surged. Anything or anyone who wanted to hurt Emily would be going through him first.

Two more thuds, then a sound like papers being shuffled came from the floor above.

He and Emily shared a look of bemusement.

"I'm going up," he mouthed.

She shook her head, brown eyes wide. Was that concern?

"It's fine. Stay here," he whispered.

He trod with silent footsteps up the next flight of stairs and crept towards the noise, his heart hammering at the volume of about a thousand decibels.

"Luke."

Her whisper made him jump.

Another bump and a fluttering sound.

Their gazes locked, her deep brown eyes on his. She held out her hand and for a second he had no idea what that meant. Then he grasped it in his, and kept her as far away as possible as he peered around the corner, into the spare bedroom he'd used as a child…

The familiar sight of the neat bed, thin rugs, and the paperbacks by the bed met him. And in front of the open fireplace lay a large dirty-white bird, flopping ineffectually. He pulled away but Emily wouldn't allow him to let go of her hand and she came with him, gasping as she saw the bird.

"Is it an owl?"

The bird flapped weakly.

"Do you think it got stuck in the chimney?"

"Guess so. Barn owls aren't usually kept as pets, even by my odd family." It took all of five seconds to grab the coverlet from the bed and gently spread it over the panicked bird, who gave a lurch and an ear-splitting shriek before settling in the dark.

Emily blinked in confusion.

He yanked his phone from his pocket. Trish answered in two rings.

"Hey, you mentioned one of the vets in Wildbrook was a prick. Should I go elsewhere with an injured animal?"

"You're in Wildbrook?"

"Yep."

"With an animal that needs a vet?" Trish sounded sceptical, which was fair.

"Indeed."

"Huh. I happen to have a vet right here on her day off. She is in need of a distraction and can take a look straight away. Unless the animal is actively bleeding out, bring it to *Moor Café*." There was the sound of sniffly protest in the background.

"We'll be there in ten."

"Wait, we? Who is—"

He hung up, carefully bundled the owl into the blanket and tucked it under his arm. It struggled a little.

"Bonus. You get to go to the village—Wildbrook—and meet my sister Trish."

Chapter Six

There was only one thing sexier than a tall, handsome, muscled guy: said beautiful man tenderly carrying an injured animal.

The owl held gently but securely under one arm, Luke searched for a box, but came up blank.

"Do you think you can hold it on your lap in the car," he asked after several minutes. His grandmother had lived a frugal life. Everything was neat and in its place, nothing spare. Not even a cardboard box.

She bit her lip and looked at the bird bundle. "Maybe?"

He tilted his head. "More certainty than that, please. An owl loose in the car would be messy."

"I can do it." Because if he could catch an owl and hold it like a baby, she could cradle it for the length of one car journey.

Outside, he directed her to sit in the car and passed the bird in its blanket onto her lap. It was lighter than she expected, the massive wings making up most of its size, but hardly any weight.

"Put your hand over mine."

His hand was warm, and as they repeated the action on the other side, it hit her that they were working together. Her and her nemesis. And it felt good. He had her back, and she had his.

"Hold it firmly but softly, like..." he trailed off as he looked into her face. Whatever he saw there made his eyes darken. "Don't let go."

"I won't." He meant the bird, but she might have meant the feeling of them being a team. She wasn't going to let him go.

The bird was mercifully subdued during the journey.

"Wait," Luke ordered when he parked the car outside a little tearoom with the moniker *Moor Café* on a swinging sign and got out.

A woman rushed out and hugged him, and Emily's stomach did a twist of unexpected jealousy. Until she noticed the woman, who wore a deep blue fleece and walking trousers, had Luke's auburn hair.

Trish. His sister. But her stomach still didn't get the memo that there was nothing to be envious of as he gave a genuine smile, and hugged Trish back. He committed to the hug, squeezing her with a casual affection she hadn't expected from him.

"What are you doing here?" he asked Trish.

"Staying with Clara for a couple days. She needs someone and I'm back in America next week," Trish replied.

What would it feel like to be on the receiving end of his warmth?

Like that kiss this morning.

She squashed the thought as Luke's hands covered hers as he lifted the bird from her lap, his shoulder brushing her breast. There were layers of thick fabric between them, but still. Her heart thundered at the contact.

Then she slipped out her hands and he had the bird in his arms again. She followed Luke and Trish into the café, Luke checking behind for her at the door.

Inside the café were cute white-painted chairs and tables and bright pastel bunting. The door was held open by a black woman wearing a red shift dress who gave Emily a friendly smile as she ushered them in. In the corner, a brunette white woman, with streaked makeup revealing sore red spots, wiped at her pinkened eyes and sat up from where she'd obviously been crying.

"Your patient has landed, Clara," Trish said, as the black woman cleared a table and directed Luke to place the owl onto it.

"Thanks for this," Emily said to the room in general.

"You're welcome. We needed a distraction for Clara, to be honest," the black woman said. "Introductions though. I'm Keri and this is my café. That's Trish, Luke's sister."

Trish nodded and gave Emily an assessing look from head to toe that Emily didn't know the conclusion of.

"That's Clara, she's an excellent vet when she's not being heartbroken." Keri pointed at the woman with Luke, now poured over the table looking at the bird.

"Clara's ex split up with her a month ago," Trish said conspiratorially to Emily, falling into a chair and picking up a cup of tea. "And now he's engaged to someone else. *Engaged.* We're telling her she shouldn't be upset."

"Did well to avoid marrying him," Emily said. "Finding out seven years into a marriage you feel a lot more stupid."

"You're not stupid," Luke muttered, not turning.

"That does sound stupid," Trish said without sympathy nodding at the chair next to her as Keri also sat. "What tipped you off?"

"It was Luke's fault, actually." Emily gratefully took both the tea and chair offered, and glanced across at Luke, who gave her the smallest of glances from the corner of his eye.

"Most things are," Trish replied. "What did he do this time?"

"I mixed up the names of a mother and daughter when booking a viewing, and Luke *helpfully* pointed out I could avoid the embarrassment by being like a cheating spouse and calling everyone babe."

"Suddenly he'd started calling you babe?" Trish shook her head, unimpressed.

"Mmm."

"Hardly damning though," Keri said and sucked her teeth. "Babe can be a cute endearment."

"But his emails..."

"No!" Trish and Keri exclaimed together.

"Damning." She probably ought not to have hacked into Eric's email account. But he made it too easy. "Life lesson. If you want to keep your affairs secret from someone who knows your childhood pets' names, turn on two-factor authentication."

"You sound okay about it," Clara said quietly. "How long ago did you split up?"

"Six months, but it was over way before that, if I'm honest." It was odd that when she poked what had been a sore spot, she found nothing but a vague feeling that Luke had helped her.

"What you need is someone to rebound with," Trish said to Clara's back. "May I suggest my brother, since he's here?"

"Trish," Luke said warningly, not looking up from the owl.

"He's single, and not that ugly if you ignore his face," Trish said with sisterly understatement, and Keri snorted. "He'll treat you right. He's been planning romantic weekends away with his imaginary girlfriend and not doing them for almost a year. And I happen to know that he won't cause you any problems with getting attached because he's in love with his—"

"Thank you, sis, that's enough."

A look passed between Trish and Luke and Trish's gaze darted to Emily, then back to Luke. Trish mouthed, "Sorry".

He was in love with his... work? He did spend a lot of time at work. Or had Trish been about to say, friend? Himself?

"How is the bird?" Emily asked to fill the awkward pause.

"It's a barn owl," Clara said. "And I'm still finding out."

"Where did you get a barn owl?" Keri slanted one eyebrow.

Emily told the story as briefly as she could.

"I didn't realise there were still owls there." Trish grinned. "That's amazing. I'll enjoy them as housemates."

"Not if they're living in the house," Luke interjected. "Or chimneys."

"You're going to live there?" Emily asked.

"Sure. It has most things I need. Water. Fireplaces. Owls."

"Owls are crucial for human habitation," Emily said deadpan, taking up Trish's joke. For some reason she wanted Trish to like her. "Every home should have one. I always recommend to my clients they install an owl as a first priority after moving in. Who needs heating when you have an owl to scare warmth into you?"

Emily had a swell of pride when Trish chuckled.

"You need electric. And I thought you were staying with Ros next visit." Luke scowled over his shoulder.

"Change of plan." Trish shrugged. "I'm used to doing without. I need somewhere to crash for a few weeks when I come back from America, and we have to clear that house and fix a few things. Perfect coincidence of needs."

"I think it has a broken wing," Clara said. "It'll be okay with some care, but you probably have to take it to the surgery. I'm sure Dan will help." Her voice wobbled on the name.

"We'll take him to the vet now, thanks Clara." Luke smiled and Emily's heart did a twisty knotted thing. It was like a bonfire, his smile. So warm and bright.

She wished he'd smile at her like that.

By the time they returned to the house, it had started snowing. At Keri's insistence, after delivering the owl to the vet practice and waiting for reassurance it would be fine, they'd returned to Moor Café for lunch. They'd sat far too long with Trish, Clara and Keri, chatting. Luke as ever was taciturn, but less so with his sister.

Nothing more than a few magical flakes that drifted to the ground, but Luke glared at them. "We should be quick. Don't want to get stranded."

Emily laughed. "Sure. Those few spots are going to prevent us getting home. I don't think."

"Exmoor weather changes fast."

The cold air fizzed between them as they took measurements and photographs of the land and barns, but the snow showed no signs of getting worse and they headed into the house.

They worked well together, him seeming to sense when she needed something or when she was too short to get the right shot of a room. When he came up behind her and took the camera from her hands when she was on tiptoes in a doorway his thigh brushed hers and she nearly spontaneously combusted, despite the snow and the lack of heating in the house.

That kiss in the car this morning played through her mind like an ImPhoto video caught in a glitchy repeat. Her mind jerked between the feel of his hands in her hair, the throaty growl he'd made when she'd pulled away, and his tongue touching hers.

"I think we're done," Luke said eventually, and glanced around with something like nostalgia. "We should go, it's getting... Oh shit."

She followed his gaze out of the window. Where earlier a smattering of snowflakes had settled, now there was a thick layer of white. Fat little flakes of snow floated down from the grey-white sky. Neither of them had noticed, so focused on each other and the job in hand.

"It'll be fine." Luke broke the silence. "I'll get you home. But we need to go now."

Ten minutes later, Luke pulled the car into a passing place.

"We're going to get stuck, aren't we?"

Luke grimaced.

They looked at each other and despite the snow, the memory of their kiss vibrated through her again.

"We can push on, but there're still miles of small lanes between here and the motorway." He sighed. "And even that..."

"Want me to Google?"

"Mmm."

"The M5 is a slippery car park," Emily said a moment later. "What's the alternative? Go back to the house and stay there? It's freezing." They'd have to snuggle together for body heat.

The idea was not entirely unappealing.

In fact, it appealed in every single way.

"Hopefully it won't come to that." Luke rubbed his jaw, pulled out his phone and tapped for a minute. The handsfree sprang into life with the sound of a dialling tone.

"Hello?" A woman's voice.

"Do you have The Old Applehouse available for tonight?"

A confused silence, then, "Yes, but—"

"Great. We're five minutes away. Can we come now?"

"Yes. Do you know where—"

"We'll be with you soon." He hung up.

"The Old Applehouse?" Emily asked.

"It's a little rental nearby. It'll be warmer than either the car or the house." He hesitated. "There's only one bed, but..."

A thrill sang down her veins. One bed.

"Better than hypothermia." He glanced at the sky, now entirely white speckled black.

"Fine, but let me pay." That didn't reveal her excitement. Would he want...?

"No."

"You've bought me coffee every day for almost a year. I owe you."

"No." His tone was implacable. "Put your contribution towards a new car. Besides, this is a business expense."

He pulled the car back into the road, and they drove in silence.

The snow kept falling, harder and harder. It was inches deep and Luke was driving in third gear, all his focus on the road.

So it was with some relief that Emily sighed when Luke said, "We're here, right at five o'clock. End of the workday."

Their snowed-in refuge. With one bed.

Chapter Seven

"I've lit the wood burner and the heating is on, so it should warm up pretty quickly." The owner gave them a key after they'd sorted the obligatory paperwork. "I need to get back to the kids, if you wouldn't mind letting yourselves in?"

They murmured they didn't and Luke led the way into the converted barn.

Emily actually gasped as they entered. It was decorated in a modern but warm style, all white walls and pale wooden furniture. The ceiling was double height, with skylights covered in snow, and a mezzanine floor from which a peek of a massive bed. An enormous Christmas tree stood in the corner, draped in gold ornaments and lit with white lights.

"How did you know about this place?" she asked in wonder.

"I thought about booking to stay here."

"With who?" With a girlfriend? Must be. There was only one bed, and it wasn't the sort of place you stayed on your own. Not unless you were indulgently a loner. Which, come to think of it, she supposed Luke might be. That was better than him coming here with a girlfriend.

She'd never heard him speak about friends. She hadn't known before today anything about his family, and in fact he had two sisters he was close to.

He didn't answer, just shaking off the snow from his jacket and taking hers. His fingers brushed her neck as he eased it from her shoulders. And Emily could have sworn that minuscule contact lit a fire in every part of her. She turned and they were close, so close. He was ridiculously tall, but it would still only take her standing on tiptoes and him leaning down a little and they'd bridge the gap easily.

For a moment, Emily thought Luke might kiss her. He watched her with a strange expression, eyes dark.

Then without another word, he knelt and it took her a second to realise he was undoing the laces on her boots.

She made a noise of protest.

"You need to warm up," he said in a tone that accepted no argument.

Big, brawny, powerful, and kneeling at her feet. Her heart skipped. He indicated for her to remove first one foot then the other, imperious as a king. He wasn't doing her a favour, he was demanding. She wobbled a little as she stood on one foot to allow him to take off her boot and when they were off she felt even shorter than usual.

"Go on." He stood, towering over her. "Sit by the fire."

She hesitated, then went exploring. The warmth of the house was perfect. She found a tiny kitchenette set up with a Nespresso machine and excellent biscuits.

He made short work of his own boots and followed. "Good to know we'll have caffeine in the morning."

Their gazes met. He always provided what she needed. Somehow, he knew.

"Knock-knock!" The owner peeked around the door, preceded by a massive tray piled high. "You'll have to forgive the food, I'm so sorry. All fresh and warm, but a bit limited. I had to throw it together."

"Thanks," Luke said, lifting the tray from her and taking it to the little nook with a table and two chairs, complete with table settings and candles.

"There's creamy leek and potato soup with garlic aioli with bread freshly baked this morning and the butter is from the local organic dairy," the woman said, unloading the items from the tray. "Those sausage rolls have meat from our own pigs—bless their delicious troublesome noisy hearts—and were baked yesterday. I've warmed them up for you. There's the promised bottle of chilled bubbly, *of course*. And I didn't have any dessert so you have chocolate truffles I made a few days ago, but they've been in the fridge and are still very tasty! I hope that's alright?"

She looked at Emily for assurance that a three-course hot banquet with fancy booze and chocolates when they'd been at risk of kipping in the cold car with nothing but some mints and body heat would be okay.

"That sounds amazing, thank you so much." Emily gravitated to where Luke was standing over the food, clearly as hungry as she was.

The woman glowed.

"If you want to put the hot tub on. The panel is here. I'm guessing you might not, given the snow, but just in case!" She pressed a button. "That'll warm it up until midnight. It's outside on the patio, but you'll need to remove the cover. Might as well use the facilities since you're here! There's plenty of toiletries and towels in the bathroom. I'll leave you to it. You know where I am if you need anything!"

And then they were alone. Just her and Luke and literally the most romantic getaway location she could imagine. She sneaked a look at him. He'd gone to the fire and was poking it, and moving something. Adding more wood.

Rebound sex.

She'd thought of it earlier when she'd kissed him and this was the perfect opportunity.

She'd have rebound sex with Luke Weston.

He was quiet and discreet at work. She'd bet he'd never tell anyone about it. He was gorgeous, and she didn't actually hate him anymore. She was close to liking him. Quite a lot, in fact.

He lacked superficial charm, but he was kind in the way an old woollen jumper was warm. Yes, a bit scritchy, but miles better than a more polished acrylic knock-off. Luke was the real thing. She watched as he rose and stalked towards her.

"You need to eat."

Emily baulked at Luke's domineering tone, but found herself nodding.

"You do too." He needed to keep his energy up for what she had planned.

For something the owner claimed to have thrown together, dinner was delicious. But once they were on opposite sides of the table, they were too busy bantering in a new word game they were still working out the rules of to do it justice. Their office snark morphed into trying to make the other person talk. She asked things she never would at work, about his family, hobbies, friends, and past. He answered with a sentence or two, then turned the question to her.

And as much as she enjoyed his attention, when she was answering his questions, Emily was hopelessly distracted by his legs. He was too tall to tuck himself underneath the little table, pushed as it was against the wall. So his legs were stretched out to the side, his torso angled towards her and the table.

How in all these months had she never noticed how long and muscled his legs were? It must have been the angle that stretched his trousers over his thighs, and tugged the fabric up slightly to reveal the smallest slither of his ankle above socks that... She had not expected. Seafoam green socks with pink flamingos.

And he just continued talking quite seriously, with that contrast on display. The whimsical socks, that tease of skin and dark hair on his ankle, and the lean strength of his quads. Even as she ate her fill, hunger grew.

She wanted to see this man. She wanted to examine him like one would a house she was buying, reading each space and alteration and crack and line until she understood the underlying structure and everything that had happened to him.

"Do you like my socks?" he asked when they had eaten everything except the chocolate truffles.

"What?"

"You keep looking at them."

"I..." It was on the tip of her tongue to deny it. But not tonight. "Yeah. I like them. They'd look even better on the floor."

He went still, then reached down, snagged first one then the other and pulled them off, tossing them away.

He had nice feet. Large, as befitting his size overall, and exactly as feet should be. But it was the casual revelation of skin that made her hot and fluttery.

"Improvement?"

They both looked at the crumpled socks. A smile gradually spread across Luke's face, and finally bubbled up in a laugh.

She soaked it up. That glow of warmth. The sound, the curve of his mouth that had kissed her earlier today. The feel of his laughter on her skin sent shudders of need through her.

"I've never understood that chat up line. But apparently it can work on me."

Did that mean he'd take his clothes off for her if she said they'd look better on the floor?

The moment stretched out, and Emily wondered if she could really do this. It was only when Luke's smile faded that her voice, as ever, went on without her volition.

"I was thinking. Would you like to give that hot tub a go? It's only on until Midnight, and it would be a pity to waste that lovely warm water."

"I don't have swimming shorts."

"Neither do I."

He was silent for long seconds, his green eyes searching her face. "What are you really asking?"

He was direct. She'd always liked that about him. That and his body, his caring, and now she'd heard it, his laughter.

"What if we tried having sex? Tonight. It need not be anything more than a one-night thing. Just bang it out of our systems. I need a rebound. And we have... Unresolved sexual tension." She cringed at herself. Way to make a proposition.

"One night?"

"Yes."

"That's all?"

"We work together." Anything else would be awkward and unfeasible. "We're rivals. I don't think it would... I don't know."

He scrunched up his face as though he was in pain. "Okay, if that's your offer. I accept."

Luke rose and walked away, leaving Emily gaping as he went first to the bathroom and retrieved towels, then the kitchen, then the patio doors which he unlocked and slipped outside.

A moment later he was back, undoing his cuffs then the front of his white shirt. Conflicting impulses hit her: watch, join, touch. Video him getting undressed on her phone so she could review it after their one night, when she was horny or lonely or pining or... Breathing.

His chest... Broad, toned, with a smattering of dark hair between his nipples. His shoulders and arms were golden perfection. Muscled without being ridiculous, he was strong. Beautiful.

It wasn't a strip tease. There was no guile in his movements, no suggestiveness. He just took off his clothes, as smoothly as he did everything, and laid each item over the back of the nearest sofa.

He held her gaze as he stripped off his trousers and boxers in one go. His cock sprang up and Emily's lungs stopped working.

She still hadn't moved. Luke strode over, pulling her to her feet, he towed her to the patio doors.

"Are you going into the hot tub like that?"

"Yes. Fully clothed."

"And be naked all of tomorrow. Good plan."

"Get in the hot tub and close your eyes. Put the bubbles on." She was nowhere near as attractive as him. Whose stupid idea was it to get into the hot tub? The him being naked part was excellent. The her being naked was... not.

He tilted his head and she thought he might argue. Instead, he turned and walked out into the snow. She nearly reached for his arse, it was that delicious. He settled himself into the water with a muted splash. The snow was still falling, light spilling out onto the decking from the house. Magical.

Luke hooked his arms over the edge. His head was at calf level in the inset water, but he looked like a lord. A mafia boss. A billionaire about to rock her world. A man so in control of the situation she couldn't do anything but what he commanded.

Which was probably why, when he whispered, "Strip", she did. Just as he had, without any show. The cold bit at her skin and snow landed in his hair, a crown of ice.

"I told you to close your eyes," she grumbled as she got down to knickers and bra and struggled not to cover herself. From the cold, yes, but that intent look in Luke's eyes was positively wolfish.

"Yeah, you did."

"And put on bubbles."

"Uh huh."

She shivered, and would have liked to say it was just the freezing temperature. But it wasn't. It was him observing her.

"Go on then. Close your eyes."

"They're as closed as they're going to be. If you think I'm going to shut my eyes for a second, when we only have one night, you're sorely mistaken."

She was beautiful beyond his wildest dreams, and she was here, in front of him, taking off her underwear. He held his breath and her hands trembled as she undid her black lace bra, then slid the matching lace knickers from her hips.

Ohhh...

"It's freezing!" She approached and stepped in, sighing with relief as the heat enveloped her. The tips of her loose curls, unbound over her shoulders, floated on the water.

"I'll warm you up," he promised as he reached for her. Then she was in his lap, cold hands on his pectorals, her pussy spread over him, the folds brushing his cock. He let out a grunt. Her perfect breasts touched his chest first, her hands having slipped up to the back of his neck, and he pulled her closer. Closer and closer still until her lips met his and she was pressed to him.

A soft kiss, gentle and sweet to befit the surreal night. Snow. Hot water. Emily naked in his arms. She was every one of his fantasies come to life. Why she was shy, he had no idea.

One night. She was using him as rebound for one night. A better man than him would say no, and insist on her not feeling the need to rebound when he slept with her. A better man than him would be able to resist her when she took her clothes off and got into the hot tub with him. A man with half a brain cell's worth of common sense would know that a one-night stand with his work colleague who hated him would complicate things horrendously. But Luke wanted Emily so damn much he didn't care about any of those things.

If he had this one night, if this was his opportunity, he'd take it and be grateful.

Yes, he wanted forever with her, but he'd wished that when she was still married, and now she was single.

A slim possibility was better than none. One night was better than never knowing.

He kissed her deep and slow, not hurrying. They had hours yet, stuck in this wonderful nowhere. A place she'd finally decided to take a chance on him. He couldn't stop touching her, the water making every movement lazy and slippery. He ran his hands down her sides, over her thighs, exploring her body as he'd always wanted to.

She was inquisitive too. Her hands smoothing down his chest and over his shoulders. She pushed the soft folds between her legs over the length of his cock and it took all his restraint not to shift her onto it.

But he didn't.

Slowly. He was going to enjoy every moment of this, and more importantly, so was she. Sex in the water wouldn't do that.

It was only when his hands found hers and he noticed her fingertips had wrinkled that he grasped her hips and lifted her off him.

"Condoms." It suddenly occurred to him that the fulfilment of his dreams might be curtailed by a fuck up so trivial as a lack of condoms. He hadn't brought any with him.

He'd never replaced the last one he'd used weeks before he'd met Emily. Laziness at first, and once they'd met he'd known she was the only woman for him, and she wasn't the type for a dirty quicky somewhere unplanned.

Except for when she was, apparently. Fucking terrible planning on his part.

"No," she said after a second's hesitation. "I have an IUD. I was tested a couple of months ago and haven't had sex since. You?"

His heart lifted. "I've been checked since my last partner." No need to tell her that was over a year of only his hand.

"Hold on," he instructed her, and rose from the water. She gave a little squeak at the cold, but he had them both in the house, the door closed, and her wrapped in a towel within seconds.

He dried himself perfunctorily and her carefully before he lifted her into his arms, shoving off their towels as he did so. Carrying her felt so right, and so did laying her on the bed, lying on his side next to her.

"Emily," he breathed.

He'd never allowed himself to hope for this. Emily, naked in bed with him.

He had one night, until the snow melted, to have her. Maybe to build something strong enough to withstand the move to the real world.

Yeah. Right.

All he could do was live this night like it was his last. Who needed sleep?

She seemed on board with that, taking things much too quickly, her hands everywhere on him. And good as that felt, her reaching for his cock, her sigh of pleasure as she felt his hardness, capturing her hands in his was better. Palm to palm. Her hands were soft and her nails manicured with pale green paint that shifted colour in the light. All delicate and pretty.

"You're so big." Her gaze flickered down to his cock, back to his hands, and settled on his face.

"You're so petite. And I'm not too big, *trust me*. We're going to fit together perfectly."

"Show me then."

"I will." He tugged her to him and without her hands to catch herself she fell gently onto his chest. Grasping her waist, he rolled her underneath him. Her whimper when he moved over her was the sexiest thing he'd ever known, until she parted her legs to allow his hips to rest over hers. That nearly made him lose it. Her willingness. The movement told him she wanted this.

"Luke," she whispered, and pushed up into his cock, the wetness of her slit sliding against him. Not just a bit wet, and not from the hot tub. She was overflowing with desire as she said his name.

Oh dear god it was going to be like this all night. He'd have to stop keeping a running total of what the sexiest things that he'd ever seen or heard or felt were, because each record would be superseded within minutes.

He nuzzled her neck with his stubble and she moaned as she stretched to allow him better access. Leaning down, he kissed his way lower.

"Your breasts are perfect," he murmured, then sucked one rosy nipple into his mouth, gently holding the tip with his teeth and laving it with his tongue. "I'm going to kiss you all over, but especially your sweet nipples."

She let out a keening sound, and her hand found the back of his neck to hold him in place. He did the same to the other nipple, then returned, lavishing her breasts with the attention they deserved as his hands explored her body, each curve and dip becoming more familiar with repetition. He wanted to know her body intimately.

Her curious, questing fingers discovered him too, a trail of electricity in their wake. The touch was what he'd craved, and also too much. She explored greedily, trying to do everything at once.

This would all be over embarrassingly quickly if she kept up this barrage of strokes and little moans as she found some new part of him she liked. His arse, his shoulders, his abdomen.

He captured her hand in his, pinning it to his cock when she strayed lower. "Slow down."

"I don't think I can."

Catching her other hand and the simple press of his palm to hers, their fingers meshed, made his heart expand to bursting point. He brought her hand up and they both looked. The contrast was delicious. Her hands were so small.

He wanted to touch and keep her captive. He moved first one hand then the other, and pinned her wrists together. Her breath hitched.

"Emily, do you like that?" He didn't let go. "Do you want me to hold you down as I fuck you?"

"You talk dirty in bed?" Her voice came out breathy rather than the snark she probably intended.

"If you tell me you want it."

She let out a little moan. "All these months you've barely said a word to me, and now you're talking dirty. You fucker. I can't believe it."

"I'll stop if you don't like it." He suited his actions to his words, remaining perfectly still and quiet. An exercise in self-restraint given how sweet and wet and willing she was under him.

"No," she panted.

The half second before his brain caught up with her body arching into him and she meant don't stop.

"Yes, I mean..." She thrashed her head from side to side like she wanted to clear her head to think past the lust in a fog between them.

"I'll make things simple for you," he crooned, and shifted so he could look into her eyes, but they were closed. "Yes-no answers."

He examined her face, so pretty. Her long dark eyelashes were enhanced by a flick of black eyeliner and this close to he could see a shimmer of colour on her eyelids. He wanted to be the one who saw her put that makeup on in the morning and take it off at night. And watch it run as they fucked so hard they both got sweaty.

"Do you want me to say dirty, sexy, wicked things to you as I touch you everywhere?"

Her nod was enough. For now.

"Do you want me to fuck you? Do you want to come on my cock?"

She jolted at the way the word fuck seemed to reverberate between them. "Yes."

"Do you like being held down?"

A gulp this time, before a softer, "Yes."

"Do you want me to take control?"

"Yes." Accompanied by a bite of teeth into that plush bottom lip of hers.

"Open your eyes. You are going to see that it's me."

She did and that nearly broke all his good intentions. Because her gorgeous eyes were soft and hazy with want. He hadn't thought it was possible for him to harden further, but his imagination had been frankly poor when it came to Emily. Every single aspect of her and him together blazed hotter than he'd imagined.

"Don't close them," he ordered. "Not when you come, not at all."

She nodded, mouth falling open.

"Me fucking you bare, with no condom, just skin to skin. Me filling you up with my come. Is that what you want?" He threw out the question, despite their having talked about it earlier, because he couldn't let her have regrets, because he wanted her to say yes to what he desperately needed, and because when he was inside her he didn't think he'd be able to stop.

"Yes. Fuck me." She tilted her hips to try to get the blunt head of his cock to her entrance. But she couldn't quite manage the angle and he was going to spin out the occasion longer. He'd only once slip into her the first time. He wouldn't hurry such a sweet moment.

He stroked his free hand down her body, and couldn't repress a moan of delight. She was perfect.

Then he eased back enough to notch the head of his cock at her entrance, and watched her eyes go wide.

"Luke, don't tease."

"Not teasing, enjoying. Relishing the feel of your soft, wet pussy opening for me." He pushed the smallest distance into her, just the beginnings of a stretch.

She panted and tried to get him to move, but he held them both in check. Then he pushed in a little more. Another pause where the urge to slide all the way into her wet heat was almost unbearable. Even though he was bigger than average, she was so ready there was hardly any resistance as he went deeper, oh so slowly, spinning it out. And all the time, her eyes searched his face.

He withdrew a little and she mewed in protest until he thrust in further. She hooked her legs around his thighs and urged him on. But he paused instead.

"You are so beautiful. You feel so good around my cock. I've wanted this for so long and I'm so crazy for you I can't think straight when you're near." Not, *I love you*, but close, so close. He would probably regret these candid words in the morning. He couldn't even use the excuse that he was drunk to pretend he'd said things he didn't mean.

Her fingers flexed in a half caress of his hand that trapped them.

He slid the last distance and they were fully joined, as close as two people could be. She writhed against him and it was his turn to gasp. His hips moving of their own accord. It was impossible to keep as still and slow as he wanted. But he managed to retain some control, even as his body roared with need.

A slow wet slide of him into her. He leaned down for a kiss as he thrust again, and again, easy but relentless.

She kissed him back a little desperately as his hand found her breast. Their kiss was almost feral in comparison to the languid pace he imposed with his thrusts.

She whimpered his name and dug her heels into his buttocks.

"You want more?" She had to say yes, because in a moment he'd lose control and pound into her.

"Yes." She squirmed beneath him.

He increased his pace from achingly slow to firm and deliberate. Kissing her again, his tongue in her mouth was a filthy, delicious echo of his cock in her pussy. He felt her shift, looking for more friction or a better angle and reluctantly gave up the kiss. Much as he wanted that, her breaking apart with pleasure was more important. She had to break a little to allow for the chance for them to be more than rivals and colleagues.

He lifted himself from her, releasing her hands and sat back, never slipping from her tightness. She looked up at him with bright, surprised eyes.

"New angle," he murmured, flexing his hips to give them the continued movement they both wanted while catching her calf and hooking her leg to his shoulder. Unable to resist, he pressed his lips to her ankle as he pushed into her again, harder this time. Her face crinkled in pleasure.

That was the right spot, then. He smiled with satisfaction. Tonight, she was his to please, and he intended to make her wild. She was spread before him, so unutterably perfect.

He dug his fingers into her bottom to hold her in place as he thrust deep and smooth. Long, rolling movements that helped him not tip over while watching her face for what she needed. She gripped the bedsheets. He wasn't going to last much longer with her looking like this. Beautiful, intense, still not having taken her eyes off him, as he'd ordered. His cock went impossibly hard at that thought.

Shifting to change his hold, he brought his thumb to brush her clit. A sweet pink little nub all glistening, and her response made him throb from his chest to groin. Her hand found his knee and gripped him, holding on like she was attempting to bring him closer or maybe anchor herself.

He increased his pace, matching circles on her clit to the rhythm of his cock sliding into her.

Her orgasm came without warning. One second this moment could last forever, the next her back arched and she shook and clenched around him.

It shattered him too. The feel of her coming tipped him over even as he tried to hold back, to keep this going for longer so she came on his cock again and again. But it was too good to see the expression on her face, completely overcome and dazed. She was too gorgeous and hot and he pulsed into her. There was savage triumph in filling her with his come, her body seeming to draw out yet more pleasure when he thought the long seconds were over.

Then eventually, they were still. His cheek pressed to her ankle, her bottom in his lap, her gaze on his face.

"That was..." She shook her head.

"Have I made Miss Chatty speechless?" He'd caused her to lose that smart, long-running mouth of hers and he couldn't be prouder.

She nodded.

He scooped her up and ignored her squeak of surprise as he carried her to the bathroom. As he wiped away his come from where it dripped onto her thighs he had an irrational wish that she wasn't on birth control and there was the potential, however minuscule, for her to be pregnant by him after this night.

He pushed the thought away.

"I can walk you know," she protested when he tipped her into his arms to carry her back to bed.

"You don't want to be carried?" He dropped her onto the centre of the bed and she let out an "oof" that turned into a laugh, then caught in her throat as he moved over her, nudging her thighs apart with his knee to make space for him. This kiss had none of the sexual intent behind it, like the ones so far. It was a Sunday morning sunshine kiss, all tender exploration and enjoyment of the slow build for its own sake.

Or it was to him. He felt her respond, moving against him in a search for more.

He rolled to the side, bringing her with him so they were still face to face.

"I can't go again for a few minutes, beautiful. But you can."

"You want to?"

"Yes."

"I don't know if I can come again. I've never tried."

"You can," he said, even though he wanted to say, *shame on your shitty ex-husband.* "I'm not letting you sleep just yet." If they only had tonight, it was going to count. He was going to make her come so many times she'd be unable to look at him without remembering the tremors of orgasm.

"I'm already wrecked."

"You do look a little dishevelled." Her usually flawless hair was at all angles, the loose curls gone fluffy. He ran his hand down her hair, revelling in the feel of it. Emily's hair, that he'd wanted to touch so many times when sitting across from her in the office.

"Come here." There was another thing he'd dreamed about in the office, and there was no way he was letting the night finish without doing it.

He eased her on top of him, him lying on his back. She sat up and trailed her palms down his chest, making a little contented sound as she did so. Then he tugged her up, and shifted himself down.

"What?" she protested weakly.

"Hold the headboard," he instructed as he gripped her hips to move her pussy to his mouth and gave her a long hard lick down her slit. He could have moaned at the sweet musk of her, and of them.

Their gazes met and her eyes were wide. He raised his eyebrows in query.

"I haven't done it like this before," she confessed.

"You haven't ground your pussy onto my tongue and made yourself come? You're right. That's not in the estate agents' handbook for sales techniques. Generally behaviour that's frowned upon in the workplace."

She huffed out a laugh. "I meant had oral sex with me on top."

Luke was filled with the conflicting instincts to say her ex was a fuckwit for never doing this for her, and savage glee that he would be the first.

"I'm going to make you come with my mouth, or maybe you're going to use my mouth to make yourself come." He ran his hands down her lower back, over the curve of her arse and to the delicious length of her thighs. "Either way, you're going to need to hang on."

Uncertainty, she reached for the headboard.

"Or you can grip my hair if you prefer."

"I can't do that!" she protested.

"We'll see, won't we?" He pulled her hips until her folds met his tongue.

Chapter Eight

Emily woke with Luke's heavy arm over her ribcage, his big hand cupping her breast, and his hard cock pressing against her bottom. And it felt right. It was still dark, so Emily assumed it wasn't long since they'd fallen asleep. Luke was insatiable. He'd seemed to have one focus —her pleasure. She'd come more times last night than she had in the last two months. It had been almost a year since she'd woken up with someone. And how long had it been since she'd been—there was no way other to describe it— snuggled with a man? Too long. A very long time. Maybe... never?

She covered his hand with hers and wiggled her bottom closer.

"My minx." Luke pressed his lips to the back of her bare neck.

Her stomach flipped with excitement.

My. The possessiveness in that word. She wanted to be his.

"Mine," she made the word with her lips and no sound.

"How do you feel about morning sex?" Luke whispered into her ear.

"I think you should close the deal." She turned her head so their lips met.

"I intend to." He shifted his hand and rolled her nipple in his fingers, softly, then harder. Just the right amount of roughness to make her whimper. Then his hand dragged over her skin, down to her mons, dipping into her.

"You feel like heaven." He eased his fingers over her clit.

No. Being bracketed between his hand and his cock, that was heaven.

He grasped her thigh and laid it over his, opening her and slipping in.

She gasped. He was big, and she was small, and the fit was tight and wet. Then he found her clit with his fingers again and began to move.

He had her twice before dawn, then again when he brought her coffee. He joined her in the shower and washed her with infinite care. She left him to finish up, dressed, and flitted to the windows that opened to the deck. Beyond, snow-covered mountains touched a starkly blue sky with a streak of white cloud.

The uncovered hot tub had a layer of snow. Next to the edge sat two champagne glasses and the bottle they hadn't even opened. They'd been so consumed with each other, everything else had fallen by the wayside. Though Luke had remembered the chocolate truffles at some point in the night, feeding them to her in bed and licking every "accidental" smear of chocolate from her body.

One night. They'd said one night, and now it was morning.

She didn't want to stop.

Luke's quick footsteps echoed behind and he wrapped his arms around her.

For a few minutes, she breathed in the scent of him, familiar and yet new.

"Tell me why you found this place." This magical spot in Wildbrook where everything had changed between them.

"No." He groaned, hiding his face in her hair and kissing her neck. "It's weird. And sad."

That was even more intriguing. "Go on."

"I don't want to."

"You're such a baby."

He grazed his teeth on her sensitive nape, making her shudder with need.

"No distracting me," she warned and he huffed a sigh of resignation and straightened slowly.

She could see the barest outlined reflection of both of them staring out at the snow-covered landscape.

"I plan what I'd do with my days off if I had a girlfriend to spend them with," he said softly. "Every week I go online and find a place to stay and things to do. I work out a restaurant, activities, accommodation. Obviously the accommodation is an interest area for me. I like it to be... Nice."

"This is a bit more than nice. This is next-level luxury. I've stayed at five-star hotels that aren't half as good as this." It said something about his taste. And maybe also about what it would be like to be his. Cherished. Valued. His highest priority, if he planned days off and was willing to spend so much on being with his hypothetical girlfriend.

She wasn't sure what that would feel like, but some creature in her chest purred at the thought of his attention to making something so good.

"Like I said. Nice. My girlfriend would deserve that." He stroked his hand down her arm. "This was one of those locations. I picked it out for Valentine's day this year."

"Every weekend?"

She felt him nod. "If I had a girlfriend, I'd want to spend every moment I could with her."

Not like Eric. Luke, for all his gruff manner, cared in a way charming Eric never had. She pushed the comparison from her mind.

"And what would you and your imaginary girlfriend have done here for Valentine's day?"

"Lain in the hot tub sipping champagne and feeding each other strawberries. We'd have pastries for breakfast and lunch at *Moor Café*. We'd walk up that hill." He gestured to the mountains in the distance.

"Which one? The really high one?" That looked like a lot of effort, and yet she was practically turning green from the inside out she was so envious of this unknown woman who Luke wanted to walk up hills with.

"Whichever she liked. I'd hold her hand in mine and we'd talk about anything and everything she wanted. Her problems, her hopes, her fears. I'd want her to know I'll always be there for her."

"An active day, then." It suited him. Her heart ached to have him there for her, and to draw out his secrets and fears too. "What about the evening?" Was last night what he'd planned for someone else?

"There's a traditional English pub in Wildbrook. We'd go there for dinner and sit in one of those intimate warm little nooks and I would stare into her eyes."

"And then?"

"I'd bring her back here and kiss her on the sofa by the fire. Eventually we'd end up in bed. Or against the wall. Or on the floor rug. And in that shower afterwards, I'd stroke her until she was gasping with need again. I'd make her come until she was so replete she just curled into my arms and slept with her head on my chest."

"You have this all planned out." She was melting at the image he drew with his words. She wanted that to be her, and him. Jealousy at the thought of the faceless girlfriend chewed at her.

"Yeah." He heaved a sigh. "I guess I do."

"Why didn't you just get a girlfriend, and take her to all these places?" She forced the words out. He deserved a girlfriend who would appreciate him.

"Join Tinder or something. You'd have a girlfriend in five minutes flat." With his looks he could have any number of girlfriends.

"I don't want a girlfriend from Tinder. It wasn't a generic girlfriend I was planning these trips for."

That stole all the air from her lungs. There was a particular girl who he'd been thinking of all this time, and Emily had usurped her place.

"Is it important to you that your girlfriend could come away with you for weekends?" Because that excluded her. Why she was torturing herself, she didn't know. He had some other girl in mind. If it were her, he'd have been nicer to her for the last year, and he'd know that aligning their days off was impossible. She had Monday and Tuesday. He had Wednesday and Thursday. Unless there was a wedding or some other incidental Saturday, there was no deviation.

"Yeah." His arms tightened around her just as she would have pulled away. "It's important to me. I wouldn't allow the woman I love to think I didn't care about her or want to be with her whenever I could."

Emily could almost see the green tint of jealousy under her skin. The snow was slowly melting in the sunshine. They'd have to leave soon and she couldn't allow it to end, not yet.

"Do you think the roads are clear?"

"No. Not for a few hours."

They still had time. The relief was hot chocolate on a cold day.

"You offered to show me your house once."

She felt his soft laughter.

"If you got a car to drive there. I remember."

"Can I see it today? When we get back."

"Yes. But first…" He turned her in his arms, cupped her jaw, gazed straight into her eyes, and kissed her.

His house was exactly as she hadn't allowed herself to imagine when he'd first told her about it. Aged red brick with the imperfections and variations giving the house character with a bay window. The original stained-glass window spilt coloured light onto the hallway floor.

They'd had a lazy breakfast with coffee in their his-and-hers travel mugs, returned to bed and then finally, unfortunately, the snow had melted in the midday sunshine.

Luke had driven them back in comfortable silence. Fairly comfortable, anyway, so long as she hadn't thought about the dream girlfriend he planned trips for.

"Are you going to give me the tour?"

He smiled and she melted like the snow, unable to hold onto what she wanted.

"No, you give me the tour," he replied. "Sell me my house. Tell me what it's worth and why I should buy it."

"I've never seen it before."

"You've never done a viewing without seeing the house? Bullshit. 'Course you have. Think on your feet."

"You're an arsehole." But it was a fun game.

"Noted. I'll put your comment on file with the hundreds of other complaints to the same effect."

"Shall we go through to the front room? I think you'll find it's exactly the same as every other Victorian terraced house in this town and the bay window is draughty and allows the neighbours an excellent view of what you're watching on Netflix."

He laughed delightedly and turned into the room on the left.

She'd been completely wrong. It was not like every other front room in the area.

The room was decorated in a deep forest green, the obligatory enormous wall-mounted flatscreen and snuggly leather sofas with seafoam green silk cushions opposite. One whole wall was covered in real oak bookshelves, stuffed with every-thing from architecture coffee-table books to modern philosophy. The bay windows were obscured to chest height with simple privacy glass inset in double-glazed painted frame sash windows and the nook held a plain bench. The original Victorian fireplace had gorgeous patterned tiles and dried flowers in the grate. A potted Christmas tree was decorated with what looked like vintage baubles.

A tiny whimper escaped her. It was perfect.

"Great space, and so cosy, no?" She attempted to recover her composure. "There's underfloor heating." Since she couldn't see any radiators and her toes were toasty. "Lots of storage." She indicated the fitted bookshelves that looked too new to be anything other than less than a year old and what looked to be storage under a window seat. Her hand went out to lift the lid, but she pulled back just in time.

"Practical. You want to look inside?" he asked.

"Of course not."

"Come on," he crooned. "You want to snoop? That's part of the fun of viewing a house."

"I really shouldn't." But she lifted the lid of the bench seat and peeked. Power tools, screwdrivers, other tools she didn't know the names of. "The current owner seems to be a DIY enthusiast. And seems to be very diligent, based on the standard of work of those shelves and this window seat."

"Bet he was pleased with those. There's no garage, so gotta keep stuff somewhere." He leaned his shoulder against the wall and watched her explore the room. "The new occupier could repaint, if they found it too dark."

"I don't think it's too dark. I think it's perfectly snug."

That satisfied smile came out again. "Shall we see the kitchen?"

"Oh!" The exclamation popped from her mouth as she walked into the kitchen, which opened up further than she'd thought, with a big kitchen island. The walls were the slightest off-white and the cupboards a deep blue like the night sky. Light poured in from skylights in the ceiling. The whole room was clean and tidy, but it was also obvious he lived mainly here.

On the kitchen counter was a barista-style coffee machine, chrome glinting. She glanced at him before she opened the cupboard next to it, and he folded his arms with a look of amused patience.

She found the packet. An organic, bird-friendly brand she didn't recognise, but was clearly artisan and expensive.

"Now you know all my secrets," Luke drawled.

Hardly. She was desperate to know more about him, and had to restrain herself from examining the contents of every shelf, trying to be satisfied with the surface things instead. The teal sofa had an indent and a book laid on the arm, as well as more seafoam green silk cushions.

"These are so pretty." She skimmed the silk with her forefinger. "It's the same colour as the coffee cup you use for me."

He nodded.

"I have a dress in an almost identical shade," she added.

"I know."

"It's my lucky dress. Never lets me down. Whenever I'm nervous about something, I wear that dress, and it all turns out well. Never failed... Until that first day we met and you barely spoke. Took an instant dislike to me."

"Poor dress. Wrongly maligned."

She laughed at that. "Why wrongly? That first day was a disaster."

"I guess in some ways." He'd walked away from her, to the French doors that led out to the garden. "Not how I remember it, though." Unlocking them, he tilted his head in enquiry.

She nodded and followed him out into the cold. Despite the snow on the ground and the bare branches, you could see it was a well-cared-for garden. A neat rectangle of lawn, a large paved area with bulky shapes covered in tarps which were presumably a table and chairs and probably a BBQ. Plants trailed up the high fences that made it private. He wrapped his arms around her shoulders when she shivered.

"Not much been done outside," he said into her ear. "Do you think it has potential?"

"Yes. Easy maintenance, though. Just cut the lawn and you're pretty much done and sitting on the patio of an evening. You could use it exactly as it is."

"I think you're right. Come on, I've seen enough outside."

"We're still pretending I'm showing you around?" She allowed him to guide her back inside.

"Are you leading the way upstairs?"

This smiling, teasing Luke was so at odds with her work nemesis, she reflected as she climbed the open stairs from the dining part of the kitchen. Except, he wasn't. They were two halves of a whole.

"Two bedrooms on this floor," she said, checking the number of doors. "And a family bathroom."

"Probably a master bedroom upstairs. Might be an en suite, too."

"Three bedrooms. Perfect for resale value, appeals to a wide range of people."

He leaned against the wall. "Yeah? Why is that?"

"Professional couples needing an office as well as a spare room, as well as young families, or retired couples looking to downsize." She said this with a polished tone, as though he didn't already know it.

"Do you think this would be an appealing house for a young professional couple thinking of starting a family?"

"I... I don't know." She floundered. What was he suggesting? "I thought *I* was giving the tour."

"Three bedrooms. This one could be a nursery." He pushed open a door, revealing a spare room. "The creamy yellow is nice and neutral. Good for any gender. And that big garden. Great for kids to play in."

"I thought you scared people into buying via silence."

"Just because I shut up doesn't mean I don't know how to talk. I think we established that last night."

Her body flushed with remembered heat, and he saw it, his eyes going black.

"Is that an attractive option, do you think? The space to have kids."

She stared at him, chest tight. "For a lot of people..."

"What about you?"

"I've not thought about it much." She looked away from him, but instead of retiring into the hallway, she allowed herself to imagine the clutter of baby wipes and paraphernalia on the surfaces. Little clothes in the drawers. Honestly, it wasn't that she hadn't thought about children. Her body clock ticked as loudly as the next woman's. It was she'd given up on the practicality. There was no way she could work full-time and have a baby and manage with Eric only around at best two months in six, and frequently less. When they'd married children had been a long-off concept.

"Liar."

She shot her gaze back to him, a denial in her mouth. But his expression was so soft, so understanding, she couldn't push him away. She shook her head in disbelief. "How do you even know that?"

"Because you wear every emotion on your face. And—you may have noticed—I like looking at you."

There was a beat of silence and the moment for her to reply disappeared in a storm of things she wasn't brave enough to voice.

A ringtone from her pocket made them both turn.

"Is that..."

It was Eric's ringtone. The specific one that rang, whatever time of the day or night because she'd bought into the idea that she had to jump whenever he called. After seven years it was a hard habit to break. He would have just arrived back in the UK after his last trip. They'd barely spoken throughout the divorce.

She looked at Luke, who was studying his fingernails.

This could develop into something special with Luke, if they could take it beyond the one night they'd said. And *if* she could put Eric finally behind her. If.

Emily snatched up her phone and gave a breathless greeting and Luke's heart broke.

"Hi. Oh. Yes."

Say no, he begged her silently. *Stay with me. I'm the one who loves you.*

"Yes, sure. I'll be there in a minute."

He'd thought they'd made a connection, but the moment her ex crooked his finger she said, yes. And he, fool that he was, had fallen in love with her.

"I have to go." She slipped her phone into her pocket. "Something I need to sort out."

He didn't look up. There was no way he could look at her without showing his desperation. "Alright."

"I won't be long. I'll message you?"

"See you at work," he muttered through clenched teeth.

"Oh." She sounded a little hurt by his tone, but dammit, he couldn't be cool with her scuttling back to her ex. "I guess it is a bit impossible, what with us working together and..."

He didn't reply. She was right, but not for the reasons she thought. They couldn't work together anymore.

She had said it was just one night, and he guessed that was really the case.

But if she wanted to be his girlfriend, he was done with planning romantic days off and spending them alone. And if she went back to that cockwomble he wouldn't be able to keep his mouth shut about it any longer, and that would make for an awkward working relationship, to say the least.

In his office, he shoved open his laptop and began to type.

Whatever happened tomorrow, everything was going to change.

Chapter Nine

As she walked into work she was as nervous as that day almost a year ago. She'd dreamed Luke was holding her hand tight in his, not letting her go. Waking, she'd realised her hand had been trapped between her chest and the bed.

Auspicious.

Closing the door once and for all on Eric last night had been the right thing. He'd given her back the keys to her flat, she'd found the teapot that apparently had been his at the back of a cupboard. She didn't give a shit about it; she'd never drunk tea anyway. The conversation had been perfectly civil.

Except, she was terrified she'd inadvertently closed the door on Luke at the same time. She'd picked up the phone to call him a dozen times, and put it down hearing his response when she'd left. That he'd see her at work.

It had just been a one-night thing, that's what they'd agreed.

Here she was. She'd thought she'd beat him into the office for once, but he was early too. Everything as usual. Luke, gorgeous as ever, staring at his computer. Her seafoam green coffee cup on her desk waiting for her.

Like nothing had changed.

But dammit, she didn't want nothing to have changed after their night together. She wanted to shout and scream that he could plan trips for her. She could be his girlfriend.

She sat at her desk and glared at her coffee.

"It's not poisoned," he said after several minutes had passed.

"Just laced with chilli powder?"

He stood abruptly, strode to Pauline's desk and placed a letter in the middle. Unmissable.

"What's that?"

"My letter of resignation." He moved into the no man's land between their desks, leaned on the edge of his desk and watched her.

"You're leaving?" He couldn't leave. She was out of her seat and in front of him before she'd thought it through, panic in her heart. They'd begun to understand each other. If he didn't work with her and he spent all his time off with his girlfriend, she'd never see him.

"Yep."

"But... Why?"

"Jones and Gough offered me a managerial position. I took them up on it."

"But they're our rivals!"

He nodded.

"You don't want to work with me after..." She failed to find the right words for what had happened. *After you turned my whole world upside down.*

"No. I don't want an hour three times a week when we snipe at each other."

"Oh." She'd thought...

"Or at least, that's not all I want," he added, shoving his hands in his pockets.

"Why do you always do that?"

"What?"

"Put your hands in your pockets when you're talking with me. You don't do it with anyone else. I don't get it."

"Been watching me, huh?"

Constantly.

"You said you'd stop when I divorced Eric. Take your hands out of your pockets."

He nodded slowly. Then he reached, grabbed her by the waist and pulled her roughly into his arms.

"This is why I put my hands in my pockets," he whispered against her lips. "To stop myself from dragging you to me. Every single day you were within reach and I couldn't have you, I had to ensure I didn't touch you. Because I couldn't trust myself. I wanted—want—you so much."

Her voice was dead. Deceased. No words could come out of her.

He stroked the small of her back even as his other arm held them tightly together. She ran her hands over his shoulders in wonder.

"Don't go back to him," he said in a strangled, tortured tone. "If you don't want to be with me, I can live with that. But don't get back together with him.

He didn't treat you right. You deserve someone who will love you and put you first."

"I'm not going back to Eric."

His sigh of relief was a hurricane.

"And you don't have to say the other stuff. That I deserve someone who'll put me first..." And he'd said, *love*.

"You didn't hear anything I said over the last two days about how I would treat my girlfriend?"

"But that's someone else..."

"Someone I've been thinking about for a year, whom I bring coffee every day we're together. Someone I've been falling in love with since we met. Someone clever and funny and stunningly beautiful, and whom I just resigned my job for so nothing would stop us spending our days off with each other, if she wanted to."

All the oxygen had gone from the room. She was lightheaded.

"Someone I hope has recovered enough from her breakup to give me a chance."

"You don't mean me." That was too much luck for her. Extravagant luck, that he might want her.

"You've listened to all that," he said dryly. "And concluded I mean someone extraordinarily like you—alike in every detail—but not you."

"But..." This didn't make sense. "You hated me. All this time we quarrelled and you gave me one word answers."

"You were married." He shrugged. "I wasn't trying to fuck up your life. But now, there's nothing not worth the sacrifice. Not my job, not my pride. Whatever has to happen for us to be together, I'll do it."

"But you gave me no hint of your feelings." She wasn't sure what she would have done with that knowledge if she'd had it, or if she would have trusted it.

"None?" He raised a brow. "There was the coffee."

"I thought you picked it up on your way to work to shut me up."

He shook his head and rolled his eyes. "I didn't mean *bringing* you coffee, though that was pretty obvious."

"There wasn't anything else. Coffee or non-coffee based."

He sighed. "There were lots of things. I can't help myself with you. But you never opened your coffee before you took a sip? Not even once? Not even when you thought I was trying to poison you."

"No..."

His gaze flicked to the coffee on the desk. A latte in her seafoam green cup. He let her go and she unscrewed the lid with shaking hands.

And there in the foam was a simple and unmistakable sign in latte art. A symbol in milk froth and the caramel colour of the coffee.

A heart.

"You did this for me?"

"Not in the first month or so. But every day after that. Once I knew you better, yes."

And like this one symbol unlocked all the others, she could see lots of signs. The new seafoam green cup, the plans for trips together, the way he'd always pushed her to be a better sales negotiator.

He covered it over with plausible deniability, but he'd even tried to give her the money to buy a new car. She'd spent it on a manicure and new shoes and with the win, her confidence had been boosted when she most needed it. Luke hadn't turned up with a new car or some gesture that would humiliate her. He'd made her work for that money and made it satisfying.

It was obvious now she allowed herself to see it.

He'd known because he understood her better than anyone else in life. He loved her.

And she loved him.

All this time she'd listened to his curt words and thought they were at odds. Watching him and finding the perfect response had become a part of her day and a part of her. She'd refused to recognise what either of them said without words. His might be a gruff sort of care, but she'd had enough of superficial charm.

He'd told her she deserved better from her romantic relationship. He was right. She deserved him, someone who'd protected and guided her without hope of return. It didn't hurt that he was the most considerate and spicy lover she'd ever had.

All this time their conflict had been the friction of sexual tension and the fun of banter. Despite their height difference, they fit perfectly.

She reached up, cupped his rough, stubbled cheek and looked into his green eyes. "I love you."

He stilled. "You complain I don't talk, but I have one thing I want to say, and you steal it."

"I'm the chatty one. If you want to get a word in edgeways you'll have to be quick, or I'll keep saying it. I love you. I love you I love you I love you—"

"I love you," he said simultaneously with her before pulling her in to kiss her deep and hard, dragging her up his body and holding her tight to him, like he'd never let go.

And that was when clapping broke out behind them and Pauline said, "I thought you two would never get it together. Best ever office Christmas present."

Fancy more Luke and Emily? Get the Exclusive one year later epilogue into your inbox.

Want more sexy enemies to lovers with lots of banter? *Her Grumpy Neighbor until Halloween* continues the Wildbrook steam and angst.

Or start at the beginning of the *Secrets of Wildbrook* series. Clara is surprised by a billionaire turning up at the vet surgery with a poorly pregnant dog and offering to be her fake date to her ex's wedding in *Her Fake Date until Midnight*.

The Spark

Kimberly Quinn

Chapter 1

Grace

The overhead lights cut out, throwing the room into silent darkness and leaving me frozen with my hand clutched to my chest, breath caught in my lungs, and pulse racing.

"What the...?"

A chorus of "Happy Birthday" started from behind me—terribly off tempo and way out of tune—and I whooshed out a breathy laugh. Leave it to this bunch of wonderful weirdos to first scare the crap out of me, then torture me with their singing.

With a smile tugging at my lips, I turned to find the small group of co-workers I now considered friends crowded around a dimly lit table. When the heck had they found the time to pull this off?

Twenty-one candles flickered above the most beautiful cake I'd ever seen. It was shaped like an artist's pallet, covered in white frosting, and decorated with a stunning array of buttercream flowers that must've taken hours to create.

Whoever made it had serious talent... and possibly a sixth sense.

The final notes of the song faded, and a small lump formed in my throat as I stared at the cluster of petals. Each one was delicate, intricately woven with the next, and the perfect shade of periwinkle.

Not blue. Not purple. Periwinkle.

It was my favorite color and had been since I'd first discovered it in the giant box of crayons my grandmother gifted to me on my sixth birthday. It was that day, and finding that color, that had influenced me to become an artist.

I'd wanted to be just like her.

When I'd confessed my decision, she'd squeezed my hand and told me to aim higher. She'd said her attempts to recreate the classics were mere scribbles, and promised I was destined for something better. Something exceptional.

She was still my idol, but now, thanks to the inheritance she'd left, I was about to follow my dream all the way to Paris—the pinnacle of artistic ambition —to study at one of the most prestigious art schools in the world.

It was exciting and terrifying all at once. And it had all started with that pretty periwinkle crayon.

I'd never told anyone that story, though. It was a private, cherished memory that made me miss her even more. Yet, someone here had made this cake with these gorgeous flowers just for me. The coincidence was uncanny.

"Make a wish!" a voice called from the group, breaking me from my reverie.

The restaurant was about to open for the night, but instead of hustling with our usual last-minute preparations, the entire staff of Tremonti's had gathered to watch me blow out my birthday candles. It was a week early, but this was my last shift, and possibly the last time I'd ever see some of these people whom I'd spent the previous two and a half years working alongside. They really were a great bunch, and I would miss them all.

All except Levi Miller.

"Okay, okay." I smiled, still admiring the cake. "But this is too perfect for words. I have no idea what else I could possibly wish for."

My stomach knotted as I lifted my gaze to the expectant group, scanning the few tear-filled but otherwise beaming expressions in front of me. Until I met his eyes.

Impenetrable electric blue. Those eyes drew me in every damn time, and like a fool, I couldn't seem to get enough—no matter how much vitriol they cast my way.

I sank into his stormy glare, allowing it to consume me. And as always, it felt good.

So darn good.

My cheeks heated, and tingles coursed over my skin, the sensation building as it traveled. It was embarrassing and unwanted, and still, I couldn't look away.

Levi stared back, unflinching. His usual scowl was set firmly in place, with his jaw a chiseled rock, lips a tight line, and a deep crease formed between the dark brows that framed his captivating gaze.

Slowly, his eyes dipped, tracing across my face before sweeping down my neck, over my collarbone, and further still. It was just a look, but the light that caught in his eyes flashed like lightning, and his mouth quirked in a slight yet wicked sneer.

Why did he have to be so ridiculously attractive? And what was it about his simple gestures that made me feel so exposed?

It was as though he could see beneath my skin to the riot of sensation lashing within me. Like he knew the havoc his attention caused... and enjoyed it... but only because I didn't.

Nothing about him or his unfriendly scrutiny should have made me feel a darn thing. After all the hostile glares, brush-offs, and mumbled curses, the only thing I should've felt was bitter indignation. Yet, his gaze was so fierce—filled with such fiery intensity—it set my body ablaze. Every. Single. Time.

It was infuriating.

He might have been the most handsome man I'd ever met, and the only one who'd ever sparked such desire within me, but he was a grumpy jerk. A big, hot, grouchy a-hole.

Also, my brother's best friend.

I'd learned long ago, their friendship was a bond I could never cross, and no matter how often I'd fantasized otherwise, Levi Miller was not the man for me.

To him, I was still the annoying child he'd grown up with. The girl who never took no for an answer, tagged along on all their adventures, and cried when she couldn't keep up. During the time we'd worked together, he'd made it painfully clear I was nothing more than an obligation he couldn't wait to be rid of.

Not that I blamed him.

When I'd arrived in Vancouver from our hometown of Copper Cliff less than six months after him, then took a job where he was working, it had probably seemed like I'd followed along uninvited, once again.

In truth, the only school in British Columbia that offered the exchange program to Paris was here, and my brother, Cade, was the one who'd told me Tremonti's was hiring. I had no idea Levi already worked here. Although, I probably should've guessed since Cade hadn't left Copper Cliff, and there was no other way for him to know about the opening.

Still, I hadn't expected to be greeted with such disdain. Or sent away with it either.

"Just promise," I said to the group, even though my eyes were still glued to Levi's glower. "You won't forget me while I'm gone."

With a jolt, his gaze snapped up and caught on mine.

Maybe I only noticed because I was staring so hard, but I could've sworn for a moment the barrier he held between us dropped, and a hint of anguish peeked through. His eyes widened, bringing the sharp cobalt outline of his irises into full glorious view, and giving me a glimpse of the misery held within.

I could've wept from the beauty of it.

But just as quickly, that impervious wall was back in place. His gaze darted away, robbing me of the connection, shutting me out once again. I'd probably only imagined it anyway.

With a deep breath, I closed my eyes, tamped down my body's absurd reaction, pushed away the futile longing... and made a wish. It was silly to wish for the one thing I could never have, but I did it anyway. And I didn't regret it.

Not even when I opened my eyes to find Levi was gone.

After all, I had Paris to look forward to and a whole lifetime of memories to make. It was probably better if my future didn't include a grump who wanted nothing to do with me.

After several attempts, I blew out all the candles and everyone clapped and cheered. Someone turned the lights back on while I held back tears through hasty hugs and well-wishes.

The melancholy moment was over almost as quickly as it began, and I rushed to snap a photo of the cake before it was cleared from the dining room.

As I was slipping my phone back into my apron pocket, an incoming text lit the screen.

There was scarcely time before the doors opened to welcome our first guests of the evening—Tremonti's was always packed on a Friday night—but I checked that message anyway.

Now the regret hit me.

Why had I wasted my birthday wish on a man who'd never want me? If I'd have known what was coming, I'd have used that wish on my future. On Paris...

If I ever made it there.

Chapter 2

Levi

If I were a smart man—a man capable of thinking with anything other than his dick—I would have booked the night off work. Or called in sick.

Or hell... quitting was always an option, wasn't it?

The job was useless anyhow. Three years of working in Tremonti's kitchen had gotten me nowhere. I was nothing but a glorified fry cook with no formal education, no prospect of moving up, and no clue how to get what I wanted.

The absolute last thing I should have done was take on an extra shift, only to watch Grace Crawford blow out the candles on her birthday cake.

Fuck, just using the word *blow* and her name in the same sentence...

Well, those thoughts were the problem. The biggest fucking complication I'd ever come up against. One I had no idea how to solve.

The fact that she was moving off the continent should've been the fix.

All I had to do was make it through one more night. *Easy.* Then I could move on with my life, put her in my past where she belonged, and no longer have to face the attraction. The constant, agonizing temptation.

It would've been a helluva lot *easier* if she didn't look so innocent and enticing. So goddamn *willing*. If the fact that it was her last night didn't make me want to say *fuck it* all the more.

Why'd she need to wear her glossy hair in that tail I itched to pull? Blush so furiously every time she caught me looking? Or pout her ruby lips in that way that made my balls ache?

If even the joy-filled tears in her eyes didn't turn me on, then maybe I could've handled her reaction to the surprise I'd cooked up for her. I could've kept my mind from wandering to all the places it had no business going when she complimented my hard work. It might've even stopped my chest from cracking wide open when those innocent, heartfelt words tumbled out of her mouth.

Promise you won't forget about me while I'm gone.

As though it were possible. Like I hadn't already tried and failed to do just that.

I'd thought leaving her behind in Copper Cliff and starting a new life in the city was going to do the trick. But then Cade had to go and mention her—had to ask me to look out for his little sister while she was here—and all of sudden I was bringing her closer, securing her a job, and putting myself directly in the line of fire.

Now, with her looking more delectable than the goddamn cake, and me, such a hopeless disaster that even a bit of prolonged eye contact made me hard... Fuck me. My only option was to be a prick. Again.

It seemed to be my go-to move anytime I'd felt myself slipping. Which meant I was a righteous asshole whenever she was around. It sucked to be that guy, but this was the way it had to be.

She'd leave for Paris hating me, same way she had most of our lives, and I wouldn't need to worry about doing something I'd regret. The one thing I'd promised Cade to never do—let anyone hurt her. Not even me.

Fuck, especially not me.

And hurting her was the only possible outcome to this thing I'd been feeling. This obsession.

Because there were things in my life she didn't know about. Things she could never know. Hell, even Cade didn't know half of it, and if any of it ever spilled over... I could never live with myself.

So an obsession was all this could ever be.

What Grace wanted—what she needed and fucking deserved—was the kind of stability and commitment her parents had. Something my broken family was severely lacking. It was that sweet slice of pie in the sky, nothing can get us down, love with fucking sprinkles and a cherry on top kind of perfection. The type of relationship I knew nothing about.

So, instead of celebrating with the group, and doing the thing I'd specifically come here for, I left the room before she even had time to make her wish. Never mind the candles or watching her enjoy the cake I'd crafted just for her. I walked out, not willing to torture myself any further, and threw myself into the only thing I should have been focused on to begin with. Work.

Maybe without the distraction of Grace and her doe-eyed optimism to get in my way, I'd finally figure out what to do with my life.

Or I'd simply spend the next eight hours sulking over a hot grill in bitter silence.

It helped that we were slammed. Friday nights were always busy, but word that she was leaving had gotten around to some of our regulars, and they all wanted a chance to say goodbye. The lineup for a table was out the door, and by seven thirty, the wait time was so long we started turning people away.

By closing, we were all dead on our feet.

Which was fine by me. I was used to hard work and didn't mind feeling bone-weary—it was better than being frustrated and horny, any day. But Grace looked beyond tired, and that worried me.

I'd tried not to notice her coming and going from the serving window all night, but the few times I'd glimpsed her, she'd seemed not only fatigued but downright bleak. Like this night and saying goodbye was punishment, instead of one more step toward her brilliant dream future.

Her sadness dug at me, and the more I tried ignoring it, the deeper it burrowed. Until finally, I couldn't stand another minute of the irritation.

The kitchen had already shut down, and my workstation gleamed like never before, but the dining room had yet to clear out. There were always stragglers, but this night seemed to be wearing on forever.

I didn't care. I was done waiting. Done wallowing.

I marched out there, not giving a shit what anyone might think. "Grace. Time to go."

She whirled on me, her tawny eyes wide with... was that shock? Contempt? Rage?

"Come on." I motioned toward the door.

"I'm busy," she hissed, her eyes darting toward a couple seated nearby who seemed content to take their time—a half-full bottle of wine between them.

My annoyance was full-blown now—my fuse burning shorter than I should've ever allowed. Why the hell did I keep putting myself in these situations with her?

With my heart pounding in my ears, I stalked closer. And closer still. Until I was so near to her, I could see the flecks of green and gold in her forlorn stare. So close, all I wanted was to bend down and kiss her.

"You've done enough." The rough edge to my voice betrayed my need.

Her brow crinkled. "But I—"

"No buts. I said you're done, and I meant it." God, I really was an asshole.

With a heavy sigh, I eased back a step and tried adjusting my attitude. "Besides," I said. "What are they going to do? Get you fired?"

The corner of her mouth tipped up, loosening the ache in my chest just a little.

"Come on." Gently, I snaked an arm around her shoulders and maneuvered us toward the door. "You and I are leaving."

She followed along a few steps, then suddenly halted. "Together?"

I huffed a laugh. She was so goddamn sweet, she'd be the death of me.

"Yes, Grace." I hugged her to my side for a moment, relishing the feel of her body next to mine. She was short and curvy and fit just fucking right in the space under my arm.

If I could've stayed like that with her the rest of the night—the rest of my life—it would've been fine by me.

But when a dish clattered somewhere behind us, she stiffened, reminding me this wasn't the right time or place. There would likely never be a time or a place for us. She would always be the girl that could've been, if only I were a different guy. A better fucking guy.

I released her from the impromptu hug, taking her hand instead. "Come on," I repeated, tugging her along once again.

For now, the least I could do was keep my promise. I'd make sure she was all right, double-check her arrangements for Paris were set, and say goodbye like an older brother would. I'd send her off with a fucking smile—no matter how big the hole in my chest grew.

"Time to get the hell out of here... *Together*. Okay?"

With tears swimming in her eyes, she nodded. "Okay."

Chapter 3

Grace

T*ogether.*

Why did that one word make me so nervous?

It might have been the determination in his eyes, the bold way he slung his arm around my shoulders, or his no-nonsense tone. Or maybe it was simply that Levi Miller had never asked me to go anywhere with him. Not together. Not alone. Not ever.

Oh gosh... We would be alone, together, and I was in the middle of an existential crisis.

My meltdown wasn't because of our situation, though. For the first time, it wasn't his proximity or my body's outrageous reaction that was causing my distress. It was Paris, my future, and the giant roadblock in my path. The fear of having nothing to fall back on when things fell apart.

And based on the text I'd received earlier, my fear was real, because everything was crumbling to pieces. *Fast.*

What the heck was I going to do?

After grabbing my purse from the staff lockers, we stepped outside to the gloomy parking lot, and my overheated skin prickled from the cool evening breeze.

The sky was dark and overcast, and suddenly I missed the warmth of Levi's big body. For that split second when he'd cradled me under his arm, I'd felt calm and protected. Like everything was going to be all right—he'd make sure of it. He'd keep me safe.

But that was just a fantasy. No one else could fix this for me, especially not a grumpy man whose only goal was to get me on a plane and far away from him.

Guess he was in for some disappointment.

"Did you drive?" he asked, his fingers still linked with mine as we walked through the lot toward his truck.

"No." I swallowed back the utter panic and clung to his hand for dear life. "I sold my car."

I'd sold my dang car.

"Good."

Good? How on earth was that a good thing? No car meant the only way back to Copper Cliff was to call my parents. Then I'd be forced to explain what a screwup I was—how I'd wasted not only my grandmother's money, but the last two and a half years of my life.

They'd understand and wouldn't place the blame on me. Heck, they'd probably be happy to have me back home. But it was the embarrassment I'd feel. The heartbreak of such disappointing failure. The thought that, if Gran were still with us, she'd be devastated for me. For the loss of my dream.

I climbed into Levi's truck with my heart in my throat, the tears I'd been holding back finally spilling from my eyes.

He didn't seem to notice at first. Or perhaps he was just too uncomfortable to mention it. But as we drove, my silent tears turned to sniffles and then racking sobs, and he quickly steered the truck off the road, parking illegally along the curb.

The glare from the streetlights filtered in through the windshield, making me feel like I was on display. So many times I'd cursed his attention while secretly wishing for more. This was not one of those times.

I turned from him, furiously wiping at my smeared makeup and tears, wishing I was as invisible to him now as I'd been most of my life.

"What the hell, Grace?"

What the hell, indeed. There was no way I could explain this to him without sounding like a child. Without further breaking down. How could a man who oozed such confidence possibly understand?

I didn't know who I was without the art. Without this pathetic little dream, I was nobody. Heck, I was nobody *with* the darn dream, but now...

"You're worrying me," he said.

In my peripheral, he gripped the steering wheel in what looked like a stranglehold. Was it the frustration of dealing with my outburst that was getting to him? Or was he worried my brother would blame him for my breakdown?

"I'm sorry," I choked out between hiccupped cries, hating that I was such a liability to him—a burden and nothing more. "I just... I don't know what you want me to say. I don't understand what's happening right now."

"What's happening is you're having a panic attack in my truck, and I don't know how to help you if you won't fucking talk to me."

Oh, that was rich. This, coming from the man who avoided speaking to me unless necessary, and even then, acted like it was worse than shoveling crap.

Anger unfurled deep inside me, more powerful and frightening than ever before.

I turned on him with my heart speeding out of control and my mouth along for the ride. "You know what? Screw you, Levi. I didn't ask you to pull me out of work or force you to drive me anywhere. I didn't ask for your help or your pity, and I sure as heck don't need it."

"Pity?" He spat the word at me like it was laced with poison, his mouth twisted from the bitterness. "You think that's what this is?"

"Yes, that's exactly what I think."

My stomach fluttered as a look of fury crossed his features. He leaned toward me—his nostrils flaring and those impossible electric-blue eyes holding me captive.

"Well..." He crowded further and further into my space, his voice a low, gritty rumble. "You're wrong."

If he thought intimidation was the best way to convince me, he was the one in the wrong, and he'd be sorry he'd even tried.

Maybe I should have retreated. Should've backed the heck down, apologized, and called it a day. But I did not. Something about being in an impossible situation, with little hope, emboldened me. There wasn't much more for me to lose.

"After all the times you've been rude or flat-out ignored me, am I supposed to believe you suddenly care?" With my shoulders straight and head held high, I followed his lead, closing more of the gap between us.

"Grace." He said my name like it was a warning.

One that I promptly ignored.

My entire body vibrated with nervous, zinging energy. Yet still, I dared, "Prove it."

His breath hitched, enigmatic eyes flared wide, and for a moment it seemed I'd beaten him at his own game.

A cocky smirk tugged at my lips, the words, *that's what I thought,* on the tip of my tongue. It was a sour-tasting victory, but where Levi was concerned, I'd take whatever advantage I could get.

But my triumph was short-lived.

Without warning, his arm shot out, his hand grasped the back of my neck, and his fingers tangled in my hair. He tugged me closer, until our mouths were brushing and the scruff of his chin tickled mine.

"Just remember..." Warm breath skated over my lips. "You asked for this."

Leave it to Levi Miller to say something callous right before kissing me senseless.

His mouth covered mine in a blaze of heat and hunger, burning away all thoughts of right or wrong. His thorny demeanor was forgotten, as was the point I'd been trying to make. Forget about winning, or losing, or anything else at all...

The only thing that mattered was the hard press of his lips, the demanding sweep of his tongue, and all my pent-up desires finally breaking free.

His hand at my nape flexed, his fingers burrowing further into my hair, and he let out a desperate-sounding groan before taking our kiss even deeper.

It was like nothing I'd experienced before. No kiss had ever been so powerful. So all-consuming. So dirty.

And I'd never been so turned on in my life.

I reached for him, my hands frantically running over broad, muscled shoulders and down the wall of his chest. He was so big and solid—a rock I unexpectedly wanted to lean on. A man I wanted...

I turned my head, tearing my mouth from his—his lips trailing across my cheek with the movement.

The tears came flooding back, my breath catching on the regret. I wanted him. More than I wanted anything in my life. More than art school. Or Paris. I wanted him in a way he'd never want me back... and I just... couldn't.

He eased off, his hand shifting down to grasp my chin, and he gently nudged me back to face him.

I closed my eyes, unable or perhaps unwilling to meet his gaze.

A finger caressed my salt-stained cheek, but his voice was flat when he whispered, "Was that proof enough for you?"

Chapter 4

Levi

Her tear-stained face was breaking me, and the only thing I knew how to do was make it worse.

Was that proof enough for you?

Fucking hell. Could I be a bigger dick?

Based on the incensed look in her eyes when they snapped open, the answer was no. My condescension had done the job. We were back at square one—right where we belonged—with her pissed off and disillusioned and me in excruciating hell.

It was for the best. At least, that's what I kept telling myself.

That mantra would need to play on a never-ending loop if I were going to move on from this. Because that kiss... That kiss was pure fucking ecstasy. From her taste, to her soft sounds, and the way she'd opened so eagerly for me. Even when she'd abruptly broken it off, I'd been intoxicated.

But that was Grace. I'd been enraptured by her for as long as I could remember—since I was a scrawny, neglected kid who went to bed hungry most nights, and she was a vivacious little cherub who believed the world was magic.

Cade might've been my best friend, but it was Grace I'd stuck around for. Grace, I got into fights for. Grace, I now made myself the villain for.

Kissing her, though? Well, that had been a mistake. One that would cost me more than she'd ever know. And even though that kiss made me want to throw my frosty demeanor into the furnace, say to hell with it all, and make the effort to be someone different—the man she needed me to be—I had no fucking clue how.

And I was too damn chickenshit to try.

She jerked her chin out of my hold, and those delicate artist's hands that, only moments ago, were lavishing me with their attention, now pushed me away. It should've been expected. But as I relinquished my hold on her, and her hands fell away, the loss felt insurmountable.

"No." She retreated to her side of the truck's cab, her tongue darting out hesitantly to skim over her lips. "*That* proves nothing at all."

So, that's how we were playing this? With stony indifference?

"Well then, seems we're at a stalemate. I say I care... have all along, by the way... and you say I don't. How else are we going to resolve this thing?"

Her sigh was more like a pained groan of annoyance, but something about it wasn't right.

She threw the seat back and folded her arms in front of her. "Guess we'll never know," she quipped. "Can you please just take me to my apartment now?"

No, something wasn't right at all.

I hadn't imagined her earlier anxiety. She'd dissolved into outright panic as we'd driven away from Tremonti's. Those tears were real. This flippant act of exasperation was exactly that—an act.

But I didn't bother challenging her on it.

What was the point? It was better if she held on to this grudge, whatever the reason—real or make-believe. If she pushed me further away and kept me at a distance, then maybe I wouldn't be tempted to do something foolish. Like kiss her again.

Or proclaim my undying devotion like a lovesick fool.

It was after midnight when we rolled up to her building, but the streets were still busy with late-night partygoers. Most of them were students trying to soak in the last minutes of summer. School would be back in session soon.

And Grace would be gone.

I parked my truck, and without waiting for her to agree, jumped out and ran around to open her door.

She looked at me, bewildered. "What are you doing?"

"Walking you up to your apartment."

As though by reflex, I took her hand in mine, helped her down from the cab of my truck, and guided her toward the walkway. Surprisingly, she didn't argue. She remained quiet as we entered the front lobby, waited for the elevator, and rode up to her floor—our fingers entwined the entire time.

It wasn't until we'd reached her door that she finally broke the silence.

"Levi?" She hesitated, her eyes downcast and her grip on my hand loosening just a fraction. "There's something I should probably tell you..."

This was the moment. I could feel it. My make-or-break opportunity. And I was still sitting firmly on the goddamn fence.

Before either of us could take that chance, the door cracked open and a frazzled-looking girl poked her head out. "Grace! Thank goodness you're here!"

Her fingers, still laced with mine, squeezed tightly, while at the same time, her other hand landed on my arm, and she tried to turn me away from her unit.

Too late.

The frantic girl swung the door wide and threw her arms around Grace, enveloping her in a weepy hug. And I stood staring, with my arm awkwardly captured between them.

But it wasn't the stranger's seemingly over-the-top greeting that had my attention—it was the wrecked apartment.

This wasn't the mess of a busy college student who couldn't find time to clean. Or any kind of decorating style. And it certainly wasn't the organized chaos of someone preparing to move across the world in the next day.

The place had been ransacked.

Bare wires hung from the wall, where I was guessing there was once a TV, dirt and debris were scattered over the hardwood, and the couch cushions had been shredded. And that was just what I could see from the hall.

"Grace." I yanked my arm free of the unwieldy embrace and stepped inside her doorway to take a closer look. "Fucking hell. You've been robbed."

"Oh." The girl finally moved away from Grace, and smoothing a hand over her frizzy hair, acknowledged my existence. "You didn't tell him?"

"Tell me? You mean you knew about this? And who the hell is this person?"

"I'm Sinclair." Her face was a mess of tears, her clothes rumpled, and her hands wouldn't stop wringing, but the smile this girl gave me was so bright, I almost forgot to be suspicious.

Almost.

Grace interjected, her eyes darting between us and the ruined apartment. "Levi, this is my roommate, Sinclair... Sin, this is Levi."

"Yeah, duh," Sinclair tittered. "I kinda put two and two together."

Roommate? Fuck, this is how far I'd pulled away—how much of a barricade I'd placed between us—other than what I'd seen of her at work, I knew nothing about her life. No wonder she thought I didn't care. I'd gone out of my way and done everything in my power to prove to her I didn't.

This is what happened when I was too worried about shielding myself, and not focused enough on the one thing that mattered—protecting her. I'd tried to stay detached, and in the process, let her down.

"Okay..." I beat back my building frustration. Feelings of failure and remorse were useless right now. "What did the police say when you called them?"

"Police?" Grace winced, looking to her roommate.

I wanted to yell, but losing my cool wouldn't help. So I kept my voice low and tried to stay fucking calm. "You didn't call the cops?"

"So, this is all kinda my fault." Sinclair took a step toward me, her hand raised as though answering a question in class.

"No, it's not." Grace sounded sweet as always, but I could see the exasperation in her eyes. "Sin, would you mind if I had a moment with him?"

"Of course! I'm so silly. I'll just grab my purse and go for a little walk. Maybe head over to Zahara's place." Fuck, this girl was something else.

Grace gave her a pointed look.

"Okay, then. Bye!" The girl, Sinclair, bolted down the hallway toward the stairs and was instantly out of sight.

This time, it was Grace who initiated our hand-holding. Her elegant, talented fingers curled around mine, easing the apprehension, swirling in my gut.

"It's not her fault." Grace's head swiveled as we walked into the apartment, and she surveyed the ravaged room. Off to the side, the open bedroom doors revealed more of the same. "It's mine."

"Explain that to me, please."

Her attention flew back to me, a smile playing on those luscious lips. Lips that—if I could figure out what the hell was happening here—I planned to feel again.

"I think that's the first time I've ever heard you use that word."

I quirked an eyebrow at her. What the hell was she talking about?

"Please." She laughed. "It's the first time you've ever said please. Are you feeling okay?"

No. Fuck, I was nowhere close to okay, and nothing about this situation was, either. But she was smiling and laughing... And somehow, that made me feel better. Like the two of us, together, could make this all right.

The only question was, how?

Chapter 5

Grace

He did not laugh.

The furrow in his brow smoothed, and his shoulders relaxed just a little, but my attempt to lighten the mood had basically failed. Sure, his eyes may not be flashing murder at the moment, but the ticking at the corner of his jaw was a good indication it wasn't far off.

Admittedly, I was stalling. No part of this situation was amusing, not even his awkward use of manners, but it seemed a heck of a lot easier to make untimely jokes than to face reality.

Because the truth was, I was scared.

The damage to my apartment was worse in person—the hastily snapped photos Sin shared in her text hadn't captured the full extent of the loss—and I wasn't prepared for the brutality of it. Or how violated and helpless I would feel now that I was standing in the center of the chaos.

Yet, this mess and dealing with the repercussions paled in comparison to the prospect of facing my feelings for Levi. My belongings were gone, and I was on the hook financially for the damage, but all I could think about was him and the way he made me feel.

It was terrifying.

"Tell me." How was I supposed to pretend his growled words didn't affect me?

Especially when his fierce gaze kept diverting to my lips.

"This happened because of my bad decision," I said, pulling away from the enticing comfort of his big, warm hand.

The physical contact was too tempting right now, and it was better that I face this on my own. Even though he said he cared and was here showing signs that it might be true, I couldn't rely on anyone else to clean up my mess.

"I needed someone to take over my half of the rent while I was away, and Sin had mutual friends with this guy, Clint, who needed a place. He had references, but I should have trusted my gut because something about him just seemed off, and Sin has a habit of... Well, that doesn't matter and I'm not judging her."

The hand I'd been holding was now a tight fist at his side, and that tick in his jaw had intensified.

But I carried on, despite the growing tension between us, because this trouble couldn't be avoided any longer. "He moved in a couple months ago, and things have been... difficult."

"He was living here? With you?" On the outside, he was calm, but I could tell under his stony exterior, he was fuming.

He always seemed to hold back such unruly, passionate energy.

What would he be like if he ever set it free?

A shiver ran through me at the thought, and I wrapped my arms around my middle to try and stop the tremors. "I mean, we were all living here at the same time, yes."

"Where did he sleep?"

"Really? That's your concern right now?"

He was so darn overbearing. It frustrated and annoyed me, and yet, it was nice to think he might not be so apathetic after all.

The space between us quickly disappeared as he invaded it once again.

I did nothing to stop him. Maybe it was because his intense stare pinned me in place. Or maybe it was just that I liked being close to him so darn much.

I'd always liked it. Even when I pretended otherwise, I'd always wanted more.

Incapable of resisting his magnetic draw, I reached out to him. I needed his strength. His stability. His unwavering determination. Even if I had no idea how I'd survive needing him so much.

My hand landed on his chest, and his turbulent gaze intensified. But he didn't enclose me in his arms the way I'd imagined—the way I yearned for. Instead, he simply placed his hand over mine and flattened it over his heart.

Under my hand, his heartbeat was a violent echo of my own.

"You are my only concern." The words were matter-of-fact, but his voice was strained—filled with an edge of pain I'd never heard before.

But what the heck did it mean?

"He was on the couch at first..." I explained, trying my best not to succumb to my body's greedy response. "Then after about a week, he was sharing Sin's room. And I don't need a lecture about it or more of your questions or your domineering tone."

He opened his mouth as though to argue, but I held my other hand up to stop him. I honestly couldn't handle any more criticism right now.

"I know I messed up, all right? Clearly." My face felt hot and flushed, and the white button-down I'd been wearing all night suddenly felt like it was sticking to me.

"And I'm paying for it because he took all my bags, including the one with my passport. I can't leave for Paris on Sunday like I'd planned. Plus, it's my name on the lease, so I'm on the hook for all this damage and the rent if Sin can't find someone else to move in here. I can't afford all this and the cost of living in Europe."

I swallowed, my throat feeling tight and raw, but it was his heart beating so steadily under my palm that had me on the verge of tears. "Everything I've worked for is gone... So, I don't need you or anyone else to tell me what a failure I am. I already know it. I've already beat myself up plenty."

His merciless expression didn't shift. "You done?"

"What?"

His lips descended over mine, catching me off guard again.

This kiss was not hard and fast like the one before. It was soft, almost sweet. Yet the intensity was still there, vibrating beneath the surface, just waiting to be unleashed.

His hand came up to cradle my face, his thumb brushing along my jaw, and I melted.

But the kiss didn't last. He pulled away; his hands were still holding me, still stroking me, but his mouth was so far away—leaving me drowning in my own need.

"You're not a failure, Grace. And you're not a fucking quitter, either. You're the bravest, most beautiful girl I know. Inside and out." His low voice stroked the flame burning within me, but his words...

How long had I waited to hear him say words like that? "This is just a tiny fucking blip—one that's in no way your fault—and we're going to fix it. Okay?"

Unshed tears blurred my vision, my body at war with my emotions. "Okay."

"Good. Now tell me everything you know about this guy, Clint."

"What are you going to do?"

"I'm going to get your stuff back and make damn sure you get on that plane to Paris tomorrow. Whatever it takes."

My stomach sank, and those repressed tears released, dripping in a steady, unstoppable stream.

That kiss. Those words. His lust-filled stare. Maybe I *was* more to him than just a liability. He was offering to help me, and based on the determination in his voice, he'd succeed.

So why did I feel like everything was falling apart, instead of finally coming together?

Despite how tired I was, I couldn't rest. I'd been pacing the room for the last hour or more, worrying about all the things that might have gone wrong.

After telling him as much as I knew about Clint—where he was from, who he hung around with, and how Sinclair had kicked him back to the couch a few nights ago—Levi took charge.

He'd done it with his usual gruff and demanding attitude, swearing up a storm with each new detail I'd revealed. But he said I was in luck because he knew a guy who knew another guy who could find anyone. It was no problem. He'd find Clint and my stuff.

I didn't understand who all these shady-sounding people were or how he knew them, but I didn't question it. I was just happy to have some hope. Even if that hope came with a big side of confusion and a healthy dose of fear.

Once he'd left, I'd spent an hour or so cleaning. The damage wasn't as bad as it had first seemed. Most of it was superficial—dirt, garbage, and some broken dishes. There were a few big losses, like the ruined couch and all the food dumped on the floor, but thankfully, my room was untouched. I could sleep in my bed tonight and not worry.

Sin's room, on the other hand, looked like a tornado had gone through. Her clothes were in tatters and strewn around the room, which smelled a bit like a urinal.

What happened here was obviously personal, and it frustrated me that she'd let it come to this. But I couldn't blame it all on her. Not when everything in my gut had told me from the start that letting him in was a bad idea.

Finally, after too many anxious hours spent worrying about Levi's safety, someone banged on the door.

A shock of excitement sparked in my belly.

It could be anyone on the other side, but that didn't stop me from flipping the lock and opening it wide.

Levi stood in the pale-yellow lights of the hallway, looking like a pissed-off god. "Did you even look to see if it was me?"

"Yes," I lied. "Are you okay?"

"I'm fine. Now, let's go." He held out his hand for me to take.

I ignored it and launched myself at him instead, forcing him to catch me in a hug. His arms wrapped around me, squeezing me tightly, but he let out a short, pained grunt as he did it.

"What happened?"

"Doesn't matter," he said. "I have your things."

I pulled back to look at his incredible electric blues. "You did it? You found my stuff?"

"Fucking right I did, sweetheart. I even got the rent. Now let's get the hell out of here."

Chapter 6

Levi

"Where are we going?" Her soft gaze traced over me. If it weren't for my bruised ribs and aching shoulder, that look would've made me feel invincible.

I hadn't been prepared for her to fling herself into my arms at my arrival. Not that I was complaining. No amount of pain could make me object to physical contact from Grace. I craved it too damn much.

But fuck, I was hurting.

Clint was a mouthy little shit, and he'd been sitting with a truck's worth of stolen goods when I'd found him. At his mother's house, no less. Right where I was told he'd be. Part of me wanted nothing more than to teach him a lesson. To show him that messing with Grace would always result in a beating from me.

It wouldn't have been the first time I'd hurt someone to protect her. There'd been more than one asshole who'd learned the hard way to show some respect and leave her the hell alone. But this time, my fists weren't necessary.

Sure, it might have been satisfying to punch the cocky smirk off his face, but it didn't seem worth the trouble. Not when all it took was one snarled warning for the bastard to hand over her things. And not when I knew how much she'd disapprove of the violence. Plus, it felt wrong in front of his mom.

I hadn't needed physical force in order to deliver the message, so I chose not to use it. My injuries weren't from fighting, but from missing a step on a flight of stairs with my arms full.

"You can't stay here." I smoothed my hands down her back, savoring the feel of her curves pressed against me and wishing like hell she were even closer. "I doubt Clint will try anything else. Hell, the cops might've even picked him up by now. But it's better to be safe."

"You called the police?"

I gave her a sly smile. "I did."

It was cute that she was so easily impressed. Although, if she understood how unusual it was for me to be on this side of the law for a change, she might've had different feelings about it. And if she knew that I'd demanded the money from Clint's wallet right before I'd called in my anonymous tip...

Yeah, I doubted she'd appreciate that part much at all. But I couldn't feel guilty about it.

Not when it had solved her problem. Especially not when she kept looking at me like I was her goddamn hero. Like maybe I wasn't so much of a villain after all.

Still, it wasn't lost on me that the part of my life I'd wanted to hide from her—the things I'd worried could hurt her—had actually saved the day. The unsavory people I knew, the connections I had, and some of the favors I was owed, had suddenly come in handy. Without them, I might've never found Clint.

On the other hand, if it wasn't for all the secrets I'd been keeping, I might've been around to prevent the entire drama from happening in the first place. I could've been here to protect her—to keep my promise, and maybe even enjoy my time with her in the process.

God... All the ways we could've indulged in that time...

"You didn't answer my original question."

Was it any wonder? With the blush back in her cheeks, the teasing lilt in her voice, and my mind firmly in the gutter, it was a fucking miracle I could form a coherent sentence.

She laughed at my confused silence before asking, "Where are we going?"

"Right... A hotel." It seemed the obvious choice. The safest one for me, anyway. Because the only other option was my place, and if Grace were to lay her head on my pillows, I'd never want her to leave.

She tensed, and the sweet expression she'd been wearing turned rigid.

"But just you. I'll drop you off," I rushed to explain, not wanting her to get the wrong impression. "Hotels are relatively secure—no one will bother you—and if you're closer to the airport, it'll be easier to make your flight."

All good, logical reasons. Yet, she didn't seem convinced.

The color had drained from her face, and her gaze darted away. I knew she was tired—she had to be after all she'd gone through—but this wasn't exhaustion shutting her down. This was Grace retreating. Protecting herself. Hiding her beautiful light. From me.

"Is that okay?"

The weak smile she gave me nearly broke my damn heart. "Yeah... perfect."

Was it?

It sure didn't feel perfect. Not the catch in her voice, the weary resignation in her eyes, and definitely not the detachment I could feel slowly growing between us.

She pushed out of our embrace, and I let her go.

It was the last goddamn thing I wanted to do, but what alternative was there? As much as I wanted, I couldn't keep her in my arms forever. Even if I'd hoped things might end differently. After everything we'd said and done, I'd hoped...

Ah fuck, that was the problem. I'd pinned it all on hope. Something I should've learned by now was a waste of goddamn time.

There was no point wishing or dreaming—I'd never be the right guy for her. She had her whole life in front of her, packed with so much damn potential. She was smart, gorgeous, and headed for Paris.

And I was... still going nowhere.

Without wanting to drag things out any further, I made short work of driving her to a decent hotel. I waited while she checked in, then escorted her to the room. All in total silence.

I felt more like a hired thug or a bodyguard than I did her brother's best friend. *Her* damn friend. Which was probably for the best. If I could pretend we were strangers—if I could shut off these damn emotions, the same way I'd ignored them all along—then I had a chance of surviving this. The devastation of saying goodbye might not fucking kill me.

The luggage cart was emptied, and I watched as she fussed with a few of her bags. She was here. She was safe. And in just over twenty-four hours, she'd be gone.

"You all set?" I asked, reluctant to go.

Her head popped up, a look of anguish crossing her delicate features. "You're leaving?"

"That was the plan." Fuck, I still sounded like a heartless dick.

"Please don't." Her words were barely a whisper. So soft, I wondered if she'd really said them or if I was making up something I'd only longed to hear.

When I didn't budge, didn't respond, she made a bold move toward me.

I stood frozen—sparks of hope building inside me once again.

"Levi..." She advanced with slow, steady strides. "I want you to stay. With me."

Still, I couldn't answer. I didn't know what to say. Didn't want to risk breaking this exquisite fucking spell I was under.

Instead, I waited, my heart ready to burst out of my goddamn chest and my arms itching to hold her. I watched and endured the desperate plea of my body as step by cautious step, she came to stand before me.

Apprehension flared in her tawny gaze as it searched mine. "I need you, Levi," she murmured and bravely curled her fingers around the buckle of my belt.

"Grace," I groaned, the pain of wanting her almost more than I could bear. "I can't... We shouldn't."

She shook her head, tears forming in the corners of her eyes. "Why not? You said you cared. Heck, you went out of your way to prove it. Am I reading you wrong?"

"No, sweetheart..." I pulled her hands from their loose hold, up to run my lips over her knuckles. "You read me just fucking right. I'd like nothing more in this world than to lay you in that bed, take you nice and slow, and then watch the sun come up with you beside me."

"Then why don't you?"

Unable to resist, I pulled her into my arms. "Because I couldn't live with myself. You mean more to me than that... You are *worth* so much more than that. More than one night in a cheap motel room."

Her head fell forward on a groan until her face was buried against my chest. I cradled her there, running my hand over the silky tail of her hair.

"Will you stay anyway?" she asked, her voice muffled but not at all timid. She shifted to look up at me, piercing me with her sorrowful gaze. "We can just sleep. Or watch the sunrise. Please."

What could I say? Goodbye would hurt either way.

And for Grace, the agony was worth it. "How could I say no when you used my favorite word?"

A genuine, glorious smile spread across her luscious lips, and I couldn't help but return it.

I smiled so wide my face felt like it might break. It was a foreign fucking feeling—this giddiness. It felt infectious. It felt incredible. And for one sublime moment, I wasn't only in love with her... I was almost happy.

Chapter 7

Grace

The smile on his handsome face was real. It wasn't his usual snarl or smirk, or even a forced condescending grin. This was the smile of a man who'd spent so much of his time in self-imposed misery, I thought he might've forgotten how.

And it was wonderful.

"I think you just like hearing me beg." My face flooded with heat at the realization of how those words must sound. When had I become such an intolerable tease?

"Fuck, sweetheart." His gruff voice sent a shock of lust running through me. "You have no idea. But right now, I'm the one who's begging... Please, please don't make this harder than it already is for me."

That wonderful smile slipped—replaced by a look of pained conviction.

"I'm sorry." *So sorry.* Sorry I'd ever allowed him to push me away. Sorry I hadn't seen clearly from the start...

He wasn't a snarly jerk for the fun of it or because I was a nuisance he couldn't stand. Or even because I was an obligation he resented. He acted like a miserable a-hole because he thought that's all he deserved.

Levi Miller didn't believe he should be happy.

How had I never seen this before? My heart hurt both *for* him and *because* of him. Because no matter how much I wanted to stay and help him discover the joy he'd been missing—to explore whatever was happening between us—I couldn't.

He'd never let me.

But he was right not to. I respected him all the more for that.

I'd been chasing my artistic dreams of Paris for too long and had worked too darn hard to simply walk away from it. Especially after what he'd done to help me make it this far. I had to go and make Gran proud. Make Levi proud.

And I had to do it for myself.

But I felt the same way about him. How could I turn my back on him? On what this could be for us?

The warmth of his mouth was moving over the backs of my hands again, reminding me I was cherished and protected. Like a queen. But I didn't much appreciate the view from up here—from this pedestal he'd placed me on. How long had he been propping me up, without me even noticing?

How much lower would he let himself sink?

"Why does it have to be all or nothing?" I asked, dizzy from the whirlwind of emotion tearing through me.

The line of his jaw seemed to sharpen as a dark look passed over his features. "Because there's nothing in the middle but uncertainty."

"That's not true." I dragged my hands from his, moving to grip his broad shoulders and bringing our bodies flush. "What's between us right now?"

His arms encircled me as though by reflex—his pained look intensifying as he shook his head. "I'm not sure."

"Me neither," I admitted. "But that's not uncertainty, Levi... That's possibility."

It was a spark of something good and a chance I was willing to take.

"What are you saying?"

To me, the answer was obvious. I could see the future stretched out before us, like a painted canvas on display. I could see all the soft lines and hard edges. All the unexpected twists and hints of inspiration. Up close, it was messy and hard to interpret, but from a distance, even the mistakes became a beautiful work of art.

But could Levi see it?

I lifted up on my toes and skimmed my lips over his hardened jaw, hoping like heck I could show him.

"I'm saying..." I kissed the slight divot in his chin, delighting in the rough feel of his scruff against my lips. "I understand if sex is off the table. You've respected my boundaries when I've drawn them—it's only fair that I do the same for you. So I'm not asking for that... Not right now, anyway... But I'll be gone for less than a year."

His arms flexed, pulling me impossibly closer. "A year's a long time."

"It is." My mouth danced a short path toward his, pausing just below the curve of his bottom lip. "But it's not so long that we shouldn't try. We can work on this thing between us. We have phones and can video chat."

His eyebrow raised and I smiled at the image of Levi gabbing on the phone with me. "We can work on our communication," I said through a laugh. "Long-distance relationships can work."

"Sweetheart, I'll talk to you every damn day if that's what you want. I just don't think you should make any promises. You'll meet new people and see things..." His voice hardened, and my breath seized. "Things I'll never get to see. You might change your mind, and I wouldn't want you to feel bad about that."

He was going to say no. He was going to deny himself, and in the process, punish me.

I brushed a kiss over his mouth, blocking the rest of his protest, and whispered, "Please stop trying to shelter me from every little harm. It's not your job, and it's an impossible one, anyway. Trying to guard my feelings is only hurting them."

He reared back, his hands flying up to clasp my face in a desperate grip. The electric-blue gaze that I was so infatuated with searched... For truth? Or meaning? The secrets of my darn soul?

Whatever he was seeking, he could have it. I'd give it to him willingly.

"Fuck... I'm sorry. You're right, and I'm so fucking sorry."

"Don't be," I said with a smile. "Despite all my tears, I'm not that fragile."

"No, you're not." With a heavy sigh, he spread his hands wide over my back, his fingers tangling and tugging at my hair. "You've always been strong and brave. Braver than me, anyway."

"Oh, I don't know... I've never been brave enough to admit my feelings for you. I always just pushed myself in front of you and hoped like heck you'd notice me."

A wicked smile tugged at the corner of his mouth. "Trust me, I noticed. I have *always* fucking noticed. You've always had my undivided attention."

"*Always?*" I teased.

"Yes, Grace... I think I've always wanted you." His voice broke over the words, and I thought my heart might've cracked along with it. But then he kissed me.

His mouth fused to mine in a hard and urgent rush, sending a quake of desire straight through me.

But the firm line of his lips softened as he kissed me, roaming in a languid, lingering path across my own. He sipped and savored. Every slight shift of his mouth, like an erotic, intoxicating adventure.

He kissed me until my lips felt raw and both my mind and body had yielded.

"Did you want a shower before bed?" he asked, running his fingers through my hair.

What I wanted was more of him. More of his kisses, his touches, his body. But I'd already promised not to push him for more than he was willing to give, and even if it was torture, I had to honor that.

"I'm not sure it's such a good idea... You're the only thing holding me up right now."

"Come here, then." He lifted me into his arms and carried me to the bed, placing me gently on top of the covers.

I held firmly to him, trying desperately to drag him down beside me, but he straightened like a shot, a look of sudden panic on his face.

"Shit, I almost forgot... Wait here."

Before I could protest, he was striding across the room and out the door.

As the minutes ticked by, my heart stuttered and stalled and my breath became a nervous pant. What the heck was he doing? Was he leaving me here? Had he decided I wasn't worth the effort after all?

I held back my sob as a single tear carved a jagged path down my cheek and dripped from my chin.

But then the door banged open, and Levi was stalking into the room toward me with a large Tremonti's cooler bag in hand.

When he saw the look on my face, he froze. "What the hell, Grace?"

Yes, what the *hell*. "Nothing... I'm just really tired."

With a skeptical look, he climbed onto the bed, holding out the cooler for me. "Well, I hope you're not too tired to enjoy this."

"What is it?" I asked, my pulse finally returning to normal.

"I went back for it after I got your stuff from Clint. I figured you should have more than a photo."

My hands shook as I slowly worked the zipper—Levi's electric blues watching me the entire time. With my breath held, I flipped the lid.

Rows upon rows of pretty periwinkle flowers greeted me from under a plastic lid.

"You stole the cake for me?"

"Fuck no, I didn't steal it," he said, the conviction in his voice making me shiver. "It's yours... I made it for you."

"*You* made this?" Now my entire body was vibrating, and new tears joined the one that was drying on my cheek. "Levi, it's so perfect. This color is my favorite... How did you know?"

He shrugged. "You carried that damn crayon around with you for years."

Carefully, I moved the cake aside and then launched myself at him, throwing my arms around his neck.

He caught me in a solid hug, just like always. He was always catching me. Always there for me. Even when I hadn't known it.

"Does this mean you're willing to try with me? You'll wait for me, and we'll make this thing work?"

"Sweetheart, I baked you a fucking cake; doesn't that prove I'm willing to do anything?"

We spent the few hours left before my flight talking, sleeping, and eating delicious cake. For the first time, we were on equal ground. And even though my departure loomed, and I'd cried more times than I could count... I was happy.

When we finally said goodbye, I knew the sad smile on Levi's face wouldn't be the last I'd ever see. Besides, I'd waited most of my life for him.

What was one more year?

Want to know what happens after Paris?
Get Burn for You, book one in the Copper Cliff series, to find out.

Kimberly Quinn is a steamy romance author, born procrastinator, and grumpy hero lover. For news about her steamy heartfelt stories, exclusive excerpts, give-aways, and more, sign up for her newsletter. www.kimberlyquinnbooks.com

Wheels vs Blades

Echo Grayce & Melissa Ivers

Chapter 1

Weston

I need to get laid.

Especially when I was looking up sex tricks for dummies and stumbled on a webpage that said your nuts could shrivel up inside your body from disuse. After I got that horrifying image out of my brain, I decided it was well past time to get rid of my v-card.

If the guys found out—if the media found out—I'd be the laughing stock of the NHL. The only twenty-three-year-old virgin in existence. Okay, maybe not the only one in all of existence, but the only one in the NHL.

These guys are all notorious playboys, and while I don't ever see myself living up to that status, it's time to take that card out of my wallet and set it on fire.

I've paid my dues, I've dedicated my entire life to hockey, and now that I finally got my first two-year contract with the Nashville Devils, it's time to live my life a little.

We're out of town in Boston, and I can't think of a better place to let loose and have some semi-anonymous sex.

Okay, maybe not all that anonymous considering we're only a few blocks away from the hotel, still wearing our game day suits, and most of these guys surrounding me are big time hockey players. Not me, but I'll get there.

"Hey there." A pretty little blonde sits next to me, giving me a sly smile. She has on the classic little black dress, emphasis on little.

"Uh, hi." I wave because I'm obviously shit at talking to a real woman and have no idea what I'm doing. I'd have better luck talking to a puck. I glance across from me to Dimitri Kozak, our goalie, who gives me a thumbs-up and grins, nuzzling into the giggling brunette in his lap. He's awkward as fuck too, and I should in no way, shape, or form consider him a role model.

"So." Her smile widens, and she puts her hand on my thigh—high on my thigh, like we're talking inches from my dick—and gives it a squeeze. "So you play for the Devils?"

"Yeah. I'm Weston. Weston Gray." I clear my throat, squirming in my chair as her nails dig into my dress pants, and she runs her other hand over my chest.

All sorts of alarm bells start going off in my brain. I'm not sure if they're telling me to get up and run or sink down in my chair to force her hand to go higher on my thigh.

"That's nice." Her hand continues to go back and forth across my pecs, and she leans in to whisper. "You're a hockey player, and I fuck hockey players. That's all I need to know."

Okay, the alarms are definitely telling me to get the fuck out of here.

Easy isn't going to get it. I know I said I want to set my v-card on fire, but maybe I want the other person to know my name. Maybe I want them to fuck me for a reason other than my NHL status.

I look over at Dimitri who is now completely entranced by the bunny on his lap, and before I turn back to the lady beside me, I catch sight of my teammates Tag Harris, Foster Craig, and Rhett Remington. Those three used to have a reputation as playboys, but are now very happy with their wives and girlfriends.

Maybe I need something in between an anonymous one-night stand and a committed relationship.

The woman next to me toys with the top button of my white dress shirt, and I push her away and stand. "Sorry, I've got to ... not be here."

Without waiting for her response, I grab my beer and hightail it over to the bar, slipping on the barstool Rhett vacated seconds ago.

"Hey, guys. I think I need help," I blurt as they each grab a beer from the tattooed hipster bartender.

"With what?" Tag turns around, his brows raised.

Foster eyes me, taking a sip of his beer. "Your slap shot?"

"Your skating?"

"Your choice of clothing? Your personality?"

"Your new Vanilla Ice hair style?"

"Yeah, looks like your barber might need a new pair of glasses or something."

"Whoa." I hold up my hands, anything to get them to stop all the insults, and run them through my hair—the hair I thought I liked. "What's wrong with my hair? And my personality?"

"Eh." Foster shrugs, taking another sip of his beer.

Tag looks me over, rubbing his stubbled chin, looking like he's deep in thought, and I know I'm about to get insulted again. "Don't worry... Baby Ice? Little Vanilla? Hanging out with us long enough will make you more likable."

I let my head fall back and groan, my fingers tightening around my beer bottle. Maybe this isn't the night and this whole thing is a mistake. Maybe I'm meant to die a miserable virgin with way too much lube in his nightstand and arthritic fingers on my right hand.

"Well, this was fun—"

"We're only fucking with you, rookie. What's going on? Tell your Uncle Tag what's bothering you."

Yep. Big mistake. "Forget I said anything. I'm going back to sit with Dimitri. Maybe he'll have some advice."

Foster nudges me with a laugh. "You know he talks to the goal post. Our advice will be better than anything he has to say. Come on. Out with it, mate."

"I just..."

"It can't be that bad."

"It might be." I sigh and then finish my beer while Tag and Foster stare at me expectantly. I sigh again, fiddle with my empty bottle, put it on the bar and avoid all eye contact.

Yeah, this was a pretty fucking bad idea. Am I ready to tell someone I'm a virgin?

Tag slaps my shoulder, hard I might add, and points in my face. "If you don't spit it out, I'm going to punch you in the face. I don't care how nice this bar looks–I will fuck you up."

I take a deep breath, and the words come out of me in a rush. "I've spent my entire life dedicated to hockey. I've never had sex, and there's a good chance my balls are going to shrivel up and die."

"Wait..." Tag's mom-arm shoots across my chest, cutting off my words and almost hitting me in the throat. His voice lowers as he says, "Did you seriously just imply that you're a virgin? Is that what I'm hearing?"

"The rookie is a virgin?" Foster bumps into my shoulder, looking way more amused than he should. "How old are you, rook, twelve?"

"Okay, fuck you guys," I mumble, trying swivel around on the barstool, but Tag's arm remains firmly in place.

He rolls his eyes and glances over to the table where the rest of the team are seated. "I can't believe you were going to ask the goalie for lady advice. He's as appealing as a fence post. Yeah, he's got a bunny on his lap, but he's got his arms all over her like he thinks he's an octopus, and if you've ever seen one in person, they're not sexy. And look at her face. He's trying to kiss her, and she's trying to maneuver around so he doesn't poke her in the eye with his big nose."

I blow out a frustrated breath and loosen my tie. "It's not a big deal, okay?"

"Not a big deal," Foster repeats slowly, shaking his head. "Spoken like someone who needs to get laid, and I say that as a practically married man."

"How did this happen?" Tag passes me a second beer, nodding toward my face. "You're not a terribly unattractive guy."

"Gee thanks." I glance around the bar and ignore the glare from the blonde who's now cuddled up to another one of the guys. See, she's doing just fine without me. "You guys know how it is. Hockey, hockey, hockey. My parents were pretty strict growing up, and I was barely allowed to even have friends. They wouldn't allow anything that would interfere with my hockey schedule, and when I went to college, I stayed at home. I kept my head down and worked as hard as I could to make it into the NHL."

And now that I'm here it's time for a change. I *need* to change.

Losing my virginity is just the start. A way to take my life back because outside of hockey, I'd like to have one.

"I get that." Tag huffs a breath, running his hand through his long blond hair and tossing Foster a look. "Hockey's tough, but you made it. So, what's the problem now? There are literally bunnies everywhere, and all they care about is your name on that roster. Maybe not that blonde one talking to Victor, she's giving you a death glare."

"And if talking to women makes you nervous, most of them don't give a flying fuck what you have to say," Foster adds, his gaze traveling over to the rest of the team where the bunnies have, in fact, descended. "They just want a ride on your knob. Something to either tick off their bucket list or give them hope you'll keep them around and buy them shit."

"Yeah..." I run a hand through my hair, casting a quick glance back to the blonde and Victor. "I don't know. Is it too much to ask for a girl to actually be interested in me?"

Tag laughs and slips his hands in the pockets of his dress pants. "That depends. Are you looking for a connection or a quick fuck?"

"Both?"

Foster has his phone in front of him, his fingers flying across the screen when he says, "Avery says you need to find someone you're attracted to and start with a conversation. See if you have chemistry, things in common. Sorry, rookie, I had to pay her to fake date me and before her, I had a lot of one-night stands. No connections. No strings. Nothing."

"What do you like?" Tag points around the large open bar. "Maybe not blondes? Redheads? Brunettes?"

What do I like?

I let my gaze wander around the bar, taking in the multitude of women, but none of them really catch my eye. This seems a little counterintuitive to finding a girl who actually likes me, but I guess I need to start somewhere. Make sure there's at least a base of attraction first.

Looking far away from the bunnies surrounding the team, I check out the pool tables toward the back of the bar and nothing. This clearly isn't my night.

I really should... Holy shit.

She's gorgeous. Different from all the other girls in here. She seems confident in her own skin. Her shoulders are back, her smile is genuine, and there's a little evil glint in her eyes as she points her cue at her opponent's face. I bet she knows exactly who she is and what she likes. I bet she wouldn't compromise her morals and settle for anything less than what she deserves. I bet she's not afraid to try new things, not afraid to break away and walk her own path.

"That's the one. That's what I like." I gesture toward the pool tables, keeping my eyes glued to every single one of her curves, and for the first time tonight, my blood's pumping through my veins, sparking my entire body into overdrive.

My dick twitches in my pants. Him too.

Tag squints, looking in the right direction, but the pool tables are crowded and the light is a little low. "The busty redhead in the football jersey?"

I shake my head, watching her rub a hand up and down the pool cue, imagining what it would feel like to have that hand on my cock. "The one with the purple hair, tight jeans, and an ass that's just..."

She bends over to take a shot, and that's all I need to lose my train of thought. That denim molding her ass and thighs is enough to drive me crazy. The rips in the fabric, giving me teasing views of the pale skin underneath, has my hands itching with the need to feel it beneath my palms.

My heart races, my mouth waters, and I need to know her name. What makes her tick. What makes her come.

I'm getting ahead of myself, I know, but I almost need to get her beneath me.

She's my exact opposite in every way, and she's fucking perfect.

"Bloody hell," Foster mutters. "I feel like I should be the responsible one and point out that you're still in training wheels, and being with that girl would be like jumping on a Harley with no clue how to ride a bike."

"She's out of your league."

"She'd break you in half."

Tag puts his hand on my shoulder and glances across the bar and then back at me. "She looks like a badass super villain, and you're like Captain America and Vanilla Ice had a love child."

"She's going to tell you to fuck off."

"Probably. And then threaten to cut your dick off."

I shrug, my eyes never leaving her delectable curves and whatever that black lacy thing is under her white tank top. "I'm a big bad hockey player. I can do this. Let's go play some pool."

Chapter 2

Emerson

"I'm up, rack 'em," Coach calls over as he grabs a cue from the wall. He stands it on its handle, runs his gaze up the length, shakes his head, and puts it back and reaches for another.

I snort at his picky ass as I rearrange the balls in the triangle. "Good. I've been waiting to kick your ass. You benched me, you shithead." With three quick glides of the triangle counter-clockwise, I come to a smooth stop on the footspot. A flick of my wrist later, I'm ready to whoop Coach Hung-Like-A-Horse's sweet ass.

His ass is taken–very taken–if how quickly he and Maisy started shacking up together is any indication, but as long as there are eyes in my head, I'm not going to hesitate to soak in its yumminess as often and for as long as I want.

It might be the only thing that keeps me from killing his bossy ass some days.

He finally settles on a cue and leans against the window ledge, glancing at people scurrying past the pub as the rain and wind picks up and fat raindrops splatter against the glass.

"You sure you got just the right cue? I wouldn't want you to try to use your warped wood as an excuse for your imminent embarrassing loss."

"Says the chick clutching the most warped pole of the bunch."

With six quick swipes of the chalk, I glide the cube in his direction and blow off the excess caking the tip. "I like my wood warped. Hits all the right spots. Warped or straight, you're going down, Coach."

He gestures at me with his beer, that fucking brow of his quirked, before tipping back the bottle. "I did you a favor. You were taking shit personally out there. It wasn't personal."

"I fucked Doublewide's brother after we kicked their asses in the finals last season." I get perverse pleasure watching the coach choke on his gulp of beer. "*In her bed*. I assure you, every time we go head-to-head on the track now, it's personal."

"I knew you fucked him! I told you. All. Of. You. You were so confident placing bets on it. You owe me fifty bucks." Maisy slaps Eve's arm with the back of her hand, before holding her palm out and wiggling her fingers. "Pay up."

Marty takes a slow step toward the bar.

And another.

"Uh, uh," Maisy says, snapping her gaze to Marty as she tries to slink away. "And you owe me twenty-five, cheapskate."

Marty, the best fucking accountant in our hometown of Galloway Bay, and least likely to gamble out of all of us, rolls her eyes and reaches into her bra. "Calculated risk. Which is why I'm only taking a light hit. I knew our little *Come Queen* had an itch to scratch that night," Marty says, using my roller derby name as she slaps the cash in Maisy's hand. "And who could blame her... did you see the brother?"

"A corpse would come back from the dead in the presence of that dude." I huff out a breath and grab my beer, downing three gulps. "He likes pain too. And I like to bite. We had a good fucking night."

It's the most I've ever revealed to my derby team about my personal life, but tonight, something is shifting in our group, and it just feels like the right time to maybe finally let my guard down.

I've been on the team for three years now. With the influx of younger blood moving in, I've gradually gravitated to the core team, the originals, especially with how many bouts Eve has missed in recent weeks with turmoil at work. Being number two blocker in terms of skill set, I've slipped into the void she leaves on the track.

Maybe that's why we've landed here at this bar while our younger teammates hit up a dance club a few blocks away.

"Ooooh, Cain likes–"

Coach's hand snakes around Maisy's waist and drags her back against him. "Don't you dare finish that sentence." His lips brush over the shell of her ear, his voice low whispering God knows what kind of fuckery. Whatever it is, it's gotta be good since it makes Maisy slump against him, her teeth digging into her bottom lip as her cheeks and neck flush red.

I mean, if he wants to do any of that to her right here and now, I might be convinced to let his ass whoopin' go if they let me watch. The man is a cop for fuck's sake. He has cuffs.

And one hell of a nightstick. The Devil knows we all spent our fair share staring at it during practice last winter when he trained us for the banked track exhibition in Philly.

The itch Doublewide's brother scratched that night… It's nothing compared to the one brewing now watching these two rub against each other every chance they get. My clit is sick of the bullshit monogamous relationship I've forced her into with my right hand. She's looking for a little three-way action, a little unpredictable finger, but her owner has been cock blocking her at every turn, and tonight will be more of the same. Kick some ass at pool, drink a few beers, and when I'm back at the room, a little solo service before I close my eyes.

Utterly. Fucking. Forgettable.

I survey the crowded pub and see way too many couples and not a lot of prospects. And puck bunnies. Puck bunnies everywhere which means somewhere in the masses, we've got hockey players.

Cocky fuckers thinking they're God's gift to women. Hard pass.

I put in almost twenty hours of overtime at the shop this week so I could get the time off for this derby match, aka a bout, and night in the city. I didn't do it to wind up in some conceited prick's bed where I need to stroke his ego harder than his cock just to get a shot at a little individual attention.

Chances are, he wouldn't be able to find my clit with a magnifying glass anyway.

I need to figure out a better schedule now that our team is fielding invites for bouts all over the east coast. The hours at the shop were a whole lot more flexible when I was just working on cars, but the minute word got out about my experience with motorcycles, my schedule turned into never-ending overtime and a six-month waitlist. My new popularity slashes away at the eligible bachelor pool in my town since I refuse to shit where I sleep, leaving me boner-hungry in Boston with only hockey cock on the menu.

And I think it's safe to say I'm not touching any of them with this pool cue.

I shake off a mountain of sexual frustration and set my beer on the window ledge, a tad too hard, earning a questioning look from Eve. "You guys done fucking over there?"

Shit, just last year she and Maisy were a couple. Shouldn't their PDA be pissing her off at least a little?

"Fine, he's all yours," Maisy says, giving him a shove in our direction.

"Gee. Thanks. You wanna break, Coach?"

"Nope, do the honors."

"Such a gentleman." I try to make it a joke, but it comes out as more of a sneer. He really is genuinely a good guy which pisses me off when I'm hellbent on being mad at him. Doublewide winked at me six fucking times while my ass warmed the bench, and it was his fault.

Gripping that flash of anger, I bend over and line up my shot. Out of the corner of my eye, I spot a bunny sidling up to a dude in a suit at the bar, bumping his arm with the tits she's aimed his way.

God, that could have been me. Before I decided to take control of my life. If my mother had her way, I'd be coming in hot with that beauty queen energy, where every move is calculated and hungry. Maybe I'd be here, shoving my tits in some bleary-eyed exec's face just waiting for him to rain a few dick crumbs on me.

I want to rage at the sight. Rage at the girl I was when my mom tried to mold me into her dainty little mini-me. The woman I am now watches the bunny with jaded glasses and wants to scream at her to find some fucking dignity already.

He turns to her, a lecherous grin on his face, his wedding band winking in the light, and I growl low in my throat and snap the cue, sending the balls scattering. Two striped balls sink in the side and corner pockets respectively.

I snap my gaze up to the coach and grin. "Game on."

Turn after turn I sink two balls to his every one until I'm ready to chase the eight ball. "How's that straight rod working out for you?"

"Atrociously. I'm better with handcuffs," Coach mutters.

I stifle a laugh, shove my tongue in my cheek, and enjoy this side of him playing out. Hardly anything rattles the coach. He's mostly quiet unless he needs to be loud. Private. Reasonably controlled.

I've only seen him unhinged once when he let Maisy's personal and derby rival on our team to train for a special exhibition. They held it together longer than anyone expected. Until one whispered barb. A big one about Maisy's dead mom. Maisy took Tilly down in one lunge, straddled her, and whooped her ass, forcing the coach to pluck her off.

When he tried to stop her, she took a swing at him too, shocking the shit out of all of us. Who knew Maisy had it in her.

He bellowed and carried Maisy off caveman style. Hate fucked her against the wall on skates and everything.

Lucky bitch.

I jerk my chin in the direction of the corner. "Eight ball, corner pocket." I snap my wrist and send the ball sailing, but miss seeing it drop into the target entirely, when I catch sight of a group of hockey players headed our way.

Fucking great.

Chapter 3

Weston

I take off my suit jacket and toss it on a nearby chair as Foster racks the balls, gliding them around the table until he gets to a spot that makes him happy. Maybe there's a spot where they're supposed to go, but I have no idea.

Guess I should have thought about my lack of skill before I decided to play pool at the only other table in the bar to impress my purple haired temptress with my pool playing.

It's too late to turn back now. Foster already has everything lined up, and Tag's handing me a cue. Shit. I hope I don't look like a complete and utter idiot. I played pool a few times in college, and I'm pretty sure I was buzzed each time.

With any luck, she'll think my ineptitude is cute.

Don't mind me, I'm a big ass idiot, but I think you're very pretty.

I casually glance toward the other table and meet a pair of slightly hostile and vaguely familiar olive green eyes. Odd. We've been to Boston a few times for games, but I've never been to this particular bar, and I definitely would've remembered seeing her before. My eyes roam down to her almost see-through tank top, her killer tits, the tattoos covering her arms, and those damn thick thighs I want wrapped around my head. There's no way I could ever see her and forget.

"Like what you see, hockey dick?" Her lip curls into a sneer, and I think she growls at me before leaning down to take another shot.

Tag laughs, and laughs, and laughs some more, sitting at the circular high-top table on our other side. He glances at me and then looks behind me, still chuckling it up. Fucker.

Foster hangs his head and chuckles. "I told you, mate. She's a Harley, and you haven't even gotten on a tricycle to see if you can ride. Are you breaking or am I?"

"You can," I mumble, glancing her way one more time and earning some curious looks from the other girls at their table.

Foster shakes his head and breaks, scattering the balls in every direction but sinking none. "Alright, rookie, time to put on your big boy pants and make an impression."

With a nod, I step up to the table, my heart pounding and my palms sweaty. I can't believe I'm actually doing this. I grab the cue with my right hand and lean over the table to line up my shot.

I'm about to hit the cue ball when I hear her behind me. "I hope you don't hold *your* stick like that."

I turn, glancing at her over my shoulder. She's behind me, one hand on her hip and the other holding the pool cue like she wants to stab me with it. "Like what?"

"Limp."

Tag nearly spits out his beer, and Foster gives me a look that says, told you so.

I do my best to ignore...well...everyone, and take the shot, sinking a solid ball in the left corner pocket. With all eyes on me, I walk around the table, line up my next shot, and miss. Of course.

"Better luck next time, pretty boy." One of the other girls, this one petite with short blonde hair, tips her beer in my direction before draining it. Well damn. Who are these girls?

Foster walks by me, patting my shoulder. "So ladies and gent, are you from here or on holiday?"

The girls give us a bit of a side eye before blondie answers. "We play roller derby. We're here for a bout. But the skating you guys do is...cute."

Tag chuckles, and I swear he mutters, *of course the rookie picks a fucking derby girl*, before taking a lengthy sip of his beer.

"Cute?" I puff out my chest a bit and stand a little taller. "It's endless invasions of privacy, traveling all over hell, exhaustion, constant muscle aches, spasms, busted lips, black eyes, stitches—"

Blondie smirks and swirls her highball glass with her eyes on the ice as it clanks along the bottom. "And a big fat payday...don't forget that part."

"That's the difference between us." Purple steps up to me, and I almost stop breathing. She smells good, like leather with a hint of cinnamon, and I have a strong urge to see if she tastes just as nice. But I won't, because I'm pretty sure she'll punch me. "We don't just play roller derby. We are roller derby. At the end of the day, there's no fat check. No people adoring us or buying cute little jerseys with our names on them. Our sport doesn't make us a dime. It costs us money. It's easy to be dedicated while you're fanning yourself with your stacks of cash."

"You think we weren't dedicated long before the payout?" I hang my head with a shake. She doesn't have a fucking clue. "You think we didn't eat, breath, and sleep hockey to get where we are? Let me tell you, the millions didn't come without a shit ton of hard work and sacrifice."

"But at least they came. You guys go out there with endless medical staff to keep those bodies running tip top. Tonight, I get to go back to my hotel room and see if I can squeeze out enough ice from the ice machine so maybe I have a chance to sleep with this beauty."

I'm staring right into her eyes, full of fire and passion, that is until her hands slide to the snap of her jeans taking my gaze right along with them.

Blood rushes to my dick at the sound of her zipper, and before I can catch my breath, she has one side of her jeans pulled down–*where the fuck are her underwear*–and holy shit, she definitely needs medical attention for whatever the hell happened to her hip.

She reaches up and nudges my jaw closed with her knuckle. She touched me. She fucking touched me.

"You're looking green, dude. This is nothing. We all get them, derby kisses. Multiple times a season. While you're darting all over the country playing your little hockey games, we're out there doing our second jobs in fishnets and no paycheck."

"Little hockey games? We skate on ice with knives on our feet. Balancing on literal blades. What do you skate with? Four wheels. No balance on a razor's edge required."

"Yeah wheels. The forty-five degree banked track we roll on begs to differ about the balance. And we do it all in half the padding." She steps even closer, her chest brushing against mine and fuck. Me. I swear to Christ, I stop breathing. "You willing to give up some of that protection? Let's start with your cup," she says as she presses her pool stick right against my growing erection. "I sure as hell don't use one and let me tell you, catching a skate in the vagina when we go down isn't something you'll forget. I'm not sure you can handle it..."

I lean down and brush my nose alongside hers, relishing the feel of even the tiniest bit of skin against mine and the hitch in her breath. Not sure what came over me, be if this is the most I'm going to get to touch her, I'm going to take advantage. "West. My name is West."

"Just what I thought. Boring."

We stare at each other for several seconds, the air thickening around us. She refuses to back down, but I'm not going to step back and put the space between us. Her eyes flash with surprise before they soften, and she smirks.

"Christ, Emerson, give the guy a break." The tall guy with dark hair and a good amount of scruff who was playing pool with purple steps up behind her and puts a hand on her shoulder. "You're pissed at me, not him."

Emerson. Again, something about that seems vaguely familiar, but I just can't put my finger on it. What is it about this girl?

She takes a step back, and I can finally take an easy breath. "Don't underestimate my ability to multitask, Coach. I can be pissed at you both."

"I benched you. You firmly kicked my ass at pool. We're even." Their coach turns to us and reaches out a hand. "I'm Cain. Good to meet you guys."

"Interesting to meet you and your crew." Foster jumps in and shakes his hand. "We have a lot of roller derby in the UK, but I haven't had the pleasure of watching it in person. I'm Foster, the lurker back there is Tag, and this is our new rookie. You wouldn't know it from his hair, but he's a pretty good lad."

Emerson scoffs but moves back to whisper something to one of the other girls.

"You guys play with Rhett Remington?" Cain eyes us after he shakes my hand. "I think he was in here earlier."

"We do. Are you a fan?" Tag hops off his stool and decides to finally grace us with his presence. "He was here for about five minutes before his wife flew in for a surprise visit."

Emerson scoffs again, and I cross my arms, leaning against the pool table, keeping an eye on her while she watches me with a scowl on her face.

Cain huffs a laugh, shifting on his feet before rubbing his scruff. "I used to be on the Boston PD. Last season, we were briefed every time the LA Stars would come to town because of his ass. Can't imagine seeing him married and walking the straight and narrow."

"I'm sure he's still hopping from bed to bed when his wife isn't in town." That's scoff number three for Emerson, and her eyes narrow even more, moving between the three of us.

I uncross my arms and gesture to her, eyebrows raised. "Remington would cut his own dick off before he'd cheat on his wife. You really don't think much of hockey players, do you?"

Scoff number four while Tag and Foster move to stand by my side. "I don't like cliche guys who cheat on their wives or fuck anything that moves."

Her olive green gaze flicks over me one last time before she turns around, completely dismissing me.

"I'm not married."

"And doesn't fuck anything, period," Foster says, disguising his laugh with a cough.

Chapter 4

Weston

"**O**h shit," the redhead with the tattoos says in awe as all eyes swing in my direction.

Fucking big mouth Foster.

Damn, I'd love to be mad at him, but I'm the one who blabbed my secret to begin with. I should've just accepted the fact that I was going to retire from the NHL with my virginity untarnished and kept it at that. At least my hand knows what I like.

"Motherfucking burn," the blonde whispers next, quickly burying her face in her glass and draining the rest of her drink.

Foster tosses me an apologetic look while Tag glances at his phone and busies himself with a text. Cain narrows his eyes as he studies my face—probably trying to figure out what's wrong with me—and Emerson, well, now it's her mouth hanging open.

I don't want to nudge it closed like she did mine. I really want to fill it with something. I bet she'd be surprised then.

"You're a virgin?"

I try to swallow the groan, but instead it comes out strangled and ends on a high-pitched squeak. A manly high-pitch, but still.

"You suck as a wingman," I mutter over my shoulder before spotting the dart board behind us. "Look, darts. That's more like it. You guys up for a game?"

Tag passes me a fresh beer. "You sure you want to give her sharp objects? She just jammed that cue stick right into your–"

"Yes. I was there," I snap, shooting him a look over my shoulder and then giving Foster a similar one. The little smug fucker can't stop laughing. He must think he's real cute after waving my v-card in front of everyone. That's the last time I ask either of these guys for help.

"Wait, you're a virgin and he's your wingman? So no bunnies at all?" she says with a glance at Foster.

"He's afraid of them. All goes back to that one Easter when he was just a kid in short pants...something about taking a picture with the rabbit and he touched his no-no zone. Just the word bunny has him clenching his ass cheeks."

This time I do manage a groan. He does know he can shut the fuck up at any time, right?

"And you're what, trying to make a play for me? Oh, that's rich. Baby, you can't handle this ride. Why don't you stick to the low hanging fruit over there. The brainless kind just looking to rub their cat on something in skates." Next thing I know, she bursts out laughing, her head thrown back, and sure, it's at my expense, but shit, I don't want her to stop. Her laugh is just like her, free and uninhibited.

There's no way I can walk across the bar and even look at another woman. She's the one I want. She's the only one I see. She's the one I won't forget. "No can do. I'm allergic."

The blonde leans around her friend and scans the room. "I'm pretty sure all you'll find over there is the hairless variety. You're good."

"Have you seen those things? Calculating little shits ready to gnaw off your face the minute you close your eyes." I glance over at Victor and tonight's conquest just to find she's taken the upper hand, clutching his head in her hands. Her blood red fingertips digging into his scalp, and her mouth—it's everywhere. I hitch my thumb in his direction. "See, where's his nose? Maybe it's behind the bleach blonde hair. Maybe she ate it. Odds aren't good for Victor."

She chokes out a laugh and glances over at me, shaking her head. "I—shit, you're making it really hard to stay pissed."

"I'm glad I could entertain you," I deadpan, handing her the set of yellow darts while keeping the blues for myself. "Around the World. We take turns. The one who hits each number in order first, one to twenty. You know it?"

"Please. This is my game." She's wiping her eyes now, tears of laughter giving them an even deeper green glow.

Between the hair, the eyes, the tattoos snaking over her skin, she's full-on color and mystery. And fun. She just looks like she could be fun. If any part of this turned out awkward, at least we could count on that. If I can convince her.

"Good. If I win, we go back to the hotel. Together."

"Funny."

"Am I laughing?"

Those eyes of hers I love so much widen, and she stares at me for a few seconds, studying my face before giving me a sharp nod.

"Fine. And if I win, you put on Cain's skates–"

"I hate it when you guys fuck with my skates." Cain glares as he digs at the label on his bottle.

She throws her hands in the air with a sigh. "Your replacement wheels are on me. Happy?" Turning back to me, she plants her index finger in the middle of my chest. "And you skate your sweet virgin ass back to our hotel. All recorded. We have a YouTube channel that could use fresh content. Win-win." Hooking her thumb over her shoulder, she grins. "Just make sure you give the coach his skates back, or he might do to you what he did to Maisy."

Tag leans over to the blonde and redhead. I really should have caught their names. "I really need to know which one of you is Maisy and what he did to you with skates."

The blonde snorts and sinks back in her chair, her gaze landing on Cain. "Fucked her so hard she qualified as a human condom."

"Damn, Eve... Guess you are well and truly over Maisy then."

Foster rears back. "You two were..." He's all hand gestures and waggled eyebrows as he glances between them.

Maisy laughs. "Quite a while ago now, but yes."

Foster props his chin on his hands and gazes at the both of them, fluttering his eyelids. "You ladies paint the prettiest pictures."

Removing Emerson's finger from my sternum, I bring her hand down between us, and I don't let go just yet. "Sweet ass, huh?"

She glances down at our hands. Her lips part on a subtle gasp when she realizes she's naturally beginning to lace her fingers with mine.

All too soon she snatches her hand back. "It's an expression."

"Sure it is. Fine. You've got a bet. Ladies first." I take a step back, giving her space. When I win–and I will win–I don't need her having any excuses for her loss.

She taps the flight of each dart against the edge of the pool table one at a time before she takes her stance, and I freeze.

I can't stop staring at her profile, the purse of her lips, the way she squeezes her eyes shut just a bit as she studies the board.

The noise of the bar blends and fades as the roaring fills my ear.

Tap. Tap. Tap.

She knocks the tip against her bottom lip three times and flips it in her grip until the point's out. With one smooth flick of her wrist, she lets the dart fly.

With a slight shift, she leans forward, the light casting a halo over her purple hair, bathing her in golden yellow for the briefest second before she straightens her spine. I suck in a hard breath as the final piece of the puzzle slides into place.

"Emmie?" The name is hardly more than a whisper on my lips, but it's enough for her to jerk to a stop.

She pierces me with a glare. "If you treasure your balls, you won't call me that."

Reaching for her, I take her arm gently and turn her toward me. She trembles beneath my touch, such a contrast to her tough exterior, and I want to see what else makes her quake. "You're Emmie Walsh from Charleston, South Carolina."

She takes a step back and looks me up and down. "How the hell do you know that?"

"Because you used to babysit me. Holy shit. It is you."

The chatter between our friends dies a quick and violent death. Someone whistles low. I have no idea who because I can't stop staring at her.

She had blonde hair then, and braces. She let me stay up past my bedtime, and we'd eat strawberry ice cream in the game room and shoot darts for hours. Before every single shot, she'd tap the flight and bounce that metal tip on her lip just like she did tonight. Thousands of times, never missing a step.

Tag huffs a laugh and chugs the rest of his beer. "And just like that, folks, we've gone from zero to Pornhub."

Foster grins and sits up straighter. "Rookie wants to shag the babysitter. Didn't know he had it in him."

"Where's the damn popcorn when you need it," the redhead whispers.

"Sorry, show's over. I need a drink." Within seconds Emerson hands off her darts to Blondie, mine to Foster, and is dragging me not toward the bar, but toward the bathrooms.

We have to weave our way around the table with the rest of the team. Victor comes up for air, red lipstick smeared from his mouth all the way up to his nose, and gives me a thumbs-up as we sail by. When I turn my head away from him, one of the bunnies catches sight of me. "Aren't you a hock–"

Emerson whips around, goes chest to chest with the startled blonde in the little black dress, stares down at her hard. "Mine."

One growled word has the girl stumbling away on her high heels.

And me puffing out my chest, because even if I do manage to lose my v-card to her, that single moment in time might be the one I remember above all the rest. I'm all for equal rights, and if she wants to lay claim on me, even if it's only for five minutes, I'll take it.

"I thought you'd see it my way," Emerson mutters before yanking me along with her until we leave the main bar area.

"Hold on." I pull us to a stop. "There's no drink this way, and if you're planning on dunking my head in the toilet and giving me a swirly, I think I'll pass."

She rolls her eyes. "How old are you again?"

She pulls me down a dim hallway, bulb flickering horror movie style, and I wonder if this is how I'm going to die. "The Emerson I was all those years ago is dead and buried in South Carolina, and the last thing I need is for my past to start bleeding into my present."

"Come on, was it really that bad?"

"You have no idea." She takes a deep breath and crosses her arms over her chest. "My dad was fucking half of the moms in the PTA."

"Mr. Walsh? Seriously? Shit. I—wait, my mother was in the PTA."

"Yeah," Emerson huffed. "Tell me about it."

"Emerson," I squeeze the bridge of my nose, the image in my head enough to shrivel my balls on the spot, and for the rest of the night. "I'm going to need you to tell me your dad did not do my mom. In the next five seconds or less preferably."

"Breathe, kid. I don't mean that. Your mom is safe."

I shove my hand through my hair, wondering what the hell I'm supposed to say here. She's defensive. By her stance, sure, but it's those wary eyes studying me, just waiting for me to say something awful. "I would've never guessed. He always seemed so unassuming. Quiet. Polite. Boring even. No offense."

"Nothing screams more boring and unoriginal than fucking a PTA mom. So that tracks."

I shrug. "Since everyone now knows about my nonexistent sexual history, I'll have to take your word for it." Her repetitive sneer earlier all of a sudden makes more sense. "Or maybe not, since you think all hockey guys are cheaters and man whores."

"Okay, that was—well, not my best assessment. I just. I've seen this before. Too many times. And sometimes it's hard to accept just how much I saw then, but didn't speak up about. I knew. Well, not knew, knew, but there was something that wasn't quite right. A look. A brush a bit too close at school events. Just enough that I should have said something."

"You were just a kid, Emerson. It wasn't your responsibility to be the adult."

"No, but it's my responsibility to myself to never become one of them. So I went my own way."

"I get it. I've let how many years slip away while I chased hockey. I love it. Don't get me wrong, but I've been going in the directions my parents set."

She finally drops her arms, opening herself a bit more to the conversation. To me. She leans back against the wall and searches my eyes. "So, if you've held onto your virginity for so long, why now? Why tonight? And why me?"

"Because tonight I wanted something of my own." I cock my shoulder against the wall next to her and lean in. "The second I laid my eyes on you, I knew you weren't one of them. You wouldn't care about my NHL contract and maybe, just maybe, you would actually give a fuck what my name was. You're not like any other woman here, and that makes you special." I reach out and drag my knuckle over the sweeping swirls of smoke snaking up her arm and swirling around a skull. "And I thought... I thought that maybe there was a chance that if I was with you for my first time, it could be special too. Not something forgettable like I would have with anyone else out there." I sigh. "Sorry, that was stupid."

"No, you've got a point. Those bunnies would be a shitty lay. Totally forgettable. Fake orgasms all the way."

"I bet there's nothing fake about you. Not even an orgasm to make me feel better about myself."

"Nope. I'll make you work until you give them to me. I'm not about setting up the next woman for shitty sex. If I do this, you're going to learn something. Actually, several things."

I pause for a second, my gaze roaming over her face, searching for anything that might tell me this is all one big joke. "Wait. Are you actually agreeing to this?"

"My babysitting days are over, kid. But..."

"I feel like you're about to say, just kidding, and push my head in the toilet for good measure."

She purses her lips and flips her purple hair over her shoulder. "You do understand I can crack that skull of yours with my thighs, right? And if you want to avoid that fate, your job will be to be good enough that I don't want to."

"Yes, ma'am."

"I'm not that old. Stop it."

"Just old enough to babysit me."

"And punish you. Come on." She takes my hand and drags me out of the hall, but now she has a hint of a smile and a whole lot of determination in her eyes.

I take a deep breath, my heart racing and holy fuck me, I can't believe it. First, the purple-haired vixen is my damn babysitter, the first girl I had a crush on. And now she agrees to sleep with me even though my experience is very limited.

When we get back to the pool tables, their coach is all hand gestures and laughing it up with Tag and Foster on either side of him. They don't notice us as we approach, but the derby girls do. They glance at our interlaced fingers before Emerson leans toward them, a smile painted on her face. "Don't wait up."

"Wait, you're going to do it?"

"Awe, she's throwing him a bone," the redhead says with a laugh.

"By the looks of it, he's throwing her one." Foster turns around, casually sipping on his beer.

"We'll be at...wait, where are you staying?"

Ah, shit. I'm here with the team, which means I have a roommate. Victor, to be precise, and I have a feeling he's going to be needing his space for a few hours. He might not be very disconcerting when it comes to picking up women, but he never goes to their place when we're traveling the next day. "Your room."

"You want to go to my room?"

"Unless you want to be in the bed next to Victor and the bunny trying to lick his face off. I figured you might want a little more privacy."

"I think I'll pass. I don't want to see your goalie's dick tonight."

Foster clamps a hand on my shoulder and gives me a slight shake. "You're going to feel really good for about fifteen seconds, and then it's going to be over for you."

Tag leans around Foster, his face lit up with a cheesy grin. "Remember to think about grandmas, baseball, ball sweat, Coach Weller."

"What would you like on your gravestone? I don't think your teammates can be trusted with that detail," Cain tosses in.

"Oooh, look at the derby coach gliding in with the burn." Tag laughs, nodding to Cain. "We're going to be good friends. Let me buy you another beer."

I grab Emerson's hand, wrap my fingers around her, and pull her closer. "You guys are the worst."

"First lesson, West," Emerson says, tugging me toward the exit. "You don't let them get away with that shit. It doesn't need to be now, it doesn't need to be tomorrow, but at some point, you make them pay."

Chapter 5

Emerson

Fucking little West Gray.

I never imagined any part of my childhood in Charleston would bleed into my adult life. Especially after I burned it to the ground and moved to Maine ten years ago for a fresh start and, well, beer. The last time I saw West was right before he turned eleven. I was almost eighteen. My friends and I shared a limo for prom and stopped for pictures at the Waterfront Park. He was there with his mom, and she stopped to say hi to mine while we stood for pictures in front of that ridiculous pineapple fountain.

Little West was so watchful that day, and I don't know what he saw, really saw, but letting myself be put on display like that, I cringed at the thought of him seeing me, almost an adult, and still my mother's little doll. So I snuck a middle finger into the next shot and when he spotted it, I winked at him.

He grinned at my act of defiance, but it was more than that...it was one more step toward becoming the version of me that managed to so thoroughly catch the attention of adult West to the point he was willing to risk the certain promise of total and utter humiliation to have a shot at me.

That day was the last time I looked the way my mother wanted with the pink chiffon and tulle ball gown with a skirt big enough I swear the whole football team could fit under. She had no clue I'd been dating the town's bad boy. Dating—er, well, fucking.

And that tiara. That stupid fucking tiara. She spent more on that tiara than the dress, and to this day, the few times I've facetimed her out of obligation and guilt, she makes sure she sits in the chair right next to the display case she has it in. Like some passive aggressive reminder of what she hoped for me and my future.

She had no clue the minute I graduated, I'd be hopping on the back of that bad boy's bike and hightailing out of the South for good with nothing more than my backpack and the sweet rush of freedom.

I never thought I'd see West again or be the one to dirty his good boy nature. But somehow, when I think back to prom, he's what I remember. It's like we were destined to end up here at some point, and it's the heaviness of that, the responsibility of it, and the idea that fate might just have secret roadmaps of our future that fills me now with this weird energy. Like it's daring me to go down the road it's set.

Like fate knows I won't be able to resist the challenge.

I throw open my hotel door and try to ignore the fact that I can feel his heat at my back. I'm still angry—between the rough day on the track and resurrecting my lingering resentment toward my parents, especially my dad—but that tension is slowly morphing into something much bigger, much more volatile, making me jump when the door clicks shut behind us.

Soaked from the rain, my tank top caresses my girls in all the wrong, or right, places. Depending where I want his eyes to land.

The still air in the room is buzzing with awareness between the two of us and fuck, I need to get a handle on this. "Look, kid," I start as I spin around.

My words die in my throat at the way his eyes devour me. Next thing I know, his hands frame my face and he backs me up a step at a time until I'm trapped between him and the wall.

His chest heaves as he slants his mouth over mine and sucks whatever the hell I was going to say straight out of my lungs.

Fucking. Damn.

His lips are hard against mine. His kiss is so aggressive, so hungry, it's like he's a different person than the shy Weston Gray I met at the bar.

My brain scrambles, grasping for control, but my body? That ho is vibrating hard enough to shake my clothes clean off.

I need to get a handle on this before all reason goes straight out the window. There are things we need to address.

"Hold up." I slap a palm to the damp shirt clinging to his chest. His hard fucking chest. His wide, hard, Jesus Christ Mr. and Mrs. Gray had to be slipping this kid pure protein at every meal chest. "I thought you said you haven't done this before, because that kiss suggests otherwise."

His lips twitch and his eyes practically dance before dropping to my mouth. "You think virgin means I've never kissed anyone?"

The fucker is laughing at me. "Okay, fine. Good. I, um…you've got that part down. Maybe let's move on."

"Move on to what?" He cocks his head, his brows practically raising to his hairline.

"You jerking off."

His eyes shoot wide open and he rears back, looking at me like I just told him I want to peg his muscular ass. "What?"

"You heard me."

He slides his hands in the pockets of his dress pants and rocks back on his heels, a lock of light brown hair flopping over his forehead. "I've got that part down too."

"Yeah, I remember your mom warning mine about boys and crunchy sheets. My mom made sure my little brother was stripping his own bed by the time he was eight."

West's cheeks flame, and he shoves his hands through his hair. "Great. That's awesome that she shared that with you."

I grab a bottle of water from the desk and toss it to him before snagging one of my own. I settle across the room, leaning back against the heater under the window ledge and pop the top. "So how long has it been anyway?"

"Twelve years. You guys moved when I was eleven."

"No, hotshot, since you rubbed one out?"

He chokes, a gulp of water dribbling down his chin. "Uh…"

"Okay, I'll go first. It's been…" I slide my cell out of my back pocket and swipe the screen, "About ten hours for me."

"So you–here–before?" His eyes dart over to the rumpled bed.

"You got it, hotshot. Now you? When?"

He tilts his head to the side. "Yesterday."

"Then you've got some prep to do."

"Is this really necessary?"

"If we have any hope of you lasting longer than thirty seconds, then yes. Lucky for you, I like to watch, so we can just call this foreplay." I back up, leaning against the dresser and crossing my arms.

"Ummm, maybe–"

"West…" I wait for his eyes to meet mine. "Lose the pants."

He doesn't move, he just studies me with those piercing blue eyes, and right about the time I'm ready to shake him, he flicks the leather of his belt from the buckle. His baby blues never leave mine, and he looks so fucking confident, so fucking hot, and it's so goddamn unexpected for someone who's never done this. Just watching his fingers pull down the zipper in this slow dance of seduction has my skin ready to burst into flames.

With his pants hanging open giving me a scant glimpse of black underwear, he drags the tails of his dress shirt from the waistband and flicks open a button.

Then another.

All the way up his chest until he's peeling the shirt from his shoulders and tossing it over a nearby chair.

I'm not sure what gets me hotter, the fact that he didn't just toss it on the floor or the dusting of golden hair sprinkled over his broad and heavily muscled chest leading to a damp happy trail heading straight down the valley of his chiseled abs to his...phew.

My stomach bottoms out and my heart climbs into my throat, making it damn impossible to speak.

And since fucking when have I ever been speechless?

I haven't. If anything, I don't know when to shut up. It's a whole fucking problem.

I'm the experienced one here. Me. I've got to get it together.

But son of a bitch, the rain still dotting my skin trickles down my chest, disappearing under my tank, and I'm suddenly desperate to shed my clothes too. I compromise by grabbing the hem and dragging the cotton over my head.

He reaches for his slacks and misses when his eyes roam over the lace bralette covering my breasts. He swallows hard and I know if I take it off, he'll be a goner.

Hello, upper hand. It's about time you decided to join the party.

"You're shit at following directions." I motion to his pants which are still sadly perched around his hips. "That's not the boy I used to know."

"I haven't been a boy for a long time."

"Well, except for one pesky little thing."

His lips quirk up into a crooked smile as he runs a hand down his abs, ridge by fucking ridge. "Baby, there's nothing little about what I'm about to give you."

"Well, well, you certainly can be a smooth fucker when you want to be, can't you? If you're going to get my hopes up, you better deliver." I gather my hair and flip it with several twists and secure it in a messy bun. "Maybe a visual aid will help you loosen that grip on those pants."

He sucks in a breath, his gaze zeroing in on the finger I'm gliding along the band of my bralette. Back and forth I tease him until his cock grows harder, climbing straight out of his underwear.

Jesus. He wasn't kidding. I can't see the entire thing, but the head of his dick is thick. So thick it makes my jaw ache just thinking about taking him in my mouth.

Fuck. And now I'm just as invested as he is. Criss-crossing my arms, I drag the lace over my head and toss it. I'm not graceful about it, and maybe that's the best part–with him I don't have to be. He'll take away far different memories from tonight than I will.

I shiver at the feel of the air on my damp skin, and my nipples tighten almost painfully. Dragging my fingers over the tip, I swirl and pinch, grinning at him. "So I'll ask you again, like what you see, hockey dick?"

Oh, look at that Adam's apple gliding up and down his throat.

"Yeah." His voice dips, the one word grating like he had to tear it from his throat. In seconds he's ditched the pants and underwear, tossing them on top of his shirt. With a flick of his wrist, he spins the desk chair around to face me and takes a seat. Splayed out in the chair with one muscular leg stretched out, the other knee casually bent, he gives himself one long stroke, never taking his eyes from mine. "This good?"

"Oh, you look like you've had plenty of practice."

He huffs out a laugh, tightening his grip around his cock. "I've been fucking myself for a long time."

There's something about that—the gravelly way he says fuck—that makes my clit throb with need and because I can't fucking help myself, I brush my thumbs across my nipples and a moan breaks free. I keep my eyes on him as he licks along the length of his hand. Fuck. Me.

I suck my bottom lip between my teeth, biting down as his hand travels the length of his cock, root to tip and back again.

His low groan fills the room as he lifts his hips, fucking his hand, his abs tightening with every thrust. He's so long, so thick, and I can't wait to feel him in my pussy, my mouth...everywhere. I want him to come on my tits and then rub himself into my skin, marking me as his. It's clear that neither one of us will leave this room completely unscathed.

Minutes, hours... I'm not sure how much time has passed, but there's one thing I'm sure of—there's no fucking way I can stand here and let him do this himself. I need a taste. I need to feel his cock in my mouth. I need to feel him let loose and fuck my face, to lose control.

With his hand, he cups his balls, massaging them as he continues to stroke himself, his gaze glued to mine as I push away from the dresser and make my way to him.

"Change of plans, West. I want you in my mouth." I drop to my knees in front of the chair and replace his hand with mine. "I need to taste you."

His gasp sends a shiver down my spine as I lick along his length, swirling my tongue around the head of his dick, relishing the salty taste of his pre-cum. I grip the base of his cock and take him between my lips.

"Fuck, Emerson. That mouth." He groans, sinking down in the chair, brushing the stray hair away from my face.

I moan, taking him deeper, working him faster, sucking him harder. He pulls my hair free from the bun, wraps it around his fist, and uses both hands to push me down on his dick, forcing me to take him as far as I can.

He hits the back of my throat, and I swallow around him, breathing through my nose as tears sting the corners of my eyes.

I shift on my knees, desperately trying to rub my thighs together, anything to get some relief for my aching clit. I didn't expect to be so turned on, to want him so badly.

West tightens his grip in my hair, working me up and down his shaft, letting loose a string of profanities that would make a sailor blush. While he fucks himself with my mouth, I cradle his balls, rubbing them and the sensitive stretch of skin behind them.

His thighs tense, his body trembles, and I swallow him down, taking him impossibly deep as he loses himself. My name is a groan on his lips as he empties down my throat, and I drink him down, not wanting to waste a drop.

"Jesus Christ." He loosens his grip on my hair, and I lick my way up his cock, cleaning the tip before I lean back and admire my handiwork.

His head falls back as he reclines in the chair, his eyes closed, and his breaths come in shallow pants. He really is a thing of beauty, everything from the muscles he clearly works for to the perfect amount of chest hair decorating his sternum.

With a low hum, his eyes pop open, pinning me in place with those baby blue orbs. "Are you okay?"

I nod and lick my lips with a smirk.

"Good." He gives me one of those All-American lopsided grins and motions to the bed. "Now get the fuck on the bed. I think it's my turn."

Chapter 6

Weston

"You think you're in charge or something?" She smirks, getting to her feet and making her way over to the bed.

"Or something."

But she saunters away, her ass swinging, and glances at me over her shoulder just a second before her jeans slide off her hips.

Christ.

I watch her crawl to the middle of the bed, every last part of her on display from this angle, before turning over to lie on her back. I should be nervous, but I'm not, not with her. Her tits are perfect–soft and full–her curves mouthwatering, and damn that mouth of hers.

With one arm up, her hand tucked under her head, she crooks a finger my way, and I'm more than happy to oblige–crawling up her body, sucking her nipple in my mouth, and biting down tentatively.

She bows up with a hiss, her fingers sliding along the back of my head holding me to her. "What made you do that?"

"It just felt right." I kiss the damp spot where I sank my teeth into her. "Too much?"

"God no." She shoots up, her mouth meeting mine in an aggressive kiss that leaves us both panting. "Your instincts are good. Let's see where they take us."

I grin down at her. "You sure you're ready for that?" I don't wait for her answer as I work my way down her neck, kissing, nipping, flicking my tongue along her skin, committing her flavor to memory, until I'm kneeling between her legs, staring at her bare cunt.

Curling my fingers around her soft thighs, careful of the deep bruise blooming on her hip, I spread her legs apart and take in every part of her.

Her blazing eyes are fixed on me. "Instincts, kid."

The breathy sound of her usually confident voice prompts me to keep going. I run my knuckle over the wet slit of her pussy, watching for her reaction. When she lets out a low moan, I continue my ministrations, paying attention to everything she does. What makes her sigh, what makes her hips chase my fingers, and what makes her suck in a tight breath. I stroke and pet, exploring every part of her there, and by the time I feather my thumb over her swollen clit, a cry tears from between her lips unlike anything I've heard.

I want to hear it again and again until she falls apart.

Every porn I've ever watched got this part all wrong.

There are no sultry looks, no calculated moans. It's more primitive. There's just her, at her body's mercy, the almost crazed look in her eye, and the animal sounds she can't hold back.

I glide over her again, pressing my thumb into her clit harder, and her gaze takes on an edge while she pants under me. I don't know if she's close. I don't know how long this takes. But her body tells me I'm on the right track, and I know for sure when she finally loses it, really loses it, I want to taste it on my tongue.

Eyes on hers the entire way down, I drag my nose along her inner thigh and breathe her in.

My eyes drift closed, her scent engulfing me in musky heat unlike anything I could have imagined on my own. I dive in and drag my tongue along her slit, close my mouth over her clit, and flick my tongue across it. God. Fucking. Damn.

Her thighs flex, and she holds me there. I can't breathe, but I don't give a single fuck. If I died right now, I'd die a happy man. Settling in, I wrap my arms around her thighs and hold her there.

A taste isn't enough. I want my mouth wet with her. My chin. Everything. I'm so fucking hungry. I circle her clit with my tongue, sucking it into my mouth, and she bucks against my face. Her hands grip my hair and yank me even harder into the warm, wet heart of her.

Her rolling hips tell me she loves when I spear my tongue deep into her. Her hands fisting the sheets tell me she loves when I use the flat of my tongue to swipe the full length of her slit. But it's the way her heels dig into the mattress, the way her ass comes off the bed, and how her thighs squeeze around my ears that tells me her absolute favorite—the key to her losing total control.

"Of course you'd be a fucking overachiever," she says with a strangled gasp.

My laugh rumbles against her, making her gasp. I drag the tip of my tongue along the side of her clit, back down the other side, then close my lips over her and suck. Over and over, increasing speed each time, until she's fighting for air and beating the mattress with her closed fists.

God, I need to watch her break. I need to feel her. Letting go of her thigh, I sink two fingers inside her. Her greedy pussy grips me the minute I do. I close my mouth over her clit and mercilessly suck at the tight bundle of nerves, thrusting my fingers in and out of her quickly, fucking her at a frenzied pace. A jagged scream tears from her throat, and a warm gush floods my hand and the mattress beneath us.

My face is covered in her. The sound of our mutual gasp fills the room as we suck in some much-needed air.

I should check on her. Kiss her. Something, but I can't stop staring at her pussy. The fucking thing is magic. The taste, how it feels wrapped around my fingers, the sounds she makes as I touch her a certain way, lick her in particular spot. Incredible.

She tugs at me, pulling on my hair, but I continue feathering my thumb over her swollen flesh.

"You told me to trust my instincts. They're telling me to stay here a while."

A tortured laugh bubbles from her throat, and she tightens her grip on my hair, dragging my face up to look at her. "None of the girls are going to want to let you go." She pauses to take a breath. "I'm going to need you to fuck me. Now."

"As you wish." I push up from the bed and grab a condom from my wallet. Emerson is splayed out on the bed, her purple hair spread around her, her legs open, and she looks like a wet dream.

As I approach the bed, I try to tear open the condom wrapper, but my fingers are shaking and I can't quite get it. Shit. I was doing so good. Reality is sinking in, and this is fucking real. This woman, this beautiful woman, is going to let me fuck her, and I haven't a clue what I'm doing.

What if I'm horrible? What if I can't last more than thirty seconds? What if she—?

"You need some help?" Emerson asks softly, taking the condom from my hand and ripping it open in one swift movement. "Don't forget, you always wear one of these." Her gaze drops to my dick, and she licks her lips. "I can't wait to get on this ride."

I groan the second her fingers brush against my dick and then again when she grabs it and slowly rolls on the condom. My heart races, and my whole body is humming with energy; it feels like my body is a live wire and I'm about to explode.

With a quick kiss, she smirks, gesturing to the bed. "Lay on your back, Weston Gray. It's my turn."

I take a deep breath and do what I'm told, lying back and watching her crawl up my body. Her eyes are wide as they sweep up my thighs, the ridges of my abs, and over my wide chest. Never have I been so grateful for hockey and all the conditioning we have to do.

"Like what you see, derby girl?"

She throws her head back and laughs, running her nails down my thighs. "I thought my motorcycle was my favorite thing to straddle, but...your body is giving my bike a run for its money."

I open my mouth to reply, but the words die on my lips as Emerson lifts her hips and sinks onto my rock-hard cock. "Fucking hell."

Her pussy grips my dick as she slides all the way down, and I close my eyes. Warm and wet, she feels impossibly good wrapped around me. Too fucking good. I run my hands up her thighs, my fingers digging into her flesh as I try to steady my heart rate, try to breathe, try to think of everything and anything except how good her pussy feels.

"God, West." She leans forward, planting her hands on my chest and begins to move up and down, back and forth, rotating her hips in small circles.

Ah, fuck.

My hips thrust, meeting her strokes, and her nails scratch down my abs. I meet her gaze and hold it as I run my hands over her curves, loving how she feels beneath my palms.

Emerson sits up, leaning back a little, and moves my hand down to her clit. "Right here. I need you right here."

Pressing my thumb into her clit, I rub in small tight circles as her entire body trembles and her pussy clenches around my cock. She whimpers and groans my name, as she quickens her pace, rocking herself on my cock like her life depends on it.

"Fuck. Fuck," I growl, gritting my teeth and grinding into her, increasing the pressure on her clit.

Lightening zings down my spine, and my balls tighten as she clamps down on my cock, tremors running though her body. She cries out as her orgasm rolls through her, and after a few more thrusts, I let out a string of expletives and empty inside her.

She collapses on my chest, and I hug her to me, pressing a kiss to the top of her head.

We lay like that for several minutes, skin to skin. I stroke the valley of her spine over and over with me still deep inside her until our heavy breaths return to normal.

I want to hold her. I want to stay. She keeps telling me to trust my instincts, but right now, they're at the mercy of her warm body draped over mine.

I'm damn reluctant to let her go.

I'm going to replay every bit of this thousand times over. I'm going to compare it to every experience to come. Emerson didn't just take my virginity, she gave me her trust. After what she told me about her parents, it's definitely not something she hands to just anyone.

In a perfect world, I'd be able to have more time with her, get to know her. Hell, I'd love to take her out on a date and catch up, but God knows I just got my first NHL contract. I don't have time for dating. And Emerson?

Well, she doesn't strike me as a girl who's ready to settle down anytime soon.

Emerson rolls over with a huff, linking our fingers together, and glancing at me with a smirk. "You're a good student. All the gold stars."

"Gold stars, huh." I laugh, lacing my finger with hers. "Wonder what my mom would think if during my next visit I slapped that accomplishment on the fridge?"

She busts out laughing, a full-on belly laugh right there on top of me. So I hold her tighter and grin into her neck, in no rush to leave this bed.

Chapter 7

Emerson

Well shit.

Who knew that little virgin Weston Gray would make me orgasm so hard I can't feel my legs? Honestly, I wasn't expecting much. He's a virgin for fuck's sake, and they're supposed to be the worst lays. Boy was I wrong.

Eve and Maisy are going to know the minute they see me that the kid broke me about as much as I broke him, and they're never going to let me forget it.

I bite back a grin and throw on a t-shirt, while I watch West pull his jeans over his very yummy hockey butt. It's just the beginning for him. His body will only get better.

And those bedroom skills—the boy was going to be dangerous. A devastating lady-killer.

He grabs his dress shirt and turns around, a lopsided grin plastered across his face.

"Don't get cocky now, hockey boy."

With a chuckle, he shrugs on his shirt but leaves it hanging open, giving me a very delicious view of his chest and abs. Damn. A woman could get used to that view. Not me, of course. I'm not the commitment type, and West has that white picket fence, two point five kids, and a golden retriever energy coming off him in waves. He doesn't realize it yet, but he will.

He deserves a nice girl, a girl who conforms to society and would look good next to him on the front covers of a magazine. A woman who will join the PTA and bake cookies and shit for their kids. That will never be me.

Never.

"Well, uh..." He runs a hand through his hair and gestures to the space between us. "I'm not sure what to do here. Thank you doesn't seem like enough."

"Don't sweat it. It was as good for me as it was for you."

He glances toward the ground before meeting my eyes, his clouded with uncertainty. "Can I ask you a question?"

"Of course."

"Is it always like that? That good?"

His cheeks flush and turn a cute shade of pink. I open my mouth to respond, close it, and open it again. My first instinct is to say yes, but the more I think about it, the more certain I am that it's a lie. Sure, sex is usually fun, but that was more. Maybe it's our connection from the past, maybe he's just a really good student, but it was way better than anything I've experienced in the past.

"No." I shake my head and grin at the memory of his face after he made me come. His instinct wasn't to get a nut off. Nope. He wanted to give me more. "But with the right connection? Mind blowing."

He shoves his hands in his pockets and nods. "It was really good to see you again, Emerson. I, uh, I guess I should get back—"

I remain silent, watching him button up his shirt and put on his shoes. The closer he gets to leaving, the more something inside me tugs at my heart. That bitch doesn't want him to leave, but this was never meant to last beyond tonight.

Still, I can't help my stupid mouth from opening up. I grab a pen and the pad of paper by the phone and scribble my number. "Hit me up if you make your way back to Boston. Maybe you can show me some new moves you pick up along the way. Earn yourself some more of those gold stars."

He nods, turning to leave, but changes his mind and doesn't stop until he's directly in front me. West frames my face with his hands, kissing me with such ferocity, such passion that I feel it in my toes.

"You're something special, Emerson." He pulls back, pressing a kiss to my forehead. "I hope we run into each other some day."

"Yeah." I don't recognize the sound of my own voice. I take a step back, creating a little distance between us. West gives me one last heated look before he brushes his thumb across my lower lip and leaves.

As the hotel door closes behind him, I sink down onto the mattress, running my fingers along my lip, following the trail of his thumb. Just like that, he's gone. Back to his life in Nashville, far away from my home in Maine.

I'm still sitting there when my phone vibrates in my pocket. With a swipe of my screen, I open the text from the unfamiliar number.

"Add me to your contacts. Call me Hockey Dick. The nickname is growing on me."

Laughter bubbles up, and I flop back on my bed and promptly add him to my contacts.

Looks like little Weston Gray decided not to bank on hope to bring us back together one day.

Smart boy.

About the Author

Meet a whole new mashup...
USA Today Bestselling Author Echo Grayce
&
Hockey Romance Extraordinaire Melissa Ivers

When Echo isn't on the track alongside her roller derby girls creeping on Coach Yummy Pants and his big stick and Melissa isn't on the ice or lingering in the locker room with her shameless voyeuristic gaze on the naughty bits of her sexy ass Nashville Devils–they can be found in each other's DMs–Melissa with her strong AF GIF game and
Echo's penchant for punctuating everything with emojis.
Melissa, the realistic one, can count on Echo to skid in hot with last minute fuckery–like fitting a mashup in their tight writing schedules–and convince her to set her voice of reason on fire and say, "Why the fuck not?"

For more from both worlds, check out Echo and Melissa's websites:
www.echograyce.com
www.melissaivers.com

Grown Up Words

Lauren Stewart

Chapter 1

Gillian

3.21.23

Gillian

Damn it. Why weren't they all fat? Statistically speaking, that should have happened by now. Anyone who peaked in high school should be about halfway down the other side of the mountain at the ten-year mark, right? Sure, a few hairlines from the truly mediocre football team had receded, most of the cheerleaders had lost their annoying perkiness, and nobody looked anywhere near as hopeful and idealistic as they once did. Including me.

But if I had to wait until our *twenty*-year reunion for all these assholes to understand what it feels like to be called "fatty," I might as well not even bother.

Of course, I wish I'd thought of that yesterday or—even better—the day I received the animated evite to this shitshow. Four animated dancers in gradua-tion robes celebrating a time best forgotten by high-kicking and twirling in front of a sparkly Riverside High School Class of '13 banner. Yep, I should've known better, especially because the dancers' faces had been replaced by those of our head cheerleader, class president, and prom king and queen. Seriously, it was the stuff of nightmares.

But no, I'd somehow convinced myself—probably after a few too many glasses of wine and Hallmark movies—there was still good in the world. That people grew up, bettered themselves, and that teenage assholes and bullies could become rational, considerate adults.

Such bullshit.

Add that to my list of accomplishments since graduation: Gillian Thomas graduated Summa Cum Laude from the University of California at Long Beach, got her law degree from USC, joined a non-profit organization to support women's rights, opened her own law practice, and set out to change the world all before turning twenty-eight. All while doing her best to keep her little human healthy, happy, and well-adjusted.

And between all that, she still had time to become delusional enough to believe the kids who bullied her in high school might have become decent human beings. The joke's on her. I mean me. Yep. The joke was totally on me.

I'd actually been excited to come here tonight. To get all dolled up in new high heels and a sexy-yet-tasteful dress that hugged the curves I'd grown to appreciate and minimized the ones I still wished I didn't have. I'd even had my nails and toes painted in the same dark red as my new Mac lipstick, a color that made me feel dangerous and all-powerful—two things I would need to make it through tonight.

At least the music was decent. There may not have been a once-a-century monumental shift in music during the 2010's, but nostalgia is a funny thing. It was impossible not to feel a connection to the songs and artists we listened to and loved, who helped keep us sane during our teenage years. All I can say is: Thank you, Adele. Thank you for being there for me—then and now.

I flicked the edge of the paper name tag stuck to my beautiful dress, wondering if I should just rip it off and go home now, or if I should stay a few more minutes to really let my mistake set in—so I wouldn't forget it and decide to do it again in another ten years.

For what? I'd had one real friend in high school, and even *he* had blown me off shortly after graduation.

Of course, a lot about that first year after graduation was different. I'd wanted—no, I'd needed, oh so desperately needed, to start over and forget every awful experience in this town. Elementary school to senior year. Not a single year had included anything I wanted to remember.

Well, the *last* night in this town wasn't one I could forget, as it had directly led me to who I was today—a slightly dysfunctional, highly successful, independent, happy, single mom with a checkered past of relationships and trust issues. But I'd leave all the others to those who wanted to remember them.

The only things I'd held onto from high school were thirty pounds and the nickname my best-and-only friend had given me when we were nine: Gills, pronounced with a hard G sound instead of how most people say it: Jillian. Alec had renamed me so I didn't have to think about the nickname the *other* kids gave me: Jelly-in or—when they were feeling particularly creative and cruel—some combination of "Gillian," "jelly," and "jiggles."

As soon as I left Riverside for good, I told my dad, my stepmom, and everyone else I met that I pronounced it Gillian with a hard G. "When you're trying to remember my name, think of a shark's gills. If you need to remember my attitude, think of their bite." As an attorney, introducing myself that way was always good for a chuckle or two.

I cringed when I saw Denise do a double-take and walk toward me. The girl voted "most popular everything" looked excited to see me. Unfortunately, her entertainment always seemed to come at my expense. Sure, she could've turned into a nice person who regretted all the years of torture she put me through, but more likely her smile was due to the thrill of having another chance to hurt me.

I heard she was a yoga teacher now though, so that could have changed everything. You can't be a bitch and be a yoga teacher, can you? Is that even allowed?

Unfortunately, teaching yoga for ten years also meant her body had only gotten better since graduation. And I think she was one of those people who started shooting up Botox at twenty-five as a preservative. I have always preferred my preservatives to be taken orally...in yummy things filled with far-off expiration dates and unpronounceable ingredients.

"Wow, Jelly-in. You look so different!" She took both of my hands before I could step out of her reach and swung our arms out to examine me better and make me even more uncomfortable. "You're, like, two whole pounds lighter than you were senior year, aren't you? How'd you manage that?"

My fake smile grew even bigger. "Just one pound actually," I lied. I weighed exactly eight pounds less than I had senior year, plus I'd gotten a little taller and learned how to dress to enhance my body shape. No one would ever mistake me for thin, but I grew to love myself *and* my body. So Denise could go fuck herself.

Bitchy yoga teachers. Wow. What was the world coming to?

"You haven't changed a bit." I yanked my hands back from her. "You're still the same bitch you were senior year. How'd you manage that?"

The Botox prevented her face from showing any reaction, but I could tell she was unprepared for me to snap back. Since she hadn't change over the last decade, she probably assumed I hadn't either. That I was the same shy wall-flower whose greatest wish was to be ignored and forgotten, at least by the popular crowd.

But unfortunately, and ironically, Denise and the people like her were what brought me here tonight.

"*Kid-ding*," we said in unison, complete with the head tilt and singsong voice I knew she would do. Shit, I even giggled with her. Just because I was lying didn't mean she was, right? Maybe she really was just kidding.

"Did the reunion committee get the magazine I sent?" I asked, eyeing the nearest exit. "Did you have a chance to read the main article?" If she said no, there was no reason for me to stay another second.

"I did. Thank you so much for sending it," she said excitedly. "When I showed it to my dad, he was so excited he went online and bought his own copy." She laughed. "It's just mind-blowing to think that one of California's Top 30 Under 30 got their start in our tiny, little town."

I took a sip of my drink in the hopes the ice would cool down my cheeks. "Honestly, it's been a pretty humbling experience overall."

When California Magazine had included me in their list of the "Top 30 Under 30 Professionals to Watch," I bought as many copies as I could get my hands on. Since it came out the same day I received the evite for the reunion, it seemed like a sign from the universe that it was finally time to stop being so afraid of this place and everyone in it. It was time to be the confident, mature woman I claimed to be and go home. You know, to rub my success in all their jerk faces.

"I feel exactly the same way."

She did? Why?

"I just wish he could've come tonight, you know?" she asked.

My stomach dropped. The other reason I was brave enough to come tonight—because *he* wouldn't be here. Then the second hit landed. Denise had said *one* of the Top 30 under 30.

One.

"My dad watches tech industry news like my kids watch Bluey on Disney Plus." She rolled her eyes, completely ignoring the woman slowly crumbling in front of her. "Not that you can miss Alec—he's everywhere now, isn't he? Well, Dad would've freaked the F out if I'd gotten Alec's autograph. I swear, he thinks that man walks on water."

"Alec, right." Obviously, I knew Alec also made the list. The jerk had been number one in the damn 30 Under 30 list. But as number twenty-nine, my name was listed before his in the magazine. *Way* before his. Pages and pages before his. So how could she have missed it? Missed *me*?

And here I'd thought sending the magazine with a post-it stuck to the page with my name and face on it lacked subtlety.

"Trust me," I said after taking a long breath, "he doesn't walk on water."

"If you say so," she trilled. "You'd know better than me." She pursed her lips and got serious for a second. "I wish I'd gotten to know him better back then."

"Why?" If she'd gotten to know him back then, she would've had to see him as a real person with real feelings who could feel real hurt versus just someone to pick on and belittle. And where was the fun in that?

"In all the time you two were together, did you ever think he'd be the one to finally give Apple some real competition?"

"We were *never* together." I winced, pissed at myself for letting that comment hit a little too deep.

She laughed. "That's probably a good thing. I don't know what I would do if my ex-boyfriend turned out to be one of the richest men in America, *and* one of the hottest." She shook her head. "That part is almost more incredible, isn't it? Like, he was so skinny and awkward in high school. He sure grew up well, didn't he?"

"Honestly, I haven't had much time to think about him," I said tightly and truthfully—in the last five years, I'd gotten incredibly skilled at clicking away from or ignoring anything involving him. "What with running a successful law practice, raising a child, and appearing on MSNBC." Only twice, and only because I was representing a celebrity, but it was two appearances more than *Denise* had done.

"That's too bad because his story is fascinating."

I growled internally. "A lot of people's stories are fascinating. For doing more than making a lot of money."

"He's F-ing hot too."

"Right," I agreed tightly. "Can't believe I forgot that part."

"I still can't believe he couldn't make it tonight," she pouted.

"Yeah, that's...too bad." For her, anyway.

"You live in California too, right?" The fact that she asked meant my post-it had definitely been too subtle. "Do you think you could ask him to sign my dad's magazine the next time you see him?"

"Do you have any idea how big California is? I live in Southern California, and I assume"—fine, I knew, but I didn't have to admit that to her—"he lives in Northern California. No one drives eight plus hours to bump into an old friend at the grocery store like you do here."

"But you guys were besties," she said, squinting at me. "Why don't you see him?"

"It's complicated." I sighed internally, wondering how I could explain how badly he'd broken my heart to someone who would never understand...or care.

Sadly, that seemed almost easy compared to explaining the *reason* my heart had been broken ten years ago. How one night altered every moment of my life since. And how it would've done the same to Alec's...if he ever found out.

Chapter 2

Gillian

Before Denise could destroy any more of my ego, there was a commotion by the entrance. Alumni were peering out the double metal doors into the small vestibule where the check-in table had been set up.

Denise groaned. "What did they F-up now?"

"You know you're old enough to say 'fuck', right?"

"Huh?" she asked distractedly.

"They probably need you to help with whatever they F'ed up."

"Isn't that the F-ing truth?" She shuffled across the gymnasium as fast as her tight little yoga ass and four-inch heels could take her.

"Namaste," I mumbled, thankful her attention span hadn't expanded, and her need for control hadn't diminished.

I watched the crowd near the door grow, wondering how obnoxious it would be to open one of the other doors to make my escape, the ones with alarms attached to them.

I'd come here for nothing. My big moment of retribution had disappeared before it began. I hadn't felt this invisible since...high school.

"Motherfucker," I said out loud, emphasizing the second part of the word. With absolutely no desire to get sucked into whatever drama was happening, I realized now would be a great time to swing by the bar and grab a drink or three while everyone else was distracted.

I didn't turn around to check out what had happened until I held a double vodka tonic in one hand and a tiny plateful of sad *hors d'oeuvres* from Costco in the other.

"You couldn't have gone with the *good* Costco *hors d'oeuvres*, Denise? Really?" It may have been a petty thing to criticize, but it was better than nothing and, God help me, I needed something to feel better about. If it had to be the frozen food options at Costco, so be it. At this point, I was above nothing.

While I was getting my snack, the crowd had come all the way into the gym and formed a circle with all of them facing inward, as if whatever was in the middle was magnetic.

When a hole appeared in the wall of people, I saw a flash of the magnet. Just the side of his face, but no way could anyone be that gorgeous. It just didn't happen, especially not in puny towns like this one.

I'd been meaning to get my eyes checked, and the gym was lit only by string lights and the radiance from the spotlights pointed at the DJ onstage, so who knows what I saw. The man might not have been the most beautiful man I'd ever seen. The sharp edge of his jawline and perfect straightness of his nose might've been a result of shadows and not at all as strong as they looked.

In the time it had taken me to blink a few times, the crowd had constricted again, and I couldn't see anything. It was probably Gus the janitor anyway. He'd been older than God ten years ago, but I wouldn't be surprised if he was still working here. I laughed at the idea of him clean shaven, his giant ball of keys ruining the lines of his fancy suit.

Unfortunately, that laugh happened at the exact moment I popped a baby quiche into my mouth. Coughing like mad, I spit bits of egg and spinach into my napkin, thankful I didn't choke on it, and that no one was paying any attention to me at all.

Just like in the old days.

I flashed back to something similar happening in this very place sophomore year. A chunk of carrot had briefly lodged itself in my throat. The whole school sat there, staring at me while I turned bright red from both the humiliation and the lack of air until the carrot dislodged. Then a loud commotion by the lunch line had swung everyone's attention away from me. Alec had tripped and knocked over the big, black trash can, sending old food and half-empty milk boxes skittering in every direction.

"Ta-da!" he yelled, going down on his knee, sticking his scrawny arms out to the sides, and shaking his hands. "I'll be here all week. And the week after that. And the week after that. And the next one. And sadly, the next and the next. Because high school is a never-ending torture chamber."

His "accident" had given me the time I needed to get through the coughing spell and regain my composure without the eyes of the entire school staring me down.

When he winked at me, I knew he'd done it on purpose, drawing the judgmental eyes and laughter to himself and off me. It didn't even matter we had to spend the rest of the lunch period picking up garbage. I owed him. Alec had saved me twice that day.

I missed that guy—the one he'd been back then.

Denise and everyone else could have who he was now—the "new and improved" version. Although, even if I could have the old Alec back, I wouldn't want to see him here tonight. It had been too long since we'd seen or spoken to each other and so much happened since. Those kinds of reconnections were awkward and painful enough without the added pressure of long-held secrets.

Thankfully, the reunion's RSVP list had been public, and his name hadn't been on it, so I figured it was safe. Plus, I didn't see his name tag on the table when I checked-in—proof he opted not to come tonight and was therefore still smarter than me. Taking over the tech industry, doing whatever it is gorgeous, rich people do, and being the number one person to watch in California, probably kept him busy.

I looked back over to the crowd and saw the back of a man's head this time. His hair looked a little too dark and healthy to be Gus'. When he turned his head to say something, and I could see him more clearly, I started choking again.

It couldn't be him. He wasn't coming. They hadn't made a shitty name tag for him, so how could they possibly let him in?

Plus, Denise's views on his hotness aside, I'd seen a recent picture of Alec in the California Magazine article. Sure, he looked amazing, but hello! That was why God had created Photoshop and filters—to make someone look a hell of a lot hotter in a picture than they were in real life. Hell, my own mother could barely recognize me once the magazine editors had finished photoshopping the already-photoshopped headshot I'd sent them to use.

Come to think of it, maybe that was why Denise didn't know I was the twenty-ninth most important professional to watch. She hadn't recognized my picture. And that, ladies and gentlemen, was the unintended danger of filters and Photoshop.

I'd gone to school with a lot of what I used to call "beautiful people," but now I knew I'd given them too much credit. True, they were the most beautiful people in a town of five thousand, but they weren't even in the same league as people like this man. And they knew it. All of them did. They looked at him the way I used to look at *them*—with far too much awe than was healthy or even rational.

If in doubt, look at how everyone was fawning over the poor guy. He was still human, for goodness sakes. And he was probably a total dick. A suit that fit as flawlessly was probably made by small, incredibly skilled children in a sweatshop somewhere. People like him were what I fought against every day. Good looks let people get away with all kinds of things the rest of us weren't allowed to, and money only made it worse.

If that rule worked on levels, this guy could get away with murdering someone in the middle of the dance floor. Hopefully he'd start with Denise.

Why would someone like him even be here? There was nobody that attractive in my graduating class, and he was too well-dressed to be making a teacher's salary. He had to be someone's plus-one. A husband or significant other of one of my old classmates.

Well, whoever was standing next to him in that circle of admirers was probably feeling how I'd hoped to feel tonight. Vindicated. Proud. Able to look her former classmates in the eye and enjoy the shock on their faces for how far she'd come, even if in her case, her big accomplishment was landing a hot husband. That couldn't be easy to do. Certainly *keeping* him had to be tough.

Wait a second! Maybe she wasn't actually keeping him. Maybe she hired him just for the night. An escort. Damn it. Why hadn't I thought of that?

Miraculously, I swallowed the next baby quiche without choking on it and spun around as the man slowly made his way out of the circle of admirers and headed toward me.

No. Not me. He was heading for the bar. Or the buffet. Definitely *not* me.

Of all the terrible reasons I showed up here tonight, hooking up with an old classmate's husband or male prostitute wasn't one of them.

I turned my head subtly, just enough to be able to see a fuzzy version of him out of the corner of my eye. He made his way across the room, dismissing people at least politely enough not to make them run off crying. But boy did they seem disappointed, walking away with their heads lowered. I might've been able to enjoy that a little if I didn't already hate everyone.

He stopped about halfway, cursed, and took a phone out of his suit pocket. I turned back to the food to distract myself and avoid being caught gawking at him like everyone else. What was wrong with me?

Having given up on the *hors d'oeuvres*, I moved to the small dessert table and popped a mini profiterole with chocolate drizzle into my mouth. Blech. Is there anything in the world more disappointing than bad-tasting dessert? I think not.

I chucked the plate into the garbage and grabbed a new one.

"Let me give you my number," a voice I instantly recognized as Denise's said behind me. "We can catch up."

"I don't think so." The voice was low, firm, and dismissive. "You don't seem to have changed at all, and apparently, you already know everything there is to know about me. So what could we possibly have to catch up on?"

I chuckled under my breath, already liking whoever she was talking to. But if I looked to see who it was, I'd have to reengage with Denise. I'd just give them another minute and hope he said something that made her cry.

"Maybe..." Denise whined. "Maybe later then."

Out of my peripheral vision, I saw a man step up to the table, uncomfortably close to me. The gorgeous stranger who apparently *was* an alumnus of Riverside High after all.

"Like in ten years or so?" He shrugged. "Maybe."

Denise laughed nervously as if she had a hunch he wasn't kidding but still wanted to take it that way. "Okay then. I'll be around all night if you need anything." Was there anything more enjoyable than hearing the clicking heels of someone you don't like as they walked away?

His shoulder bumped into mine. Rude or accidental? That was the question. Rich men always took up more space than they should, so I decided it had been an accident, at least until I heard what he said next.

"A lot can change in ten years, right, Gills?" *Gills.* Not Gillian, not Jillian, not even Jill. He said *Gills*, complete with a hard G. Like a shark.

Only one person in this place ever called me that. My best friend, the person I grew up next to, who, back then, knew me better than anyone else.

The one who wasn't F-ing supposed to be here tonight.

Chapter 3

Gillian

I took a step back, creating not nearly enough space between us, and kept my gaze level with his chest. I wasn't ready to see his face, his eyes, because nothing made sense. Up was down. Inside was out and all that.

I knew Alec had changed—a pact he made with his college roommates or something—but after he blew me off, blew *Lucas* off, without a word, I'd done my absolute best to forget about him. It hadn't worked—I thought about him way more than I wish I did—but I refused to let myself Google his name or company. I had no desire to make myself feel worse than I already did.

Look at him, Gillian. The least you could do is look at him in the eye.

Apparently, even my eyeballs were out of shape because it took a lot of effort to move them up his broad chest, over his classic gray tie to his clenched jaw, the fullness of his lower lip, then his upper one, to his perfectly straight nose, and finally to the brown eyes I spent my teenage years mesmerized by.

The only things about him that hadn't changed were his height and his dimples.

"Wow." I'd missed a lot. Denise was right—the man in front of me was unforgettable—and I was wrong—the magazine editors had photoshopped my picture within an inch of my life, but they hadn't touched-up his picture *at all*.

"Alec." The stupid, flimsy, hand-written name tag on his lapel made it all too real. "Alec? Oh my gawd, what happened to you?"

"That bad, huh?" His voice was lower, more masculine and richer, but also exactly the way I remembered it. When I *let* myself remember it.

"Bad? No. Good." Very, very good. "But you're so..." I reached up to touch his face and check if he was real, stopping myself just in time. As impossible as it seemed, he was. He was so... He was just so damn... "Gorgeous."

"I was thinking the same thing. I thought I remembered how beautiful you are. Now I feel like I should apologize for underestimating you."

I felt the kind of blush only real redheads can manage rush from my chest to my cheeks, hating how quickly I'd turned back into a nervous teenager.

"You aren't supposed to be here," I snapped to regain a bit of my pride. Anyone could give you a compliment. They might even mean it. But if it wasn't backed up by respect and decency, you were better off without it.

"I switched a couple things around at the last minute and got here as soon as I could." He'd probably chartered a plane. Or maybe he had his own plane. I didn't ask. I didn't care.

"What the hell happened to you?" It was impossible not to stare at him—now more than ever. He looked like a completely different man until I caught his eyes and saw his dimples as he smiled. "Was it steroids, or that stuff they gave Captain America in the Marvel movies?

"No. No. And it was Steve Rogers who got Erskine's serum to become Captain America. Plus, it was in the comic books way before the movies." He cocked his head to the side just like he used to when discussing something random he cared about. "But also, no, unfortunately, I didn't get that either." He pulled his wallet from inside his coat as he went up to the bar. "What's the shittiest wine you have?" After a moment of confusion, the bartender held up a bottle.

"What do you think, Gills? It's not Boone's, but it's probably close."

I sighed dramatically and acted as if I wasn't going to need the entire bottle to deal with this unexpected reunion. "After ten years of not seeing me, you're going to buy me the cheapest wine you can find? Wow, you sure know how to treat a girl."

He shrugged. "I figured it would help put us in the mood to reminisce. Remember the night we graduated?"

I almost choked again, this time on nothing. Did I remember grad night? Dumbest question ever.

"Not which wine we drank." I swallowed. "Do you?"

"I remember every single second of that night—from swiping your mom's wine to..." His gaze lowered and ran the length of my body. My involuntary shiver made it clear we *both* remembered what happened that night. "To saying goodbye to you the next morning."

Neither of us had known that would be the last time we spoke or saw each other. I'd left to spend the summer at my dad and stepmom's house like I'd done every summer since I was seven. And like every other summer, I expected us to write to each other constantly and then reunite before school started. None of that happened.

"Anyway…" After he paid for our drinks and tipped the bartender well, he handed me one. "A toast! To the sweetness of bad wine and good memories."

"What about bittersweet memories?"

"Nope. Not tonight. Tonight is only for the good ones." He raised his glass, smirking. "Bottom's up." He really had changed. Whatever transformative event he'd gone through that had put forty pounds of muscle and sixty pounds of confidence on his frame, had also made him more seductive and wicked. Did that make it better or worse that he never replied to my letter?

It wasn't anything like the Boone's Farm wine we drank a decade ago, but without a word, we both held our noses closed exactly as we'd done that night, downed the whole glass, and then burst out laughing.

"I missed you, Gills." He took my cup, tossed it and his into the garbage, and pulled me into a hug. "I missed you a lot."

"I missed you too." Closing my eyes to avoid tearing up, I pressed my cheek to his chest, feeling all his warmth encircle me. It had been too long since I felt the touch of someone who'd loved me for me, not just what I could give them.

It was just like the old days—me and Alec against the world.

Except his hugs were better now. A lot better. He'd always been able to wrap his long arms all the way around me, but now they were thicker, warmer, more protective. His chest was hard against the side of my face, now hard like muscle not just bone. And instead of being able to practically feel every one of his ribs and the random jab of an elbow, his body filled my arms, and the only hard thing jabbing me was his—

Oh my.

As soon as I pushed back, we both looked down to the bulge at his crotch.

"Really, Alec?" I grumbled. Apparently, he was still the same teenage boy in some ways after all.

"Sorry 'bout that," he said. "Hang on. What am I apologizing for? It's your fault."

"You're blaming me for that?" I snorted. "That's not fair."

"It is what it is, Gills. I don't make the rules."

I tore my gaze away from his cock and saw how small my hand looked in his. Wait. Why was he holding my hand? Why was I *letting* him hold my hand?

Just then, a tiny blonde came up, stopping a few feet away and waiting for him to notice her. The woman was stunning and probably not the type accustomed to being ignored. In fact, Alec was the only man in the room not staring at her. Because, for some reason, he was too busy staring at me.

"Alec?" After a quick, possibly genuine smile at me, she motioned for him to come over.

He sighed and dropped my hand. "Excuse me for a second."

I nodded even though I didn't think it was a question or something I could say no to. Maybe it was shock. It's not every day you discover your nerdy high school best friend had turned into someone who could be Chris Evans' better looking body double.

Even with the help of the blonde's four-inch heels, he had to lean down so she could whisper into his ear. I didn't recognize her, and her name tag was handwritten like Alec's, so he must have brought her. As his date.

Alec might not have stood a chance with a woman like that ten years ago, but now he could have whoever he wanted. And look who he picked. Someone who looked as different from me as possible. This proved all my worst fears true—all men, even the ones who'd been on the other side and should've known better—would pick a tiny, beautiful-since-birth, blond woman over someone who'd had to learn that, despite what everyone told her, she was worth something.

Damnit. They would make beautiful children together. And unless Alec had made a deal with the devil to look like that in exchange for all his intelligence, their kids would be brilliant even if the blonde was a moron.

Why did that thought hurt so much?

I had a brilliant and beautiful kid who'd inherited my freckles, his dad's eyes, and both our intelligences combined. No way would their kid be able to compete with mine, so there was nothing to feel jealous over.

Alec's brow tightened. "Well, that's the end of that, I suppose." Any trace of his smile was completely gone when he pulled away from her and looked at me. "You'll keep me company, won't you, Gills?"

"For a little while, I guess." I quickly added, "Unless you get drunk and obnoxious."

"Thankfully, I only plan on doing one of those things tonight."

I raised a brow. "Are you going to make me guess which one?"

"Yoohoo?" The woman held up her palms. "What about me?"

"You can take off," he said dismissively. "I won't need you anymore tonight, but thanks for coming."

I flinched at the remark. Regardless of how much jealousy, deserved or undeserved animosity, and judgment I felt toward her, women needed to take care of each other.

"Don't you dare talk to her like that."

Both of their gazes flew to me.

The woman held up her hand. "It's okay—"

"No. It's not okay," I said, stomping over to my old best friend. "You really *have* changed, haven't you?"

His eyes narrowed but still looked amused. "You think so?"

"I don't mean how you look. Well, not *only* how you look." I grabbed the blonde's arm to stop her from fleeing but kept my glare focused on him. "The Alec I knew would've never spoken to a woman like that."

His stupid smile just grew. "He wouldn't have."

"No, he wouldn't. He treated everyone with respect." Whether they deserved it or not. "He wouldn't have dismissed someone just because he found someone he wanted to talk to more." Not that there wasn't a tiny sliver of me that wasn't happy he saw me as more appealing than the blonde, of course.

"He didn't dismiss me. He—"

This time, Alec stopped her. "Don't you want to hear about the man I used to be, Shelly?"

The woman chuckled. "With every cell of my being."

I shook my head disgustedly. "I would never have imagined the guy I knew would give up who he *was* just to be hot."

"The guy you knew didn't have the option," he said seriously. "So how could anyone know what he'd do?"

"I could." I shook my head again. "At least, I thought I could." All those painstakingly handwritten letters back and forth every summer while I was stuck at my dad's place outside Los Angeles. Or during the school year when he'd come to my house and sneak into my room late at night. All that damn talking about what our futures would be like, how different from our present. But in the end, I realized I didn't know him as well as I thought I did.

"I did too." He motioned for me to continue, but my fire had quelled. Or gotten confused by his lack of anger or defensiveness.

"What am I missing?"

Alec glanced at the woman. "Shelly, do you want to explain or should I?"

"I will. You've already blown it." She cleared her throat. "Alec is way too smart to dismiss me. Because he knows he wouldn't make it three days on his own."

"Oh." I'd heard about these kinds of relationships. Hell, I'd even had one a few years ago. Co-dependency, I think my therapist called it.

"Shelly is my executive assistant, Gills. I begged her to come with me tonight for backup—in case I needed to get out of here in a hurry. Since that is no longer something I need, I told her she could go back to the hotel if she wanted to."

"Oh."

"Where her husband is staying."

"Oh."

"Would you like me to go away too?" he asked calmly.

"No." I felt dizzy when I finished shaking my head. "I mean, you should stay if you want to."

"The other option is we could *all* leave. Shelly can go be with her husband, while you and I go catch up somewhere with fewer balloons and better food."

"You forgot to mention fewer and better people," I said as I noticed Denise speed walk toward us, holding up a copy of California Magazine. "Let's go."

Chapter 4

Alec

Gills played with her phone while I spoke to Shelly in front of the school. The place was so much smaller than I remembered. Then again, maybe it was the angle I was seeing it from this time that changed my perspective. A member of the football team hadn't shoved me to the ground and left me there to flounder like a flipped over turtle—my backpack rivaling my entire body weight and keeping me down.

Yep. After leaving this hellhole everything had changed for the better. And tonight, if I was very lucky, everything would change again.

Shelly peered around my shoulder to look at Gills. "How do you think it's going?" She'd been my assistant for the last four years and had spent the last four days prepping me for tonight. It hadn't been nearly enough time.

"You asking that makes me think the potentially fatal level of panic I'm feeling isn't showing on my face, so that's good, right?"

She pressed her lips together to hold in her laughter while she adjusted my tie. "I'm still having a hard time believing a woman can cause an incredibly confident, successful, charismatic man to completely lose his shit so quickly. Maybe I should stick around and learn her secrets. Honestly, if Darren was half as excited to spend time with me as you are with Gillian, I'd be a much happier woman."

"You already *are* a happy woman."

"True. But who doesn't want to be happier than they already are?"

I would have to think about that. I could spend my entire morning commute listing all the things I had to be grateful for. That the software company I'd started right out of college had been consistently growing, blowing past the goals we set at the beginning of each year. Having a team of professionals to handle all the jobs I didn't have the expertise for. Being able to live in an apartment straight out of a magazine in a city I adored. Having a mom who loved me no matter what, and a prick of a father who'd been kind enough to bail on us early. My four best friends—my brothers in every way that mattered—who'd gone with me on the bizarre journey that led me to where I am.

And, of course, the woman who'd made me a man—in both the biblical sense and in helping me define the man I wanted to be.

All so that tonight, ten years later, I finally had the balls to tell her.

"Now remember," Shelly said, "you're a total catch who could have any woman you want."

I chuckled, still not believing it, despite the proof. I hadn't done much to test the theory, but women did respond favorably to me now. A hell of a lot better than they used to. The three hundred bucks my buddies and me each chipped in to learn how to talk to and treat women had been the best investment any of us would ever make. Like a bootcamp for nerds. A bunch of geniuses were finally smart enough to realize we weren't up to the challenge on our own; therefore, hiring an expert just made sense.

"And we're absolutely sure she's not married, right?" Just because it felt wrong to Google my first real friend, love, and lover more than three times didn't mean someone else couldn't. "Or in a serious relationship?" That's all I needed to know to prepare myself. So I could grieve what-might-have-been-mine far away from other people, especially her. Because no matter what, I wanted Gills to be happy, and it's hard to feign happiness while you're ugly crying.

"No marriage. No serious relationship," she said, smoothing my lapels. "Stop worrying, Alec. From what I could tell with my superior cyberstalking skills, her dating life is just as pathetic as yours." Shelly got serious for a moment. "I just hope she realizes what she could have." She patted my chest as if she'd done all she could. "Go have fun."

Fun. Right. I hadn't smiled since Shelly showed me the stupid reunion evite. She knew how hard high school had been for me. I guess she thought I would want to come back to my dinky hometown and show off how far I'd come, how much I'd *over*come.

Did it feel good to see all the people who'd treated me like shit before suddenly look at me with a bit of awe, speak to me with respect, treat me like I was special? Sure. How could it not? Those days were awful.

But that's not why I came tonight.

From the moment I saw that evite, I couldn't get rid of the thought of how easy life was when you never thought about what was missing from it. Or who was missing from it.

After Gills left for her dad's place the summer after graduation, I wrote her so many letters—our normal way of communicating while she was away because her dad lived off-grid. But after a few replies, she stopped. So I wrote her *more* often, kept asking when she'd be coming back to her mom's, hoping we could spend some time together before we left for college on opposite ends of the country.

She didn't reply. She didn't come back. And I spent the rest of the summer miserable and lonely. When I got to MIT, I tried to shove all thoughts and memories of Gills and Riverside High out of my conscious mind. Honestly, it worked for a little while—everything was new and challenging, and I had to focus on what I was doing if I wanted to get anything out of it.

But even now, when I was tired or frustrated or couldn't sleep at night, an intense need to talk to her took over, and nothing I did would shake it loose.

"Remember what you promised," Shelly said as she slid into the back of the hired car. "I get four days to spend with my husband and your credit card, and under no circumstances will I be answering any calls or texts."

I cocked my head to the side. "I don't remember mentioning anything about my credit card."

"Well, it's a good thing I remembered for you then, isn't it?" She smiled, knowing I wouldn't refuse. "But I will still have my phone, so if you wanted to, say, text me good news later..." She winked. "Or tomorrow, that'd be great. But no work stuff!" Shelly lowered the window and waved. "It was nice to meet you, Gillian."

Gills fumbled with her phone as she looked up. "You too."

When the car was gone, I turned back to look at her. She'd always been beautiful—the kindest blue eyes, lots and lots of freckles, a mass of red hair she always complained about. But now? Now she had all that plus grace, wisdom, and presence. She wasn't hiding anymore. Her self-confidence was the sexiest thing about her, and that was saying something.

"We should probably talk." The way she gnawed on her lower lip sent a signal straight to my cock.

"Absolutely." *I can do this.* I run a billion-dollar company and have people who depend on me for their livelihoods. I have everything material I could ever want, and friends who've been with me through thin and thick. Literally.

Gills and I were inseparable for all four years of high school. She loved me back then. I know she did. Granted, it wasn't how I *wanted* her to love me, but things were better now, *I* was better now. And I could do anything I set my mind to.

This was me setting my mind.

"Where would you like to start?" I asked as we walked back toward the muffled sound of "Blurred Lines" playing over the ancient sound system in the gym. But since neither of us had anything to say to our former classmates, we hung a right and walked toward east wing of classrooms.

"Denise called you hot."

I blew out a breath. "Did she?"

"The most beautiful and popular girl in our graduating class thinks you're hot, and that's your reaction? If you went back in there"—she flicked her head back toward the gym—"and told her to get on her knees and suck your cock in front of all those people, she'd totally do it. All she'd want in return is for you to sign her magazine."

I smiled, ignoring all the shit about Denise. "Congratulations on making the list, by the way. I was so proud when I saw your name. At first, I wasn't sure it was you because the picture was..." I grimaced a little.

"Bad?"

I shook my head. "Not bad. Just not a good representation of how incredible looking you are."

"That's because it was photoshopped and then photoshopped on top of the photoshopping. Like yours should've been."

"What does that mean?"

"Never mind," she grumbled. "Besides we're not talking about me. We're talking about you..." She exaggerated a wink. "And Denise."

I knew she meant it as a joke, something to distract from the awkwardness of two inseparable friends meeting up again after a decade of separation, so I gave it to her. But I hadn't come here tonight for Denise.

"Tell me about your life," she said. "I want to know everything."

I'd told my story so many times to so many reporters and peers, it bored the hell out of me. But talking to Gills made everything exciting again. I could go deeper, be more open and honest than I could with anyone else because I knew she would understand. And even when she didn't, she wouldn't judge me.

So, as we wandered down the halls I never thought I'd see again, I told her about the deal my friends and I had made with a dark-haired, nineteen-year-old devil in our second year of college and a little about the torture and humiliation Maddie had put us through.

"It all started on a Friday night when the five of us were feeling particularly pathetic. Maddie came by to sweet-talk her twin brother into giving her some money. Twenty minutes later, we'd each coughed up three hundred bucks to hire her as an expert in the one thing none of us were smart enough to master."

Gills popped an eyebrow. "Women?"

I smiled. "Maybe for my friends, but my goal has never been to master a woman. I just wanted to know how to talk to and treat them." That was a lie. At the time, I was pining over Gills and trying to figure out what I'd done wrong, why she'd ghosted me after the only time we'd been together as more that friends.

"Maddie told us what clothes to buy, how to cut our hair, what skin products and colognes to use, and—because she watched too much reality television —if we were that week's VIN—"

"Vehicle Identification Number?"

"Very Important Nerd." I shrugged. "She thought she was funny, and it wasn't a lie—we *were* all nerds. Plus, what she knew, and the rest of us finally figured out, is that the attributes that got us picked on in high school turned out to be pretty handy as adults."

"If only bullies could learn that."

"Bullies are the way they are because they're scared someone will find out how weak they really are. They're trapped in their own cycle of fear. That's the last thing I would ever want to be—afraid of being discovered as something I'm not."

She knocked on her old locker, the loud tinny sound reverberating through the sad, empty hallway. "Think it's the same combo?"

"I hope not." I shoved her over a little so I could get to mine.

After we'd both tried a few times, we gave up and kept walking, our conversation broken up by random memories brought on by classrooms, bulletin boards, and bathrooms.

"So what did you get as a VIN?" she asked.

"We got to ask Maddie any question we wanted. Nothing was off-limits, so you can imagine what topic we spent the most time on."

She nodded. "This went on for over a year? I didn't think there were that many positions. She must be a knowledgeable girl. Maybe I need a coach like that."

"Maddie was the only one who referred to herself as Coach. All of us called her a sadist."

"I'd call her a genius. She took five insecure, skinny-yet-adorable nerds and turned them into well-dressed, confident, fairly attractive men with—"

"Fairly attractive?" I laughed. "Gee, thanks."

"Okay." She rolled her eyes dramatically. "I don't want to fight over modifiers. How about well-dressed, confident, *moderately* attractive men, at least one of whom has a great big sensitive ego?"

"That's accurate." I stopped and looked at her with my best sad puppy eyes. "Is it too much to ask you to add the 'yet-adorable' back in there somewhere?"

"Yes, Alec, you're still adorable." She shrugged. "And you've always been moderately attractive...I guess."

"Awww, that's so sweet." I nudged her with my shoulder. "But I'm still a nerd. I just grew up, did a lot of weight training, learned how to eat properly, and bought some new clothes."

"Is that really all that changed about you?"

I couldn't tell if her expression meant she was afraid I *had* changed a lot or disappointed I hadn't changed more.

Either way, I had to be honest. Tell her how I felt and let the dice fall as they may.

"Come on."

Chapter 5

Alec

"Tell me where we're going first," she said skeptically, although she didn't even hesitate to follow me. Until she realized I was leading her back to the gym. Luckily, whoever had been sitting at the check-in desk was gone and only two nametags remained on the table.

"I don't want to see those people again, Alec. Like ever."

"We don't have to." I shushed her with one my finger to my lips, then relaxed the rest of them to expose the key I had hidden in my hand. "But we have to pass it to get to the yearbook room."

"Where did you get that?" Wide-eyed, she grabbed my hand as we snuck past the reunion, keeping our backs to the open doorway the whole way.

"Remember Gus, the janitor?" I waited for her to nod. "Shelly helped me track him down today. All I can say is that he has enough money to finally retire now, and it's also the last time anyone will ever use this key because I may have agreed to replace all the school's ancient door locks with the digital keyless entry kind."

"Alec, you didn't!"

Her laughter stopped me in my tracks. "I love making you laugh." Always had. Even if it came at my expense, it was a price I'd pay a thousand times over.

"Stop staring at me, creeper." She smoothed her hair off her face. "I want to find out if Gus played you and took your money in exchange for the key to the bathrooms."

"Shit. I hadn't thought of that." I took her hand again and started walking. "We'd better find out."

When we got to the yearbook room, I handed her the key and stepped out of her way. "Go for it."

We both held our breaths. Not sure about her, but at least part of the reason I couldn't breathe was that I was standing directly behind her, her neck exposed as she slipped the key into the lock on the doorknob. It would be so easy to lean in and run my lips across her skin, race my tongue down her neck. I couldn't think of anything else until she spoke.

"I think Gus ripped you off."

"What the fuck?" I blurted. "Seriously?"

Laughing, she stepped out of the way so I could turn the handle and curse a few more times.

"Oh, Alec." She shook her head slowly, crossing her arms over her chest and popping her hip out. "I can't believe you forgot the wiggle and push."

"How did I forget the wiggle and push?" It was one of the few high points in my high school career.

The school was built in the 1950s and had only gotten cosmetic repairs since. This meant there were so many layers of paint built up on the doorframe and latch plate, the latch wouldn't release without a decent amount of force being added. That was why Gills had created the wiggle and push, and why I couldn't believe I'd forgotten it.

"Let me," Gills whispered. "For old time's sake."

"I'd have it no other way." I watched her with the same wonder as I had as a seventeen-year-old as she wiggled her ass along with the doorknob and then swung a hip into the door to pop it open.

Whatever else happened tonight, just seeing that again made the trip worth it.

"Still got it." She strutted into the room we'd spent every lunch break and afterschool hiding in.

"Yes. Yes, you do," I said, appreciatively. "You may even have developed *more* of it."

She swung around to glare at me. "Are you calling me fat?"

"Of course not," I spat, closing the door behind me. "I would never... You're not..." Then I saw the corner of her mouth curl. I sighed in relief and mumbled, "I might call you cruel though."

I didn't turn on the overhead fluorescents because someone might see the light through the high windows on the hallway side, but there was just enough light coming through the drapes covering the windows on the side of the room that overlooked the quad.

"I was kidding," she said. "I know you'd never call me that. Besides, while I may not have hired a Maddie, I did learn how to dress to feel good about myself. That plus lots and lots of therapy and the ability to choose who I let into my life has done wonders for my self-esteem."

"I'm glad." There had never been any doubt that when our former classmates called me a nerd, they weren't lying. But they'd always been wrong about Gills. They picked on her because they could, because she had always been too afraid to fight back. And maybe because she chose to hang out with the kid they enjoyed picking on most, whose attempts to fight back only made them laugh harder.

Gills went to a bookshelf, dragged her finger along a row of yearbooks until she found ours and pulled it out.

"Are you sure you want to look at that?"

The yearbook committee consisted of four whole members, but Gills and I had picked out each picture, done all the typesetting, organized all the pages. For her, yearbook was something to put on her college applications and an excuse to hang out in this room all the time. There was only ever one reason I worked on the yearbook—because she was working on the yearbook.

"Just one picture. It's my favorite." She set the heavy book onto the long worktable in the center of the room and started flipping groups of pages without looking at them, as if she knew the exact page she wanted.

"Your senior portrait?"

"Nope."

"*My* senior portrait?" Even I couldn't keep a straight face when I said it. No one on earth—not even my own mother—would say my portrait was their favorite. I looked as clueless as I'd felt—the only glasses we could afford were bulky black plastic circles a la Edna Mode from *The Incredibles*, and with a prescription as strong as mine, the cheap lenses distorted my eyes, making them look abnormally large. My hair had been too long and too unkept, and the suit my mom had gotten me for the photo was two sizes too big but also somehow too short in the sleeves and cuffs.

I took the plastic chair next to her, leaning in until she shooed me away. "Denise's senior portrait?"

Since we hadn't been in any clubs or on any teams or gone to the dances or done much of anything at all, our class photographer hadn't taken any candid pictures of us.

"The yearbook group shot?"

"Stop guessing," she said sternly. "You're just embarrassing yourself."

"It doesn't take a lot for me to do that." As soon as she slid the book in front of me and sat back, I laughed. "Fuck, I'd blissfully forgotten how tragic I looked back then. Thanks for the reminder."

It was the only picture Gills had taken herself—me sitting at this very same table, my big, worshipping puppy eyes taking up most of the shot.

"I think you look great." She chuckled when I elbowed her in the arm. "I mean, I can't lie—you look better now."

"Stop, you're making me blush," I grumbled.

"But your eyes are the same, and that's what I love most in this picture. I don't even know what you were working on or thinking about right before I snapped the picture. But I adore the way you're looking at the camera."

"I wasn't looking at the camera."

She furrowed her brow. "Of course you were."

I shook my head. "I was looking at *you*."

After a moment, she sighed. "Look, Alec. There's—"

I caught the side of her plastic seat before she could scoot away.

It was now or never.

"You want to know what I was thinking about just before you took the picture?" I asked. "I was thinking about you. I know that because I *always* thought about you." I dragged her chair out and shifted my own so we were facing each other properly. "Every time we were in here, or at your house, and every moment in between."

"Alec, I should've told you—"

"Whatever it is, I want to hear it," I said quickly. "I do. But I should've told you all of this a long time ago, and I didn't. Because I was too afraid. And now..." I swallowed. "Now I'm still afraid, but it needs to be said. I don't want to wait another ten years for you to know." I paused. "Plus, I started first, so it's only fair..."

She pursed her lips and thought about it. "You should've written me a letter."

I nodded. When we'd started swapping letters, it had been just for fun—two little kids who didn't have computers or cell phones writing multi-page letters filled with their dumb thoughts, bad handwriting, and countless misspellings. As we got older and learned how to write cursive, she'd tell me what it was like spending the summer on a self-sufficient, off-grid farm in the middle of nowhere, and I'd fill her in on what movies I'd seen, and if they were worth going to again when she came back to Riverside before school started. As teenagers, it felt more like writing a diary entry than a letter, each of us expressing thoughts and ideas and pain we couldn't speak aloud.

"I tried," I said. "It just... I could never get it to come out right."

She nodded, her gaze falling back to the picture. "I always imagined you were fantasizing about tech systems or power suits."

"Nope." Just her. "I can't believe you didn't figure it out. I mean look at that face." I tapped the photo, right on my greasy, clueless teenage forehead. "All I can say is thank God no one will ever find out how much time sad, little Alec spent in here fantasizing about kissing you. It would completely ruin my reputation. Probably cause stock prices to fall too."

"Yeah, right." She laughed.

"Fine. Nothing would happen to my rep or the stock, but that first part..." I blew out a breath. "That first part's true."

"If you spent that much time wanting to kiss me"—she turned her head to look at me—"why didn't you?"

"Uh..." I chuckled. "Because I was scrawny, and I thought you would've kicked my ass?"

"I would not have kicked your ass... any more than you deserved." She laughed, shaking her head so hard a few more curls escaped from the hairclip. Fuck was she beautiful. No wonder I could never forget her.

"Exactly."

She adjusted her chair then smoothed her dress. "I didn't kick your ass the night of graduation."

"Depends on your definition of 'kicking my ass.' Not that I would've wanted it any other way of course." Grad night. "That was the best night of my life. Seriously, never in the history of pity fucks was there a better one. Since you left the next day, I don't know if I ever officially thanked you but—"

She snapped her head up to glare at me. "Excuse me?"

"Oh, come on. You know that was a total pity fuck." Not that I'd minded. Hell, that night had given me jerk-off fodder for years. Literally.

Her eyes intensified, proving she'd wildly misunderstood what I'd meant.

"Oh geez! For *you*. You did the pity fucking. Not me." This was not coming out as I'd planned. "Shit, are you kidding? You were incredible. You were..." I blew out a long breath of air, wondering how to express everything she'd done for me that night. Beyond the physical, which was spectacular albeit on the short side—my fault not hers—she'd made me feel loved, accepted, surprised as hell that someone might actually want to be with me.

"You saved me from being the only virgin in our graduating class who wasn't saving themselves for marriage."

"I didn't fuck you out of pity, Alec."

"I shouldn't have used that expression. I'm sorry. It wasn't fucking. It was—"

"I didn't sleep with you out of pity, you moron! I was a virgin too."

That stopped me. "I thought..." She'd had a boyfriend part of senior year. He went to the school one town over. I hated him with a passion previously unknown to me, so she stopped bringing him up around me. "What about Kyle?"

"Seriously? Eww, no. Would you have wanted Kyle to be *your* first?" She laughed under her breath. "He drooled on me more than my Boxer did."

"Nobody drooled more than Hercules did."

"Except Kyle."

"I was your first." I wasn't sure if I'd meant it as a question or a statement. I needed a minute to process. For the last ten years, I'd believed she'd put up with my inexperienced fumbling because it hadn't meant as much to her, but it was her first time too.

"Why did you sleep with me that night, Gills?"

Her brow tightened as she looked between our feet. "You were the only person outside my family who I ever loved or could imagine ever loving. We only had that night before I left to spend the summer at my dad's, and then you would spend the next four years in Massachusetts."

"But you were supposed to come back here before we both left for college. You didn't. Not even to pack up all the shit at your mom's house." Let alone to say goodbye. "I wrote you." Once a week to start, but as her letters became shorter and more superficial and then outright stopped coming, I started wondering if she had outgrown me. Or if she actually *had* minded my sexual bumbling and having sex had ruined our friendship like everyone said it did. "You were the one who stopped."

"You know that's not true." She slammed the yearbook shut and got up to put it back on the shelf. "Maybe not that summer. I had a lot going on. But I wrote to you in the fall. A few times. I got the address of your dorm from your mom. And you never replied. Not once. About any of it."

"You wrote me back? In the fall?" It felt as if muscles that had been clenched for a decade finally released their grip all at the same time. A single summer I could've understood, but since I hadn't heard from her at all, I figured she'd decided to move on. At that point, the only thing I could do was honor her decision. "My scholarship didn't cover housing, so as soon as I got there, I talked to the bursar about it and started looking for cheaper places off campus. I was only in the dorms for a couple days. And since no one but us sends letters anymore, and you had access to technology by fall, I guess I thought that if you wanted to get hold of me, you'd email." I smiled. "You know, like a normal person."

"You swear you didn't get them?" She stayed facing the bookshelf, her head lowered, until I took her arm and turned her around.

"Gills, this is dumb but great news." I held her by the shoulders. "I spent the last ten years thinking I was so terrible in bed you didn't want anything to do with me ever again."

"Yeah, well, just because you didn't get my letters doesn't mean you weren't terrible in bed too."

"Ouch." I knew she'd said it to lighten the mood, but she hadn't been wrong. "I promise you I'm better now. In fact, all that guilt forced me to up my game and educate myself."

"Education is important." She stifled a laugh.

"Some might say I'm at the top of my class in this arena," I said, smirking. "Summa cu—"

She threw her hand over my mouth. "Don't you dare say it."

Chapter 6

Gillian

I took my hand off his mouth, both of us groaning and grinning at the terrible pun that had almost come out of his lips.

A decade ago, when he didn't reply to the most vulnerable letter I'd ever written, I was angry. Hurt. But that's not actually what landed me in this mess. No, this mess was all mine. He hadn't been reminded of me every single day since. He hadn't chosen not to deal with it, putting it off longer and longer, until any reasonable excuse was long gone. I had. Me.

I'd been waiting ten years for the perfect time to tell him. A time when it would be easy and make sense.

But he seemed so happy to see me again. Should I ruin that for him too?

Unsure what to feel after his revelation about my letters, I'd studied Alec go through a deluge of emotions—relief, embarrassment, joy—hoping I'd be able to pick one to settle on and start feeling again.

"If only there was a way to prove to you how much better I am now, Gills." Apparently, *he* settled on cockiness, along with a bit of the sarcasm I remembered and loved.

"Prove...?" It took me a second to catch up. "How much better you are sexually?" I put my hands on his chest to stop him from getting any closer. "I couldn't possibly ask you for that big of a sacrifice, so I guess I'll just have to take your word for it."

"Will you really be satisfied if you never know for sure?"

I paused. "I honestly don't know how to answer that question." Because I wasn't sure I would. I wanted to know, wanted to remember a time when things were pure and simple. And if I were completely honest, it didn't hurt that he looked like he'd been created on Mount Olympus and smelled like he'd just showered out on a cattle ranch somewhere.

For some reason, I still hadn't lowered my hand from his chest. I stared at it slowly slide down his tie.

"Gills?" He whispered it, reminding me of all the nights we spent laying on my bed, sharing gummy worms, and talking about the future, Alec terrified our laughter would wake up my mom, me occasionally flinching as if I heard her coming down the hall, just to freak him out.

"I've had way too much time to think about that night." He shuddered when I reached his abs, felt each ridge of muscle.

I yanked my hand back, embarrassed. "Me too."

"Mostly, I remember how fucking terrified I was. I was so worried I'd disappoint you."

"You didn't," I said, tossing up my hands. "I really don't remember you being as terrible as you seem to think you were." I shrugged and made a face. "I mean, I've had better since, but I'm pretty sure I've had worse too. Does that make you feel any better?"

"Not really," he said, smirking. "Now I just feel bad for *you*."

I slumped back against the bookshelf. "Me too actually."

"Honestly, it was a miracle I didn't come the second I touched you." He walked to the door and flipped the lock, glancing to me as if checking to make sure I didn't mind. I didn't. "But what do you expect from a teenage boy whose vision of the perfect woman is laying there next to him, completely naked?"

"You thought I was the perfect woman?"

"I still do." When he turned all the way around, the intensity in his eyes sent a pulse through me, and we let out a quick breath at the same time.

"That's..." I blinked a few times. "That's the nicest thing anyone has ever said to me."

"Then you need to stop hanging out with idiots."

Damn it, a girl could only take so many compliments, and he was definitely pushing my limit.

"Why are you being so nice to me?"

He just studied me for a minute, not giving anything away. "I was never good enough for you. Anybody who was paying attention knew that. I came here tonight..." He ran his hand roughly over his mouth, curling it to a fist before dropping it. "I came here hoping you'd think that wasn't true anymore."

It wasn't every day a gorgeous, successful, brilliant man cared what I thought about him, let alone made himself so vulnerable I could break him with a single word.

I never, ever would.

But holy shit, was it a turn-on.

"I guess I wasn't paying close enough attention then." I took a deep breath, let it out slowly, and walked right up to him. "Because the thing I loved most about us is that we didn't have to be anyone other than who we were. Equals. Nobody looking up or down on anyone else." I smiled at the dumb irony that I was saying that to a man five-and-a-half inches taller than me, eight when I wasn't wearing heels.

"I loved that too. Like you wouldn't believe." After tucking an escaped curl behind my ear, he slid his hand around to the nape of my neck and pulled me closer. "Gills, I know this is too fast, and, unlike me, you haven't been dreaming of this moment for most of your life."

My heart was beating double-time. "Well, it's not exactly what I'd planned on happening tonight, that's for sure."

"Let me guess: You thought you'd have a couple drinks, show all those assholes what they missed out on, and then go home and never think of this place ever again."

"Pretty much, yeah." I swallowed and reached out to loosen his tie. "But you know, now I'm thinking I might want the evening to end differently."

His eyes flashed. "You sure?"

I answered by pushing his jacket off his shoulders. "I'm always open to alternate endings." I undid his belt and yanked his shirt from his trousers while he shook off his shoes. "You know, if something comes up." I gasped dramatically. "Well, would you look at that." He groaned as I ran my hand the length of his erection. "Something came up."

He slipped his arms under my ass to pick me up, my heels dropping to the floor as he took me to the long worktable in the middle of the room and set me down on the edge. I pulled my dress up to my waist to get it out of the way so he could stand between my legs and grind his cock against my core.

"I'm not a fumbling virgin anymore, Gills." Yeah, that was evident by how he seemed to already know where the zipper to my dress was—something that had baffled me for a good three minutes at the store.

"Neither am I."

"Good." The fabric gathered on top of his hands as he slid it over my hips and yanked it over my head in one motion. "Then I don't have to be gentle."

I wasn't prepared when his lips met mine, my gasp leaving my mouth open just enough to make it easy for his tongue to slip in. He ripped the clip from my hair, fisting what he could and using it to keep me exactly where he wanted me.

His kiss, the way he cupped my breast, the smooth muscle I felt under my fingertips as I reached for him, even his scent was nothing like I remembered. The last decade had stripped away any sign of the sweet, timid boy he used to be. I opened my eyes, pushing him away to give myself a chance to recenter, remember that this incredible man was still the boy I'd loved.

"You alright?" he asked breathlessly.

Fuck, his voice made me want to do all kinds of dirty, dirty things.

"Gills, are you okay?"

"Do I not look okay?" I teased, leaning back on one hand and pushing hair out my eyes with the other.

"You look fucking delicious." Unhurried, he dragged my bra strap over my shoulder then yanked down the cup, his lips warming my skin as soon as it encountered the air. I moaned when he took my nipple into his mouth and rolled it with his tongue. When I reached behind myself to unclip my bra, the arch of my back forced him to take more of me in his mouth.

With my breast in one hand and his mouth on the other, he paused long enough to catch my eye and mumble, "Delicious."

I'd never thought of myself as delicious before, but I kind of loved it.

When he kissed me again, I grabbed hold of his boxer briefs, unsure if I wanted to yank them off or use them to pull him tighter to me. A second later, the choice was taken away as he quickly slipped free of them.

Thank goodness.

While Alec kicked the pile of our abandoned clothing to the side and pulled a few chairs out of the way, I had the chance to jump off the table, wiggle out of my panties and stockings, and then jump right back up. Luckily, this was school grade furniture which meant it was incredibly ugly but was made to last through the apocalypse.

"Please tell me you have a condom."

"I do," he said, "but we're not ready for that yet."

"We're not?" I pouted. I mean, I was definitely ready for that.

"Nope." He put his hand on my sternum, spread his fingers, and slowly but firmly pushed me flat on my back. His short, well-manicured nails dug into my skin as he dragged me to the edge of the table. "I've owed you this for ten years."

"You don't owe me—" I shut up when I felt his lips, flinched when he added his tongue, and thanked the gods when multiple fingers joined in.

"Delicious," he mumbled from between my thighs.

My moans grew louder and louder the higher he took me, until I almost cared if someone at the reunion could hear. *Almost.* But didn't.

When I went over, everything stopped, even my ability to breathe. All I could do was hold onto him and let it happen. The subsequent release felt just as incredible. My arms and legs flopped down as if my body had just been drained of all the muscle I'd ever had.

"*Now* we're ready for the condom."

"You mean there's more?" I panted. "But you've already ruined me. See?" I lifted my arms a little and let them thud back onto the table. "Nothing's functioning properly anymore."

He chuckled as he licked his lips and wiped me from his mouth. "Are you saying you want to call it a night?"

"God no!" I popped my eyes open and struggled to sit up. "I just want you to do all the work."

At least, his laughter didn't stop him from grabbing the condom from his jacket and slipping it over his erection.

"Remember how hard it was to figure out how to get the damn condom on?" he asked, leaning over to kiss me. "God, I felt so inept."

The reminder might've bothered me more if he hadn't been rubbing the tip of his cock along my slit at the same time.

"At least you're better at it now," I mumbled against his neck.

"I'm better at a lot of things now."

"Show m—" I sucked in a breath when he thrust into me, my body opening and taking him all the way inside as if it was meant to be. It definitely wasn't like this the first time. If virgin-me had known how big the average cock was, I would've reconsidered starting with Alec's. Back then, he was skinny everywhere but there. Now, he was big everywhere.

I tried to hold onto him, to keep our mouths close enough to kiss, but after a few minutes of luxuriously long strokes, he increased his tempo, and I fell back, catching myself on my hands.

"Fuck, you're beautiful." The sight of my breasts distracted him and forced him to slow down so he could hold them, run his thumb over my tightened nipple.

I closed my eyes, tilting my head back when I felt his hand on the nape of my neck. With his new grip, he pressed deeper into me, rolling his hips against mine at the end of every stroke to increase the pressure on my clit until I was gasping for air.

Looking for something to hold onto as my pleasure intensified, I grabbed his arm, squeezing the tight muscle and cursing more than I had in years. He thrust into me harder, faster, the hand at my neck tightening until it was almost painful. When he slipped his hand between our colliding bodies, finding my clit and pressing it with his thumb, my body locked around his cock so hard, he groaned along with me.

But he didn't let up, rocking me through my orgasm until all the after-shocks were done.

"Hi." I grinned at him like a fool, a very satisfied fool.

"Hey," he said, smiling. He pulled me closer and kissed me, both of us catching thin gasps of air in the brief moments we separated.

I pushed his abs back, hinting I needed a break. He understood immediately, but as he pulled out, his groan held a tinge of disappointment. Hopefully, that wouldn't last long.

Without a word, I scooted off the table and turned around, arching my back and sticking out my ass.

"Oh fuck, Gills." Good. He got it.

But just in case, I turned my head and, with a raised eyebrow, said, "No butt stuff."

His laugh held no disappointment.

When he slid inside me, I leaned on my elbows and dropped my head to the table. "So *goooood*."

His first thrust knocked me forward, but by the third, we'd inched all the way in, until my thighs were hitting the edge of the table. I was locked in between it and him. I felt his heat against my back as he wrapped his arm around me, one hand holding my breast, the other on the table beside me, his fingers splayed as if he'd really have preferred to have something to hold onto.

As his strokes sped and grew harder, he straightened and grabbed my hips.

Every time he slammed into me, I let out what I hoped was a cute, feminine kind of grunt, if such a thing existed. I just really didn't want either of our memories of this moment to include any embarrassing noises.

A few minutes later, I stopped caring, focusing on the far more pleasant things happening behind me, enjoying every second of him I had.

Neither one of us could last much longer. I knew he was close when each stroke shortened but intensified, and he started repeating my name under his broken breath.

One thrust separated my orgasm from his, our final moans blending together until both of us collapsed.

"Sorry," he mumbled into my hair, starting to push himself back up.

"Wait." I reached behind me and held him still. "Don't go."

"But I'm crushing you."

I couldn't properly shake my head because my cheek was smooshed against the table and he did actually weigh a lot, but I think my message was received. We lay there silently recovering for a few minutes.

I groaned when he straightened, then whined pitifully when he slid his cock out of me. When he came back from taking care of the condom, I hadn't moved.

"Congratulations," I said. "You were right—you have absolutely upped your game. Like, by orders of magnitude. Well done."

"Gee, thanks." He chuckled. "Will you be giving me a letter grade at some point too?"

"Am I not supposed to?" I teased.

"You can do whatever the fuck you want to do, Gills." With a hand on either side of me, he leaned over and kissed my back. "I'm just happy to be here."

"Me too." I slowly hauled myself onto the table and then laid down and closed my eyes to rest a bit.

There I was, all comfortably laid out on a table naked. In the last few years, I'd worked hard to be the woman I wanted to be. I loved myself, was proud of myself, *knew* myself. But I didn't think I had ever felt this accepted, this loved, this beautiful. All without judgement, not even of myself.

When I opened my eyes, he was still standing there looking at me with a sliver of a smile.

"What?"

All he did was smile. I'd missed that smile.

"I think we owe them a new table," he said. "Maybe a new room." He climbed up and stretched out beside me, pulling me toward him so I could rest my head on his chest.

"Maybe." I curled closer into him and sighed. "I think all those new muscles made you warmer. I like it."

In fact, I would've been happy to spend the rest of the night just like that. The rest of tonight. Tomorrow. Next week. Forever.

But good things always end faster than you want them to.

And the bad shit always took too long.

After we were dressed and the table had been thoroughly cleaned with hand sanitizer, we snuck back past the gym, the only part of the reunion we couldn't avoid being Katy Perry's voice, which made the evening pretty damn perfect in my opinion. After agreeing how lucky we were to miss the sight of our former classmates dancing and singing along to Roar, we switched to talking about my law practice, his tech company, and a little about our parents. Both of our smiles were so damn big, it seemed right not to ruin the afterglow with anything more serious than that and let this entire night be one we could both look back fondly on.

Without deciding what happened next, or if anything was going to happen next, we took the path to the north corner of the employee parking lot where we used to meet every day after school to walk home.

He stepped in front of me and tipped my chin up to look at him. "I always fantasized about kissing you here too."

"In front of the whole school?"

"Yep. In front of God, Denise, and everybody," he said softly. "I guess I'm a bit of an exhibitionist that way." He didn't hesitate this time. This time, he kissed me like he owned me, parting my lips with his tongue and pulling me in so tightly, my feet felt like they lifted off the concrete. I followed his lead, wrapping my arms around his neck and absorbing his passion for as long as I could, knowing this was the end of something that couldn't last. Nothing this good lasted.

When his lips lowered to my jawline, I took in a full breath of air and opened my eyes.

"Alec?" I asked softly, still undecided on whether I wanted him to listen to me or keep kissing my neck.

But the worst part of anything good is the moment you realize it had to end eventually. Once that really hits you, all the good instantly disappears.

"Alec." Better. Louder.

"Mmm?"

I tapped him on the chest. "It's late, and I'm going to get cold if I'm out much longer."

"We should definitely do something about that," he mumbled as his lips made their way up my neck and back to mine. Miraculously, he managed to keep our lips together as he took off his suit jacket, swung it around, and put it over my shoulders.

"That's enough there, big fella." I stepped backward, pushing on his chest so he wouldn't just follow along. "I actually do have a problem with Denise watching us."

"Come back to my hotel," he said, his eyes never leaving my lips. "We can order burnt popcorn and jelly bellies from room service, curl up naked in bed, and watch zombie movies until dawn like the old days."

"In the old days, we burned our own popcorn," I said, ticking off my fingers as I went through each. "Sat fully clothed on opposite ends of my mom's busted up couch, and you had to go home by midnight. Plus, I thought you hated zombie movies."

"I did, but I was young and dumb back then. I know better now. I'm willing to try anything that involves us staying up all night naked and gives me an excuse to grab you whenever I get"—he did air quotes—"scared."

"Sounds fun, but I can't." I looked at my phone, wishing my mom would pick that exact moment to bug me or that one of my clients would get arrested and call me to ask how bail worked. Unfortunately, my clients weren't the type to get arrested, and my mom had the supernatural ability to only call when I *didn't* want to be interrupted. "It's way past bedtime, and my mom is expecting me—"

"You're a grown woman, Gills. A beautifully grown woman. Your mom's not going to ground you for staying out too late anymore."

"You say that as if you've never met my mom."

"Point taken." He conceded with a nod, then got serious. "It's not just your mom though, is it?"

I rubbed my lips together and handed his jacket back to him. "My life is complicated." Ugh. That sounded a lot more like a brush-off than I wanted it to.

"You know, I don't think I've ever met anyone who would say their life is *un*complicated. I think we all need to accept that's just how life is." The light in his eyes dimmed a little as he watched me wring my hands like a nervous kid. "But yeah, I get it."

"It's been good to see you again though." That was even worse. "And I'm really happy you're doing so well." Oh my God, will someone please put me out of my misery?

"Don't..." He held up a hand. "It's okay if you're done with this"—he motioned back and forth between us—"and want to move on. That's how reunions are supposed to go, right?"

I didn't know how to respond.

"But don't say shit that makes everything awkward and cliché. Not between us, okay?"

"Okay," I whispered, feeling even more foolish and immature. It wasn't as if this was the first time I ever said goodbye to someone after sex, but everything was different with Alec. Everything had always been different with him.

I nodded and looked toward the parking lot. "I have my mom's car. Can I drop you off at your hotel?"

"Thanks, but I'll wait." He glanced at his watch. "My driver should be back pretty soon."

We stared uncomfortably at each other for another moment. It was hard to know what Alec was thinking. It always had been. But I knew if I spent one more second here with him, I wouldn't have any excuse not to tell him everything.

But it was late, and we were still in that post-great-sex mellow where the last thing you wanted to do was think too hard.

Maybe tomorrow. Actually, that wouldn't work because Lucas and I were flying home tomorrow. It probably took at least a month to get onto Alec's schedule anyway. So, next month then. I could figure out how to tell him in a month.

Did I know these were all lame excuses to cover up my lack of courage? Yes. Yes, I did. Did it make me feel bad? No. Not bad. Terrible. I was a terrible human being. Did knowing that change anything? Nope. It didn't change one damn thing.

"Take care of yourself, Alec. I mean it. I'll be in touch soon."

"Hey," he said, stopping me by grabbing my arm. "It's okay if you're not looking for anything serious, you know? I've been told I make a decent friend."

"Good to know." Smiling, I raised up on my tiptoes and kiss him on the cheek. "I'll write you soon."

"Write me. Sure." He smiled sadly. "You don't even know my address."

"I know your name, I know where your offices are, and I have this impressive looking stationary that tends to get to the right person when I hire a process server to deliver it."

He burst out laughing. "When you run a successful business, being sued for all kinds of shit is part of the deal. But guaranteed, this is the first time I've ever looked forward to being served."

"Goodbye, Alec."

"Bye, Gills."

Chapter 7

Alec

After Gills left, I walked the perimeter of the school then sat down on the rusty metal bench near the bus pick-up. The tour gave me just enough time to remind myself how far I'd come, all I had yet to do, and try my best not to think about Gills. She'd been fairly clear about what she wanted, or rather, who she didn't want. And I accepted that. I'd done what I came here to do—I told her how I felt. I could've been clearer about how good I thought we could be together, but she'd never been able to hide her feelings from me. And it was obvious that once her orgasm was gone, she was very clearly looking for the nearest escape hatch. Honestly, if she hadn't also been so expressive *during* the sex, I would've worried about my performance again.

I glanced at my watch for the hundredth time, trying to estimate out how long it could possibly take to drive Shelly and her husband wherever the hell they were going. Unless they decided to drive all the way to that little vineyard she was talking about earlier.

Shit. Of course they were going there—she was using my car service and credit card. Good for them. At least someone was living their best life tonight.

Speaking of... If I stayed out here any longer, one of two horrible things would happen. Horrible Scenario Number One—my ass would go numb on this goddamn metal bench while I mentally relived all my shitty high school days. Or Horrible Scenario Number Two—Denise and the other assholes I hadn't come here to see tonight would find me and my numb ass out here after the reunion ended. Of course, I would probably be crying at the end of both scenarios.

I sent the driver a text telling him I was taking a walk and to let me know when he was heading back this way so I could tell him where to pick me up. Worst case, I would walk the six miles through town to get to my hotel.

Anything was better than staying in my least favorite spot in America.

My mom had struggled as my only parent, which meant I had long stretches of time to myself. I spent most of them with Gills. I'd always enjoyed taking the long way to her house at night. I missed it. Not that I couldn't go out at night in San Francisco, but when you said, "It's dark out" in a small town, you meant it. Walking the old neighborhoods gave me time to stretch my legs and close some of the open threads in my mind. Over the past few months, even before I knew if I could make it or not, I'd been preparing for tonight. Going through what-ifs and what-the-fuck-did-I-dos. Hell, some threads had been open since high school.

I didn't regret coming. Apart from the sex, which was absolutely worth the price of admission, I now had ten years' worth of new and better fodder for jerking off. I believed her when she said we'd keep in touch, and I was pretty sure I believed myself when I'd suggested being her friend would be enough.

I had to laugh when I realized where I was. Without planning on it, I'd gone straight to her old street and was three doors down from her old house. Like a fucking pigeon, I knew my way home.

Unfortunately, just like last time, Gills was done and ready to move on. Maybe in ten more years, I'd get another shot. I should just be grateful I had the chance to see her, touch her, relive an old memory that we actually made better. Now, I needed to let her go live her complicated life and be happy.

Wait a second.

"Fuck that." We could've spent the last ten years having something amazing. Why would I waste the next ten not knowing for sure?

I groaned when I saw the two-person swing on the front porch. The fabric looked new, but I remembered when Gills' mom installed lights that turned on at dusk and off at sunrise, thinking it would keep her daughter from sneaking out at night. Little did Ms. Thomas know Gills never snuck out... because I always snuck *in*. But never through the front door.

I kept my eyes pointed at the sidewalk in front of me until I was out of the sightline of Gills' doorbell camera and the security cameras at the house across the street.

As soon as I was out of range, I quickly veered toward the house, cursing when I felt the wet grass soak through my pant cuffs. Ms. Thomas used to be particular about her lawn. I knew because she had paid me four dollars a week to cut it for her. Four dollars. But how could I refuse the mother of the girl I loved?

I stopped ten feet away from the house and looked up to the second story window farthest from the front door. Had I really hauled my scrawny ass up a wooden trellis to get onto the roof under her window at least three times a week for most of my teenage years? I might be in better shape than I was back then, but there was no way that thing would hold me now. I could still get up—finally a real-life reason for doing all those damn pull-ups at the gym—but it was an old house, I could also end up pulling off the rain gutter and falling through roof.

Shit. Being too proud to ask for her number proved to be a stupid mistake earlier than I thought it would. I thought, at least, I'd make it until tomorrow.

I glanced to my right, hoping Ms. Thomas hadn't changed too much of her landscaping in the last ten years. She had, but it was still something I could work with. The wood bark that used to cover her flowerbeds had been replaced by small stones running from dime to golf ball sized. I scooped up a handful, picking out the big ones and tossing them back.

Even though the remaining rocks were small and probably wouldn't break a window, I tried lobbing them underhand to soften the strike. After the first two misses, it became obvious I should start a company softball team to learn how to throw. Or have had a dad to teach me how to do this kind of shit.

"Yes!" I whisper-shouted when the third stone hit the window hard enough to wake her but not enough to do any damage. I tossed another one. Another hit. And another. Hell, yeah. I was better at this than I thought. Who needs a dad anyway? I definitely planned to start a company team now. The only thing that would make me happier is Gills waking up and coming to the window.

I froze when the light inside the room turned on. It was faint—more likely a bedside lamp than the overhead room light. Good. The last thing I wanted to do was wake up her mom. She still scared me a little.

"Gills, it's me." Unfortunately, I didn't consider what *else* to say to her until the curtains were ripped open, and she unlocked and lifted the window.

"What's going on?" asked a confused, unrecognizable voice that was *not* Gillian's.

I used a very un-kid-friendly word when I saw him. Not having or knowing any children since I *was* one, I sucked shit at guessing ages, but from his voice and stature, I'd put him somewhere around nine or ten, I guess. His hair was sticking straight up on one side, but since the light was at his back, I couldn't see much more of him. Like, for instance, if his facial expression was one of absolute terror.

"Oh shiiii—ooooot!" I threw my hands up as if the light from his bedroom was coming from a cop car. "I'm so sorry! I thought somebody I knew lived here." Most things about the house were the same, but enough was different to have at least thought to check to make sure Gills' mom still lived here before chucking rocks at some poor family's windows.

But I hadn't because my head had contained one thought and one thought only from the second I saw her. And that thought proved to be very unhelpful.

"Do you live here?" I called out.

What the fuck? Of course, he lives here. He's inside the fucking house, you idiot. While you're standing in the dark outside his window trying to get in. Way to make yourself seem like a pervert.

"Who are you?" the kid asked, wiping his eye with the back of his hand. "What do you want?"

"Nothing. I don't want anything"—I backed up with my hands still raised —"from you...or anyone. Anywhere." I jerked to a stop when I saw the doorbell camera. Motherfucker. Someone was going to be watching this video tomorrow or the ones taken from across the street. If I ran off without explaining myself, the whole neighborhood would be talking about Alec Benson, CEO by day and Peeping Tom by night. Then somebody will post it on Twitter, and my company's stock price will plummet. Because that was exactly how shit like that happened.

"Look, kid. Do me a favor, okay? Tell your mom or dad—"

"I don't have a dad."

That stopped me for a second. There was a reason they referred to this sensation as "a punch in the gut."

"Sorry for bringing it up, little man." I was younger than him when my dad took off, and I'd taken it poorly for a long time. I didn't know what had happened to *his* dad, but loss is loss and comparing was useless. "It's tough, but trust me, you'll be okay without one." I got lost in my own thoughts for another second before remembering how many nosey neighbors lived in this town. "I need you to tell your mom that I'm not a creep or a pervert or any—"

"Mom!" The kid wailed.

"Not yet! You were supposed to wait until I was gone." So I wouldn't have to speak to a sleepy-eyed, panicked women and explain what I was doing outside her kid's window in the middle of the night.

"Mom!"

"Don't... You don't have to call her, little man."

The overhead light turned on, brightening his room up well enough to see him and all the trouble I was in.

"Let her know it was all a big misunderstanding," I said desperately. "I'm really—"

Shocked. Confused. Disoriented. I felt all of it and more as soon as I saw

Gills stick her head out of the window. The one that used to be hers but was now used by some kid.

No, not some kid.

Her kid.

Her nine or ten-year-old kid.

Oh fuck.

"Alec?" she asked, pushing the boy behind her. "What are doing here?"

I didn't respond, hoping my brain would be able to quickly fit all the pieces of this situation together until something made sense.

Gills had a kid. I should've known that.

Her LinkedIn bio didn't mention children nor did the article in California Magazine, and if her website did, I'd missed it. But those sources all reflected her professional life, and sadly, it made sense for a woman to not include information about her private life for a bunch of reasons. When I'd asked Shelly to look into her for me, I hadn't specifically asked about children, only marriages and serious relationships, so if she'd found anything, she'd kept it to herself.

"Who's out there?" someone yelled from the front door as the whole house lit up. "I'm calling the police!"

"It's okay, Mom!" Gills leaned out the window. "It's Alec. You remember Alec, right? From high school?"

"Alec? Of course I remember him." She didn't seem overly happy about it either. Maybe because she already knew the thing I was just starting to.

"Hey, Ms. Thomas!" I shouted numbly, wondering if the night had suddenly gotten darker, or if I was going to pass out. "Looks like your grass needs a trim. Maybe I can…"

"Alec?" Gills asked with real concern in her tone. "Are you okay?"

"What's wrong with him, Mom?" The kid pushed her arm out of the way and adjusted his glasses as he looked down at me.

Nope. Not the kid.

My kid.

Chapter 8

Gillian

Alec's eyes darted from Lucas to me to Lucas again. I pushed Lucas' hair off his face so Alec could get a good look at his son.

A second later, he started talking about mowing my mom's grass again.

God, I hoped I didn't break him.

"Don't pass out, Alec. I'll be right down." Then I called, "Mom, can you help him to the swing? And maybe get him something strong to drink?" I shut the window and closed the drapes without waiting for her reply. I knew she would. She'd been mad at Alec for a long time after I told her who Lucas' dad was, but she'd been equally mad at me for not telling him. Since I'd eventually been forgiven, I knew Alec had been too.

"Come here, sweet boy." I sat on my old bed and patted the spot next to me. I'd been successfully avoiding this moment for over nine years, but I knew it would happen eventually. Secrets never stay secret. I was just hoping for a little more time, imagining it would be when Lucas wanted to know more about his father. Or, now that we'd reconnected, I could break it to him slowly. Build up trust again first, and then sit down for the unpleasant conversation.

"Am I in trouble?" he asked as he plopped down.

"Nope, but I am." I kept it age appropriate, telling him I kept something from an old friend even though I knew it was wrong. That I was scared of his reaction and hadn't been brave enough.

"It's okay, Mom. We all make mistakes. I'm sure he'll forgive you."

"I hope so, baby. I hope so." I hugged him tight and helped him back into bed, taking his glasses from him and tucking him under the handmade quilt. "I'm going to need your help tomorrow, so get some sleep."

"Ok-aaaay," he said on a yawn. "Night."

I kissed him on the forehead and turned off the lamp and the overhead light. "Night, love."

Here we go.

"He's already on his second glass of my favorite whiskey," my mom said quietly as I spied on him through the peephole on the door. He hadn't taken his hands or his eyes off the glass either.

"I'll buy you another bottle, Mom," I grumbled. "That's hardly the biggest issue here."

"I just meant you need to get out there and talk to him before he's too drunk to hear you."

"Actually,"—I glanced at her—"I think that sounds like the best solution for everybody."

"Gillian," she threatened, using the old pronunciation of my name. "Get your butt out there and tell the poor man the truth."

"Fine," I whined like my fifteen-year-old self. What was it about being in the house you grew up in that makes people revert to the brat they used to be?

I'd changed into my pajamas as soon as I'd gotten home, so I grabbed my sweater from the back of the sofa and put it on as I shuffled outside in my slippers. Nothing like fuzzy slippers and an oversized cardigan to make a grown woman feel strong and capable.

Alec looked up from his glass, his eyes wide and a little glossy. After asking if I could sit next to him on the swing and watching his head bob up and down, I settled into a diagonal position with my torso turned toward him and only one leg touching the ground.

"Alec," I said. Good way to start, I thought.

"What's his name?"

I was shocked the weight of his simple question hadn't caused the swing to come down.

"Lucas, after—"

"Luke, your grandpa." He nodded. "It's a good name. Good man from what I remember."

"He was." I should've known Alec would remember my grandpa. He'd died when we were in middle school, and I was a wreck. "He was the best father figure I ever had, so it made sense to name my son after him."

"*Our* son."

"Our son." I felt the first of what I believed would be many tears fall onto my cheek. "I know you're mad, and..." God, why was my mouth so dry? "And you have every right to be. I just could never come up with a good way to tell you, and I know how pathetic that sounds, how ridiculous, but it's true."

I pulled the glass of whiskey out of his hands and took a big sip before handing it back. He didn't even move, his head tilted forward, his forearms resting on his thighs.

"When you didn't reply to my letters—before I knew you never got them—I was hurt. Not to mention confused, scared, and *seriously* hormonal, so I dealt with it the only way I knew how—I put my blinders on and muscled through it alone. Then Lucas was born, and even though my parents weren't happy about it, I wanted to tell you..." I blinked the tears away. It was literally *years* too late for Alec to give a shit about my tears. "But what could you have done? Give up a scholarship to MIT and come back to California to change diapers? That would've been the dumbest decision of your life. Plus, somehow, not telling you was preferable to risking the chance that my best friend would reject me... reject his son.

"Time just passed so quickly," I continued, knowing I was babbling but afraid to stop. If I stopped, he might start, and I wasn't sure I was ready to hear what he had every right to say to me. "I had college classes at night, daycare, then law school, work. I was so tired. I figured I'd wait until I got on my feet and had the emotional bandwidth to tell you, but that never happened. Somewhere in the middle you and your company started showing up in all these damn magazines. I mean, seriously? Who does that straight out of college? It did make my mom finally change her mind about you, by the way."

He let out a thin chuckle, still not looking up. "Too bad it didn't change *your* mind about me too."

I stood up and leaned against the wall opposite him. "I didn't want to be that woman, the one who comes out of the woodwork once their baby daddy hits it big. I worked too hard to be my own woman by that point, and I knew what would happen to me and my career if I said anything. It's not a good enough reason—"

"Stop." He lifted his hand, his eyes hurt and intense. "I don't care."

I swallowed. "What?"

"It's been a hell of a night, Gills." He finished the rest of the drink in one gulp and slammed the glass down on the plastic side table. "To be honest, I'm not exactly sure what I'm feeling right now. All I know is that ultimately, I don't care about any of that stuff." He motioned toward my face as if swatting away all my excuses.

I shut my eyes and took a breath. "I'm so sorry, Alec."

"For what? Raising my son on your own?" He stood and took my hands in his. "Putting yourself through hell to make his life the best you could?"

"That's one way to look at it, I guess." Not one I would've imagined, but since it made me sound a lot more noble than anything I'd ever come up with, I let him continue.

"You were young, scared, and alone. Right or wrong, you made the decisions you thought were best. While sometime soon I may feel some resentment that you didn't tell me, I can't say for sure I would've done anything differently in your position. But that's for our therapists to help us figure out."

"Therapy" I nodded. "Good idea."

"Lots and lots of it," he said, his eyebrows raised. "But for right now, let's focus on the most important things."

"What are those?" I asked carefully.

"First"—he blew out a quick breath—"I want to meet my kid." His smile was gigantic, and nervous, and excited, and quite possibly the most beautiful thing I'd ever seen. "I can't believe I have a fucking kid. I have to stop saying fucking, don't I?" He pulled me in and wrapped his arms around me. "Then I have to come up with a way to convince you to marry me and find us a place to live that's close to your office and wherever my new company headquarters will be."

"Is that all?"

"We have ten years to make up for, so what do you think?"

I wrinkled my nose. "I think it sounds like an awful lot of work."

"Don't worry. It's nothing two people on California's 30 Under 30 list can't handle."

"Good point." I raised up onto my toes to meet his kiss, knowing I could finally let go of all the fear and shame I'd held onto for so long and replace it with forgiveness, love, and the good kind of Costco *hors d'oeuvres*.

He pulled back just enough for our lips to separate, his curling into a grin. "If we have an obnoxiously big wedding, do you think we should invite Denise?"

"Not a chance in hell." I cocked my head to the side. "But I'll make sure to send her a magazine article about it."

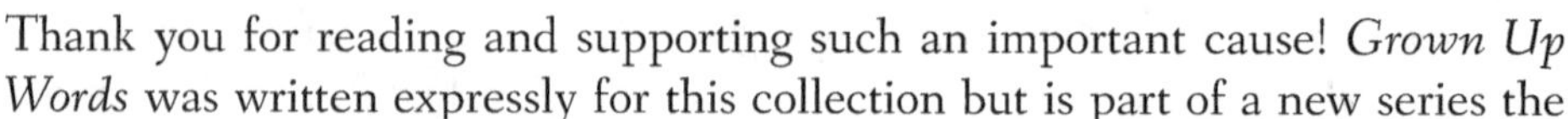

Thank you for reading and supporting such an important cause! *Grown Up Words* was written expressly for this collection but is part of a new series the author came up with after watching one too many girl-needs-a-makeover-to-get-the-guy movies and wondering why it so rarely was the *guy* who needed to change. Look for more to come! In the meantime, laugh and cry with the book that started it all: *Darker Water*, a friends to lovers, bad boy twist on The Frog Price.

About the Author

Lauren Stewart is a USA Today bestselling author of contemporary romance and urban fantasy. She strives to make readers think, laugh, and cry (not always simultaneously, although it's great when it happens). Inside each of her books, you'll find elements of other genres, always with a drop of angst, a splash of humor, and a bucketload of sarcasm.

Because what doesn't kill us should make us laugh.

Keep up with Lauren and receive exclusive extras when you subscribe to her newsletter: http://bit.ly/LS_news

Reload

Tara Wyatt

Chapter One

Brandon Clarke-Davies took a long, slow sip of his pint of Guinness and laid an arm across the back of the red leather booth nestled into a quiet corner of the pub. His eyes dropped to the white folder on the table in front of him, the light blue MI5 insignia in the top left corner.

He tapped it with one finger. "Not that I'm complaining about the free pint, but what are we doing here?"

Harry leaned against the booth and glanced around the small pub. Despite the fact that it was just shy of 2:00 PM on a Thursday afternoon, The Red Lion was bustling with patrons.

"She should be here any minute." Harry drummed his fingers on top of the folder.

Brandon glanced out the windows on the opposite side of the pub, watching the traffic crawl by on Parliament Street. Weak summer sunshine filtered through the parting clouds, glinting off the puddles dotting the cobbled sidewalk. With an arched eyebrow, he shook his head at his boss's secrecy and picked up his pint. As a highly trained MI5 Intelligence Officer, he was used to discretion.

He'd just tipped the pint glass to his lips when the sharp click of heels against the scarred wooden floor got his attention and he froze, shock turning his blood to ice water in his veins. Chiding himself for his minuscule slip in composure, he set the glass down and leveled his gaze at the woman standing in front of their table. Wrapped in an elegant Burberry trench, her hands shoved casually in her pockets, she tipped her head and gave them each a small smile before sliding into the booth right beside Brandon.

"Gentlemen."

Her voice, just as low and husky and feminine as he remembered, hit him like a kick to the gut.

Harry shot Brandon a look. "Thought you might want to have the meeting here, as opposed to the office. In front of...you know. People. "

"You're a bloody saint, Harry," he said, his jaw wound so tight he was surprised he could speak. He forced his shoulders to relax, unclenched his fists, and didn't allow himself to reach for his pint. He dared a glance at the gorgeous woman sitting beside him, her legs crossed, her hands folded on the table as if sitting next to him were the most natural thing in the world.

But it wasn't, because he hadn't seen her in six years. Natasha Rowe. His ex-wife.

"Nice to see you, Brandon," she said, the hardened consonants of her American accent sharp against his ears. As a wave of nostalgic desire crashed into him, he looked at her with what he hoped was a bemused expression because he had no idea what the hell to say. He sucked in a deep breath, which was a terrible mistake, because it brought with it her lavender scent, as warm and familiar as ever. Memories, most of them happy and exciting, floated to the surface, but he squashed them and plastered a thin smile to his face before they could suck him under, a tsunami disguised as a gentle wave.

Harry's eyes flicked from Brandon to Natasha. If he picked up on the surprise, the anger, and goddammit, the *lust* crawling beneath Brandon's skin and threatening to burst out, he didn't let on. With quick, efficient movements, Natasha unbuttoned her coat and shrugged out of it, letting it pool around her waist. Her red tank top cupped her ample breasts perfectly, leaving a subtle amount of cleavage on display. She ran her fingers through her chin-length dark blond hair and suddenly he was half-hard, watching her breasts strain for freedom beneath the red fabric. God, those tits. As if he'd ever forget how good they felt in his hands. In his mouth.

No. He couldn't let his mind go down that path. He needed to focus on other things. Like the fact that two years into their struggling marriage, she'd walked out on him without a backward glance. *That's* what he needed to be thinking about, not her glorious rack.

"Shall we?" asked Harry, leaning forward and flipping open what Brandon now realized was a mission dossier.

Bloody fucking hell.

Without waiting for an acknowledgment, Harry plowed ahead, spreading several pages and photographs across their sequestered table. "Last week, the

United States Army Medical Research Institute of Infectious Diseases in Maryland was breached."

Natasha cut in. "We believe that Sergei Silayev, one of Europe's biggest arms dealers—"

"I know who Sergei Silayev is." Brandon's skin crackled with angry impatience.

She nodded and continued. "We're certain that Silayev's agents were responsible for the breach."

"What was stolen?" asked Brandon, his eyes narrowed as he studied the image of Silayev in front of him.

"Several vials of Marburg virus." Brandon's eyes met Natasha's as the magnitude of what she was telling him sunk in. One of the biggest arms dealers in Europe—if not the world—had stolen several vials of a highly potent and deadly biological weapon.

"Fuck me," muttered Brandon, finally allowing himself another sip of his Guinness. Something flashed in Natasha's gray eyes, a hot, searing spark, and she rubbed her thighs together, almost imperceptibly. Almost. "How did you lot cock-up so bad that you let one of Silayev's agents infiltrate an Army base?" He was deflecting, trying to cover his own arousal at seeing Natasha again. She didn't bat an eye, not allowing herself to be baited.

That was new.

"The chatter we've picked up indicates that the vials are here, in London. Silayev has just bought a house in Belgravia, and we believe he's holding the vials there until he can find a buyer," she said.

"Obviously, the Americans are keen to regain possession of the virus," said Harry, leaning forward and interlacing his fingers. "Which is why we're assisting the CIA on this mission."

"*You're* CIA?" Brandon turned in his seat, angling his shoulders toward Natasha. "You're not still at Aegis?"

In response, she pulled a CIA badge from the inside pocket of her trench, flashing it at him before tucking it away. "I haven't been at Aegis for years now."

"But you loved it there. Why did you leave?"

"I'm sorry, but that's classified." She tipped her lips up in a half smile. God, that half smile was maddening. It made him want to strangle her and kiss her, and damn the consequences of both. Instead, he smiled smoothly.

"Of course. Apologies." Brandon kept his voice deliberately flat. "Seeing as the vials are on British soil, and the mission falls under the MI5 umbrella, why doesn't the CIA leave it to us?" He glanced at Natasha. "No offense."

She smiled sweetly. "Because the CIA doesn't trust anyone, not even MI5. No offense."

The doors to the pub's kitchen swung open, and the heavy scent of deep fried foods wafted through the air. As a waitress rushed past carrying a tray laden with several orders of fish and chips, all conversation paused, an involuntary ceasefire.

Harry cleared his throat and lowered his voice. "Silayev is having a cocktail party tomorrow night and will be feeling out several potential buyers for the virus," said Harry. "Your mission is to infiltrate the party, retrieve the vials, and return them to the U.S. Embassy. There are officials from the CDC on standby who will ensure the virus's safe transport to America."

"Harry, I have to ask..." Brandon shook his head and blew out a slow breath through his nostrils. "Why me? Given our..." He gestured between himself and Natasha. "History. Wouldn't another agent be better suited to the job?"

Harry tented his fingers and studied Brandon, narrowing his eyes. "No. Given your skills, experience, and the cover necessary to infiltrate Silayev's party, it's got to be you. Additionally, you've never worked a mission involving him or any of his known associates before, so there's no chance of him making you for MI5."

Resigned, Brandon nodded, scanning the pages and photographs in front of him. He glanced at Natasha, who he knew was deep in thought, running her index finger along her bottom lip as she studied the dossier contents.

"Agent Clarke-Davies, I've secured you an invitation to the party tomorrow night." Harry slid a sealed envelope across the table to Brandon, who took it and slipped it into the inner pocket of his suit jacket. "You'll find your cover and all necessary information in that envelope. You know the drill." He turned his attention to Natasha and slid a matching envelope to her. "Agent Rowe will be working the party as a waitress; we've secured the cooperation of the catering company. Agent Rowe will secure the vials while you, Clarke-Davies, make sure Rowe is able to do so without any hindrance. We'll go over the finer points of the mission tomorrow. Questions?"

Brandon and Natasha looked at each other before shaking their heads. Harry stood and nodded once, his eyes darting back and forth between them. "Best of luck, agents." Shaking his head, he pushed open the door and set off down the sidewalk in the direction of the MI5 offices.

"So why did you leave Aegis?" Brandon asked.

"Why did you?" She threw the question back at him like a live grenade.

Why had he left Aegis, the private, international intelligence organization where he'd met Natasha almost eight years ago?

Because after their marriage had fallen apart and she'd left him, the shine of international espionage and adventure had lost its allure. Without his part-ner, his heart hadn't been in it anymore. Coming home to London and joining MI5 had seemed the best option at the time. But he bloody well wasn't going to tell her any of that.

So instead, he smiled, aiming for charming. "I'm sorry, but that's classified."

She laughed, her full lips pulling up into a genuine smile. She slid out of the booth, pulling her trench on as she went. "See you at headquarters tomor-row, C.D.," she said, tossing out a nickname he hadn't heard in years.

He found himself smiling as he watched her walk out of The Red Lion.

Bollocks.

Chapter Two

"No, the plan is that *I* secure the vials while *you* look out for *me*. That's the mission, and we're not changing it!" Natasha spoke through clenched teeth, arms crossed, not caring that she was yelling at her ex-husband in the middle of MI5 headquarters.

"Listen, you lot already lost those vials of Marburg once. We can't risk another bout of incompetence." Brandon leveled his cool gaze at her, and she wanted to scream in frustration.

Why did he have to look as though he'd just stepped out of the pages of *GQ*? He looked so good that she could've cried at how unfair it was. Unfair that she had to work with him, and unfair he had to look like that while she did.

His chestnut hair was shorter than when she'd last seen him, with a hint of a wave that she knew turned into curls if he let it grow long enough. Piercing blue eyes looked at her, framed with thick, long lashes that most women would kill for. His nose had a bump in it that hadn't been there six years ago, indicating it had been broken at least once. He wore a simple white dress shirt that emphasized his broad, muscular physique. It was unbuttoned at the collar and tucked into gray dress pants. At six-two, he was nearly a foot taller than her, and a good seventy-five pounds heavier.

"So, what?" She jabbed her finger at the blueprint of Silayev's house spread before them on the illuminated table, focusing on her frustration. "You're going to sneak upstairs, crack the safe, and secure the vials while I'm *your* lookout? Ha! And let you take all the credit? Right. No fucking way, C.D."

"Is that what you're worried about? That I'll get all the glory?" He braced his hands on the table and leaned toward her. "That would be a shame, wouldn't it?"

She opened her mouth to tell him exactly where he could shove his glory when he smiled, and it wasn't just any smile. No, it was the wolfish one that never failed to disintegrate her panties.

And he knew it. Her heart knocked against her ribs and her scalp prickled with the intoxicating mixture of lust, passion, and competitiveness that only Brandon could elicit, and she saw the flash of triumph in his eyes.

So much for not letting him get to her. Ever since she'd seen him in the pub yesterday and had nearly lost her lunch at the shock, she'd been fighting against the current of memories threatening to pull her under, trying desperately to exude cool indifference. But under that gaze, and with that smile, she was quickly melting into a puddle of nostalgia and hormones.

Her mind flashed back to the beginning of their relationship. They'd met on an assignment for Aegis, and their highly competitive natures had found them at each other's throats—and in each other's beds—before the assignment was over. They'd fallen hard and fast, the intensity of their feelings heightened by youth, by the danger around them, and by the exotic locations to which they'd traveled. Thanks to Brandon, she'd had orgasms on every continent except Antarctica.

God, the sex. She'd never been able to get enough of him, and in the years since, no man had come close to satisfying her the way Brandon had. She gave her head a small shake, sweeping away the memories like broken shards of glass.

"No," she said, leaning over the opposite side of the table and mirroring his posture, giving him a generous view of her cleavage. His gaze dipped. "I'm worried you'll fuck it up and make me look bad. Then I'll have to rescue your ass, and I don't have time for that. This time tomorrow, I'll be back at Langley."

Something flickered across his face that looked a hell of a lot like disappointment, but before she could be sure, it was gone. In an achingly familiar gesture, he raised a hand to his face, thumb under his chin, his index finger stroking the bridge of his nose. He ran his tongue over his teeth, and in another familiar gesture, let his tongue linger on the slightly crooked eyetooth on the right side of his mouth. British dentistry jokes aside, it was his only imperfection.

Only visible one, anyway. The others only became apparent when one knew him on a deeper level.

The moodiness, the competitiveness, the cockiness. Granted, they'd been twenty-two, and if memory served, she hadn't been all rainbows and sunshine either. She'd like to think that now, at thirty, she'd matured somewhat.

"Fine. Yes. You're right. We'll stick to the plan." He rubbed a hand over the back of his neck, shooting her an apologetic smile. He crossed to her side and propped a hip against the table, facing her with his arms crossed. For several long seconds, he studied her, and then sighed. "It's not easy for me to trust you, Tash."

His words hit her with the force of a hurricane, almost knocking her over. She took a step away and folded her arms in front of her. "That's fair."

His brows knit together. "You're bloody right it is." He lowered his voice to a fierce whisper. "You just fucking *left*. I returned from that mission in Baghdad and you were *gone*."

"Let's not pretend we weren't making each other miserable, C.D."

His expression softened at the old nickname. "I wasn't miserable."

She snorted and rolled her eyes. "We fought constantly."

He leaned in close, bringing with him the warm scent of his woodsy after-shave. "We fucked constantly, too." Butterflies exploded in her stomach as heat curled over her thighs, and she fought the urge to rub them together. "It wasn't perfect, but it was *us*, Tash."

"It was dysfunctional."

Hurt flashed in his eyes, replaced quickly with anger. "So your solution was to walk without giving us the chance to fix it?"

She ducked her head, blood rushing to her cheeks. They'd hit a particu-larly rough patch and she'd panicked. She'd run, giving in to her immature, selfish fears and by the time she'd realized the magnitude of her mistake, it had been too late. She couldn't put the pin back in the grenade. She'd wrecked the best thing that had ever happened to her because she'd been too young to handle the complexity of marriage.

She could've tracked him down at any point over the past six years if she'd wanted, but she hadn't, too terrified he hated her guts for bailing. But it didn't seem like he hated her. And she wasn't sure what to make of that.

Harry cleared his throat as he approached, rubbing his hands together as though warming them. "All set for tonight then?"

Brandon pushed off the table and returned to his side, putting distance between them.

Not that she could blame him.

Natasha skimmed her hands down the front of the skintight, revealing black dress that all of the catering company's waitresses wore and sucked in a steadying breath. She smoothed her hair over her ears, further concealing the nearly invisible micro earpiece in her right ear that linked her both to Brandon and to headquarters.

She hadn't initially understood why Harry had insisted on Brandon for this mission, but seeing him now, she understood perfectly. He'd assumed the identity of William Drummond, heir to a European banking fortune with several semi-illegal investments in his portfolio. Drummond was exactly the type Silayev's people would invite to a party like this: rich, connected, and crooked. She had to give MI5 credit—given the short notice, they'd done an excellent job of creating a deep and convincing cover for Brandon. Googling William Drummond brought up pictures, several news articles, a Linked-In page, and an investment profile, all courtesy of MI5's Digital Intelligence team.

And now, chatting with guests, a tumbler of scotch in hand and wearing the hell out of a navy blue Hugo Boss suit, complete with light blue dress shirt and deep red silk tie, he looked perfect.

For the role.

Right.

She lifted the tray of champagne glasses from the counter and pushed through the kitchen's swinging door, her eyes scanning the open living and dining space currently filled with several dozen guests, all drinking champagne and feasting on toast points smothered in caviar. The decor of the large Wilton Street townhouse was opulent and over the top, with marble floors, intricate crown molding tracing across the ceiling, and lush, textured wallpaper in rich browns and blues hugging the walls. The entire place screamed wealth, power, and questionable taste.

She wove her way through the crowd, her eyes landing on the curved staircase by the kitchen that led to the second floor. Silayev's office and the safe within it were upstairs, and the next step in the mission was to get into his office undetected and start working on the safe. A guest's stray hand squeezed her ass in passing and she ground her teeth in disgust, suppressing a snarl.

"I saw that. What a cheeky bugger. I should break his hand." Brandon's voice came crisply through the earpiece, his accent having the same effect on her as always, sending sparks dancing across her skin.

She turned her head to the side as she spoke softly. "No. Focus, C.D." She smiled, covering the flash of irritation burning through her. Irritation at the creep who'd squeezed her ass and irritation at herself, because Brandon's words had tugged at something soft and warm right in the center of her chest. Something she had no right to feel, given the way she'd treated him.

"Hard to focus with you in that dress, love."

More sparks. "Suck it up. I need you on your A game. If I get shot, we're going to have a big problem."

"Bigger than what I've got in my—"

She turned her face to the wall, speaking in a whispered rush. "I swear to God, I'm going to rip you out of my ear."

"There was a time when you liked having me inside you." Instantly, her traitorous mind conjured up memories of just how much she'd liked it. How wild he'd driven her, how safe and treasured and whole he'd made her feel. When they hadn't been driving each other insane, that is.

She brushed by him, her bare arm grazing the soft wool-cashmere blend of his suit jacket. In a movement so small that everyone around them but her would've missed it, he dipped his head slightly as she passed and inhaled. His eyes closed briefly, and her stomach did a slow turn. Maybe if, after the mission, they snuck away, and didn't talk, and just...

She shook her head. Talk about a spectacularly bad idea.

She smiled, her teeth clenched together with such force that if she didn't let up, she was likely to crack a molar. "Now isn't the time." She kept moving through the crowd, and could feel his eyes on her ass as she strode away.

Through the earpiece, he laughed, his deep rich voice sending a wave of heat rippling along her spine. Her stomach fluttered, and she swallowed thickly, fighting to regain her composure. He was unraveling her, probably on purpose. Probably as revenge for running scared and bailing out on their marriage.

She shook her head again, refusing to get sucked in to the lust simmering through her veins. She needed to get upstairs, crack the safe, and recover the virus so that she could get the hell out of here and away from Brandon before she did something incredibly stupid.

Again.

Chapter Three

Natasha slipped into the kitchen and set down her now empty tray, poking her head around the corner and glancing in the direction of the living room and the staircase to her immediate right.

"I'm heading up," she whispered, edging closer to the stairs, her gaze scanning every direction before she darted furtively up the stairs two at a time, not slowing her brisk pace until she reached the top. Finding the hallway dark and quiet, she headed straight for Silayev's office. It was locked; slipping her lock picking tools from a garter under her dress, she made quick work of the simple pin and tumbler mechanism. Closing the door behind her with a quiet click, she crossed to the far side of the office and began her search for the safe, locating it in a low cabinet nestled into the wall. She pulled her phone out of her bra and started the process of hacking into the house's wireless network.

She snorted out a quiet laugh. "The network's not even encrypted."

Brandon chuckled in her ear. "What is this, amateur hour? I guess we can be grateful that he hasn't had a chance to put in all the upgrades yet."

She smiled, and then a pang of longing and loneliness slipped between her ribs like a knife. God, she'd missed him. She'd known that, but she hadn't realized just how much; seeing him again, arguing with him, flirting and laughing with him brought home the fact that without a doubt, she was still completely in love with Brandon Clarke-Davies.

The enormity of her mistake sat on her chest like a lead weight. It was a mistake for which he'd likely never forgive her. Hell, she'd never forgive herself for leaving him the way she had.

Once she'd accessed the house's wireless network, she opened the CIA's customized safe cracking software on her phone. She tapped a series of numbers into the safe's electronic number pad, connecting it to the wireless network as well. With a swipe of her finger, the software connected to the safe, interfacing with it directly. The program began running through sequences of numbers at lightning speed.

For several tense minutes, there was nothing she could do but stay silent, let the program do its job, and listen to Brandon flirt with some Eurotrash socialite. When she excused herself to go powder her nose—probably with cocaine—Brandon checked in with her.

"How's it coming?"

"I'm still cracking the safe. All clear downstairs?"

"Maybe."

"Maybe? I don't like maybe." She stared at her phone's screen, willing the program to work faster, the prickling threat of sweat teasing along her hairline.

"Two blokes headed upstairs. I'm on it."

The safe emitted a series of beeps and popped open as the locking mechanism released. Triumph surging through her, she tucked her phone away and swung the small safe's door wide open.

"Hel-*lo*," she murmured to herself, pulling free both a small metal briefcase and a silver Walther PPK covered in garish scrollwork. She flipped open the case, verifying that it contained the vials. It did. Then she checked the Walther's clip, and found it loaded.

The office door swung open, cutting a swath of light across the darkened floor. Briefcase in one hand, gun in the other, she dove behind the heavy wood desk as the first bullet, muffled by a silencer, dug into the wood paneling to the left of the window, inches from where her head had been.

"C.D., I need you. I've got company."

Brandon's heart pounded furiously against his ribs. As soon as those men had gone upstairs, he'd excused himself from the party, made for the loo, and then charged up the stairs the second he was sure no one was watching. Natasha was unarmed. He couldn't let anything happen to her. Not that he'd let anything happen to a fellow agent, but this was different, somehow. The idea of something happening to Natasha sent him spiraling into a near panic, urged on by the sound of her laugh skimming along the surface of his brain, her lavender scent ghosting through his nostrils. Even now, after all these years, after the way she'd left, she had the ability to utterly and completely captivate him, even when he wanted to strangle her.

Bloody fucking hell. He was still in love with his ex-wife.

On silent feet, he approached the open door of the office. Two muffled shots reached his ears, and he broke into a sprint. Like Natasha, he was also unarmed—it hadn't been possible to sneak any weapons into the party. Two men stood just inside the room, advancing on the large desk. Swiftly, he grabbed the first assailant's arms from behind, slamming his hands against the door frame and forcing him to drop the gun. Brandon moved in front of him and landed a hard right hook to his jaw, sending him sprawling backward. Brandon dove for the gun and recovered it as a shot whizzed by his ear, splintering into the wood paneling behind him. He rolled to his back, sat up, and squeezed the trigger. The bullet hit the first man square in the chest, and he slumped heavily to the floor.

Brandon pushed to his feet, the gun trained on the second man, whose own gun was aimed directly at Brandon.

"Drop your weapon," Brandon said, knowing he was going to have to kill him. He couldn't leave him alive and risk having both his identity and Natasha's exposed. Out of the corner of his eye, he saw her rise from behind the desk, a gun clutched in her hands. He kept his eyes on the man in front of him, not giving her away.

"Drop yours," sneered the man in a thick Russian accent.

Suddenly, Natasha was behind the man, the barrel of her gun pressed against the base of his skull. "You're outnumbered. Drop it."

"Fuck you," he spat, and spun, knocking Natasha away. Her gun flew from her hands, and the thug now had his gun trained on her. Without hesitating, Brandon fired two shots into the man's back, and Natasha scrambled out of the way before he fell.

"Did you get the vials?" he asked. Without a word, she dipped behind the desk and emerged with a small metal briefcase. He stuffed the gun into his waistband and closed the distance between them, his hands landing on her shoulders. "You're okay?"

She nodded. "Thanks to you."

He pulled her into his arms, unable to stop himself. She laid her head against his chest, and something deep within him settled, blood flowing like liquid gold through his veins. She pulled away and their eyes locked in the dim room, heat pulsing between them. He tucked a strand of hair behind her ear, letting his thumb trace along her cheekbone. She was so beautiful it almost hurt to look at her. Beautiful, and smart, and brave.

"You gonna go all James Bond on me and sweep me off my feet?"

Mentally, he added smartass to her list of attributes. Funnily enough, it also went in the pro column.

God, he'd never told her that, had he? No, he'd only given her grief for what he now realized were some of her best qualities.

He'd been a royal prick at times, but he'd been too young and stupid to realize the extent to which he'd pushed her away. Small wonder that she'd left when he could've done so much better by her.

"Let's get the hell out of here." He shoved the window open and scanned for guards, but the alleyway at the rear of the house was empty. He eased his feet out onto the narrow ledge and grabbed the drainpipe, climbing down quickly. Once he was safely on the ground, Natasha tossed the briefcase to him and then followed, her athletic body making quick, graceful work of the short descent. Without a word, he took her hand and they started to run, their feet slapping against the pavement as they wove their way toward St. Peter's in Eaton Square, where a car had been left for them.

The towering wrought-iron street lamps cast a warm glow against the darkness, reflecting against the puddles dotting the sidewalk and street. Within minutes, they'd reached the black Fiat parked in a far corner of the church's car park.

Both Brandon and Natasha stepped up to the driver's side, and just as she yanked the door open, he pushed it closed again.

"What do you think you're doing?"

"I'm driving. I'm the better driver. I'd like to get to the Embassy before, oh, I don't know, tomorrow."

He laughed. "I don't think so, Top Gear. You'll drive on the wrong side and kill us. My country, my agency's car. I'm driving."

"I think—"

"Shut up and get in the fucking car, Natasha." He leaned his hands on the roof of the car, caging her in as he beat back the urge to kiss her until neither of them could think straight. Jesus Christ, the woman was infuriating. Sexy, and smart, and irritating as hell.

He fucking loved it.

She inhaled sharply and pulled her bottom lip between her teeth. "Fine. You're right. You drive."

Before he could fully process the miracle that was Natasha telling him he was *right*, headlights flashed as a car turned around the corner, and she scurried around to the passenger side. In what he felt was a generous compromise, he pulled the stolen gun from his waistband and handed it to her as he dropped into the driver's seat. She tucked the small briefcase containing the vials under the passenger seat.

He started the car, threw it in gear, and gunned it, heading toward Belgrave Place. The same headlights flashed again and then disappeared as the driver extinguished them. Brandon's stomach knotted and he flexed his fingers around the leather steering wheel.

He floored it and took a sharp corner toward Belgrave Square Garden, and the sedan followed, tires squealing. "Shit," he hissed. "They're on us."

"Don't worry. I've got it." Twisting around in her seat, Natasha opened her window just enough so she could wedge her head and upper body out.

"What the bloody hell do you think you're doing?" If he hadn't been so intent on steering and keeping them in one piece, he would've reached over and hauled her back inside.

She ducked back in, frustration pulling at her features. "You saved us. Now I'm saving us. You really do want all the glory, don't you?"

"For fuck's sake. Not everything is a competition."

"Sorry, can't hear you. Too busy being awesome." She eased back out the window, the stolen gun clutched in her competent hands as she took aim at the black sedan pursuing them. Trying to avoid the main roads, Brandon swung around Hyde Park Corner, keeping the yawning darkness of Hyde Park to his left and avoiding the bright beacon of Buckingham Palace. Cutting his gaze to Natasha, he watched as she squeezed off several shots, pumping her fist in victory when the sound of squealing tires and then crunching metal pierced the night.

He tightened his grip on the steering wheel, the leather creaking beneath his hands. "Did you just—"

"Shoot the tires out in almost complete darkness?" She sent him an adorably cocky smile. "Sure did."

Something tugged painfully in his chest, and he fought the urge to curse. God, he was so angry with himself. He should hate this woman for what she'd done to him, but he couldn't. She might drive him mental, but, idiot that he was, he *liked* it. *Needed* it. In the six years they'd been apart, he'd dated plenty of women, and not a single one of them had challenged him, frustrated him, impressed him, and turned him on the way Natasha did without even trying.

The simple truth was, there was no one else for him except Natasha Rowe. Never had been, and never would be.

"Hey, you okay? You look upset." She laid a hand on his thigh and his knuckles went white on the steering wheel.

Now wasn't the time to process the confusing jumble of emotions churning through him, so he simply nodded and focused on getting them safely to the American Embassy in Grosvenor Square.

Chapter Four

"It's fine, C.D. I can get to my room on my own." Natasha shot Brandon a tired smile. After barely getting away from Silayev's men, they'd turned the briefcase in at the Embassy, and then headed over to MI5 headquarters for a lengthy debriefing. Brandon must've sensed her fatigue because he'd insisted on driving her to her hotel.

"I wasn't trying to be chivalrous. I need the loo."

"Oh. Okay."

The elevator doors slid open on the fourth floor, and she led him along the hallway, her limbs heavy. Her eyes stung and her throat thickened when she realized that the heaviness wasn't exhaustion, but sadness. Tomorrow, she was headed back to Langley. Home, and out of Brandon's life.

He shut the door to the bathroom and although she wanted nothing more than to flop on the bed, she paced to the window. She looked out onto the lights of Grosvenor Square, leaning her head against the cool glass as rain pattered softly against it.

Tired though she was, her brain spun at a hundred miles an hour as she wrestled with whether or not to say anything to Brandon. Whether or not to tell him how she felt about him, to tell him how sorry she was for leaving all those years ago. Would he even want to hear it, or was she simply looking to ease her own guilty conscience?

She turned as he stormed out of the bathroom, his chiseled features taut with a thrilling combination of anger and lust. "Why do you still have this?" His voice was a low growl.

With long strides, he ate up the distance between them, a slim gold ring clutched in his strong fingers.

"Did you go through my stuff?" Her voice rose, sharp with incredulity.

"Of course I did."

She laced her fingers together and twisted them, anxiety shooting through her and mingling with hope.

"Natasha." His voice was low, the three syllables of her name a warning that his restraint was fraying like worn rope. Excuses tumbled against each other in her brain, but she knew she owed him honesty. Owed *them* honesty.

"Because I couldn't bear to get rid of it."

"Why?" Something wild and desperate shone in his blue eyes, and she broke, unable to stop herself from being selfish and telling him the last thing he wanted to hear.

"Because I never stopped loving you. Because I regret leaving you with every fiber of my being."

"I see."

"I hurt you, Brandon."

He closed his eyes briefly. "Yes."

She licked her lips, and then spoke the words she owed him. "I'm so sorry. It was so..." She blew out a long breath. "It was so wrong for me to leave like that. I know that now. God, I'm so sorry for hurting you, C.D." Her heart pounded in her chest as she spoke.

He inhaled sharply and then extended the ring to her. "Put it on." It wasn't a request, but a command, and a hot thrill chased up her spine. With a trembling hand, she took the slim gold wedding band and slipped it onto her left ring finger. He took one final step toward her, backing her into the window. Her breasts pressed against his chest, and he looked at her, that wolfish smile she loved curving his lips.

With excruciating slowness, he raised his hand and traced his thumb over her cheekbone, her jaw, and then down to the hollow of her throat and over her collarbone. He dipped his head and buried his face in her neck, dragging his lips over the sensitive skin behind her ear. "Tell me why you left." He nipped at her earlobe, and she could feel herself melting. Only Brandon had ever had this effect on her.

"Because I thought it was the right thing to do. I thought we were making each other miserable, and I—" She sighed out a moan when he bit gently at the juncture where neck met shoulder.

"You what?" His hands skimmed over her waist, tracing up her back. He found the pull of her zipper and began easing it down.

"I didn't know how to fix it, and I thought you'd be better off without me. If you weren't peeling my dress off right now, I'd think you must hate me."

He let out a chuckle, the sound rumbling deliciously over her skin. "You drive me mental, but I could never hate you, Tash. I know things were hard between us. God, we were young. We didn't know what we were doing. You messed up, leaving like that, but I didn't know what I was doing either. I could've been better to you. We could've been better to each other." He pushed the straps of her dress off her shoulders and she wiggled out of it, letting the material pool at her feet.

She reached behind her and unhooked her bra, freeing her breasts.

"Sweet Christ."

She gasped when his strong hands cupped her ass and lifted her just as his mouth crashed into hers. There was nothing gentle, or tender, or sweet in Brandon's kiss. It was the kiss of a man staking his claim; hard and hot and ravenous. His tongue stroked into her mouth and she sighed against him, wanting to dissolve into him. She twined her legs around his hips and he tumbled them onto the bed, his weight solid and reassuring above her. He deepened his kiss as they worked as a team to undress him, his fingers pulling at his tie, undoing the buttons of his shirt, while she wrestled with the buckle of his belt.

"Bloody fucking bollocks," he swore, his mouth still against hers. He pulled back just as she freed his thick, hard cock from his pants.

"What?" She stroked him and he hissed out a breath, closing his eyes.

"I haven't a condom."

"So? I'm on the pill. Brandon, Jesus. I don't want to use a condom with you."

The wolfish smile reappeared and he pushed off the bed, shucked the rest of his clothing and then pulled her panties off, tossing them on the floor before crawling back on top of her. He notched the head of his cock at her entrance and rocked his hips, giving her only a taste of what she needed. He sucked a nipple into his mouth before raising his head to look at her.

"If we do this, if we try again, we have a lot of shit to work out. I need to know you're on board with that."

She nodded, swallowing around the lump in her throat. "I want to make it work with you. I promise to try harder, to be better. For better or for worse." Her voice shook and cracked on the last word.

"For better or for worse, Tash." His voice was hoarse, his eyes bright as he looked at her.

Happiness, relief, and hope filled her at the same time as Brandon eased himself all the way in, not stopping until he'd buried himself deep inside her.

He slid his hands up and pushed her arms above her head, intertwining his fingers with hers. Over and over again, he filled her with slow, sensuous strokes that gradually gave way to harder, faster, deeper thrusts that all too soon had both of them crying out in bliss, sweating and shaking and panting.

As the sun rose over London and they lay sweaty and sated in each other's arms, she felt whole in a way she hadn't in years.

"I love you," she whispered, pressing a kiss over his heart, his chest hair crisp against her lips.

"I love you more," he whispered back, nuzzling into her hair.

"Are we going to turn this into a competition too?" She propped up on one elbow, and he looked at her, one hand behind his head, the other sliding up her waist and to her breast. He looked so devastatingly sexy it took her breath away.

He shook his head. "No point. We've both already won."

She laughed and kissed him. Just this one time, she wasn't going to argue.

About the Author

Thank you so much for reading Reload! I hope you enjoyed it. If you'd like to find out more about me and my books, check out my full booklist at www.tara-wyatt.com/books, or say hi on Facebook at www.facebook.com/tarawyattau thor.

Snowed in With the Lumberjack

Lee Savino

Chapter One

L*ainey*

Fat snowflakes fly at my car, too fast for my windshield wipers to clear away. To my right, hemlocks bow under the weight of several blizzards' worth of the white stuff. The dark forest and snowy drifts create a winter wonderland, as picturesque as a Christmas card.

My car's chosen a beautiful place to skid off the road.

I press the gas pedal and the engine whirs. My tires spin. I've just made my predicament worse.

One more attempt, and I turn off the car. The windshield wipers switch off and snow sticks to the glass. The cold seeps in, too. Pretty soon the interior of my car will be below freezing.

I fight to open my door. My car is canted towards the passenger side, half in the ditch. I swing my legs around and land in shin-deep snow. The fluffy flakes aren't so pretty when they're coating my jeans and falling into the tops of my Ugg boots. I clamber out of my Kia, grabbing my purse as I go.

My little car makes a sad sight, stuck in the ditch. Soon it'll be a white lump and no one will be the wiser. Snow covers everything and makes it beautiful, hiding the sorry state of affairs underneath. My accident will be hidden until things thaw.

I followed truck tracks to get this far up the mountain, but a new layer of snow is obliterating them. This road doesn't get plowed much, if ever. If you ask folks in town who lives up here, they'd say, "No one."

They'd be wrong. Up somewhere on this side of the mountain is an old hunter's cabin. That's where I'll find warmth, and help. That's where I'll find someone who can make a call for me. My cell doesn't get service in this remote part of town.

The wind picks up and drives the snow faster into my face. The flakes stick to my eyelashes and I blink, fighting to keep my eyesight clear. I duck between the hemlocks, gripping my parka tighter around me and wishing I had brought gloves.

Maybe this wasn't such a good idea. I didn't even make it halfway up the mountain, and it's colder out here than I expected. My winter coat might as well be a bikini for all it's doing to keep me warm.

I trudge through the shadowy woods. A hundred steps in, and I have a hitch in my side. I read somewhere that tracking through snow on cross-country skis burns more calories than any other activity, and I don't even have the skis. My body heats up fast, making my skin itch with exertion and sweat. My boots are clogged with snow and my thighs ache with the extra weight.

The forest is silent, all life buried under the white shroud. The only sounds are the huffs and hitches of my breathing and, under my coat, my thumping heart. I follow what looks like a path through the pines. With any luck, it'll bring me to safety. If not...

The last of the light is disappearing through the trees when the trail turns and reveals a dark wooden hut. Its sides are mounted up with snow, and the windows are dark too, but a thin wisp of smoke trickles from the chimney.

A thwacking sound breaks the quiet. For a second I think I've imagined it, but it comes again, a hollow thud. The sound of an ax hitting wood.

"Hello?" I shiver in my boots, resisting the urge to dance back and forth. I can't feel my toes.

A shadow slants between the black tree trunks. In the low light, he looks like a frost giant with an ax in hand and snowflakes clinging to his beard. Joel Adler, the man I hoped to see.

The man of my dreams.

"Lainey," he asks in a deep voice, "what are you doing here?"

Chapter Two

J*oel*

"My car broke down," she says. It's Lainey Stevens from town, shivering in a snow drift, with flakes crusting her clothes. Her teeth clack together.

I swear before I can stop myself, and sink my ax into a log. I stalk forward, watching her closely, but she never flinches. Other people in town give me a wide berth, but not Lainey. She works the register at her aunt Gemma's grocery store. I see her every time I drive down to buy supplies.

"Jesus, it's freezing out here." My voice sounds harsh, unused. Not many people to talk to up here. Not many people want to talk to me when I'm in town. Only Gemma Stevens... and Lainey. "Where are your gloves?"

She stares up at me, her wide eyes fringed with black lashes. Her lips are tinged with blue.

I jerk my head towards my cabin. "Get inside."

She stumbles and I reach for her, stopping myself at the last moment. No reason to put my hands on her.

"Sorry," she squeaks, and my soul wilts a little. She's intimidated by me, even though I've been as gentle and considerate as I can be. But of course she is. Everyone knows I'm an ex-con. A felon.

And now she's on my mountain, fifteen feet from my home. Alone. Any woman would be nervous.

"I'm not going to hurt you," I growl. I sound like a psycho.

"I know." She stops and stares up at me, and a line appears between her brows. Is she glaring at me? "You would never hurt me, Joel Adler."

She's scolding me.

"All right." I can't stop my smile, and I'm glad it's hidden behind my beard. I've never been berated by someone a foot smaller and a hundred pounds lighter than me. "As long as we're clear."

I take her hand. If she's not afraid of me, she won't mind a gentle touch.

Her fingers are little icicles in mine. I suck in a breath.

"Sorry," she says again.

"Don't apologize." I propel her forward, practically hauling her off her feet in my haste to bustle her inside. When she staggers again, I scoop her up into my arms and carry her across the cabin threshold like a groom with his fairytale bride.

I kick the heavy door hard so it swings open without sticking. Snow spills off the roof, narrowly missing us. I duck inside and carry my precious bundle straight to my butt-ugly orange couch in front of the fireplace.

"Stay here," I order, and rise to shut the door and knock snow off my boots. I return and tug hers off, tossing them to dry by the fire. I'll mop up the piles of melting snow later.

I help her out of her coat and hang it up close to the hearth. "What were you thinking, hiking up here?"

"I couldn't get cell service on the road."

I bite back another curse. I need to watch my foul mouth. "Why were you even driving in this?"

"It wasn't so bad in town." Her gaze is fixed on the floorboards at her socked feet. She's like that when I visit her aunt's shop, peeking out from behind the books she reads in between dealing with customers. She's shy, and looks young for her age. I'd think she was in her teens if I didn't know she was only a few years behind me in high school. We were in a junior English class together, because she was advanced and I was a senior with straight Ds in every class, barely scraping by. That was Lainey—smarter than the whole school, and better than me by a mile.

Ten years, and not much has changed.

"Let's get you warm." I can't think when she's shivering. I pull an old quilt off the couch and wrap it around her, then crouch to rub her hands.

"I'm okay," she whispers.

"You could've fucking died," I growl.

She has nothing to say to that. We sit in silence, her on the ugliest couch ever made, me on the floor.

My hands are battered and scarred, marred with the blue tattoo ink I got in prison. More of my bad decisions, written on my skin.

Her fingers are perfect—small, and tipped with glossy nails filed to neat crescents.

I can't stand the contrast between her hands and mine, so I leave her side to throw more logs on the fire. When I turn back to her, she's pulled off her snow-dusted hat, releasing a waterfall of silky dark hair. Her cheeks are pink under the black crescents of her eyelashes. In the firelight, Lainey glows like a jewel.

My breath saws in my chest. Next to her angelic perfection, my home is worn and dingy, one step away from decrepit. I spent the last year renovating it, fixing sections of rotten wood. My grandfather used it as a hunting cabin. There's no mention of the structure on the land deed he willed to me—either he'd forgotten it, or thought it had rotted away. I furnished the place with castoffs I found at the dump. I knew it was no palace, but I see it now through Lainey's eyes, and I'm ashamed.

No one's been up here for years, no one but me. The closest anyone's come was Lainey, six months ago, in summer.

Shame makes me snap. "You shouldn't have been on the road tonight."

"I was going to see Aunt Gemma," she stammers. "It's Christmas."

"You're from here. You know what the storms are like," I chastise her.

She bites her lip and looks to the window. The glass panes are choked with white, but there's a small dark center that shows white flakes flurrying through the night.

I want to do a lot more than scold her so I force myself to head for the door.

"I'm getting more wood," I say without turning. "Stay by the fire. It's snowing like crazy, and there's no way a truck can get up here before they plow the road. Looks like you're here for the night."

Lainey

Ten minutes in Joel's house and I've already screwed up. He scowls as he tells me to stay, as if the thought of sharing his home with me for the night disgusts him. The door slams behind him.

I palm my cheeks. Am I so repulsive? Such awful company?

My hair is tangled and the ends are wet from melting snow. I push the mass back and adjust the old quilt he threw over me. I'm wearing my nicest sweater and favorite pair of jeans. The fuzzy wool and denim are buttery soft and fall nicely over my curves, highlighting the swell of my breasts and butt, hiding the rest.

In high school, Joel was a chick magnet. He didn't have to chase girls, they flocked to him. Blondes or brunettes, pink-haired emo goth wannabes or the most prissy cheerleaders—he didn't seem to have a preference. He didn't care if you had a boyfriend or were flirting with him to make your crush jealous. He'd be down for a quickie in his old Corvette, the one he bought at auction and pieced back together with parts he scavenged from the junkyard. It had different colored doors but was still an awesome ride.

No one was surprised when he got busted for jacking cars. What was more surprising was that after he did his time for grand larceny, he came back to our little town.

"Where else would he go?" my aunt Gemma snorted when a customer gossiped about this in front of her. "He always liked the woods."

I'd always had a crush on Joel Adler, the coolest boy in school. But that was the first time I saw him for more than his facade, the sexy charm boy who was always down for a fuck or a fight. I remembered how he created works of art in shop class: birdhouses and stools and even a cradle, made with honey-stained wood.

The next time he came into Aunt Gemma's store, I summoned my courage and gave him a smile.

The cabin door swings open, letting in a blast of frozen air. I summon my habitual smile but it falters in the frozen stare of my host. He comes in, blowing smoke and glowering at me like a frost giant who's found an intruder in his lair.

His cold stare doesn't cool his hotness one degree. If Joel was gorgeous as a boy, he's breathtaking as a man. Tall, with lean muscles, and thick brown hair striated with red and blond like rare wood. Eyes a striking, crystalline blue.

He stomps past, carrying a stack of wood that looks like it weighs more than I do. The only sounds are the crackle of the flame-eaten logs, and his harsh breathing.

I knot my fingers together. I've messed up and I don't know how to make it right. So I sit in silence and watch Joel stack wood. Once he's done, he strips off his coat and toes off his boots, and my own breaths grow heavy. He's got a flannel shirt on, and while I watch, he loosens the button and rolls up his sleeves. He's not bulky, but he's strong. Sleek as a mountain lion. Even the indigo smudges of his prison tattoos lurking under the crisp, gold-tinted hairs on his powerful forearms are sexy. Another layer to the enigma that is Joel Adler.

I've always liked puzzles. Mystery novels, or romances with anti-heroes. Chapters with layer upon layer of intrigue my intellect can sink into. The blessing and curse of the voracious bookworm: a life lived sitting in corners, hiding between the pages, reading instead of living life.

One more semester, and I'll graduate with my Masters in Library Science. I'll move out of my parents' summer home, find a job, wear frumpy sweaters and pencil skirts, adopt a succulent and a cat. Become a cliche.

The only blip on my horizon, the only piece that doesn't fit, is Joel Adler. Another woman would know exactly what to say to him. She'd be cuddled right up with him on the couch.

"Are you cold?" he asks, staring at the fire as if it'll give him the answers.

"I'm good." My voice is soft.

Coming here was a mistake. I know that now. Some adventures are best left to heroines in books.

I shift on the couch, and a paperback flops from the quilt's folds to the floor. The cover's torn off, but I recognize the font.

I slide off the couch to my knees to rescue the book, a familiar friend. *"Secrets of a Summer Night."* I pick it up and smooth the pages. "I love Lisa Kleypas. Were you reading this?"

From my position kneeling on the floor, Joel looms even taller. His blue eyes burn and his nostrils flare.

"Get up." He motions me back to the couch.

I catch my apology before it escapes and obey, but he's already moved away to another part of the cabin. This place is one open room. He can't escape me, not unless he goes back out to chop wood. And he's already used that excuse.

He stands in the kitchen area of the cabin, as far away from me as he can get without heading into the cold. I've made him upset. How? Why?

I clutch the book to my heart. Books are easy. Books, I understand. "I love this book. I reread it all the time."

"I know," he says, his back still to me. "I've seen you read it. You gave me that copy, remember?"

"Oh…" I do remember. I keep a stack of paperbacks by the register to read and reread. Sometimes I give them to customers. Why didn't I remember I gave this to Joel?

I'm so flustered, I open the book and read a few lines. I don't look up until Joel's shadow falls over me.

His voice echoes in my ears and I realize he's been calling my name.

"Sorry—"

"No apologizing," he corrects me gently, and plucks the paperback from my hands. I would protest and clutch it to my chest like a safety blanket, but he replaces it with my second favorite thing in the world: a mug of tea.

So that's what he was doing in the kitchen corner of the cabin. Making me tea. Loose-leaf Earl Grey, from the smell of it, in a carefully knotted teabag. I bury my face in the fragrant steam.

Joel remains standing, cradling the book in his palms. His fingers are long and elegant, even rough with scars and tattoos. A craftsman's hands. "And yes. To answer your question. I was reading this."

"Really? I mean..." I stammer. "I didn't mean to imply I didn't think you'd read it."

"It's okay. I didn't used to read like I do now. Picked it up in prison." He glances at me then, checking for a reaction. Does he expect me to shy away from the reminder he did time?

"If you like that book, you'd like the whole series. I have a whole list of favorites."

"A whole list?" There's a hint of a smile under his beard. He's teasing me.

"She's good," I defend. "Everyone loves *A Devil in Winter*. But my favorite is *Marrying Winterborne*."

"I'll check it out. Drink your tea."

I sip the hot liquid. It occurs to me that he keeps issuing orders and I obey without thinking. "This tea is really good." The kitchen takes up one corner of the cabin, to the right of the door. The fireplace and couch are opposite. In the middle of the room is a wooden table with a single chair. Beyond that, in the far right corner, is a big bed.

I snap my gaze back to the fire and meet Joel's ice-blue eyes. My cheeks burn, knowing he watched me snoop.

Awkward girl is awkward. Why did I think tonight would be any different? It would take a lot of Christmas magic to fix my dorkiness.

"I've never been here before," I mumble to my tea.

"No one has." Joel sets the paperback on the mantle. "Kinda the point of living alone on a mountain. The privacy."

I set my mug on the floor, feeling ill. "You're angry with me. I shouldn't have come."

"No, Lainey." He crouches in front of me and closes his hands around mine. "I'm an asshole."

Chapter Three

J*oel*

Lainey looks so miserable, I'm ready to banish myself from my own home. Instead, I warm her fingers between mine. She's not as frozen, and a lot of my tension eases out of me knowing she's warming up.

"You scared me," I admit.

"What?"

"It's dangerous for you to be out on the road, in the snow. You could've died. Why aren't you with your family?"

"My parents are in Arizona."

"Right." I knew that. It's wrong, how much I eavesdrop on Gemma and Lainey's conversations. How much I keep tabs on Lainey. "They own a place there now."

"Yes."

Acid fills my mouth but I make myself ask the next question, "Why aren't you with your boyfriend?"

"With Landon?"

Landon. A frat boy with no chin who thinks he's hot shit because his dad owns some strip malls a few towns over and dips his toes into politics. When

Landon visits Lainey at the store, he parks his red Mercedes in the Reserved for the Disabled spot.

"We broke up."

"You dumped him?" I settle beside her on the couch.

"I... It was mutual." Her gaze drops away, her shyness tinged with shame. "He wanted more than I wanted to give."

Heat flares in my chest. "Did he do something to you?"

"I'm okay, Joel," she says quickly, as if she recognizes there's a monster inside me roaring to be let out. "He didn't do anything."

I make a note to check if she's telling the whole truth, or downplaying it to be nice. If Landon hurt her, I'll kill him with my bare hands.

It'd be so easy. Hang around one of the ratty college bars on a Friday night and wait for him to stagger out drunk. Hit him over the head or choke him out, and secure him in the trunk of a throwaway car. I live on a ton of private land. It's easy to hide a body in these woods.

"Joel." She puts her hand on mine, and my murderous visions fade away.

"It's fine. It just wasn't working out."

"You're too good for him." Her hand is delicate, pure, in my dirty palm, but I can't let her go.

"It's nice of you to say that."

"It's true. You're too good for anybody in this town."

Her long lashes flutter. She doesn't believe me. I shouldn't touch her but I can't let this pass.

"You're perfect." And she is. Dark hair, dark eyes, pure skin. Lush curves under the bulky sweaters she wears. She zoomed through high school and college, graduating early. She's only working at the grocery store to pay the bills and help out her aunt. Soon she'll have her Masters and be done with our small town.

Lainey Stevens is going places. Me? I'm an ex-con, living like a hermit on a deserted mountain. I might as well be a million years older than her. I fix up old cars and sell them at a profit, making enough so I don't have to count coins when I buy ground beef and tomato sauce at Gemma's store. Lainey's so high above me she might as well be in the clouds.

But she doesn't seem to understand that. She shrugs off my compliment.

I grasp her chin, forcing her to look at me. "It's true. Lainey, listen to me." I wait until her gaze meets mine. "You are perfect. You are. Don't let anyone tell you otherwise." Our faces are inches apart, her breath sweet on my lips. "Do you understand? Say *yes, Joel.*"

"Yes, Joel."

Damn, if that doesn't get me hard.

Her tongue darts out and licks her top lip, glazing it. She has a perfect mouth with thick and curvy lips. I bet her pussy looks the same.

I'm so busy fantasizing about her pussy, I almost miss her little laugh.

"You're always lecturing me. Remember the last time my car broke down?"

I do, vividly. The summer heat, and her bent over to check her tires, her dress hitching up the back of her curvy calves and delicious rear. She wore a white cardigan and looked modest and sexy at the same time. "You were driving up here with bald tires. You deserved a lot more than a lecture."

She's looking at the floor again, instead of at me. "You said if it happened again... I'd be in trouble."

"I said more than that. I told you if you ever drove on bald tires again, I'd turn you over my knee." I wait for her to run, screaming. Instead, her breath hitches and her lips curve.

I save us both from the silence. "I'll take a look at your car before they tow it. I might be able to fix it. Your car and I have a good relationship."

"You're always rescuing me."

I rise, because I can't sit close to her any longer. My dick makes it too uncomfortable. "Right. You're going to sit cozy. I'm going to feed you. And in the morning, I'll trek out to call for a tow. If the roads are good, I'll take you home. I can try to text Gemma now, so she's not worried."

"Okay." She sounds reluctant. "I texted her too. She won't be worried."

Something about her tone strikes me as off, but I don't think too hard about it. After I've fired off the text, I serve her a bowl of beef stew and hover over her to make sure she eats. "You're lucky I was here tonight," I say, picking at my own stew. I don't want to think about what would have happened if she'd been stuck up here alone.

"I heard you tell Gemma you'd be home for Christmas," she blurts, and ducks her head.

I rock back on my heels, feeling amused that she eavesdropped on me, just like I do with her. I might go grocery shopping more than I need to, just to see her.

I take her bowl and hand her back the book to read while I wash up. I'm mopping up the wet spots where the snow melted on the floor when what Lainey said earlier lands.

I might not be book smart like Lainey, but I have my own brand of smarts. Lainey's good at a lot of things, but lying isn't one of them.

Chapter Four

L *ainey*

Joel looms over me. "You lied to me, Lainey." He looks so stern. "Gemma isn't in town for the holidays. She flew out to be with your parents."

I swallow. I've spent the last few minutes trying to think up excuses and pretending to read.

He takes the book out of my hand and sets it aside. "What's really going on here?"

"You said you'd be alone." I knot my fingers together. "It's Christmas."

His brows slant down.

"No one should be alone on Christmas." I resist the urge to squirm under his fierce stare. *Be bold.* "So I came up here."

"You came up here," he repeats slowly.

"I want to be with you." And I put my hand on his leg. A tremor runs through me. Or maybe him. Or both of us.

"Fuck," he breathes. "You did this on purpose."

"I didn't mean to break down. I was hoping to find the road."

"You could have been hit by a car. Or gotten lost in the woods." The tops of his cheeks flare red. He lets out a gust of air and motions sharply. "Stand up."

I rise and he takes my place, immediately grabbing my hand to guide me down into his lap.

His *lap*.

"Wh-what—"

"It seems my first lecture didn't take hold. So I'm going to give it again... with a little reinforcement."

"Reinforcement?"

"Oh, yes." His hand skates up my back. "It's time you learned your lesson. I promised you punishment, didn't I?" When I don't answer, he gives me a squeeze. "Isn't that right?"

I nod.

"Use your words, babygirl."

My face has to be bright red. I squeeze my thighs together. "Yes. That's right." I'm breathless and my heart's galloping. I'm on Joel Adler's lap, staring into stern blue eyes inches from mine. I have no idea what's going to happen, but there's no place I'd rather be. "You said you'd turn me over your knee."

His grip tightens but his face is calm. "Good girl. Tell me, Lainey. Have you ever been spanked?"

I shake my head before I remember to answer. "No."

"In a minute, I'm going to help you up. I'm going to unbutton your jeans, but I won't undress you yet. You're going to lie across my lap. I'll spank you over this," he rubs the denim stretched over my hip, "first. Warm you up. Then, you'll get punished."

"Will it hurt?" I squeak. I'm six seconds away from hyperventilating.

"Oh, yes." His breath ghosts across my ear. "That's why it's a punishment. "But if you take it like a good girl..." he leans back and tucks a thick strand of hair behind my ear, "I'll give you a reward."

Did I know this was going to happen when I drove up the mountain? Some part of me knew that even if I made the first move, Joel would take me on his terms. But I never imagined this, not even in my wildest fantasies—most of which starred Joel.

"Are you ready?" He doesn't wait for the answer. He's already guiding me up and doing exactly what he said he'd do.

I can't stand to look at him when he undoes my jeans button and pulls down the zipper. His knuckles brush the soft bulge of my belly and there's a sharp ache right in my core. I need him to go further. But I'm afraid of what will happen when he does.

He eases me over his lap, face down this time, so my stomach rests on the hard and powerful muscles of his legs. He tips me over so I'm a little off balance. I'm two sides of a triangle and my ample rear end is the apex, pointed up right at him. Not a flattering position. I'm used to hiding, using sweatshirts to cover up my softness and size.

His fingers ghost up my thigh, and my skin prickles under the thin layer of denim.

"You're so beautiful," he mutters. Each pass of his hand wakes my body up, bringing it to life. I never knew my bottom had so many nerve endings. "I can't believe this is happening."

Same, Joel. Same.

Something prods my stomach. It's his dick. I shift so I'm not crushing it, but he steadies me with a hand in the small of my back. I'm clutching his leg, off balance, and wait for his hand to descend.

The first few smacks over my jeans are underwhelming. His palm claps down with a thuddy sound. There's sensation but there's no pain.

"Ready for more?"

"Yes."

He chuckles. "I should have known. Let's get these jeans off you."

I start to rise and his hand on my back turns to steel.

"No." He holds me down and yanks off my jeans somehow, scooting them over my hips. Now my face is really red. I'm ass-up and totally exposed. I wore my best underwear—a blush-pink bra and panty set. I didn't anticipate this happening, but I'd hoped *something* would.

"Pink." He sounds like he's been punched in the gut. He trails his fingers across my bottom, exploring. My panties are so thin, I feel everything. The way his rough callouses catch on my soft skin. There's reverence in the way he touches me.

His palm crashes down, and the air goes out of my lungs. He peppers my bottom with sharp, stinging smacks. Tears spring into my eyes.

But a part of me is satisfied. *This is more like it.* He said this was punishment. Punishment shouldn't be fun. This is the way I earn my reward. And I love to strive and earn things. To prove myself.

"This is what happens to naughty girls who disobey me." He spanks in a rhythm, harder when he wants to emphasize something. "You'll remember my lecture this time, Lainey. You'll never put yourself in danger again."

Yes, yes, yes. I can't speak. I can't breathe.

The flat of his hand claps my bottom, hard, sending fire shooting through me. "Your ass is getting nice and pink for me."

My breath rushes out of me in a half gasp. Am I laughing? Crying? This is so weird. The humiliation and intimacy all rolled into one.

He pulls down my panties and I freeze up again, imaging my big dimpled bottom on display. His hand skates across my skin, barely touching me. I want to wiggle away from him but he catches me before I even try.

"You're almost done with your punishment. And then..." He dips his fingers between my legs, brushing the pouting lips of my pussy. All the air leaves the room. "Breathe, Lainey."

He lets his palm crash down on one cheek and then the other, covering every part of my bottom and even the tops of my thighs. I kick my feet and writhe, but he winds a leg around mine, pinning me so that I'm still. He's way stronger than I am.

The part of me that's fighting gives up and lets go. My thoughts float away, too. There's nothing but Joel's body wrapped around mine, and the punishing kiss of his hand on my skin that sparks heat and pain.

I float in a warm haze. I don't realize he stopped spanking me until he strokes my labia again and a different sensation sings through me. His skilled fingers dance over my intimate parts, finding my clit and painting it with my own wetness. This is so different to when I touch myself, or the few fumbling attempts my ex made. With Logan, if my clit was in Kansas, his finger would be at the North or South Pole.

"You did good for me, taking your punishment." He takes one of my lower lips between his thumb and forefinger, and rubs. "Now it's time for your reward." I'm restless, shifting on his legs again. He clamps his limbs down and holds me so that I can't slide away. Unable to move, I'm forced to focus on the feelings. He tickles my clit and circles it, rubbing at the itchiest spots, making the neediness build in my limbs until a little golden pulse flares through me and satisfaction floods my core. My lips part and my breath comes in a rush. The first pulse is followed by another, and another. And all the while, Joel rubs my back, murmuring, "Good girl."

I'm wobbly when he pulls off my underwear and jeans and eases me back up. My face is flushed from being upside down. My hair is a lost cause.

"Whoa," I breathe, and his eyes crinkle.

He holds my gaze as he licks his fingers. I'm too blissed out to feel embarrassed.

"There's another reason I came up here tonight," I tell him. He's clothed, and I'm naked from my hips down. Not quite my fantasy, but we're a quarter of the way there.

He inclines his head, the flinty spark in his Arctic gaze warning me to tell him the whole truth. My bottom throbs.

"I wanted to give you a gift." I pause but he doesn't guess what I wanted to give him. I'll have to spell it out. Problem is, I don't think I can say it out loud.

I grab the hem of my sweater and pull it over my head. It drops to the floor.

I wait, wearing nothing but my blush-pink bra. *Please, please, get what I'm trying to tell you.*

Understanding lights his eyes. He grips my hips and pulls me closer to him. "This is what you want?" There's a rough edge to his voice. Underneath my burning bottom, his dick surges.

"Actually," I say, "it's more like a gift you could give me. Because..." the word sticks in my throat, "I've never done it before."

His eyes flare, then narrow. "Lainey... are you telling me you're a virgin?"

I bob my head up and down, and remember to use my words. "Yes."

"Holy hell." His hands fall away from me, shocking my skin with a sudden rush of cold.

Chapter Five

J*oel*

Lainey sits on my lap, her bare skin glowing in the firelight. She looks like an angel, an apparition, an emissary from heaven come to bless the faithful. Except I'd be the last person an angel would visit.

And yet here she is, midnight eyes and hair, unwrapped in my lap like a gift.

She came up here to seduce me.

I can't move. I can't speak. I can't think.

After a moment, she shivers and wraps her arms around herself. Her chin drops. "Please don't say no."

I gather her to me immediately, sliding my arms around her. "No. No. I'd never say no to you." She collapses against me and I encourage her to, pulling her chest flush to mine and stroking her hair. "I don't think I'm capable of it."

She shudders, and I feel the emotions filling her to the brim. She's been through a lot in the last hour. I keep her cradled against me for a while, stroking my hand up and down her back. Eventually, I can't resist rubbing her bottom, exploring the marks I left on her, but she doesn't seem to mind. She relaxes further.

I glide my hand over her body, finding my way to the seam between her legs. I shift her in my lap, easing her thighs apart and soothing them until they relax and fall open.

The scent of her arousal rises, and I grit my teeth so I don't come in my pants. I haven't had to fight an orgasm like this since I was a teen, and even then I didn't have to fight this hard. Lainey destroys my control.

"You're going to give me this," I cup my palm over her sweet pussy, "for Christmas?" She's hot and pulsing and oh so wet in my hand. My rough, tattooed hand. The contrast of her perfection against my ugly flesh should make me want to look away. Instead, it gets me hotter. "This most perfect gift... for me?"

She squirms but her lashes lift and she looks squarely at me. "Yes. I want you..." her voice wobbles and she musters more strength, "I want you to have it. To have me."

I wait for her to change her mind. *She's not drunk. She's alone but she drove up here. For me. She hasn't said no. She took off her shirt.*

And as I stare, her chin lifts another inch.

She wants this.

I can't wait a second longer. I scoop her up and stride to my bed, where I lay her out like the virgin offering she is.

As I stare down at her, I know two things: I'm going to hell for this. But it'll be worth it.

She's so soft and sweet—chubby thighs and belly, lush breasts spilling out of the top of her sexy bra, lying on my faded flannel sheets. I can't resist her.

This is a dream. In the morning, she'll be gone.

But right now, she's here. My angel. My miracle on a dark and sacred night.

I lean down and kiss the inside of her knee. She squirms and kicks, unused to being worshiped. If I get my way, she'll get used to it. I'll work my way up her gorgeous body, pleasuring every inch of her. I'll tie her down if I have to. My bed posts are sturdy. And tomorrow—

No. There'll be no tomorrow. This gift, this miracle, is only for one night. I need to make the best of it.

So I get comfy between her legs. When she tries to inch her knees closed, I part her thighs so her pussy blossoms. The scent of her is the sweetest perfume. I kiss a line from her knee to inches from her dripping center, my beard scraping up the sensitive flesh until it's chafed pink. I like my mark on her.

"Joel," she breathes. Her hands come to rest on my head. If she tries to push me away, I'll pin them down, but for now I like how her fingers tangle in my hair, ready to hold on tight. "You don't have to go slow for me. You can—"

"Shhh, babygirl." I stroke two fingers up and down her outer pussy lips, rubbing them with the lightest touch. She's shaved smooth, and ultra sensitive. She torques her hips one way, then the other, and I steady her with a hand at her waist. "There's no rush. This is for me."

"But—"

"No talking." I make it an order, and don't miss how her pussy gushes in response. *Beautiful.* I scoot further to the apex of her thighs. "I'm going to get to know you. Inside and out." I take one labia between a thumb and forefinger and rub until she can't catch a breath. I nuzzle the inside of her knee, nipping her tender flesh. She's spread before me like a book, and I want to read every chapter. Study every paragraph. Memorize every line.

There are faint stretch marks on the curves of her hips and insides of her thighs. I trace them, first with my fingers, then with my tongue. She makes the most adorable little whimpers and squeals. Is she embarrassed about her body? Her responses? At one point she tries to roll on her front. I spank her sweet ass. "No. No hiding from me."

It takes her a moment to obey. I give her another swat and her rear jiggles so nicely, I spank it some more. The redness from her spanking has faded to a pink flush. It'll be interesting to see how much punishment she can take. She rocks back into position before I can imprint a red mark in the shape of my hand on her bottom.

Her eyes are dark as night, her lips glossy from biting them.

"Relax. I'm going to make this good for you." I slide my palms under her ass, gripping her punished flesh in a reminder of what happens when she disobeys me. I need her to let go, to give me control. Erotic pain can unlock some people better than pleasure can. I suspect it works that way for Lainey.

I let my beard brush over the crease of her thighs, teasing her, circling her wet center. Her scent envelopes me until I'm drunk with it. I thumb her pussy lips until she's restless and desperate, not for escape, but for more.

That's when I lick her. She tenses up but I wear her down, massaging her intimate folds with the lightest touches of my fingertips and tongue. I tickle her clit and taste her from the top of her labia to the bottom. I prop her hips up higher and lick in long, rhythmic strokes. Up and down, up and down, until her hips rock with each pass.

Every so often, she lets out a little coo or sigh. She's been such a good girl, keeping quiet this whole time.

I take a break and lean back, spreading her labia to drink in the view. Her little clit is swollen and needy.

"I want you to come. You can cry out if you want, but the only thing you say is my name. Got it?" I punctuate my command with a light smack, right on top of her clit.

She gasps.

"Nod if you understand."

She nods so hard, her hair flops into her face.

"Hang on, babygirl." I dive back in, licking her in the same rhythm until she's at a simmer.

"Joel," she hums my name at a volume barely above a whisper. I lick lower, and delve a thumb to massage the shiny skin around the knot of her anal entrance. All of her is mine. Mine to explore. Mine to possess. Mine to fuck.

"Joel!" She clenches her bottom cheeks, trying to squeeze herself shut, but I press my face to her pussy, driving my tongue into her channel to lick up all the juices there. Her hips judder, her whole body vibrating at peak intensity. She turns my name into a moan. I squeeze her ass in rhythm to my tongue fucking her.

She finds my head, digging her fingers into my hair and tugging hard enough to rip it out by the roots. I don't stop. She's panting my name, singing it out as her muscles clench.

"That's it, baby," I say, my mouth filled with her pussy. She jerks, coming undone on my tongue. Her cries are the sweetest music.

I rise up, beard dripping, and crowd closer, making her legs stretch wide. Her pussy is hot and sopping wet in my palm. I've penetrated her with my tongue. She's loose from her orgasms, but she needs more preparation before I give her my dick.

I slip a finger inside, collecting the wetness. I add another and watch her face—the flutter of her eyelashes, the tiny wince in the corner of her mouth.

"You can take me," I tell her, and the wrinkle between her brows disappears. She's so damn responsive to my commands.

We stay like that, joined by my fingers inside her. I toy with her, exploring her wet heat, hooking a finger around to find the rough patch on the front wall of her pussy and swirling over the ridges until it swells.

She's already come twice, her pleasure painted pink on cheeks and chest. The next time she comes, I'll be inside her.

"I'm going to put my dick here," I tell her, being crude on purpose. I have three fingers at her entrance, stretching her. "Inside you. I'm the only man who will have you this way."

Now and forever. The thought flashes through my mind, and I push it away.

She nods, looking nervous and eager at the same time. It's too much. I slide my fingers out of her and yank off my flannel shirt so fast, I lose a few buttons. My undershirt and jeans get tossed on the pile. Her eyes widen at the sight of my dick but she doesn't scramble away.

I fist my cock, squeezing hard to stay my orgasm. This isn't about me. It's about her. I've gotta make this good for her. I can't forget myself.

I get close enough to run a finger over the soft pad of her lips. "One day, I'll fuck you here."

Her eyes grow heavy and her lips part, allowing my finger to penetrate her mouth.

Fuck. If I don't stop now, I'm going to blow.

She reaches for me then hesitates.

"You can touch me, baby. I want you to."

"Like this?" She runs a finger up the side of my dick and it jerks. She pulls away, so I take her hand and guide it. Her fingers are small and dainty, and the sight of them clutching my cock threatens to make me explode.

I cast about for something to distract me. Anything. "The last time you tried to come up here. This summer, when you got a flat. Were you...?"

"Trying to give you my virginity?" She nods. "That was attempt number one."

And I lectured her about her tires and sent her home. "I'm an idiot."

"My seduction technique needs work." She touches her thumb to the head of my dick, gathering the precum and spreading it around. Then she wraps her fingers around the shaft and gives it a tug.

My thighs tremble as I fight the urge to spill in her hand. "Your technique is just fine." I pull her hand away. "You're too good."

She narrows her eyes like she doesn't believe me. I trace her soft lips again.

"Before, when you were on your knees... I couldn't stop thinking of this. Then I hated myself for it," I tell her.

"Why?"

"How can someone like me ever hope to deserve you?"

She grabs my hand and kisses it. "I want you."

I shift so I can line myself up with her pussy. It's now or never, or I'm gonna come on my sheets.

I stop. "I don't have a condom." How could I be so stupid? This cabin has been my haven, my place of hibernation. I live like a monk. "I've never had a girl up here."

"It's okay." Lainey's hips jerk towards mine, silently begging. "I'm on the pill."

"I've been tested. I don't have anything. Any STDs."

"Neither do I," she tells me, solemn.

I pass a hand over her, memorizing the curve of her belly, the generous swell of her hips. My work-rough hands are tanned and stained with ink, obscene beside her pure flesh. An angel and an abomination. The sacred and the profane.

There's no redemption for a man like me. Lainey is as close to heaven as I'll ever come.

But I'm damned if I can't stop myself from possessing her all the way.

Chapter Six

L *ainey*

Joel looms over me, his hands on each one of my knees. He sits between my legs like I always imagined. My thoughts are slow and loopy as my body sinks further into the comfortable bed. I want to stay here forever.

"I'll need to go slow," he rasps. "I don't want to hurt you."

"I don't want you to hold back. I want it all." I've risked this much and come so far. We're not stopping now.

I prop myself up and reach for him, draw him down, and kiss me. His beard scrapes my face. I taste myself on his lips, a musky and sharp flavor, with a hint of Joel underneath.

"I want this," I whisper into his mouth, and that seems to be enough.

He shifts himself over me. "All right, Lainey. All right." His hand comes to my left breast, the ragged nap of calluses catching on my soft skin in a rough caress.

He dips his head and kisses me deeper. I open to him, inviting him to give me more. We fall back into each other as easily as if we were born to do it.

His dick probes my entrance. I'm wet enough, he can push in. The stretch burns in the best way. I make a little sound and he pauses but I arch my hips up, letting him sink in a little more.

He holds himself over me, not quite all the way inside me. His broad shoulders fill my vision. All I can see is him.

"Breathe, Lainey."

I pant against his mouth. I scrape my nails down his back, scratching lightly. He's left his mark on me and I want to leave my mark on him.

Will he remember this night? Will he think of me fondly? Or will this barely be a blip on his radar; the faintest memory?

"Lainey," he calls. "Come back to me."

I blink, and study the glacier ice in his eyes. I tip my hips up and dig my nails into his back, pulling him closer. I want my skin to meld to his.

He rocks over me, moving deeper. His weight comes down on me slowly, and I breathe to better accept the pressure. Finally, he's sheathed fully inside me, his hips cradled in mine. I feel him deep in my belly. We're together as close as people can be. It's everything I've ever wanted.

"You're going to come for me again."

"I don't know if I can." I've read that it's difficult for some women to orgasm vaginally.

He pulls out a little and slides back in, angling his hips somehow so he drags over a sensitive spot in my pussy. Sparks fill my vision. "Don't think. Just feel."

His body works over mine in a rocking, easy rhythm.

"So tight," he mutters. "So beautiful. My angel."

Pressure builds in my belly. With each drag of his cock, a hot flush comes over me and my muscles draw up tighter and tighter.

The fire's burned low but the temperature's rising. The heat builds between us.

I writhe under him, needing to move, needing more. "Joel..."

"That's it, babygirl. Say my name." He glides in and out of me. "Look at me. I'm the one who's fucking you." His cock swells inside me, stretching me until I can't take any more. "Give over, Lainey. Give everything to me."

He lowers his head and nips my lip. The combination of the pain, his scent, the way his cock rubs me—it's too much. Something inside me snaps, and golden warmth fills my limbs. Joel shudders over me, his cock pulsing deep inside me. For a moment, he lets his full weight press me into the bed. He kisses my brow, my right cheek, my lips. Then he pulls out and gathers me to his chest.

For a moment, we simply breathe.

There's nothing left of the fire but a few glowing embers. The sweat's cooling on my skin but I don't want to move. "Is it true? You've never had a girl up here?"

"Only you." He kisses my temple.

"I like that."

"Possessive, are you?"

"You have no idea. I've had a crush on you since high school." The darkness makes it easy to spill my secrets.

"You were too good for me in high school. Still are." He draws away and prowls naked into the kitchen. I squint but can't see what he's doing until he returns and presses something warm and wet to my sore pussy.

He cleans me up, wiping away the traces of himself. But part of him is deep inside me. When he's done, he tosses the washcloth on the floor, but doesn't return to my side.

I'm shivering. "Come back to me."

He fixes the quilt so it's covering me, and stretches out beside me. Other than a few pops and crackles from the dying fire, it's so quiet, I imagine I can hear the falling snow. Joel's breathing is deep and soft, but his body is tense beside me. What is he thinking?

"Joel?"

"I'm here, babygirl." But he sounds distant.

"Did... did I do okay?"

He rolls to me, gathering me in his arms. "You did perfect. You are perfect."

I settle back against him. This is what I've wanted for so long—to be in Joel's arms.

"I have a confession of my own to make," he says. "I don't need to buy groceries half as much as I do."

I knew it! I smile into the darkness. "I was wondering what you were doing with all that ground chuck."

"Sometimes I'll just drop it off at the soup kitchen. Whenever my day's too long and grinding me down, I drive past Gemma's store. And if I drive past, I have to go in. Because nothing in my life goes so wrong that it can't be fixed by seeing you."

I hum and snuggle closer. "After prison, why did you come back to town?"

"Because I was done searching for what I already had. You make your life and your happiness."

Exactly. I trail my fingers over his skin. I can't see them in the dark, but I know he has some freckles here and there. I've studied him for so long but I barely know him. It'll take me a lifetime to educate myself about this man.

"I wish..." His voice cracks.

"What?"

"I wish I could spend every night like this."

"But we can."

"No. I'm not in your plans, babygirl." His fingers stroke my belly. "You're going to finish school and move on to bigger and better things."

"Working at a library isn't necessarily bigger and better."

"You're too smart for this town, too smart for me."

"You're plenty smart."

"Lainey, please." He catches my hand, stilling it. "I have to let you go."

"Do you want to let me go?"

"I want to hold on forever." His hand flexes, gripping my fingers tighter before releasing them. "But I have to do what's best for you."

I decide what's best for me, I want to say. Instead, I look out the window. The snow's mostly stopped falling. A few errant flakes drift through the dark blue square. "What time is it?"

I feel him shrug. "Probably after midnight."

"So it's Christmas."

"Yes."

I got my wish. It's time to make a new one. I yawn, fighting off a rush of tiredness. It will be so nice to fall asleep in Joel's arms. It'll be a dream come true. But I want a few more moments to savor it. "Thank you for my gift."

He drops a kiss on my bare shoulder before tucking the blanket over it. "This was the best gift anyone's ever given me. I'll never forget this."

He makes it sound so final. And now I understand: he doesn't think he deserves me. *Oh, Joel.* "You think I'm smart, right?"

"Smartest one I know."

"Then trust I know what I want."

"Lainey—"

"It'll work out."

His sigh stirs my hair, but he doesn't argue. "Go to sleep."

Obedient as ever, I relax against him.

You make your life and your happiness.

Joel thinks we can't last. He thinks that when the sun comes up and the snow stops falling, he'll have to let me go.

But there is magic on Christmas. Maybe it'll be enough to work another miracle.

So I close my eyes, and make another wish.

Epilogue

Joel

I swing the ax above my head and let it fall. The log splits with a satisfying thunk. The temperature's falling below freezing. My breath is white on the wind but the work warms my muscles until I'm sweating and tempted to strip down to my shirt sleeves. I'm almost done, and it's a good thing—the clouds overhead tell me a blizzard's on its way.

I hustle to chop the rest of the wood, setting aside the best pieces to sell online. Turns out woodworkers will pay premium dollar for New Hampshire hardwood. I spent the last year building up my online shop, finding the best wood and planting trees to replace what I've cut down. Between that and the jobs I get fixing cars, it's been a good year. I made enough to add a room to the cabin, and that's a good thing too, because I'm not the only one living here now, and we need the room.

The snow's starting to fall when the door swings open and Lainey steps out. The sight of her makes me catch my breath, the same as it always does.

The same as it did years ago, when I came back to town and she greeted me with a shy, soft voice in the grocery store.

Her cheeks curve, pink where the cold nips them, and her smile lights up the gray day.

"There he is," she coos to the little bundle in her arms. "There's Daddy."

"It's too cold to be outside."

"He wants you," she says, tipping the bundle to show me my son's tiny face. He has blue eyes the exact color of mine, but his round cheeks and angelic smile are all Lainey.

"Go inside. I'm almost done."

She obeys. The door shuts but I can still hear her talking to Joel Junior, singing a lullaby off-key.

I savor the sound. It's been one year since she trekked up here to give me the most precious gift anyone's ever given me. A gift that keeps giving. Our son was born in September. We got married in June, after Lainey graduated. She got a part-time job in a nearby college town, and helps me with the store on the side.

Lainey thinks there's magic on Christmas, but I have another theory. There's nothing supernatural about my wife's determination and a car that won't stop breaking down. It's Lainey.

She's the magic.

Thank you, I mouth to the frozen air. To whoever's listening: God or angels or just the snow-filled clouds in the sky. *Thank you.*

I set my ax under a tarp and head back inside to my home and my wife and my son. My angel, my redemption.

My miracle.

About the Author

Author's Bio

USA today bestselling author Lee Savino loves writing super spicy romance with wild, one-of-a-kind plots and world-building, plus all the feels. Her favorite heroes are hot, dominant alpha-holes–the type of men who can handle the hot-mess heroines who crash into them and turn their lives upside-down. Lee's books have been translated into multiple languages and she's still amazed she can make a living writing what she loves to read.

Want more sexy lumberjacks? Check out Beauty and the Lumberjacks: https://leesavino.com/books/beauty-the-lumberjacks/

Scorched Turf

Cadence Keys

Chapter 1

Daniel

Chaos reigns as Tommy and I move through the crowd of football fans on our way to the field. Sweat builds underneath my shirt, and it's not because of the heat on this warm Southern California night. Tommy is yammering on about how excited he is to meet the Fierce Four—the key players on the LA Wolves' defensive line who have become legends in their own right. I'm more excited about seeing their coach—Alison Fairbright.

The first female defensive coach for the LA Wolves.

And the love of my life—even if she's convinced herself we should be broken up.

Nothing will be right until I have her back in my bed with my ring on her finger.

My steps feel heavy with trepidation that she'll continue to push me away, but also light in anticipation of seeing her in person. It's been two weeks since I've breathed the same air as her, and that was only because her Pop invited me over for dinner without telling Alison. At least her grandad is on my side.

I understand why she bolted. You don't work in my line of work as a firefighter without seeing a vast array of experiences from loved ones. Some can handle the danger and the long shifts. Others struggle. It takes a special strength to love a first responder.

And sometimes it only takes one tragedy to break even the strongest.

I knew I wanted to be a firefighter when I was five years old and saw those flashing red lights come down my street to save my friend Joel's house from burning to the ground. His teenage sister had tried to smoke a cigarette, and instead of putting it out all the way like she had thought, it set her trashcan on fire—the same trash can that was right under her long curtains.

I joined the firefighter academy right out of college. I'd already been a part-time EMT through school. I met my best friend, Mark, on the first day of academy and we even got jobs at the same station. Every shift working with him was always my favorite, and anyone who knew us knew the pranks we'd play on each other, or how where one was, the other wasn't far behind.

When he introduced me to his sister, Alison, he secured his position—not that he was really at any risk of not being my best friend—and he definitely gained bonus points for helping me convince his sister to go on a date.

It wasn't hard to get Alison to say yes. Our chemistry was off the charts from the very first moment we met. Her eyes sparkled with joy and mischief as she schooled me on football. She'd been watching religiously since she was a little girl, and it was hot that she knew more than I did and was just as invested in the game as I was. She could call how a play was going to pan out before the ball had been snapped. It was like football was her chess, and she observed the game like a chess master at the board.

It certainly didn't hurt that she also filled out a pair of jeans in a way that made me bite my fist and was without a doubt the most beautiful woman I'd ever met. Her long dark hair fell straight to her shoulders with bangs that were right above her eyes. Her hazel eyes were more green than brown, but the brown flecks were prominent and mesmerizing.

But her laugh sealed my fate.

She laughed with so much pure joy, it made everyone else in the room light up too. I was convinced her laugh could heal almost all ailments.

If only it could heal a broken heart.

I can't remember the last time I heard her laugh. She's been serious and withdrawn every time we've run into each other these last five months. And by run into each other, I mean I do everything in my power to go to places where I know she'll be because I miss the shit out of her. I'm surprised—and thankful—she hasn't filed a restraining order for stalking.

But it's the only way I can check in on her directly without going through Pop.

It's been five months since Mark died in a fire, and my whole world shifted on its axis. A week after he died, Ali broke up with me. She gave a bunch of bullshit excuses about not really loving me, but I could see the devastation in her eyes. I could see the self-preservation too. Not only was I a reminder of her only brother—and her only family apart from Pop—but I was also in the same line of work and therefore at the same amount of risk. She could lose me just as easily as she lost Mark, and that wasn't a risk she was willing to take—not anymore.

I understand her fear and her reasons for ending it, but I also know her better than anyone else, and I know she lashed out to protect herself from further pain. While I can't always guarantee my safety, I can guarantee that no man will ever love her the way I do.

Even Mark knew that. In fact, I'd gotten his blessing to propose only three days before his death. I even had the chance to show him the ring I'd picked out for her. It's the same ring that I keep on me at all times. It's a reminder of what I'm fighting for.

I've been patient for five months and given her space, but I know better than most that time is precious, and I'm done letting her sabotage our happiness.

Tommy and I pass a large group of police officers, also here for "Hero Night," which is a yearly event the team puts on where all first responders get free seats and can meet some of the players. But unlike the other people milling around, I didn't come for the players this year.

My breath catches when I spot Alison less than twenty feet away from me. She's standing next to one of her players—Gabe Romero—and nodding as a man talks to her and Gabe.

I came for her.

And fuck, it's good to see her, but my heart aches when she smiles and it doesn't reach those gorgeous eyes of hers. I'd give anything to take away her hurt and promise she'd never have to experience that kind of pain again.

"Holy shit, that's Gabe Romero!" Tommy exclaims next to me.

"Yeah." I'm being a terrible friend right now, but I'm too distracted by Ali.

We move closer, my gaze eating up every inch of her in her tight jeans, tennis shoes, and an LA Wolves sweatshirt. Her dark hair is up in a ponytail, and the headset she normally wears during the game has long since been removed, but some loose strands of hair fall around her face from wearing it during the game.

She turns her head, her eyes sweeping over the crowd before they land on me, and my body warms from the heat of her gaze. A spark of recognition and happiness lights her eyes for the briefest moment before immediately shuttering, but it's enough to feed the flame of my determination.

The man finishes talking to Gabe and moves on to the next player right as Tommy and I reach them. Tommy shakes Gabe's hand with all the exuberance of someone who's meeting their idol for the first time. My gaze stays locked on the only person in this stadium who matters.

"Hey Ali," I say, my voice soft like I'm trying to put a spooked animal at ease.

"Danny." Her pained gaze scans my face as her arms cross over her stomach and her shoulders curl inward. Her eyes sweep across my features and my body as if she's cataloging any changes since the last time she saw me—like she's reassuring herself that I'm okay. I'd be better if she'd stop being stubborn, but her stubbornness is also one of the many things I love about her, so I suppose I have to take the bad with the good.

"I didn't expect to see you here," she says, her voice now completely neutral as if I'm just an acquaintance. With another breath, she drops her arms to her sides and stiffens her posture. She's trying to look put together, but I can see the cracks in her veneer.

"I would never pass up a chance for a free football game. Plus I couldn't pass up the chance for the meet and greet. My favorite Wolf is here."

"Who's your favorite?" Gabe asks conversationally, but with a faint trace of a smile. We've met before at events Ali used to bring me to. I know he's loyal to her, but he's not giving me a death glare, so I'll take that as a good sign. He nods at the small football I bought at the gift shop to toss around at work when I'm procrastinating on paperwork. "I bet we could get that signed."

I look down at the football and then back up at Alison. Extending my hand with the football toward Ali, I say, "I'd love to have it signed."

Emotion flickers in her eyes, but it's too brief for me to figure out exactly what she's feeling. Until she nibbles on her bottom lip, which has been her tell for as long as I've known her. She only does it when she's feeling vulnerable and unsteady.

I just need one of those cracks in her armor to widen enough for me to find a way back in.

In my periphery, Gabe's head swings back and forth between us like he's watching a tennis match, but my gaze is still locked solely on hers. She reluctantly grabs the ball, clears her throat, and says, "Did you want me to get it signed by someone who's not here?"

"No, I want you to sign it, since you're my favorite Wolf."

She swallows hard, the motion moving her delicate throat that I've kissed hundreds of times. I even left a hickey once, which she covered up with makeup for the few days that it lasted because she didn't want the players to razz her. My fingers itch with the desire to trace her throat and pull her to me so I can kiss her as hard as I used to. My whole body aches being this close to her and yet feeling so far away.

"Can I have a word with you?" she says through clenched teeth. She doesn't wait for my response, but instead just turns and walks away toward a more secluded corner of the field where not as many people are congregating. She doesn't look back to see if I follow—she knows I will.

I'd hope she'd know by now that I'd follow her anywhere.

When we're far enough away not to be overheard, she spins on her heel, facing me. Her expression is filled with the kind of determination that used to get me hard but now fills me with dread because I can already tell she's about to dig her heels in further and refuse to talk about us.

"I need the rest of my stuff back from your place. I've been asking since"— she catches herself—"for months, and you conveniently never remember to bring it when Pop invites you to dinner." She rolls her eyes at the mention of Pop, and I fight the smile tugging at my cheeks.

God bless her Pop and all the ways he's tried to help me these past five months. That man loves me as much as he loves Mark and Alison, and he's been an avid supporter of me even as Alison has worked hard to freeze me out.

"I can bring it by tomorrow night."

She opens and closes her mouth like a fish out of water, her eyes hesitant as she watches me like she can't believe I'm giving in that easily.

I'm not, but I'll let her think I am.

It's all part of my game plan to win her back. To convince her not to give up on us, even if my job scares the shit out of her.

I'm a firefighter to my core. It's what I was born to do. I can't live without it.

But I can't live without her either.

"Just like that? You'll bring it over tomorrow, and we can finally end this for good."

I shrug, trying to play nonchalant, even if my entire body feels like it's bracing for a blow. "If that's what you want."

"It is," she says with a nod, but there's the faintest waver that gives me hope. "We're never getting back together, and it's time we finally tie up all the loose ends. Once I have my stuff back, we can call it good."

She says it almost like she's trying to convince herself. Maybe she is. Maybe that's exactly what she's doing every time she adds a crack to my heart with her words—as if it's so easy for her to be done with us.

I really hope it's not, because it's been nothing but hell for me.

And yet, I know she's suffering through the loss of Mark, and I hate the idea of her in any kind of pain. Especially trying to deal with it alone.

"Tomorrow night then?"

She nibbles her lip, and for a minute she lets all her sadness fill her hazel eyes. "Tomorrow night."

She looks at me one last time, as if memorizing my features and saving the image for later, and then walks back across the field toward her players.

I remain where I am, watching her go, knowing she's the only woman I will ever love and there's no way I can give up on her, and praying with every ounce of my being that my plan will finally be enough for her to give me another chance.

Chapter 2

Alison

*I**n...2...3...4, hold...2...3...4, out...2...3...4, pause...2...3...4*

I close my eyes and count in my head, completing the square breathing exercise my grief counselor recommends for when I'm feeling particularly panicked and unsettled, but it does nothing to steady my racing heart.

Daniel will be here any minute, and I need to remain strong. He looked so good yesterday, his sandy-blond hair cut close to his scalp and his tattoos barely visible underneath the sleeve of his shirt. Seeing him was so painful I had to go straight to my office and lock myself away until I could stop the tears that burned in my eyes.

Breakups are never easy, but this one has been particularly brutal. Maybe because in the year we were together, I never envisioned breaking up with him. But that all changed when Mark died in a fire.

I always knew there was risk in Mark and Danny's job, but I'd thought PTSD would be a bigger concern. I'd seen more than one first responder struggle with the trauma they see on a daily basis—one even succumbed to their PTSD, leaving behind a wife and two teenaged children. It was a devastating blow for their department, and was the last casualty they had before Mark.

I remember being out with Danny when I got the call from Pop, and the way he struggled to get the words out over his broken voice. I've never felt such terror and utter devastation as I did in that moment. That is, until I looked at the man standing next to me. The man who, without hesitation, pulled me into his arms, hugging me tight as sobs racked my body. The man who held my hand through the worst week of my life and helped organize everything for Mark's funeral. The man I thought I'd spend the rest of my life with, until my nightmares about Mark's death morphed into Danny's face and his mangled and burned body instead of my brother's. I was barely getting through the loss of my brother; I knew I'd never survive losing Daniel.

Which probably makes it all the more ironic that I pushed him away. A week after Mark's death, I broke up with Daniel in the hopes that ending things would mean I'd never have to feel such heartbreaking, soul-crushing pain again.

But being apart from him hurts in a different way. And as hard as I'm trying to stay strong and keep my resolve that we're better off apart, each time I see him, my resolve grows a little weaker. He's too handsome for his own good, and it certainly doesn't help that he continues to look at me with such love and devotion in his eyes, even after I broke his heart.

I pace my living room, continuing my square breathing even though it's not doing a damn thing to calm me down. I need tonight to be our last interaction. It's too hard to see him all the time and still be tied to him. We need a clean break so I can finally let him go and move on. Then maybe it won't hurt to breathe, and I won't miss him quite so fiercely.

Maybe.

I hope so.

The doorbell rings, and I force myself to stay put for one...two...three seconds before I take one step at a time in some weird, twisted version of a bridal march, extending the time it takes me to reach the door as long as I can. If I open it too quickly, he'll think I'm excited to see him, and I can't give him false hope.

I take one more last breath—wishing it would actually give me strength—then steel my spine, lift my chin, compose my face, and open the door.

Goddamn him for always looking so good.

Whatever breath I had in my body is stolen as my gaze scans him from head to toe, admiring his fitted navy T-shirt that's tight around his thick biceps and chest, but hangs looser down his abs. He's wearing a well-worn pair of jeans with frayed ends over his brown steel-toe boots. When my gaze makes its way back to his face, his blue eyes are filled with longing and heat. The same determination I saw on the field is present now, and I cross my arms in a pathetic attempt to create some kind of barrier between us. When it doesn't ease my quivering insides, I nibble on the inside of my lip until I taste the coppery flavor of my blood. But even that small bite of pain can't compete with Daniel and the way he always sucks me into his orbit.

I used to love that look in his eyes. It made me feel like I was the only woman in the world and no one would ever be able to tempt him away from me. And having worked in an industry with a lot of men who aren't always faithful to their women, I knew how special and significant that look was. Now, it's a reminder of what I can't have—or what I refuse to allow myself to have, as my grief counselor has so kindly pointed out.

"Hey," he says, his deep voice washing over me and sending sweet tingles down my spine and filling me with warmth.

"Hey," I say back, proud of myself for not sounding at all fazed. "Come on in."

I move aside and give him plenty of room to walk past me without touching, but of course he still manages to graze my arm. In his hands is a big cardboard box, and I'm filled with a confusing mix of surprise and disappointment. I don't know why I thought he'd find a way to drag this out. It's been months. He's obviously given up.

Which is good.

That's what I want.

So why is that thought so depressing?

He moves past me and sets the box on my coffee table before standing up and looking around the room. I close the door and make my way over to him, trying not to fidget.

"Thanks for bringing this over."

"Hmm," he murmurs as he moves to the mantel over my small decorative fireplace. His eyes linger on the picture of him, Mark, and me when we ran the Los Angeles Half Marathon last year. I swallow the lump building in my throat and turn my attention to the box in front of me. I peel away the top flaps and look inside.

"What the fuck is this?" I ask, my accusing gaze darting up to glare at him.

He glances over like he hasn't a care in the world and raises his eyebrows in faux surprise. "Oh, that's your favorite sweatshirt."

I hold up the offending article of clothing. "It's *your* sweatshirt."

He smirks, and damn him if it doesn't set my panties on fire to see that confident look on his face. "Okay, so it's my favorite sweatshirt that you always love to wear. I figured you were probably missing it."

My glare deepens, and then I let out an exasperated huff and look down at the other items in the box.

Un-fucking-believable.

"Are you serious right now?"

He leans back against the wall—casual and cool like this is all some kind of joke—and I swear to God I'm about to have smoke billowing out of my ears.

"Danny!"

"What?"

"This box is filled with *your* stuff, not mine."

He sticks his neck out and glances into the box with a confused little furrow on his brow that is all for show. "Is it? I could've sworn that was all your stuff." He looks up at me with an aw-shucks grin and has the audacity to say, "Oops. My bad."

That's it.

Months of pent-up emotions explode in a stunning display as I mash his sweatshirt into a ball and chuck it at him.

"You."

Then an old band T-shirt that I used to sleep in.

"Infuriating."

Then the CD he bought when we went to Hawaii that I loved listening to while I took a bubble bath in his claw-foot tub.

"Stubborn."

Then the earmuffs I stole skiing at Big Bear.

"Man!"

Each item he catches casually with a shocked, yet giddy face. "You call *me* stubborn? I'm not the one who's been pushing everyone away for the last five months."

"Everyone? *Everyone?* Try just one person. *You!*"

His eyebrows shoot up to his hairline. "Do you actually believe that lie? What about Mark's girlfriend, Grace? Or my sister, Sadie? Huh? What about when Ronan kept reaching out to you. You know he was close to Mark and how much he looked up to him. Mark's the reason he became an EMT and has been studying to become a firefighter himself. Don't you dare lie to my face and say you only cut me out when you cut anyone with any connection to Mark. Grace was devastated when he died. And my sister loved you like you were already family. Does Sadie deserve your silent treatment?"

He steps forward, and I step back to keep a distance between us, but that only works until he corners me.

He's only a breath away from me when he leans down until our lips are almost touching, and my heart is pounding so hard I'm convinced he must hear it.

His voice is deep and low when he speaks, and I can't help the goose bumps that prickle along my skin. "You're not the only one hurting, Ali. We all miss him. Why won't you let us all grieve together? Why won't you let *me* be there for you when you need me most?"

"I don't need you. I don't need anyone," I choke out, my voice a hoarse and unsteady whisper, and I regret the words immediately because they aren't true. Not even a little bit.

But I regret them even more when I see how the blow lands on Danny's shoulders. They sag heavily as his eyes turn down, and he stares at me with all the heartbreak I see reflected in the mirror every morning when I wake up. This look is different from the look he gave me when I broke up with him, or even the look on his face when we found out about Mark.

I can't take it. I can't stand watching his pain and knowing I put it there.

I wrap my hand around his neck and pull him into a fierce kiss. He's stiff for only a second before he wraps his hands around my waist and hauls me against his body, holding me firmly against him while my legs automatically wrap around his hips. We kiss with such desperation it's like it'll be the last kiss of our lives.

For the first time in five months, I let go. I let go of the heartbreak, the pain, the fear. I let go and breathe him in. My lungs feel like they're taking their first full breath in months, and it feels so good to be in his arms that I let my body do whatever it wants. I don't want to think, I just want to feel.

Feel him.

Feel this.

Feel us.

God, I've missed us. I've missed the way we fit together like two perfect puzzle pieces. The way our mouths mold together and our tongues swirl around each other in a dance they've perfected over months of make-out sessions. The way his big, strong hands carry me as if I weigh nothing.

The way he loves me with every ounce of himself.

He carries me through my house and straight to the bedroom where he lays me down and kisses my neck in the one spot that always made me weak in the knees for him. We don't speak—I don't know that I could find the right words anyway—and for once we let our bodies do the talking.

He kisses his way down my throat and chest before he sits up and pulls my shirt over my head, unhooking my bra and pulling it off before pushing me back against my soft comforter. His hands are a tender caress against my heated skin. Our eyes connect, an intensity shining in his that makes me wish I could allow myself to have him like this always.

I could, if only I could keep the fear away long enough.

He must see what he's looking for—permission most likely, because even though he knows me better than I know myself, he would never force me to do something I didn't want to do—and then he removes my shoes, socks, pants, and underwear like he's unwrapping a long-awaited Christmas present. He takes his time kissing every inch of my body from my toes, up my toned legs, bypassing that spot between my thighs that's absolutely desperate for him, and then up my stomach until he reaches my breasts.

I've always had sensitive breasts, but no man had ever taken the time to find exactly what kind of breast play got me off.

Daniel did, and it quickly became his favorite way to give me my first orgasm. Tonight is clearly no different from all those other times. He laves my right nipple while tugging on my left, then switching sides and repeating his actions until stars explode behind my eyes.

My fingers claw at his shirt, anxious to get him as naked as I am. I need to feel him.

I need him. Period.

He stands up and rips his shirt over his head before his lips come back to mine, our tongues tangling as he kisses me with all the passion he possesses until we're both panting. He pulls away only long enough to strip out of the remainder of his clothes and grab a condom from where I've always kept them in the nightstand—even if I haven't used them since the last time we were together—before he's back on top of me and my legs are locked around his waist, my ankles crossed and pushing on his ass in a desperate attempt to get him inside me.

He slides home, and I suck in a sharp breath, relishing the stretch of him inside me after so many months of feeling achingly empty.

"Fuck, I've missed you so much. I love you, Ali. I fucking love you, and this is killing me. Please don't push me away anymore."

His thrusts are slow but steady, like he's soaking in every slide inside while I fight back tears from his words. I want to give him what he wants, but I'm so fucking scared.

And fear is a powerful demon to overcome.

But right here, right now, wrapped in his arms as we find pleasure with our bodies, I can almost pretend I'm strong enough to overcome it.

Chapter 3

Daniel

The morning light filters in through the windows, and the gentle rise and fall of the soft body next to me reminds me that I never made it to my own bed last night.

I don't mind.

I'd rather wake up with Ali in my arms than sleep in my own bed ever again.

Her breathing loses the regular rhythm, giving away that she's awake, and I fight against the tension that wants to build in my shoulders as my body braces for her to push me away again. I'd give anything for her to roll over, smile at me, and tell me she loves me and she's been just as miserable these past few months as I was. I want her to tell me she's done hurting us both. I don't want her to question the perfection of last night.

Or worst of all to regret it.

I don't want her to dash the small flicker of hope that settled in my chest when she ravaged me with a hunger she's never had before.

Neither of us move, and I start to believe that maybe the magic of last night will carry through this morning—until my phone alarm goes off, signaling that I need to head to the station in an hour for my next shift.

I roll over, turn off the alarm, and then roll back, wrapping my arm around her again.

"Do you have to go in?" she asks.

Of course she knows. We were together for over a year, and no one knows my routines or schedule better than she does.

"Yeah."

"I'm guessing since you didn't work yesterday or the day before, that this is the end of your four days off."

"Yeah. I'll be alternating twenty-four on, twenty-four off for the next five days." I hesitate—the words I'm desperate to ask clogging my throat. I drop a kiss to her shoulder, close my eyes, and push the words out. "Can I see you again when I get off shift tomorrow?"

The seconds tick by in slow motion as I hold my breath, waiting for her response, fearing I already know what it is.

"Yeah," she whispers so low I almost don't catch it. She clears her throat. "I'd like that," she says a little louder, but her voice is still soft and maybe even a little unsure.

But it's the opening I need and a step in the right direction. I can work with unsure.

Happiness fills me until I think I might burst from it. "I would too," I tell her, keeping my voice low so she can't tell how giddy I am at the idea of spending more time with her. I kiss her shoulder one more time—because I can't help myself with her this close—and then pull away, even as my body aches to remain wrapped around her.

"Just maybe not right when you get off. Seven in the morning is too early to go on a date."

I drop my forehead against her shoulder as my body shakes with a laugh. "Noted. How about brunch then?"

"It's a date," she says, her voice soft and her words a balm to the ache that's been in my heart all these months without her.

"I should get going. I gotta pick up some stuff from my house before going in."

She turns over and her beautiful eyes trap me in their gaze. "I'll see you tomorrow."

"You can count on it."

I get dressed and then head toward her front door when her voice calls out my name, causing me to turn around. She's right there, covered only by the oversized shirt that was in the box I brought over last night under the guise that it was hers. It falls to midthigh and teases me with the nakedness I know is underneath.

With three steps, she's in front of me, her hands sliding up my chest and only stopping when they graze the short hair at the back of my neck. She pushes up on her tiptoes and plants a kiss to my lips that isn't nearly enough.

"I don't regret it," she whispers against my lips.

Tension I didn't know I'd been holding immediately releases, and with a groan, I wrap my arms around her body and plunder her mouth, kissing her with a hunger and desperate need that rivals her own.

Leaving is torture, but this time is different from all the other times I've had to walk away from her the past five months.

Only a little over twenty-four hours before I'll have her back in my arms. If the last five months have taught me anything, it's that I can be patient.

I'll wait a lifetime for her if that's what it takes.

I enter the station with an extra spring in my step and a smile on my face.

"Well, looks like someone had a good night," Tommy says with a wide, knowing grin.

I keep my mouth shut because what I do with Alison is no one's business but ours, but I can't wipe the smile from my face to save my life. Tommy just shakes his head and lets out a chuckle before slapping me on the back.

"It's good to see you happy again."

"Thanks, man."

He leaves the room, likely to get started on checking equipment, and I put my things in my locker. My phone rings, and I glance down at the caller ID to see my sister's name flashing on the screen.

Sadie and I didn't have the best upbringing. Our parents divorced when I was ten and Sadie was five, just old enough to remember the fallout. They used us like pawns on a chessboard—not important enough to protect, but useful for their end goals. Our only constant source of unconditional love and support was each other, and I vowed never to make Sadie feel like she wasn't important. My parents did that enough with the both of us.

So, of course, I answer her call.

"Hey, Kid, what's up?"

"You realize I'm not actually a kid anymore, right?"

"Spoken like a true smartass. What can I do for you?"

"I wanted to see if you were free to grab some lunch or something."

I lean against my locker. "Can't. I just got on shift."

"Bummer. Okay." I can hear the disappointment in her voice that she tries to hide with her verbal acceptance.

"Is everything alright?"

It's been a long time since I've felt the need to worry about Sadie, but there's something in her voice that tugs at that brotherly concern in my chest.

"Yeah, everything's fine."

"Why don't I believe you?"

She huffs out a laugh, but then sighs. "Probably because you know me too well."

"You gonna make me guess?"

"How's everything going with Operation: Get Ali Back?" There's something in the way she says it that rubs me the wrong way, but instead I focus on her avoiding my question.

"I know what you're trying to do."

Her voice gets low, borderline pleading. "I'm not ready to talk about it, okay? So will you just let me change the subject and focus on you for a minute?"

I scratch at my jaw, torn between wanting to share with her that Ali's giving me a shot but also wanting to make sure my sister's okay.

"You're sure you'll tell me when you're ready?"

"Don't I always?"

Yeah, she does. So instead of pushing further, I tell her about Ali—not the sex stuff because she's my sister and that's gross, but everything else. I expect her to squeal with excitement, but instead the line is silent.

"Sadie?"

"Are you guys getting back together?" There's a hint of concern in her otherwise neutral voice.

"That's the goal. It's always been the goal."

She hesitates again, and the concern is crystal clear when she speaks this time. "I love Ali, you know that, but it's been hard to see you hurting so much these past five months. I really don't want her to string you along and then have to watch you heal all over again."

My good mood threatens to disappear, but I hold on to the hope I woke up with this morning. "It's not going to be like that. She loves me, Sadie. I know she does. She's fucking scared, and she has every right to be. What I do is dangerous, and she just lost her brother. She's allowed to grieve however that looks for her, even if I hate it. But I belong to her. My heart is hers and has been since the moment we met. That's not going to change whether she's ready for us to get back together now, or if I need to wait another thirty years. Although I hope I don't have to wait that long, I sure as shit will if it means I get to be with her in the end."

She hums, but it's clear she doesn't get it. She's never loved anyone like this. All her boyfriends have been weak little shits who didn't appreciate how amazing she is.

But someday she'll find the love of her life and she'll understand. She won't be able to let him go any more than I can let Ali go.

The heart wants what the heart wants, and all that nonsense.

"I don't want to argue with you about this, Danny. I love you. You're really the only family I've got that matters. I don't like to see you hurting, that's all."

"I know you don't." My chest squeezes painfully as all the hope and conviction I had this morning starts to wane. What if Sadie's right? "It'll all work out," I say, less confident than before.

It has to.

I don't want to live my life without Alison by my side, because what kind of life is worth living if you can't be with the person you love?

A couple of the guys getting off shift come in to grab their shit from their lockers, and I say a quick goodbye to my sister and then hang up. The guys look exhausted.

"Long night?"

They both nod. "Arsonist struck again. Hardin is going to debrief you once you get out there."

Two months ago there was a fire at an abandoned building that had some telltale signs that it could be arson. Stacy Everett was the arson investigator on call and agreed with the initial assessment that things weren't quite right, primarily the burn pattern, color of the smoke, and evidence of accelerants that wouldn't have been natural to the building. Two weeks later, there was another fire. Then another one. Each fire has increased in intensity and size and not only become more dangerous for us to fight, but have been started in buildings that are increasingly populated.

We've got to find this guy before someone gets hurt. I slap my comrades on the back in solidarity and then head out to find our captain.

Captain Hardin is a burly man who's been doing this job longer than I've been alive. He's slightly taller than I am, with a gray mustache that always makes me think of Sam Elliott. He probably could've been promoted up to one of the chief positions, but he always says he prefers being closer to the action. No one does more for his firefighters than he does.

When I find him, he's talking to Stacy, who took point on the investigation and is leading a team as they examine any of the fires that we suspect are tied to this arsonist.

"Captain," I say with a nod.

He turns to me, his lips curving up in a slight smile but his eyes weary. "Hey Daniel."

"I heard the arsonist struck again."

He nods, rubbing at the back of his neck, but it's Stacy who answers my unspoken question. "It was pretty bad. He's escalating dangerously, whoever he is," Stacy adds, her face set in a somber expression that immediately puts me on alert.

"Was anyone injured?" A frisson of fear tingles down my spine—something that got worse after Mark died.

"Not this time, but it was too close for my comfort," Hardin says.

We move toward the kitchen where the other firefighters on this shift are grabbing coffee before we get to work checking inventories.

"I'll make this quick so you guys can go home," Hardin says. "The arsonist struck again—this time on an apartment building that was fortunately cleared out due to a severe water pipe leak on the upper floors that had just been repaired. Residents were supposed to move back in today."

"The building is a complete loss," Stacy adds. "We've been taking pictures of the crowd from the past three fires hoping this firebug wants to watch his work, but don't have anything definitive yet. He is definitely escalating; to what purpose, we aren't sure yet. There's no apparent rhyme or reason to the buildings or locations, at least none that my team's been able to find. "

Captain clears his throat. "Long story short—be vigilant on fire calls. If anything seems off to you, get out of there until we can assess if it's safe."

We already take lots of precautions, so his comment shouldn't even be necessary. "Is there something you're not telling us, Captain?" I ask.

He and Stacy share a look, and she nods at him, albeit reluctantly. "It appears that whoever this fire starter is, he might be targeting firefighters, specifically."

"What makes you think that?" I ask.

"The last three fires have had evidence that an electrical timer of some kind was used to set off an additional point of origin. The last one went off as soon as our guys were inside the building."

"We suspect that it went off earlier than it was supposed to, but the intention was to cause more damage and potentially even casualties."

"What makes you think it went off early?"

"One of our guys thought he saw someone. He went to check it out in case they needed a rescue and nearly got trapped. We later found that door had been secured from the outside, and two eyewitnesses reported seeing someone dressed in dark clothes running from that direction. If that was our fire starter, I don't think they planned for it to go off while they were still inside the building," Hardin says.

"I know that's not much to go on, but with how this person is escalating each fire, we'd rather play it safe than sorry and consider all questionable instances suspect," Stacy adds.

Captain clears his throat again. "Alright, let's get back to work. You've all got inventories to do." It's not surprising that he wants us to focus on our daily tasks. Arson cases rarely get solved, and there's no point worrying before something happens.

Chapter 4

Alison

Walking out onto the field used to be the most awe-inspiring feeling in the world. Not many women can say they are professional coaches for an NFL team. The number is increasing, but it's still predominantly a man's world. I feel honored to be among the first of many women to stand on this field in a leadership position that can shape the success of our team. Watching my players find victory in game after game gives me the greatest sense of pride I've ever experienced.

It's one of the few places where my life makes sense. Even when everything felt topsy-turvy after Mark's death and my breakup with Danny, this field—this team—gave me focus and purpose.

Danny's arms have always been the other place that made me feel secure. I was so sure ending things was the right decision, but after last night—and waking up wrapped in his arms this morning—I can't deny that I'm regretting how I've behaved these past five months. I don't want to hurt him anymore, but I don't know if I'm strong enough to take the risk he wants me to take.

Being with him means possibly reliving the worst day of my life all over again—the memory of the phone call about Mark's tragic death is as fresh in my mind now as it was when it happened. I don't think I'd survive losing Danny.

Before I can linger on it too much longer, my four favorite players come running onto the field in their practice jerseys. I know I'm not supposed to have favorites, but these guys have been mine since my first day. They never questioned my authority or my knowledge of the game. They followed my advice immediately and took over if other players ever tried to second-guess me. They've had my back and always made me feel like part of the team, regardless of my gender.

So, yeah, they're my favorites.

And despite the moniker fans have given them—The Fierce Four—they're a bunch of softies. Gabe Romero, Dominic Smith, Romel Watson, and Tyler Russell tower over my five-foot, nine-inch frame and arrive with take-no-shit expressions on their faces.

"Hey Coach," Gabe says as a smile quickly breaks on his face.

"Hey Gabe. How's the houseguest situation going?" He's got some girl staying with him, which I think is crazy since he met her at a bar and then offered his house when he played a role in her getting fired. But who am I to judge someone else's life when my own is a chaotic mess?

His eyes soften and his smile turns tender. "It's good."

I opt not to ask more because I'm self-aware enough to know I'm not in the best headspace, and if he's in a good mood I don't want to ruin that for him with my attitude. Although clearly there's something more going on with this woman than I originally thought. I hope he knows what he's getting into.

"You guys ready to run the new play?"

They nod eagerly and we go over the logistics, breaking down each of their roles. Our next game isn't for a few days, but it's against one of our biggest rivals, and we've been watching tape for hours a day to learn all their tells. We're as prepared as we can be, but that's not the time to get lax—it's the time to double down on preparation.

We're playing better than we ever have, and I can practically taste that conference championship victory already—although none of us will breathe a word of it out loud out of fear of jinxing it.

The first few times we run the play, it's a mess, but we keep making minor adjustments until they work like a well-oiled machine.

Practice runs smoothly after that—despite one of the rookies trying to get snarky with me. Gabe, Dom, Romel, and Ty stare him down until he shuts up and puts his head down, and he never says another bad word after that.

At the end of practice, I release them to the showers and then head to the bench to jot down some notes for things I want us to review tomorrow. I normally write out my practice plans in my office, but there's something about sitting under the warmth of the sun with the cool breeze brushing across my skin and the calming quality of the green turf that convinces me to sit outside to finish my notes.

"Coach?"

I glance up to find Romel still on the field, even though the rest of the guys are already halfway to the locker room.

"Hey, what's up?"

"Everything okay with you?"

I stiffen for a moment before responding. "Yeah, it's fine. Why?" I thought I kept it together during practice, but maybe I was more scattered than I thought. That would not be good. Coach Denton would never fire me, but he's getting older, and if the GM ever decided to switch things up, I'd likely be the first to go if there was even a hint that I couldn't be completely focused at all times.

"I know you've had a hard time these past few months. It's been a while since I checked in." He takes a step closer, his voice radiating care and sincerity. "The guys and I worry about you."

My shoulders sag, and I slouch against the backrest of the bench. Romel comes over and sits next to me, both of us facing the field, now mostly empty apart from the trainers dealing with the equipment.

"It's hard...moving on," he says, his voice somber and filled with a depth of sadness only someone who's experienced gut-wrenching loss can carry. If there's anyone who I can talk to about what I'm going through, it's Romel. His wife, Sydney, died from cancer shortly after their daughter, Kaylee, was born. It was the Fierce Four and me who kept Romel afloat while he fought to overcome his grief and raise his innocent newborn daughter by himself. But it was ultimately Kaylee that made all the difference. I've never seen a more devoted father than Romel. That little girl has no idea how lucky she is because he's always going to put her first over anything—or anyone—else.

"Yeah," I say, but it still hurts to talk about Mark—even with someone who understands grief. Instead, I confess, "I saw Daniel last night."

I see his smirk in my periphery. "It's about time."

I snap my head toward him. "What's that supposed to mean?"

"We've been waiting for you to get back together with him. You two were too perfect for each other to stay apart for long. I'm surprised you've lasted this long."

A heavy sigh escapes me as I look back out at the field—the only place that makes sense right now. Everything is clear. Our goal is to win. To keep the other team from getting that pigskin into the end zone.

Unfortunately, it's not nearly as cut-and-dried with my feelings toward Daniel. "I'm scared," I say.

He nods but doesn't say anything at first, as if he's chewing on his words. Then he says, "I get that. But five, ten years down the road, is it going to be fear you're still feeling, or regret?"

His words land as he intended them to—that knot in my stomach turning into despair at the idea of not having Daniel in my life for the next ten years—and we sit there in silence while I process them for several minutes.

"I really hate you sometimes, you know."

I can hear the smile in his voice even if I don't look at him. "No, you don't."

"No, I don't," I say softly. "Thanks."

He bumps my shoulder. "Just returning the favor. We have your back, Coach. No matter what. I just don't want you to let fear keep you from what makes you happy. You always tell us not to be afraid to take risks and challenge ourselves. Maybe it's time you take your own advice."

I send a pretend glare his way. "I didn't realize that advice would get thrown back in my face."

He lets out a light laugh, nothing like the belly laughs he used to do before Sydney died, but it's a laugh, nonetheless.

"It's good advice."

"Yeah, I suppose it is."

"Think about it, Coach," he says as he bounces up from the seat and starts an easy jog back toward the locker room, leaving me on the bench with my thoughts.

The rest of the trainers and coaches head back as well, but my body feels like dead weight so I remain seated, staring out at the green turf and thinking about all the choices I've made since Mark's death.

I went scorched earth on my life—destroying anything that had any connection to Mark in some weak semblance of trying to protect myself from further hurt. Except the only thing that accomplished was making me feel like a raw sore for the last five months.

I don't want to feel that way anymore. I want to feel whole.

I want to be happy.

I want Danny.

Chapter 5

Daniel

My fingers tap against the table with impatience, and I check my phone again—both for the time and to see if I missed a message from her.

"She'll show."

I glance up at Agnes, the older woman who owns this little hole-in-the-wall diner that makes the best brunch in the world, as she tops off the coffee I've barely touched. She looks down at me with a twinkle in her eye like she's thrilled to have both of us back in our old regular booth.

Ali and I used to come here for brunch every weekend she was home during the season, and every weekend during the off-season. She hasn't been here since we broke up, which I know because *I've* been here every weekend on my day off, and Agnes would have told me if she'd been in.

"I know she will," I respond, but even I can hear the doubt in my voice.

It's been over twenty-four hours since we've seen each other. What if she took that time and talked herself out of giving us another chance?

Agnes gives me a sympathetic smile and opens her mouth to say something, but before any words come out, the bell over the door rings and both of our gazes shift toward where the love of my life has just entered.

Alison's gaze locks on mine, and my chest feels tight from how much I love her. There has to be a way I can convince her to take a chance on me. That it'll be worth it, even if she's scared.

I honestly don't think I'll survive without her in my life. My heart has been hers since the very beginning.

A small smile graces her lips, and that tightness in my chest loosens. When she reaches our table, her gaze swings to Agnes, and her smile brightens as her eyes soften with warmth.

"Agnes. It's so good to see you."

Agnes pulls her into a hug, and Ali stiffens slightly before wrapping her arms and hugging the woman back. I can hear Agnes murmuring something, but not the words. Alison tears up and then looks over at me, and there's so much love in her eyes that I have to actively fight my body's urge to get up and pull her into my arms.

I promised myself I wouldn't push today—at least not as much as I have been lately.

Agnes finally releases her. "Alright, I'm bringing your usual," she says and then bustles away. Ali watches her go with a peaceful smile on her face before she turns back to me. I stand as she steps closer to the table because it feels rude to stay seated, but it takes great effort not to touch her.

"Hey."

Her eyes have a spark in them that they haven't had in a long time. "Hey," she says. "Brunch was a really good idea. I've missed Agnes's eggs Benedict. Every time I've tried to order it, they just throw ham on there."

I gesture to the table as I talk, and we sit down across from each other. "You know she adds the chorizo to yours because you love it, right?"

Ali looks affronted. "You're lying."

I struggle to hold back a laugh. "Not in the slightest. She told me once she overheard you talking when we were sampling all the different menu items before you landed on eggs Benedict. She remembered how much you loved the chorizo, so she thought she'd give it a try, and you acted like it was the best thing you'd ever put in your mouth. So she just kept making it for you that way."

"You're serious right now? Eggs Benedict doesn't actually have chorizo on it?"

"Google it."

She hastily pulls out her phone and her fingers fly across the screen while she types. I know the moment she realizes I'm right because her entire body sags against the backrest.

"Holy shit. I can't believe it."

"I can't believe it took you this long to look it up. It's been a year since we found this place."

"Why would I? That was the first time I ever had it, and I never thought to question it. I'm shook right now."

I barely stifle my laugh, but I can't hide my smile. "You've got weird tastes, my love. Agnes just happens to like feeding them."

Her cheeks flush and it takes me a second to realize what I said.

My love.

I grab my coffee and look out the window while I take a sip. I need something to occupy my mouth so I don't accidentally say something else that hints at how close I am to bending down on one knee and proposing to her right now.

She clears her throat. "How was work?"

I almost tell her about the arsonist. She'd know if she watched the news—it's been all over the headlines—but I know she doesn't. She's always said the world is depressing enough without watching the news. Instead, I say, "It was uneventful." It's not really a lie—we hardly had any calls and no fires. They were mostly car accidents and one fall at a retirement home.

"The team's looking really good this year. Lots of murmurs about them going all the way," I say.

She smiles wide, pride glowing in her eyes. "Yeah, they're good guys and have found a stride this year that's made them unstoppable."

"Every interview I've seen them do, they've given you large credit for that."

She keeps her shoulders back and her head held high, confident in her position, and suddenly I'm the one who's proud—proud of her and all that she's accomplished. "It's nice to be listened to. It's not always easy for female coaches in a male-dominated field."

"You proved yourself a long time ago. They're only giving you the respect you more than deserve."

She shakes her head and rolls her eyes. "You and Mark were always going on about that." The smile slowly slides off her face, and her gaze turns serious. She opens her mouth to speak, but Agnes interrupts by placing down a coffee mug and filling it up with the pot of coffee in her other hand.

"Your orders will be right out." She steps back and glances between the two of us with a happy smile on her face. "It's so good to see the two of you back together again. I knew you kids would work it out."

"Oh! Um..." Alison sputters, glancing at me. I probably shouldn't let her flounder the way she is, but I'm curious what she's going to say.

I don't want her to deny it, but my body braces for her refusal.

Alison's gaze stares at my face with something that almost looks like longing. When she speaks, her voice is soft. "He's been more patient with me than I deserve."

My heart nearly stalls out—afraid to hope that she is really willing to give us another chance. No more hiding from her feelings or denying what we have.

Agnes leans down and says quietly—but loud enough that I can hear—"He knows a good thing when he sees it." Then more pointedly at Ali. "Do you?"

God, I love Agnes.

Ali blushes, but then nods. "Yeah. I just forgot for a minute."

Agnes hums, pleased at Ali's response, while I remain speechless in my seat, afraid to look away from the love of my life for fear this might all be a dream.

I couldn't tell you exactly when Agnes walks away—I'm too mesmerized by Ali—but eventually I realize she's not standing next to our table anymore, and Ali and I have just been staring at each other. There's a lot to be said, but there's also so much being communicated with just her eyes.

The guilt filters into her expression, and my heart drops to my stomach. She's going to do it again. I knew it was too good to be true.

"I owe you an apology."

"For what?" My throat feels dry and scratchy as the words come out. I don't know if I'm ready for this conversation. After all these months of trying to win her back and being *so close*, I don't know if I can take her pulling away again.

"For how I handled things after Mark died. I...well, I didn't handle it well. Losing him was a blow I wasn't prepared for. Although I suppose you can never really be prepared for that kind of call, can you?"

"No, I don't suppose you can." My muscles ache from me clenching them as my body braces for her to vocalize my fear.

"I knew his job—your job—was dangerous, but that danger didn't seem real until Mark died." She smooths down her ponytail quickly before dropping her hand and rubbing one finger along her thigh. It's a nervous gesture I haven't seen from her in a long time. Mark said she did it all the time after their parents died, but I'd only seen her do it once or twice when she was afraid of losing her job because there was talk of Coach Denton retiring. New coaches are notorious for making changes to the coaching staff based on their preferences.

"I was completely blindsided by his death, but when I walked up to his casket, it wasn't his face I saw lying there. It was yours." Her voice cracks as tears pool in her eyes.

All the tension fades and is replaced by an ache to hold her, comfort her, and give her all the love inside of me that's only ever belonged to her. But I don't know how receptive she'd be to that, and the last thing I want to do is make her uncomfortable. She has a hard enough time expressing herself.

"All I could think about was getting that same call, but telling me you were the one who would never come home again. And it broke me, Danny. It was devastating to lose my brother, but the thought of losing you was unbearably terrifying. It seemed like more than my heart could take, so I did the only thing I thought I could. And then I spent the last five months missing you and more miserable than I've been in my entire life. I am so truly sorry I let my fear destroy us-"

"It didn't," I cut her off as a tear slides down her cheek.

"What?"

I lean forward and reach my hand out across the table. She places hers in mine, and I give it a gentle squeeze. "It didn't destroy us, Ali. I'm still right here waiting, and I'll be here when you're ready to give us a chance again. I'm in love with you—completely. I've loved you since the moment we met. I have no doubt that you're it for me, but if you're not sure because my job is dangerous, I understand. I'll wait until you're sure. But I'm not giving up on you, or on us."

The words are so honest, it hurts.

"Even after everything I've put you through these past five months?"

"I'm not gonna lie and say it's been easy. It's been hell. I miss you, love. More than I could ever put into words. But I also get it. I've seen other first responders go through similar situations with their partners. But I'm telling you that you're all I want. If you decide you want to give us another chance, I'm in. I'm in one hundred percent. My heart is yours, and only yours."

Tears spill down her face, and I can't take the distance anymore. I slide out of my side of the booth and sit next to her, immediately wrapping her in my arms. I hold her close, soaking in the feel of her and enjoying this moment where she's not pushing me away. She nuzzles her face against my neck, and I shiver as goose bumps go up and down my arms.

It feels so good to have her in my arms, to have her close, where she belongs. I kiss her forehead, and then she tilts her head up as she slides one hand up my chest until she's cupping my neck.

"I want another chance," she whispers, her eyes filled with hope and fear and all the love I know is mirrored in mine. "I'm still scared, but I love you so much, and I don't want to keep pushing you away anymore."

My lips descend on hers instantly, giving her every piece of me with a kiss that evaporates any distance she's put between us over the last five months. She moans quietly into my mouth and slides her fingers into my hair.

A throat clears, interrupting our brief make-out session, and we pull away, both a little dazed from the haze of lust that just took over us.

Agnes watches us with a knowing smile.

I simply grin back and say, "Check, please."

Chapter 6

Alison

We crash through Daniel's front door, our lips smashing together while our hands rip greedily at each other's clothes. My nails scrape across his abs as I push his shirt up, and he lets out a deep groan before reaching behind his head and pulling it off. I don't know why that move is so sexy, but my clit throbs, and I can feel how embarrassingly wet I am. His shirt lands in a pile on the floor, and I allow my gaze to meander across the artwork that is his upper body. His long hours working out—both on and off the clock—are evident in his thick muscles that bunch and flex as my fingers glide over them in admiration. Desire licks across my skin until I feel hot with the need to make this man mine again in every way possible. My heated gaze moves up his body until it connects with his gorgeous blue eyes that make my heart ache from all the love in them.

"I want you." My words are barely a whisper, but they're said with such fierce desire that there's no way he could miss all the depth of emotion behind those three simple words.

He reaches out and slides his fingers through my hair, tugging slightly, just how I like. "I'm yours."

He says it like it's the most factual thing in the world—like saying the sky is blue—and I can't stop myself from launching my body at him. I wrap my arms around his neck and my legs around his hips, locking my ankles together at the base of his spine. His thick arms hold me tight against his body, while his hands grip my ass and squeeze.

His hard, thick cock rubs against where I want him most, and I let out a sigh, dropping my head back. I can't stop myself from grinding my clit along his erection, and even through our clothes, it feels heavenly.

"Fuck, babe. I'm gonna need you to stop doing that if I'm going to last until I get inside you."

"I don't want to stop," I murmur before kissing his mouth. I don't know what's come over me. I've never needed him like this. I've never had such an overwhelming ache that felt like it was crawling under my skin, and he's the only one who can satisfy it. My hips start thrusting faster, my breaths coming out in heavy pants. "Oh God, I'm going to come."

He groans like he's being tortured, but holds his body still while his hands hold me against him so I can rock mindlessly against his erection until a shattered sob rips from my throat as my orgasm crests over me. I shake in his arms as the aftershocks slowly fade and then open my eyes. My head is only slightly clearer than it was a moment ago, but that need to feel him, to be completely connected with him, is still there, pulsing and needy.

His gaze is filled with lust and so much love I can't do anything but kiss him and pour all the love inside of me into it.

His arms move up to band around my waist, instead of holding my ass, while I keep my legs locked around his hips, even though they're still shaking slightly from my orgasm.

"I fucking love you, Ali," he says, his voice hoarse and nearly broken.

"I love you too. I'm so sorry for everything I put you through the last five months."

He shakes his head. "You have nothing to apologize for."

"I do," I say, desperate for him to understand how remorseful I feel. "I hurt you and that kills me. I never want to hurt you again."

He kisses my lips—just a quick peck—before doing the same to both cheeks and then my nose. Each kiss seems to soothe my desperation until the tension starts to seep from my body.

"Make love to me," I whisper. "I need you." I'm always going to need him. He's the other half of my soul; that much was made clear during our time apart.

"You've got me. Forever," he says before leaning down and taking my mouth in a kiss that eases the final threads of desperation I was just feeling.

He carries me to my bedroom, and within moments, we've stripped off the rest of our clothes and are back in each other's arms.

His lips trail down my body in languorous movements, not missing an inch, until I'm a bundle of nerves waiting to explode. My clit throbs painfully between my legs, but no matter how much I whimper and beg, he doesn't relieve the ache he's building. If this is his way of torturing me for what I put him through, I accept it completely.

He blows gently on my mound, just above my clit, but I feel the faintest hint of it as if he was touching me. Goose bumps pebble my skin, and every nerve ending comes to life.

"Please," I nearly sob. It's too much. It all feels like too much.

"Please what?" he murmurs, back to kissing and licking me everywhere but where I want him most.

"Make me come." I'm well past having a delicate response or trying to play coy.

"Is that what you want?"

"Yes," I cry as my body shakes from sitting so close to the precipice with no end in sight.

"Well, why didn't you say so?" he says darkly.

I glance down and see him watching my face intently. The second our gazes connect, he drops his mouth to my clit and sucks at the same time that he slides three fingers inside my soaking wet heat. It only takes two thrusts of his thick fingers and his talented tongue before my body explodes like a supernova. It feels like a rebirth, like everything is shiny and new and glittering.

I spend the next several hours making him feel the same way until we're both spent and exhausted. I fall asleep with his arms wrapped around me and his chest against my back, feeling more peace than I've felt in a long time.

The past few weeks have been bliss. No one ever told me make-up sex was so delicious—or that we'd be so insatiable for each other. We had a healthy sex life before our breakup, but it was nothing like now.

It's not just the sex that feels transformed. Our conversations are deeper, our time together more focused on each other. I'll be the first to admit, I wasn't always present when we were hanging on the couch watching TV after a long day. I'd usually scroll social media on my phone or check my emails and he'd do the same, but now we soak in every moment together. We talk about everything and nothing, deep topics, light topics, things we agree on and things we don't, and everything in between.

Our relationship now is fuller, and more fulfilling in every way—which is saying something because I never had any complaints before. It feels as if our time apart made us both realize how important the other person really was to us, and we want to honor and respect that time instead of getting complacent like we were.

I've even managed to keep most of my anxiety about his job in check. It helps he's had fairly mundane shifts—at least based on what he's told me. There's a moment every time he leaves for work that my heart beats faster and I cling to him a little tighter as the thought that this could be the last time I see him flits through my mind. But just as fast as it comes, it's gone.

Tonight, though, anxiety swirls in my stomach unbidden. Work has been fine. Danny doesn't work again until tomorrow. Everything is as it should be.

And yet, the anxiety is there.

I cuddle closer to Daniel as the movie plays on the screen in front of us. I refuse to let my irrational fears ruin a perfectly good night at home.

A buzz comes from Danny's pants, and he digs in his pocket to pull out his phone. As soon as he glances at the display, his body stiffens.

"It's the station. I gotta take this. Be right back," he says, standing and heading for my kitchen.

I can hear the muffled conversation, but only enough to pick up bits and pieces of his side, but the surprise call from the station only causes the knot in my stomach to tighten. Rationally, I tell myself I'm being ridiculous and everything is fine, but when he comes back into the living room with a frown on his face, I know something's wrong and *this* is what's had me anxious all night—whatever this is.

"I need to get to the station. There's an emergency."

"Okay." I hesitate, afraid to ask because I'm not sure if it'll make my worry worse. "Is everything okay?"

He stiffens so briefly that I'd question if it even happened if I hadn't been watching him so closely.

When he doesn't answer right away, that knot grows until the only thing I feel is dread.

Chapter 7

Daniel

"What's going on?" Ali asks before she begins chewing on her lip in obvious nerves. I've been dreading that question since I got the call and knew I'd have to tell her I needed to go to work for an emergency.

I can't lie to her, but I know the truth is only going to worry her. I've been careful not to mention too many of the hazards of my job since we got back together.

"There's a five-alarm fire and the Battalion Chief for our district called all hands on deck." I hold up my phone. "That was Captain calling to tell me he needed me to come in early."

Stacy is already at the scene with concerns that it could be the arsonist again. She's got her team dutifully taking pictures of any bystanders watching the fire since any other evidence she could get from the scene won't come until we get the fire out. Our entire district has been put on notice to get to the site.

She wrings her hands together until her fingers turn white. "A five-alarm? That's the really dangerous kind, isn't it?"

I stare at her, trying to exude a calm exterior while my gaze memorizes all the lines of her face. "We're all trained and know what to do. We don't take unnecessary risks." This is just another day on the job.

She watches me carefully like she's searching for a lie in my words—she won't find one—and the worry in her eyes slashes my stomach like a knife to the gut. "You didn't answer my question."

I clear my throat. "Yes, it's dangerous." Technically any fire is dangerous. If you forget one safety step, the result could be catastrophic. It's why we regularly train and take safety courses. It's why they changed the firefighter schedules so we'd be better rested and more focused on the job—and therefore less likely to miss those small, but critical steps.

She doesn't say anything else, and after a few more seconds, it's clear she won't. I check my watch—I can't stay any longer. Moving toward where she sits frozen on the couch, I lean down and drop a kiss to her lips, then her forehead. But it's still not enough. I can't stop myself from clasping the back of her neck and pulling her mouth to mine. I will never get enough of her mouth, her body.

Her.

"I love you. I'll come back as soon as we get the all clear, okay."

She nods stiffly, her eyes now wider and the fear she's tried not to voice shining in her eyes. I brush my lips against hers once more and then reluctantly head to the door, grabbing my keys and wallet on the way. I'm halfway to my car when she shouts my name. I spin around to see her standing in the doorway, her arms wrapped protectively around her body, while her eyes gaze at me like she's memorizing every inch of my face.

"I love you," she says, her voice clear and strong but tinged with urgency.

Smiling, I blow her a kiss. "I'll see you in a few hours."

Then I get in my car and take off. A ladder truck flies by me as I near the station, sirens wailing, but the engine is still in the garage when I arrive. That's my ride, and I haul ass to get my gear on. To an outsider, our movements would appear chaotic, but it's all systematic and there's a method to everything we do. I throw my gear on, trained to put it on in a hurry, and am joined by two other members of my company. We nod grimly, unsure exactly what we're going to, but knowing it's bad, then get on the truck and drive to the site.

When we arrive, I look at the scene before me with determination and years of training. There's a scent of something in the air that has the hair on the back of my neck standing up. The fire doesn't smell right, but I can't put my finger on why it's different. Black smoke billows out of the windows of the multistory building, licked by orange-and-yellow flames coming out of several windows in the upper floors of the building. It doesn't mean the lower floors are safe. Without knowing the origin point, it's hard to know how bad it is, but by the turnout they know something I don't.

Our captain finds us quickly. "Engine 87 guys are already inside. There were a couple of businesses open on the bottom level with apartments above, but they haven't been rented out yet. They're still finishing some of the construction, so folks weren't due to move in until next week."

"That's good news."

"Yeah, but I don't feel good about this one. The construction issues were last minute. All the residents who'd already rented were supposed to move in three days ago. The building manager said everything had been on time until suddenly last week it wasn't. Maybe I'm being paranoid, but I don't believe in coincidence. Be safe in there and stick together. Keep your head on a swivel and be by the book. Got it? Anything seems suspect, get the hell out of there."

"Got it," we all say in unison.

"McKay," he says, grabbing my shoulder. I turn around to face him. "I'm not losing any more guys. Don't take any unnecessary risks in there."

I nod. I have no intention of putting myself in any more danger than I already am. I have more to live for than I ever have before.

Tommy and I pair up. "Ready for this?" he asks me. This is his first five-alarm since joining our squad. His first *ever*, but I trust him. We've worked together on other fires, and he's smart and knows how to think clearly under intense pressure.

"Ready as always."

And then we walk into the burning building.

The heat hits me like a blow to the face. I've gotten used to it over time—you learn to expect it and brace for it, but this one feels more intense. There's a weight to it, just on the edge of suffocating, and I look over at Tommy to check in. His eyes are focused, and his expression seems calm but determined.

Exactly how I need him to be. We pass by another pair of firefighters who I recognize from an engine at a station near ours. In the arms of one is a man covered in black soot.

"We've cleared that whole left-hand side. The right still needs a sweep."

"We're on it," I tell them as they take the man out to be evaluated by the EMTs who are waiting near the engines.

Tommy and I make our way along the right side of the building. We clear two rooms easily, but the farther we get into the building the louder it becomes. The roar of the fire makes it nearly impossible to hear, and now that we're deeper in the building, it's clear the fire isn't contained to the top floors we saw from outside.

I can feel the heat coming from beneath my feet.

"Is there a subfloor in this building?" I shout into my two-way radio, hoping someone's outside with access to blueprints. Since this is a newer build, they should, but sometimes it takes too long to get access to the PDFs to be of any use to us.

The radio cracks and I have to hold it close to my ear to hear them. "Yeah, looks like the furnace and some other maintenance rooms are located in the basement."

I look at Tommy who's heading for the door to the stairwell, but before he reaches it the door bursts open and another pair of firefighters from a different station come rushing out.

"Get out! Get out now!"

Before any of us have a chance to move, the ground beneath my feet shifts as the building shakes with a deafening roar. Another boom comes at the same time that I'm thrown backward, a blast of heat pounding into me. I land painfully on the ground, my head spinning and my ears ringing, but I can't move. I stare up at the thick layer of smoke rolling over the ceiling, then glance to my right where I last saw Tommy. There's a beam where he was standing, but no sign of a body.

Thick sludge impedes my vision—wait, not sludge...blood.

Fuck.

I have to get out of this building.

I need to get to Alison. I need to hold her one more time. I need to kiss her and tell her I love her—that I've only ever loved her.

But I can't move.

Spots dot my vision, and as my consciousness fades, I hear the loud beep of my PASS device, alerting anyone who might be able to hear that I haven't moved in thirty seconds.

I struggle to stay conscious, until finally I can't fight it anymore and the darkness takes me under.

Chapter 8

Alison

Cleaning is supposed to be therapeutic—or at least that's what I'm told. But standing here scrubbing my bathroom floor is doing nothing to ease the knot that's been growing in my stomach since the moment Daniel left for the station.

I check my phone for the four millionth time and then sit back on my heels and brush aside a loose hair with my hand while I stare at my now clean floor.

It's been over two hours since he left. I have no idea how long it takes to put out a five-alarm fire, and now I'm wishing I had bothered to ask those questions in the year that we were together, or all the years before that when Mark was a firefighter. It might help with some of this anxiety if I knew whether or not I should've heard from him by now.

I stand up and grab my phone, turning the volume up to its loudest setting so I won't miss a call or text from him. Then I slide it into my pocket so I can grab my cleaning supplies to return them back underneath the kitchen sink.

When I get to the kitchen, I put everything away, wash my hands, and then pour myself a tall glass of water. The cool liquid slides down my throat only to land in my hollow stomach. Setting the half-empty glass aside, I lean against the counter and put my head in my hands.

He's alright. He's alright. He's alright.

He's trained and will be safe. He's fine.

The words repeat in a loop but again do nothing to ease the pit of anxiety in my stomach. All I can think about is how my brother was trained. How he was fine.

Until he wasn't.

It was only a second. One single second that took his life and completely changed mine. I can't go through that again, but that's the risk I've taken by getting back together with Daniel.

Is this feeling better or worse than the empty devastation I felt after Mark died?

Am I strong enough to love Daniel despite how much his job scares me?

Yes.

I have to be. Because there's no one else in the world for me but Daniel. And as scared as I am right now, I'm not the one putting my life on the line to save other people. If he can be strong enough for his job, then I can be strong enough for him.

With resolve that comes from somewhere deep within me, I take a deep breath, releasing some of the ball of nerves in the pit of my stomach. It's not all of my anxiety, but it's a start.

He's alright. He's alright. He's alright.

My phone rings loudly in my pocket, and I jump, then pause when I see an unknown number on the screen. My stomach clenches, but I still answer the phone instead of letting it go to voicemail like I usually do for unknown numbers.

"Hello?"

"Alison?"

"Yeah."

"It's Captain Hardin," he says, even though I recognized his voice. My brother worked with him, and Pop often invited him to Sunday dinners. He came to several when he was available.

"What happened?" My voice doesn't sound like my own. It's scratchy, hoarse, and vacant. "Is Daniel okay?"

I know the answer before he even speaks. Why would he call if Danny was fine?

He lets out a sigh that's weighted with so many words he's not saying. "No, he's not."

Those three words bring all my greatest fears to life, and my heart sinks to my stomach at the same time that I grip the counter to keep myself standing.

"What happened?"

"They just took him to the hospital." It's not an answer to my question, but it's just as important.

"Which hospital?"

He tells me, and I hang up before he has a chance to tell me anymore. Nothing he says right now matters anyway. All that matters is getting to

Daniel's side. I operate on autopilot, my emotions shutting down as I grab my keys, purse, and slip on my shoes. I speed to the hospital, not caring that I'm breaking traffic laws as long as it gets me to Danny faster.

I run into the ER and straight to the nurse at the desk. "I'm here for Daniel McKay."

"Are you family?" she asks.

I stare at her in complete dismay and heartbreak because the answer is so much more complicated than a yes or no. We may not be family by blood or law, but he's mine in every way that truly counts, and I'm his.

Completely.

"Yes! She's family," I hear a frantic female voice say behind me. I turn to see Sadie, Daniel's sister, standing with tears in her eyes. She doesn't stop in front of me like I expect her to, but instead immediately wraps me up in a tight hug. After a second's pause, I reciprocate, holding her tight and fighting back tears as we comfort each other the only way we can.

"I'm still waiting on an update," she says, pulling me toward the waiting room where a few other firefighters are sitting with equally worried expressions on their faces.

"Do you know what happened?" I ask her.

She shakes her head. "All the captain told me was that there was an explosion, but he didn't want to say any more over the phone."

An explosion? Was it just a byproduct of the fire or was it intentional? I've heard snippets in line at the grocery store or in the newspapers about an arsonist, but often tuned out whenever anything fire related was mentioned because it had been too much for me. Now I'm hating that I haven't been paying more attention to what was going on.

We sit in the waiting room for hours waiting for answers, as more firefighters that I recognize from Danny's station trickle in and join us for the wait. As each one arrives, they fill in a few more of the blanks. The explosion took out three floors above them, and considering how weak the building was already from the fire in the basement and the fires in the upper levels, it's a miracle it didn't all come tumbling down on top of them. Danny and three other firefighters were rescued. Tommy Barnes, who was partnered with Daniel, was rushed to the ER with burns and a crushed leg from when a beam fell on it. The two other firefighters had moderate concussions, some pretty nasty scrapes, and one punctured a lung. Danny had been thrown back into a cement wall, and there was a concern he had severe internal injuries on top of a likely concussion from hitting his head. They try to fill in the gaps as best they can, but only the doctors working on him now will be able to tell me if I'm going to walk out of this hospital as a shattered shell or if I'll still be whole when this awful night is over.

This is my worst nightmare, but instead of fear and anxiety and the need to run, all I can think about is how much I'll regret all the time I wasted pushing him away if he dies. How much time we've already lost because I was stubborn. Too fucking stubborn.

I hope he knows how much I love him. The words don't feel like enough, and I vow to step up my actions so he feels it with every breath he takes.

He can't die.

I don't want to live without him, not when we are finally back to a good place. Tears slide silently down my face until there are none left. And then the doctor walks through the door and a hush falls over the room, now packed full with firefighters, Sadie, and me.

Sadie and I stand up, gripping each other's hands, both of us squeezing tight while we prepare for the worst and hope with every beat of our heart for the best.

The doctor looks weary, but a small smile graces his face as he says, "It was touch and go, but he's in stable condition."

You can hear the sigh of relief that escapes from everyone connected to Danny in the waiting room.

"He's resting now, but we can let one of you come on back to sit with him until he wakes up."

My heart sinks that I'm going to have to wait even longer to see him, until I glance over at his sister only to find her already staring at me.

"He's going to want to see you first," Sadie says, a kind smile on her face. She may only be twenty-two, but she always seems so much older than that.

"Are you sure?" I ask. I know how much her brother means to her, and if I were in her shoes, I don't know that I would've been able to lose the chance to make sure my brother was alright. But she gives me a reassuring nod and squeezes my hand again, so without hesitating anymore, I step forward to follow the doctor to Danny's room.

My palms are sweaty, and my hands have a slight tremble to them as the doctor leads me through the hospital down several halls and then pushes through a closed door across from the nurses' desk.

It's a single occupant room, and lying on the bed is my heart in human form. I push past the doctor and rush to Danny's side, immediately grabbing his hand and holding it delicately in mine. His dark-blond lashes rest against his pale skin.

"His coloring should get better over the next few hours," the doctor says reassuringly.

I don't take my eyes off Danny as my free hand brushes his blond hair away from his forehead and then slides down to cup his cheek, my thumb rubbing tender circles.

"Thank you," I say, emotion choking me and tears slipping silently down my face as it hits me that I almost lost him.

"I'll give you some time with him," he says before exiting.

The room is silent except for the sound of my sobs as I cry grateful and relieved tears. I pull the chair closer to his bed and sit down, kissing his knuckles, while my gaze traces every line of his face. My heart leaps every time his lashes flutter, hoping that will be the time he opens his eyes.

I hope he's not having nightmares. I'm not even sure how much he'll remember, but no matter what, I'm not leaving his side. The only thing that matters is that he's okay.

It's at least another hour before his lashes flutter open and his gorgeous blue eyes lock onto me.

"Ali," he says, his voice soft, hoarse, but still filled with love and affection.

I stand up and lean over, dropping a soft kiss to his lips and cupping his face in my hands. "I love you," I say, my voice thick from all the tears I've cried in the last several hours. "I love you with everything I have. You're not allowed to leave me, and I promise I won't leave you ever again. Okay? I love you. I love—"

Sobs rack my body, and he pulls me against him until I'm forced to actually get up on the bed and lie next to him so he can hold me tight.

It takes a few minutes before I can compose myself enough to realize I'm probably hurting him. "I'm so sorry," I say, pulling away slightly and scanning down his body searching for signs of injury.

"Don't ever apologize for telling me you love me. I've never heard sweeter words than those."

"I'm not sorry for that. I'm sorry if I'm hurting you. Where are you injured?"

The words that just came out of my mouth register slowly, but when I finally realize exactly what I said, I realize I have so much more to apologize for.

"You're not hurting me, babe. I'm okay. Just a bit sore, and my head feels like I got hit by a two by four, but as long as I've got you in my arms, it's not that bad." He says it with a flirty smile, and there's only a hint of pain in his eyes so I relax against him.

"Maybe I should be apologizing for all the months we spent apart because I know I hurt you then."

His gaze softens, and he nods before cupping my face and staring into my eyes. "But you were hurting too. I knew where you were coming from. I was willing to wait as long as I had to because you're it for me, Ali. You've always been it for me."

"You're it for me too," I say, resting my head against his chest where I can hear the beating of his heart. "Now tell me where else you're hurting so I don't accidentally hurt you again," I whisper, knowing he wasn't completely forthcoming when I asked before.

He chuckles but keeps his arms locked tight around my waist. "Just my head, mostly, but I also feel like I tweaked my back."

Before he can say more, his doctor and a nurse come in the room, and I quickly slide out of the bed and stand next to it, still holding his hand tightly in mine. "Mr. McKay, so happy to see you awake. You have quite the entourage in the waiting room wanting to know how you're doing."

"How's Tommy?"

The doctor glances at the nurse and then says, "I can't go into specifics due to HIPAA laws, but I can tell you he's going to be just fine."

Danny's head rests against the bed as if it's too heavy to hold up, relief evident on his face.

"How much do you remember?" the doctor asks.

Daniel shakes his head. "Not much." He looks down at the cream hospital blanket, his eyes darting back and forth like he's trying to remember.

"Tommy and I were heading toward the stairwell, but something stopped us—or someone. I think there were other firefighters there." He looks up to confirm with the doctor who nods.

"They're okay too."

"Then there was an explosion and…" He trails off, but his gaze moves up from the blanket and locks on me.

"It's okay if you can't remember all the details. You had a deep, three-inch gash to your head that we stapled. You were also hit with some shrapnel from the explosion and needed a significant amount of blood. We need to run some tests to check for concussion, but overall, you got pretty lucky."

"Yeah, I did," he says, still watching me.

"Well, I'll leave you to rest. The nurse will check on your pain in a bit to see if you need more meds."

"Thanks, doc," Daniel says as the doctor and nurse walk out.

When they're gone, he turns to me and grabs my hand, playing with my fingers like he always used to when we'd be lounging in bed together.

"You were all I could think about. The last thing I remember was thinking about your smile. I knew I had to make it out of that building for you because we have our whole future in front of us, and I wasn't about to let a fucking arsonist steal my future with you. I hate that he almost did."

So it was the arsonist. I'd wondered.

"All that matters is that you're safe and okay," I say, kissing him again because how can I not?

He pulls me back into the bed with him, and instead of worrying about if we're going to get yelled at, I soak in the feel of his body and rest my head near his heart, soothed once again by the steady beat I can hear just beneath his skin.

When you almost lose the love of your life, you don't question whether or not it's frowned upon to snuggle together in a hospital bed when he should probably be resting. You just appreciate the simple gift of being together, being alive, and thinking of all the beautiful things your future holds.

Chapter 9

Daniel

I knew what I was signing up for when I became a first responder. I've had concussions, I've been put in situations that exposed me to dirty needles and people not in their right mind willing to attack anyone in front of them. I've had a couple of falls when getting out of a burning building. I've even had to face a gun a time or two.

But it was different when it was just me that it affected. Now it affects Alison, and the whole time I was in the hospital, I kept waiting for her to realize it was too much for her. That she couldn't live through losing another loved one the way she lost her brother.

I should've known she'd surprise me. It wouldn't be the first time. Not only did she never suggest that what happened was too much for her, but the more days that passed, the more she talked about our future together—trips she wanted us to take, plans she was making, if I wanted pets, kids, and how many.

The answer to that last one was a resounding yes and however many she wanted.

Now, I'm finally getting discharged, and she's insisted on me coming to her house so she can take care of me while I'm still healing. She'll hear no complaints from me. I'll take any excuse to wake up next to her every day, especially now that I'm off on medical leave for the next few months.

"Here," she says, digging around in a bag next to the window. "I think this bag has all your stuff they took off you when you came in, or at least what they didn't ruin. I don't see any clothes in here, but there are some socks and your boots."

Her gaze is locked on the contents of the bag as she pokes around, pulling out items one at a time, and my heart starts to beat frantically as I realize what else she's going to find in there.

"There's a necklace..." Her tone is confused, and as her words die in her throat, her gaze shoots to mine before dropping once again down to the necklace now resting in her hand.

"Daniel."

"Yes?" I say like I have no idea what she's holding.

"What is this?" Her voice is high pitched in a way I've never heard from her before, and I have to fight back a laugh as calm comes over me.

"It looks like a ring on a silver chain, but you'd need to bring it here so I can get a closer look."

She walks over, her gaze locked on my face and her motions robotic as she hands it to me.

I hold the sparkling one carat—I would've gotten her more, but I knew she'd never wear anything that large—diamond ring with a halo of smaller diamonds on a white-gold band.

Her brother actually helped me pick this ring out. Back then, I had plans to propose on the beach, but maybe this is better.

Maybe this is how it was always supposed to go.

I'm already standing, leaning against the bed, but my body is still stiff, so when I go down on one knee it's not nearly as smooth as I imagined it to be in my head. But maybe that's perfect too. The tears glistening in her surprised eyes make me think she doesn't mind.

"I've carried this ring next to my heart for over six months, waiting for the moment that I could give it to its rightful owner—the same woman who owns me. Every piece of me is yours. Completely. I love you, Alison—everything about you. I love the way you challenge me, the way you laugh, the way you push yourself and fight for your dreams no matter what. I love your strengths, your weaknesses, your brain, your beauty, and every other facet that makes you *you*. You're the love of my life, Alison. There's no one else I want to spend the rest of my life with, and I've been waiting for six months to pour my heart out and show you how much you own me. Please don't make me wait anymore. Will you marry me and make me the luckiest damn man in the world?"

Tears started trickling down her face halfway through my speech, but she starts blubbering completely as she throws her arms around my shoulders.

"Yes! Yes, yes, yes," she chants, kissing my cheeks, my nose, my lips. "You're all I want, Danny. I love you so much. I want to be your wife."

My own eyes start to water as I slide the ring on her finger, and my heart feels so big it could burst.

"I'm yours," I tell her as I push it all the way on—right where it has always belonged.

"And I'm yours," she says, placing a passionate kiss on my lips.

Before we can say anymore, the door to the room opens and Captain Hardin enters. "Sorry to interrupt you lovebirds." He sees the ring on her finger, and his face lights up with a happy smile. "Well, it looks like congratulations are in order. It's about time you two kids got engaged."

We all laugh softly, and I drop a kiss to Ali's head, grateful to be alive and have this woman standing at my side with my ring on her finger.

"I'll make this quick, so you two can celebrate. I just wanted to let you know we caught him—the arsonist."

My brows rise in surprise. It's rare to catch an arsonist, and even harder to get enough evidence to put them away. "How?"

"A man was seen fleeing the scene. A bystander thought it was weird because he saw him coming out of the building and wrote down the license plate number. We were able to trace the number to a man who'd applied to be a firefighter and didn't make it. When we showed up to the house, his dad answered the door and was on the phone with 911. He was in the process of turning in his own son because he suspected he was the serial arsonist. We found all the evidence we need to put him away in his room and the trunk of the car that matched the license reported by the bystander. He was arrested on the spot."

Relief floods through me faster than a flash flood. It doesn't change the everyday dangers of my job, but it's a relief to know we aren't being targeted anymore. Ali's shoulders relax and I can tell she's also relieved.

"I just wanted to make sure you heard it from me instead of the news. I'll let you rest."

I reach out to shake his hand. "Thanks, Captain."

He nods and then exits, leaving Ali and me alone again. She wraps her arms around me, hugging me gently, and then places a kiss to my chin before forcing me back into bed so I don't overexert myself. I let her fuss over me with a smile on my face, feeling more content than I knew was possible.

She makes every day worth living, and I plan to spend the rest of my life making sure she never doubts how much I love her.

We've been through hell and back, and I know it won't always be easy. Marriage, relationships...hell, life never is. But if love is a spark, then what I feel for her is an inferno, and that's one fire I plan to never put out.

. . .

Thank you for reading Scorched Turf! If you're curious about the LA Wolves guys, Gabe's book comes out late May, but you can start with *In the Grasp*, which is FREE on all retailers and the first book in the LA Wolves Football series. To learn more about me and my books, check out my website: www.cadencekeysauthor.com and join my newsletter for exclusive discounts and bonus content.

The Perfect Dilemma

January James

Chapter One

K*eeley*

I stared at the email and tried not to vomit all over my keyboard. Was she actually kidding me? My boss had asked me – and the rest of our brow-beaten team – to collate a spreadsheet of daily actions that we needed to tick off hour by hour, in between all the actual *doing* that our jobs entailed. We had to note down the number of emails we sent, the number of phone calls we made, the exact changes we made to each line of merchandise, the specific wording used to describe every single aspect of a product that we could possibly think of. It was micro management at its absolute finest, well below my paygrade, one of many instances, and I was sick of it.

I wouldn't have minded if said boss was marginally older than me, substantially more experienced and significantly more qualified, but she wasn't. She was Jessie Minchin, my senior school nemesis, whose boyfriend just so happened to be one of my best friends. She was jealous of our friendship, and this was her way of paying me back – by messing with a career I'd set my sights on since the time I received a 'Fashion Wheel' toy for my eighth birthday.

I inhaled deeply and added another line to my never-ending to do list. Fine. If the boss said I had to do it, then I would do it. But I was determined to get out of there. If not the department, then the company. I didn't want to leave, but I couldn't take much more of the silent treatments, the rude dismissals in meetings, the constant eyeballing, and the completely unfair negative performance review she gave me last month. I just needed a few more months of working at Glimmer on my CV then I could hotfoot it to the next nearest high street retailer to do the sort of work a real merchandise assistant would do.

"Did you read it yet?" Bali, another member of the team, rolled her eyes at me across the desk.

"I'm pretending I didn't."

"Where does she get off? Seriously?" Bali shook her head, sending bronze curls flying about her elfin face. "How are we supposed to get any damn work done if we're constantly writing emails about the emails we've sent, or having meetings about the meetings we're about to have? It's crazy. We work in fashion. It's supposed to be more fun than this."

I felt terrible. I was the only one who knew Jessie before I started working at Glimmer. I could only assume her unreasonable expectations of the whole of our ten-strong team were for my benefit. "She has issues, clearly."

"Well, lunch is looking way more appealing right now. Fancy a walk down the high street?"

"I'd love to, but I've actually had an idea I want to work on."

"Sounds cool, babe. Just don't let the witch get her hands on it, otherwise it won't be your idea for long."

I winked in the affirmative. I was sort of thankful it wasn't just me Jessie vented her issues on – everyone felt it. It would have been mildly amusing had it not been for the fact we were starting to lose some really good people. We could have been doing some awesome things, making waves in the fashion industry, but our greatest minds were leaving in droves. I waved a hand as Bali left and returned to my screen. A new email flashed up, from none other than Jessie herself. I took another deep breath and opened it.

"I didn't receive your end of day report yesterday. Send now."

A flicker of panic shot up through my chest. I'd sent it to her. I swore I had. Shit, I hoped I had. I checked in my sent items and there it was. I opened it, clicked forward and typed in her email address with a metaphorical middle finger held up at the screen.

"Hi Jessie, here it is. I sent it to you at 5:02pm. Maybe it slipped into your spam folder. Best, Keeley."

Silence dragged its feet until I gave up expecting a reply and turned back to the idea I'd had. Ever since I set up my first Barbie shop and sold makeshift clothes to my friends' Barbie dolls, I'd wanted to help people look their absolute best. I loved watching people try on clothes they wouldn't have looked twice at, then looking back at themselves open-mouthed because their reflection was knock-out gorgeous. I loved experimenting with new fashions and unexpected accessories to add a unique twist to someone's style. Part of my job included designing the looks worn by the shop mannequins, and I would have a field day in the warehouse dressing and undressing what were, in effect, life-sized dolls. But, all that being said, I wasn't playing anymore. I was deadly serious about my career, and so good at it, sales of all the items I dressed the windows with sold out within days, if not hours.

Fashion stylists were my heroes, but I knew as well as anyone, only the rich and famous could afford to spend the sort of fees the good stylists charged. My dream was to create some sort of virtual personal stylist that anyone, of any budget, could use. I'd already scribbled down a few basic points, but I didn't have much of a clue about building apps or using technology and data, so I parked that while I continued to dream about the perfect solution.

My thoughts were rudely interrupted by an email, finally, from Jessie. But, I could see it wasn't a direct reply before I clicked on it. In fact, it looked like a conversation I hadn't been a part of at all. The subject line read: "RE: Not long now... (evil laugh)"

Before I had chance to open the email, another one came through, titled: "Recall: RE: Not long now... (evil laugh)"

And of course, whenever I saw someone wanting to recall an email, I wanted to open it straight away, so I did. And if I'd suspected Jessie Minchin was a nasty piece of work before the email, it became as clear as day now.

"Hey babe, I got the paperwork through from Jilly, so it's now only a matter of time. That little bitch won't know what's hit her. First, the 'casual' updates to my marketing director, then the shitty review, and now this. I'm going to performance manage that girl out of here in no time at all."

I scanned down the thread. I knew she was talking about me, but I needed to see my name in black and white. The recipient seemed to be a friend who worked somewhere else, no one I recognised, but she certainly knew me by name.

"How's it going with *Operation Get Keeley The Fuck Out Of There?*"

I nodded my approval at the ingenious project title, then read further down to an older message.

"The review couldn't have gone better – for me anyway, lol. I could tell she was trying not to cry. I laid out everything she's doing wrong – embellished of course – and she couldn't get a word in. Hopefully, this will be enough to make her resign. If not, I have more tricks up my sleeve. I don't want to be looking at that face every day for longer than I have to. It brings it all back, the fact she cheated with Rhys."

I grit my teeth. I did not cheat with her ex. He was like a brother to me – it would have been plain ick. But this was stupid. She was stupid. Who in their right mind would write all of this on a company email? I had everything I needed now to get Jessie fired, and she knew it. I saw two more emails pop into my inbox from her, asking me to go see her immediately. She was having a laugh. Not a chance. I clicked print, swiped the copy from the printer and practically ran to the stairwell. I took the steps two at a time until I reached the exec floor, where all the HR managers sat.

I paced down the corridor, fury seeping into my bones. Down the corridor I saw a sign above a door saying "Norbert McCarthy, HR Manager." I made a beeline for it. The door was partly open but I knocked anyway. I might have been fuming, but I still had manners.

I heard a shuffling of papers and a throaty cough. "Um, yes? Come in."

I pushed open the door, hardly seeing what was in front of me, and strode up to the desk. I had it all memorized – everything I'd intended to say – which was just as well because the man sitting at the other side of the standard issue cubicle desk was, frankly, disarming. His blue eyes were wide, as though he was half-surprised, half-amused by the hastiness of my entrance. His suit jacket pressed flush against a seemingly hard chest, looking way more expensive than it probably was. I mean, an HR Manager was hardly likely to make more than fifty thou a year, right? Maybe I was in the wrong job? His dirty blonde hair was curled in such a way it could have been trimmed by Charles Worthington himself, and the hand that tapped a pen against the desk was soft and uncalloused, meaning this guy worked behind a desk, hard. That last thought sent a flush of heat through my body and I shook my head to get rid of it. Focus. I needed to focus.

"How can I help you?" The man smiled like I'd just made his damn day and I didn't know whether to be infuriated at his apparent arrogance or swoon because I'd never seen a smile so devastating in all my life. Seriously... wrong job.

"Mr. McCarthy..." I began.

"Please," he interrupted, with a look that said – weirdly – he was thoroughly enjoying this. "Call me Norbert."

I opened my mouth to continue, but the idea that this incredibly beautiful man had been graced with a name like Norbert threw me for a loop. I cleared my throat. "Um, yes, Norbert. Well, I'm here to make a complaint about my boss, Jessie Minchin."

At those words, the smile fell from his face, and he sat up straight, filling his suit even more than I would have thought possible, and clicked open the pen, which I now noted was a very expensive Caran D'Ache. "Go on," he said, with a slight frown.

I sighed out a breath, relieved to have someone's attention. "I hate doing this," I said, quietly. Because I actually did. As miserable as Jessie made our lives, and as evil as her actions had been, she was still a human being with sensitivities, issues, buttons and weaknesses. If I'd thought she would be receptive to help, that's the route I would have taken. But sometimes, people can't be salvaged; they just have to be removed. "Our boss is sabotaging our efforts to make this company money." *Get straight to the point, Keeley. The one with a bottom line drawn beneath it. HR professionals claim they're all about the people, but really, they're all as driven by profits as the next person.*

"How?" he squinted as he looked up at me. His voice was soft and here was no judgement behind it. It was as though he knew I wasn't reporting Jessie to be vindictive; I simply wanted to do my job.

"She's giving us unreasonable, unnecessary, time-consuming admin tasks to do, and then demanding we re-do the spreadsheets and timesheets in our own time. Most of us work overtime, long hours, because we love what we do and we care about the store and the customer experience. We give everything we can. So, when we're asked to carry out these non-essential, nonsensical tasks that don't contribute to the bottom line, it feels like our time isn't respected, like we don't deserve a life outside of Glimmer."

I looked down at my fingers curling around each other and drummed up the courage to continue. "And... well, I think some of it is personal." I handed him the email and waited, bracing myself, as he read down the page.

I felt his eyes flick up at me, then return to the email, then he breathed out slowly. "We'll need to look into this," he said, after a painfully long pause. "In the meantime, I'm moving you to a different department."

I almost choked on my own saliva. "What?" At the most I had expected they would pull Jessie up on a few things. I even expected some sort of revenge on her part that would lead to me resigning anyway. I did not expect this: to be moved to another part of the business. It felt... extreme. "Where?"

Norbert leaned forward and clasped his hands together on the desk. I noticed his chiselled cheek flutter as he ground his jaw. He really was beautiful. How had I never seen him around? Why wasn't there some sort of Norbert Fan Club amongst the employees? He had to be gay. No one who was that gorgeous *and* worked in fashion was heterosexual, or – my eyes strayed to his ring finger – unmarried.

"That's up to you," he said, the corner of his mouth twitching as though he wanted to smile but was stopping himself. "Where would you like to work?"

"Um, I..." I couldn't believe he was asking me this. Surely he couldn't just put me in any department without checking with the director of it first? Besides, I wanted to keep doing what I loved: styling and merchandising. "Well, I like what I do. I love to dress people, advise them, empower them to be their unique selves."

"It that how you would describe merchandising?" He looked back at me, quizzically.

"Well, no. Not exactly. But it's where I think the fashion world is heading. People want to embrace their individuality but don't know where to start. They want to try new things but don't have time to shop around. They want an expert's opinion on what looks good, but they don't know who to ask."

Norbert cocked his head. "And you think we can offer that?"

"I'm not sure yet," I replied, honestly. "I'm still thinking through the details... how we might create something digital. You know, an app or something." I almost shrivelled up hearing myself talk. I sounded naïve, uninformed and idealistic, but this HR Manager didn't seem to agree.

"Then I suggest we place you in digital development," he said, seriously. "You can shadow the developers, learn how to make software programmes, understand what's possible. Then you can design a product or service you think our customers would pay good money for."

My hand roamed around for something to hold onto and gripped the nearest chair. "Why?"

"Because it took guts to come up here. Because you've raised a serious issue on behalf of your colleagues. Because you've brought to my attention something that could have been significantly damaging the effectiveness of a whole department. And because..." he glanced at the paper on his desk, "no one deserves to be treated like this."

He looked back at me with an expression of such sincerity I almost drowned in it. I also hadn't failed to notice my heartrate had racketed up and was now vibrating inside my chest. Not only was he gorgeous, he'd further ingratiated himself by handing the opportunity of a lifetime to me on a platter.

"Thank you," I said, in almost a whisper, glancing down at the floor.

"I'm pleased to see you didn't cry in your review. She doesn't deserve your tears."

I lifted my head and stared at him, my throat suddenly dry.

"It isn't true, you know, what she said. I didn't cheat with anyone." I didn't know why I was telling him that; it wasn't any of his business and it had nothing to do with my work, but I felt as though I needed to lay that out there. I couldn't have this Adonis believing I was ever the 'other woman' in anyone's relationship.

When he spoke, his voice was also quiet. "I believe you."

He watched me steadily then stood suddenly and walked around the desk. He towered over me, making me feel like a waif. "Take a long lunch break while I get security to collect your things. There'll be a desk waiting for you on the floor below. Will you be coming to the company update later?"

I shuffled towards the door in a daze. "Um, yes. I haven't been to one before. I wouldn't miss it for the world."

He chuckled under his breath. "Don't get your hopes up – it's mainly a financial update, but it would be good to see you there."

"Great," I forced a smile onto my bewildered face. As I stepped through the door, a thought occurred to me. "Um, who will I be reporting to?"

His face was perfectly poker-like when he answered. "Me."

"You? Since when do HR managers get involved in digital development?"

"They don't," he replied.

I narrowed my eyes. "But, I'm confused. You're an HR Manager..."

"Actually, I'm not." He placed a hand to the small of my back as he followed me out.

"But it says right there." I pointed to the sign secured to the door of his office. "Norbert McCarthy, HR Manager."

One of his cheeks hollowed as he bit back a smile, and his hand slid around my waist as he stepped past. "Yeah, Norbert doesn't work here anymore." He strode off in the other direction and I spun around to face his retreating back.

"What?"

He kept on walking. "Three months ago to be exact."

"So..." I had to raise my voice so it carried down the corridor after him. "Who are you?"

He thrust his hands into his pockets and spun back towards me on one heel, a grin stretching from ear to ear. "James," he said, walking backwards.

I failed to hide my annoyance that whoever this man was, he'd duped me into thinking he was someone else. Who exactly had I just complained about my boss to? Who knew my own manager hated me because she thought I'd cheated with her ex? Who was actually working for? Had it all been a joke? I couldn't help but pout when I asked him. "Well, that's cute, James. Now come on. Who the hell are you?"

He stopped suddenly and cocked his head to one side. "Cute? I've been called many things, but cute is not one of them..."

I opened my mouth to correct him. I didn't mean I thought *he* was cute, just the little joke he'd just played on me, but his next words, which he delivered before turning back on his heel and walking away, shut me the hell up.

"Most people just call me the CEO."

Chapter Two

J*ames*

I waited backstage for the room to fill. Events like this, where I had to speak in front of several hundred people, usually got my blood pumping, but today was even more exciting. In fact, today was shaping up to be one of the most interesting days I'd had in a long time.

It started off like all the rest. My secretary plying me with my morning coffee while I caught up on emails. A weekly meeting with my directors, then a conference call with the area managers, then an update from the finance team. Then a reminder about some leadership training course I'd agreed to attend. That was the reason I was in Norbert's office. He booked me onto the course months ago, saying the mindfulness-based one-day retreat was the latest in leadership development, that it would be transformative. I'd completely forgotten about it, and it was this weekend, so I had to rummage through his old folders for any kind of paperwork that might have been helpful.

But, less than five minutes into my rummaging, the course had been plain forgotten, all because some raven-haired firecracker burst into the office, assuming I was HR, and let rip about her boss. It was perhaps a little unethical of me to not correct her straight away, but it was kind of amusing that she didn't know who I was. Refreshing. Usually, people either avoided me like I carried some plague or other, or they practically chased me down wanting to get my opinion on something or to grovel for a promotion. I realised this girl was either very new or had been purposely sheltered from the various goings on in the company.

To be fair, I wasn't a Philip Green or a Richard Branson. I didn't particularly like attention or the spotlight. I was ok with doing things like this – standing on a stage in front of my employees to update them on the state of the nation, as it were – but I didn't want to have my face plastered everywhere, not even on the 'About Us' section of the website. So, it wasn't entirely weird this girl didn't know who I was. It was, however, enjoyable.

First, there was the outfit. She wore a tight little grey pinafore dress over a crisp white shirt, and a tie – an actual tie. She wore black boots that reached up over knees with little heels raising her up to about five foot three. After my eyes had grazed over the outfit, which was a little crazy, but cute, they landed back on her face. She looked like a quirky doll. Big, red-rimmed glasses over big brown eyes, and long dark hair pulled back into a low ponytail. As she talked, her full pink lips moved at a million miles an hour, making the little freckles on her cheeks come to life. I had never seen anyone look like this before – like a cross between Britney Spears in her *Hit Me* days, and Christina Hendricks in *Mad Men*. It was the edgiest look I'd ever seen, and as the CEO of a fashion business, I guess that was saying something. And tight as it was, the dress was still conservative. It covered her completely. But, as the ache in my pants testified, it was sexy as sin.

Within seconds of being in the same room as her, relishing her spark, inhaling her soft floral fragrance and trying not to drool over my desk, I decided I needed more of her. It was handy she'd come to complain about her boss, because I had a genuine reason to move her. Closer. Create a special project for her. The ideas she had were bright, but they weren't developed and may not ever be; I couldn't know for sure. I'd enjoy a few weeks having her work for me, then reluctantly move her back downstairs to continue in a role she was clearly good at.

I chose not to think about the fact this would likely be a temporary arrangement as I stepped up to the stage. The lights pointing at me were so bright I could hardly make out anyone beyond the first five rows. I stepped up to the podium, glanced at the clear Perspex autocue then proceeded to ignore it for the next ten minutes. I didn't need a script. I spoke from the heart instead; I always did. The autocue was merely a formality – more to make my staff feel better than anything else. I generally flew by the seat of my pants in most scenarios, something that brought the majority of my team out in hives. But, it hadn't failed me yet, and as this business and several others before it would agree, it wasn't likely to.

I began by thanking everyone for taking time out of their day to be there, then got straight into the performance figures. I celebrated the stores that were performing exceptionally well, and those that had been floundering, covering off the plans I had to inject some life into them. I talked about the new flagship concept and how it was going to put our well-placed Carnaby Street store on the map for good. And throughout all of this, my eyes roamed the room. She said she was going to come but I couldn't see her anywhere. After about five minutes of looking and not finding, my chest hollowed out. Maybe I'd freaked her out telling her who I really was.

Just as that thought began to make me feel like a prized idiot for taking advantage of her ignorance and duping her, my eyes found hers. Like magnets across a crowded room, her brown eyes met my blue ones and for a second, I lost my train of thought. She was gazing back at me, riveted. I couldn't believe that what I was saying was all that interesting, but she looked as though she was watching a box-office smashing blockbuster movie. My previous wilted chest puffed out immediately and I regained my composure. I didn't just regain it, I damn well smashed it. Coming to life, I strolled across the stage, gesturing, making impromptu jokes, calling out individuals who'd done amazing work that quarter. None of it had been scripted and I could feel the anxiety pouring off the stage manager standing in the wings.

I overran by ten minutes, because I didn't want to lose the feeling of having her eyes glued to me, even as I walked up and down the stage. I knew, in a way, it was unprofessional, but I'd never taken such liberties in my entire career, and what the hell? The teams were entertained, so why not? As I stepped down from the stage, I glanced at her once more and quirked a smile. I was buzzing with adrenaline but another sensation had also settled in my belly. It was the realization that I cared what she thought. I cared about her opinion more than anyone else's. Which was new. It was also absurd. And if the Group HR policy about relationships between colleagues being forbidden was set in stone, quite unfortunate.

I was, in a word, fucked.

Chapter Three

K *eeley*

I dressed with even more care than usual and entered the office building with my heart thrumming against my throat. I couldn't sleep, instead replaying the memories of meeting James – the CEO for crying out loud – in an HR Manager's office, and then watching him outright own a room filled with about a thousand people. And not only own it, but slice through it with his eyes until they held mine rigid. I think I sucked my breath in through the whole thing, and I certainly had to watch the replay on the intranet because I couldn't for the life of me remember anything he'd said. God, I was screwed. I fancied my boss. Not just my boss – my CEO!

The lack of sleep gave me more time to plan my outfit. I wore a plaid mini kilt, black tights and patent Mary Janes, with a cashmere boatneck sweater I'd snagged at a sample sale – a merchandise assistant's salary would never have paid for *that*. I'd wrapped my hair up in a giant bun on the top of my head hoping it would add a couple of inches to my height. If I had to keep craning to look up at my new boss, I was going to get a crick neck.

With my signature blood red glasses perched on my nose, I settled down in front of my new computer and sipped my takeout latte.

"Well, you're new," came a voice beside me. I looked around and found I was being gawped at by a guy, around my age, ginger-haired, a little spotty, but with a wide, white-toothed smile.

"Not new exactly," I said, holding out my hand. "I came from merchandising, Keeley."

He reached over and shook it. "Greg. Or Ron, as most people call me." He rolled his eyes.

"Harry Potter?" I winced.

"Damn that franchise."

"Why do you have so many screens?" I nodded to the three giant ones hemming him into his desk.

"Because I have so many brains," he winked. "Actually, this one is for the running sales figures from the website; this one is user activity on the home page; and this one..." He turned the screen towards me. "This is just for my own personal viewing pleasure."

I squinted at approximately four different YouTube windows playing different music videos, another window playing what looked like Fortnite, and another that looked like Spotify.

"You're doing the millennials proud, I see."

"Yeah, terrible attention span. Need to consume *everything*, all at the same time." We grinned at each other. "So, what brings you up here?"

"Oh, well. Weird story," I replied, not quite knowing where to begin. It wasn't the typical tale of career advancement. "I had an issue with my boss, I talked to James about it..."

"James?"

"Um, yeah. James—" I realised with a surge of embarrassment I didn't know his last name.

"James Royce?"

I shrugged, hoping that was the right answer.

"The CEO?"

"Yes," I rushed out. James *Royce*. So, that was his name. I would consider it tattooed across my brain. "He put me here to learn about digital development."

"Do you know anything about digital development?"

I shook my head. "Nope, nothing."

"Ok, well, I'm a millennial. I like to have a million different plates spinning in the air at once. Tell me what you want to know. You have my full-*ish* attention."

Chapter Four

J *ames*

I'd managed to avoid her for a whole week. I even managed to only think about her maybe fifty times during the relentlessly boring leadership development day. Once I'd made sure she was settled and knew who everyone in the digital team was, and how she could reach me if she needed to – via my secretary – I'd purposely kept my distance. And yes, I realise how nonsensical that sounds. I fired her old boss so it wasn't like Keeley needed to be moved; I'd moved her to be closer to me, in work and location. And now I was backtracking like a moon-walking pony and trying to avoid all possible human contact with her. But, as it turned out, absence does make the heart grow fonder, which is why I found myself hovering over her desk at ten a.m. one morning waiting for her to come back from a training workshop with Ron Weasley.

I heard her glittering laugh before the sparkles appeared before my eyes. And I mean that literally. She was wearing sequins. A genuine eighties batwing sweater with a giant rainbow-coloured star across the front. And stone-washed jeans. I mean, ok, we worked in fashion, but it was hardly a party. For a second there, I thought I'd just employed Tiffany. Her face flushed the second she spotted me waiting for her.

"Did we have a meeting?" she asked, hurriedly.

"Not a planned one, no. But I would like an update from you," I said, forcing myself to sound professional – stern even. I couldn't afford for anyone to see through me to the truth. That there was a lot more to me placing her here than her sheer willingness and a good idea.

"Um, of course. When? Now?"

I glanced around the faces all looking up at me and held their gazes until they blinked away, back to their own business.

"I'm pretty busy, but I can talk over lunch?"

She hesitated, then bent down to reach into her bag. She pulled out a florescent pink lunchbox and packet of prawn cocktail flavoured crisps. "Ok."

I had to shake my head in disbelief. She dined like a thirteen-year-old. "You can leave that here," I said, kindly but firmly. "My car's waiting outside."

I held open the door to Pollen Street Social, pleased I was able to get a last-minute table. Not that it mattered – she seemed to have no idea how exclusive this place was. Put it this way, hers was the only batwinged, sequinned sweater in the place. And I *loved* that.

The host pulled out a chair and she sat and glanced around. The second I sat opposite her, she leaned towards me and stage-whispered with the excitement of a child on Christmas Day. "Is that Simon le Bon?"

"The singer from Duran Duran?" I followed her gaze. "Yeah." I spun back to face her, shaking my head. "How do you know Duran Duran? You must have been born about twenty years after their last hit record."

She curled a hand over her heart. "I'm an old soul," she smiled.

My eyebrows shot up. "Less of the 'old soul' please. I'm probably closer to his age than yours."

She blushed instantly. "What can I say? I'm a bit of an eighties nut."

"I can see that." I glanced down at her sweater and swallowed. Close up, I could clearly see the mounds of two pert breasts beneath, so I quickly looked down at the menu. With both our eyes overly occupied with the Specials, I felt on slight safer ground, though I still questioned my sanity, and why on earth I thought bringing her to lunch was a good idea.

"So, what's good here?" she asked.

"What's good? I glanced up briefly. "It's the Pollen Street Social. Everything's good."

She sighed, put down her menu and batted her eyelashes at me through her glasses. "I don't doubt that, Mr. Royce. But I thought, seeing as you clearly frequent this place, you might have some recommendations." She finished with a sweet smile that alone would have made my stomach flip, but hearing her call me Mr. Royce was almost a turn-on too far. I swallowed – again.

"The ravioli is good, and the sea bass. I like the ox cheek personally."

"Great!" She dropped her menu onto the table. "I'll have the ox cheek too."

My eyebrows shot up in surprise. "Really? I would have had you down as a seafood girl."

She sat back and crossed her denim-clad legs. "You don't think I like red meat?"

My eyebrows couldn't shoot up any further so a flush of blood crept up my neck instead. "No, I... I just figured..."

"That being a girl and all, I would be more into fish?"

"No," I pouted. That's not what I was thinking *at all*. I took a long sip of water in an attempt to wash away the current conversation.

"I had beef sandwiches in my lunch box," she continued. "So, I guess ox cheek is the next best thing."

I clapped a hand over my mouth to stop the water I spat out from flying everywhere. *Next best thing?* This place had a Michelin star. After mopping myself up with a napkin, I noticed a quirk of a smile on her lips. She was winding me up.

"So, tell me, Keeley. How are you getting on with this idea of yours?"

Instead of shrinking backwards like a lot of my employees would when put on the spot, her eyes brightened and she sat up, gleeful. "Oh my gosh, I've learned so much just by sitting in Digital, and I think I've come up with a way to make this work."

I smiled politely, and prepared to fake some gushing. While I didn't doubt she'd developed her idea, it had initially sounded like little more than a glorified personal shopping service. But I owed it to her to give it my full attention.

Half an hour later, my jaw was on the table, my plate had been cleaned and I'd hardly tasted a bite.

"So, it has the potential to expand into other offerings," she went on. "Like light cosmetic surgery, diet and lifestyle coaching, hair consultations – pretty much anything related to personal image."

She had just outlined an idea that no one else was doing. Her concept was a virtual image consultation. She envisioned an app that would take a whole host of personal details like height and waist measurements, as well as lifestyle information – the kind of work someone does, their hobbies and other responsibilities like children – and turn it into a fully personalised image plan. It would give people advice on the type of clothes that would suit their body shape, the kind of exercise regimes that would fit into their lives, all within their budget.

Not only that, it could increase revenue by allowing other brands to sell through the app.

In short, it was a virtual fairy godmother that might well make Glimmer more money than it had made in a long time. She finished and looked back at me with wide eyes, awaiting my verdict.

"I think it has amazing potential," I said, honestly.

"Really?"

"Yes I do," I replied in all seriousness. "But, we don't currently have budget for it. We'll have to go cap in hand to the Group and ask if they will finance it."

"The... the group?"

"Yes... Glimmer Fashion Group – GFG. In Boston."

"Boston? As in Boston, Massachusetts?"

"Yes."

"Right. Ok." She furrowed her brow, deep in thought. "And you need to go there to ask them for more money? You would do that?"

The next statement, for some inexplicable reason, made my chest swell. "Well, as a matter of fact, I'm scheduled to travel there the day after tomorrow for some meetings." But the next statement was not planned by any part of my brain. It just came out and it was too late to retract it. "Why don't you come with me? You could explain the concept to Lucas yourself."

"Lucas?" Her cheeks paled and I noticed her knuckles – the ones belonging to the hand gripping her water – had turned white. I gently prized the glass out of her fingers. I didn't want to have to explain a crushed crystal tumbler to the staff here; I wanted to come back again at some point.

"Yes. Lucas Hannigan. He's my boss in the States."

"You... your boss?"

"Yes," I paced a hand on top of the one I'd just released the glass from. She was shaking. "He's a pussycat. You don't have to be nervous. And I can coach you." Acutely aware I was touching her hand, I pulled away and ran my fingers through my hair instead.

She didn't bat an eye. "How do you know he's a pussycat?"

"I worked with him in the States for a year before moving back here. He's not just a boss, he's a good friend. Working for him didn't even feel like work, you know? You'll be fine, trust me."

"So, you liked working for him?" She sipped again at her water while I watched her glistening pink lips rest on the glass.

"Yeah, I really did."

She held my eyes, a slight frown clouding her brow, as she placed her glass back on the table. "If you enjoyed it so much, why did you move back?"

My head suddenly felt very heavy. I didn't often talk about the reason I'd returned, mainly because it was pretty upsetting. "My father has Alzheimer's and my mum is... well, physically challenged. She has severe arthritis, so she can't move far or lift things. I couldn't live three-thousand miles away knowing they needed me, if only to help pay for some bills. Care can be very expensive."

My eyes flicked up from where they'd been focused on the tablecloth and I was shocked to see she had tears in her eyes. "Anyway, I've managed to move them both to a wonderful home. They're looked after very well, but they only have me. I made a promise to visit every week. I can hardly do that if I'm living in the States." I grinned to make light of the situation.

"But... your dreams and goals..." she said, quietly.

I cocked my head slightly. "I can still achieve them here."

"But isn't America the heart of retail? The place to be if you want to make it big?"

Without thinking, I reached across the table to put my hand over hers again, as much to reassure myself as her. The warmth that rose into my palm was instantly settling. I always felt a torrent of emotion when talking about my parents. I felt sadness, despair, but mostly guilt. Guilt that I wasn't there more often, and that I'd already spent so many years away, first at university, then working all over the country, then in the States. They'd done so much for me but had hardly seen me since. Those feelings had risen again but one touch of Keeley's hand melted them, completely.

"Not all dreams have to be about having a career," I smiled, reluctantly pulling my hand back again. *What was with that? This strange need to be in contact with her?* "Yes, there are still things I want to achieve but I can do all of it here, in London. I don't know if you heard but we have this thing called the internet now..."

At first she looked confused, then she picked up her napkin and threw it at me. A bold move for a junior employee.

"I was trying to be sympathetic," she retorted, supressing a smile.

"You succeeded. And I appreciate it. Now, what do you say? Fancy flying with me to the Land of the Free?"

Chapter Five

K *eeley*

I'd hardly had chance to recover from the most perfect lunch I'd ever been treated to, and the mind-shattering verdict on my rookie idea, before I was sitting in the first class cabin of an A350, heading to Logan International Airport.

When I finally stopped talking, I realised, shamefully, I'd been rattling on for about three hours about my idea and everything Ron and other members of the digital team had taught me. But James – Mr. Royce – was so easy to talk to, I couldn't help myself. And he seemed to be as excited about the idea as I was. Well, he must have been because here I now was, sitting across the aisle from him, gawping out the window at a beautiful horizon while he tapped away on his computer and flicked through several libraries-worth of documents.

He lifted his head every ten minutes or so to check I was ok, but other than that, we barely spoke on the flight. I didn't mind one bit. I had only ever visited Europe for summer vacations. I had never travelled for business, and absolutely never in the first class cabin of a brand new airliner. I was more than happy to skim through the inflight magazines, flick through the million different films and TV series on offer, and simply stare out of the window at the bright morning sky and deep blue ocean beneath.

Occasionally, I snuck a glance at his profile and watched him as he worked. He was deep in concentration, with a frown furrowing his brow. I watched out of the corner of my eye and noticed when he ground his jaw lightly or chewed his lip or a fingernail. And I felt the giddiness inside my chest grow more vivid with every second that passed.

After our lunch, Mr. Royce had dropped me back to the office before his driver ran him over to another building for more meetings. He touched my hand again as I climbed out of the car. The very same sizzle I felt both times he touched my hand in the restaurant returned, making me feel light-headed as I stepped onto the pavement. I realised, as I watched his car drive away, what I was feeling was more than a mere crush. Yes, he was hot. Yes, he was my boss. Yes, he was possibly one of the nicest men I'd ever met. But, there was more to it than that. He'd shared some of his personal life with me. He'd confided in me about his parents. I'd shared more of the story about my relationship with Jessie. There wasn't much more to tell, but he listened intently anyway. I felt like we knew each other more than we would have if we were nothing more than boss and employee.

In the few days that had passed since then, he'd sent me exactly two emails: one replying to the summary of my app idea, and one forwarding information about travel arrangements. Both were signed off 'Best, James' which I had figured was his usual sign-off until I walked past Ron's screen and saw an email from our CEO, which had been signed off, 'Regards, JR'. Both were fairly informal sign-offs, I told myself. I was reading too much into it.

"Ladies and gentleman, we will shortly begin our descent into Logan International Airport," came a voice through the small speakers. I buckled my seat belt and packed away my magazine and notebook. When I looked up, he was staring at me. It was a look that reached through my bones to my very soul, and even the hottest of blushes couldn't tear my gaze away. He blinked as though suddenly realising we'd locked eyes, then gave me a firm smile before stowing away his laptop. A gasp was flushed from my lungs as I turned back to the window. I was in so deep.

After landing, we headed straight for GFG's offices in central Boston, and I followed my boss through the revolving doors to the main reception desk. Both receptionists looked up as we neared.

One of them, a petite woman with bright blonde hair and ginormous breasts, beamed at him. "Hi James. It's so good to see you again. You look great!"

"Thanks Ronnie, so do you," James replied, grinning. "And Beth, that new hair colour looks great on you."

"Oh James, you're such a darling. When are you coming back?"

He opened his arms wide. "I'm back now aren't I?"

"For how long?" the blonde frowned.

"Only today," he said, gesturing towards me. "We leave tomorrow. Flying visit."

"That's too bad," the brunette said, looking at me with what appeared to be genuine disappointment. Wow, Americans really are super-friendly, I thought. "What's on your agenda?"

"Well, Keeley here has come up with an incredible idea that I'm convinced is going take Glimmer in a new direction, or at the very least add a bow to our arrow that no one else has even thought about shooting yet."

The brunette's frown deepened. "Well, that sounds... great." She had no idea what he was talking about, but who would?

"That's partly why we're here now – to talk it through with Lucas."

"Fantastic," she replied. "He just finished a meeting with the board so you can go right on up."

"Thanks, Beth." James smiled again, leaving the two of them with a parting look I would have cherished forever, and led me to the bank of elevators. Once behind the sliding doors, he looked at me with a softness that made me want to melt. "You ready?"

An hour later, my boss took me on a tour of the building, introducing me to all his former colleagues and anyone I might find to be a useful contact in the future. It felt like incredibly special treatment and I wondered what the hell I'd done to deserve it. Sure, Lucas Cramer had liked my idea, and I mean, *really* liked it. He'd agreed to fund some initial development to see what it might look like, and that was all I could have hoped for. I was on cloud nine, but James was sending me higher with every fresh second I spent in his company.

He'd let me do most of the talking, only answering questions about topics he knew I wasn't familiar with. He was generous with his own praise but not so gushing it might have raised eyebrows. And... he'd placed his hand on my knee beneath the meeting room table, sending fireworks through my thigh and up into my torso. He did it so casually and easily I knew he wasn't thinking. When he eventually realised where his hand was, he whipped it away, almost angrily, and my body temperature plummeted.

As we left the building to check into a nearby hotel, his hand on my back made me shiver, and I stopped, involuntarily.

He turned to face me, with gritted teeth. "Will you dine with me at the hotel?" he asked, his voice gravelly. "I think we need to talk."

Chapter Six

J*ames*

I spent most of the afternoon, after we met with Lucas, kicking myself. No, not kicking myself, cursing myself to hell and back and metaphorically clouting myself around the head several times, for practically feeling up my goddamned employee. What was wrong with me? She had to be ten years younger than me – at least – and was someone I'd taken under my professional wing. And here I was, abusing my authority. Not only that, if anyone from HR found out I was salivating over a young female exec, they'd have my guts for garters. It wouldn't matter that I was their boss; they had personnel law on their side. We had a company policy, and a strict one at that. No romantic relationships between employees. It had been drilled into me so vehemently, I wouldn't have been surprised if it was punishable by death.

I'd always thought it extreme, but never had a personal problem with it until now. Now, I cursed the man who created that rule. Jerry Gold, the president of GFG. Rumour had it, he hired his wife to be a personal assistant to one of the execs. She ended up getting a little too close to her new boss and thus, the rule was born. He was bitter that his wife had run off with one of his colleagues, and so everyone else had to pay.

But, was I really arrogant enough to think that even if it weren't prohibited,

Keeley would want any sort of relationship with me outside of work? Actually, here's where I could allow myself a little cockiness. I was never short of opportunities. The number of ballsy women who approached me in bars, restaurants, hell, even on the streets, told me I was attractive. But, what did they see beyond what I looked like? They didn't know me and may not even have cared. But, Keeley... Keeley was different. She talked to me like I wasn't her CEO. She looked at me like I was a real person, not just someone who looks slick in a good suit. She listened to me like I was about to reveal the Holy Grail. And she didn't try to be someone she wasn't. She was defiantly, unapologetically herself. And most worrying of all, she drew my skin to her skin like a butterfly to the sun. And I was her boss, which made her even more dangerous than the flame of a burning star. Which was why I was now sitting opposite her, about to lay my cards on the dining table and hope she didn't singe them to ashes.

Her eyes were wide, her face pale but for a sweet blush in the apples of her cheeks, as my words settled nervously in the air. *I like you, Keeley.*

"Um... well, um... thank you. I... um... well, I like you too." It came out like a question. Like she hadn't grasped the true meaning of my statement.

I spoke more slowly this time, enunciating every word. Not because I thought she wasn't bright enough to get it, but because I really needed her to hear me. "No. I don't think you understand. I *really* like you, Keeley. And I'm sorry."

"S—sorry?"

"Yes," I said, working overtime to keep my voice calm, despite wanting to rip out my jugular because I hated the words I was having to say. "I'm sorry because I've overstepped the mark a few times with you. There is no excuse; I knew better, but I couldn't help myself."

Her voice shivered. "Why are you telling me this?"

"Because I'm going to have to distance myself, put a new manager in above you, and I didn't want you to think it was because you'd done anything wrong. You haven't at all. You've done everything right, and I've let my feelings get carried away."

Her gaze dropped to the side as though she was thinking intensely. I noticed the light from the ceiling reflected in her glossy hair which hung loose down her back. How I would have loved to drag my fingers through it and hold her in place while I tasted that sweet mouth and did treasonous things with her tongue.

A few seconds passed then her head snapped up and her eyes narrowed, like a cat's. "What if I like you too? Would that be a problem?"

Gone was the blush and in its place was a cheek pulled taut by bright teeth nipping at her bottom lip. *Fuck me, if this wasn't already difficult.*

"The problem would be magnified, believe me." Even I could detect the pain in my voice. "It's against company policy to have any... *romantic*... involvement with another employee. We would both lose our jobs."

Her teeth retreated and her lip sprung back, a little darker from the blood pumping to where she'd bitten it. It mirrored the engorgement of my cock which was blissfully oblivious to the conversation happening above the table.

"Are you serious?"

"I'm afraid so." *Afraid so? I'm actually fucked-offly-incapacitated-with-fury so.*

She put down the menu she'd been scouring and clasped her hands together as if forming a physical barrier between us. At least there was one thing to be almost thankful for. This revelation proved she did have feelings for me – I wasn't imagining it.

"Well," she said, scooching her chair backwards. "Thank you for clarifying that, and thank you for an amazing day, an amazing trip, an amazing opportunity. I understand you have to do what you have to do. Thank you, Mr Royce."

She stood up, avoiding my stunned expression. "What are you doing?"

"I'm sorry, I've lost my appetite. I'm just going to head on up, get an early night."

"Keeley—"

She paused and lifted her eyes to mine. There was a sadness in them I couldn't begin to describe if I tried, and that made my stomach crumble. I was doing the right thing – for both of us – but there was nothing I could say. When nothing else came out of my mouth, she sighed a pained breath and walked away.

I must have sat for a minute or two, staring at her discarded menu and wallowing in the bitterness of knowing I'd done the right thing but it felt so unutterably wrong. Then I became aware of a pit in my stomach growing heavier with each passing second. I couldn't leave things like this. We needed to talk about this. *I* needed to talk about this. I needed her to understand why I simply couldn't risk bending the rules on this one. I rammed my own chair backwards and traced her steps out of the restaurant. The second I saw the elevator doors open, I broke into a run.

Chapter Seven

K*eeley*

I barely registered the sound of footsteps running down the long corridor behind me. I was still trying to process the last twenty minutes. Mr Royce – James – just confessed he liked me more than a boss should like his employee. And because it was *him* – a man I'd fantasised about since I thought his name was Norbert – it should have made me the happiest girl in the world. But it didn't. Because what he said after that, shattered me.

It broke me in places I didn't think breaks could occur. I had no idea of the depths of my feelings for him until he laid it all out, in black and white, on the damn silk tablecloth between us, that nothing could ever happen. I had never thought it would, but now that I knew in another world it could, I wanted it more than ever.

I blinked back tears as I swiped the key card in the door and pressed my weight against it. I was about to fall through and collapse in a heap on the floor, but two giant hands stopped me. Or, more accurately, they spun me around and forced me to look into the eyes of the only thing I'd ever wanted but could never have, even if I worked hard for it, just like my mum and stepdad promised. They said if I wanted something badly enough, if I worked hard enough, it would be mine. Clearly, they had never met James Royce, the most beautiful, unattainable man on the planet.

"Keeley..." his voice was rasping. "I need you to know that if things were different, I wouldn't be stopping you from entering your room right now. I'd be dragging you into it."

I almost collapsed at the knees.

"Please hear me when I say what I'm about to say."

His hands cupped my shoulders and pressed me back against the wall. The key card hung limp in my fingers as my eyes drowned in his desperately furrowed brow and cheekbones that seemed even more perfectly chiselled in the dim light of the hotel corridor.

I nodded, though I didn't want to hear it. It felt like when I was back in the first year of high school, picking up the water bomb that hadn't burst, only to hand it back to the senior year bullies for them to throw it at me again.

"Glimmer isn't doing well," he said, breathless. "Lucas is laying people off. Right now, there is a CEO for the UK – me – and a CEO for western Europe. He has to merge the two territories. We have to go head-to-head for one job."

He waited for me to digest what he was saying. He had a fifty-fifty chance of remaining CEO of anything at Glimmer in the near future.

He closed his eyes as though he didn't want me to look beyond his next words to anything resembling vulnerability. "I can't lose my job," he breathed out. "My parents... I need to be able to continue paying for their care. They have nothing..."

His jawbone jutted out as he ground his teeth. It had pained him to say that much and my heart wept for him. I reached out and placed a palm against his cheek. To my surprise, he leaned into it and a soft moan escaped his lips. I stifled a gasp at the feelings it elicited in me. Electricity was literally humming through my fingers at the contact with his skin.

"I'm so sorry," I whispered. "I don't want to cause you any pain."

His eyelids pinged open, and he speared me with an intensity that crumbled my bones. "Pain? You think you're causing me pain?"

I couldn't decipher what was going on. We'd entered a small world in which conversation was, essentially, meaningless. We were talking around in circles, neither of us saying what really mattered. Until he did.

"You don't cause me pain, you heal me. I've known you for only a matter of weeks but you bring a light to my life I didn't know was missing. Before you came along I was just Mr Royce, CEO and son of two ailing parents who desperately need his help. Then you arrived, and suddenly I became James, hilariously stuffy chap in a suit, completely enamoured by an eighties nut in a sequinned sweater with more bright ideas than a shooting star. You make me feel more alive than I've felt in years, and I don't want to give that up just because of a thin black and white line on my contract."

His words engulfed me. All I heard in them was what everything I acutely felt: need. "So... don't."

His Adam's apple bobbed. "What?"

"Just have me. One night. No one needs to know."

He stared at me. The intensity of his glare made me vibrate. Then everything – time, space, movement, feeling – stopped.

And all I saw, and felt, was him.

Chapter Eight

J ames

The corridor swam around me. She had just given herself to me for one night. Every beat of my heart told me it was a bad idea. Like heroin. Just one dose, they all say, not expecting it to be so utterly blissful they can't live without it. That's what my brain screamed to me as I leaned into her, our eyes hooked as my lips brushed against hers.

I sucked in a gasp of air at the tingling sensation that erupted across the whole of my skin when my nerve endings connected with hers.

Holy fuck, I'm screwed. And I can't stop.

I pressed down, slowly, then firmly, almost crushing her into the wall. Just when I thought I was going to be too much for her, she let out a desperate whimper, like she needed more.

More.

She was going to damn well end me.

Our lips opened and my tongue slid into her mouth, lapping at hers with a decadence that astonished me. I had no idea I was capable of such a slick manoeuvre. Her lips went limp, so I did that thing I'd fantasised about. I pushed my fingers through that ebony sheen and gripped it, holding her in place as I bore down on her, working her mouth like a precious jewel. She tasted divine, as though every emotion had seeped into her taste buds and she was feeding me with them. Another moan made my boxers feel instantly several sizes too small.

"God, you have no idea what you do to me," I murmured into her mouth.

Her eyes opened, lazily, as though she'd been drugged. "If it's remotely near to what you do to me, you'll be about ready to pass out."

How the fuck do I respond to that?

Simple. I scooped her up, eased the key card from her fingers and swiped open the door, walking us both inside. She covered my neck with small, searing kisses as I laid her down on the hotel bed. It was plain and functional, but with her on it, it became the most alluring, decadent, delicious thing I'd ever had the pleasure of kneeling on. And I did just that. I straddled her limp form, dipping my tongue into her mouth and dining out on the gorgeous sounds that leaked from those fucking lovely lips.

"Please don't pass out, baby," I whispered. "At least, not until I make you come."

She gasped, hotly, and my cock stiffened. I felt wetness pearl at the tip and marvelled at how fast my body was ripening itself for her.

"Let me see everything I can't have," I said, my voice low, deep and unrecognisable. I pushed her sweater up and over her breasts, then she tugged it the rest of the way, over her head. Thankfully. Because I couldn't move. The sight of her, bra-less, her nipples peaked like diamonds, was paralysing.

"You are so fucking sweet," I groaned, then I wrapped my lips around each one, relishing the way her back arched, pressing the soft domes into my face. I inhaled deeply, every one of my senses on fire. The sharpness of her nipple against my tongue, the smell of her natural fragrance, the warmth of her flesh against mine, the sound of her moans as I stretched her peaks into my mouth and swirled my tongue around them. I couldn't get enough. She was giving herself to me for one night and I was going to drag it out for as long as my stiff cock would allow.

I came out of my trance to find she'd unbuttoned my jeans and snuck her hand inside my boxers. I gasped as her warm palm curled around me. *Oh my God, what I wouldn't give to keep her.* I would have given anything. Except the two people on this earth who'd done everything they could to get me to where I was.

"James... you're so hard."

"Because of you," I murmured, silencing her with another deep, engulfing kiss. "This is all because of you."

She pulled me back and forth, sending ripples of warmth up and down my spine. My hips thrust into her hand, the rhythm matching the speed with which my tongue plundered her mouth. We were becoming one.

But it was too fast.

I needed to hear her scream.

Chapter Nine

K eeley

Without warning, he sat back on his heels, pushed my pleated skirt up around my thighs with one hand, and grabbed the waist band of my tights with the other. With an animalistic growl he ripped them over my hips and the sound of tearing fabric filled my ears. Before I could protest, his burning fingers eased between my folds and his jaw unhinged.

"Fuck, you're so wet." He swallowed, audibly.

"Of course I am," I pouted. "It's *you*."

He shook his head without answering, like he couldn't believe he was the reason I was more turned on than I'd ever been in my life.

His eyes returned to mine and his voice broke. "What do you want?"

"Everything," I said, without hesitation.

And so he began.

First, it was a finger slipped into my heat, pushing slowly, slowly, as far as it would go. My eyes rolled back in my head and an enormous gush of relief issued from my chest. "James," I sighed, like a prayer.

His own breathing became laboured, even more so when he circled his finger, feeling every ridge and curve inside me until he found a spot that lit me up. Like a feather, he stroked me with painful softness until my thighs gripped his arm and my head snapped to one side.

"Right there," I gasped. "*God.* Something... right there... *oh...*"

I felt his weight shift down the bed, then the fire of his mouth on my pussy, stretching my clit into his mouth as he stroked that scorchingly tender place inside me. I cried out like a wild animal, and like an out of body experience, watched my entire torso lift off the bed, my head hanging back against the mattress, my face contorted into one of pure, filthy desire. "James!"

He growled, as consumed by the moment as I was, and licked me ferociously through the most intense orgasm of my life. As I collapsed in a haze of bliss, he entered me, a thin sheath of latex the only thing between us. My loosened flesh let him in further than I thought possible and my eyes widened at the pressure against my cervix. He buried his face into the flesh of my throat. "Oh God, you're gorgeous."

I panted with the sensation of him filling me completely, knowing at once it was the most intense feeling but also the most perfect feeling in the world.

"Wait," I whispered. "Just let me feel you like this."

He lips found mine in the darkness and he kissed me deeply, softly, ravenously, all the while letting his cock lay inside me, lengthening and thickening with every swipe of his tongue. He was absolutely going to eat me alive. Like a cat playing with a mouse before going in for the kill.

Suddenly, I was ready.

"Fuck me, James."

"With pleasure," he murmured. Then, with a grunt of pent-up desire, he pulled out then thrust into me, closing his eyes against the onslaught of sensation.

"Yes," I coaxed. "Just like that."

He moaned again, as though words escaped him. Instead, his hands and mouth did all the talking, One hand gripped my thigh, wrapping a leg around his waist, angling him deeper. The other fisted my hair, tugging sharply, to the point of pain, rendering my head immobile. His pounding rocked me back and forth and I cocked my hips, willing him deeper.

"God, James," I gasped, right on the edge.

"Wait for me, baby," he breathed, pumping hard and deep. "Fuck, I'm almost there."

"I can't James... it's too much."

"I'm there," he cried. "I'm gonna come..."

"James, oh *Christ...*"

"Yes," he hissed. "Come for me, Keeley. I can feel you... *God...*"

The world disappeared. I felt him swell and abate, swell and abate. I heard his cries in my ear, in my chest, in my soul. I felt his grip on my thighs, on my hair. I felt his teeth on my shoulder as his hips ground me into the bed. And all the while I was rolling, rolling. Every pulse of his cock thundered through me like an electric shock, setting off sparks in every nerve ending. By the time the tremors had passed, I could barely breathe.

And I wished I couldn't.

Because the question hit me like a ton of bricks. How the fuck was I going to live without *that*?

Chapter Ten

J*ames*

"How have they been?" I asked Jenny, the nurse charged with looking after my parents in the home.

Her laboured sigh said the words I didn't want to hear. She said them anyway.

"There's been some deterioration in your father's memory. Your mother is keeping a brave face but it's hard for her, I can tell."

"And mum? How's her arthritis?"

"She's doing ok, James. The medication is helping but you know, with her age, and the stress of Mr Royce's deteriorating condition, she is likely to worsen."

My heart ached. I wished I could visit more but the home was an hour outside London, one of the best I could find. "Is there more we can do to make them more comfortable?"

"Not a great deal really. You're already providing so much for them." *It would never be enough.* "The only other option is to move them to their own managed apartment. They would have their own space there and it would be modified to help with you mothers physical requirements. And having space if their own might help your father hold on to his memory a little longer. There's nothing scientific behind that, it's just a hunch I have after doing this job for many years."

"Ok, let's do it."

"Mr Royce... um, there will be quite a substantial fee increase. I should talk you through the costs before you agree to anything."

"No," I replied, placing my Amex in her hand. "Whatever it costs, I'll find a way to afford it. I owe my parents everything. The least I can do is make their final years as comfortable as can be."

I sat at my desk, numb and unable to remember the last time I smiled. Actually, I did remember and I remembered it very clearly. It was the night that never happened. The best night of my adult life. The night I spent with Keeley. Two weeks ago.

Ever since I first laid eyes on her, I knew she would be special. She was so different, so funny, so brazenly confident yet so charmingly shy at the same time. I missed her bonkers fashion sense and her wide smile, her kind words and her electric touch. What the fuck had I been thinking? That night I indulged in the most delicious narcotic known to man and now I was suffering from the world's biggest comedown. And the worst part about it was I doubted I would ever recover. I got a taste of perfection that no one else could match.

I couldn't ask her to wait for me while I fought for my job and worked night and day to pay for my parents' care. I couldn't ask her to give up her own job either. She was driven, determined, and oh so clever. Her idea was a stroke of genius. Despite Glimmer being in financial strife, Lucas still saw fit to siphon off some money for her to explore it.

My phone buzzing beside me tore me from my depressive wittering.

"James Royce," I barked, without looking at the screen.

"James, it's me, Lucas."

"Oh hey, boss. Apologies, I was a bit distracted there. Got my head in numbers."

"No problem. Listen, I need to talk to you about Keeley's idea."

My chest hollowed. I knew what he was going to say. He couldn't afford to fund it. Not now the job cuts had been announced and all eyes were on how we could save pennies to avoid job losses. "It's ok, I get it, Lucas. We need to put it on hold. I'll tell her."

"I hate doing this, James. It's a great idea, but at the rate we're going, we won't have much of a business to enhance. I'm sorry."

"Don't be. It's not your fault."

His voice quietened at the other end. "I'm the president of the entire company James. If it's not my fault, whose is it? The buck stops with me, remember?"

I was shocked at his uncharacteristic negativity. "To an extent, yes. But it's not your fault the economy has tanked, and world politics is in disarray, and online businesses are taking over the world. You're doing your best under very challenging circumstances."

"You're a good friend, James."

"I hope I'm as good a friend to you as you've been to me." I was itching to tell him about me and Keeley. It was natural, wasn't it, to tell your friend you might have actually fallen for someone? Crazy as it sounded, I quite possibly had. But, that would be driving the final nail into a coffin the current economic climate had burdened me with. I needed this job. I needed that special care for my parents. If Keeley was still single when all of this ended, there'd be no question I'd fall on my knees for her. But that wasn't going to happen. She was too special. Some lucky guy would snap her up long before then.

"You are, bud. Unfortunately, that doesn't make my decision about the CEO job any easier."

"No, I understand. You do what you have to do Lucas."

"Please relay my regrets to Keeley. She's a true talent."

"Will do." I hung up the phone. *She absolutely is.*

I stared at the phone for what I thought was five minutes but actually turned out to be twenty. How was I going to break this to Keeley? It burned that I had to. She'd worked so hard and she'd put up with that mean girl manager for too long before that. She didn't deserve this. She should take her idea, get some funding elsewhere and make it her own. Make herself rich. It was completely online, where all the major retailers were heading. With the right technology, the right connections and the right people, she could make a fortune. Right then, a name popped into my head. Not just any name. It was the name of a buddy from university who went on to found one of London's biggest investment banks. I rammed a large foot into my shin. Why hadn't I thought of this before?

I swiped open my phone and scrolled through my contacts. It was a recent enough friendship that I hadn't deleted his number. I pulled up his name and pressed the call button.

An highly efficient, classically clipped voice answered. "Marcus Armstrong."

"Marcus. Hey. Long-time-no-speak. It's me, James Royce."

There was a long pause and then, "Jim? Jim Beam Royce?"

"Ugh, don't remind me. That stuff makes me wanna puke these days."

"What a pleasant surprise! I've been meaning to call you for ages, but... well, you know how things are."

"Yeah, I do. You've been busy building an empire and swanning about on yachts with Annabelle Gainsborough. Don't think I haven't seen the headlines."

"Ah man," he groaned. "Anyway, cut to it. To what do I owe this pleasure?"

I took a deep breath and steeled myself. This was for Keeley. "Well, I have something of a proposition for you."

Chapter Eleven

K *eeley*

"James, I don't think I can do it!"

We were standing on the pavement outside the offices of Falcon Investments, and I was clutching at my boss's lapels like they might save me from drowning in lava. He laughed lightly and the sound hummed through my veins, making me laugh, even though that was the last thing I thought I was capable of.

"I'm being serious. I can't stand in front of a boardroom of people and ask them for money, all to pay for a little online shopping service. I can't do it James, I can't."

"Woah, woah, woah," he said, placing a finger over my lips. "First of all, it won't be a boardroom full of people. It will be my old friend Marcus and one or two others. Second, you are not asking for money. You are given them an opportunity to invest in your business before you take it to other interested parties. And third, it is not a little shopping service. It's a cutting edge, online image enhancement platform designed by experienced system architects." He gripped my shoulders firmly and I tried to ignore the fizz that shot through my skin from the familiar pressure of his touch. "Now is not the time to downplay what you've done here, Keeley. It's a great idea and you owe it to your damn brain to show it off."

I tried to breathe while he stared at me.

"Okay," I whispered, placing one hand on his chest. "Okay. But can I ask you one final thing?"

His Adam's apple bobbed as he swallowed. "Anything."

"I think I need to go in there alone." I watched his expression for any small sign of disappointment but there was none, only a slight hint of pride. "Is that okay?"

"Of course it is. I know you can do this."

"It's not that you haven't been helpful," I rushed out. "I mean, I would never have brought it this far if you hadn't believed in it. Or in me." I implored him to listen closely to what I was saying. "It's just that... when you're with me..." I glanced down at the ground. "I can't think straight."

A second passed, then he scooped me into his arms and I felt his lips against my crown. "If it's any consolation," he murmured into my hair, "you do the same to me."

He held me close until I forced myself to pull back.

"I'll wait out here for you," he whispered.

I nodded and placed my hand to his cheek just like I did that night in Boston. He closed his eyes against it, then took it in his.

"Keeley?"

"Yes?"

"Whatever happens, I'm so damn proud of you."

At that, I rose onto my tiptoes and pressed a yearning kiss to his warm lips. A hand crept around the back of my neck, holding me there while he deepened the kiss, tasting me once last time. I was almost dizzy when he released me.

"No go kill it."

I was nothing but a collection of stunned and confused cells as I stumbled back out of the rotating doors. James was on me like a shot.

"Well? How did it go? What did they say?" When I stared wide-eyed at the ground instead of answering, his questioning swiftly moved on to, "Are you ok? Do I need to call an ambulance?"

I placed a hand on his arm, as much to steady myself as to reassure him. "I'm fine. Can we sit?"

I let James guide me to a bench beyond the offices and sit me down beside him.

"They loved it," I said, still staring into thin air, and not believing a word of it. "They want to invest."

"I knew it!" James punched the air before wrapping his arms tightly around me. "I knew it, I knew it. Congratulations baby."

I gently pushed him away, a small shadow of darkness passing over my brow. "I can't be your baby," I said, casting my eyes up to his.

His face fell. "Okay."

"Well, you said it yourself. We can't be together. Not while we work at the same firm."

James' mouth twitched like he wanted to smile but had to appreciate the gravity of where my head was at in that moment.

"They're going to invest, right?" he asked.

"Yes."

"Did they say how much?"

"Um, I..." I looked down at my hand and uncurled my fingers. I vaguely remember Marcus scribbling a figure onto a post-it note and passing it to me. I think I nodded and said that would work but I was floating at that point and could barely take anything in. We both looked down at the note.

"Two million," James gasped.

I squinted. "Is that what that number is?"

He laughed again, infusing me with a warmth I hadn't felt for weeks. "He's going to invest two million. Jeezus. That's some seed investment, Keeley. He must really believe in you."

"But... that still..." I tried to argue for why he couldn't call me baby but I totally lost my train of thought. Luckily, he hadn't.

"Keeley, you don't need to work for Glimmer anymore. In fact, I think Marcus will insist you don't. He'll want you working full-time on this. It's *your company*, do you understand?"

He watched his lips move, then repeated. "*My* company."

"Yes. All yours."

He watched in fascination as the reality sunk in.

"So, I can call you baby, if you want me to."

"You can?" I asked, then shook my head. "You can. Yes. You can call me baby any time you like."

He cradled me chin in his fingers and landed a searing hot kiss to my lips. Slow, languid, but full of promise. When he finally released me, I stuttered. "Do you, um, know of any hotels around here?"

His eyes glittered. "Yes, ma'am, I do."

"In that case, Mr. Royce," I angled my body towards him and hardened my expression. "You can go fuck your job."

A flash of alarm crossed his features then he realised what I meant. He cupped my face and ran a thumb across my lips. "Nah," he whispered. "I can think of far lovelier things to fuck."

The end.

Follow January here:
www.januaryjamesauthor.com
facebook.com/januaryjamesauthor
instagram.com/thejanuaryjames
tiktok.com/@thejanuaryjames

Diamond Solitaire

Alix Key

Chapter One

ALIX

Sometimes loving someone means you want to kill them.

My brother was supposed to meet me on campus an hour ago. Late lunch, just the two of us. Twins united against the world, because we turn twenty-six today. I even wore my favorite skirt, the one with roses on it.

But Leo stood me up.

He isn't using again. He can't be.

He swears Barney fired him last month because some niece or cousin or long-lost goddaughter needed a job waiting tables. He promises he'll find something else soon, any day now.

So why wasn't he waiting for me outside Barton Library?

Maybe we got our wires crossed. Maybe he's upstairs in our tiny apartment, fidgeting on the sway-backed couch that doubles as his bed. Maybe he forgot to charge his phone; that's why he didn't answer my texts. Didn't pick up when I called.

He was fiddling with his dark-blue chip this morning, tapping the plastic against the lip of his coffee mug. He got the Narcotics Anonymous token at his meeting last week, marking six months of sobriety.

He isn't using. He can't be using.

I slam my keycard against the ancient entry pad for the third time, finally finding the sweet spot that makes the release buzz. Pushing open the heavy glass door, I step into a lobby that smells like day-old pizza and sweat. I cross to the line of mailboxes and force my key into the gritty lock. The key cuts into my palm, but it finally turns.

Nothing. No birthday cards. No slips telling me to pick up a package at the post office. Not even a coupon pack from every sorry business with a storefront on the south side of Dover, Delaware.

The elevator wheezes like the June heat has melted something important in its gears and cables, but it shudders me up to the fifth floor. For just a second, with my key set to turn the deadbolt, I wonder if Leo has a surprise waiting inside.

Maybe he's made up with our father. Or our stepmother. Maybe this is all a major Step Nine—NA's instruction to make amends—and every one of the family members and friends who've cut me off for trusting my twin is waiting to shout "Surprise!" before singing "Happy birthday, dear Alix-and-Leo."

I shoulder the door open, pushing hard when it sticks in the June humidity. Of course the apartment's empty. The hot afternoon air hasn't stirred for hours.

"Leo?" I ask anyway, because I want to be wrong.

Silence.

He isn't using. He can't be using.

I loop my heavy hair into a loose knot and cross to the scratched coffee table, looking for something to use as a fan. Three books are stacked there: *Clinical Textbook of Addictive Disorders, Individual Psychodynamic Psychotherapy,* and *Neuroimaging in Addiction.* They match two dozen other books stacked on the shaky nightstand in my bedroom. Finishing my dissertation is the only thing left between me and my PhD. I'm through taking classes at Sherman University, through teaching them as well.

A bright white corner of paper peeks out from beneath the largest book. I ease it free, hoping I can use it to fan dry the sweat prickling at the base of my throat.

Bright red letters glare from the top of the page: EVICTION NOTICE.

In black, below: "To tenants Alix Key and Leo Key, all other residents, and unnamed occupants at…"

"…tenancy is hereby terminated due to non-payment of rent…"

"…required to quit and vacate the subject premises…"

"…thirty (30) day legal notice…"

"…midnight cancellation of electronic access to premises…"

"…dated: May 21…"

I reread the page three times, like the words might change if I stare at them long enough. Leo must have gotten the notice a month ago. He's hidden it for the past thirty days.

But at midnight tonight, my keycard turns into a pumpkin. I'm out on my ear, along with my brother and every last stick of the broken-down furniture around me.

He's using. He has to be using again.

Chapter Two

ALIX

I want there to be some mistake.

Leo moved in six months ago, the day I picked him up from Spring Valley Renewal Center in a rented Honda. We celebrated with Oreo Blizzards before I dropped him off at St. Bart's for his first NA meeting—ninety meetings in ninety days.

Three months ago, red chip shiny on his sweaty palm, he asked if he could drop off our rent check at the landlord's office, halfway between our apartment and Leo's job at Barney's Grill. He promised a receipt. I could follow behind him, watch him every step of the way. He begged to be trusted. To help with something, anything.

I love him.

He's my brother.

My twin.

I *did* follow him the first time, staying far enough back that he didn't see me, even though he looked over his shoulder every ten steps or so. But he brought me a receipt, signed and dated. And he was so, so proud. He kept going to meetings every day, even though he had his red chip, even though he'd done his ninety.

Now, I carry the eviction notice into my bedroom. I put it on top of my psych books as I wrestle open the drawer of my nightstand. It sticks in the midsummer humidity, but I'm persistent. I fumble beneath my nail scissors and my hand lotion, shove aside a handful of cough drops and a tube of cherry-flavor ChapStick.

The receipts should be here. I keep them as proof of payment because I'm the responsible one.

They're gone. Which makes me pretty sure they were never any good. Leo forged them or photocopied them or...I don't even know how else he could come up with fakes.

"Dammit, Leo..." My words bake in the stifling room.

I don't have the money to pay three months rent, even if I can reach our landlord before midnight. I *had* a grad student stipend, funds that were supposed to get me through my doctorate. It ended when I finished winter quarter, when I stopped taking classes and teaching. Knowing I'd be "ABD"—all but dissertation—I'd planned, saved a little. But I'd counted on Leo's wages from the restaurant.

I have two hundred dollars in my bank account. Another forty in my wallet, if...

I dig my wallet out of my frayed backpack.

My student ID is there. My driver's license too. I don't carry credit cards—for so many years they weren't safe, not when Leo was using. I scissor open the bill slot with my fingers.

Empty.

He took my change, too, even my lucky Eleanor Roosevelt quarter.

Anger feels like a live animal chewing its way out of my belly. But I'm embarrassed too. Ashamed that—once again—everyone else was right. Leo has betrayed me.

I'm going to be sick. I run to the bathroom and lean over the toilet, retching and choking, but nothing comes up. I give up and go back to my bedroom, collapsing on the edge of my sagging bed.

My heartbeat pounds in my ears. My numb fingers take a while to figure out how to get my phone out of my skirt pocket. They take even longer to text my dad, using full sentences because that's the kind of thing he likes.

Alix

Sorry to reach out this way, but I've fallen behind on rent. Any chance I can borrow $1000?

Three dots float, and I allow myself to breathe. But the dots disappear and five minutes later there's still no reply.

Fine. I'll text Aunt Cindy, my mother's sister.

Alix

Alix here—sorry it's been so long. Long story but my stipend's run out, and I still have a month or two before my dissertation's done. If I could borrow $1000, I'll pay you back in two months. With interest, of course.

I add a smiley face and tap send. The message flashes Delivered, then Read. But there aren't any dots, and five minutes later I'm reaching out to my stepsisters.

Olivia first. Then Ava. I'm waiting for answers when the screen turns to black broken by angry white letters. Wicked Stepmother is calling.

It seemed funny when I put her in my contacts under that name. And it's not like she'll ever see my screen. My stomach executes a triple axel before I tap the green icon. "Candace!" I say, stretching my lips into a fake smile to keep my voice bright.

"You know the rules."

"But it's been so long—"

"No calling or texting from you or Leo."

"Leo's not even here!"

"We can't help you anymore. We won't."

"I just—"

"Not your father. Not your aunt. Not your stepsisters. You made your choice, Alix. Now you have to live with the consequences. Don't bother calling again. Everyone just blocked you."

A crash on her end tells me she slammed down her landline.

I clutch my phone, desperately swiping through my contacts. It's been years since I added a new name. There's a handful of entries for friends from high school. Maybe a dozen from college. Only one from grad school, because by then I'd learned the truth—Leo ruins everything.

He takes and he takes and he takes, and one by one, each of my friends had enough. It wasn't Leo's using, they said. It was me, standing by him. Enabling him.

I try to swallow the red-green taste of enraged shame as I stare at my last possible lifeline: Jason Carter. We met my first week of grad school at Sherman. He was my first—my only—boyfriend. We dated for three and a half years. The last time he was in this apartment was Thanksgiving, eight months ago.

Leo showed up three hours late, stumbling into the rickety kitchen table as he lost his balance. He shattered a thrift-store bowl because he thought the cranberry sauce was blood, then he threw our turkey off the fire escape to protect us from supposed poison.

Jason was a saint. Together, we talked Leo down. We got him to stop shouting, to stop sobbing, to—finally—fall asleep in my bed.

And when Jason asked if he could see me the next night, I thought he was finally going to propose. We'd worked so well together. We'd shared so much.

He wanted to meet at Ondine's, the little bistro where we had our first date. I braved the Black Friday sales in Dover for a killer outfit—little black dress, matching bra and panties that made me blush, and actual high heels—the only ones I'd ever owned.

His eyes went wide when I walked in the door. He waved off the waitress when she came to take our drinks order, and I waited for him to reach into his pocket, to bring out a ring. Instead, he took my hand and said, "Alix, these are the hardest words I've ever said. But I can't stay with you, not if Leo's in your life. He's an addict. A user."

"He's going to a meeting tomorrow!" I said. "He feels terrible about last night."

"He always feels terrible. And nothing ever changes. How many times has he been to rehab?"

Six. No, seven. But I said, "This time is different. He'll do it for *us.* For you and me."

Jason shook his head. "I'm sorry," he said, and he *did* sound sorry. "We both know that's not enough. So there can't be an 'us.'" He stood and pushed his chair in very carefully. "I'm sorry," he said again and left, just as the waitress came back to the table.

So, yeah. I can't call Jason. I jam my phone back into my pocket.

I'm livid about Leo. Desperate. He's lied to me more times than I can count. Cheated. Stolen.

But I can't give up on him. He's my brother. My *twin.*

When we were babies, we slept in one crib. We spoke our own private language before we spoke English. We still finish each other's sentences, and it's freaky the number of times I take out my phone, knowing he's about to call.

When our mother died, he was the only one who understood why I couldn't cry. And at the wedding reception when Dad married Candace, Leo slipped me a miniature voodoo doll, complete with half a dozen straight pins.

We started at University of Delaware at the same time. I flirted with anorexia my first semester, trying to make it through an entire day of classes on an apple and eleven raw cashews because calories seemed easier to control than my impossible freshman classes. He made me go to Student Counseling, where I got better and fell in love with psychology.

But by the time I was ready to thank him, he'd found drugs.

It started with Ritalin his roommate gave him—enough to get a buzz and study all night long. Adderall got him through first semester exams. The first time he took meth seemed like a big deal, but soon he was hooked, with ecstasy and ketamine and God knew what else on the side.

I should have been there for him, the way he was there for me. But I wasn't. So I tried to make it up by staying loyal, even when it cost me my friends, my family, even the man I thought I'd marry.

Now Leo's rewarded me by getting us evicted.

I have two hundred dollars in the bank. I have no clue where I'm going to live. No one to turn to. Nowhere to go.

I'm so angry, my fingers shake as I text Leo.

Alix

Call me, buttface.

Now.

Don't be a baby.

But he doesn't call, and he doesn't text back.

And suddenly, I can't stand the idea of being in the apartment anymore. It's too hot. The walls are too close. I'm too furious.

I haven't had a drink since Leo got out of Spring Valley. I've been supporting his sobriety, trying to make it easier. Make him stronger.

My mouth is suddenly full of saliva, like I've already taken a huge gulp of a lemon drop martini. I swallow hard as I yank open my closet door.

I'm tired of saying *no*. *No* to drinks. *No* to friends and relatives who say Leo's a disaster. *No* to my thesis advisor who wants to know if I'm close to finishing my dissertation. *No* to the crazy voice deep inside my skull that says I should walk away from Dover, from Sherman U, from Leo, from *everything*, and just start over.

But tonight...

Tonight I'm celebrating my birthday. Tonight *no* isn't part of my vocabulary. Tonight I'm saying *yes* to every opportunity that crosses my path.

Chapter Three

ALIX

I'll never tell a living soul, but I'm broken. I've tried touching myself *down there* since Jason left. I thought maybe I could do on my own what never happened with him.

Nothing.

I know enough psychology to be certain my brain is the problem. I've created a terrible feedback loop: I don't respond sexually, so I worry about ever being able to respond, which stresses me out, so I don't respond sexually.

At this point, I can't even make myself think real words—clinical ones *or* slang ones. *Down there* is the most I can manage, and that leaves me feeling embarrassed. Ashamed.

I'm a mess.

But maybe *yes* is my ticket out of this vicious circle.

I don't know if I feel light-headed because my brother has pulled the rug out from under me or because the apartment is hotter than Hades' left armpit or because I've decided to spend my last two hundred dollars on cocktails in some bar trying to solve the problem of my broken body. I need to put together some vaguely appropriate outfit, but first I manhandle the window in my bedroom, punching the sash with the heel of my hand until it finally shrieks and slides open.

A lazy breeze drifts in and I immediately feel a thousand times better. I stick my head outside and gulp fresh air like this is my last day of freedom. I don't even mind that heat radiates off the iron fire escape.

It's midsummer eve, the summer solstice, so the sun won't set for a few hours. Leo and I used to love celebrating our birthday on the longest day of the year—it makes it last even longer, Leo used to say.

Forget about Leo!

At least for tonight.

Before I can pull back into my room and start ransacking my closet, a squawk shreds the air and a massive crow lands on the fire escape. As he shifts from foot to foot, tilting his head for a better view of me, he's joined by three of his buddies.

I laugh, because the last week has been full of long days at the library. I haven't seen my bird friends since last weekend, but they haven't forgotten me. I reach for a jar that I keep on my nightstand and unscrew the lid, taking out a handful of shelled, unsalted peanuts.

"Hello, Gorgeous," I say to the first crow, placing a peanut on my windowsill.

He hops over to collect my gift before I have a chance to step back. Gorgeous flies off, but the other birds approach, bobbing their heads as I greet them by name—Nosy and Grabby and Caw—and give them their own treats. The birds make short work of their nuts, craning their necks as they search for more.

It's my birthday, and my black-feathered friends are the only ones who'll share my celebration. I'm about to duck back inside to grab another handful of peanuts when Gorgeous returns.

His wings flap wide as he settles on the fire escape. When he tilts his head, I see something in his beak. "What's that, Gorgeous?" I ask.

He hops over to my window, as if he understands every word I say. Ducking his head with perfect precision, he drops his prize on the sill. He retreats to his fellow crows, but he cranes his neck, pointing to the gift and fluffing his feathers with pride.

I pick up the present and turn it to catch a better angle in the sunlight. It's a battered metal heart, the kind a careful owner would put on their dog's collar, with a name and a phone number so a lost animal could find its way home. The heart used to be red, but it's so beat-up, I can't make out any of the letters or numbers engraved on its surface.

Closing my fingers around the charm, I nod gravely to Gorgeous. "Thank you," I say, and I'm surprised that tears thicken my words.

Before I can say anything else, my little murder of crows takes flight. I watch them fly toward the park, one block over. When they're gone, I turn to take stock of my closet. It's not like I've got a fairy godmother. I have to make do with whatever I already own.

I have a pair of pencil skirts and a trio of tops, the ones I wore when I taught. I have the never-worn bridesmaid's dress I bought for my stepsister Olivia's wedding, the Barbie pink one with the gigantic bow across my butt. She uninvited me when Candace found out I was in the wedding party, but the dress couldn't be returned.

Now that I'm done with teaching, I live in a handful of jeans and yoga pants, with equally casual tops. I consider pulling on a stretched-out pair of leggings and knotting a T-shirt at my waist, but I don't have the swagger—or the rail-thin body—to pull that off.

The answer, of course, lurks in the back of my closet, on the very last hanger. I pull out the dress I bought for Jason's proposal, the one I wore the night he broke up with me.

Why not?

It's not like I'm going to see anyone I know.

I dig out my fancy bra and panties, rescuing them from the very back of my dresser drawer. They fit like a dream, and I remember all over again why I spent a month's food budget on them.

Shimmying into my dress, I suck in my breath so I can wrestle the hidden side zipper into place. On my first try, it catches an inch shy of the top, and I have to twist like a seal to ease it back down.

Forget about a fairy godmother. I need a flock of happy bluebirds to get me properly dressed.

I glance back at the fire escape, but Gorgeous and his friends haven't returned. That's okay—I can't imagine how many peanuts I'd have to spend to train them to be my personal maids. I close the window and nudge the lock into place.

The zipper slides home on my second try. Barefoot, I pad into the bathroom where I have to hunt for the crimson lipstick I bought for my non-existent proposal. I finally find it, behind an empty bottle of Leo's body wash.

Forget about Leo. Seriously. For just one night.

Lips shiny and red, I tackle my hair. It's too heavy to stay in any up-do. I brush it until it shines and leave it down around my shoulders.

My shoes are waiting in the back of my closet, narrow stilettos with sky-high heels. My ankles are strong. I've spent the past five years walking two miles a day to campus, and two miles back.

Good thing, too, because my fancy carriage has gone the way of my fairy godmother and my bluebird attendants. I find the tiny clutch purse I bought for Proposal Night, and I drop in my phone, my apartment key, and the scratched keycard I'll need for the front door.

My last stop before I leave the apartment is the kitchen. I know better than to drink on an empty stomach. I open the cupboard, but the offerings are slim—a couple of Cup O' Noodles and a blue box of macaroni and cheese that I won't take time to cook. The refrigerator isn't much better—some limp carrots, a carton that used to be leftover beef with broccoli, and an apple.

But I find a hunk of cheddar cheese at the back of the deli drawer. Miraculously, it hasn't begun to sprout green mold. I cut thick slices and eat them with the apple. Something's better than nothing.

Okay. Time to go. I have to be back by midnight—any later, and I'll be locked out of the apartment for good. I'll pack my meager belongings in the morning.

Out on the street, I make a quick detour to withdraw cash from the ATM—ten crisp twenty-dollar bills. I fold them carefully and tuck them into my clutch.

I've already chosen where I'm going. It's an underground bar, literally below ground level, a few blocks from campus. It's called Debasement, which made me laugh the first time I saw it, but made Jason scowl. I've seen people go down the steps there. They seem happy. They seem fun.

I walk through the muggy evening, wondering if people are looking at me, worrying that they know. *That woman is being evicted.*

She doesn't have a single friend to call, not even family.

All she has is a brother who lied to her. Again.

I grit my teeth and run my fingers through my hair. No one is looking at me. No one cares.

Forget. About. Leo.

I'm a block away from Debasement when I see the flashing lights—red and blue bouncing off the plate-glass storefronts. As I reach the bar, I realize a pair of patrol cars is parked directly in front.

Two policemen are wrestling a man up the concrete stairs that lead to the underground bar. He's twisting like a strung-up catfish, his hair sticking out like broken pretzels, his face the color of plums. His hands are cuffed behind his back.

"You'll pay for this!" he shouts down the steps. "Your ass is mine!"

The police pause as they reach ground level, adjusting their grips on a man who truly looks—and sounds—deranged. The criminal jackknifes in their grip, stretching his neck to hawk a huge gob of spit down the stairs.

"That's for you, asshole!" he shouts. "Think you're a big man? Getting the cops to do your dirty work? Fuck you! I'm gonna kill you!"

The closest policeman yanks hard enough that I hear the screaming man's teeth clang shut. "Hey, scumbag! That's assault, on top of everything else." The cop looks down the stairs. "Do you want to press charges, sir?"

"No thank you, officer."

That voice is as smooth as melted copper, warm and fluid in the evening breeze. It washes over me like a physical thing, stroking my spine from the nape of my neck to my tailbone.

I gape as a man tops the stairs, a perfect man, a man with the ideal body to match that molten voice. He's taller than either cop or the squirming guy in custody. He's broad, too—his shoulders stretch the seams of his sleek black T. His black jeans fit like they were sewn just for him.

Green eyes flash beneath spiky chestnut hair, and he steps too close to the man between the cops. A tiny white rectangle slips between his fingers, and I realize he's holding a business card.

"You can try, motherfucker," he says, and now his flowing copper has been forged into a sharp-edged spear. He shoves his card into the other man's breast pocket. "My name's Prince. Travis Prince. And you can find me at Diamond Freeport—if you fucking dare."

Chapter Four

TRAP

I talk big, but the loogie on the steps behind me woke the fucking Beast inside my head.

My pulse is racing. My palms are slick with sweat. My lungs need more air, and pain clamps my skull like a charley horse, but I refuse to pant like a goddamn dog.

Instead, I clench both hands into fists, squeezing until my knuckles bulge like stone.

Once.

Twice.

Three times.

Four.

Five.

The Beast retreats.

The fucking nightmare fizzes into a rage that makes me want to break the asswipe's face. But the cops are loading him into one of the black-and-whites. Going after him now will only punch my own ticket to the station. If I land in a holding cell with that cocksucker, I'll end up facing a murder beef.

I narrow my eyes as the car door slams. The asshole throws himself against the window, screaming something I can't hear. I shoot him both middle fingers, waiting until the car takes the corner to drop my fists.

It's time to tighten security around the freeport. That shit-for-brains won't make it past the front gate, but we need to bring the biometrics online anyway.

I turn back to the bar, steeling myself to get past the mess on the steps. Beast or no Beast, I have a fresh-poured shot of WhistlePig waiting downstairs.

That's when I see her—a woman standing on the sidewalk.

She's staring at me like I'm Christmas, Easter and her fucking birthday all tied up in a bow. Her made-up face is pretty, but she's trying too hard, like she found that lipstick in her mother's bathroom drawer.

This is not a girl who spends a lot of time in bars, watching dirtbags get dragged out by Dover's finest.

Some part of my lizard brain kicks me in the balls, and I force myself not to stare at her tits. Instead, I start looking at her legs and the invitation of her fuck-me shoes, which I'm only too happy to oblige.

So I miss the expression on her face when she says, "Let me guess. He left a lousy tip?"

That catches me by surprise and I laugh, even though adrenaline still smokes the back of my throat. "Fucker waited for one of the college girls to go to the john and then he tried to roofie her drink."

"Tried?"

I flex my fingers. My knuckles are bruised, but the skin isn't split. "I got in his way."

"My hero," she says.

And the funny thing is, I feel like a good guy when she says it.

I want this little princess. She's exactly what I need. After all, I'm celebrating. Five years of legal hell, and I finally got government clearance to run Diamond Freeport as a tax haven.

Not one of the girls downstairs looks old enough to drink, much less consent to my twisted demands. But this little number, in her painted-on dress... Those red, red lips are killing me. But the thing that really shoots steel into my cock is the sense that she hasn't played this game before.

I can't say how I know. It's nothing she does, nothing she says. Hell, I don't think she's *said* a dozen words.

But I'm suddenly certain she's the reason I came to Debasement tonight. We'll have a drink together. Maybe two.

And then I'll fuck her on my terms—bound, gagged, and gone by dawn.

Chapter Five

ALIX

I should be scared of this guy.

He towers over me, even though I'm wearing heels. When he flexes his fingers, I see his knuckles are red. He *punched* the guy the cops took away.

But he did it to protect a woman. He took a risk for a stranger. So I say, "Your name's Prince? Like Prince Charming?"

"More like the Prince of Darkness."

His slow smile lights a Fourth of July sparkler deep inside my belly. No. Not my belly. *Down there.*

Not breaking my gaze, he edges back, clearing a path for me to approach the steps. "You were heading to Debasement?"

The copper's back in his voice, warm and fluid, like honey glinting in the sun. I catch the wry twist of his lips, the insinuation in his tone. I smile past my nerves and say, "I should take the fifth on that."

"Take whatever you want. That's what I do."

He's not talking about corny legal terms. The sparkler settles into a steady flame, low and slow. My body loves his sly words, even as my mind says I should slow things down.

But I don't have time to go slow. I need to be home by midnight. I've only got this little pocket of time, this magical space where nothing matters, where nothing is real. Six hours of freedom, before I turn back into a responsible, care-burdened woman.

That's when I decide to change my name—just for tonight. Here, at Debasement, I won't be Alix. Tonight, I'm...Ella.

Ella is fun. Ella is light. She knows how to make a man—how to make Travis Prince—look at her with hunger in his eyes.

"Can I buy you a drink?" he asks.

Alix has never dreamed of accepting a drink from a stranger. But Ella knows exactly what to do. She smirks and says, "Just one?"

"You think you can handle more?"

He's not talking about alcohol. I almost lose my nerve and tell him I made a mistake. I need to go home. But he gestures for me to precede him down the stairs, and that's exactly what Ella wants.

Ella wants his eyes on her butt.

That's nasty and wrong and I've never wanted a stranger to ogle me before. But when I walk past Travis, I expect to feel his palm brush the small of my back. And when he doesn't touch me, I'm actually disappointed.

The air-conditioned bar feels icy after the summer heat outside, and I blink hard to help my eyes adjust to the dark. Everyone applauds as Travis steps in behind me. I turn to catch the mountainous roll of his shoulders under his tight black T. He's uncomfortable with the attention.

The redhead behind the bar waves him over. "Your money's no good tonight," she says.

"Not necessary, Caitlyn," he says.

She ignores him with a saucy smile, selecting a bottle from the mirrored wall behind her. I admire her easy grace, the way she teases, striking a pose with the liquor. "Your first glass didn't make it through the war. Still want the Pig?"

He nods and she gives him a generous pour over a single baseball-size sphere of ice. He inclines his head toward me and says, "And my friend will have..."

Ordinarily, I'd say a lemon drop, or maybe a cosmo, something sweet and fruity. But as Travis's hand closes around his rye, I want something simpler. Something more mature. "Grey Goose," I say. "On the rocks."

Caitlyn smiles like I've made the best choice in the world but before she reaches for a bottle, she says, "I'll have to see some ID."

"Sure, um, of course." I find my driver's license in my clutch and hand it over.

"Oh!" Caitlyn says. "Happy birthday!"

I blush, even though I haven't done anything weird. As Caitlyn pours my drink, Travis slides a hundred-dollar bill from his wallet and shoves it deep inside the beer mug holding tips.

Who is this guy? A crime-fighting millionaire super-hero? I bet he rescues stray kittens from trees and helps little old ladies cross the street.

But the look he gave me outside, at the top of the stairs, told me loud and clear he wasn't any Boy Scout. I wonder what it would take for him to give *me* a hundred-dollar tip.

I can't believe I even thought that.

"Trap!" Caitlyn says, digging out the bill and trying to hand it back to him.

"What happened to 'the customer's always right?'" he asks. He flashes her a smile that is somehow friendly and feral at the same time. I want him to look at me the exact same way.

She holds up her hands in resignation. "Okay, okay. You win."

"I always do," he says levelly.

He salutes her with his glass before returning his attention to me. I've never met anyone like him before, anyone with his brash confidence, his absolute certainty. Here in the bar, his eyes are the almost-black of forest underbrush, and I look down, needing to escape their intensity.

My fancy lace bra is doing nothing to keep my nipples from straining against my dress. I try to tell myself I'm reacting to the chill in the air, but that's Alix's lie. Ella knows the truth.

"Join me?" Travis—Trap?—asks, gesturing toward a booth in the back.

I shouldn't. I don't know this man. I shouldn't follow him into a dark corner.

Ella says yes.

Crossing in front of the bar, we pass a woman who's crying at a table for four, a sweating glass of ice water at her elbow. A friend is comforting her, saying, "It wasn't your fault. He was a creep. You had no way of knowing."

The crying woman must be the one whose drink was almost doctored. I'm still looking over my shoulder as I approach the booth Trap indicated, and I stumble over the step up to the private alcove.

Before I can lose even a drop of my icy vodka, Trap's hand closes over my elbow. The hungry thing inside me presses hard *down there*, making me gasp a little. "Thanks," I say, trying to catch my breath.

He doesn't answer. Instead, he takes a seat opposite me, setting his glass on the table with a precise thud. He spreads his right hand, the one that just rescued me from sprawling on Debasement's floor. He taps his thumb against the table, then moves each finger in turn—index, middle, ring, pinky—like he's playing scales on an invisible piano.

After he finishes, the silence stretches between us, lumpy and awkward. So I say, "Trap? Not Travis? Trap sounds like something to avoid."

He shrugs with one shoulder. "My father's name was Travis too. 'Trap' kept things simple."

"Then you're not as dangerous as you seem?"

"I wouldn't say that," he growls.

The thing inside me rolls over and I realize, once again, that I was wrong about his eyes. They're jungle eyes—green and gold and wild.

Before I can answer his declaration—is there *any* way to answer that?—the college women from the four-top approach. "Excuse me," says the one who was crying.

Trap looks at her calmly.

"I just wanted to say, like, thank you. I *know* I shouldn't have left my drink there. I mean, they told us that in *Freshman* Week. But I never thought anyone would do something *here*. It's like, *Dover*, you know? We're supposed to be *safe*. We're, like, not even a *mile* off campus. I mean, who would think a creep like *that* would be in Dover?"

Her friend elbows her, a tight little gesture that finally puts the brakes on the runaway train of words.

The woman Trap rescued swallows hard, then raises her chin. She offers Trap her hand, like she's sealing a job interview. "Thank you," she says, her tone grave.

"Take care of yourself," Trap says, nodding curtly. But her hand still hangs there, fingers trembling just a little. He sets his jaw and shakes, his palm engulfing hers. I wonder what his heavy fingers would feel like, surrounding mine like that.

The two women scurry away. Trap puts his right hand back on the table and plays his imaginary musical scale—thumb, index, middle, ring, pinky.

His scowl makes Alix think about following those two freshmen out of the bar. But Ella raises her glass and takes a delicate sip.

The vodka is snowmelt off a glacier, so cold it glides down my throat without a hint of alcoholic burn. It settles in my belly like a crystal star of courage and I drink again, a healthier swallow this time.

Trap curls his fingers into a fist, like he's barely resisting the urge to play more notes. He doses himself with a healthy gulp of rye.

I've got five years of graduate level psychology courses under my figurative belt. I know not to throw around words like obsessive-compulsive disorder—OCD—but I recognize a tic when I see one.

He needed to ground himself after he saved me from falling. And again, after shaking hands with his damsel in distress. Touch is his trigger. Touching someone makes him seek escape.

I look up from his fisted hand, and those jungle eyes are waiting for me. "Wh—" I start and have to clear my throat. "Where were we?"

"You were making the mistake of thinking I'm not dangerous. I was correcting you."

Correction. Something in Ella—in me—wants to test him. Wants to see what will happen if I make another mistake. Wants to know exactly how far he'll go in *correcting* me.

Before I can act on such a crazy thought, I grab for my vodka, barely taking time to match my lips to the scarlet print on the glass's rim.

"You have an advantage here," he says. When he watches me swallow, it feels like he can see through my dress, past the lace of my bra, all the way to my flushed and feverish skin. I don't feel like I have any advantage here. I don't have any control at all.

His teeth flash white as he says, "You know my name, but I don't know yours."

"Ella," I say, cementing my lie by finishing my drink with a gulp. I make up a last name. "Ella Locke."

"Would you like another drink, Ella?" he asks.

I shouldn't. The roof of my mouth is already buzzing. I'm much too interested in the curve of Trap's lips, in his shark-like smile as he waits for my response.

But *no* is off the table till midnight. So I square my shoulders and say, "Yes, please."

He raises a hand and gets Caitlyn's attention. We talk while we wait, about the weather maybe, or how the Phillies are doing, or recent studies in how the perihypoglossal nuclei function as part of the brain's complex circuitry related to eye movements.

Something like that. The humming in my ears distracts me.

By the time the bartender finally brings my drink, I'm digging deep for a fresh topic of conversation. "Diamond Freeport," I say, folding my hands around my new glass. "You told the jerk that's where you work?"

"Not exactly," Trap says. "I *own* Diamond Freeport."

It sounds like something in *Star Wars*, a place where spaceships dock to trade goods with aliens. So I ask, "And that is...what, exactly?"

There's that one-shouldered shrug again. "Basically, it's a warehouse."

"What's the not 'basic' part?"

His smile strokes me like I'm a cat. The thing *down there* wants to arch toward him, to twist and curl to get closer to his touch. "We have a special tax status. As of midnight tonight, deals inside Diamond are tax-free. That's why I'm here. I'm celebrating."

"Wait!" I say. "I'm celebrating too!"

"Imagine that," he drawls. And the wild thing in his jungle eyes dances with the yearning thing inside me. I have to press my thighs together to keep from trembling *down there*. And try as I might, I can't think of a single thing to say.

Chapter Six

TRAP

I'm bored by the bullshit.

I want to lean across the table and plant my thumb on her bottom lip. I want to tell her, "Look, little girl. You're begging to be fucked, with your big-girl makeup and your painted-on dress and your sky-high heels. And I *need* to fuck—that's the whole reason I'm here. So we both know it's gonna happen and we can forget all about polite conversation and have another drink."

Point of pride, though: I've never forced a woman. And there's no way a drunk woman can consent to the things I plan to do.

But I'm not opposed to stacking the deck a little in my favor.

If I can get her to the freeport, if she sees my house, sees the way I live, she'll be more inclined to accept the way I need to fuck her. Even if—*especially if*—I give her a chance to sober up once she's there. I just need to get her loose enough to take that first step, to come home with me.

So, it's back to the bullshit.

"If I'm a billionaire..." she says. The phrase must strike her as funny, because she cuts herself short to laugh.

"If you're a billionaire..." I salute her with my glass, like she's on to something special. She answers with another gulp of Grey Goose.

Good girl. She's a very good girl. I shift on the booth's upholstered bench, easing the pressure of my jeans against my cock.

Ella polishes off the last of her second vodka and sets the glass on the table with a decisive clink. She frowns. "Impossible. I'll never be a billionaire."

"Never say never."

She shakes her head with a vehemence that tells me it's time. She's ready. "Not gonna happen."

I give her my best good-guy shrug. "That doesn't mean you can't see the freeport."

She pins me with a shrewd look. She's not as far gone as I thought she was. "What d'you mean?"

"Come home with me. Let me give you a personal tour of Diamond. I've got paintings and jewelry and luxury cars…"

She laughs, sitting back in the booth. "Do a lot of woman fall for that?"

It was a long shot. But I match her laugh and say, "Come on. I'm celebrating. You're celebrating. Let's celebrate together."

Too much, too fast. She frowns. "My mother told me never to get in a car with a stranger."

I think about asking what her mother would say about how her tits are falling out of her dress, but I don't think that'll get her any closer to gagging on my cock. So instead I say, "Then ask me a question. I'll tell you whatever you want to know, and we won't be strangers anymore."

She tilts her head, considering. "I can ask anything?"

I spread my hands wide. "I've got nothing to hide."

"What's the deal with your counting to five?"

Every sip of rye I've had turns to a separate brick of ice in my belly. The Beast roars its evil laugh. "Five?" I ask, pretending to be confused.

"When you touched me. When you shook hands with that student. Why'd you have to play five notes after that?"

The Beast snarls as my fingers fold into fists.

There are plenty of other women in Dover. Some of them will come to Debasement tonight. I can chain one of *them* to my bed.

I don't want some other woman. I want Ella. I want her wide wicked mouth and her thick dark hair and her timid, tempting body.

But the price is going to be telling her the truth.

Or part of the truth, anyway.

I take a deep breath and exhale slowly. "I saw something when I was a kid. Had to touch it. When I think about it now, I need to move to make the memory go away."

It's the first time I've ever said the words out loud. The first time I've told a soul.

She's quiet for so long I think I've lost her. I've said too much. I'm too fucked up—and she doesn't even know what I'm going to do to her back at the freeport.

So I steel myself and take her hand. I fold my fingers around hers deliberately. I feel her warmth against mine, the softness of her skin, the pulse at the base of her thumb.

The Beast howls, but I wait for Ella to meet my gaze, to acknowledge that I did this just for her. Finally, she nods, a tiny dip of her chin.

I swallow and say, "Come home with me, Ella. Nothing will happen that you don't want. I promise."

Chapter Seven

ALIX

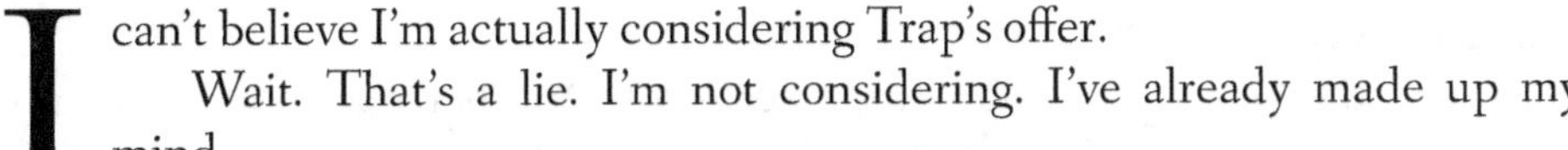

I can't believe I'm actually considering Trap's offer.

Wait. That's a lie. I'm not considering. I've already made up my mind.

I just have to figure out how to protect myself.

I think about the college woman, the one who nearly had her drink roofied. She wasn't safe, even with her friend here at the bar.

I don't have any friends. All I have is Leo.

It feels foolish to trust my safety to my brother. He's already proven he can't be relied on.

But there's a big difference between earning a dark blue chip at NA and keeping his sister safe. Leo may be back at square one with his recovery, but he can still be my back-up on this. He'll be there for me if I really, truly need him. If it's life or death.

I take out my phone and say to Trap, "I'm telling my brother where I'm going."

"Good idea," he says.

I tap the screen. "I'm sending him your name."

"Smart."

"And the name of Diamond Freeport."

"Excellent."

"What's the address? Where're you taking me?"

I feel the weight of Trap's jungle gaze as I type in the destination. He gives me the zip code too, even the plus-four. I stare at the screen after I send the last line, waiting, hoping, praying that Leo writes back.

Nothing. No three dots. No response at all.

"Anything else?" Trap asks. "Anyone else you want to tell?"

I don't want him to know the truth. I don't want to say I'm alone in the world. I put my phone back in the clutch. "Nope. I'm good."

He nods and climbs to his feet, making a sweeping gesture toward Debasement's front door. I walk in front of him, hyper-aware of how my hips sway as I plant my feet, courtesy of my high-heel shoes.

As I walk by the bar, Caitlyn is polishing a glass with a white towel. "Have a good night," I say, purposely drawing her attention.

She gives me a knowing smile. "You too."

I wonder if she's walked the same path I'm taking right now. Has Trap invited her back to Diamond Freeport? Is that the reason they're on a first-name basis? Do I care?

If I'm honest, the idea bothers me.

But I have zero right to make that claim. Alix is a woman who dreams of dedicated boyfriends, of committed relationships. But I'm Ella tonight. And Ella doesn't care.

I lead the way up the stairs to street level. Another man might take my hand as we move down the sidewalk, might even pull me close to his side. But I already know Trap won't do that.

Which makes me wonder: If brushing my hand was enough to trigger a traumatic compulsive response, how can Trap possibly expect to make love? Because I have no delusions—he absolutely intends to take me to bed.

I consider asking him, right then and there. But this is my night of saying *yes*. Whatever answer he gives, I'm not changing my mind. I've made that promise to myself.

Am I actually brave, or are the two shots of Grey Goose doing the talking? I set my jaw. What difference does it make? The result is the same.

I'm going to Diamond Freeport with Trap Prince.

I follow him down a narrow alley, between the building that houses Debasement and the boutique clothing store next door. I cross the tiny parking lot, weaving between cars. My ankle starts to turn on the uneven surface, but I steady myself against a gray Camry.

So I'm barely paying attention when Trap stops beside the most beautiful car

I've ever seen. It's a dark shimmering blue, as if the paint is lit from deep inside. Its body is low to the ground, sculpted with the grace of a hunting panther. Everything about the car says power and speed, masterful control of the road. Of the world.

I realize Trap has opened the passenger door. He's waiting for me to move forward, to finalize his invitation.

I wish I'd insisted on a third drink. I wish I had more courage.

Forcing a laugh, I ask, "Who'd you sell your soul to, for this?"

His answer is pitched low, just for me. "Who says I ever had a soul?"

The car is very beautiful. The seat is very low. Trap shifts his weight. He extends a hand, beckoning, welcoming.

Yes. This is the night for *yes.*

With my left hand, I twitch my dress higher, raising its hem to the middle of my thighs. With my right hand, I steady myself, using Trap's outstretched fingers as my anchor.

He trembles when I touch him, but his hand closes over mine. Strong. Steady. Stable.

He waits until I'm settled before he closes my door. If he needs to tap through his five-point ritual, he does it before he slides into the driver's seat.

The engine roars to life—fierce and bold instead of the tamed purr I expect. I wonder if this is how Cinderella felt, settling in her crystal carriage with a matched team of horses and a uniformed footman attending to her every need.

Cinderella's ride was just a pumpkin, I remind myself. She stayed out past midnight and nearly ruined everything. I don't have that luxury. Not tonight. Not if I want to maintain the few possessions I still own.

I glance at the dashboard, at the smooth, orderly gauges. A clock displays the time: 6:27. Five and half hours left of *yes.* Trap shifts gears, and the needy thing inside me shifts as well, flooding *down there* with warmth.

Maybe I'm supposed to make small talk. Tell jokes. Say something about Trap's muscled forearm as his fingers caress the gearshift.

But I'm afraid if I talk I'll break the spell. I'll lose my nerve. I'll forget about *yes* and tumble back to *no, no, no.*

We pass the Sherman campus. We reach the edge of town. We leave behind Wal-Mart and Home Depot. Orderly rows of corn march beside the road.

If Trap is nervous, he doesn't give any sign. His hands are steady on the wheel, not a tremor in sight. He scans the road before us with casual competence.

I concentrate on breathing.

We've been in the car fifteen minutes when Trap turns into a private drive-way. Trees arch over us as we approach an iron gate.

He brakes to a stop and lowers his window. Reaching toward a metal box, he types in a combination. It looks long, eight or nine digits at least. After a moment's hesitation, the gate glides open.

Glancing over my shoulder, I see a towering brick wall on either side of the gate. An iron cage is built into the wall, the type of one-way revolving door that guards inner-city subway stations, letting riders exit while keeping fare jumpers from breaking in. Concertina wire curls on top, metal teeth glinting in the evening sun.

Trap pulls into a paved courtyard. A construction site spreads to our left, a gaping hole ringed by wooden fences and guarded by a pair of bulldozers. Directly in front of us stands a four-story glass and chrome office building complete with another security box.

But Trap guides the car to the right.

A neatly trimmed lawn sets off a two-story building. It's made of white brick, I think, or maybe perfectly stacked stone. The walls are stark, sharp with precise right angles. About one third of the way from the driveway, there's an alcove, a diagonal slash that might lead to a door. There's not a window in sight.

Trap guides the car to the right, around the side of the shimmering white building. A garage waits for us, dark and spare. Trap parks in the middle of the open space, taming the engine with the quick tap of a button.

I could wait for him to circle the car, to open my door and hand me out like a princess, but I'm perfectly capable of exiting on my own. I shut the door care-fully, maybe more gently than it requires.

I can't imagine living in a pile of stone—cold and bleak, not a single sign of life. What happened to Trap when he was a child? What—or who—was he forced to touch? What broke this man, and how did he put himself back together inside this silent castle?

Trap moves to a featureless door. He types another passcode into a panel, pausing long enough for some inner electronics to work. The door sweeps open.

I need to move. I need to walk. But once I cross that threshold, will I remember how to shape my lips around tonight's word—*yes*?

The jungle is back in Trap's eyes. He takes in the rucked line of my skirt, the twist of fabric exposing my right thigh and the edge of my black lace panties. His gaze pokes the creature inside me, sending another hopeful shiver *down there*.

He steps back to let me enter before him. I'm still feeling Caitlyn's vodka, so I settle my palm against the door frame as I step inside the house. And I almost collapse against Trap's broad chest behind me.

I'm standing in a kitchen, but it's like no kitchen I've ever seen before. There's a granite island large enough to land a 747, with a spotless steel sink bigger than the bathtub in my dingy apartment. There's a pair of ovens, in case anyone needs to roast a couple of buffalo, and an induction cooktop the size of a soccer field. I don't see a refrigerator, but I bet one or two are hidden in the wall of honey-colored wood that stretches from floor to ceiling to my left.

But none of that is the most amazing thing about the kitchen. The most amazing thing about the kitchen is the curved wall of glass that swoops around a courtyard, a hidden oasis invisible from the driveway at the front of the house. I'm drawn to the windows like a swallow flying home.

The wall of glass continues beyond the kitchen. The entire back of the house is clear, a swaying organic shape. On the ground floor, I can glimpse a book-lined library and an austere office, computer screens erected in a forbidding fence. A living room offers leather couches and sleek chairs, arranged around a thick white rug that makes my toes curl inside my shoes. A dining room table is large enough for twelve.

I can't see the rooms directly above us, but a bedroom waits on the upper floor, directly across from the kitchen. A stern black comforter stretches over a Montana-size bed, corners made crisp against matching iron headboard and footboard.

Swallowing hard, I turn to see Trap watching me. His fingers curl easily by his sides. He carries his weight on the balls of his feet, like he's ready to spring, to catch me if I stumble or to drag me to his lair.

There isn't enough air in the kitchen. My knees tremble, and for the first time that day, my ankles forget how to support me in my shoes. I wonder what I'm doing here. Whether *yes* is really right for me.

I want to ask him for a shot of vodka, a booster for the drinks I had at Debasement. I want to tell him I need a minute; my brain has to catch up with my body. I want to say I'm overwhelmed, that I thought I could do this but maybe I was wrong, and I might want to go home.

He steps toward me and my breath catches, freezing somewhere deep inside my chest. I close my eyes, but I can still feel the drinks Caitlyn poured for me, and the floor rolls beneath my feet. I open my eyes and steady myself with a palm on the kitchen island's endless plain of granite.

Yes, I remind myself.

Yes, I want this.

Yes, I need this.

"All right," Trap says, and his voice sounds different now. There's a snap of command, a hidden core of iron that makes me wonder if I imagined the honey-melt of copper outside Debasement. "First things first."

I brace myself. This is it. This is why I'm here. This is what I chose.

"You," Trap says, and every muscle in my body tenses. "You need a glass of water."

Chapter Eight

TRAP

The look of relief on Ella's face is so transparent that something hitches inside my chest. I almost regret that she's the one I brought here.

Almost.

But she's here and she's mine and my cock is tired of waiting. She needs to sober up so I can fuck her blind.

Two drinks. Two hours. And it's already been thirty minutes since she took her last sip at Debasement. Plus, I don't need her stone, cold sober. Just clear-headed enough to make an honest choice.

Call it an hour of waiting. 7:40.

"Make yourself at home," I say, and my smile is real. She takes one of the bar stools, like she's not certain how much longer she can stand.

I want to know if her knees are shaking. I want to make her thighs tremble. I want to feel the slick of her pussy against the palm of my hand as she grinds her clit against my wrist.

I want a thousand things I'll never have, even if she stays after I tell her everything she'll have to do.

"Water?" I ask, like I'm not picturing her spread-eagled on my bed.

Her eyes shoot to mine, and I read an entire novel there. She wants another shot of vodka. She wants to numb herself, to take herself away. I

1107

can't figure out what brought her out tonight, why she's wearing that fucking dress, why she chose those shoes. But whatever demons she's fighting, she wants a security blanket, a barrier between her desire and mine.

Too bad that's the last thing I intend to give her.

Finally, she nods. I open the fridge and pull out a bottle of Berg. I crack the cap and put it on the island in front of her.

"Ice?" I ask, retrieving a glass from one of the hidden cupboards.

She nods again, and I slide open the unseen icemaker. The cubes are clear as air and cold as my scarred heart. I fill her glass to the rim.

"Hungry?"

Her eyes are wide, and if I hadn't been with her every second of the past hour, I'd wonder if she was riding some sort of chemical high. But her chin dips again, so I open the disguised fridge.

I'm glad she wants to eat. I want to feed her. I wish I could give her bread and cheese and a bottomless bowl of rice to soak up the alcohol in her blood, but those are frat-boy tricks that don't really work. The only thing that will get her sober is time.

I pull out a basket of strawberries. For just a moment, I imagine crushing them against her skin, starting with her lips before I move down her throat to her tits, to the high tight nips I caught a glimpse of when she first walked into Debasement.

The Beast growls. That's another thing I'll never get to do—rub fresh juice into her, skin against skin. At least I can watch her eat, hear her breath catch as the first bright taste of a berry explodes across her tongue.

I won't imagine anything else exploding across her tongue.

Not now.

Not yet.

"So..." she finally says, and I wonder what *she's* been thinking while I've been imagining the sounds she'll make when she comes for the fifth time.

"So," I answer, tossing back the conversational ball. I press my hands against the cold granite island. I'm a twenty-nine-year-old captain of modern industry, not a hard-dicked high-school geek.

I can't remember the last time a woman got to me this way.

Who the fuck am I kidding? No woman has ever gotten to me this way.

She drains her glass, letting the ice cubes nudge the soft spot between her lips and nose. Without my prompting, she pours herself more water. I resist the urge to glance at the clock set into the cooktop's control panel. I promised her an hour.

I'm a sick, twisted bastard, but I'm a man of my word.

"So," she says with a little more force. "This freeport of yours. There are other ones, right? Your competition?"

Jesus fucking Christ. Are we back to talking about business? But maybe that'll make my cock stand down.

"A handful right now. More should open in the next few years."

"Why would anyone work with you?"

I consider being offended, but it's a good question. "My environmental controls were designed by the top experts in the world. Temperature in the fine arts galleries will fluctuate less than one one hundredth of a degree."

"Okay..." She doesn't sound convinced.

"The construction out there," I say, nodding in the general direction of the plaza. "It'll have state-of-the-art conference rooms." That sounds even more boring than HVAC, so I quickly rattle off key facts and figures—my communication systems and recording facilities and the trio of Michelin-starred chefs I've hired full-time.

"All right," she says, clearly unimpressed.

"But?" I prod.

"Can't billionaires hire their own chefs? What makes Diamond Freeport special?"

"Sounds like you have something in mind."

"Diamond..." she says. "The hardest substance in the world. One of the rarest, right?"

She's stringing ideas together, adding up scraps of knowledge. If I can't fuck her yet, the next best thing is watching her think. "Right," I say.

"And one of the most valuable?"

I shrug. "Sure."

"So what's more rare, more valuable than time? No one—not even your billionaires—can make more of it. Invite your best customers to spend time together. Keep it exclusive. An even dozen."

I laugh. "Why would they do that?"

She ignores my challenge. "Call it...the Diamond Ring. Each month, invite the Diamond Ring to an exclusive event. Here. In your private home."

My refusal is automatic. Voice flat, I say, "I keep my private life separate from business."

She shakes her head like she knows me. Like she knows what I am. "Not anymore. Not if you want to make Diamond Freeport the most elite business venture in the world."

"What the *fuck* would I do with clients in this house?"

She's shocked by the *fuck*, but it only takes her a moment to shrug. "Throw a dinner party. Host a poker game. I don't know, give them pony rides and birthday cake and fireworks at midnight. The important thing is they're the only ones who ever set foot inside the door. They're the only ones who get that side of you. They're special. They're yours."

I poke the idea like a bruise. It's absurd, opening my home to *strangers*. That's why I built the office tower. That's why I'm investing in the conference center.

But my clients won't be strangers once we've shared business strategies. Once we've invested our fortunes together. Once my millions direct their billions and the freeport yields profits beyond my wildest dreams.

My dreams are fucking wild.

I study Ella's face. She's more animated than she's been since she entered Debasement. Engaged. Confident. I say, "You seem pretty sure of yourself."

"I am." She doesn't seem to realize how her spine straightens with her simple declaration.

"Because..." I prompt.

"Because people love being part of an exclusive group. The more exclusive the better. It's simple psychology. The dorsolateral prefrontal cortex, ventrolateral prefrontal cortex, and anterior cingulate cortex mediate the modulation of emotion-elicited activation in limbic regions."

I stare.

"What?" she asks.

"I love it when you talk brainy to me."

She blushes. Her cheeks stain red like I've told her how much I want to bury my face in her snatch, eating her out until she loses her voice screaming my name.

Like the Beast would ever let me do that...

I can't help it. I look at the cooktop clock. 7:46.

Shit. I've wasted six minutes. Six minutes I could have spent...

I lean across the island and take away the berries. "It's time," I say.

She swallows hard, and she's back to being the girl I met at Debasement. Shy. Nervous. Determined. "Time?" she asks, and my cock twitches as the quiver in her voice.

"Time for me to tell you exactly what I'm going to do to you. And time for you to decide if you're going to stay."

Chapter Nine

This must be what whiplash feels like.

One moment, I'm eating the sweetest fruit I've ever tasted in my life, sipping water that probably costs fifty bucks a bottle. The next, I'm spouting off psychology theory like I'm in the middle of a graduate seminar.

And now I'm facing a man who looks like he's stripped me naked in his mind, like my sexy dress and my lacy underthings have melted away from the heat of his blazing eyes.

I'm scared.

But I'm excited, too, excited like I can't remember ever being before. Certainly I never felt like this in bed with Jason. Jason was a boy. This is the first time I've ever been with a man.

I lick my lips. I take a deep breath. I force myself to meet Trap's gaze, and I say, "Yes."

"Yes, what?"

"Yes. I'll do whatever you want."

He shakes his head. "That's not the way this works. You can't say that until you hear exactly what I'm going to do you. What you're going to do to me. With me. For me."

Every time he says "me" the thing *down there* pulses. I'm pretty sure my pretty silk panties are damp, which they've never been before.

He doesn't know tonight is my night of *yes*. But this is his house. His rules. And the first rule seems to be I have to listen and agree. "Okay," I say. "Tell me."

He plants his hands in front of him, spreading his fingers wide on the granite island. I catch a flicker in his wrists, like he's fighting back the urge to play his imaginary scales.

"You'll walk upstairs to my bedroom," he says.

I nod.

"You'll take off all your clothes."

I nod.

"You'll enter my bathroom and turn on the shower, where you will wash exactly the way I order you to."

Order.

The word shoots through me. Alix wouldn't take orders from a stranger. She'd say *no* and leave.

But Ella likes the idea of being told what to do. She likes Trap being in charge. She trusts that he has a better imagination than she'll ever have.

I start to ask if he'll be watching me in the shower, but I already know the answer. I try to imagine what it will be like, if he'll order me to touch myself. If he'll make me wash *down there*.

Of course he will.

He's the victim of childhood trauma, apparently untreated. He's spent years developing workarounds to defuse the mis-firing of his traumatized brain. This elaborate ritual is apparently how he functions sexually.

Plus, it sounds incredibly exciting.

I nod.

"Say it out loud. Tell me you'll follow my orders in the shower."

"I— I'll follow your orders in the shower."

He must have been afraid I'd say no, because he exhales a huge breath. Then he comes to stand behind me. He leans in, his T-shirt pressing against the back of my dress, against my bare shoulders. He plants his arms beside mine, wide enough that we don't touch.

And he starts to whisper in my ear.

He tells me the rest of what he's going to do to me, every filthy word. My heart starts to race as I imagine giving up the control he demands. *No, no, no,* warns Alix.

Yes, sighs Ella.

I can feel the heat of his body. I can sense the wire strung through his limbs as, item by item, I consent.

"Yes, I'll follow your orders when you bind me."

"Yes, I'll follow your orders when you're gloved."

"Yes, I'll follow your orders..."

"Your orders..."

"Orders..."

Yes, yes, yes.

His voice is raw by the time he's finished. I'm shaking so hard he has to shift his arms, spread them wider to keep from touching me.

Everything he demands is sick. Perverted. Wrong. But Ella makes sure I say yes to every last command.

Finally, he grits: "And you'll be out of here by midnight."

"M—midnight?" I sound like I've never heard the word before. Somehow, I forgot my own limit on tonight. I forgot I need to be home before my keycard dies.

"No one sleeps over," Trap says, like it's some sort of punishment.

He's saving me from myself. "Yes," I say. "I'll be out of here by midnight."

Trap shudders at my final acceptance. I feel the ripple go through his chest and down my spine. He pulls away, releasing the cage that's held me, and I embarrass myself by moaning when the cool kitchen air kisses the nape of my neck.

He smirks as he rounds the granite island. He waits until I raise my chin, until I meet his jungle gaze.

"Are you a virgin, Ella?" he asks.

"Of course not!" I answer quickly, like that would be a terrible thing.

"Don't lie."

"I'm not lying!" And I'm not. Technically.

He waits for me to back down, but I don't. "I need to be sure," he says.

"If I were a virgin, would you send me home?"

"No," he answers slowly. "Not unless you ask to go. But if you're a virgin, I'll go more slowly. I'll do my best to keep from hurting you."

"I'm not a virgin," I confirm again. But I hear the warning, clearer than all the things I've already accepted. What Trap plans might hurt.

He nods, but I'm not sure he believes me. "We'll use a system," he says. "A code. If I ask you your color, green means you're fine. We can continue whatever we're doing. Yellow means you need more time. I'll slow down. Red is your safeword. Red means stop. Immediately. With those rules in place, with those protections, will you stay with me tonight?"

*Yes. This is the night of *yes*.*

"I'll stay," I say.

"Good girl."

I should bristle. I should fight. I'm not a girl; I'm a strong and independent woman.

But I think about the long nights since Jason walked out on me. I think about how I've touched myself. I think about all the books I've read and movies I've watched and how easy it's supposed to be to induce a sexual climax.

My brain knows Trap's proposal is a heart-stopping minefield. But my body wants to try. It wants to follow Traps rules, his commands. It thinks this controlling man might be the only person in the universe who can make it work the way it's supposed to.

"My good, good girl," Trap says, and the flutter *down there* is so strong I have to clutch the counter.

Chapter Ten

TRAP

Sweet holy fuck.

She'll do it.

She's not the first, of course. Four other women have listened to my rules and been brave enough to stay.

The blonde who brayed like a donkey.

The pharmaceutical rep with the mole behind her knee.

The marathon runner with thighs like steel.

The brunette who screamed for Daddy when she came.

I should remember their names, but they're nothing to me. Each of them was nothing the moment I called a car and got her out the gate.

But Ella is different. She's special.

I don't know her story, why she's dressed like a whore but acts like she's dedicated her pussy to God. Maybe that's what sparked, the moment I saw her at the top of the Debasement steps. She's innocent. Clean. Pure enough to sing the Beast to sleep.

She's smart, too. The smartest woman I've ever dragged back to Diamond. She's got a secret or two, just like me.

She's sad.

"Hey," she says. "I want to do this. I really do. But can I have a drink before we start?" Her laugh sounds a little crazy. "Just one, for courage."

I should tell her no. She should be stone-cold sober. She should have every last wit about her so her safeword's really safe.

Oh, fuck it. One goddamn drink.

"I don't have Grey Goose," I say. "How about Belvedere?"

A quick frown flicks across her face. I realize she doesn't recognize the brand name. I could tell her it's made from rye, that it's unfiltered and heavy on botanicals, floral with a citrus edge.

Or I could pour her a fucking drink.

I fetch two glasses from the cupboard. Ice cubes, three each. I pad into the dining room for the bottle, but I'm back before she thinks about following me.

I pour with a steady hand, like I'm measuring ingredients for a bomb. After I pass her a glass, I raise my own, swirling the clear liquor around the ice. Once. Twice. Three times. Four. Five.

Fuck. I haven't even touched her and the Beast is stepping in.

Ella follows my motion, flexing her own wrist like there's a right way and a wrong way, and she's determined to follow the rules. I salute her, just raising my glass between us, and she answers with her own.

Before I can sip, she tosses back her entire shot, downing it like it's medicine.

Medicine.

Belvedere is eighty proof, forty percent pure alcohol. If we were soldiers on a battlefield, we could use it to sterilize our wounds.

She sets her glass on the counter with a decisive clank, still shuddering from the vodka hitting the back of her throat. Her lips part, and the tip of her tongue emerges, soft and pink and ready to swipe clean the last film of Belvedere.

I surge forward and crush her mouth with mine.

Heat.

Soft, wet, heat.

She opens to me, offering up her timid tongue, and I savage her lips against her teeth. I need her, all of her. I need her pressure. I need her breath. I need her startled, muffled squeal that changes to a hum when I pull back enough to find her tongue with mine.

A normal man would fold his palm behind her head. He'd turn her head to a better angle, softening his lips in an invitation for her to press her body against his. He'd use his other hand to trace her curves, to make her feel good, to gain her trust.

I'm not normal. I'm broken and jagged and barely holding on to what passes for sane.

I grip the metal back of the stool she's sitting on, clench it tight enough that I hear my knuckles pop. I turn the chair, the whole chair, so I can deepen the kiss for both of us.

She stays with me. She tilts her head. She presses forward, breathing an urgent, wordless plea for more. Her hands move toward my shoulders, but she stops herself with a tiny gasp that I drink down with all the rest.

Fuck. I can't remember the last time I kissed a woman like this. Who am I kidding? I've *never* kissed a woman like this, not with this heat, not with this desperation, not with this bottomless, shattering need.

I want to devour her. I want to suck the breath out of her lungs. I want to drink the blood out of her veins. I want, I want, I want...

Gradually, my brain stirs back to life. I realize that I'm standing in my kitchen, hulking over a woman who's trapped between the iron back of a bar stool and a hard stone counter. I'm *kissing* a woman, mixing her spit with mine, breathing her breath with mine, exposing myself to everything she's brought into my house.

I soften my lips. I pull back. But before I lose her completely, before she pulls away, I catch her lower lip between my teeth. I feel its plump heat, its soft, wet weight, and I hear the moan that rises from her throat.

I bite her. My jaw tightens and my teeth close, hard enough to cause real pain. I tug, knowing it'll hurt her. I start to turn my head, to yank her lip between my clenched teeth, sharp enough to draw blood.

But I make myself step away.

Breathing like a stallion, I can't meet her eyes. I break my death-grip on the bar stool, loosening fingers that ache like they've been forced through the holes on a cheese grater. Flexing both hands, I force myself to grit out two damning syllables, "Color?"

She doesn't answer right away, and I know I'm a monster. I made a big show out of saying she'd have a choice, out of telling her every single way I was going to touch her, make her touch herself. And then I throw the entire fucking lie under the bus, jumping her like a rutting dog.

We had a deal, and I broke it. I lost the only thing I wanted before I even had a chance to see what it was.

"Wh—what?" she asks, her voice tiny and breathless and stunned. The back of her hand is pressed to her lip, and I realize I lost more control than I thought. She's bleeding.

"Color," I grit out. "Red? Yellow?"

"Green," she whispers. And then, as if she can't quite believe it herself, she says it again, full voice this time. "Green."

I see the question in her eyes. If I broke that rule, am I breaking all the others? Did I throw the entire playbook out with the booze?

For just a moment, I think about what that would be like. How it would feel to have a woman move under me any way she wanted. How her fingers would pull my hair as I ate her out, how her lips would close around my throbbing cock...

The Beast storms back like a Category 5 hurricane. Roaring, I pound the counter with my fist—once, twice, three times, four, five. I want to hurt myself. I want the bones in my hand to crack. I want to drive order back into my life. Power. Control.

When I can push words past the screaming monster in my brain, I repeat her single syllable. "Green."

She nods.

I swallow hard. "Then get your ass upstairs. In my shower. Now."

Chapter Eleven

ALIX

I brush my lip with my fingertips as I climb the stairs to the second floor. It feels tender, bruised, and I want to never stop touching it.

I've never had a man kiss me like that before. Like he's dying. Like he's drowning. Like I'm the only thing keeping him from spinning out in space.

At the top of the stairs, I turn to the right, to the master bedroom I could see from the ground floor. My knees do something funny when I see the huge bed; they buckle, and I have to take a quick three steps forward to stay on my feet.

When I turn around, Trap is filling the doorway. His arms are crossed over his broad chest, and his biceps pop in his tight black T. His feet are planted wide, like he's anchoring the world.

"Okay," he says. "Strip."

I look at the wall of windows. It's summer, so it's still light outside, but the sun is sinking into the thicket of trees at the far end of the sculpted lawn. No one can see inside. Yet. But the overhead lights are on a dimmer; the room is already filled with a golden glow. As twilight advances, Trap and I will be on display like actors in a play.

"You saw the gate," he says, as if I've spoken my fears out loud. "No one's getting back there. No one will see you but me." When I continue to hesitate, his voice cracks with command. "Ella! Strip!"

Alix is horrified. But Ella whispers *yes* as I work the side zipper on my dress. My fingers shake, triggered by equal parts of fear and anticipation. I've never done anything like this before. I've never *imagined* doing anything like this.

I wriggle out of my dress, letting it fall onto the thick white rug like a snake's shed skin.

The air in the room is cool, and my arms and legs immediately sprout goosebumps. They're not the only things reacting to the chill. The tips of my breasts harden so fast they hurt.

I catch my breath the same time Trap does. Part of me wants to close my eyes, to take myself away, to put miles and years between us.

But part of me wants to know what he's seeing. Part of me wants to know if I'm doing this right, if I'm being the woman he needs me to be.

His fingers tighten on his biceps as I twist for the back clasp on my bra. The two hooks break apart like he's bribed them. My breasts spill free as I slip the straps down my arms. I drop the bra on top of my dress.

"Shoes," Trap breathes.

I step out of the left stiletto, and then the right. The arches of my feet weep with relief as my bare soles settle onto the rug. I curl my toes, relishing my moment of freedom.

Trap's gaze strokes my legs, smoothing over my calves, my thighs. He settles hungrily on the scrap of lace around my hips. His intensity yanks the leash on the creature inside me, and I realize I'm more wet *down there* than I've ever been in my life.

He nods, and I slip my fingers beneath the edge of my panties. The lace feels like it's printed on my skin. I pull the soft silk over my hips and let it slide to the floor. I take a single step forward, completely naked.

I want to cover myself. I want to spread my fingers across my breasts. I want to hide the soft curls *down there*.

But more than that, I want to see the jungle light in Trap's eyes. I want him to be hungry. I want him to be mine.

Without waiting for his reminder, I skirt the bed. He's already told me what he needs next.

A wavy wall covered in tiny tiles separates the shower from the rest of the bathroom. As I round the bend, I see an array of four chrome controls. A rainfall shower head broader than my shoulders is suspended from the ceiling. Two jets are set in the wall, chest-high and waist-high. A hand-held spray snakes along beside them.

Remembering my instructions, I work the nearest control, waking the rainfall head. I set the temperature a notch short of scalding, just like Trap said I should. It seems like years have passed since he stood behind me in the kitchen.

It only takes a moment for steam to curl above the rainfall, a far cry from the ancient pipes I fight with every day at home. Trap has followed me; he's standing in the open doorway that leads out of this watery paradise. "Wash your hair," he prompts, his voice strangled.

Shampoo waits in a stone alcove, a sleek silver bottle from a brand I've never seen before. Conditioner stands beside it. My throat tightens when I see the other things on the shelf, but I ignore them for now.

I gasp when the scalding water hits my head. I start to reach for the control, to dial back the temperature, but I decide to give myself a moment, to see if I can adapt. After the initial shock, my body settles into the battering heat. My muscles soften like flame-licked candles, and a little of my nervousness swirls down the drain.

It's strange to wash my hair in front of someone else. The shampoo smells like rosemary, sharp and clean and cooler than the water turning my skin pink. I'm conscious of my fingers massaging my scalp; I wonder what it would feel like to have Trap's hands in my hair.

I lather and rinse, repeating just the way it says on the bottle. The second time I work in the shampoo, it foams up in billowy clouds that cascade down my body. I finish by conditioning, finger-combing the rich cream from scalp to tips.

When I've rinsed again, my hair is as heavy and sleek as the pelt of some wild animal. Nearly languid, I look to Trap for my next instruction.

"Razor," he says, like the single word costs more than he can afford.

I knew this was coming. He told me downstairs: "And then you'll shave." I retrieve soap from the alcove, a creamy white bar that feels like it's made of buttermilk and dreams. A few turns between my palms builds a thick lather. I use my right hand to smooth suds over my left armpit.

The razor is heavy, fashioned from steel instead of the cheap plastic throwaways I've used all my life. The head rotates like a precision surgical tool, and I glide it over the lather, slicing away the soap along with invisible stubble.

I make short work out of shaving under my right arm too. When I'm through, I return the razor to its shelf.

"Legs," Trap says.

Of course he wants my legs smooth. I should have realized that. I retrieve the soap and make more lather. It's awkward, bending down to work the razor around my ankle. I'm sure he's watching my bottom, but I can't make myself look up. I take my time, careful not to knick either knee.

When I finish, I look at Trap, eager for his nod of approval.

"Your bush," he says.

"Wh— what?"

"Shave your pubes."

I've never used that word in my life. I've certainly never shaved my pubic hair. I know some women get waxed, and I've read about something called a Brazilian. But I've never even considered doing that to myself.

"Color," Trap snaps.

I could tell him red and leave forever. But the hibernating beast *down there* chooses that moment to turn over, sending a lazy, rolling ripple from my neck to my knees.

It doesn't want red.

It doesn't even want yellow.

"Green," I breathe.

"Trim first," he says. "Short." And I finally understand why the nail scissors are waiting on the shelf.

I grab a deep breath, pick up the scissors, and trim. Short.

When I finish, Trap tells me to use the shaving gel. "Stroke down with the razor. The direction the hair grows."

There's something about his tone—patient, calm—that makes me stare. He's asking me to do revolting things, but he's taking care of me at the same time. He's almost—I test the word in my mind and it fits—*kind*.

I shave carefully, rinsing the last of my hair down the drain. When I finish, I cup water against myself with my fingers, taking care to wash away the last of the shaving gel.

I gasp in surprise at the heat against skin that hasn't been bare since I was a child. Every nerve has been jolted awake. I run my fingernail over the surface and a tremendous shiver rolls from the crown of my head to my toes. Every muscle in my body tightens, and I laugh in wonder.

Trap, though, is nowhere near as amused.

"Wash everything," he commands. His voice is strained, barely evolved from a groan. I stop splashing water against my smooth, smooth skin and really take the time to look at him.

His hands are planted on his hips. His feet are locked hip-width apart. His jeans bulge at his zipper.

I've seen an aroused man before. I once asked Jason if it hurt. But judging from the line of Trap's jeans, his thing is huge. My mind scrambles, and I try to remember everything he said he wants to do with it. A tremor of panic crawls across my belly.

"Start with your face," he says, like I haven't just been gaping at him. "End with your toes. Use the wall jets."

The instructions are exactly what I need. They give me something to concentrate on instead of my growing realization that this night with Trap will be my first with a total *man*.

I follow Trap's directions and use the soap. The shower's side jets have a lethal pressure. I lather and rinse my face, my arms, my belly.

"Wash your tits," Trap says, and I was foolish to think he wouldn't notice what I skipped.

"But the jet—" I start to say. If I finish the sentence, he'll ask me my color, and I already know I'll say green. So I soap my breasts, hoping Trap doesn't realize how small they are. The jet of water pounds my nipples exactly the way I feared it would, but the pain quickly ripens into something close to pleasure.

I wash my feet and my calves, knowing I'm ignoring Trap's demand to end with my toes. One glance confirms his tolerant smile; he understands exactly what I'm doing. My delay won't make a bit of difference in the long run.

I soap my shaved skin, nearly mesmerized by the new sensation. Before I can lose my nerve, I reach between my legs.

"Spread your lips," Trap says.

Obediently, I stretch my mouth into an O.

"Your pussy lips," he snaps. A wicked blush roasts my face, and for just a moment, I wonder if it's possible to faint from embarrassment.

To give myself time to recover, I roll the soap between my palms, slipping the bar over and over the mountains of suds. It squirts from my grasp, skating to the far corner of the shower. Instead of chasing after it, I ease my left hand between my legs. I use my index finger and my middle finger to part my folds. My right hand follows with the lather, slipping, sliding, smothering myself with foam.

"Rinse," Trap says, the word almost a groan.

I turn toward the jet that's targeted at my waist. I arch my back to frame the water's spray with my pelvis. Bracing myself for what I know I can't escape, I expose everything *down there* to the full force of the water.

Soap cascades down my thighs. My left hand plays the music it learned just a moment ago, my fingers angling, stretching. The jet pounds against me, pounds *into* me, a searing column of liquid heat.

My bottom grows tight. My hips push forward. My left hand splays wider, as if it's possible to bare more of me to the water. I realize my right hand is gripping my breast, cradling my aching nipple against my palm.

I want...

I need...

I'm so close...

I'm almost there...

And the jet of fire turns to a piercing spear of ice.

I yelp at the invasion, jackknifing forward. My hands shoot out, blocking the freezing spray. My entire body trembles like I've just completed a marathon, and I barely find the coordination to turn toward the temperature controls.

Trap is there, his huge hand covering the lever. His message is clear: He's the person in control. He's the one who decides what I do and when and how I do it.

I start to shiver as he snaps, "Wash your asshole."

"Th— the water's too cold."

"Get the fucking soap."

The rainfall from above is freezing. The jet directed at my chest is a javelin. The one I rode below is a solid rod of ice.

My teeth start to chatter, but I cross the tile floor and retrieve the bar of soap. I roll it over my hands quickly. My fingers shake as I force myself back to the icy jets.

"P— please," I start to beg for an exception.

Trap's eyes are colder than the water. "Wash. Your. Asshole."

Humiliated, I spread my legs. I bend forward. I spread my cheeks with one hand and use the other to clean myself. My embarrassment is almost hot enough to counter the freezing water.

When the suds finally circle the drain, Trap turns off the spray on all three controls. I splutter and gasp, shuddering like a spent horse. Trap moves outside the tiled wall, only to return with a stack of terry towels. He hands me one and hangs the other two from hooks on the wall.

"Dry off," he says. "Then back to the bedroom. You're clean enough to fuck."

Chapter Twelve

TRAP

I circle the bed, testing the leather restraints I've anchored at each corner. It never crossed my mind Ella would try to get off in there. She seems too...naive. Too pure. She doesn't have a clue how she looked in there.

The Beast cranks its vise around the base of my skull, but I argue I'm following the rules. Ella's clean now. She's safe.

The Beast says no. Ella took the reins. She managed her own pleasure. What will she do next? Touch me when I least expect it? I have to put her in her place. She has to know who's in control.

The Beast can gag on my ten-inch cock.

I talk a big game. But I know from past experience that the Beast can melt my rod with a single swipe of its slimy claws. It can kill a day-long hard-on with just one whisper about the worst memory in my life. It can lock me in a light-less room for days, weeks, months.

Fine. I'll do what I have to do. I'll show Ella who's boss.

She comes in from the bathroom, swaddled in a towel that covers her from chin to knees. She's done her best to dry her hair, tousling the ends till they curl above her tits. She looks vulnerable. Sweet.

I'm even gruffer than I need to be. "Drop the towel and get on the bed. On your back."

She climbs onto the mattress, giving me a clear view of her ass. My mouth fills with spit, and I barely resist the urge to bite her hard enough to mark.

Before I can imagine what the Beast would demand for that improvisation, Ella finds the middle of the bed. She's precise, like she calculated her spot with a tape measure. I've left her a pillow, a cradle so she can watch everything I do. I don't want her craning her neck.

She thinks she'll be safe there. She thinks she's out of harm's way. Her knees are pinned together like a Mother's Day corsage and her arms are two-by-fours nailed to her sides.

I stride to the headboard and snap my fingers. She jumps like I've fired a rifle. "Wrist," I order.

She closes her eyes, but she presents her hand. I close her into the cuff, tugging hard to make sure she can't free herself. The Beast demands its due because I touched another person, even a clean one, and I play a quick one-two-three-four-five on the headboard.

I walk around the bed and snap again. Good girl. Ella learns fast. I take the hand she offers and tighten the cuff, pulling a little harder than I have to. When I'm done, I trace my thumb across her palm, pressing just enough for her fingers to curl in. I'm making a promise. Or maybe I'm saying I'm sorry.

The Beast isn't impressed. It makes me answer twice, playing double penance above Ella's bird-like wrist.

At the foot of the bed, I snap for Ella's right foot, but her knees stay locked.

Impatient, I snap again.

Nothing.

"Ella," I warn, my voice liquid steel.

She whimpers a little, but she slides her heel across the bed. I'm vicious with the cuff, determined she'll never break free. The contact costs me another five notes, this time played against the footboard.

Ella's little rebellion is over by the time I reach her left foot. Her heel has already crossed the bed. She's waiting.

After she's secured, I run my index finger down her sole. Her foot twitches, and a shiver runs all the way up her leg. She smells clean, like rosemary and soap.

Of course, the Beast doesn't care. It makes me pay for the contact, three times for good measure.

Ella's pussy is bare to the world, flawless orchid folds beneath her swollen clit. Her breath catches, and my attention is dragged from the paradise between her legs to her face. The flush of the shower has faded from her cheeks. Tiny folds crease her forehead.

"Color?" I ask, almost choking on the fear that I've already pushed her too far, too fast.

She swallows hard and I think she'll tap out. But then she whispers, "Green."

My good girl. My good, brave girl.

My cock surges, heavy as an anvil.

The Beast mutters in my ear, insisting Ella can't be trusted. If I had any other woman in my bed, I'd circle around to the nightstand now and take out a pair of gloves—black silk to keep me clean. Safe. I'd climb onto the bed. I'd kneel between my clean girl's legs and use my covered hand to…

The Beast says fuck that. I have to make sure Ella knows who's in charge.

My cock thinks the Beast is on to something. Usually, it has to wait its turn. Ladies first, after all. But tonight, it's heavy as a log, my heart buried somewhere deep inside, pounding a drumbeat that shakes my balls.

I tear off my shirt. I rip the belt from my jeans. I shove my boxers to the floor and free my eager dick. The Beast crows its approval.

Scrambling onto the bed, I ignore Ella's gasp of surprise. I spit into my right hand and close it around my eager cock. My left hand clutches my balls, squeezing hard enough to make even the Beast happy.

I stroke myself from root to tip, my fingers tight. My breath comes in short, sharp huffs like I've just come off a six-minute mile.

Ella pulls away, stretching toward the far side of the bed, but I did my job well. There's no way she's escaping. I want to tell her this is the only way I can keep her safe, the only way I can appease the Beast, but it will take too long to say the words, and she might never believe me anyway.

Another stroke, a vicious tug, hating myself, healing myself. One more, and my balls seize up, high and tight and hard as baseballs. I bellow as I pull again, a wordless shout of rage and glory.

I come.

Spunk arcs from my cock to Ella's belly. She freezes at the first hot splash, and then I paint her, thick shiny cords lashing her soft, clean flesh.

She's mine. She's helpless. I'm the one in absolute control.

I work my cock until I'm pumped dry, until I shiver, until I'm ashamed. I crash forward on hands and knees, my head hovering over Ella's belly. The bleachy smell of cum drowns out my sweet girl's rosemary and soap.

The Beast is cackling like a hyena. I brace myself to ask Ella her color, to find out if this is the end of our night together.

But when I find her eyes, they're gleaming. Her frown has somehow transformed into a brilliant, close-lipped smile. She looks like someone has told her a secret. Like she just learned the punchline to an ancient, dirty joke.

"Green," she says, before I can ask. "Oh my God, green."

Chapter Thirteen

I should be disgusted. I entered Trap's bedroom the cleanest I've ever been in my life. Now, I'm a filthy mess, a woman's who's been used like a life-less sponge.

And I'm happier than I've ever been in bed with a man.

I made him that excited. *I* pushed him beyond his control.

I don't think he even realized the things he was saying, the words he chanted as he hulked over me. Eff me. Eff himself. Eff the effing eff in his brain.

But that moment when he actually reached his climax? He was free. He was broken and open and almost blindingly pure.

I can smell his semen on my skin. It's like sunshine and fresh-cut grass and it makes the creature *down there* more than a little crazy.

As soon as I give him my color, he climbs off the bed. He yanks open his nightstand drawer and pulls out a pair of gloves. They're black fabric, the sort of thing a serial killer would wear.

But Trap's not a killer. Trap's a man wrestling with some horrific trauma. I want to tell him not to use the gloves, to try touching me without them, but I'm not his therapist. I'm not so naive that I think pleasuring himself over my body will cure his compulsive state forever.

He mounts the bed again, climbing over my leg so that he's kneeling in the triangle between my thighs. He rests his weight on his forearms, bringing his face so close I think he's going to kiss me.

I squirm, desperate to cover myself with my hands. Jason said I was smelly *down there*. I can't imagine why Trap would possibly want to stare at me. But this is one of the things he told me about in the kitchen. I don't understand why he wants to do this, but I'm ready.

He taps me, and my body tries to jump three feet into the air, stopped only by the bonds on my wrists and ankles.

I guess I wasn't really ready.

"What—" I start to say, but he's doing it again, tapping the most private part of me.

He sets a rhythm, steady and fast. He flutters his fingers, one to the next to the next, like his compulsion ritual but faster. Then he settles into a steady, insistent drumbeat—*tap, tap, tap*.

"Oh my God," I say without thinking. "That feels amazing."

"Good, Ella. Talk to me. Tell me what you like."

I don't have words for that. But he shifts back to triplets, and my ankles strain against their bonds. I want to close my knees because the things he's doing are too intense. I want to keep my knees open forever.

I have to move. I can't move. He tied me to the bed, and I let him do it without a word of protest.

I'm bad. Dirty. I should tell him to stop. I should tell him we're done.

He drops a finger, or maybe it's his thumb, on the sensitive ridge of flesh between my front and back. The weight is amazing. It stretches me *down there*. It makes every touch at the front echo through my body, every tap of his finger.

The hungry animal inside me insists I arch my hips. I know that puts my private parts closer to his face, which he must find disgusting, but I can't stop myself.

"Please," I beg, tears leaking from my eyes.

"More," I plead.

"Faster. Faster. Faster."

My toes point. My calves stretch. My thighs petrify into stone.

This is better than the water jet in the shower. This is better than anything I ever did with Jason. This is better than any dream I've ever had of helping myself, of freeing myself, of unlocking the door to pleasure.

I'm close, so close. My head thrashes. My fingers curl into fists, fighting to break free from the headboard.

Trap delivers a single, devastating tap.

The creature inside me pulls into a tiny, fur-wrapped ball.

Another tap.

The creature whines.

One more tap.

The creature explodes, gasping and flailing, firing every neuron in my brain at the chaotic speed of light. I'm clutching, I'm gasping, I'm screaming an endless, everlasting *YES!*

I ride the waves back to my body, back to the bed. Trap hasn't stopped. His fingers still work their impossible magic, softer and gentler, tapping flesh too sensitive to tolerate his attention.

No. Not too sensitive.

Just sensitive enough.

My body pulls together, tighter, tighter, tighter, and this time when I explode, I fall through an endless pile of cotton clouds.

After a century, sensation rushes back to my ankles and my wrists. I can feel a thousand tiny abrasions where I struggled against my bonds. My right calf twitches, threatening to seize up in a painful cramp, but I flex my foot and it subsides.

Once I asked Leo was meth was like. He thought a long time, and then he said, "Like sex with a person who knows what you need before you even think to ask for it."

I pretended like I knew what he was talking about.

Now, I finally do. And maybe for the first time in my life, I understand why my brother is an addict.

"Oh my God," I say, and my voice sounds very far away. "That was amazing." I force myself to open my eyes. "*You're* amazing," I say to Trap.

He's sitting back on his heels, eyeing me with a smug grin. "Welcome back," he says.

"I never..." I struggle to sit up. Somehow I'm still bound to the bed. It seems like the restraints should have incinerated when my mind left my body.

"Okay," I say, and my voice is a little steadier. "I need to clean up. I'm a mess."

"You're perfect," he says, and he runs his gloved fingers down the inside of my thigh. I can feel the streak of wetness he leaves behind, *my* wetness, and I consider dying of embarrassment.

"Come on," I say. "Let me go."

"No." His voice is steady. Absolute. He's back in full command. "Not yet. We're only starting to play."

Chapter Fourteen

TRAP

She has her safeword if she really wants me to free her.

The sight of her pussy quivering in aftershock makes my cock twitch. I catch the moment she realizes I'm staring at her snatch. There's the blush I've come to expect, the hot wash of color over her cheeks.

I've never heard a woman scream the way she did when she came. She said she wasn't a virgin, and I took her at her word. But I'll bet the entire freeport that was the first time she ever came.

It won't be the last.

I climb off the bed and make my way to the bathroom. Behind me, I hear her little mew of disbelief, and I smile. The towel I want is hanging beside the sink, but I take my time slipping it from the bar.

"Trap?" she calls. And then, with a little more urgency, "Trap!"

I run water in the sink, soaking half the hand towel. I use my left hand, letting my silk glove flood with water. I keep my right hand free. I don't want to wash away the scent of Ella's pussy.

She's panting as I come back to the bedroom, yanking at the bonds that hold her wrists. "Hush," I say, the terrycloth hot and heavy in my hand.

She's a good girl. She falls silent the second I climb onto the bed.

A drop of warm water falls from the towel to her belly, rolling into the sweet divot of her navel. I want to trace its path with my tongue, but the Beast would throw a fit.

Instead, I wash my Ella clean.

Some of my come has dried, flaking like pearly glitter. The thicker ropes, though, are still liquid—heavy and sticky. I clean her belly first, using broad swipes of the towel. The terry and my gloves keep the Beast at bay.

The towel is warm, but Ella's clean belly cools quickly. I measure the temperature by the peaks of her nips—two bullets rising out of soft brown targets.

I wash her small tits, bunching the towel so I can make quick, short strikes. She moans at the attention, arching her back like she's offering me a feast, but I know I can't indulge. Her head falls back on the pillow and her knees twitch, trying to draw together.

Pinching her left nipple between folds of cloth, I tighten my fingers to scrub away the last of my come, twisting hard to do the job right. She gasps, and her eyes fly open.

"Yellow!" she barks.

I pull back immediately, dropping my towel-covered hand to the thousand-count sheet. My good, good girl, keeping herself safe.

Some twisted part of me, something deep inside my lizard brain, is grateful she used the safeword. If she said *yellow* now then I can have faith she'll say *red* when she needs to. I can push her. I can trust her. The Beast won't win tonight.

"I'm sorry," she says. "I shouldn't have—"

"Stop." I cut her off. "You did exactly the right thing."

"It was just so intense. My erogenous zones have never been so sensitive."

She sounds like she's reporting symptoms to a doctor. From the blush on her cheeks, she feels about as sexy as a hospital patient, too.

I want to scrub the formal words from her mind. I want to tear her down to single syllables—tits and nips, clit and cunt, cock and balls and hard, hot, fuck.

"I'm sorry," she says again, and a desperate panic rattles beneath her words. She doesn't want to leave my bed. She's not ready to be done.

"No apologies," I say. "Breathe."

She takes in a short, sharp gasp.

"No," I say. "Relax. *Breathe.*" I take my own deep breath, showing her how it's done. My cock thinks I'm calling a meeting; I'm hard again, and I can't imagine how much I'd ache if I hadn't shot my load before I started playing with fire.

"That's right," I say, as she imitates me. "You're fine. You're safe. Keep that up. I'll be right back."

I take the towel back to the bathroom and collect another one from the rack. Soft terry. Warm water. I know exactly how to finish the job now.

"There you go," I say, returning to find her exhaling on a four count. "I'm almost done here. I promise this won't hurt."

I wash her right tit like I'm polishing an opal—soft, soft, feather-soft swipes. Her nip gets just as dark as the one I pinched, just as hard, but I treat it like a treasure. Just a touch on the side... A brush across the top... A soft, sweet stroke all around.

Her breath catches and, out of the corners of my eyes, I see her hands curl into fists. She's so responsive, so tightly strung...

If I were a normal man, I'd take that nip in my mouth. I'd roll it with my tongue. I'd suck on it hard, then soft, letting her moans tell me just how much she can take. I'd get her so turned on she'd *beg* to feel my teeth. I'd wedge my knee in the hot, wet V between her legs, give her something to ride while I pinched the left side, bit the right side, taking away the burn with my hot, wet tongue. I'd stretch her. Pull her. Back away and laugh as she begged and then I'd flick her with my fingers, again, again, again until she opened beneath me, folded around me, coming hot and hard and heavy, screaming my name.

Fuck.

I'm not normal; the Beast sees to that. But I'm hard as a diamond, my cock aching with every pulse of my heart.

Ella's clean now.

Safe.

And with my soft touch and her sensitive *erogenous zones*, she's ready for anything I need.

It's time now—even the Beast agrees.

I take the towel back to the bathroom and slap it down beside the sink. My hard-on is in charge now, making it difficult to think. It pulls me back to the bed.

I intend to go straight to my dresser, to the bottom drawer with its combination-locked chest, but I make the mistake of looking at the wall of windows. The sun has set. It's dark outside. I can't make out a hint of the patio, the lawn, the distant line of trees.

All I can see is Ella. My Ella. Spread-eagled and waiting. Her legs must be getting tired now. Her arms must be starting to ache. She's raising her head from her pillow, and she's watching me, waiting for me, trusting me.

The windows blur her beauty. They turn her skin to gold. They darken the shadow of her pussy so I can't make out the dark pink home it's time to claim as mine.

The Beast growls, making sure I haven't forgotten its rules.

I tear my gaze away from the windows and yank open the dresser drawer. It takes me three tries to work the combination. My right glove is slick with Ella, the left with the water I used to bathe her. It's almost time to take them off. Almost time to be free.

The lock finally clicks, and I raise the lid to stare at all the tools the Beast has taught me to use.

"What are you doing?" Ella calls from the bed.

She's a good girl. She deserves to know. I lift the box out of the drawer and carry it over to the bed.

My cock is as hot as a fireplace poker and every bit as hard. It twitches when I take out the string of foil packets that will keep it safe.

I show Ella the rubbers, and her face floods with relief. I can read her so easily now, pick up on all of her emotions. I know the way her mind works. Any man who thinks of protection at a time like this is a man who can be trusted.

The box has tools for other times, other uses. I take out the gag, the one I told her I'd use, when we were down in the kitchen. The silicone ball floats in its leather harness, looking big enough to choke her. I won't use it now. I don't want to take away her choices. She's already said *yellow* once, and I need her mouth free to say it again.

Setting aside the gag, I show her the dildo. Its ridged rubber is half again as large as my own huge cock, traced with massive veins designed to push against her clit. Ella's eyes grow wide, and she shrinks away. I could teach her. I could coach her. I could get her to take the whole damn thing, but that won't give me the release I need tonight.

I put back the dildo and take out the vibrator. It doesn't try to look real; it's got a bulb no woman could manage and a panel with three speeds, along with a snaking electric cord so it never gets tired. Ella looks interested, and for a heartbeat I consider giving her what she wants, but my cock jerks hard, and the vibrator goes back in the box too.

My fingers close around the tool I need. I'm not sure Ella will recognize it. I don't want to scare her. I hope it won't hurt her. Because this is what the Beast commands.

The black rubber looks evil. The ridges look hard. It looks longer and thicker and far more brutal than any body can take. The flared base is as wide as my palm, a mercy, another way of keeping her safe, but Ella might not understand.

I take out the lube first. She needs to know I'll help.

I didn't think my cock could get harder, but it's had enough with my delays. Steeling myself with a steady breath, I meet Ella's trusting gaze.

And I show her the butt plug she needs to take before she's clean enough, safe enough that the Beast will let me fuck her sweet little cunt.

Chapter Fifteen

ALIX

"No."

The word is out of my mouth before I can stop it. It's like my body is completely separated from the brain that came up with the whole "we're saying *yes* to everything tonight" idea. My arms try to contract, to cross over my chest, even though I can't move an inch. My hips rotate in as my knees fight to touch. Every cell in my body rejects that rubber monster instinctively.

Trap flips open the cap on the tube he showed me. It's lubricant, and he squirts a generous dollop on top of that black nightmare. I shake my head more vehemently. There's no way that thing can fit inside my vagina.

I find my words. "You didn't tell me about this downstairs."

He didn't. He told me I'd have to wash. He said he'd tie me to the bed. He said I'd orgasm—*come*, he said—when he touched me. But he didn't say he'd impale me with that terrifying black thing.

"You're right," he says. "I should have. But I didn't want to scare you. You can take this. I'd never ask you to do something you aren't capable of doing. You already know I'll slow down when you need me to."

I shake my head again. "No."

But I don't say *yellow*.

And I don't say *red*.

I want him to know I'm scared. I want him to know I've never had anything close to that size inside me. I want him to set it aside, to say it's a joke, to say he really means to use his own impressive thing, that's the way we'll make love.

But he's told me the rules. I know the way to make him stop, and it's not by saying *no*. *No* doesn't count. In this room, *no* is the same as *yes*.

"Please," I say. "Don't put that thing inside me."

I mean the words. I don't want it anywhere near me. But I realize this is part of what *he* needs—me pleading with him. He needs me to pretend I want him to stop.

I pull on my bonds, acting like I want to get away from him. His thing leaps like I've touched it. He's excited by my pretended fear.

And so am I.

I know I can stop him any time; he proved that when he hurt my breast. So I can afford to play this game now. "Please," I beg. "It's too much."

That's true. And there are more true things I can say. "I've never done this before. I don't know what sort of woman you usually bring here, but I don't do this kind of thing."

The words tumble out, faster and faster. I breathe harder, like I'm terrified.

I'm ashamed to admit it, but this game is…fun. There's power in saying the words, in playing the role. Now I understand why my safeword isn't *no*, why we aren't using *stop*. When I'm certain I'm safe, certain I'm in control, it's exciting to pretend he's forcing me.

"You can't," I say, purposely breaking my voice, like I'm sobbing. "Please. Let me go. I promise I won't tell anyone."

Trap is kneeling between my legs. His thing is engorged. He's more excited than I've seen him tonight, and that makes me excited too. He puts a hand under my thigh, spreading me even wider than the cuffs around my ankles. He slides his fingers up, spreading them, supporting me, supporting my bottom until I'm arched as far off the bed as I can possibly be.

"Don't make me do this," I plead. "I'll do anything else. Anything you ask. Just not this. Please, please, please…"

He shoves the black rubber against my anus.

I yelp.

The sound pops out of me, like a dog or maybe a seal. I thrash in my bonds, really fighting, really trying to get away.

My *bottom*? He thinks he can put that thing inside my *butt*?

He must be surprised by my fighting because he swears, combinations of words I've never heard before. He's calling me a beast, which doesn't make sense. An effing, GD beast.

His swearing doesn't make sense. His gloved grip on my thigh doesn't make sense. His thinking he can fit that monster rubber *thing* in my butt doesn't make sense.

Yellow. The word's right there. I can say it.

But I don't want to.

He gave me my first orgasm ever. He made my body do things it's never done for anyone else.

I owe him.

And I want to make him happy.

And if he thinks I can take that thing, then he must be right.

I make a conscious effort to stop pulling away. I try to relax my legs. I do my best to ease the trembling that's taken over my arms.

"Good girl," he says.

I've never wanted to be anyone's *girl*. I'm a woman. A grown, thinking, perfectly competent woman.

But when Trap says *girl*, I know exactly what he means. He's taking care of me. He's protecting me. He's helping me be the best person I can be.

He brings the rubber back to my bottom. Every muscle from my belly to my knees squeezes tight in rebellion. I can't help it. It's like my body knows what he's asking his wrong. Is impossible.

"Relax," he says, pressing steadily.

"If you think this is easy, then *you* try it!" I'm as surprised as he is when I snap. Our little game is over.

He chuckles and pushes harder.

It hurts.

Without my giving my body permission, it tries to squirm away. I can only move a few inches in any direction. My arms are really shaking now, like I've been out in a snowstorm for hours. My hips flex left, then right, desperate to escape his grasp.

"Just...stay...still!"

He's more determined than ever and fire sears inside me and I know how much this much means to him and my body can't stretch any more and there must be a reason he's doing this and I'm splitting in two and he's hollering again and I'm tearing apart and he calls me a beast and this will never end and it hurts, it hurts, it hurts...

"Red!" I shout, knowing that if he doesn't stop, I'll die.

Chapter Sixteen

TRAP

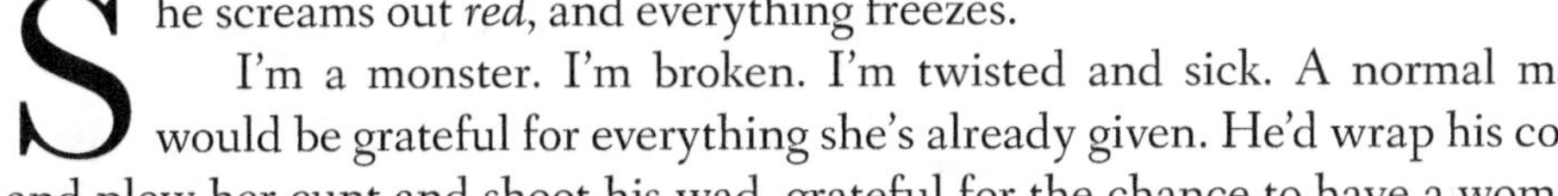

She screams out *red*, and everything freezes.

I'm a monster. I'm broken. I'm twisted and sick. A normal man would be grateful for everything she's already given. He'd wrap his cock and plow her cunt and shoot his wad, grateful for the chance to have a woman like Ella in his bed in the first place.

The Beast says I can't do that.

The Beast says Ella has to be clean.

The Beast says Ella has to take the plug.

Red.

I need to plug her ass.

Red.

I need to prove that I'm the one in control, I'm the one who makes the rules, I'm the one who decides who can and cannot fuck.

Red.

I need to scrub the Beast out of my life, I need to strangle it, shred it, kill it fucking forever.

Red.

Kill the Beast. Kill the Beast. Kill the Beast.

Red.

Chapter Seventeen

ALIX

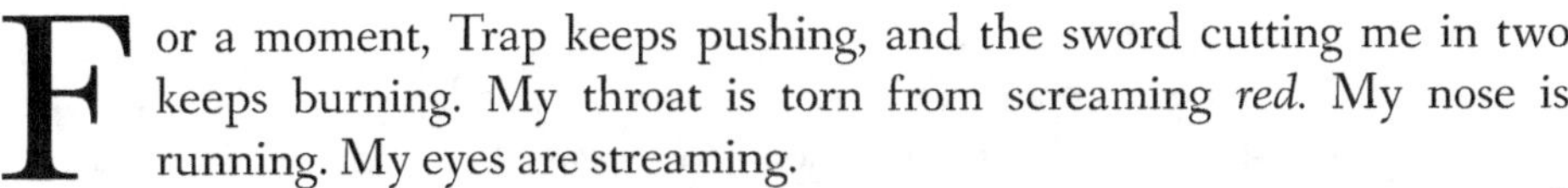

For a moment, Trap keeps pushing, and the sword cutting me in two keeps burning. My throat is torn from screaming *red*. My nose is running. My eyes are streaming.

Through my tears, I can see Trap's face. His mouth is twisting around horrible words. His eyes, his jungle eyes, are on fire, a rim of flame around pupils so wide I wonder if he's drugged.

He kneels there, magically turned to stone. His hands don't move. His arms don't move. He's balanced on the edge of a ravine so deep I can't imagine the floor.

And then, with a bellow like an elephant dying in a pit, he pulls that thing out of me and throws it across the room.

Gasping for breath, he fumbles at the bonds around my left ankle. His fingers slip, and he tries again; he squares his shoulders and makes one more try.

My left leg is free. My right. He scrambles to the top of the bed and releases my right wrist. Hurries around to free my left.

It hurts to bring my arms to my sides; they burn like they'll never move that way again. I want to be brave; I want to be good, but a sob rips out of my throat.

Trap is back; I didn't even realize he'd left the room. He's holding a glass of water in one hand, and there's a sky-colored blanket draped over the opposite arm. I really must be out of it, because I didn't even see when he pulled on a pair of boxers. He's taken off his gloves, too.

He puts the water on his nightstand and climbs onto the bed with the blanket. I try to move, intending to give him room, but every muscle in my body protests. I settle for curling into a ball.

He whispers something, nonsense sounds, the type of things a jockey mutters to a frightened horse. He unfolds the blanket and covers me, which is when I realize I'm shivering hard, my teeth clattering together like a bad Halloween toy.

"You're safe," he says, tucking the blanket in closer. "You're fine." He repeats the words, over and over, like a child's spell against monsters in the dark.

"I— I'm c—cold," I say, or try to shape the words with my clumsy lips.

He scoots up to the headboard, retrieving the pillow that was under my head and stashing it behind his back. He leans toward me, and I'm not sure if he lifts me, or if I crawl toward him, but suddenly I'm cradled against his body.

My spine curls against his belly, only the blanket between us. I sit in the V of his bowed legs, my knees tucked almost beneath my chin. His arms fold around me and my head nestles in the hollow between his chin and his shoulder. He squeezes me tight, supporting me with his arms and legs. The blanket feels like a cloud between us.

"You're fine," he whispers. "You're safe. My good, good girl."

When I finally stop shivering, he leans away and I manage to mew a protest. But he's only reaching toward the nightstand. He brings me the glass of water, tilting it gently so I can take one swallow, two, and then he lets me drain the whole thing with greedy little grasps.

He leans away again, and this time I believe he'll be back. He fumbles for something beneath the lamp, and he comes back with a golden packet the length of his thumb. Reaching around me, keeping me close, he fiddles with it until he's released a tantalizing dark-brown square, which he promptly breaks in two.

He places one of the pieces between my lips, centering it on my fledgling tongue, and the taste of chocolate shoots to the base of my brain. It's creamy and dark, with notes of coffee and smoke and just a hint of the berries he fed me a lifetime ago.

When it's melted, he feeds me the rest of the square, and another whole piece after that. I feel each individual molecule of the chocolate hit my bloodstream. My brain comes online, module by module. Fingers. Toes. Arms. Legs. Motions. Memories. Words.

"What was it?" I finally ask. "What *happened* to make you need that?"

He stiffens beneath me. He already answered my question, at least in part —back at Debasement a lifetime ago, when I was trying to decide if it was safe to get in his car. He was hurt as a child. I understand that. But I have to know more—what kind of hurt. What made him be this way. When he stays silent, I ask, "Why are you *so* afraid to touch?"

I think he'll pretend not to hear me. Pretend not to understand. Maybe he'll distract me with another piece of chocolate or a second glass of water.

But he shakes his head, a single terse twitch. "Not touch," he says after a long pause. "I'm not afraid to touch. I'm afraid of germs."

Mysophobia, my brain immediately supplies. I can picture the page in my freshman year *Abnormal Psychology* textbook—the cycle of compensating behaviors that get worse and worse when the root cause is left untreated.

"Germs," I say, so he knows I'm listening. I hope he knows I care. I don't want to push him, but he said the word out loud and from the weary disgust in his voice, he's been holding it in for a very long time.

He says, "I told you I touched something when I was a kid."

He hesitates for long enough that I think he's changed his mind. Afraid of shutting him down completely, I wait. And wait. And wait.

"I was twelve," he finally says. "My parents got divorced the year before. I did screwy things after they split. I'd sort my baseball cards for hours, like if I got them in the perfect order, Mom and Dad would get back together. I had a ritual for eating, all the red things first, then green, white, brown. I had a plan for bedtime—take a shower for exactly five minutes, read exactly five pages of a book, turn my pillow over exactly five times."

"You were trying to control your environment."

"My mother would have agreed with you. Dad called me a faggot and told me to get my shit together."

"That wasn't fair!"

"Dad wasn't real big on fair."

He falls silent again, and I wonder what memories he's working through. I hate the fact that he suffered as a child. I want to find his father and tell him off.

Trap goes on, like I've actually figured out something useful to say. "Dad had a major business opportunity come up, in DRC, Congo, and he decided to take me with him. I didn't know it at the time, but he broke his custody arrangement with Mom. On the plane, he said he was going to toughen me up. Make me a man."

"You must have been terrified!"

"He was my father." Trap's voice is bitter, like he needs to spit. "He had to know what was best."

Another pause, this one the longest yet. Even through the blanket, I can feel the tension in Trap's body. His chest is as tight as the corners on a hospital bed. His fingers clench and release like he's scrubbing filthy laundry in a stream.

He's said all he can. He can't push himself more. So *I* do the pushing. I ask, "What happened?"

He sighs, and I never knew human lungs could hold so much air. "Dad had a couple of business partners—two guys from South Africa who scared the shit out of me. All the white men were armed—rifles to cover the workers, with handguns just in case. People—children—hauled tons of earth out of holes fifty feet deep, day after day after day..."

"What were they doing?"

"Mining diamonds."

Diamonds. Like Diamond Freeport.

"How long were you there?"

"Less than a year." He seems grateful for the easy answer. But then he says, "The mine was shut down. Quarantined. There was an ebola breakout, and ninety-seven workers died."

"Oh my God!"

"My father decided it was time to bug out. But first he stole from his partners—a ten-pound bag of the finest diamonds the mine produced."

"Ten pounds—" I start to say. Not much. Not worth haunting Trap for decades.

"Cut and polished, worth about a hundred mill."

I'm too shocked to respond.

But he's rolling now. "One hundred million dollars. In a kid's backpack. *My* backpack."

"The partners caught you with the diamonds?"

He shakes his head. "My father hid me where he knew they'd never look."

I wait. He seems to think I already know the answer.

When I can't come up with anything, he blows a short breath through stiff lips. "He put me in the morgue."

"Oh, Trap!"

"He put me in the aluminum hut where they stored the bodies. He left me with my backpack, five gallons of water, and a stack of army surplus field rations."

"But *ebola*. How did you survive? Isn't it one of the most contagious viruses in the world?"

"Only if you touch a corpse. It isn't transmitted by air."

"You poor..." I'm too horrified to finish. I start to imagine the heat, the stench, the *terror*... I try to stop before I'm overwhelmed.

"He taped out a square on the floor. He told me not to move outside it, no matter what happened. He said if I did, I'd die bleeding from every hole in my body. He told me to wait for him, and he'd be back when the coast was clear."

"And did he? Come back?"

Trap shakes his head. "Ten days later, the spacemen came."

"Spacemen?"

"Relief workers, in hazmat suits."

"What happened to your father?"

I feel him shrug, the same one-shoulder twitch I thought was casual in Debasement. "He was in the field hospital when the relief workers found me, already in a coma. He died the next day."

"What happened to *you*?"

"They kept me in quarantine for a month. Then they passed me from government agent to government agent. I didn't have a passport or visa. Dad had greased palms every step of the way to get us in country. I think they finally sent me home because I was too fucking weird to keep around."

I'm offended for the lost and frightened child he'd been. "How were you weird?"

"I already had a bunch of bad habits before I left—the baseball cards, the eating, the bedtime crap. While I was in the morgue, I came up with more. If I tapped my canteen five times, the water would be safe. If I stirred the MRE five times, the food couldn't hurt me. It was stupid. But I thought it saved my life."

"Compulsions aren't stupid."

His lips quirk in a bitter smile. "Seventeen years later, those same *compulsions* rule my life. The Beast. That's what I call them, in my mind. The goddamn animal that keeps me alive. That keeps me crazy."

Beast. He hadn't been calling *me* a beast. He'd been wrestling with the tics that kept him sane.

I make my voice as gentle as I can. "So, what happened tonight?"

"Tonight? Tonight, I tried to celebrate the biggest business milestone of my life with a beautiful, willing partner."

My cheeks heat, and I'm glad I don't have to meet his gaze. I don't think we could have had a word of this conversation actually facing each other. "Until I freaked out," I say.

"This was some pretty messed-up shit," he says.

"But you told me the rules downstairs. None of it came as a surprise."

He huffs a short laugh. "None of it?"

"Okay," I amend. "Some of it." I let my admission sit between us for a minute. But then I ask, "What happened, though? What changed?" I start to sit up, to pull away from his broad chest. "How can you stand to sit here with my head on your shoulder?"

He reaches across with one hand and presses me back to my place. His palm is gentle on my head. His fingers tangle in my hair. "The Beast doesn't seem important anymore. Not when it threatened someone I care about. Seventeen years was long enough. I don't need it anymore."

I love the warmth of his hand and the firmness of his chest. But I have to dispute his words. "Phobias don't work that way. People don't just snap their fingers and say, 'I'm done.'"

"Who the fuck knows?" he says. "Maybe when I wake up tomorrow, I'll be back to square one. But I pushed you too far, and the Beast couldn't care less. *You* trusted me. *You* needed me. So, screw the Beast. I'm done."

I want it to be that simple. I want him to feel as safe as he's making me feel.

I suspect it's going to take more than a single conversation for him to process everything he's feeling. But it seems cruel to make him say more tonight.

I don't want to leave here. I don't want to give up this circle of comfort. I have to keep him talking about *something*, so I reach back to the heart of the story he's just told me. "What happened to the diamonds?" I ask. "The ones your father gave you?"

Chapter Eighteen

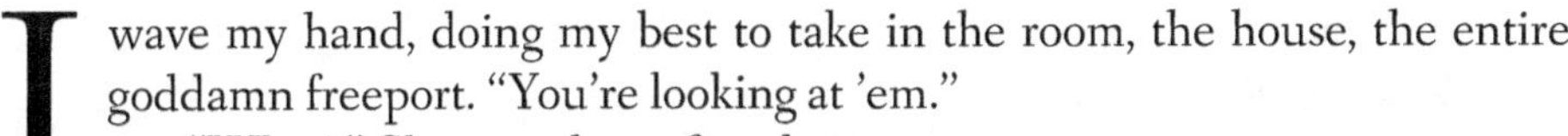

I wave my hand, doing my best to take in the room, the house, the entire goddamn freeport. "You're looking at 'em."

"What?" She sounds confused.

"No one takes away a kid's backpack when it's the only thing he owns. And there's no security to speak of, on a military flight out of Congo. Mom never asked what I brought home, and I was smart enough to keep my mouth shut till I was old enough to use them. My father's diamonds, a hundred mill... They're Diamond Freeport now."

The admission feels good. Right. No one else knows how I started this business. I'm glad Ella knows the truth.

Which makes me realize how much I want to make things right with her. How much I want to give her what *she* wants. What she needs, now that the Beast is dead and gone.

I work my fingers through her hair, making my way to the nape of her neck. When I knead the tiny muscles there, she purrs like a kitten. I lower my head to whisper by her ear, "What would make you feel good?"

She stiffens, for just a moment. I wouldn't have felt it if her entire body hadn't been curled against mine. Before I can react, though, she says, "What you're doing right now is pretty amazing."

It's a coy voice, and I should probably drop my question, but I really feel I owe her. She spent the past four hours with the biggest asshole in the known universe. I want to prove to her—and maybe to myself too—that I actually know how to make a woman happy.

"Don't tell me you're getting shy now," I tease. My fingertips skate past her tits and down her belly, pausing over the mound she shaved for me. I brush against that soft smooth skin, and she shudders.

She whispers, so quiet I can barely hear, "I like it when you touch me down there."

"Down there?" I say, starting to laugh until I realize she's serious.

Indignantly, she says, "I don't have as much experience as you do."

I keep my voice light. "Then tell me what you like."

She shakes her head.

"Then tell me something that worked tonight. Something we did before..." *Before I tried to ream your ass with a horse-size butt plug.* I don't say it out loud, of course.

She covers her face with both hands. I feel her rocking, just a little, shifting back and forth like she needs to run away.

"Ella?" I ask, closing gentle fingers around her wrist.

"I'm not—" she starts to say, but she stops herself. It seems forever before she finally comes up with, "I'm not good at this. I don't know what to say."

"Bullshit."

"I'm scared!"

"Of what? You were brave enough to get in my car. You were horny enough to get in my bed. Why is it so terrifying to tell me what you want?"

"I don't know the words!"

She shouts, and I'm stunned.

"I don't know what to say!" she gasps. "You'll think I'm desperate. Or stupid. I don't want to sound disgusting or crude."

My sweet, good girl... "There's nothing you can say that will make me think less of you," I assure her.

She moans, still hiding behind the screen of her hands.

"Ella..." I cajole, but that only makes it worse. She's pulling inside herself, shrinking away. Her pulse pounds beneath my fingertips like she's a jackrabbit fighting a snare.

I'm losing her. I have to say something. Do something. So I try the only thing I can think of before she falls apart completely.

Gently, determined not to hurt her, I pull her palm from her face. I shift my grip on her wrist, moving my fingers to weave between hers. I guide our hands down her body, ignoring the sudden intake of her breath. Squeezing her fingers beneath mine, I say, "This is your *tit*."

I push the word as I say it, purposely making it short. Sharp. I squeeze again, like that will help her remember.

Moving my fingers with hers, I pinch them together, tweaking her hard enough to get her attention. "This is your nip."

When I pull our hands south, she resists just a little. She knows where we're going, and she has to be afraid. But I cup her firmly, and she has no choice but to do the same. "This is your mound."

We move lower. "Your clit," I say, and she gasps when we slide our knuckles over the firm little knob.

We part her lips. She's wet there, soaking, and I almost breathe a prayer of thanks, because if she hated me for touching her, I don't know what I'd do. "Your pussy," I say, circling our fingers around her opening.

She whines a little, a sweet needy whimper, and I slip one of her fingers inside. "Your slit." I add mine next to hers, both of us dipping together. "Your snatch." Again, as her spine melts against me and she offers up a perfect little moan. "Your cunt."

I move our soaked fingers lower, following the slick path she's already made for herself. "Your taint," I say, gliding front to back, once, twice, a third time.

Her thighs grow tight above our still-joined hands. I want to give her what she's asking for. But more than that, I want to set her free. So I take our sticky fingers and brush them over the tight rosebud I savaged earlier tonight. "Your ass," I whisper.

Before she can think about it, I lean to my left, shifting her weight to my thigh. I guide our hands inside the fly of my boxers. Cupping her hand in mine, I press against the cotton, stretching to reach low. "My balls," I say, showing her how to squeeze them. "My nuts."

I'm hard now, long and heavy. Hands together, I guide her in stroking me from root to tip. "My cock," I say. And just in case she missed the point, we tug it again. "My dick."

I squeeze her fingers in mine, feeling every knuckle around my cock. "We fuck," I say. "I go down on you. I eat you out. You give me a blow job. A hand job."

You take it up the ass. I don't say that. Not tonight.

Instead, I say, "We come."

She needed to hear the words. But I needed to feel them—every single one. I needed to touch her, every inch, to confirm the Beast is nowhere in sight.

Not once did I flinch. Not once did I feel the urge to count, to tap, to play.

Whatever Ella says about phobias and therapy and the impossibility of instant cures, I'm free.

I pull her back to rest against my chest. I raise her hand to my lips. It's still sticky, her juices caught in the lines between her fingers. I suck them clean one by one, tracing them with my tongue.

When I'm done, I place my still-damp thumb against the soft O of her mouth. She opens for me with a greedy little gasp. I fuck her lips with my thumb as she sucks me clean and only after she swallows do I bend down to her ear.

I exhale softly and wait for her to shudder. Then I whisper, "Tell me how to fuck you. Tell me what you want."

Chapter Nineteen

ALIX

"I want..."

The two words hang there.

I want to say more. I want to use the words Trap gave me.

But I've been silent for so many years.

Jason and I had sex every Saturday night, because we weren't too tired from the workweek, and we didn't have class the next day. He thanked me like a gentleman, and he wiped me dry with Kleenex, every single time.

"Ella..." Trap says.

I should tell him the truth. I should tell him my name is Alix.

But Ella's the woman who went to Debasement. Ella's the one who dared to visit this castle in the woods. Ella let a stranger do incredible things to her, with her.

Ella's the one who came.

I swallow hard, and then I decide Ella can do this too. Ella can trust. Ella can say, *does* say, "I want you to go down on me." I don't fly apart in a million pieces from embarrassment. So I go on. "I want you to eat me out. And then I want you to f— fuck me with your cock. Hard. I want you to squeeze my tits and suck my nips and fuck me till I come."

The room is silent, except for the pounding of my heart. I stare at my twisted fingers—the fingers that found my pussy, the ones that have been in Trap's mouth. But I can't sit like a statue forever.

I twist around until I'm facing him. I force myself to raise my head, to find his eyes. I see the wild jungle there, hot and dark and full of life.

He reaches out one of his giant hands. He doesn't hesitate. Doesn't flinch. He cups my face, his touch impossibly gentle. "Good girl," he says.

And then he rises on all fours. He closes his hands around my ankles and tugs me toward the foot of the bed, sending the cloud-soft blanket over the edge of the bed.

He growls like a wild beast, and my pussy squeezes hard with desire. He runs his hands up my thighs, and I know I'm supposed to open to him.

I want to. I trust him. But I can't help myself. As my knees fall to either side, I cover myself with my hands.

He traces my legs like I've given him a present. His thumbs find the exhausted hollows behind my knees. He follows the lines of long muscle, stroking my thighs until I start to melt.

"Please," he says, settling his fingertips in the creases at the tops of my legs. "Let me look at you, Ella."

A sound comes out of me, part exasperation, part laugh. He could force me move my hands. He could make me to do anything he wants.

But this isn't about what Trap wants. This is about what I need.

I shift my hands to the bed, clutching the sheet on either side of my hips. It takes all of my willpower to keep from slamming my knees together.

"Such a sweet pussy," Trap says, staring at me like I'm something beautiful. "Such a brave girl."

I'm proud when he says it. But I don't have time to think of a response, because he buries his face in my snatch.

His tongue is magic. It can be hard, driving against my clit without a hint of mercy. It can be soft, licking my pussy lips like they're the most exotic ice cream ever made.

He does things with his mouth I can't define, and his teeth, too. He's drinking me, eating me, consuming every inch of me, and I'm soaring, soaring, soaring, until he delivers a single, devastating tap to my clit with his thumb.

I collapse in on myself. I clutch and clutch and clutch. My knees slam tight, keeping Trap's face deep in my pussy, and he rides the wild tide, fucking me with his tongue as I come until I cannot see.

It seems like centuries before I return to my body. I can hear my breath, long, deep pulls that do their best to anchor me. I can smell sex, my pussy's briny scent mixed with good, clean sweat. I can see the ceiling above me, and if I tilt my head, the wall of windows, black against the night outside.

My legs are trembling, still clamped shut to lock in the final, stuttering waves of my orgasm. I feel the weight of Trap's face against me, the soft lap of his tongue as he drinks my final shudders.

"Oh my God!" I make my knees open. "Did I hurt you? I'm so sorry!"

He pushes himself up on his elbows, eying me over my shaved mound. His face glistens, soaked by my juices. "I'm not," he says. His kisses along the inside of my thigh make me giggle.

Me. Giggle.

This is *fun*. I know I told Trap I want him to fuck me next, but I've changed my mind. I'm adding to the menu.

I scramble to my knees, feeling the stretch and sigh of muscles that I know will be sore tomorrow. With hands that seem to have taken lessons on their own, I push Trap down to the bed. I slip my fingers under the elastic of his boxers until I've pulled them past his feet. I crouch between his legs and watch his cock rise in eager greeting.

When I cup his balls, I'm surprised by their weight. I worry about crushing them, about hurting him, but I remember the pressure he placed on my hand as he led me over his body. He grunts as I gather the sack in one tight hand and squeeze.

I use my fingernails to trace the veins on his cock. He gets harder as I learn him. Longer too. "Sweet Jesus fuck," he says when I measure the rim beneath his even more sensitive tip.

He tapped my clit and I came. I wonder if I can do the same to him, tease him, tap him, play him to the end. But it's not enough to touch him. I want to taste him, too.

I need him in my mouth. His cock is too long for me to take the whole thing. I close my lips over the rounded end, sliding down until he hits the back of my throat. My eyes water, and I start to gag, so I pull up, tightening my lips to make up for the lack of depth.

His fists tangle in my hair, pulling hard enough for me to know he wants me, but not enough to hurt. I use my own hands to tickle his balls, and he almost slips out of my mouth when he leaps in surprise.

We find our rhythm—short, sharp darts of my head, taking him as deep as I can, then long, slow pulls as I draw back to his tip. He talks the entire time—encouragement at first, then beautiful, filthy words about how I look swallowing his cock.

I stretch my neck, managing the deepest thrust yet, and his fingers tighten on the back of my neck. I freeze, terrified I've done something wrong. "One more like that," he says through gritted teeth, "and you won't get the rest of the show."

I want to feel him come inside my mouth—pulsing and hot, shooting down my throat with the pearly ropes he painted on me hours ago. But I want to feel him fuck me, even more.

I take my time rising off his beautiful cock, relaxing my lips and easing my fingers from his balls. He has more control than I feared, or he purposely stopped me early. As I sit back, he groans and fumbles for something on the nightstand.

I'd forgotten about the condoms he showed me ages ago. For just a moment, I hesitate, wondering if he expects me to put one on him. I've never done that, and I don't want to do it wrong. I don't want to hurt him. I don't want to ruin everything we've got.

He tears the foil with steady fingers and takes out the round of rubber. He rolls it onto his sturdy erection the way he does everything else—with absolute, unshakeable certainty. His quick glance lets me know he wants me to see, wants me to learn.

When he's good and wrapped, he pulls me close for a kiss. His hand spreads across the back of my head, fingers twining in my hair. His lips are hard on mine, asking, promising, demanding. When I open to him, his tongue meets mine, and a satisfied rumble rises from his chest.

When we come up for air, he pulls away. I'd whimper, complain, but his hands are on my tits now. He squeezes them hard, just the way I asked him to, and then he closes his lips over the tight, hard peak of my right nip.

I squeal at the pressure. He laughs, but he doesn't let me go, brushing me with his teeth. He switches to the other tit, squeezing, sucking hard, and the pressure of his tongue almost makes me come.

He edges a knee between mine, making room for his body. He matches his hips to mine, letting me feel his weight. He rises up on one hand, using the other to bring the tip of his cock to the soaking wet lips of my pussy.

"Ready?" he asks, and I don't trust myself with words, but I nod.

He eases in, steady and slow.

I stretch around him, hovering on the point of pain. I tilt my hips and find a better angle. My breath catches because I've never felt this full.

He brushes the hair off my face. He tells me I'm his good girl, his beautiful girl, that I can take this. He settles home, and the tight curls above his cock tease my sensitive, shaved mound.

And then he starts to move.

Slowly at first, raising his hips. He's leaving me, pulling away. I ache with emptiness even before he's gone. But then he pushes back, sliding home faster, deeper, even though I thought I'd already taken all he has to give.

Once he sets the rhythm, I instinctively rise to meet him. My body knows this dance, or it learns as we go.

Faster.

Harder.

More.

My toes stretch to needy points. My thighs tighten into desperate steel. My eyes close and my breath stalls and I need need need...

His fingers flash between us, scissoring around the hot tight pearl of my clit. He flicks once and a fuse sizzles through my body. Fire sparks up my spine and detonates in my brain at the same time my cunt explodes.

I thought I'd found nirvana the first time I came in this bed. But now I'm carried to an entirely different universe. Now, my muscles tighten *around* Trap's velvet cock. The sensations inside me multiply, echo around themselves until I don't know if I'm coming or screaming or begging or crying and the perfect spiral goes on and on and on.

Just when I think I can't take any more, that I have to faint or disappear or explode in a cloud of glittery dust, Trap drives home one last time. His chest pins mine, his legs anchor mine, his arms press against mine as every muscle in his body turns to stone.

I feel him pulse inside me, the rush of liquid heat as he comes. He bellows against my shoulder; his teeth clenching until I know they'll leave a mark. I hold him as he bucks, as he strains, until the aftershocks finally fade to a feather-like tremble.

"Ella..." he sighs, pulling out and rolling off to lie beside me on the bed. His dangling hand brushes my tit; he rolls his fingers over my nip, but my nerves have fired past the point of any response.

I'm drifting toward sleep when I feel him push off the bed. He pads into the bathroom. Water runs, and he comes back with a washcloth. He wipes between my legs gently, and my spent body registers nothing but soft warmth. He eases a pillow beneath my head.

My brain is stripped, its gears left in melting pieces. I know there's something I need to say, something I need to do, but when I try to string together words, Trap mumbles a kiss against my temple.

"Sleep," he says, the single word little more than a sighing breath.

That's not what he said in the kitchen. That wasn't the deal we made. Trap Prince never lets a woman spend the night. He told me that.

But he's told me so many things tonight, taught me so much more than I ever thought I could learn.

So I close my eyes.

I sink deep into my pillow.

I sleep.

Chapter Twenty

ALIX

I startle awake, sitting up like someone rammed a cattle prod against my tongue. For just a moment, I don't know where I am, but then I see the wall of windows, the endless bed, the leather cuffs still fastened to the iron uprights. The entire night floods back into my brain.

Trap is sleeping beside me. He's sprawled on his back, legs splayed, one hand over his head. His tired cock rests against his thigh. I don't know how long we've been out, but given his utter exhaustion, I don't think it's been long.

As I shift to the edge of the bed, he mutters my name.

"Go back to sleep," I say. "I'm getting a drink."

He mumbles something, but he's out before he manages actual words.

There's a glass on the nightstand. I could get my drink in the bathroom, but I've already woken Trap once. After the night he's just had—the physical, but the emotional too—he deserves every second of sleep he can steal.

I slip into my panties before I realize there's no way I can put on my dress without disturbing the sleeping man. I settle for pulling on his boxers and his soft black T-shirt. I collect my dress and my bra to put on downstairs, snagging my shoes for good measure. I tip-toe down the stairs and into the kitchen.

I'm about to search the cabinets for a glass when I glance at the stove. A clock glows balefully in the moonlight from the wall of windows. 11:32.

Crap!

Everything rushes back to me—Leo missing our birthday and the eviction notice and my midnight deadline before I lose everything I own. For one blinding moment, I think about running up the stairs, about startling Trap from sleep and begging him to drive me home.

Before I can move, though, a wave of shame washes over me, so intense I almost retch in the sink. My life is an absolute mess. If there's something to do wrong, I've done it. I've got no family. No friends. No degree in sight. All because of a brother who has lied and lied and lied again.

But I've learned something tonight, in the magical world of Diamond Freeport. I've learned how to use my words.

I'm going home right now. I'm telling Leo I don't want to hear his excuses. I don't care why he blew off our birthday lunch. He can get clean on his own. Get a job on his own. Prove he's worth me on his own.

I'm through twisting my life for Leo.

And tomorrow, when I've said all the things I need to say, when I've said the words I've swallowed for far too long, I'll tell Trap what he's really done for me. I'll explain what tonight really meant.

Because then I'll be worthy. Then I'll deserve to be with him.

I glance at the clock again. 11:36.

I grab my clutch, where I left it on the counter hours ago. My phone is waiting.

No Uber, no Lyft, because Leo's kept me from having a credit card for years. But I've still got ten crisp twenties in my bag, the last from the ATM. I tap a stored number for Dover Yellow Cab.

They say they can be here in ten minutes. I beg them to hurry and hang up the call. Only then do I realize I have seven voice messages.

I tap the red badge and see they're all from Leo. He's going to beg me. He's going to lie. I delete all seven without listening.

He's left me texts, too. Nine of them. I have to scroll through those to delete, and I glimpse his growing panic.

Leo
Sorry about lunch
Hope u didnt wait 2 long
Can we talk
A - got 2 talk
Call me
Rlly need 2 talk now
Come on A
Im not kidding

ALIX

I jam my phone back in my clutch and gather my belongings. I look around the kitchen, but there isn't a scrap of paper anywhere.

I pad into the office, figuring even a Prince living in an ultra-modern castle has to have a pen where he works. I'm halfway to the desk when I hear the double-tap of a car horn.

The gate!

I've completely forgotten the iron gate. The cab dispatcher must have heard the urgency in my voice and gotten a car here faster than the ten minutes she quoted.

Forgetting the note I want to leave, I juggle my clothes, throwing the lock on the front door.

The car honks again.

"Ella?" Trap calls from the bedroom.

What was I thinking? Why didn't I just wake him and ask him to drive me home?

But the cab is waiting, and my keycard will die in twenty minutes and my phone is filled with my brother's incoherent rambling, the very thing I didn't want to explain to Trap.

I throw the door open and run across the driveway, in front of the office building, past the construction site. The cab is waiting by the front gate, its headlights slicing through the night.

My bare feet scrape against the paving stones. Ground lights flare to life behind me, outlining the driveway.

"Ella!" Trap calls again from the house's front door, louder, more commanding.

The cab starts to pull away. I scream, "Wait!" and break into an all-out run.

I start to drop my clutch, scramble for it, and my dress begins to drag. I bunch it into a ball, crushing my bra, and one of my shoes falls.

I start to go back for it, but the cab is leaving, so I forget about the shoe and fling myself at the gate. It takes me a moment to find the revolving door, the curved metal that will let me out while keeping any invader from breaking in.

I stumble into the road, three feet in front of the cab, and I'm blinded by its headlights.

"Ella!" Trap hollers, somewhere to my left.

"I'm sorry!" I call into the darkness. "I didn't mean..." I can't remember what I did or didn't mean. "I have to..." I can't explain everything I have to do. "I'm sorry," I shout again. "I'll call you! I promise!"

I stagger to the cab and yank open the door. Tumbling into the back seat, I tell the driver my address, and I beg him to get me home by midnight.

Chapter Twenty-One

ALIX

1 1:57.

I give the cabbie a massive tip because I can't wait for change. I slam my keycard against the reader, half expecting it to refuse to open. It takes three tries, but the door finally buzzes, and I tumble into the lobby like a boxer collapsing on the ropes. As always, it stinks like pizza and gym socks.

For once, I'm grateful the metal panels in the elevator are too dented and scarred to cast back a reflection. I swipe at my eyes, not certain when I started to cry. I bend down and wipe my nose with the hem of Trap's shirt.

I've made a huge mistake. I should have stayed with Trap. Should have trusted him. Should have explained. I acted like Alix, a woman afraid to use her words, afraid to tell the truth. I should have been Ella.

He would have understood.

My brain was paralyzed by the thought of losing everything I own as the clock struck twelve. But I should have realized nothing in my lousy apartment is worth what I left behind.

As soon as I'm inside, I'll call him. How hard can it be to track down a number for Diamond Freeport? I'll say I made a mistake. I'll take the blame and beg him for a do-over. I'll offer to meet him at Debasement. Whatever he wants. Whatever he needs.

My key sticks in the lock, but I know exactly where to kick the door and how hard to shove with my shoulder. I slam it shut behind me.

"Alix!"

Leo sits on the swayback couch. His pillow and sheets must still be in the closet. He hasn't set up his bed for the night.

"Leo," I say, trying to keep my tone even.

"Didn't you get my messages?" he asks. "I left them on your phone."

He's nervous, glancing over my shoulder, looking at his hands, keeping his gaze from anywhere but me.

"I deleted your calls," I say. It feels good to speak the truth.

"You shouldn't have done that," he says. His voice shakes, and I wonder when he last used.

"There's a lot of things I shouldn't have done." I know precisely what I want to say and how I want to say it, but the words are still hard. I've held them back for so many years. I clutch my clothes to my chest.

"I'm sorry," Leo says, the two words blurring together.

"I'm sorry, too," I say. "I'm sorry you didn't tell me about the eviction sooner. I'm sorry you didn't—"

"No!" Leo cuts me off. "This is important!"

"I know. It's always important. You didn't mean to start using again. You thought you could handle just one hit. You didn't know you were slipping until you fell—"

"I tried!"

"You always try!"

"You're not listening to me!" He's sobbing now, frantic.

I've always been the one person who understands. I've always been the one person who believes him. I've loved him. He's my twin.

"I'm through listening to you," I say, trying to make my voice gentle. "You need help, Leo. A lot more help than I can give you."

"Please!" he cries, dropping to his knees. He waddles across the floor, hands clasped in front of his chest, like a bad movie's stereotype of a man with nothing left to lose.

Despite everything, I'm crying again. I've always wanted to protect him. Always wanted to make him whole.

"You've been to enough meetings," I say, even though he's gasping so hard I doubt he can hear me. "You know how this works. Maybe if you actually reach rock bottom, you can finally—"

"No!" he cries, and I suddenly remember a day when we were eight years old. We took kites to the Washington Monument, and his caught an updraft.

The kite swept high above the obelisk, stretching, straining, until the end of the string slipped free of the spool and it was gone forever.

Leo screamed then the way he just screamed now. Like he's losing everything in the world.

I don't want to wake the neighbors. I glance over my shoulder to make sure the door is closed.

For a second, I can't parse what I'm seeing. A man stands there, a stranger. He's wearing black jeans and a black T and his hands are covered by jet black gloves. He could be Trap, but he isn't.

He's shorter than Trap. He's got acne on his cheeks, angry red pits, and his lips cave in like he's missing most of his teeth. His muddy brown eyes are dead.

I open my mouth to scream, but he gets an arm around my throat, yanking my head back against his shoulder. I twist and try to knee him in the balls, but he anticipates me and jerks me off my feet.

"Leo!" I scream—or try to. The sound is cut off by the arm crushing my larynx.

"Get the hood, motherfucker," the man snarls near my ear. I thrash like a dying fish, trying to see his accomplice. I land an elbow in my guy's ribs, and he huffs like a wild boar. "Let's go, cocksucker—the hood!" And then, wheezing, stinking like onion: "Don't make me go for my knife."

I turn toward Leo, trying to warn him. I don't know if he heard the part about the knife.

But Leo doesn't need a warning.

Leo is standing in front of me.

Leo is sobbing like the day Fluffy McFluffster went to kitty heaven.

Leo is holding a rough burlap sack, his hands shaking so hard I think he's going to drop it.

"I'm sorry," he babbles. "I'm so, so sorry. I owe him so much money. He said he was going to kill me. He said he'll only keep you a few days. You'll be okay. He promised. I made him promise, Alix. I did!"

He puts the hood over my head like we're going trick-or-treating, his hands shaking so hard he can barely pull it past my eyes. The guy behind me uses his free hand to yank it down harder, muttering, "Fucking junkie pussy."

"Oh my God, Leo," I gasp, because jerking the hood loosened the guy's hold on my throat. "What did you do?"

I ask the question, but he's already told me. With diamond-sharp clarity, I'm certain: the brother I love has just sold me to pay his drug debts.

Before I can beg, I feel a sting like a fist-size hornet launching an attack on my neck. It must be a needle, because my blood turns to fire, torching a path from my neck, down my arm, to my heart.

Alix Key

I open my mouth to scream, but I'm gone before I can force out a sound.

Afterword

Can't wait to find out what happens to Alix? And how Trap reacts to her running out before midnight? Rough Diamond is available now!

Visit Alix today at https://www.alixkey.com.

Afterword

We hope you enjoyed all the stories in *Backed by Love*. Thank you so much for supporting this anthology and giving to such a worthy cause.